Alathea

Pamela Belle was born and bred in Suffolk, the daughter of a local prep. school headmaster. She went to the University of Sussex, and has now given up her teaching post to write full time.

Alathea, the heroine of Pamela Belle's third novel, is the daughter of Francis and Thomazine Heron who featured in the author's first two books, *The Moon in the Water* and *The Chains of Fate*, which are also published by Pan.

Also by Pamela Belle
in Pan Books

The Moon in the Water
The Chains of Fate

PAMELA BELLE

Alathea

Hang love, for I will never pine
For any man alive:
Nor shall this jolly heart of mine
The thoughts of it receive:
I will not purchase slavery
At such a dangerous rate,
But glory in my liberty
And laugh at love and fate.

(Aphra Behn, *The Jealous Bridegroom*)

Pan Original
Pan Books London and Sydney

First published 1985 by Pan Books Ltd,
Cavaye Place, London SW10 9PG
9 8 7 6 5 4 3 2 1

ISBN 0 330 28942 X

Printed and bound in Great Britain by
Richard Clay (The Chaucer Press) Ltd, Bungay, Suffolk

For the shades of John Wilmot, Mary Beale and Aphra Behn: in the hopes that I have not done them any disservice herein.

FAMILY TREES

HERONS

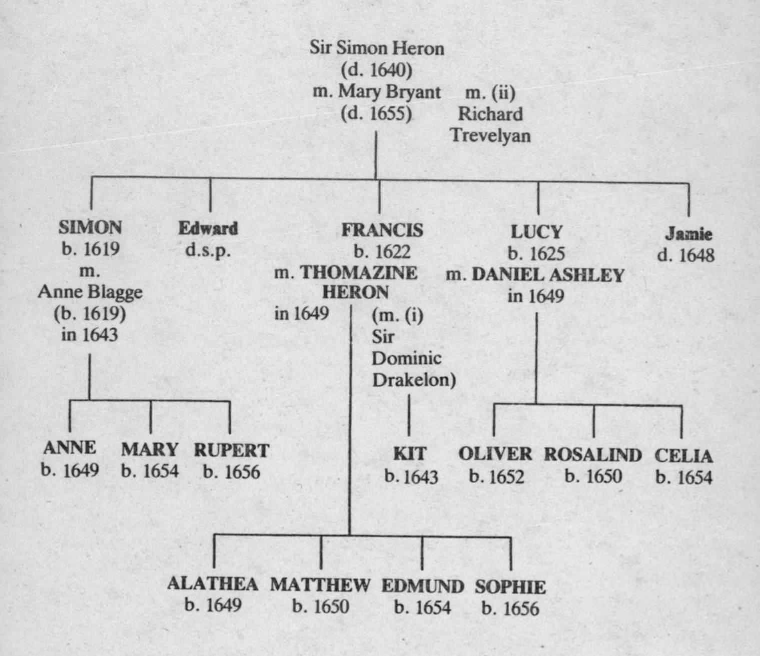
Sir Simon Heron
(d. 1640)
m. Mary Bryant
(d. 1655)
m. (ii)
Richard
Trevelyan
SIMON
b. 1619
m.
Anne Blagge
(b. 1619)
in 1643
Edward
d.s.p.
FRANCIS
b. 1622
m. THOMAZINE
HERON
in 1649
(m. (i)
Sir
Dominic
Drakelon)
LUCY
b. 1625
m. DANIEL ASHLEY
in 1649
Jamie
d. 1648
ANNE
b. 1649
MARY
b. 1654
RUPERT
b. 1656
KIT
b. 1643
OLIVER
b. 1652
ROSALIND
b. 1650
CELIA
b. 1654
ALATHEA
b. 1649
MATTHEW
b. 1650
EDMUND
b. 1654
SOPHIE
b. 1656

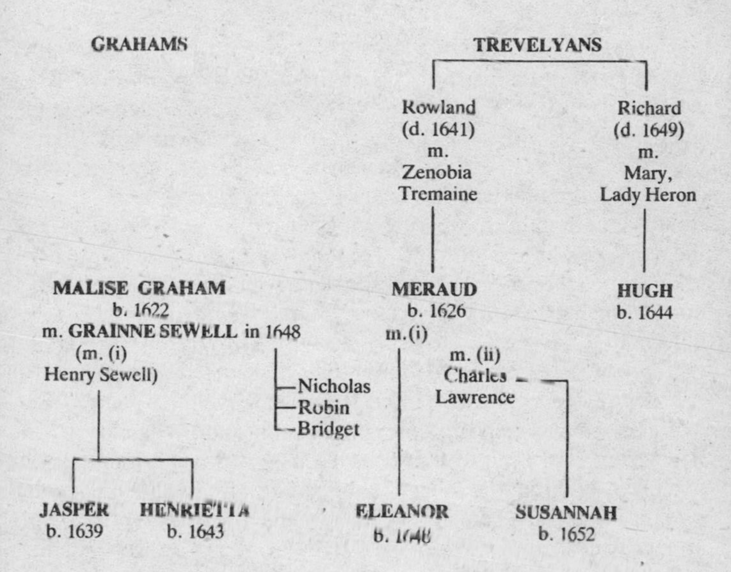
GRAHAMS
TREVELYANS
Rowland
(d. 1641)
m.
Zenobia
Tremaine
Richard
(d. 1649)
m.
Mary,
Lady Heron
MALISE GRAHAM
b. 1622
m. GRAINNE SEWELL in 1648
(m. (i)
Henry Sewell)
Nicholas
Robin
Bridget
MERAUD
b. 1626
m. (i)
m. (ii)
Charles
Lawrence
HUGH
b. 1644
JASPER
b. 1639
HENRIETTA
b. 1643
ELEANOR
SUSANNAH
b. 1652

HISTORICAL NOTE

The obscurer byways of the history of Western art are littered with the paintings of female artists, long forgotten; many of whom, like Alathea Heron, began full of bright early promise, famous and feted, only to fade away under the pressures of marriage, male prejudice and competition, the vagaries of fashion. Mary Beale's long and successful career was one of the few exceptions, and even she disappeared in the shadows of Lely and Kneller. So although the name of Alathea Heron will probably not be found in any work of reference, her career does reflect some of the problems faced by most women artists in the past, and anyone wanting to explore this field in detail is advised to read *The Obstacle Race*, by Germaine Greer, whose research and theories I have shamelessly plundered.

I also owe a great debt to all the scholars who have struggled over the years with the complex character of John Wilmot, Earl of Rochester, and I am well aware that my portrayal presents only one facet, and that the most likeable, of a man who has fascinated me since my teens. I am also well aware that the famous portrait of him crowning his monkey, still hidden in the bowels of the National Portrait Gallery, is usually ascribed to Jacob Huysmans: but since there is no signature, and no certainty, I felt free to assign it instead to Alathea. Rochester's poems, however, are all his, and the order in which they appear in the story corresponds to the order in which most scholars consider he wrote them. The delightful letter in Chapter 21 is also genuine.

As in my previous books about the Herons, I have woven my fictional family into the fabric of a real society, and many of the other characters actually existed. Charles Jermyn, like the rest of his family, lived and died as described in the story; but his marriage to Henrietta Sewell is not a matter of record.

Finally, I would like to acknowledge once more my indebtedness to my mother, and her gimlet eye for errors; to the encouragement of my father and other members of my family and friends; and last, but not least, to that most splendid gentleman Samuel Pepys, without whom any study of Restoration England would be a pale shadow of the rich and fascinating reality.

Contents

PART ONE

The Apprentice 1660-66

PART TWO

The Picture-drawer 1667-74

PART THREE

The Artist 1674-7

PART ONE

The apprentice

1660–66

. . . an unlesson'd girl, unschool'd, unpractis'd:
Happy in this, she is not yet so old
But she may learn: happier than this,
She is not bred so dull but she can learn.

(Shakespeare, *The Merchant of Venice*)

CHAPTER ONE

First meeting

The childhood shows the man
As morning shows the day.

(Milton, *Paradise Regained*)

The day, the momentous day that changed Alathea Heron's life for ever was a most beautiful one: high summer in the soft green Oxfordshire hills, thick with grass and flowers and butterflies and silly, denuded sheep, filling the air with scent and colour, sound and movement. No cloud marred the limitless, hot sky, and the afternoon sun poured down on the child's back as she sat, her green skirt almost invisible in the deep grass, and turned her ash-fair head to a cap of wild silver.

Below her, the house lay somnolent amid the still greener grass of the water-meadows around the little River Swere: a golden house, ancient and rather dilapidated, built of the local Oxfordshire stone more than three hundred years ago, and hardly touched since. There were fresh scars, though, where the Parliament soldiers had dismantled the fortifications after the late Civil Wars, when Ashcott had held a King's garrison, and suffered for it. The encircling wall had gone, and the gatehouse and the tower and the remaining structure had a very desolate, lop-sided look, not improved by the riotous growth of grass and ivy and nettles all around it.

Alathea's mouth tightened as she stared at it. Doubtless to many this still substantial manor house seemed a palace, and her father had pointed out their good fortune in having such a place to live, but only a month before they had all been at Goldhayes, and, compared to Goldhayes, humble Ashcott was pottery after amber. She had been born there, so had her younger brothers and her sister, and it was her home, the place that her heart yearned for, despite the unwelcome, undeniable truth that it in fact belonged to her Uncle Simon. So, her parents had cared for Goldhayes until the King, and Simon Heron, could come into their own again: and on a glorious May day in 1660, the King and Simon

Heron and thousands of other Royalist exiles had joyfully, triumphantly ridden into London amid the wildly celebrating populace, and Alathea and her family must leave Goldhayes, the lovely rose-brick, moated mansion that was the jewel of all Suffolk, and go to Ashcott, the neglected mutilated old house that had belonged to her mother.

Even now, a month after the move, she longed and yearned for Goldhayes. She only had to shut her eyes to take her mind away from the hillside above Ashcott to the park at Goldhayes, to wander up the drive to the bridge over the moat, to lean down and drop twigs and bits of grass on to the still murky water to see if they moved (they never had), to stroll between the clipped flowerbeds over the gravel of the Front Court, to open the heavy oak door in the porch and smell again that strange, warm aroma unique to Goldhayes, sunshine and flowers and polish and herbs, and hear the hard, flat, dearly familiar Suffolk voices of the servants, so different from the soft rolling Oxfordshire drawl.

But her Uncle Simon, newly made Lord Bradfield in recognition of his years of exile and his devoted service to the King and to Prince Rupert, lived there now with his ailing wife and his three unlikeable children, and Goldhayes was Alathea's home no more. Nor could she reckon to return on the occasional family visit, for her father had parted on very acrimonious terms with his older brother (they had apparently never liked each other very much anyway), and accusations about mismanagement and profligate spending had flown thick and fast, even within her hearing. Lord Bradfield had objected very strongly to what he considered to be unnecessary expenditure on improving tenants' cottages and raising wages, and the extraordinary newfangled practice of planting turnips and clover for winter and spring fodder, which he considered to be a complete waste of time: and Alathea's father had at first answered in his usual reasonable, rather ironic style and at last, when making no impression, had unspectacularly lost his temper. Despite herself, Alathea grinned as she remembered it: her father's icy, quiet rage as he pointed out his brother's ingratitude with some force, and Lord Bradfield's fierce fury-reddened face as he shouted back, becoming more and more undignified as he grew louder. In the end, their wives had calmed them and the cracks were superficially covered over: but Alathea knew, as did they all, that Goldhayes would not welcome them, ever again.

And they had all come to Ashcott, so that her father could put the knowledge he had acquired with Goldhayes and a goodly slice of Suffolk, into setting right crumbling Ashcott and a few hundred acres of neglected land and a hamlet of apathetic peasantry. All of them: her parents, her brothers Matthew and Edmund, her sister Sophie, her half-brother Kit, and her orphan cousin Eleanor, who was six months older than Alathea and had always been part of their family. Together, they must make Ashcott comfortable and the land productive, and there were months and years of hard work ahead. But this afternoon, Alathea had managed to escape here, out of reach of all of them, with the little dog, Mab, who was an ancient and respected member of the family, for company: to indulge her great and secret passion, which was drawing.

The boy riding the hired gelding was half asleep, lulled into a state of daydream by the heat, the swaying ease of his horse's gait, and the somnolent murmur of the bees and the swish of grass. He had long since let the reins drop and the animal made its own leisurely way along the hillside path from Barford St John; lazily avoiding the occasional sheep or grass tussock: and his rider dreamed, revelling in this unique day of freedom. In a life planned to the last detail by mother and tutors – the grammar school at Burford, a student at Oxford at the age of twelve, then the obligatory nobleman's tour of the more dubious areas of Europe, and an assured place at Court at the end of it all – with his future laid so plain before him, a spontaneous excursion such as this, undertaken purely for curiosity's sake and unsupervised by overbearing parent or officious tutor, was his idea of paradise, and he was making the most of it. No pressure to conform, to direct his mind along the narrow rigid paths ordained for it by insensitive adults, to behave with the stiff formality expected of an Earl, even a thirteen-year-old Earl: a blessed chance to be himself, and let his mind rove free.

And because his mind was always full of words and rhymes, and the wild flood of exhilarating talk he heard at Oxford among tutors and students alike, it was words that jostled undisciplined in his head, arranging and rearranging themselves in fantastic patterns that somehow never seemed to achieve the facility, the graceful fluency he so greatly desired. He had read poetry in Latin, in Greek and in English, he knew large portions of Horace and Shakespeare by heart and their rhythms and language were as much a part of him as his own: and yet when he tried to translate the silent exuberant song inside his head, all that seemed to emerge was dull, pedestrian, ridden with cliché and conceit. One day, he knew, the elusive tantalising key would turn at last and true poetry would flow, but for now the lame verses that struggled from his pen did not seem sufficient for his imagination and ambition. Robert Whitehall, one of the sycophants and hopeful ageing Cavaliers who had attached themselves to him at Oxford – for his title's sake, for his father's sake, never for his *own* sake – had 'polished up' some of his childish verses on the King's Restoration and sent them to His Majesty. Two months older, he grew hot with embarrassment at the thought of those stilted couplets being perused by royal eyes: but Whitehall was a good enough fellow, with his rough talk and refreshingly advanced ideas about learning at hidebound, prosy Oxford, and his enormous capacity for beer and tobacco. Whitehall, the boy decided with a reminiscent, slightly guilty grin, might be what his mother would describe as bad company, as bad as his poetry, but to his mind was very good company on hot summer nights in Oxford taverns.

He was nearly there now, only a mile or so from his father's house at Adderbury, that he had not seen since he was small: his mother lived at Ditchley, her jointure-house, and its long low mellow frontage, the green park and trees, were engraved on his heart for ever as home. But in going to Adderbury he was in some strange way moving closer to the shade of his father, that fat, bluff, jovial, hard-drinking, hard-loving caricature of a Cavalier whom he had met only once, long ago in France when he was six: he could still remember, when he wanted to, his disappointment at the coarse reality of the fabulous being he had worshipped from afar. He thrust that inconvenient, unpleasant memory from his mind and concentrated on guiding his ambling nag around a clump of hawthorn bushes.

Something tiny and black-and-white leapt up from almost under his horse's hooves, barking furiously. Startled out of its somnolence, the gelding squealed and reared, and its rider, equally surprised, was nearly thrown. It took most of his not inconsiderable skill to calm his mount as the little dog fussed indignantly around, still protesting at its narrow escape. Then a hand whipped it out of reach by the scruff of its neck, and a furious, breathless voice ordered it to sit, following up this command with a brisk tap on its rump. 'You may nearly have been trodden on, but there's no call to make things worse!' said the voice severely to the dog, which lowered its head and cringed guiltily.

By this time the boy had leisure enough for a proper view of the owner of voice and dog: which proved to be a child, a girl not much younger than himself, with lint-fair hair tangled round her face and wearing a grass-green linsey-woolsey dress and an apron that had seen better days. She said defensively, 'Can't you look where you're going? You nearly ran us down!'

He had immediately assumed her to be some villager's brat: the sharpness and tone of her voice, with a faint accent he could not recognise, told him different. Angry after his alarm, he attacked in return. 'That's not a thing I could have avoided very well, is it? What were you doing, anyway, skulking about in the bushes with your unmannerly cur?'

'That's none of your business! And Mab's no cur, she's a dear old lady even if she is a bit deaf, and she's seen hard times and deserves more respect than you've given her – so if you're a gentleman you'll say you're sorry and be on your way!' And with an angry flourish, the girl stood aside to let him pass.

And he would have done, had not a flash of white on the ground caught his eye and his attention. The girl followed his gaze and then snatched it up and held it behind her back, her face, reddening, daring him to comment. But he had seen what it was and, his interest held, said quietly, 'I'm sorry if I was rude. Have you been drawing? Can I see?' His curiosity grew: it was, at the very least, a strange thing for a young girl of (presumably) good family to be doing up here on the sheepwalks above the River Swere. Who was she, and where did she live?

The girl stared at him intently, suspiciously. He noticed her eyes: they were long, a smoky green colour, watchful and wary, incongruously adult in her pointed, freckled, sun-flushed child's face. Evidently her assessment of him was favourable, for she gave a sudden wry shrug and grinned. 'Yes. I was drawing Ashcott, that's the house down there, that's where I live.' And the white paper was thrust out at him and her eyes, as he took it, all the while daring him to laugh, to sneer, to make cruel comments. But he remembered, with a pang of mortification, his own childish efforts at creation that had doubtless been the subject of much adult amusement behind his back: and knew that, if necessary, he would lie kindly.

But there was no need. He knew very little of drawing or painting: words fascinated him, it was words he could control and manipulate and one day, perhaps, join into poetry. But even his inexperienced eye could discern that the detailed pen-and-ink drawing of the little golden house below them in its green growing valley, was quite exceptional: and from the hands of a girl perhaps twelve years old, truly astonishing. Something of his admiration and surprise must have shown in his face, for she said, hesitantly, as if such appreciation rarely came her way, 'Do – do you like it?'

'Like it?' He looked down at the drawing, tiny and jewel-perfect, and then at the distant house – what had she called it? Ashcott? – that had been reproduced so faithfully, and with such care. 'Like it? I think it's beautiful . . . it really is. I don't know much about drawing, though – who teaches you? Is your father an artist, or something?'

'No – oh, no, it's my brother who's the artist, Kit, my half-brother, he's good at drawing – but he doesn't teach me,' said the child, with some bitterness. 'He doesn't think girls can draw.'

'But you can.'

'I know,' said the girl, sitting down abruptly – all her movements were quick, sudden, but curiously graceful – in the long grass. She heaved a sigh and stared unhappily out across the distant valley, her chin on her knees and her arms, thin, brown and freckled, wrapped around her legs. After a moment the boy slid down off his horse, tied its reins to a part of the bush and sat beside her, the drawing still in his hands. 'Mind the ink,' said the strange child without looking round, and he picked up the little jar and the quills and the penknife and placed them out of harm's way under the hawthorn. 'And you did this drawing with one of those? A pen?'

'Yes.'

'You haven't made a blot or a smudge or a scratch anywhere.'

'No. I was very careful, once I knew it was going to be good. Sometimes I ruin it if I don't think. In that book – you can look if you like – there's a sketch I did of my brother, and I spoilt it when it was almost finished, because I wanted to get it done quickly.'

The paper, perhaps a dozen thick and crackling sheets, had been loosely sewn together. The drawing of the house was nearly the last: he turned back a page, to discover the arresting portrait of a young man staring belligerently up at him. Black-haired and light-eyed, with a hint of powerful emotions barely kept in check, the image presented was a most uncomfortable one, the ink-blot across his hairline somehow enhancing that impression, and the boy was aware of a brief hope that he would not come across that face in reality. 'That's Kit,' the girl explained.

'The one who draws?'

'Yes.'

'Is it like him?'

The child screwed her eyes up in thought. 'I suppose so,' she said at last. 'But it does make him look rather ugly.'

It certainly made the unknown Kit look rather unpleasant. The boy turned over the pages, glad to be rid of those faintly malevolent eyes. Other faces presented themselves to his interested gaze, done in pen-and-ink or red smudgy chalk, highlighted in white and black. There were adults and children, obviously family and servants, and all most remarkably accomplished for a child of her evidently tender years. He said impulsively, 'Could you – could you draw me, do you think?'

'Now?' said the girl. 'Why? Don't you think I really did them?' The defensive note, he was sorry to hear, had returned to her voice: Kit's habitual disapproval must have struck very deep.

Quick to reassure, he said, 'Don't be silly, I *know* you truly did them . . . but I'd love it if you could draw me . . . no one ever has, before, and I think my mother would like it, she's always complaining that I don't write to her enough.'

The soft freckled face cleared. 'All right, then . . . it mightn't be very good, though. Sometimes I go wrong, and I don't know why. Would you mind if it went wrong and you couldn't send it to your mother?'

'No,' he said, with perfect truth: and with a friendly conspiratorial grin the girl took up paper, pen and ink, and settled herself a few feet away in the grass, the little rough-haired black-and-white dog curling up beside her.

'Good girl, Mab, and don't you *dare* jog me . . . she upset the ink once, all over the best picture I'd ever done, and I was so cross I didn't speak to her for days . . . but it's all right, Mab old girl

I'm not cross with you now, not at all.'

The dog thumped its tail. The girl made some quick gestures with her fingers that looked like measurements, and dipped the pen into the ink-jar. After an industrious interval, she went on. 'Mab was in Colchester you know, in the siege in 1648, and my mother rescued her from being a soldier's dinner, and she caught rats for them to eat, so she's very lucky and very special and everyone loves her, don't they, old girl.' A quick glance upwards to study his face, and she added conversationally, 'Have you got a dog?'

'No,' he said, thinking wryly that his mother, that formidably organised lady, would never allow any canine untidiness, smell and mess to mar the sleek old-fashioned beauty of Ditchley. And suddenly, with a wrench of his heart, he realised that he envied this child, with her shabby, defensive, abruptly friendly manner, her dog and her family and the evident informality of her unrestricted life: and above all, that lovely flowing untaught gift that had descended on this girl from the capricious gods, and would most certainly be wasted. For who had ever heard of a female artist?

As if in answer to his thought, the girl said softly and exultantly, 'There. My very first commission.'

'Is it finished? Already?'

'I never take very long. Somehow I don't seem to need to,' said the child, the warning tone back in her voice. 'And one day when I'm in London and rich and famous and all the Court are clamouring to have their portraits painted and I'm turning away almost all of them . . . *then* you can come to me with this and tell me to do it again properly and I will, because you were the very first person to *ask* me to draw you.' And she grinned at him, her hair blinding in the brilliant sunlight, and he took the paper as abruptly as she had held it out to him, moved by something, some prophecy, some glimpse of the future, that he did not understand.

And there he was, the beautiful, fair-haired, sensitive boy with those incongruous, dark eyes that always watched back at him from mirrors. In a few quick lines with a badly cut quill, that child had laid his self down on the paper to perfection, too close for his comfort. 'Do you like it?' she asked, suddenly anxious. 'I can spend a bit more time . . . perhaps your eyes aren't right . . . '

'Oh, no . . . no,' said the boy, ruefully. 'No, they are . . . oh, it's myself to the life, and I'm well pleased. Maybe I won't send it to my mother after all.' For the thought had occurred to him that the story behind the drawing would strike her as bizarre and unfortunate, and that the picture itself might not be as good, to her practical adult eyes, as it seemed to his. 'I would rather keep it for myself,' he added, with truth.

'And as it's a proper commissioned portrait,' said the girl, 'I must put your name to it.' She dipped the quill in the jar of ink and held out her hand for the paper. 'So what shall I write, sir?'

'John Wilmot,' he said: his liking for this chance-met companion had grown too great in their short time of acquaintance to put her at a disadvantage by quoting all his titles at her. For now they were just themselves, two creative spirits in their own shared world, and there would be no intrusion of unwelcome reality. 'John Wilmot, aged thirteen,' he added, watching, with amusement, her careful inscription, in writing far more childish than the drawing, with the proper use of Latin, and the date. Underneath, as an afterthought, she added a monogram: an A and an H, simply and neatly joined. 'What's your name?' John asked, suddenly surprised that he should still be in ignorance of it: he felt as if he had always known her.

'Alathea Heron. We live at Ashcott, but we used to live at Goldhayes in Suffolk; we had to move here when my uncle came back with the King. He's Lord Bradfield, have you heard of him?'

He had, vaguely, as one new title in a list of many, but his nod delighted her. 'He was one of Prince Rupert's most faithful friends, though I don't like him very much, he's very stern and disapproving and he doesn't like my father.' Obviously that was Lord Bradfield's most unforgiveable quality. She went on, 'It's very hot, you look as if you've been riding a long time, do you want to come down and have a mug of beer or elderflower wine? Please do, it won't take long and somehow it seems a shame to say goodbye just yet.'

He knew exactly what she meant, and her guileless face, innocent of flattery and ulterior motive, persuaded him. He had his wish: he was liked for himself, as John Wilmot without burden of title or paternal ghost, and somehow the fact that his first true friend should be this talented oddity of a child made it all the more worthwhile.

'Of course, lady,' he said, with a mock courtly bow. 'I shall be most honoured to accept your gracious offer of hospitality.' And with laughter and with Mab, John Wilmot and Alathea Heron set off down the hillside path.

Thomazine Heron, on her knees with a trowel in what had once, twenty long years ago, been her grandmother's herb garden, viewed her elder daughter's approach with a certain resignation. Alathea, the child that held so special a place in her heart that she had always had to conceal it from everyone save her husband Francis, was at once a joy and a worry: moody, defensive, secretive as well as friendly and intelligent and thoughtful. In the last year or so, since it had become likely that they would have to leave Goldhayes, the moodiness and secrecy had become more marked, and Thomazine, reluctantly and with grief, had realised that she could no longer communicate with Alathea, could no longer tell what her beloved child was thinking or feeling. And yet, with irony, the girl grew daily more and more like her father: tall, already nearly as tall as Thomazine, with long legs and a long pointed face, deceptively angelic, and pale fine hair whose haphazard curl was the most obvious mark of her inheritance from her mother. One day, if she grew out of that coltish, abrupt, unselfconscious grace, she might be conventionally beautiful, with those long green eyes: but Alathea had never, ever been concerned with her appearance. Thomazine, looking at the shabby yet striking child walking towards her with some chance-met companion in tow, realised that with luck her daughter might turn out to be one of those fortunate women who would not have to.

She got to her feet, dusting off earth, and surveyed Alathea's latest stray: people, children and animals somehow tended to attach themselves to her, just as Mab and her baby sister Sophie and her cousin Eleanor had done. This was a boy a little older, quietly but expensively dressed, travel-stained, with a fairly ordinary horse, but every line of that high-bred, aristocratic young face spoke 'Quality'. He bowed, and introductions were exchanged, and Thomazine knew, as soon as she heard his name, who he must be. Doubtless he had a good reason for not inflicting his rank on Alathea, and she would not give away his secret. Smiling, she indicated the horse. 'And so my graceless daughter has invited you to partake of my elderflower wine? You're a brave one to accept: the family swears it was my brewing that finally carried off Lady Penelope Hervey last year. You'd best come in –

and tie your horse to the rose-tree, it won't matter if he eats any of it.'

'It's a lie,' said Alathea to John as they passed under the carved arched doorway. 'Lady Penelope never drank any of Mother's wine – she never came to Goldhayes, she used to sit in state at Hengrave Hall and wait for all the County to go to her and play bowls, and if people weren't careful she'd have a prospective husband or wife waiting for them as well. Father used to call it the Marriage Mart.'

'And I went there only rarely,' said Thomazine, laughter in her voice. 'I've never been very good at bowls and I might have been tempted to apply Henry Jermyn's solution to the problem.'

'He put moles on the bowling green,' Alathea explained to John, with satisfaction. 'Henry Jermyn's in the Duke of York's household now, and he's trying to get a place for Hugh, who's my uncle except that he doesn't seem like an uncle because he's only five years older than me . . . mind your feet!'

The Hall at Ashcott had never been altered since the medieval year it was built. Hopelessly old-fashioned, it was two storeys high, cold, musty and echoing, with screens, a passage and stairs at one end and a door at the other. 'Don't worry,' said Alathea, as he avoided the pile of trestles stacked against the screens and followed her through the door at the foot of the stairs. 'The masons have been engaged and it's all going to be altered. It's like living in a barn at the moment. Oh, how I *wish* we were back at Goldhayes!'

Thomazine Heron had stopped to give instructions to a pert, neat little maidservant. John wondered, rather bemused by this cheerful informal hospitality, how that small, spare, shabby woman, all brown, brown hair, brown eyes, brown skin and a slightly beaky nose like a hedgerow bird, could ever have given birth to the tall fair child by his side. Then they entered a wide parlour that seemed to hold, at his first startled gaze, more books than he had ever seen before. On the floor, on the two heavy old-fashioned court-cupboards on either side of the hearth, on the window-sill, in tottering piles balanced precariously on the settle . . . there must have been hundreds. In the middle, two girls, one about Alathea's age and the other a tiny dark-haired child of three or four, were apparently engaged in sorting them, in a sea of leather and gilt covers, bits of binding, torn pages, and dust. They jumped up as Thomazine and the children entered, and the elder girl, mousy-haired and regrettably plain, said, 'We've nearly finished the poetry books, Mother.'

Sufficiently awed to forget all else, John's hands and eyes were pulled irresistably towards the piled volumes, a world of knowledge, of love, of arts and dreams in each one. There was Shakespeare, probably all the plays and the Sonnets as well, Donne and Spenser and Jonson, Wyatt and Chaucer, Lovelace and Cowley and Waller: and beside this mound, a still greater one of music books, all with the worn look of things much loved and used. As if of their own accord his hands picked up the Shakespeare Sonnets and opened it at random: the words on the page leapt to his eye and joined all the chaotic jumble of other men's songs inside his head:

Two loves I have of comfort and despair
Which like two spirits do suggest me still . . .

Someone was talking: a hand, thin and freckled, was laid on his sleeve. 'I said, elderflower wine or beer?' Alathea's voice repeated, half-way between laughter and exasperation. 'You're as bad as Math.'

'The wine, please,' John said, putting the book hastily down.

Alathea grinned at him. 'Math is my younger brother, one of them, he's ten and he's never seen without his nose in a book, he even reads when he rides up to Deddington. Sit down, there's a space on the settle, Mother's moved some of the books, and that's Nell, my cousin Nell, she's an orphan and she lives with us, she always has, and *that*,' said his friend with deepening exasperation, 'is my little sister Sophie. Make your curtsey, infant.'

The tiny child, all glowing cheeks and shiny black hair and dancing smoky eyes, sank into a wobble of a curtsey, giggled, and sat down. At once Mab bounced up and put a paw on her shoulder: the infant pushed her away, stood up, and with commendable determination tried again, this time with much greater success. All the time her eyes were fixed meltingly on John's face, and he realised with amusement that here was a child destined to be the scourge of the opposite sex, a taking little thing who was already, apparently, well aware of her attractions. Without a trace of the shyness he might have expected, she rose and trotted over. 'What's your name?'

'John Wilmot, at your service, Mistress Sophie,' he said, joining in the game with an elegant bow.

In her forthright fashion Alathea caught his arm. 'Don't encourage the little minx, she makes eyes at anything in breeches and she's only just four. Sophie! Go and sit on that stool *now*.'

With a pained look at her sister, and a flutter of very long dark eyelashes for John's benefit, the infant flirt meekly crossed to the stool and sat down. He accepted the cup of cool clear liquid that Alathea's mother held out to him, and took his place on the cleared settle. The elderflower wine was delicious, fragrant and refreshing, a little like fine Rhenish and yet with a flowery flavour all its own, that spoke eloquently of England and summer. Politely, Mistress Heron showed an interest in him: where was he going? Was he at Oxford? Which college? She had little knowledge of Wadham, her father had been a Christchurch man himself, but her family had a house in Pennyfarthing Street and she knew Oxford very well: if he was ever in that part of the city he must make himself known to the Widow Gooch, an old family friend who kept the house for them. 'For her October is the best in all the town,' Alathea's mother explained: and John answered courteously that he would be delighted to do so.

And that delight was not entirely feigned, for these four Herons had already cast their spell over him, and for the afternoon he was enchanted. Mistress Heron was an amusing, individual woman, with a dry direct style of speech and wide interests: her talk ranged through poetry, plays and music to politics and affairs of state, and although he had thought himself well-informed from all those hot smoky candle-lit nights in the taverns, listening to the students and fellows, he was stretched to the limit to keep pace with her. And though he was fairly sure that she knew his identity, she took care never to betray it. Alathea, whose startling looks must descend almost wholly from her absent father, joined in impulsively with anecdotes or comments, and once or twice the little Sophie tried to draw attention to herself with some pert childish remark: but the cousin Nell, her lank mousy hair almost hiding her face, remained completely silent. The male members of the family, he learned, were out on some excursion to Deddington Market, and he commented idly that it was the crowds and press in that town that had caused him to make such a wide detour, and so come upon Alathea on the sheepwalks above Ashcott. 'And I'll remember it all my life,' he added, his habitual circumspection entirely evaporated in the charm of this conversation, 'for she was kind enough to draw my portrait, and though I know very little about such arts, Mistress Heron, I'd say she could one day make a living at it.'

He was astonished at the reaction his casual praise received. Alathea gave a gasp and turned her clear face towards his with a look of such agonised, betrayed reproach that he flinched: Nell jerked upright, roused from her daydream at last: and Alathea's mother said in total disbelief, 'She *drew*? She drew your portrait? But . . . but I thought you'd cast all that aside long ago.'

'No . . . no, I didn't,' said the child, miserably. 'I was drawing Ashcott, and Master Wilmot all but fell over me, and we talked for a little . . . '

'She showed me the pictures she had done,' said John, still utterly bewildered. Surely a pleasant, intelligent woman such as Mistress Heron would not deliberately crush this flowering talent in her own daughter? But if that were not the case, why had Alathea hidden her art for so long? His mind racing, he went on. 'And I thought they were good, very good, and I asked if she could draw me. And she did. Would you like to see it, Mistress Heron?'

Alathea, her face flushed, looked close to tears. Her mother, after one very sharp glance at her, turned to John. 'Yes, indeed I would, Master Wilmot, very much indeed.'

He drew the rectangle of paper from within his doublet, unfolded it and passed it to her. She took it in her brown, still earth-stained hands and stared at it for a long moment: the quiet in the little book-filled room was so intense that he could hear the birdcalls outside, and Alathea's disordered breathing as she fought for control. The silence dragged on, seemingly for ever, and then Thomazine Heron raised her head. Her eyes, he was unhappy to see, were brilliant with emotion. She said, her voice very low, 'Oh, Thea, why didn't you *say*?'

'I couldn't,' said Alathea, almost as quietly. 'You know why . . . I *couldn't*. So I did it in secret.'

'I knew,' said Nell, speaking for the first time. 'She told *me* . . . she made me swear never to tell anyone else.'

'But there was no need,' Thomazine Heron said, with a quick casual brush of hand across eyes that did not deceive the observant John. 'No need, at all, ever, to hide that kind of light under a bushel of secrecy. Master Wilmot, you were right, it *is* good, very good . . . too like you for your ease, I suspect.' She grinned at him, preserving her cheerful front, but he could sense her distress. 'Thea . . . he said there were others . . . can I see?'

There was a long silence. Alathea, by no means as experienced in dissimulation as her mother, had two shiny tear-tracks tracing a clean path down her rather grubby face. She stared unhappily into her mother's eyes while John wondered anew at the obvious undercurrents between them, private family concerns that he could not hope to understand: and then, with that abrupt gesture, pulled the book of drawings from the sagging, capacious pocket of her apron and thrust it into Mistress Heron's hands.

And with that, almost all the fraught tension in the air fell away. Nell got up and came to look: Sophie clambered on to the settle with the aid of a fistful of her mother's skirts and leaned heavily over her arm. Even John, though he had seen them all before, was quick to follow, and feast his eyes again on the swift accurate portraits that had flowed from Alathea's pens and chalks. There was Sophie, her charmingly angelic little face given the lie by those mischievous, sideways-sliding eyes: Nell, in a plain coif which did not suit her wide bony countenance and large eyes, smiling feebly: Mistress Heron, obviously sketched unawares and from a distance, sewing, every brief penline speaking eloquently of her absorbed concentration. There were others he did not know, two fair-haired boys, one dreamy, the other bold and vigorous, who must be her brothers Matthew and Edmund, and an ancient witch-like lady with, obviously, a spry and malicious sense of humour, whose picture provoked delighted comment from Mistress Heron. 'The Widow Gooch! Her to the life, as well – when did you draw her?'

'When we went to Oxford last, and you went shopping, and I stayed behind,' said Alathea, her shy abruptness still evident.

Thomazine gave a wry shrug. 'Oh, Thea, I wish you had said . . . I could have kept your secret as well as all these.'

Alathea stared at the floor: surreptitiously, a hand smeared across her face. 'I'm sorry,' she said at last. 'You know why I couldn't, except in secret . . . and I can't give it up, I can't stop drawing, I love it, and, oh, Mother, do you think I *could* make a living at it? Like Mistress Beale?'

There was an astonished silence. Thomazine Heron, her eyebrows raised, stared long at her daughter in amused disbelief. 'Mistress Beale was taught to paint by her father, she has a husband to help and support her, and pay for her materials, a house in London where she can paint and plenty of people she knows from Suffolk to come and be painted by her, just as we were. There's no one in this family who can draw, who can teach you: not even Kit is good enough, on this evidence. How are you going to learn all the business of painting? There's so much knowledge and labour involved, stretching canvas, grinding colours, mixing paint: you saw that, when your father and I sat to Mistress Beale last year.'

'I know,' said Alathea. 'She let me watch everything. I . . . I talked to her, I helped her . . . I thought that if I practised hard enough, if I drew as much as I could . . . perhaps one day I could persuade her to teach me, if she thought I was good enough.' The memory came back to her as she spoke: the wide light room at the top of the Beales' lodgings off Fleet Street, the thick tangy smells of paint and linseed oil, Mistress Beale's soft round face and curly light-brown hair, her kindness in welcoming the enthralled Alathea, and listening, and answering her eager questions in that quiet voice with the so-familiar Suffolk accent, the rising note at the end of each sentence, that contrasted very oddly with the squawking London sounds outside. They had been in London, she and her parents, to visit her Aunt Lucy and Uncle Daniel Ashley, who lived in Fleet Street; Master Ashley had his clockmaker's workshop there, and the Beales were just around the corner. Aunt Lucy had had her portrait done, and her children's, and had suggested that Alathea's parents do the same. And Alathea, free of Kit's jealous, malicious, watchful gaze, had gone with them to the sittings, and seen that a woman could, and did, paint with freedom and talent, and make money from it. She had not had the confidence to speak of her hopes to Mistress Beale, but she knew that she would be favourably received, should she ever return to the lodgings in Hinde Court.

'That's something we'll have to talk about, and soon,' said Thomazine, smiling.

Alathea looked at her mother, and suddenly delight took wings on her face, and she flung her arms around her. 'You will? You won't just say no? You'll think about it, you'll talk about it? Oh, thank you, thank you!'

In her exuberance she jogged her mother's arm and the book of drawings slid off Thomazine's lap. The loose bindings, abused beyond endurance, finally gave way, and in a dozen different directions, the pages spun across the smooth wooden floor. With a cry of dismay, Alathea plunged after them: and the door opened.

John, gazing, thought it was like some scene in a play, the guilty felons caught in the act, frozen with horror at the entry of Justice and Constable: except that it was not the minions of the Law that entered now, but a tall, dark young man he instantly recognised from the drawing. The quick malicious eyes, a vivid, passionate and uncomfortable blue, took in all the implications of the little scene in a second or two, and then, abruptly, Alathea's half-brother Kit flung himself back out of the doorway. His loud angry footsteps could be heard retreating down the passage: an exchange of voices at a distance: and then silence.

'Oh dear,' said Thomazine, with a mild ruefulness that did not quite conceal her real concern. 'That was rather unfortunate.' She glanced at John, standing bewildered beside her, and added in explanation, 'That was my eldest son, Kit. He is sometimes a trifle . . . abrupt in his moods, please forgive him.'

Alathea, her hands full of drawings, took more from Nell and put them tenderly on the mantelshelf. She looked utterly defeated. Her mother said quickly, 'It's all right, chicken. He was bound to have found out sooner or later; and he's a grown man now, he can bear some competition from his little sister. Your father and I will make him see sense.'

'You don't understand,' Alathea whispered miserably. 'You don't really know what he's like . . . how he can be . . . it *isn't* all right, and nothing you can do can make it!'

'We will find a way,' her mother assured her urgently. 'We *will*, I promise you. I'll talk to your father tonight, and when he's seen your drawings, when he's seen what you can do, he'll agree with me . . . Thea, listen, you must go on drawing because you are *good*, I don't know where your gift comes from but most assuredly you have it in abundance: and a gift is not to be spurned or cast aside, or wasted: it is to be *used*, for your joy and others', and Francis and I will do all we can to help. Understand? We are your friends, Thea, not your enemies.'

'*You* weren't my enemy,' said Alathea.

Thomazine sighed. 'I know. But nothing is impossible: one day you might even make your living at it, as Master Wilmot suggested, and nothing would delight me more. But you need a great deal of will and determination, chick: not that you could have less than a great deal, with your heritage.'

' "No Surrender",' said Alathea. She looked suddenly much happier: a beleaguered soldier assured at last of adequate reinforcements. 'That's the family motto, John,' she added, turning to him. 'And none of us ever have. The undefeated Herons, that's us! And keep my drawing safe, won't you, and don't forget what I promised – one day I'll paint you properly, when I'm a famous artist, and I'll make no charge at all!'

He judged it then a good time to take his leave, for he had still to see Adderbury, and he must be back at Oxford before dark. Also, he was not at all sure that he wished to see the mysterious, ominous Kit again: for Alathea's sake, he might be tempted to say too much of what he thought. And it was plain that in some way mother and daughter had rediscovered each other, and needed time to explore new ground between them, and talk over the day's events. He said goodbye to Nell and Sophie, who flashed her smoky eyes at him and dimpled prettily: and to Alathea and her mother, in the doorway of Ashcott, he gave a longer farewell.

'Thank you, Master Wilmot,' Thomazine Heron said. 'Chance meetings are sometimes most fortunate, and this one more than many; for I now know Alathea's secret, and I think we're all the better for it. And if you should ever come this way again, ride down and see us: you'll always be welcome.' She smiled, and added softly, 'And I much admire your tact, my lord: it's a rare thing, and much undervalued, to be modest. I thank you.'

'See you in London, in ten years' time!' said Alathea, grinning up at him as he sat his hired horse. The sun sparkled in her pale hair, and in her soft freckled face showed the ghost of the woman she would be then. 'Keep my portrait safe, and don't lose it, because I won't paint you for nothing without it!'

'I won't lose it, ever,' he said; and farewells were exchanged at last, and with reluctance he turned the horse and rode slowly away from Ashcott, up the long hill under the marching elms to the Deddington Road. He looked back, once, and they were still there, watching, two figures planted in his memory then for all time, the small brown woman and her strange and gifted daughted close together by the door of the ancient house. And then resolutely he cast the extraordinary events of the afternoon from him, and set his face towards the real world, that somehow for himself, as well as for Alathea and her family, would never be the same again.

'Look,' said Thomazine Heron to her husband, Francis, and passed over the portrait of herself, done when sewing.

John Wilmot, second Earl of Rochester, had been gone some hours now, and Ashcott was settling down for the night. The younger children, Sophie and the boisterous Edmund, aged six, were in bed and the elder three, Alathea, Matthew and Nell, were hunched at the other end of the West Parlour over a makeshift card table made of books with a rug thrown over, playing three-handed whist. In his lighter humours, Kit would normally have made a fourth; but since the moment when he had returned from Deddington ahead of the others, and seen Alathea's secret inadvertently revealed, no one at Ashcott had laid eyes on him. At the back of Thomazine's mind was the nagging, brooding, threatening thought that soon a storm would blow up from that quarter: and when Kit's volatile moods turned black, she knew from bitter experience how extremely unpleasant life could become for all of them.

But for now it was calm, and the warm summer dusk was drifting with the moths in through the open windows, kept at bay by the few yellow candles placed strategically around the little book-piled room. The children muttered and laughed over the game, relaxed and carefree, and with an inward sigh of resignation she pushed the painful thought of her eldest child to the back of her mind and devoted her attention to the new and fascinating problem of Alathea.

Francis Heron studied his daughter's picture of his wife with a faint, amused smile on his face. The years had treated him a good deal more kindly than his elder brother, Simon, Lord Bradfield, who was forty-one and looked fifty. His long Heron face with its wide mouth and shadowy green eyes had changed little since he and Thomazine had first fallen in love, nearly twenty years ago, when they had been scarcely more than children and full of joyous illusion and hope for the future. That future had held pain, grief, separation, bereavement for them both, during the years of Civil War: thinking him dead, Thomazine had married, briefly and unhappily, her cousin Sir Dominic Drakelon, and Kit was the child of that disastrous union. Only after Sir Dominic's death, when England once more had relapsed into a somewhat uneasy peace, had Francis and Thomazine at last been able to marry, after nine long years of loving: and the eleven succeeding years of their marriage, despite the infant deaths of two of their children, had been as quiet, secure and utterly happy as ships safely harboured after long storm and peril. Even the forced move to Ashcott, after Francis's quarrel with his brother, had not seriously disturbed the peace and delight they found still in each other and in their children, and as she studied his face, Thomazine felt again the same surge of love and desire she had first known as a girl of sixteen, before the war: unseemly, some might think, in a mature wife and mother now turned thirty-five.

'You're right,' Francis said softly. 'She *is* good, remarkably good . . . where does it come from? The only person in the family who's ever been able to draw was Dominic: so you'd think the obvious artist would be Kit.'

'And that's precisely what Kit thinks. Oh, he's dabbled in it, he likes to play the limner, but his talents lie elsewhere – if he'd only practise as he should, his music would be outstanding, I've hardly heard his like on the lute.'

'He has that from you,' Francis said, smiling. 'I never thought music was Dominic's forte.'

'It wasn't: he was all but tone deaf and couldn't play a note on any instrument. But he *was* good at drawing, he had a talent for portraits, and I don't doubt Kit feels that because of that, because his father drew well, he ought to be just as good if not better. I can understand how he feels, I can see that he's always at the back of his mind been jealous of Alathea. She supplanted him in my affections, after all, and although I did my best to hide how much I cared for her, I never succeeded very well. And now, for him to discover that not only has she entered *his* field, but that she is far better, even now . . . oh, I can see *why* he is jealous, but I can't condone it . . . and I can't forget her face either, when he burst in. She looked like a miserable, hunted criminal, not our brave Alathea . . . she's terrified of him, and that's why she's kept it a secret all this time.'

'Kept it very well, too,' said Francis reminiscently. 'She used to scribble and doodle all the time a few years ago, didn't she? And then it seemed to stop – presumably because Kit was making life unpleasant for her. But she must have been very clever to have done this without your knowing.'

'She had the paper and chalk hidden behind a book, apparently.' Thomazine caught his eye and grinned. 'She's not without invention, is she? And there are others that she's done, of the children, Martha, villagers, Mistress Gooch, Kit – she must have been exceptionally devious for that one – people at Goldhayes . . . and all quite out of the common run, absolutely true to themselves and to life, like this . . . I'll persuade her to show them to you tomorrow, she doesn't even know I kept this one.'

'But it makes me feel most uncharacteristically humble,' Francis said reflectively. 'Don't you feel the same? That we two with all our heritage and our faults should have produced out of the blue a child with such a gift. And it also makes me worried for her future. The world is not kind to ladies with original minds and extraordinary talents, as you have found yourself. And if she decides, ever, to go her own way and devote herself to her art, she'll have a hard time of it. Mary Beale has friends and a husband to support her, but I have a feeling that Alathea is the single-minded sort and will be determined to fight on her own without the distractions of running a household. Or, of course, she may change her mind and beg to be married to her true love at sixteen.' He glanced at his wife, who had done just that, and added, smiling, 'I hope somehow that she will not. It would be criminal to waste it, don't you think? Perhaps Mistress Beale would undertake to teach her. She'd be a brave lady if she did, for lovely though our Thea is, she's as blunt-spoken as her mother, and if she doesn't like what she's told to do, she'll say it plain. But in a few years' time, if she's still set on it, perhaps we can take her to stay with Dan and Lucy and she can renew her acquaintance with Mistress Beale. Or maybe we're all wrong and she's really nothing out of the common run at all.'

'In which case,' said Thomazine tartly, 'Kit is no more than mediocre.' She had a twinge of guilt as she said it: all his life she had felt little else for her eldest son but that. She had abandoned her husband and Kit, one month old, after less than a year of marriage, and run away to Francis: and when the hated Dominic's death had sent Kit back to her, he had been a sullen, spoiled, beautiful brat of four, his emotions warped and twisted by adult pressures he could not understand. Eventually she had won him over, only to betray his trust and love by marrying Francis and bearing other children to displace her eldest son. She could feel sorrow for Kit, and guilt, and regret; but love was harder, and she knew that the lack of it, and his unconscious sensitivity to its absence, was the cause of all the trouble.

But it could not be altered, nor could his nature now be changed: and her beloved Alathea had been caught up in it, an innocent victim of a sorry chain of deceit and lust and guilt that had begun twenty-five years ago at Goldhayes, when the young Dominic Drakelon had first beheld Thomazine Heron, aged ten, and taken a fancy to her, and asked his parents to arrange a betrothal with her. Ironically, their acquaintance had begun with his drawing her portrait unawares; she had it still, a reminder of the man who had married her by trickery and parted her from her lover, Francis.

But Kit was a more potent reminder by far, being now, at close on seventeen, the image of his father at that age, black-haired, blue-eyed, vigorous and vivid and handsome, a charming and cultured companion in his good moods, a disturbed and malicious devil too frequently for comfort. She wondered where he was now: sulking somewhere doubtless, and she felt again the guilt that she did not love, did not even really like, her first-born son.

It was full dark when, their games ended and their goodnights to their parents said, the three children left the parlour and made their way up to their chambers by the fitful light of Nell's guttering candle. Ashcott boasted a cook, grooms and farmworkers and kitchenmaids, as well as Thomazine's personal maid Martha Squirrell, but the children had no nurse now: she had been left behind, with much else, at Goldhayes. So there was no one to undress them or tell them stories, no reproving Suffolk voice to scold them for leaving clothes on the floor; and no one to prevent Sir Christopher Drakelon, third Baronet, from lying in wait for his sister in the chamber she shared with the two other girls.

When she entered, quietly so as not to wake the slumbering Sophie, he was sitting in the stone window seat, the cold night air coiling his black hair, two cushions propped comfortably against his back. Nell, startled, gave a squawk of panic and nearly dropped the candle; Alathea, despite the sudden lurch of her heart, was determined to stand her ground. The approval and praise she had earned that afternoon had greatly enhanced her confidence, and with the memory of her mother's wondering face and John Wilmot's delight, she felt far better protected from his malice. 'What are you doing here?'

'Waiting for you,' said Kit. Nell, after one frantic glance at his face, had begun to cry silently: pathetic tears were her usual answer to a situation which frightened or bewildered her. There was no sound from the small hump in the bed that was Sophie, quiet for once. Alathea was alone, unshielded from the infinity of malevolence she saw in her half-brother's blue eyes, but her pride would not allow her to retreat.

'Well, I'm here,' she said belligerently. 'Hurry up and say whatever it is you want to say and then go, we're tired and we want to get to bed.'

'Did you do these?' Kit demanded, and to Alathea's horror brought out her precious drawings from behind his back. She had thought them safely hidden within the clothes-press, concealed between the scented, carefully folded layers of their best satin dresses, but Kit had obviously had ample opportunity to poke and pry to his heart's content.

For what seemed like eternity, she stared at him as he flicked through the loose pages, the dreadful, familiar little sneer curling his lips: and her voice, when it came, was a meek shadow of her earlier, angry tones. 'Yes, they're mine. Can I have them back, Kit? Please?'

'Perhaps,' he said. 'Not very good, are they, little sister?'

'That's not what Mother said,' Alathea whispered. 'She thought they were good.'

'Well, she was wrong. Anyone with an eye to see can tell that you've no knowledge of perspective, nor anatomy –'

'Neither have you!' Alathea retorted, feeling her confidence seep back, a slow, comforting trickle of gratifying memory. 'Now can I have my drawings back?'

'Not yet, little sister, not yet. You really can't catch a likeness, can you? With a bit of practice I suppose you might just manage it, but of course you won't get much more practice: with all the work to be done here there's no time to doodle, is there? All the cooking and cleaning and sewing, and then when you're married no husband in his senses would approve of *this* . . . I should give it up now, little sister, there's no future in it.'

'Well, I'm *not* giving up, ever, and certainly not on your say-so!'

'Oh, aren't you? You're only a girl, after all, you ought to do as I say. You'll have to do as your husband says, when you get married, so it's as well to practise now – and I'm telling you give up this silly scribbling now, there's no sense in it.'

'I won't,' said Alathea. 'And who said I was going to get married? I'm not going to get married, ever, if it means just doing what my husband tells me to do – I want to be free, I want to go to London and learn painting from Mistress Beale and one day I'll make a living at it, you see if I don't!'

Kit laughed, a sarcastic, jeering sound that raised Alathea's helpless, desperate rage to boiling point. 'Mistress Beale? Mistress Beale? Whatever makes you think Mistress Beale will even consider you, you stupid little girl?'

'I'll show her my drawings, they're good enough to persuade her,' Alathea said furiously. 'Now give them *here*!'

'Persuade Mistress Beale? With these? Not very likely, I'm afraid,' Kit said, smiling mockingly, and his hands tightened on the thick paper. 'No, little sister, *this* is all these are good for.'

The thin pale hands, artist's hands, clenched again, twisted and tore. Alathea screamed with anguish as her drawings were ripped viciously apart again and again, with a furious passion that gave the lie to his shallow sneering mockery. 'Oh, no, no!' Nell cried, and burst into fresh tears as Kit, with a contemptuous, throw-away gesture, opened his hands and let the fragments drift to the floor, floating and fluttering, twisting gently in the flickering light of the candle; a dream torn with them.

And at the sight of Kit's satisfied, assured face, secure in his victory, something inside Alathea's mind broke, and flung off all restraint. All the hidden hatred, the years of torment, the sneering contempt with which he had treated her, burst to the surface. Suddenly, all she wanted to do was to hurt, to injure, to wipe the smile off that loathed face, and there was only one way she could do it. Without even really thinking about it, she gave a moan of rage and launched herself at him, kicking, scratching, hitting, biting, without any science but with a strength doubled by grief and fury: and for a moment Kit, incredulous, staggered under the impact of her attack. She had the utter satisfaction of seeing her nails rake across his cheek, and the bright blood spring out in their track. Behind her people were screaming, someone cried her name, but she was beyond noticing anything but the wonderful, exhilarating feel of her fists hitting Kit's face, chest, neck . . . And then she felt her wrists grasped, saw the madness in his eyes, a killing madness, and his free hand raised to strike her.

'Kit.' It was her father's voice, low and sure and confident of its authority. 'Kit. Let her go. Now.'

Alathea began to shake, all her rage evaporated into terror. Someone behind her, Nell probably, was snivelling. Kit's eyes held hers still, their dreadful vivid blue boring implacably into her soul, sucking out all her will, her resistance, her determination, her gift. He had won, he had destroyed her drawings, herself, her individuality. Surely all that was left now for her, at the age of eleven, was the meek wifehood that would be no threat to him.

'I said, let her go,' Francis repeated, a good deal closer. Alathea could see him reflected, clear and tiny, in Kit's glaring eyes. She was abruptly aware that all feeling in her hands had gone, that her wrists hurt where his hands gripped her. An involuntary whimper escaped her as she tried in vain to move her fingers. 'Let her go,' her father said, for the third time, and quietest of all: a sign of danger.

And suddenly Kit, who knew that sign as well, obeyed his stepfather. With a gesture of contempt, he tossed his sister aside and flung himself past his family to disappear through the door.

It was a long time before its usual night-time calm overtook Ashcott again – the children asleep, Alathea only after much hopeless, defeated sobbing; Kit vanished, none knew where; and Thomazine and Francis alone at last in their draughty stone-built chamber above the book-crowded parlour.

Alathea's mother was brushing out her hair, a difficult task at the best of times to coax the bristles through the thick cloudy tangle of brown locks, but tonight it seemed to have taken on a malevolent life of its own and snarled and twisted around her fingers. Francis got off the bed and came to stand behind her. He took the little silver brush from her hand and began to smooth down the wild hair at the back of her head with long, gentle strokes. They had the desired, calming effect: Thomazine felt the tension ebb away and a feeling of drowsy peace soaking through her body. She said thoughtfully, 'What shall we do with them?'

'Keep them apart,' Francis said promptly. Under his practised, rhythmic brushing, Thomazine's hair began to smooth and straighten, gathering gloss and colour in the soft light of the candles. It was almost possible to believe that nothing unusual had happened that evening, but no effort of will, no enchantment of oblivion, could ever erase the dreadful moment when she had thought that Kit would kill her daughter: and for what reason, save his own tormented, twisted jealousy?

'Keep them apart? I can see the sense of that,' she said slowly, 'but how? I know Kit has gone off to sulk somewhere, that's always been his way, but he'll be back tomorrow, large as life, and I can't bear . . . oh, Francis, I can't bear to see her face looking at him like that, like a little frightened rabbit when it sees a fox . . . not Alathea . . . he'll break her heart and her spirit if it goes on like this.'

'Well, it won't,' Francis said, his brushing moving now to the side of her head, stroking out the tangles. 'We have two people to think of – Alathea, who has a talent to be nursed and nourished, who is loved and knows it . . . and Kit, who has no such gift, or none that he will accept, and does not feel sure of any love.'

'And so?'

'And so we keep Kit, perhaps encourage him to Oxford or Gray's Inn in a little while – and send Alathea to London.'

Thomazine jerked round to face him, her dark eyes wide with surprise. 'Send Thea to London? Why? Why send her away?'

'Because she can stay with Lucy, Lucy will be delighted to have her. And have you forgotten, Mistress Beale is just around the corner? Alathea won't have forgotten.'

Thomazine took a deep breath. 'So . . . you're saying that if we send her to London she'll be glad? She won't see it as a punishment?'

'I doubt it, particularly if we explain about Mistress Beale. And Kit won't feel threatened any more; especially if we *don't* explain about Mistress Beale to him. I don't think Alathea would crow about it, that's not in her nature at all. She's mature enough to keep quiet, and to understand the need for it. Sometimes, owd gal, it is better to let go at the right time than to hold on to people for too long . . . do you remember when I was sent to Scotland, when I was little older than Thea is now? It was the best thing that could have happened to me, it gave me experiences that have influenced the course of my life, and I made a great friend I have still.'

'Yes,' said Thomazine, her dry tone concealing her distress, 'but your father disliked you and your mother didn't care. I most emphatically *do*.' Tears sparkled suddenly in her eyes, and she swallowed. 'I care most desperately for her, she means so much to me, and to you, I don't want to do the wrong thing – and from the purely selfish point of view, I don't *want* to let her go. She's only just eleven, after all, and that's a trifle young, to be decided on your life's path.'

'But not everyone has their route mapped out for them so clear,' Francis said softly. 'I managed to make sense of some of those poor mangled pieces of paper – come and look.'

He had laid the crumpled fragments on the heavy brocade of the counterpane, and carefully joined four sections together: and there, looking up at them with that merry, mischievous sidelong glance, was Sophie. Thomazine drew in her breath sharply, and was silent, an enormous rush of emotion overwhelming her, just as it had done when she saw the portrait of John Wilmot, that afternoon. It was the sort of feeling that she usually experienced on hearing a piece of music played perfectly, or on seeing the sweet sleek movements of a lovely horse running free. And in a sense, this gift was her creation, hers and Francis's, and it seemed so utterly right that something so special should have sprung from the first, joyous, delightful union of their love.

'You are right,' said Thomazine Heron, turning to smile at her husband. 'We must find the strength to let her go – and not count the cost to ourselves.'

CHAPTER TWO

Mary Beale

The tender leaves of hope . . .
(Shakespeare, *Henry VIII*)

The chief thing that struck Alathea about the great and glorious City of London was the noise. Not the smell, though that was intrusive enough, even to someone inured to the reek of farmyard and midden, but the pandemonium: horses and carts and carriages, hooves and wheels striking stone, the bawl and shriek of street vendors crying their wares in voices undiminished by daylong use, and the general hubbub of talk and activity, frantic rush and bustle, of thousands of people all urgently intent upon their own business. She had been to London twice before, but as part of her whole family, shielded and supported; now, there was only her father beside her, his hand on her shoulder, guiding her through the press, with a hired man behind carrying her box. Two days' journey away was Ashcott, yellow stone and sleepy cows and, above all, the deep hot silence of summer countryside, and her mother, wryly smiling, being sparing with her advice, the boys excited, Edmund demanding a real sword of his father (he was most unlikely to get it), and Math, more quietly, requesting books; and Sophie, pirouetting in the sunshine, the light flashing on her glossy curls and her best red satin dress, donned in honour of the occasion and glowing against the warm stone walls like a flag. Nell, heartbroken at being left behind, had been snivelling miserably into a handkerchief, and Alathea had been guiltily aware that she only need ask to have Nell come too. She was fond of her cousin, used to having her shadow forever trailing after her, faithfully and loyally as Mab, and she would miss her friend and ally, but this journey to London was *hers*, and the chance to go to Mistress Beale with her drawings was something she somehow did not wish to share with Nell.

In the fortnight between Kit's destruction of most of her tiny, precious stock of portraits, and that last moment of leavetaking, she had tried to build up a body of work to show Mistress Beale, taking advantage of the end of secrecy. But it had not been the same, and she had still the sullen, silent Kit to evade. He had, rather gracelessly, apologised for his actions the next morning, and had avoided verbal contact with her ever since. Often, though, she had raised her eyes from book or drawing or sewing, to see his sombre gaze fixed on her. She sensed that his behaviour had disturbed him as much as it had her, and though at first she felt prompted to overtures of peace, her fear of him soon proved the greater, and she ignored him as best she could.

He had not been with the rest at the door of Ashcott to wave her goodbye, and the greater part of her was glad.

So, she was free, free of Nell, free of Kit, free of the boys and Sophie, and much though she loved them, they were not part of this adventure, for she was going alone to stay with Aunt Lucy and Uncle Dan and their children in the house full of clocks on Fleet Street and perhaps (she resolutely would not count her chickens before hatching), gaining the approval and even the tuition of Mistress Mary Beale.

The strange London faces pushed past her, and because faces were her stock-in-trade, she noticed them all: the confident brisk bully-boy looks of tradesmen and merchants, the sharp crop-haired 'prentice boys, white-faced nimble children, dirty, bare-foot and old before their time. Beggars shrieked and whined, their appeals for alms rising even above the noise of the street, and their expressions aroused in her a curious, disturbing mixture of pity and fear. That was also the reality of London, but it was not part of her dream.

But her father gave to them. It was the subject of many wry, exasperated family jokes, his generosity to the poor, and his care of the humbler tenants of Goldhayes had been one of the causes of his quarrel with his brother. Alathea, with a child's shuffling embarrassment, had perforce to wait while largesse was distributed. Her father had an active conscience that had nothing to do with Christian charity and a great deal to do with his concern for natural justice. He had been a Leveller in his youth, and a Corporal in one of the New Model Army's most egalitarian regiments, and increasing years and responsibilities had not blunted his ideals. That side of him was one that she loved, but not here, now, in London, delaying the moment when they would arrive at Daniel Ashley's house in Fleet Street.

It was a long walk through the smelly, noisy, crowded streets from the inn in Holborn where they had left the horses on seeing the volume of traffic all about. No doubt of it, the Restoration of the King and all his Court in Whitehall had greatly increased business in the City, and Alathea, buoyed up with excitement and impatience, saw in the faces that jostled past her, to her vivid imagination so much more hopeful and happy than in the drear days of Oliver and Tumbledown Dick, a bright mirror of her own joyous exuberance.

'If we'd taken a coach, we'd have been there no sooner,' her father said above the bawl of a woman selling lavender. He took his daughter's arm and steered her briskly past a huddle of gawping apprentices round a scurrilous ballad-monger. 'The only reason for riding in a coach in these streets is to make a fuss and a show, and since we're not interested in advertising money and quality we don't possess, I reckoned we'd do without and walk like everyone else . . . you don't mind that, maw?'

It was a long time since he had called her that, the Suffolk endearment proper for a little girl. She should have felt it beneath her, but the word only served to remind her that soon, probably tomorrow, she would be saying goodbye to him, her last link with her family, and going into the future without any of the enveloping, informal, loving, friendly support that had been hers and her brothers' and Sophie's, all their lives long. She set her shoulders and grinned up at him, a cheerful, sunny smile that was the match of his own. 'Of course I don't mind,' said Alathea Heron steadfastly. 'Is it *very* much further?'

'No, not at all. You see the end of this, which is Fetter Lane? That's Fleet Street, running across there, we'll turn left and it's only a few doors along. Remember the sign?'

'An ash tree, for Ashley,' said Alathea, and a picture of the painted sign, fresh and green in the sun of last summer, danced into her mind. She gave a skip of pure joy and adventure, her whole self bursting with excitement, and the afternoon light turned her hair to glowing, spun silver. More than one male head had turned to look, as they walked down Fetter Lane, and Francis Heron wondered anew if they were doing right, to launch this precious, innocent, talented child into the disease and squalor and debauchery of modern London.

But she would have capable Ashley support and protection. With them, more than anyone else save her parents, she would be safe.

The house distinguished by the sign of the Ash Tree was a substantial merchant's establishment occupying a prominent position in Fleet Street, a little to the east of Fetter Lane, and on the corner of one of the innumerable alleys that ran off to either side of the street. It was not of course the first time that Alathea had seen the smart tarred timbers and fresh white plaster (her Uncle Ashley was most emphatic about the need for a clean and prosperous front to present to the world), but she could not suppress a renewed surge of excitement. The door was open, and an apprentice not much older than Alathea seemed to be on watch for them. As they approached, he vanished into the dim depths of the house.

A peculiar smell wrapped itself insinuatingly around her nostrils, a smell far stronger than the noisome background odours of the street, and unpleasantly signifying charred, decaying meat. On the doorstep, Alathea and her father exchanged meaningful glances. 'Another domestic crisis looms,' said Francis Heron, with one of his dry, sideways smiles, and together they stepped into the house of the Ash Tree, that ticked and chimed to the sound of its owner's clocks.

Daniel Ashley emerged from his workshop to greet them. Even in the gloomy light of the hallway, he looked exactly what he was: a solid, respectable London craftsman, with forty years of hard work and honest business behind him. He also had the appearance of being dull, stiff and unimaginative, and that he most assuredly was not, for no man so tedious would long have kept the faithful love and affection of Francis Heron's romantic, lovely, scatter-brained younger sister Lucy. An *unexpected* sort of man, Alathea often thought: full of nice surprises.

He greeted them now with cheerful family affection: enquiries as to their safe journey for her father, compliments for Alathea about her growth and her appearance. The smell became perceptibly stronger, and she could not prevent her nose from wrinkling like a rabbit's. Dan Ashley noticed, and grinned at her. 'I'm afraid we've had troubles in the kitchen today, and we may be reduced to sending out to a cookshop for our supper, but whatever happens, I can promise you'll feast royally tonight! Now, come upstairs, the children are all waiting to greet you.'

'Dan,' said Alathea's father, as they climbed the dark steep stairs, lit only by a tiny window giving on to the alley, 'what *is* that repulsive smell? Has your cook been reduced to roast horse?'

Daniel Ashley had sufficient sense of humour not to be offended, and he had been eleven years wed to another outspoken Heron. 'I'm afraid it's Lucy's attempts at preparing the dinner. The cook left yesterday in a temper, and we've been quite unable to find another at such short notice. Lucy had to do her own shopping this morning, with no one to help her – and you know what she's like.'

Alathea wondered, as she had wondered before, how such an important man as Master Ashley could be so calm and humorous about his impractical wife, whose impulsive happy-go-lucky attitude to life would doubtless have reduced such a man as her Uncle Simon to apoplexy: but this was another unexpected facet of Dan's character. 'She's even now slaving over a hot hearth, I don't doubt,' he explained, opening the door to the high handsome parlour where he and his wife entertained their guests and favoured customers, 'but she promised she'd be up as soon as she could leave the little cookmaid to watch the pans.'

Ranged around the wide window, opening on to the noise and smells of Fleet Street, were the three surviving children of Dan and Lucy Ashley: four more, much lamented, lay in the church of St Dunstan's, towards Temple Bar. In the naming of the girls, Dan had indulged his wife. Rosalind and Celia were ten years old and six, and both of them unfortunately favoured their father in appearance, being snub-nosed and grey-eyed with brownish straight hair. The boy, eight-year-old Oliver, had been called after his father's younger brother, who had died untimely some years ago, and also after the late Lord Protector, whom Dan had known as a personal friend. He had inherited his mother's striking looks: the pale, heart-shaped face, the generous mouth and gently flushed cheeks and round blue eyes were all Lucy's, and he had, inevitably, been more than a little indulged – especially by his mother and his nurse. But Alathea greatly preferred him to their cousin Rupert, Lord Bradfield's precious heir, who even at four was a spoilt brat who whined and stamped when he could not get his way.

There was an exuberant welcome from Rosalind and Oliver, and a subdued one from Celia, who had never shared their energy and drooped pale-faced around the edge of their celebration. Alathea was ensconced in the windowseat and plied with questions about Ashcott and the rest of her family as if they had not met for years, though in reality it had only been two months or so since they had all gathered at Goldhayes to welcome Simon Heron, newly Lord Bradfield, and his family home after fifteen years of difficult, poverty-stricken exile in the Low Countries. At the other side of the parlour, their fathers watched the welcome with satisfaction.

'You see,' said Francis softly, 'she has no trouble making friendships with most children. It's Kit who is the problem, and this seemed the answer, for a while at least. She can get away from his jealousy, and work at her drawing in peace, and when she's ready, you could perhaps take her to see Mistress Beale, as I suggested in my letter, and either have confirmation that her gift *is* worth pursuing, or a rebuff. In which case I pray Mistress Beale will be kind, for drawing is Thea's obsession, and if she's thwarted of that, it'll go hard with her.'

'She'll be kind,' Dan said. 'Whatever her opinion, Mary will be kind – it's her nature, she's a generous woman. And there's something else that has occurred to me – what of Thea's education? If she does turn out to be good at her drawing, and equally if she does not, she must have other accomplishments. You'd be the first to agree that single-minded people are tedious company. I can teach her French and Latin, and how to reckon and cast accounts and write a fair hand. I tutor my own already, and she can join them. There's a music-master comes twice weekly, and a dancing-master too, but I regret she'll learn little of household matters from Lucy, though in the vital matter of dress, deportment and all those little feminine secrets of fashion and behaviour, I don't doubt she'll be well instructed!'

'And so I should hope,' said Lucy Ashley, sweeping in through the door with a swish of cornflower satin that matched her beautiful eyes. 'Oh Dan, my love, I can't make *anything* of that wretched piece of mutton, the Jacksons' dog will have to have it. I'll make sure none of this household ever goes to that butcher again, how he could have the effrontery to sell me that maggoty old flesh as fresh-killed lamb, I cannot imagine!' She tore off her stained apron and cast it over the back of an empty chair. 'Do you mind *very* much if we send out to a cookshop?'

'I don't,' said Dan, 'but your brother might: you never know.'

As if seeing him for the first time, Lucy swept round on Francis and hugged him with joyful sisterly affection. They were not much alike, save in the width of their mouths and the far-spaced Heron eyes, hers blue and his green, and Francis's fair hair had always marked him out as different from his dark brothers and sister. Two of those brothers, Edward and Jamie, had died during the war, Jamie leaving the orphaned Nell as his memorial, and Francis and his remaining brother Simon had quarrelled: so the bond between him and Lucy had strengthened still more.

'I don't mind a meal from a chophouse, so long as it's still hot,' he told her, grinning. 'And it's my bet you were too vain to wear your spectacles when you went out to shop, so the maggots went unnoticed. Come on, Lucy, I've known you too long and too well: admit it's the truth.'

'I have a cold,' said Lucy, in tones as clear as a bell. 'I can't even smell the gillyflowers in the garden.' She grinned at him in return, and then transferred her radiant attention to her niece. 'Hullo, Thea! Shall we go out tomorrow to the shops and buy you a new gown for London?'

'Told you so,' said Dan, ruefully, to his brother-in-law.

The supper sent in from the chophouse a little way up the street was good, solid, plentiful fare, mutton pies and slabs of beef and a roast chicken. A lesser man than Master Ashley might have blushed to offer such a meal to his guests, but domestic disasters seemed to be regarded lightly in that household. Thoughts and talk were reserved for the more important matters in life: politics, books, music, plays (Lucy had been devoted to the works of such as Shakespeare, Ford and Webster since her childhood), and amused reminiscence of their shared past dominated the conversation. Although Celia and Oliver yawned (behind their hands) and fidgeted, Alathea took delight in following the talk with Rosalind, who had her mother's lively sparkle. No room, in this warm affectionate company, to miss the presence of Nell, her clinging friendship at once an irritation and a comfort, or the chatter of her brothers and little Sophie, or even the sweet faithfulness of Mab; and she enjoyed sharing their huge bed with Rosalind and Celia that night, just as she had done on other visits.

But tomorrow, her father was going home, to Ashcott and her mother: and she was not.

It was hard to say goodbye, in the bright cheery sunshine of a London July. She had always been so close to her father, sharing his quick mind and changeable moods and ironic, detached sense of humour, and despite her excitement at this new adventure, and the possible attainment of her heart's desire at the end of it, the tears spilled over on the doorstep and she found herself hugging him like a very little child, instead of a mature eleven-year-old. 'Do you *have* to go?'

'You know I do,' said Francis Heron gently. 'But it's not for ever . . . do you know, your mother had to leave her home when she was younger than you and had just lost her father and her little brother, and go all the way to Goldhayes from Ashcott on her own to be faced with my grim father and my vacuous mother and the five of us, all unfriendly – at first. We'll come and see you, you'll visit us, it's not for ever . . . come on, maw, what are those tears for? Not my brave Alathea at all.'

'No, I suppose not,' said the brave Alathea, wiping her hand across her nose in a manner reminiscent, had she known it, of her mother in her hoydenish youth. 'G – goodbye. Have a g – good journey home. Write . . . please write, tell me how Mab is, and Nell and Sophie and Math and Mun and Mother . . .'

'Of course I will. You know I will . . . be a brave maw, and hold your head up, and pretend you've the world at your feet even if it's all on your shoulders instead . . . and remember, there's always Ashcott, if you're desperate.'

'I won't be,' said Alathea stoutly. 'I'm going to spend every spare moment drawing, and I'll take them all to Mistress Beale and she'll teach me how to paint and I'll be a famous artist, as famous as . . . as . . . Van Dyck, you'll see!'

'I know you will,' said Francis, and kissed his daughter goodbye, and his sister and brother-in-law and nieces and nephew all clustered around him to offer their own farewells: and with a smile and a last wave, walked off towards Holborn.

It was a moment when Alathea felt lonelier than she ever had in her life before, but the Ashleys gave it no chance to linger. She was swept back inside, given a cup of precious dark, bitter chocolate as a special treat – something she had only ever tasted in London – and organised by Lucy and Rosalind for the promised shopping expedition. 'Paternoster Row,' said Lucy, embarking with relish upon her favourite pastime, 'no common-or-garden mercers will do for you, Alathea Heron. It's the finest in London, no less, and they're all to be found in Paternoster Row.'

'All the richest people in London go there, Court ladies and gentlemen, they even have a man to direct the traffic, there are so many coaches,' Rosalind added with enthusiasm. Unlike Alathea, who had never given her clothes any thought at all beyond the labour involved in stitching them together, she had inherited her mother's flair for dress and fashion, as her neat amber-coloured gown showed. Its colouring enhanced her hair and eyes and gave her skin a golden glow. Not blessed with spectacular looks, Rosalind would always make the best of what she had.

'And of course, patronised by the richest people in London, the prices are to match,' said Dan wryly. 'Don't compel me to put up my prices, will you, my love – clocks are too expensive for most people, as it is.'

'I may be extravagant,' said Lucy, putting on her best soft black silk hood and settling the gauzy scarf about her shoulders with the satisfied air of those wholly at ease with their appearance, 'but I'll never be the ruin of you, don't you worry. And you must agree that Thea needs a new gown. Desperately.'

Her niece, embarrassed and guilty, looked down at her grubby green linsey-woolsey gown that had served her well, day in and day out, since the day she had laboriously finished sewing it, six months before, at Goldhayes. She had none of Thomazine's talent for needlework, and the prospect of embarking on another garment so soon appalled her. 'Can't – won't this one do?' she pleaded unhappily. 'It can be let down a bit more, I know you can see my petticoats, and I don't want . . . I don't want to take up time making a new dress when I ought to be drawing!'

Lucy stared at her, and then burst out laughing. 'You didn't think you'd have to make it yourself? No wonder you looked so miserable! Oh no,' said her aunt cheerfully, 'all that you have to do is to come with me to Paternoster Row and choose your material, and then I'll have Wilkins, he's my tailor in the Strand, make you up a gown of it. He made Rosalind's. Would you like yours of that pattern?'

Much relieved at this news, Alathea said enthusiastically that indeed she would, and with her aunt and her eldest cousin, and the kitchen boy Will to carry the parcels, sallied forth with excitement on her very first London shopping expedition.

They walked up Fleet Street in the sunshine, very soon passing the entrance to Hinde Court where the Beales lived. Alathea craned her neck to see the lodging at the end of the alley where one day soon she would stand with her drawings for acceptance or rejection, but there was no sign of the ordinary, kind-hearted Suffolk woman who unknowingly held the key to her future. At the bottom of Ludgate Hill the crowds grew great, and Lucy, untypically prudent, took Alathea's hand in her left and Rosalind's in her right. 'For if you got lost, either of you, God knows what might happen to you,' she warned dramatically and mysteriously.

There were more people here, packed and shouting, than

Alathea had ever seen before, so many faces, all so different, each one bearing the stamp of the personality behind it: sad or merry, good or bad, old and young, beauty and ugliness and life and sickness and health, a mixture in every swiftly passing countenance. Some she longed to stop, so that she could capture their expressions, seen only for an instant, on her paper for all time: the girl with the laces, shouting her wares from a mouth filled with irregular teeth; the stout goldsmith stamping up the street armoured in the self-confidence of wealth, a hunted-looking 'prentice boy at his heels; ladies of fashion, of leisure, painted ladies of ill repute, citizens' wives parading in masks and patches, gowns of silk and satin in a hundred different colours like a great shifting shimmering field of flowers . . . and she wanted to paint every one of them now, in an instant, with all the life and bustle and noise of a tumultuous London street.

Ludgate Hill had been crowded enough with street vendors and shoppers, but Paternoster Row was quite another matter. From end to end it was jammed with the coaches and sedan-chairs of the Quality, setting down, waiting for or taking up their aristocratic passengers, all set on making extravagant purchases from the most luxurious mercers' shops in London. One undersized maid staggered past them, almost weighed down by a stack of parcels reaching to her chin, her satin-clad mistress swishing haughtily in front, unburdened, nose in the air as if there was a foul smell somewhere, and glancing at Alathea as if she were the source of it. For the first time she was painfully aware of the lamentable state of her attire, and of the importance of keeping up appearances in this acutely clothes-conscious city, and she wished, reddening, that she was dressed as neatly and elegantly as her aunt and her cousin.

'In here,' said Lucy, and ushered the two girls into the first of many shops they were to visit that morning, all of them gloomy, piled high with bales of cloth far-fetched from Holland and France, the Levant, the Dutch Indies or Cathay: every colour of the rainbow and more, glowing with a light and life of their own to match their strange and lovely names, alamode and armazine, cobweb lawn and damassin, lustring and tabby and paragon. So much choice was worse than none at all; she stared with glazing eyes at the processing colours, flicked expertly through the mercer's fingers to display their beauty to the best advantage. There was an amber satin very near to Rosalind's, but that, Lucy declared, was not her colour. The lovely rich dark red silk would make her look like a ghost, 'But I'll have three ells of that for a suit for Oliver, he needs something new for best. Now, how about the blue tabby . . . no, that won't do at *all*. You know, Thea, you're going to be very pretty one day,'

'Am I?' said poor Alathea, faintly, with disbelief.

'Yes you are, and don't you believe any different, but I'm afraid blue just doesn't suit you either. Nor does it suit Francis, and you're just like him. He looks good in black, how useful to have mourning become you so well, but no one in our family has died since Dan's poor brother three years ago, thank God . . . now *this* is the sort of colour Francis suits . . . this grey-green watered silk. Don't you think that would look nice on her, Ros?'

Rosalind narrowed her grey, rather short-sighted eyes and agreed that it would indeed: and the silk was bought, enough for bodice and skirt with room for growth both upwards and outwards, Alathea being at an age where, as Lucy said, 'Girls shoot up all of a sudden and leave their clothes behind.'

But if she had thought that was an end of it, she was to be dismayed. Lucy, now in full flight, took them from shop to shop, and the parcels mounted up in poor Will's arms: lace and ribbons for trimmings, a quantity of fine lawn for chemises and ruffles, more material for an everyday gown, a deep blue-green paduasay of fine wool, some heavy grass-coloured velvet bought cheaply because of the season, though Lucy, uncharacteristically practical, claimed to be thinking ahead to a gown for the winter, and some apricot satin for Celia. By the time she was satisfied, it was so late that Alathea's stomach grumbled with hunger and her feet ached cruelly, but, rather to her surprise, she found she had thoroughly enjoyed the morning's shopping. Perhaps there was more to this fuss over dress and appearance than she had thought.

And she had said goodbye to her father only a few hours ago, and had hardly thought of him since, in the whirlwind of activity into which the Ashleys had considerately plunged her.

She did not, then, have much time in which to think of how she missed her family, so engrossed was she in all the hectic business of that chaotic, relaxed household where, somehow, the necessary things got done, eventually, by someone, and everything else fell without fuss by the wayside. Her Uncle Dan was his usual surprising self. Alathea, used to her mother's unobtrusive efficiency, was at first astonished at the calm and philosophical way he took his wife's haphazard running of the domestic side. She especially wondered at his failure to comment adversely on the astounding and unlicensed extravagance of that shopping expedition. The maids, Jane and Sarah, and the boy Will, contributed far more to the smooth running of the household than was at first evident, and soon their numbers were swelled, to everyone's profound relief, by the arrival of a new cook. Mistress Byrd was a large, phlegmatic, imperturbable widow who obviously took a great and practical interest in her profession, and a quick sketch of her seated at the kitchen table, sampling one of her delicious spiced cakes with massive relish, was the first drawing that Alathea produced in the House of the Ash Tree.

And that was the greatest, most luxurious freedom she found at her uncle's house: the liberty to draw, whenever she wanted, whatever subject she chose. Apprentices, maids, children, journeymen, her aunt and uncle, the French music-master with his vast ridiculous breeches and huge bunches of ribbon loosely attached to his clothing, all were immortalised on paper, in pen and ink, chalk and plumbago. And because she liked to catch her subjects as they truly were, rather than imprison them stiffly in the formality of portraiture, they were done with speed, quick sketches distilling the essence of face and character: Oliver's bold mischief, the foppish Monsieur Guinard, the intense concentration of the chief journeyman, Edward Hamilton. His Scottish accent reminded her daily, with a pang of homesickness, of Goldhayes, and her Scottish cousin Malise Graham, who still with his wife and family ran the Home Farm and lands and estate, but who was employed now by Simon Heron, Lord Bradfield.

For she found, in those first hectic weeks, that the moments of intense longing that came upon her unawares, triggered by a voice, a song, a scent of gillyflowers or the cut and colour of someone's clothes, were not for Ashcott, nor even specifically for her parents and family: they were for Goldhayes, for that peaceful, gloriously happy life they had all enjoyed there, and never would again. And with unaccustomed tears in her eyes, she vowed that she would never love any place so much as that old and lovely house in the sleepy heart of Suffolk.

And to re-create it and keep it fresh in her mind, she embarked upon her most ambitious project yet: a careful, detailed study, from memory, of Goldhayes, the amber light from the sunlit brickwork reflected in the moat beneath. The drawing was done in ink, the colour suggested with smudged russet chalks, and in contrast to the swift ease of her portrait sketches, this was done over a period of several weeks during that summer, with loving, intense concentration.

She was working on it one hot August afternoon, hunched in the parlour windowseat with her knees drawn up and her stockinged feet on the cushions and the stale reek of London filling the heavy air, when there was a knock on the door and Sarah, the older and wiser of the two maids, put her head round in some agitation. 'Oh, Mistress, there's a visitor for Mistress Ashley, but she ain't here and neither is the Master, and the lady's come a long way – could you see her?'

Alathea scowled at Sarah over the top of her drawing-board. She hated being interrupted, particularly when things were going well. There was a kind of magic, it seemed, in her drawing, for on some days her gift flowed in abundance, yet a few hours later her pen would run as if filled with grit and ridiculous distortions and mistakes would cover the paper. Good days, when her mood and her hand combined in harmony, must be nursed and cherished and indulged, and she resented this unknown, unfortunate visitor who had chanced to arrive at just the wrong moment.

'I suppose so,' she said ungraciously, and laid the board and pens down on the seat. At that moment a girl brushed past Sarah and swept into the room, beaming, and all Alathea's annoyance vanished abruptly. 'Hen!' she cried, leaping up, and rushed into Henrietta Sewell's welcoming hug.

It seemed almost too much of a coincidence that Hen should arrive just as she was drawing Goldhayes, for she, lucky, lucky girl, lived there still at the Home Farm, being stepdaughter to Malise Graham, and daughter of Thomazine's greatest friend, the Irishwoman Grainne O'Brady who had married first Henry Sewell, son of the Goldhayes Steward, and then after his death in the Civil War been wed to Master Graham, a Scottish cousin of the Herons, and Francis's friend since childhood. Alathea knew the comfortable shabby interior of the Home Farm almost as well as she did Goldhayes itself, and had played with all the children there: Henrietta and her elder brother Jasper, now studying in the

Low Countries to be a doctor, and their half-brothers Robin Graham, who was three, and Nicholas who was the same age as Edmund. There was also a tiny baby, Bridget, whose birth a few months ago had almost been the death of her mother.

'How are you?' Henrietta was saying, her hands holding Alathea's grubby chalk-stained paws. 'You've grown, you'll overtop me before long, I'll reckon. And is that a new gown? It suits you. Did Aunt Lucy buy that for you?' Strictly speaking, there was no actual blood relationship between Hen and Lucy Ashley, but she, and Thomazine, had been 'aunt' to the Sewell children since their birth.

'Turn round,' Henrietta ordered, and Alathea, used to her kindly domineering, pirouetted obediently. She had learnt enough from Rosalind over the past few weeks to hold out her skirts gracefully, and she swept into a mischievous curtsey for a finale. Henrietta, grinning, clapped her hands. 'Well done – they'll make a lady of you yet! More than anyone's done for me,' she added, with a rueful glance down at her own appearance.

It was needless, for Henrietta Sewell, even as a tiny child, had always been impeccably dressed: never a grubby apron or a torn sleeve, her abundant curly red hair firmly subdued. Now she wore a dark green riding habit that suited her colouring to perfection, and was, characteristically, hardly marked by its passage through filthy, dusty London streets. But to Alathea's newly sophisticated eyes it spoke 'country', and so did Hen's face. It had little of her mother's fine-boned Irish beauty, owing much instead to her father's yeoman Suffolk forebears: a firm jaw, a generous scattering of freckles, and tawny brown eyes under positively marked eyebrows. But today the normally calm, equable Hen was radiant, dazzling, her joyous expression lending her an unaccustomed beauty. 'You look lovely, Hen,' Alathea said, her own smiles breaking out in response. 'What's happened? Why are you here?'

Henrietta Sewell showed her left hand. On the strong, capable third finger, a ring flashed gold. 'I'm here because I'm married,' she said.

She was only seventeen, six years older than Alathea, a few months older than Kit, and it did not seem very long, suddenly, since they had shared the same pony. 'Married? Oh, Hen, who is it?' Curiously, her mind raced over various eligible and ineligible young men around Goldhayes, the boys they had all laughed with ridden with, invited to convivial evenings of whist or music or dancing in the Long Gallery. 'Who is he, Hen?'

'Charles Jermyn,' said Henrietta, her Suffolk-flavoured voice lingering over the three brief syllables like a caress, and Alathea gasped.

The Jermyns of Rushbrooke lived two miles or so away from Goldhayes, and the family had been there so long that they made their friends and rivals the Herons seem like jumped-up parvenus. They were rich, talented, had Court connections – Charles's uncle was the Earl of St Albans, his elder brother Henry was attached to the household of the Duke of York. For Henrietta Sewell, humbly-born despite her family's long friendship with the Herons, to aspire to marrying a Jermyn was astonishing, though when Alathea remembered Charles's dark, dashing good looks and attractive manner, she could not blame her. She liked him herself.

But what had Lord Bradfield said, and Charles's eldest brother Thomas, who was a prude old before his time, and even Henrietta's calm wise mother and gentle stepfather? A horrible memory of Lord Bradfield at his intolerant, bigoted worst rose up in her mind, and he had once, she knew, done his best to force her own parents apart, long ago.

'Don't look like that,' said Henrietta, smiling, 'it's the best thing that has ever happened to me, not the worst. Oh, Thea, I do love him so much, I think I always have, ever since we were little and I first went to Rushbrooke with Kit and Jasper and Hugh, and Charles was always so kind . . . and he asked me to marry him last week and I said yes!'

Even Alathea's limited experience of life could guess at the world of emotion concealed behind Hen's talk. Like her father, Henry Sewell, who had been killed before she was born; she used plain words and few, and the likeness had often been remarked. Intensely curious at this transformation through love of her prosaic, practical friend, Alathea said, 'Just like that? What did his brother think of it?'

'He doesn't know yet,' said Hen. 'Nobody knows, except for my parents. And Mother said she couldn't forbid me to marry for love, having done it twice herself, and Father told me that if we were set on it he'd help us and never mind about Thomas Jermyn . . . and so, we got married, yesterday morning, in Westminster, with a special licence that Henry got for us. He lied about our ages,' she added honestly. Alathea thought that Henry Jermyn, already at twenty-four a notorious but charming member of the Duke of York's household, was doubtless capable of lying successfully about his own decease, if necessary. But he had evidently been of great help to his young brother and his illicit bride, and had procured Westminster lodgings for the happy pair as well as a very junior post in, unsuitably, the Exchequer for Charles. 'And we needn't worry too much for money,' said Hen, her practicality asserting itself. 'When Charles's father died last year, he left him a good sum in his will, though he won't get it till he's twenty-four, so there's another four years to go. But the Exchequer position will bring in a little, and I'm sure we'll manage.'

Alathea was sure too. Managing was Henrietta's forte, which was just as well, for Charles Jermyn, cossetted youngest son, was noted for his easy, prodigal manners and his freedom with coin of the realm. But why carp about her choice of husband, when Hen's ordinary, freckled, country-bred face was transformed with her happiness?

Lucy's reaction to the news, when she heard it on her return from the shops with her family, was to clasp her hands with pleasure and rhapsodise, again, on the joys of love before saluting Henrietta firmly on her round rosy cheeks and wishing her all happiness. Dan was rather more reserved, though he too congratulated her, and added warningly, 'Don't you go drooping in this hot London weather: one Suffolker pining for Goldhayes is quite enough, thank you.'

'I'm sure Thea doesn't pine for the country,' said Lucy quickly, with a reassuring smile in her direction. 'She's much too busy here. But if you should ever feel homesick, Hen, you can feast your eyes on this and feel better.'

To Alathea's chagrin, her forgotten portrait of Goldhayes was plucked from the windowseat and paraded around the assembled company, all the Ashleys as well as Henrietta, amidst cries of delight and admiration. In vain she protested that it was as yet far from finished, that the chalk was smudged and the perspective woefully misaligned. 'I can almost smell it,' Lucy declared, staring with misty-eyed fondness at her birthplace, 'that lovely smell of beeswax and flowers and sunshiny wood . . . we must never lose touch with it, Dan, we must go back there every year.'

'That,' said Dan, a chilly note in his voice that Alathea had never heard before, 'depends entirely upon your brother, my dear, and if we regard Henrietta here with favour when her marriage to Charles offends all his ideals of conventional behaviour, Goldhayes may shut its doors to us as well. Not,' he added, with one of his unexpected grins in the direction of Henrietta, who was staring at him in some dismay, 'that it will make the slightest difference to how we receive you, Hen. You'll always be most welcome here, to all of us – whatever Lord Bradfield may think or say or do.'

Dan, as ever, was true to his word, and when the angry letters began to arrive from Lord Bradfield at Goldhayes, upbraiding his sister and brother-in-law for giving 'shelter', as he put it, to the guilty couple, Dan answered them kindly, courteously and firmly, and Hen visited the Fleet Street house just as often as she wished.

Alathea had always liked her, had been taught to ride by her, and had received Hen's usual firm, slightly maternal treatment. Now, she discovered more in common with the girl who was just like a cousin, though in actual fact no relation to her at all. They were both country-bred, country-loving people, and however much the vivid, teeming, exciting life of London might appeal, at the back of both their minds was a deep longing for the utter peace and silence and balance of Suffolk or Oxfordshire, a feeling that no jaunt in a hired coach to the villages of Hampstead or Islington or Chelsea could assuage. But Hen, cooped in her tiny Westminster lodgings, showed no signs of drooping or pining: indeed, she seemed almost too happy with her secret marriage and her handsome, charming, feckless young husband.

By the end of September, Alathea had been two months and more in London, and had a fat pile of sketches and drawings to show for it, as well as a smaller pile of letters from her parents, full of cheerful advice and gossip. There was one from Matthew, an earnest discussion of books she had never heard of, and from Edmund, in large irregular writing describing, at length, his new pony and the fight he had had with a boy in Deddington. On the bottom of this epistle Sophie, eager to keep up, had added her first attempt at a signature, and Mab's small muddy paw-print completed the effect. Kit never wrote, but there were also pallid, envious letters from Nell, usually concerned with her poor summer health ('I seem to be sneezing all the time here, and my eyes are watering so much I can hardly see. Do tell me what London is like. Are you ill too? Have you got any more dresses?'), that seemed always to arouse feelings of guilt in Alathea. But she did not want Nell with her yet – not until she had seen Mistress Beale.

The last months, despite the upheaval in her life and the strain of new surroundings, new friends, new routines, had been very happy. She had drawn to her heart's content, and loved it, but now the reckoning grew near, the day when the course of her life was finally shaped, the day when Mistress Mary Beale would say yes – or no. And because, after Kit, she had never trusted others' opinions of her work, Alathea could not rid herself of the fear that the answer would be no. She prayed, with terror, each night in the stuffy bed with Rosalind and Celia on either side of her, begging any deity that might listen: 'Please, make me good enough, let me be good enough to be an artist, for that's all I ever want to do.'

Dan went to see Mistress Beale, and reported that she would certainly be kind enough to look at Alathea's work. More than that could not be promised at all, and if they cared to present themselves in Hinde Court at two o'clock on the following afternoon, Mistress Beale would be pleased to receive them.

Needless to say, Alathea did not sleep much that night. Possible scenarios – Mary Beale hailing her as a new, female Leonardo, or the humiliating dismissal of her precious drawings as childish scribbles – haunted her dreams and her wakeful moments, and she rose heavy-eyed and unable to do more than toy with her breakfast, even a cup of hot fragrant chocolate turning to aloes in her dry throat. All morning she pored over the drawings spread out on the floor of her chamber, discarding some, then changing her mind, while Lucy grew anxious and drew her husband aside from the workshop. 'Have you looked at that child this morning? She's like a ghost, all eaten up with nerves. Are you sure we're doing right? It's not healthy for a child her age to be so obsessed with something.'

'It won't last,' said Dan reassuringly, his eyes straying past his wife's immaculate shoulder to light on a clumsy apprentice who was, very hamfistedly, trying to fit one of his most delicate movements inside a silver case slightly too small for it. He was relieved to see his senior journeyman, Hamilton, come to the rescue of the unfortunate clock and gave Lucy his full attention. 'It won't last, love. She's set on this meeting with Mistress Beale, that's all. Whether the answer is yea or nay, the pressure will be off her, and she can relax a little, spend more time doing other things and less with her nose over a piece of paper and her fingers on the quill. Music, for instance. Thomazine and Francis are both musicians, but have you ever heard a note from Thea, these last few weeks? And she plays your guitar very nicely, too.'

'That was always my mother's favourite instrument, too. But I take your point, Dan. I'm sure she'll be better tomorrow – *if* the answer's yes.'

'It may well not be. Mistress Beale is a busy woman, she has a husband and children to look after besides her painting. And she may want a substantial sum for her tutoring. But I dread Alathea's reaction if she does say no. All the life will go out of her.'

'If the fee turns out to be too great for Francis to pay – they're hard-pressed at the moment, I know – could we – could we find it from somewhere? Please?' Lucy asked, the same pleading note in her voice that had once wound all four of her brothers around her little finger. Dan, well aware of it, smiled and put a hand round her waist. 'Yes, of course I will. There's a goodly sum in gold in our name up in Cheapside, and she deserves it, does Thea, and so do you.'

At exactly five minutes to two, that afternoon, Alathea Heron and her uncle closed the door of the House of the Ash Tree behind them – it was a rather windy day, though sunny – and set off up Fleet Street towards Hinde Court. No risk of being unpunctual in that ticking, chiming house, and since Mistress Beale had, so Dan said, bought one of his most reliable bracket clocks only this April, it was tolerably certain that she would be ready for them.

Alathea did not appear to hear him. Her heart crashed loudly against her ribs, her throat was tinder-dry, and her hands clutching the precious folio of sketches, were white at the knuckles with strain. Her long green eyes stared straight ahead, unseeing of the people who brushed by them, apparently stark with terror, and held up only by her fierce pride, a quality her mother had passed on to her in full measure. Dan, concerned, took her arm to steer her into the dim alley that was Hinde Court, and once there, out of the hurly-burly of the main street, took her gently by the shoulders. 'Thea . . . listen. I know, we all know, how much the next hour or so means to you, and make no mistake, we wish you well, all of us. But if . . . pray God she doesn't, but *if* Mistress Beale should say no, remember . . . you're only eleven. Other chances will come your way, for sure, you're so young yet . . . if she says no, Thea, this isn't the end, not for your drawing, not for you . . . and whatever happens, you have our love and support.'

But if she says no, the voice whispered inside Alathea's head, then I have lost and Kit has won, for ever.

Hinde Court was gloomy, the sun striking in only at the entrance, the sides bathed in shadow. The Beales' house was at the end, a substantial building that went with Charles Beale's position at the Patents Office. There was no one else about, and despite Dan's large, solid and reassuring presence in front of her, confidently lifting the knocker, she felt very afraid, very alone. They all loved her and cared for her, she knew, but none of them could *really* comprehend what the events of the next hour would mean to her.

A little maidservant, shy and smiling, opened the door to them, and showed them into a wainscot parlour, very dim and cool, with a window giving on to the Court. Somewhere above, there was a baby crying fretfully, and the faint voice of a child. Mistress Beale, Alathea remembered, had a son four years old and another recently born. Presumably she also had a nurse to look to the children, and servants to run the house, while she painted.

There were pictures on the walls, portraits and one or two with classical subjects which she took to be French or Italian. Two were certainly by Van Dyck, whose group portrait of her father and his brothers and sister hung still in the Great Hall at Goldhayes; she had copied it once, very badly in red chalk. With a pang of apprehension, she wondered if the precious drawings, clutched so tightly under her arm, would seem as clumsy and childish to Mistress Beale as her earlier, nine-year-old efforts now seemed to herself.

The maidservant returned, bobbing a neat curtsey. 'Mistress Beale's ready to see you now, sir, madam,' she said softly. 'If you'll follow me, please.'

Dan and Alathea climbed the dimly lit stairs in her wake, both of them wondering, quite independently, how Mary Beale could possibly produce anything of worth with so little light to see by. And despite the fact that they had both seen it before, the painting room, at the very top of the house, still came as a surprise. The garret had been converted into a great long airy studio, with skylights set into the roof as well as dormer windows, flooding the whole of the room with light, diffused through the sheets of oiled paper covering much of the glass. Canvases were everywhere: laid against the walls, rolled in corners, supported on the rafters which ran the length of the room a few feet above Alathea's head. There were paints and draperies and plaster pillars and other impedimenta, and, pervading everything, the thick, aromatic, evocative reek of oils.

Mary Beale was wiping her hands with an old stained piece of cloth while another servant divested her of her working apron. Dan bowed, and Alathea curtsied as best she could, burdened with her folio, and rose to greet the lady who held the passport to her future.

Mistress Beale was a round, smiling, fair-haired young woman in her late twenties. Like Alathea, she was Suffolk born and bred, her father having been rector of Barrow, a village about six miles or so from Goldhayes, and she and the Herons shared many friends and acquaintances: Blagges, Gages, Herveys and Jermyns. It had been Lady Penelope Hervey who had suggested to her parents and the Ashleys that they have their portraits painted by her when they desired likenesses of themselves, and Alathea had seen Lady Penelope's own formidable representation, faithfully depicted by Mistress Beale, hanging in the Hall at Hengrave.

The things she had remembered best from her previous meeting with the artist, were her kindness and her Suffolk voice, and both were evident in her welcome. 'Hullo, Master Ashley. Hullo, Alathea. I reckon you'd both like something to refresh you. Betty, go bring us some coffee.'

Dan and Alathea sat down on the chairs she indicated, and Mary Beale put down the rag, her hands clean, and smiled at them. 'Master Ashley tells me you want to be a painter, Alathea – and I must say, I thought you showed an uncommon interest last year, when your parents sat to me. Well, I suppose it's only fair to warn you, child, that it's an uncertain life at the best of times, and exceeding hard for a woman. And though you may have some regard for my work, do remember, I'm not a Lely nor a Walker, though I'm honoured to count the one my friend and the other my tutor. I'm only just, I hope, at the start of my career, and still learning from my many mistakes. And as yet, portraits are all I do.

What have you done? Can I see your folio?'

With a strange mixture of eagerness and dread, Alathea got up and laid the drawings on a nearby table, directly under one of the uncovered windows. With hands that seemed suddenly uncertain, she untied the ribbons binding the folio together, and turned back the stiff card to reveal the first drawing.

It happened to be of her cousin Rosalind, reading, and was an exceptionally quick, vivid likeness. Mary Beale stared down at it for a while. Alathea, glancing nervously at her, could not tell her thoughts. She said eventually, 'It's Rosalind, isn't it . . . when did you do it? How long did it take you? Tell me about each one.'

Hesitant at first, and then with growing confidence, Alathea described each drawing as it lay revealed under Mary Beale's firm, plump hands. Gradually, her terror evaporated and her enthusiasm for her art took over, and with a boldness that surprised her, she found herself able to point out the deficiencies in some of her less successful efforts, for in the end she had discarded none of them, not even the most dismal failures. 'That's my cousin Oliver, he won't sit still for longer than five minutes and he likes to tease me with it . . . he moved before I'd finished, and I tried to complete it later and went wrong because I couldn't remember how he'd been holding his hands . . . oh, and that one, that's Uncle Dan's journeyman, Master Hamilton, working on a clock – only I can't draw clocks.'

'There's no such word as can't, especially in drawing – you've probably never drawn clocks before,' said Mary Beale, smiling. 'Remember this, Alathea Heron: drawing and painting and limning are made up of three elements – technique, which materials to use and how to use them, and that I reckon I can teach you well enough; practice, working at something till you have it right, whether it's a clock or hands or eyes or the folds of drapery and that you can do for yourself; and a native gift for drawing, without which the first two are pointless.' She turned over the drawing of Edward Hamilton and stopped, with a smile of recognition, at the last picture: Goldhayes, now completed, in all its mellow glory. 'Oh, that is lovely! Is it done from memory?' Alathea nodded. 'You must know it very well,' Mary Beale went on. 'I've only been there two or three times, but my memory of it is this, exactly.' She picked it up and held it nearer to the light her fingers gently on the very edge of the paper. 'Pen, and chalk to give the colour . . . and, I would guess, a great deal more time spent on it than on the others, am I right? How long did it take?'

'She worked on it for three weeks, intermittently,' said Dan. He put his hand on Alathea's shoulder and squeezed it slightly Startled, she glanced round and received, to her surprise, a smile and the suspicion of a wink. 'I think it was to remind her of home.'

'What used to be my home,' said Alathea, sadly. 'My uncle Lord Bradfield, lives there now.'

'Yes, so I had heard. My cousin, Nathaniel Thach, met him in The Hague many years ago. Well, I am glad he is back and enjoying his own again, though you have had to leave Goldhayes: that must have been a sore wrench for you and your parents, to bid farewell to so lovely a place. Where are they now? Do they approve of your drawings?'

Alathea found herself talking about Ashcott and her family, while the coffee was brought and placed on another, smaller table well distant from her precious folio, and Mary Beale listened attentively as she sipped the hot, bitter black liquid from a thin china dish. Alathea, who liked her coffee well-sweetened, as Lucy served it, was glad to see a bowl of sugar on the table beside the fine silver coffee-pot, and in obedience to her instructions, the maid put two generous spoonfuls into the bottom of the dish and poured the steaming coffee over it. Like chocolate, it was a drink she had only ever tasted at the Ashleys', and its restorative, invigorating quality was something she much appreciated at this particular moment, despite the tingling of her scalded tongue. Mistress Beale, her own drink already finished, gave the dish back to the serving-girl and returned her attention to her guest. 'Well, Alathea – do you *really* want to be an artist?'

Alathea swallowed her coffee with a gulp. 'It's . . . it's what I want more than anything else in the whole world.'

'And have you the will to learn all those techniques and practise your drawing and painting diligently, even though you may be sick and tired and bored with hands or draperies, or whatever it is you must study?'

With sudden, wild hope, Alathea stared at her, the green eyes luminous. 'Oh, yes, *yes*!'

'And do you reckon you've the gift, the talent for it?'

Alathea, poised to answer in the affirmative, was suddenly overtaken by modesty. She was not going to be boastful, not now, with the moon and stars almost within her grasp. Meeting Mary Beale's kind greyish eyes, she said diffidently, 'I don't know . . . would you be the judge of that, Mistress?'

'Well,' said the artist, reflectively, 'you're better than ever I was at your age – what are you, eleven? – and you've had no instruction, all of it comes from your observation alone. Oh, yes, Alathea, you have a natural gift for limning, no doubt of it, and I'd be happy to teach you all I know, and I could do with an assistant into the bargain. Would you like to start next week? Oh, child, what is it? Why are you crying?'

Above Alathea's bowed silver-fair head, Dan Ashley smiled at his hostess. 'Don't worry. People who've been under great strain often crack when they attain their heart's desire, and she's very young yet. Work her hard, Mary, make sure she does everything you ask and always gives of her best – she, and you, deserve no less.'

CHAPTER THREE

Jasper

It is my lady: O! it is my love!
O! that she knew she were.

(Shakespeare, *Romeo and Juliet*)

And so, Alathea Heron became pupil and assistant to Mistress Mary Beale, and for four days each week, made her way in the morning to the house in Hinde Court, to spend all the hours of daylight in the garret studio. She learned to grind and mix the paint in linseed oil, and to fill the pigs' bladder tubes with the mixture so that it could be more easily squeezed on to the palette. She discovered the mysteries of stretching, sizing and priming canvas, ready for use; the easiest way to clean brushes; and the curious composition of the rarer pigments, some of which were so expensive that the brushes were scraped clean of paint before being cleaned, for an ounce of ultramarine cost more than most servants' yearly wages.

But she did not spend all her time helping Mary Beale to paint. There were not very many clients, and most of them were close friends, invited to dinner after the sittings and often staying on afterwards to discuss art or poetry, politics or theology. The Beales were intellectual, serious-minded people who counted many divines amongst their circle. Alathea, unused to this type of conversation, laughterless, abstruse and intense, found her attention often wandering into daydream. Her parents' racy, ironic discourse that seemed, without taking anything seriously, nevertheless to pierce to the heart of any argument, was much more to her inclination. But her boredom was put to some use, for she found in Oliver and Rosalind a ready market for her mimicry, and some of the more pretentious divines would have been horrified to learn that the demure, pretty child who hovered in the background like a ghost, was not above entertaining her cousins with unflattering and hilarious caricatures of them when she returned home. Alathea acquired with the Ashleys a reputation as a wit, and revelled in it.

But mocking the Beales' guests behind their backs did give her disquieting pangs of conscience, despite Oliver's howls of laughter, and she was never anything less than properly grateful, willing and hardworking for the Beales themselves. Mary, quiet, calm, kind, was a good foil for her rather loud, impulsive husband, who boomed amiably at Alathea whenever he set foot in the studio, pinched her cheek and called her 'Puss'. But he took a keen interest in every aspect of his wife's art, did much of the work of preparing canvas and paint, and readily imparted his wide knowledge of pigments to Mary's eager pupil. For that, Alathea was able, just, to forgive and forget the pinched cheeks and even the 'Puss'.

And slowly, surely, she learned to paint under Mary Beale's helpful, relaxed instruction. At first the lessons were limited exercises, the study of the shape and form of the eyes or mouth, detailed examinations of folds of velvet or satin designed to improve her handling of brush and paint. It was harder than she had imagined. Drawing had come so easily, so quickly to her that the complicated process of painting seemed an unendurably lengthy one: the colours to use, the colours to be obtained by mixing, the thinning of paint to achieve the fineness of texture required for face or hands, the composition of the picture, the proper poses the sitter could adopt, the accessories of drapery or pillars or background landscape . . . it seemed unending, and the most difficult lesson of all for Alathea during her first year or so as Mary Beale's pupil, was the acquisition of patience.

At Christmas, she went home to Ashcott, unaware of the change in her, the growth of confidence and maturity, and found the house rather more obviously altered, the echoing medieval vastness of the Great Hall split into two storeys to make bed-chambers above and a dining room, new kitchens and a pleasant comfortable parlour below. Kit was there, returned for the festive season from Oxford. The time he had spent at Christchurch, where several generations of Herons had studied with varying degrees of success, seemed to have improved him considerably, and he was even quite pleasant to Alathea, though the subject of painting was not mentioned between them. Thomazine and Francis Heron congratulated each other on the overwhelming success of their strategem, and, not without a certain amount of agonised mutual discussion, told Alathea that she could continue to study with Mistress Beale for as long as the artist desired, and as long as the Ashleys would tolerate her as their guest. 'And you're happy, now?' Francis asked her. 'Not homesick at all?'

'A little bit,' said Alathea, honestly. 'But the painting makes up for that. I do miss Mab though, and Nell,' she added, more out of guilt than truth.

So when she returned to London in January, through muddy winter roads with her father's reassuring, drily humorous company, Nell was with them, wrapped in a voluminous cloak and sneezing violently into a succession of kerchiefs, and trotting alongside, delighted with the prospect of extended exercise, the neat black-and-white, foxlike figure of Mab. By the most optimistic reckoning she must be at least thirteen years old, having been found by Thomazine as a young, half-starved dog in the Siege of Colchester, in 1648, but advancing age and a dramatic past seemed to make no impression on her tough wiry little body, except for the occasional twinge of rheumatism after rain. And even that, said Francis drily, was probably more a matter of policy than actual disability, for at the first sign of a limp either Nell or Alathea would be certain to give her a ride on their saddlebows.

If any of the Ashleys were surprised at the damp, ill-assorted quartet which arrived on their doorstep a week after Twelfth

Night, they were too used to the unpredictable ways of Francis and his household to show it. Mab made herself useful by briskly and efficiently ridding the cellar of rats the following day, and Nell, though in the throes of one of her frequent head colds, was after all part of the family. And because she was Alathea's faithful shadow, she was welcomed by the Beales, and sat contentedly in the corner of the garret studio, watching her cousin at work, or learning herself how to mix paints and grind colours and prepare canvases. And when, two years after beginning her training, Mistress Beale at last allowed Alathea to embark upon a full-scale portrait, it was Nell who was the model.

Mistress Beale had not dictated any particular pose or attire for this, and Alathea, not without a certain sense of mischief, chose to portray her cousin in heroic mould, with shield and spear, as Athene. Nell, with her lank mouse-brown hair, and rather large, watery, near-sighted blue eyes, would certainly have astonished the ancient Greeks: the shield propped against her knees looked heavy enough to push her over, and it was doubtful whether she could muster the strength even to raise the spear, let alone wield it with malicious intent. Nell, unaware of irony, was delighted with the result, her insignificant, hesitant soul much heartened and uplifted by a portrait that, however ridiculous it might appear to anyone else, at least accepted her as a person in her own right, for the first time in her life.

Alathea, ever her own severest critic, was rather less satisfied. The hands were badly painted, the drapery was coarse, the shield extremely clumsy, but the face, even she had to agree, was excellently done and a most exact likeness of the hapless Nell. Certainly, the adults decided amongst themselves, the work as a whole was good enough to stand comparison with many ordinary established painters, and for a girl not yet fourteen, showed very great promise indeed.

Once initiated into the skills and delights of painting, Alathea's blood was truly up. If Mary Beale had let her, she would have produced pictures at the rate of two or three a week, but the price of canvas precluded such extravagance. Mistress Beale, who was nothing if not resourceful, and quite prepared to apply a sensible if unorthodox solution to such a problem, was in the habit of using bed-ticking or even sacking as a cheap substitute for canvas when 'study' pictures were intended, and the coarser, heavier texture presented Alathea with interesting problems of technique. She learned which paints to combine with which, those pigments so deleterious to others that they must be isolated by layers of varnish, and the hazards of using white lead and blue bice, both of which were extremely poisonous and must be handled and ground with great care. There were recipes for mixtures of oils and resins for painting mediums and glazes and varnishes, instructions for brush work, composition, poses . . . Alathea had never realised that there was so much to learn, had never thought that the process of painting in oils could be so complicated, or often so tedious. There were the frustrating moments when a detailed study of hands or drapery or a piece of sculpture defiantly failed to come right, and occasions of desperate heartache. The portrait head of Rosalind, drawn at the Ashleys' house and painted in the studio, seemed likely to be the best she had ever done, her cousin to the life and beautifully painted. But it turned quite black inside a fortnight because she had forgotten that the white in the flesh tones and the blueish shadows were incompatible. It was all hard work and sometimes, stumbling back to the Ash Tree with Nell, her eyes and nose filled with the look and odour of paint, she could wish never to see another palette or canvas in her life. But so utterly happy and absorbed was she in her labours of love that time flew past – weeks, months, years of devoted study and application rolled away, and almost unawares, lost in her own world, Alathea Heron grew and matured and changed from that intense, hoydenish, shabby child into the girl of striking, unconventional, untidy beauty that her mother and her aunt had foreseen, five years previously, and in which Alathea herself had never believed.

The young man with red hair plodded wearily along King Street in Westminster, looking for the delightfully named Antelope Alley. He had enquired after it several times, and the most exact directions he had received had been merely, 'About half-way along on the Park side.' Presumably it contained, or had once contained, an inn or tavern called the Antelope, and he peered impatiently into every narrow passageway to his left, being at last rewarded by a dim swinging sign, extremely badly painted and resembling a horned horse rather than a genuine antelope. With a sigh of relief, he turned down it. For a week he had been travelling, with hardly a respite, and he was weary of it. He had left Leyden at last, buoyed up with the approval and praise of his learned teachers, the proud possessor of a degree in medicine from a University acknowledged to be the finest in all Europe for anatomy, a qualification that was at least equal to, or better than, those of many fashionable physicians. He had achieved his lifetime's ambition after seven years of intensive, arduous study, and he had wanted only to go home, at long last, and share his delight with his family.

And of course, the fates had conspired against him. He had arrived at the Home Farm, where his mother and stepfather lived, only to find the place in turmoil: for within the hour, Lady Bradfield had suffered a desperate seizure and was on her deathbed at Goldhayes, surrounded by her grieving family. And to them the sudden arrival of Doctor Jasper Sewell, well in advance of the Bury physician who had been hastily sent for, was a miraculous coincidence undoubtedly ordained by the Almighty. Lord Bradfield, whom he had not seen for five years and whom he cordially disliked, ushered him up the wide, wooden stairs and into his wife's chamber without giving him the chance even to greet his mother, who was standing, composed and calm as usual, by the bed. 'Do what you can!' Simon Heron, Lord Bradfield, had begged the tired, travel-stained young man, now suddenly aware both of his exhaustion and of the limitations of his skill and knowledge, and Jasper Sewell, whose solid Suffolk father had bequeathed to him a stubborn fighter's spirit, had done his best.

Nan Heron, Lady Bradfield, who had been born Anne Blagge, had never been strong, and her constitution had been irreparably weakened by years of failed child-bearing, miscarriages and stillbirths, and the privations of nearly fifteen years of poverty-stricken exile in The Hague. It was beyond his power, beyond anyone's power, to save her, but he could stave off the dread day for a little while, to allow the rest of the family to gather to her bedside; for while Lord Bradfield had managed to alienate himself from his surviving brother and sister, they had no quarrel with the gentle, ailing Nan, and if summoned would lose no time in hastening to her side. And when Jasper, aided by the Bury doctor, had restored a little life to his patient and prescribed rest and pills and nourishment, Lord Bradfield, his harsh eagle's face engraved with the deep lines of anxiety and grief, took him to one side in the Long Gallery. 'Doctor Sewell?'

Jasper, who had known him all his life, repressed his irritation at this characteristic formality and said, 'Yes, my lord? How may I be of service?'

'Someone must go tell my sister,' said Simon Heron, with difficulty. 'She . . . she is fond of Nan, she would like to be here when . . . ' He paused, and turned away, studying a woodenly painted portrait of his great-grandfather, Hal Heron the pirate, at his most unconvincingly respectable. 'She would like to be here . . . and my brother too, and Thomazine . . . they must be sent for, quicker than the post . . . Jasper, would you go?'

Compassion overcame his tiredness, and dislike, and irritation. 'I will leave in the morning, my lord, if you think I can be spared from Lady Bradfield's bedside.'

'Of course you can, you've done enough,' said Simon, turning. 'No one can do any more now, but wait . . . and it is a time to be burying old differences . . . Nan always wanted to forget . . . Have you heard from your sister?'

Jasper, who had never got over his intense embarrassment at adult grief, nakedly displayed, felt some relief at the change of subject. 'Only a few letters, my lord. Henrietta is not a great correspondent, and she has been busy with the children. But she seems very happy.'

'I am glad. Neither I nor Tom Jermyn liked her marriage to that harumscarum young brother of his, and still less the part Henry played in it, deceitful as always, but I think it is time to forget all that. Give my regards to her, should you see her. You will leave at first light?'

'I will, my lord,' said Jasper, and made his escape, thankfully, to the warmth and welcome of his family.

Regardless of weariness, he had kept his promise, setting out on Lord Bradfield's best horse at dawn that lovely May Monday morning of 1665, and had gone first to Ashcott, the journey taking him two days' hard riding. He had a night's rest there before setting off south towards Oxford and London, while behind him Francis and Thomazine and their younger children made ready, at once with gladness and with sorrow, for a return to their beloved Goldhayes.

He arrived late on the Thursday after another two arduous and exhausting days, riding down the Oxford Road past Tyburn Tree, and realised abruptly that he was probably nearer to his sister's lodging in Westminster than to Fleet Street. Suddenly, the thought of a chair, a meal, a drink and a loving face was too tempting . . .

And so he took the short cut indicated by the first of many passers-by, rode round St James's Park and through Petty France, leaving his horse to be fed and watered and rested in a large inn near the Palace of Westminster, and continued on foot to find Antelope Alley.

Even when he had found it, he had no idea of where his sister lodged, until he noticed a small, stalwart, red-haired child methodically playing with a top in a patch of afternoon sun at the far corner of the alley. He could remember Hen playing like that, as a little girl, and since red-haired children were not so common, there was a good chance that this was his niece. 'Beth?' he called.

The child jumped round, startled. She was so obviously Hen's offspring that he could have laughed: orange hair, freckles, round rosy face. 'Beth? I'm your Uncle Jasper. Is your mother in?'

After that, it was easy. The little girl, with the trust of a happy four-year-old, led him up a dark flight of stairs and into a suite of rooms which, though small and basically shabby, had been transformed by his sister's hard work and good management and neatness into lodgings in which anyone could take pride. And there was Hen, his dear, reliable, sturdy little sister, quite grown up now, and rather rounder and paler than he remembered, with sewing on her lap and a baby at her feet, a dark-haired, dark-eyed baby that had a look of Jermyn about it.

'Jasper!' she cried, and put the sewing carefully on a table, the needle out of reach of infant fingers, before leaping to her feet and running to hug him. For a moment, uncharacteristically sentimental, they held each other close; the baby, jealous, began to hiccup angrily.

'Quiet, Harry!' Hen said briskly, an order which was instantly obeyed. She stood back and gave her brother a critical stare. Apart from colouring, they were not particularly alike, Jasper being tall, slenderly made with an air of fragility about him and a white-skinned oval face and green eyes that he had inherited from his lovely Irish mother – the orange hair and freckles were his father's.

'You're taller, said Hen severely. 'And thinner – didn't they feed you at Leyden?'

'Well, you're fatter than you were – you obviously dine too well at Westminster, or Whitehall, perhaps?'

'Not in my condition, you lackwit. The reason I'm so fat, as you put it, should arrive in September, another Jermyn to add to the tribe. Now, what would you like? Beer? A dish of tea? Or some wine?'

'Beer,' said Jasper, through his dust-dried throat, and was treated to the sight of Hen's devastating efficiency. At the end of five minutes, he was seated in a comfortable chair, with a footstool, and a table by his side laden with food and drink – bread, cheese, a cold pasty, and a generous tankard of cool, excellent beer – and was able, with his accustomed sensitivity, to ascertain without being told that his beloved sister was happy, and fulfilled. Not that he expected her to grumble, or complain, for Hen's was a simple soul, undemanding and unambitious, looking no further than the day or the hour, and finding sufficient joy in what she had rather than seeking ahead, unsatisfied, to what she might have. It was a quality lacking in himself, and he envied her, as she would never envy him. She would love Charles Jermyn for himself, despite his multitude of faults, she would bear and rear his children and never know or want any different. Hen was rooted in the ground, but he, unfortunately, would always be looking at the stars.

He let her give him her news first. Charles was well, in his minor position on the fringes of Government, but, through his brother Henry and his uncle the Earl of St Albans, given a wider entrée to the bright, busy, glittering, decadent world of Whitehall. It was a world in which the prosaic Hen was decidedly out of place. She related stories of Henry's escapades, the duels, the assaults, the sieges of virtuous and not so virtuous ladies of the Court, the abortive expedition to Guinea on which he had offered to serve as a volunteer, all in the manner of a fond mother or aunt telling tales of a naughty but favourite child. Jasper, who had his own memories of student frolics in staid Leyden, was highly amused, despite his feeling (he had known Henry Jermyn since they were children) that his brother-in-law's exploits were always more fun when viewed from a distance.

Mindful of his sad duty, he then informed her of Nan, Lady Bradfield's last illness and the wishes of her husband. 'So I must leave you, and find the Ashleys before nightfall – is it far?'

'No, not at all. I can't leave the children the maid's gone to see her sick father in Kensington and she won't be back until dark, or I'd come with you,' said Hen. 'Will you have time to come back? There's room here for you to stay tonight, and more than welcome.'

He accepted with alacrity, and listened intently as she described the route, admittedly fairly straightforward, with her usual precise detail. 'The sign of the Ash Tree, a few doors up from Fetter Lane – rather more than a mile, it takes me half an hour or so to walk, with the crowds,' Hen told him. 'And don't be late back or Charles will eat all the rabbit!'

He walked more quickly than his sister, evidently, for there was only twenty minutes' difference between the hour on Hen's little bracket clock, made by Dan Ashley, and the times of the multitudinous clocks in that worthy craftsman's workshop when he arrived at the Fleet Street house. Master Ashley was busy with a customer, his wife was visiting friends by the Tower, the maid told him, but, she added, Mistress Rosalind and Mistress Alathea were upstairs in the parlour and would receive him.

He remembered Rosalind as a little girl, not very well, but as a child he had played with the baby Alathea, and had later taken an interest in her, both as a playmate of his sister's and as a person in her own right, amused by the tiny scrap, hair as white as lint, who had insisted on climbing back on her restless pony despite several painful falls, and with whom, in long-ago summers at Goldhayes, he and the other children had splashed in the moat and dived for coins and stones and chased the ducks . . .

The maid opened the door at the top of the stairs and announced him as he ducked through it: he must be taller than the Ashleys. There were two girls in the room, sitting on the window-seat in the slanting amber light of late afternoon, and both rose as he entered, but after the first second's glance, there was only one.

She was tall, slender, wearing a dress he scarcely noticed, for anything would have become her, from sackcloth to crimson velvet. Her hair was as pale as he remembered, and the sun turned it white gold and struck sparks from it like cold fire, and her face was like her father's but cast in a finer mould, the clear line of jaw and cheek and chin running smoothly together under the pale skin, dusted with freckles across the bridge of her long, slightly tilted nose.

'It's Jasper!' she said and he began to feel like someone who has just come to the surface of deep water, gasping for air, but still with nothing solid beneath his feet. He was completely unprepared for anything like this. No one, and certainly not the sluttish Dutch girls he had occasionally toyed with in the company of his fellow-students, had ever had such an effect on him: a girl who must be ten years his junior, a child not yet sixteen, a child he had once played with as one might with a rather brave and endearing puppy – and yet one look, steady and honest, from those long smoky eyes and he was like some lovesick swain sighing over a rustic Phyllis or Clorinda.

'Get a grip on yourself, you sawny fule,' he said to himself fiercely, in the dialect of his childhood. But it was no good, for although he was a realist, and trained to be observant and dispassionate and objective, some part of him would always be looking at the stars.

Mab, very stiff-legged and grey-faced, came out of the patch of sun in which she had been warming her old bones, and trotted over to greet him, and he was glad of the diversion, giving him a chance to compose his thoughts and feelings. It was ridiculous, to make so much of a pretty girl. Men in plenty were seduced by a lovely face into thinking, falsely, that the person concealed behind the mask was as pleasing, and he need look no further than the King and Castlemaine for his example

But he was aware, even as he upbraided himself, that any child of Thomazine and Francis Heron would surely not be a lovely creature with the soul of a whore and a heart that was rapacious greedy and callous. Yet he knew very little about Alathea, save his memories of the child he had known, hardly nine or ten years old when he left Goldhayes to go to Holland – and children change.

Full of Hen's delicious food, he had to decline the refreshments Rosalind offered him, although he accepted chocolate. She was an attractive girl, younger, shorter and plumper than Alathea, with her father's features, mouse-brown hair and snub nose and grey eyes, but with the grace of her mother's sparkle and unaffected enthusiasm to lend appeal to what was a rather plain and ordinary face. She was also beautifully and unostentatiously dressed. Alathea wore an ancient dull green garment that looked as if someone had spilt something very dubious on it, and yet she still cast Rosalind in the shade.

Rosalind did most of the talking, another characteristic inherited from her mother, and he was free to drink the hot thick bittersweet chocolate, rub Mab's harsh whiskery nose, and look at Alathea. She would not fit easily into the mould of fashionable beauty, and yet she would be spectacular anywhere, wearing anything, with that height and grace and astonishing hair. Her voice was rather low, with an ironic quality which reminded him strongly of Thomazine, and she used her hands to illustrate her points with quick, abrupt gestures. He caught her eye, once, unintentionally, and looked away again, but not before he had seen that same wry, defensive irony in her expression. It was a long time since he had blushed.

'And so that's all our news,' Rosalind was saying cheerfully. 'There are usually more of us, but Father and Mother are visiting and Nell and Celia have both got colds and they're in bed – I never knew any pair like them for catching colds and coughs and chills, even in May – and Oliver's at school now, for as long as St Paul's will have him. And today should be one of Alathea's painting days, but the Beales are going to move away into the country and Mistress Beale's studio has been packed up.'

'Painting?' Jasper enquired with interest. Alathea went slightly pink. Rosalind rattled on. 'Didn't you know? That's why Thea's staying with us, she's been studying painting with Mistress Beale for, oh, nearly five years now. And she's very good – everyone says so.'

'You toad, Rosalind,' said Alathea without rancour. 'Doubtless you'll now point out the stain on my skirt and tell Jasper that was intended for one of Mistress Beale's experimental pictures but we had it made up into a gown instead.'

'Well, if she *will* paint on sackcloth and bed-ticking,' said Rosalind, and the two girls broke into quiet, amused laughter.

'What sort of pictures do you paint?' Jasper enquired, greatly intrigued. Because of the knowledge of chemicals and processes required by most artists in the preparation of their colours, it often happened that art and medicine and alchemy were mingled, and several of his fellow-students in Leyden had dabbled in the arts. One, in fact, had begun by studying mathematics, and had turned his attention to painting in the middle of the course. He had subsequently become pupil to the great Dutch Master, Rembrandt van Rijn, whose studio Jasper had once visited to see his friend at work, and the intricacies of paint and colour had fascinated him ever since.

'What sort of pictures? Oh, portraits, mostly,' said Alathea. 'I'll do yours if you like. Red chalk should suit you well,' she added, with a teasing grin. Jasper found himself grinning back. He had almost agreed to sit for her then and there when he remembered his sad errand, and explained.

'Oh, poor Aunt Nan,' said Rosalind quietly, when he had finished. 'I always felt so sorry for her, didn't you, Thea? Poor woman, forever ill, and Uncle Simon isn't exactly a lovable person, and I positively loathed the children, the only time I ever met them.'

'Rupert was a spoilt brat and so was one of the girls, and the other one had a face fit to turn milk sour,' said Alathea, wrinkling her nose. 'If my parents and yours are going to Goldhayes, though, I don't see why we shouldn't go too, Ros, I would love more than anything to see it again even if we do have to brave Lord Bradfield and his family and sit at poor Aunt Nan's bedside. And it's not as if I would be missing any of my painting lessons because they're finished.'

'For ever?' Jasper asked, hearing the note of sadness in her voice, and she nodded. 'Yes. They've decided to move to Hampshire. Master Beale's post at the Patents Office was becoming insecure, and I think they wanted to leave while they still had the choice, if you see what I mean. So I've had to stop the lessons for the moment, but there is a possibility that the Beales can give me an introduction to Master Lely.'

'Really?' Rosalind said, sounding impressed. 'Did she really? Oh, Thea, if you could get an entry into Lely's studio – '

'I'd be turning out three portraits a week, as alike as twins,' said Alathea drily. 'All his women look like the Castlemaine, haven't you noticed? And from what I've heard, his assistants paint the drapery and the hands and the background and he does the face only – unless you're very important, or very persistent. At least Mistress Beale let me paint whole portraits occasionally! A life spent mixing colours and boiling varnish and painting someone else's pictures for them to get the credit and the money is *not* what I want to do,' she finished emphatically, the ironic detachment quite gone and a passionate sincerity colouring her voice and her face.

Jasper, looking at her, felt the pull of that independent, young, intense spirit as if drawn by a magnet, a moth to her flame. It was becoming more and more apparent by the minute that here was a very individual, unconventional girl who could never be accused of being too feminine, too passive, a person highly unlikely to leap early into married bliss, and yet his attraction deepened with every word and gesture and look. With a feeling that he would not like the answer, he said, 'What do you want to do, then?'

'Paint, of course,' said Alathea, astonished at the obviousness of the question. 'I want to set up my own studio and paint portraits – they're what I'm best at, though I do flowers and landskips as well, and history pictures if the story appeals to me, and I want to do it all myself, without anyone's help.'

There was a short silence. 'On your own?' Jasper asked. 'Without any help *at all*?'

'I hate people breathing down my neck,' said Alathea decisively. 'And the one thing that following Aunt Lucy to every play in London has taught me, is that there is no one who breathes down your neck quite so obtrusively as a husband.'

He did not like the answer, but there was little to be done about it now, and he was nothing if not optimistic. And in any case, there was no chance to pursue it further, for at that moment Rosalind's mother returned with a rush of welcome, and the business of arranging the journey to Suffolk must be done swiftly. Dan, summoned, did not think he could leave the workshop, for there had been a rush of orders recently and they were overburdened with work, but he saw no reason why the rest of his family, and Alathea and Nell, should not go. And of course, Jasper must escort them.

'You must be exhausted,' Dan added kindly. 'I'll arrange the hire of horses and all the rest, you go back to one of Hen's wonderful suppers – what is it? Rabbit? She does it in Rhenish, it's quite delicious – and as long as you're here by seven tomorrow morning, I'll do all else. And you'll have no chance to be late – her clock's from my workshop and keeps as good a time as any!'

His head tumbling with confused thoughts, Jasper walked bemused in the dusk through the emptying streets of London, the Strand and Charing Cross, Whitehall and King Street. It was fortunate that the route was straightforward, or in his dazed state of mind he might have gone astray, but he somehow found his way to Antelope Alley without making a wrong turning, and knocked on the door. Hen opened it, smiling, her hands floury, and attended by a most delectable and savoury smell. Her smile faded a little, but she said in explanation, 'I thought it was Charles. He's much later than usual, probably drinking in some tavern with an official whose palm needs greasing. Come in, do, and if he's much longer we'll eat without him – I'm pretty sharp-set, and I reckon you must be too.'

He followed her into the parlour, carefully lit by sparse wax candles. There was no sign of the children, Beth and Harry, who were presumably in bed. Hen put her candlestick down on the table, already laid for supper, and gave him a friendly, smiling glance which lingered and became unusually intent. 'What's happened?' she said. 'You look different.'

'Do I?' said Jasper. He grinned at her, suddenly cheerful. 'How do I look different? I've only been gone two or three hours.'

'Long enough, obviously,' his sister observed. 'You . . . well, you went out of that door looking tired, and annoyed, and weary of life and all manner of what, and now you come back different . . . like the old Jasper, before he grew up and became a respectable doctor. Lighter, you look, and younger, and happier. You haven't fallen in love, have you?'

Jasper began to laugh. He would never have suspected that his matter-of-fact little sister, who had always taken things at their face value, could be so perceptive. And what she said was true. Despite his surprise and bewilderment at the astonishing effect that Alathea had had on him, the overwhelming emotion filling him at that moment was one of joy, and delight. And he did feel younger, returned to the enthusiastic idealistic boy who had been fired by a dream of becoming a doctor – for he himself owed his name, and his very existence, to the skill of an Italian physician, Jasper Despotine, who had saved him and his mother during a very difficult birth. And because he wanted to practise medicine more than anything else, because he was impelled by his ambition, he had conscientiously, deliberately suppressed his old headstrong exuberance and applied himself seriously to work and study. The new, sober Jasper had not been a persona he was very happy with, but for the sake of his dream, he had accepted it.

And then Alathea, in a few minutes' conversation, had given his old self back to him again, and in sudden, joyous acknowledgement he seized his sister's hands and whirled her round the cramped space of the little parlour. A chair was knocked and Hen, helpless with laughter, released herself with difficulty and flopped into it, hands to her sides. 'You sawny fule, remember the little mite in here, will you? I was right, wasn't I?' she added, stifling her chuckles. 'I was – who is she, then? Plain Ros who dresses so nicely, or Alathea who usually dresses in paint?'

'I hope you're not casting aspersions on her virtue,' said Jasper, mischievously misunderstanding her. 'And yes, you are right, Henny-Penny, and yes, it is Alathea who has hooked my heart, quite without intending or knowing it, by the look and sound of her, and yes, I do know that she's dead set against all thought of love and marriage and she has some extraordinary idea of becoming a portrait painter, but I find her utterly captivating despite the paint on her clothes, and I am quite prepared to wait until she grows up a little and revises her opinions.'

'She won't,' Hen observed. 'Thea is already grown up. But I wish you joy – more joy – and whatever else happens, even these few hours have been very good for you. Do you know,' she added scoldingly, 'when Beth led you through that door this afternoon, I only recognised you by your hair? You looked *old*.'

'I'm younger now,' said Jasper, and gave his little sister a hug and a generous kiss. 'And at least now I know what love is like – and I once thought I'd go through life never knowing.'

'Well, you were wrong,' said Henrietta, grinning. 'And now, since Charles seems to be long overdue, shall we make a start on that rabbit before it's spoiled?'

CHAPTER FOUR

Rupert

This wimpled, whining, purblind, wayward boy. . . .
(Shakespeare, *Love's Labour's Lost*)

'His eyes keep following you, haven't you noticed?' Rosalind demanded sotto voce of her cousin. 'Don't tell me you haven't noticed!'

'I haven't noticed,' said Alathea, keeping her long narrow gaze fixed firmly on the countryside ahead, neatly framed between the horse's ears. She was tired, they had been riding all day and she was unused to it, and after all, because of the delay caused by Lucy's gelding casting a shoe, they would not reach Goldhayes that evening. In the distance, the huddled roofs of Sudbury were visible, and the three flint towers of its churches. It was at Sudbury that they would spend the night, before setting out for Goldhayes the next morning, and it was only twelve or thirteen miles away. The longing in Alathea to set spurs to her unwilling hired horse and gallop there now, in the late red light of a May evening, was so intense that she could feel it, a lump of emotion in her throat, but she knew the idea was impossible. The effect of this frustration was, predictably, to make her sharp-tempered with Rosalind, who got short shrift for her next words. 'Oh, come on. He's been looking at you all the way from London. You *must* have seen him!'

'Oh, do give over,' said Alathea irritably. She knew who 'he' was: Jasper rode about ten yards or so behind them, chatting to Oliver, who was still bursting with his delight at being excused school, and whose behaviour during the last two days had been reminiscent of a puppy released after being chained too long. In front of the two male members of the party came Lucy, the maid Sarah riding pillion behind her, and Nell, somewhat recovered from her cold. Celia, nose and eyes still streaming and with a persistent cough, had been left behind, bitterly unhappy at being thus abandoned, at home with her father. Some part of Alathea, resentful and defensive, had refused to acknowledge Jasper's yellow-green eyes resting on her wherever she went, but she was aware of them, even so, and felt acutely uncomfortable. She had not failed to notice the growing interest of her uncle's journeymen and apprentices, male customers and visitors, over the last year or so, but had ignored and gently despised them. Jasper she could not ignore, nor was it fair to despise him. She had known him since her babyhood, his sister was one of her friends, her parents were close to his, and Sewells and Herons had been tangled with each other for three generations now. And even without these facts, she liked Jasper. He was good company, amusing and knowledgeable and considerate, and there was a wild high-spirited streak in him that emerged but rarely, and matched a similar trait in herself. In

Chelmsford there had been a fiddler in the yard below their inn, playing scratchy dance music on an out-of-tune instrument, and Jasper, suddenly joyous, had swept her into an impromptu coranto around the parlour floor, with Oliver, grasping a startled Rosalind, quick to imitate.

Yes, she liked Jasper very much – but not *that* way, and she felt annoyance at his interest in her: an annoyance she had directed, very unfairly, at poor Ros.

Rosalind, however, did not readily take offence. She only grinned, and changed the subject. 'It must be your turn to take Mab, my arm's gone to sleep, holding her.'

Mab would undoubtedly have been better left in Fleet Street, where Celia at least would have doted on her sufficiently for her due, but Alathea, well aware of her beloved dog's advancing years, was haunted by the fear that something might befall her in her absence. Lucy, ever the sentimentalist, had raised no objections, and the elderly, spoilt little dog had thoroughly appreciated her leisurely ride on a variety of saddlebows, balancing neatly and expertly on the horse like, said Jasper, a misplaced figurehead. Alathea took her now, not wanting to notice the unpalatable truth that Mab was undoubtedly lighter than a few months ago, and very much slower and stiffer in her movements. But she was still happy, still thoroughly enjoyed life despite her sixteen or seventeen years, and Alathea was determined to make the most of whatever span Mab had still allotted to her.

They had no problems finding a suitable hostelry in Sudbury, despite the presence of Mab. And that night, as she dreamed so often, Alathea dreamed of Goldhayes, that she was riding down the drive towards it, as she would tomorrow morning, crossing the moat bridge and dismounting in the Front Court. But the house was still, silent, no smoke from the chimneys, grass blurring the gravel and weeds choking the flowerbeds, and she was alone. And inside there was no one, no furniture, no pictures or hangings, just the bones of the great dusty empty cobweb-hung building, bereft of the people whose love and laughter and music had given it life, and whose desertion had left Goldhayes dead. That damage, she had been unable to bear, and woke weeping.

But it was only a dream, she told herself, and its lack of substance would be proved today.

Even so, it had been so terrifyingly vivid that she could hardly bring herself to look, when at long last they rode round the curve in the drive and Goldhayes lay before them in all its amber glory, for fear there would be no smoke, and silence.

There was smoke, and the gravel was raked and the deer-fence in good repair, and after one relieved glance, Alathea could allow herself the luxury of feasting her eyes again on the place she loved best in all the world. The 'E'-shaped house, much larger than it at first appeared because of the courtyards and ranges at the back, was all surrounded, unusually, by a wide deep moat in which the house, reflected, could double its beauty. The octagonal copper-roofed turrets on the inside of the two projecting wings, the oriel window and the lovely stone porch with the sundial and the Heron arms beneath it, all were exactly as she remembered, though it was five years since she had last seen it. And as they drew nearer, the spell the house had always cast over her began to enchant her once more, so that she felt she had never been away, and would never leave it again, that somehow, somewhere, until the end of time Alathea Heron's heart and soul would always be at Goldhayes.

There were people to greet them, clothed ominously in black. Alathea saw, with delight, the dearly loved figures of her parents, and the smaller shapes of Matthew and Edmund and, quite the young madam at nine, Sophie. She would have leapt off her horse and run to them, for she had not seen them since the previous Christmas, but she was not eleven any more, and it was a grave and solemn occasion. And as if that were not enough the grim forbidding face of Lord Bradfield appeared beside her parents, so she slid down from her mount, and sank with Rosalind into her most flowing and graceful curtsey.

But even Simon Heron's sombre presence could not quite dampen a Heron reunion. Hugs, kisses, tears were exchanged, and the news imparted: Nan, Lady Bradfield, had died peacefully the previous evening, a mercifully kind release from many years of suffering and ill-health, and the funeral would take place the next day.

So Alathea s return to her family and to Goldhayes was not an occasion of exuberant joy, glad though she was to see them all again. The house, which in her father's time had rung with music and merriment and had been filled with all sorts of people, from the humblest cottager to Thomas Jermyn or Lady Penelope Hervey, who could feel at their ease, had retreated under Lord

Bradfield's aegis into a chilly formality. Voices were hushed, people moved on tip-toe, a rigid ritual of bows and curtseys prevailed, and the dinner, in a gloomy dining-hall hung darkly with stifling black cloth, was a long-drawn-out, agonisingly tedious affair. It was enlivened for Alathea by the sight of Edmund, Matthew and Oliver, who had evidently devised an impromptu code with their fingers and were passing wordless gestured messages to each other. She wondered whose idea that had been and decided upon Math. Now fourteen and a half, he was a serious boy, famous for having his nose forever within a book, but he had the inventive and imaginative flair for such a device. Edmund, nearly four years younger, was at present nothing more than a noisy, rough and rude little boy. He and Oliver had a great deal in common, but Oliver, as his much-tried schoolmaster was always complaining, had an excellent brain if he would but use it. He had learned early how to get by on his charm, and as a consequence was appallingly lazy, but likeable.

That was more, at any rate, than could be said for young Rupert Heron, Lord Bradfield's cherished only surviving son and heir. The loss of his mother did not seem to have had any adverse effect on him, and Alathea had seen him pinch Edmund's arm as they entered the dining-hall. It was an unwise move, for Edmund was a belligerent child who would nevertheless be content to bide his time for his revenge. Alathea, looking at Rupert, thought it high time that someone took him in hand. He was nine, a skinny angular boy with straight dark hair and narrow brown eyes, a turned-up nose and a mouth full of teeth that were far too big for his rather small, pinched face, and gave him a perpetual sneer. He was sitting next to his elder sister, Anne, who was no beauty either. Almost the same age as Alathea, she was as thin as a rail and no quantity of curling-papers or paint could have disguised her sharp features and hard-held mouth, framed in dark hair unwinding heavily from its tortured ringlets. Any beauty in the family had all gone to the younger sister, Mary, who simpered by Alathea's side and languished her eyes at Jasper – and she was only eleven. Alathea hoped devoutly that Sophie would not be disposed to copy her, in earnest or from mischief: her young sister could be a cruel mimic.

The rest of the day passed in boredom. There was nothing to do save sit in the Long Gallery or stroll in the Walled Garden, which lay to the west of the house beyond the moat and was glowing with the tulips that Lady Bradfield had brought back from Holland five years before. In the haste of departure, Alathea's drawing equipment had been left behind, and she did not presume to request quills and ink and paper from Lord Bradfield, whose resemblance to all the grim villains of the stage grew greater by the hour. Lucy and Thomazine, recognising the signs of danger, had packed Oliver, Edmund and Sophie, with Matthew their constable, off in the direction of the Home Farm, where they could run wild and let off surplus energy without fear of offending their host. But games, music, laughter at Goldhayes would be unseemly at this time, so Alathea and Rosalind strolled decorously up and down the gravelled walks in the Walled Garden, admiring the tulips and wallflowers and the blue drifting haze of forget-me-nots between them. The old apple trees were still in bloom, the chamomile lawn beneath them shady and dappled with sunlight and fallen petals. Mab, panting, had made her way there already and lay frothing gently at the mouth, her eyes following the girls everywhere. It was quiet, warm, beautiful, the whole air thick with the fragrance of the wallflowers; but although she was at last in the place she loved best, Alathea did not feel satisfied, and said so, with force, to Rosalind.

'You're silly,' said Ros, spreading her hands wide. 'Look, isn't it lovely – stop wanting what you can't have and enjoy it!'

'I want to draw it,' said Alathea mutinously. She knew she was behaving childishly, but some devil sat on her shoulder and drove her on. 'I want to draw it all, and I can't, and I'm tired of those dreadful children, though when you look at their father you don't wonder why they're so awful, and it's not the *same* as it used to be – it's spoilt, they've spoilt it for ever!'

'Oh, come on,' said Rosalind, with her father's unanswerable reasonableness. 'You can't expect a merry houseful at a time like this, can you? I'll wager *you'd* have a face as grim as granite if the person you'd married had just died. I feel sorry for Uncle Simon, he must be so unhappy.'

'Then why does he have to take it out on us?' Alathea demanded angrily.

Rosalind said wryly, 'Aren't you doing exactly the same thing yourself?'

The devil gibbered on her shoulder. Alathea's hot smoky-green eyes met Rosalind's calm grey ones, and dropped. 'Sorry, Ros,' she said with difficulty. 'I don't like being disappointed.'

'Nor do I,' said her cousin drily, 'but I try to make the best of things. Come on, let's go sit in the shade with Mab – I'm much too hot in this black dress.'

The chamomile lawn was sweet-smelling and comfortably springy. Mab greeted them with one of her pleased welcoming growls that often sounded for all the world like 'Hello', and put a pleading paw on Rosalind's immaculate sleeve. Obediently, they made a great fuss of her, and were just rolling her on to her back to tickle her stomach when a child's voice said, 'That's an odd-looking dog.'

Alathea looked up, startled and annoyed, and beheld Rupert Heron, standing a few feet away, showing all his teeth in that infuriating sneer.

She said sharply, 'Who are you to judge that? She's not odd!'

'It looks odd to me,' said Rupert, unabashed. 'And it can't run or catch things. Why do you keep it? You ought to have it knocked on the head.'

'I'll knock you on the head, you horrible little brat,' Alathea said between clenched jaws. 'Now go away and leave us in peace.'

'Shan't,' said Rupert, obviously disposed to be aggravating. He sat down beside them and gave Mab a prod with his solid, leather-clad foot. 'Does it do tricks? I saw a dog in Covent Garden last year that could sit up and beg, *and* walk on its hind legs. I bet your stupid dog couldn't do that.'

'No, she has more sense,' said Alathea angrily. 'Go on, leave us alone.'

Rupert evidently had all the sensitivity of a log of wood. He leaned over and briskly pulled Mab's soft black ears upright. With an indignant yelp, the little dog leapt up and retreated behind Rosalind, her tail clamped firmly beneath her belly. Once in that position of safety, she allowed herself the luxury of a growl, peering round Rosalind's skirts. Alathea patted her and rubbed her nose, trying to calm her.

Rupert whistled a few out-of-tune bars between his abundant teeth. Then he said carelessly to Alathea, 'Did you know you're a bastard?'

'Ignore him,' Rosalind hissed urgently – too late. Her cousin turned to face the child, very upright, her eyes glittering.

'*What* did you say?' Her voice was very level, and low, and tightly controlled: a sign of danger in her, as it was in her father. Rupert, cheerfully ignorant of this, gave her one of his tiresome, sneering grins. 'I said, did you know you're a bastard? I heard Father talking to Mother about it once, he said you were born before your parents were married and you might be anyone's . . . '

He got no further. Swept on the wings of a righteous and unholy rage, Alathea leapt to her feet and pulled him up with her, one hand grasping each shoulder. The infuriating teeth disappeared most gratifyingly into Rupert's mouth as he whimpered in sudden fright. 'Ow – Ow! Let me go! Let me *go*, I say!'

'Not until you apologise,' said Alathea, a bite in her tones that surprised even her. 'Go on – say you're sorry.'

'Sorry,' Rupert mumbled.

'And go away and leave us alone.'

Rupert seemed disposed to argue. He opened his mouth, saw Alathea's face and Rosalind's stern one behind it, and visibly changed his mind. 'Oh, all right.'

'Good,' said his bastard cousin, letting go abruptly and giving him a push. 'Now disappear, or I'll set Mab on you.'

Rupert, released, scampered off to a safe distance and turned to face them. 'Set that stupid dog on me? That's pretty pointless, I bet it hasn't got any teeth. And if you dare touch me again, I'll tell my father and he'll have it knocked on the head.' And with that parting shot, he fled.

'Ugh,' said Rosalind, shaking her dress as if it had come into contact with something poisonous. 'What a horrible little boy. Are you all right, Thea? You look very pale.'

'I'm all right,' said Alathea. Her hands were shaking, she saw with a curious detachment. She wiped them on the stiff black folds of her skirts, and sat down. 'I'm just realising how easy and satisfying it would have been to have strangled him then and there – and how much I *wanted* to do it, Ros, I *wanted* to squeeze the life out of him! And he's just an infuriating little brat who shouldn't be listened to. I haven't felt like that since I was eleven, the time Kit tore up my drawings.'

'I don't altogether blame you,' Rosalind told her thoughtfully. 'Did you mind very much about what he said? About being a – a bastard?'

'That? Oh, that I knew anyway, and my parents married a

month or so after I was born, and you've only got to look at me to see I'm my father's daughter . . . no, it was what he said about Mab that made me so angry, poor Mab, after all she's been through . . . I wish *he'd* been starved in Colchester, then he might have a bit more understanding, and a bit less talk about knocking her on the head, as if anyone *would* do such a thing, yes, you dear old girl, we all love you very much – well, nearly all of us.'

Mab rolled over, restored to her normal self by her mistress's fuss and attention, and revealed most of her yellowing and untidy teeth in a ridiculous grin of contentment. The two girls took turns to stroke her, finding it a great help in relaxing from the tensions induced by the repellent Rupert. After a while, Rosalind said, 'Where *is* Kit? Why isn't he here too?'

Alathea frowned, turning a scented stalk of chamomile between her fingers. 'He's in Yorkshire, at Denby, which is the house he inherited from his father. He owns most of my mother's estates as well, except for Ashcott and the Oxford house, so he's quite rich really, and my parents are fairly poor. It doesn't seem fair, does it? But when my mother married Sir Dominic Drakelon, he gained possession of all her lands, except Ashcott and the Pennyfarthing Street house which came back to her when he died, and Kit had all the rest. So when he left Oxford last year, Father took him up to Denby and tried to give him some idea of how to manage his estates, and that's what he's doing now. I haven't seen him for about three years and I don't really want to either. I don't think I'll ever forgive him for tearing up my drawings or for all the things he used to say . . . he seemed nice enough when I saw him last, but I don't think he's changed at all, not really and truly inside himself. And I'll be quite happy if I never set eyes on him again.' She glanced at Rosalind's kind plain face and added, 'I know he's my brother . . . but I don't like him at all.'

'I know what you mean,' said her cousin. 'I don't like Oliver at all, sometimes!'

'Oh, Oliver's just a pest – and much, much nicer than Rupert. No, with Kit and me it's different, not just brother and sister fighting. I do that with Math and Mun, but that's not the same at all, it's only playing. With Kit, it seems deeper . . . and dangerous, somehow. I hope he never leaves Yorkshire.'

'I don't suppose he will,' said Rosalind soothingly. Like her mother, she disliked unpleasantness and hastened to change the subject whenever it threatened to cast a shadow on a conversation. 'Look, here comes Edmund.'

Edmund Heron, known to his exasperated family as Mun, came striding up the path whistling far more tunefully than his cousin Rupert, the gravel crunching in time under his stout shoes. He altered course when he saw his sister and stamped over the chamomile lawn, scowling. It became apparent that his dishevelled appearance – the filthy doublet, bloodstained shirt and dirty hands and face – was even more remarkable than usual. Rosalind, shocked, demanded, 'What on earth has happened to you?'

'I was fighting,' said Mun belligerently. 'I was fighting that awful Rupert.'

'Rupert!' Alathea and Rosalind exchanged amused glances. Mun nodded. 'Yes. He said horrible things about you two and Mab, so I said horrible things about him and his sisters and then he hit me so I hit him back. Knocked him down,' he added with complacent satisfaction, licking his grazed knuckles. 'Then he started howling for his father, so I left him lying there, just by the moat bridge, and came to see if you were all right. Are you all right? Was he very rude to you?'

'Very,' said Alathea, grinning at her young brother, standing there so stalwart and protective, a role he evidently relished despite its unfamiliarity. 'But you appear to have avenged our honour. The question is, Mun, what in God's name will Lord Bradfield say? Rupert's the apple of his eye, and what's more, however provoking he is, he's two years younger than you and a lot smaller. And a great deal less practised a fighter, too, I'll wager.'

'Well, he started it,' said Mun cheerfully. 'And I don't care one jot for what Lord Bradfield says.'

That, however, was pure bravado, as was proved when their forbidding uncle, acting on information received from his sobbing son, summoned Mun to his presence that evening. It was an interview which reduced Mun to tears, and was followed by an even more painful discussion with his father.

The gloomy faces in the tiny, whitewashed church at Bradfield Tye for the funeral the next morning of Nan Heron, née Blagge, were not entirely due to the sadness of her death. The prospect of yet another rift in the scarce-healed, fragile family relationships cast its own blight on the day, and everyone in consequence was unnaturally on their best behaviour. Even Mun and Oliver were remarkably subdued, and Rupert, sporting a most startling black eye, remained well in the background and showed his teeth not at all.

The company at the funeral was very large indeed, a mass of Suffolk gentlemen and ladies whom Alathea had once known well: Thomas Jermyn and his wife from Rushbrooke, Herveys from Ickworth and Gages from Hengrave, Barnadistons from Kedington, even a sprinkling of Papist Mannocks from the lovely Gifford's Hall near Stoke-by-Nayland. The funeral address, given by the florid parson, Master Hepworth, extolled the patient virtues and long suffering in exile of the deceased, and Alathea, feeling her own eyes prickly with tears, was not surprised to see the worthy ladies of Suffolk, many of whom were related to Nan, openly weeping. She at least had been loved, which was more, Alathea reflected unhappily, than could be said for her husband and children.

And then she caught sight of Lady Bradfield's elder daughter, Anne. Rupert and the other girl, Mall, sitting beside her, looked bored and fidgety, but Anne's sharp white face was glossy with tears, and as Alathea looked, with embarrassment, the girl took a black kerchief from her sleeve and mopped her eyes. With a feeling that she might have misjudged her cousin, Alathea glanced hastily away.

The funeral baked meats, as her play-loving Aunt Lucy persisted in describing them, were laid out in the Hall at Goldhayes. The customary burnt wine and biscuits and ale and cold meats had been provided without regard to expense, and all the mourners had been given rings. Alathea's was made of gold and black enamel, and was too big for any of her thin long fingers, save the first one. It hung there like an over-ripe fruit, and she wished she could take it off before it fell off. Clasping it safe on her finger with the other hand, she stood on the edge of the press of people around the food and wine, and watched them with a painter's eye. Lord Bradfield, tall and gaunt in his dead black garb, looked like an ungainly, awkward stork – or a heron, she thought suddenly, amused. *Perhaps that's where our family got its name: most of us are tall and thin and long-legged. Except for my mother, of course,* she added to herself, as Thomazine's small wiry figure crossed her field of vision. And perhaps Aunt Lucy – as that worthy lady approached her mother – also lacked that characteristic length without breadth, like a straight line, that combined with the determined, positive expression to make à typical member of the Heron family. Her father had it, so did she, so did Lord Bradfield, and his elder daughter too. She searched for Anne Heron in the crowd, and soon found her, the tall shape so unfortunately similar to her father's, the stiff awkwardness and black straight hair and prominent nose no passports to beauty. Yet it was an interesting face despite the sharpness, speaking of strength of character and firmness of purpose. No sign now of the tears she had shed at the funeral, but there was a fierceness about her that warned off friendly chatter.

'Are you planning a painting?' A familiar voice startled Alathea, and she turned abruptly to find her Aunt Lucy standing by her side, smiling in a beady-eyed way that boded no good.

'No,' she said, forcing a smile in return, 'I'm not planning a painting . . . I was seeing how many people I recognised. Tom Hervey has grown somewhat stouter since I saw him last.'

'It's only to be expected with his new importance as a knight, *and* a good position in London – he's a Commissioner with the Navy Board now, you know,' said Lucy. 'I'm surprised he hasn't been to see us in Fleet Street. I shall invite him and Isabella to dinner when we return to London.' Her blue eyes, notoriously short-sighted, scanned the guests. She could evidently focus them when she wanted to, for after a moment she said casually, 'There's Jasper, talking to Mistress Jermyn. What a nice young man he's turned out to be!'

'Yes, he has, hasn't he,' said Alathea, with a sinking heart.

'He seems to have taken quite an interest in you.'

'Has he? I hadn't noticed.'

Lucy peered keenly at her. 'Really? You are unobservant,' said her aunt disbelievingly. 'Mind you, "interest" is much too mild a term – I've seen that look too often to mistake it. The boy's head-over-heels in love with you!'

'Rubbish,' said Alathea stoutly, but, to her acute annoyance, with a blush.

Lucy beamed triumphantly. 'You *have* noticed, haven't you – don't bother to deny it, I can see it in your face. Well? Do you like him?'

'Yes, but – '

'Then that's all settled, then.

'What's settled?' Alathea's anger rose. She stared at her aunt with growing annoyance. 'He hasn't said anything to me at all – he just follows me with his eyes. Ros teases me about it. And I can't help having this face, or this hair, can I? I *like* Jasper, I like him very much, but I don't love him at all, and anyway I have no intention of getting married – not now, not ever!'

'You're very young,' said Lucy soothingly. Her niece glared at her. 'I know I am, but I don't think I shall ever change my mind on that. I want to paint, you know I do. I want to succeed as a portrait painter and make my living at it, and what husband would ever tolerate that? Even someone like Jasper. And since I want to paint more than anything else, there isn't really any choice. I want to do it on my own, I want to be a success without anyone standing behind me, supporting me, propping me up, telling me what to do, lessening any achievement I may have . . . it may sound boastful, but I know that if you set one of my portraits beside one of Master Lely's it would be as good, perhaps better, because I can make women look like themselves and not cast them all in the Castlemaine's mould. And if I am as good as Lely, I can see no reason why I can't succeed as well as him or any other male painter. My sex should make no difference.'

'It shouldn't,' said Lucy, 'but I expect it probably will. You do seem very determined, but I've never heard you speak of this before. Are you sure you've thought it all out thoroughly?'

'I've thought of little else,' Alathea told her drily. 'And I know it will be a struggle, harder than anything I've ever done in my life, and even dangerous perhaps, but I have the will to do it and that's half the battle, and even if I fail, at least I will have *tried*, and that's the chief thing.'

'Do your parents know all this?'

'Well, I haven't told them in so many words, but I'm fairly sure they know, or have guessed. And I think they'll encourage me. Why else send me to Mistress Beale?'

'Well, I think you're making a very bold decision,' said Lucy. 'But, if you're so set on it . . . well, it's not for me to say, is it? But poor Jasper – do be kind to him, Thea, he's such a nice boy, and very sensitive, I'm sure, it would be too easy to hurt him.'

'I may have to,' said Alathea bleakly. 'If only to persuade him to forget all about me.'

'I don't somehow think that he will,' said Lucy, her eyes following his tall orange-haired figure as he crossed the Hall to speak with Richard Gipps, who owned Little Horringer Hall where the Blagges had once lived. 'Anyway, Thea, I shouldn't worry – he's hardly in a position to marry anyone yet, he has to build up a practice, whether it's here in Bury or somewhere else, and establish himself before looking round for a wife.'

'He won't find one in me.'

'Well, you're very young yet,' Lucy repeated. 'And in a year or two you'll probably have changed your mind. All young girls have their heads full of love and romance and marriage, and I expect you'll turn out just the same in the end.'

'I don't think I will,' said Alathea, holding hard on her patience.

Lucy ignored her. 'And just think how suitable it would be – Thomazine's daughter and Grainne's son! They've been friends for so long, and we always used to say how nice it would be if Jasper married one of Thomazine's children, so that she and Grainne could share their grandchildren, and since that little minx Sophie is quite out of the question, you are the only other candidate.'

'And a very unwilling one,' said Alathea repressively. She lifted her head and looked her Aunt Lucy straight in the eye. 'I won't do *anything* I don't wish to – least of all, marry too early or to the wrong person – and I *hate* being put under pressure, made to feel I'm obliged to do something. It's my life, and I know clearer than most what I want from it, and though I love you all, I am *not* going to be kind to anyone who gets in my way.'

For a moment longer, their eyes held, smoky sea-green and the round bright inquisitive blue of Lucy's. Then her aunt smiled, and shrugged. 'Oh, well, it was just an idle thought – no need to get on your high horse, you know, Thea, just because I was indulging in one of my fireside whims. And I won't let it go any further, don't you worry – you're quite free to do exactly as you please.'

But she was not free of Jasper's eyes, and even after Lucy, with a coy smile that indicated she had in no way abandoned her hopes, had gone over to speak with Isabella Hervey, Alathea could not rid herself of her anger. She would *not* acceed to the desires of her aunt and her mother and her mother's dearest friend, however 'suitable' it might seem. Yes, it would be nice, from their point of view, if she would marry Jasper and settle down as the wife of a country doctor, and breed their grandchildren for them to share: for Grainne and Thomazine, Malise and Francis, had shared so much in their lives that this must seem a pleasant and comforting dream for their old age. But I will *not*, thought Alathea, with the fierce anger she had only partly revealed to Lucy, I will *not* be pushed into a future I don't want, out of family feeling and duty. My parents have been very good and I love them dearly, but I am *not* going to oblige them in this – ever.

'Hello, maw,' said her father. He had the knack of being summoned by thought; she had often noticed it. Still angry, she said 'Hello,' rather more shortly than she meant, and was treated to one of his most penetrating stares. 'I see Lucy has left you in some confusion. Could this have anything to do with a certain Jasper Sewell? Due not a little to my dear sister's efforts, rumour is flying thick and fast.'

'It flies in vain,' said Alathea wearily. 'Jasper seems to have conceived a fancy for me: it may last a week or a month or a year or for ever, I don't know and I don't care, save that Aunt Lucy has just told me that it would be Mother's dearest wish, and Grainne's too, if we were married. And I don't *want* to!'

'Lucy's not the only one making large numbers from a very small sum,' said Francis Heron. He laid a glass of burnt wine on the chimney-piece, where it glowed like a dark and delicately shaped ruby against the silvery oak of the panelling. 'You seem to be jumping to all sorts of conclusions. No one is ever going to force you, or persuade you, or cajole you, or pester you with ideas of family duty, into a marriage you don't want. Surely you can remember enough of your parents' history to realise that? Oh, Thea, don't worry about it: we love you very much, and we are not going to stand in the way of anything, anything at all, that you want to do, ever.'

'Do you mean that?' Alathea whispered, feeling the tears sting her eyes. 'Do you really mean it? You'll let me become an artist?'

'I don't think we could stop you,' her father said drily. 'And we'd much rather help you, and encourage you, and let you make your own mistakes and profit from them, than stick to old-fashioned ideas of propriety and risk estranging you from us for ever: because whatever we say, I suspect that you will still do exactly what you want to do, always.' He dropped a kiss, lightly, on the fair head that was so like his own, and not very far beneath him now, though he was tall for a man. 'And don't worry – it's a trait I fear you have inherited in double measure from both your parents, and therefore hardly your fault.'

'I suppose not,' said Alathea. She gave him a brave, though rather watery, grin and quickly wiped her eyes with a clean kerchief: no use of a sleeve, now, for this newly adult child of his, and Francis felt a pang of regret for the vanished hoyden, that as if by witchcraft had been transmuted into this striking girl who had, so astonishingly, caught the eye of Jasper, of all people. It did not make him feel old so much, for he did not look or think of himself as a man of forty three, but he was made vividly aware of the swift passage of time. All the children were growing up, and he wondered about their futures: but none more so than Alathea, brave and determined and, he suspected, completely ignorant of the problems and pitfalls she faced in her struggle to become an accepted portrait painter.

But, as he had said to her only a moment ago, she must make her own mistakes: being Thea, he had no doubt that she would learn from them. So he smiled down at her, and changed the subject. 'I know it's a sad occasion, but are you glad to be back here, mow?'

'Yes – or I would be, if there weren't so many pebbles in the bread,' said Alathea with some bitterness. 'Why are you smiling?'

'Your mother uses that expression, and I've never heard it from anyone else. Go on. Who, or what, are the pebbles?'

'Oh, they're not so serious. Rupert, the repellent little brat: he was very rude to me and Ros and Mab yesterday. He makes my skin crawl, *and* he provokes Mun, and you know what Mun's like – hit first and ask questions after. And the whole place seems so different, so sad and formal: it's not just Aunt Nan's death, I'm sure it's like that always now. But worst of all by far than any,' said Alathea, losing thread of her grammar in her vehemence, 'is the fact that I can't *draw* it!'

'Oh, is that it?' said her father, amused. 'Well, I'm sure this poor man's palace can furnish you with quill and paper and ink, and even chalk perhaps – and if you balk at the prospect of begging them from Lord Bradfield, I'll tell him I want to write a letter.'

Alathea swallowed and made a decision. 'Well, start as you mean to go on – I think *I* ought to ask him. After all, I'm going to have to learn to ask far greater things from much more important people in the future, if I'm to succeed at anything – and I'll ask him tomorrow, perhaps. When are we going home? Can I come back to Ashcott with you?'

'To the first, in a week or so maybe, if you brats don't do something unspeakable to Lord Bradfield's offspring in the meantime. And for the second, yes, of course you may: you'll ever be more than welcome there, Thea, you know that.'

'I do know,' said Alathea, smiling. She turned to survey the mass of mourners, soberly clad for this solemn occasion: but of course, with so many gathered together, there were signs of levity here and there, a smile or two and even some muted laughter. Lord Bradfield, receiving the condolences now of Sir Francis Mannock, did not look as though he knew what laughter was – Alathea had never heard any sounds of merriment pass his lips. It was strange that he should be so different from his brother and sister: and then a thought struck her, and she turned to Francis. 'I've just realised who's missing! Where's Hugh?'

Hugh Trevelyan was half-brother to Simon, Francis and Lucy Heron, being the child of their mother's late second marriage. Both his parents were dead: his father, Richard Trevelyan had died when he was four and his mother Mary, formerly Lady Heron, a few years later. Alathea had always liked her half-uncle, as she had teasingly called him as a child, and had always felt that it was very unfair that Hugh had little money and no lands to set off his undoubted wit and charm and intelligence. Since leaving Goldhayes, she had seen nothing of him, but would always think of him with affection.

'Oh, Hugh!' said Francis, with the amused exasperation that his half-brother's name always seemed to bring out in people. 'Somewhere in France, I think – he's been fairly close with Henry Jermyn, I'm surprised you haven't bumped into him in London. He's one of the Court hangers-on, runs errands, goes on missions abroad and that sort of thing, small fry as yet but he's only twenty or so, after all, and you know Hugh: by hook or by crook, and I suspect mainly the latter, he'll do his talents justice in the end.'

'I hope so,' Alathea said. A memory of Hugh at his wittiest and most endearingly cynical rose to amuse her, and she had to stifle a laugh. 'I was just thinking, how unlike Hugh, and you and Aunt Lucy, Lord Bradfield is.'

'He was born under a dark and gloomy star, remember,' said

her father. 'He's the eldest son, after all, so he had a heavy mantle of responsibility laid on him since childhood. Lucy and Hugh and I, on the other hand, could afford to be more carefree. But though we've had our differences aplenty in the past, he and I, he does have a heart under that very intimidating exterior. So when you ask him for your quills and ink and paper tomorrow, remember he's as human as I am – even if it doesn't show quite so much!'

Despite her father's reminder, Alathea could not help feeling nervous as she hovered outside Lord Bradfield's study door the next morning. She knew that the worst could only be that he would speak unpleasantly to her, but she knew herself too well, and feared that she might lose her temper: and for her family's sake, she must not do that. Setting her jaw and taking a firm hold on herself, she knocked at the door.

There was a barked 'Come in!' through three inches of stout Suffolk oak, and Alathea obeyed. Her uncle, Lord Bradfield, was seated at the plain desk her father had always used when working on estate business. The solitary window looked out on to the Courtyard Garden, a tiny well of light in the centre of the house, full of herbs and flowers but not, at this early hour, of sunlight, though if she craned her neck she would see it striking the russet tiles of the roof. Her uncle looked drawn and haggard and intimidating, the great eagle's beak of a nose jutting even more prominently from his sunken face, and his sombre dark eyes were shadowed. She gave him a very deep, respectful curtsey, and rose to stand stiffly in front of him, the very image of meek girlhood.

'Good morning, Alathea,' said Lord Bradfield. Like her father's, his voice was deep and dark, but lacking Francis's mockery or humour seemed as harsh as a crow's. He placed his hands finger to finger on the desk in front of him and looked her over with what she felt must be profound disapproval. Then he said abruptly, 'What can I do for you?'

'If you please, my lord,' said Alathea, hating the humble tone of her voice, 'I would like to borrow some paper, and quills, and ink. And a penknife, if you have one to spare.'

'Of course,' said her uncle. He indicated the side of the desk, where she saw several jars of ink, a dozen or so uncut quills in a pot, and a neat stack of thick creamy paper. 'You may help yourself: there is more in the cupboard. And I have a spare penknife which you may borrow, so long as you return it when you have done. Is the letter a long one?'

Alathea, who had at first relaxed at this surprisingly friendly approach, swallowed. 'No – no, my lord, I don't want to write a letter. I – I have a fancy to draw the house.'

'Draw?' Lord Bradfield's eyes narrowed. 'Ah, yes, I remember your mother mentioned that you had been taking lessons. Well, you may take the paper, but I would like to see the results of your labours. Pray help yourself.'

'Thank you very much,' said Alathea fervently, and moved towards the desk. As she did so, her eye was caught by three pictures hanging on the panelled wall behind her uncle. She could not remember seeing them before and her curiosity was awakened. 'Oh – may I look at your pictures?'

'Pictures?' Lord Bradfield seemed puzzled for a moment, before his frown cleared and he said, 'Oh, those pictures. Yes. My dear wife bought them in Holland just before our return to England. Of course you may see them: they are pleasant trifles, no more. I know very little about such things.'

The three oil paintings hung in an unimaginative, evenly spaced row. They were all roughly the same size, but were clearly by separate hands: two depicted women, one playing a lute, the other reading a letter, and the third was a landskip, presumably of the proverbially flat Dutch countryside. This was a very stiff, clear, formally arranged composition, and she rather disliked its artificiality: but the other two were quite different. The woman reading the letter, in the light of a window, was a deceptively simple yet lovely picture, every touch of paint as clear and glowing as a jewel. It was obviously by the hand of a rare master.

Alathea drew in her breath sharply, and said in wonderment, 'This is beautiful – who painted it?'

Lord Bradfield turned and gave the painting a cursory glance. 'That? I do not remember. Meer, perhaps, yes, I think his name might be Meer.'

Alathea, studying the cool paint, noticing the palette restricted to lemon and grey, pale blue and black, was also conscious of some irritation. This was a picture of great skill and harmony, a work she would dearly love to possess for herself, and the fortunate owner could not even muster sufficient interest in it to name the artist. She turned her attention to the last painting, a dashing, vivid lady playing a theorbolute and, obviously, singing. Complimenting the subject, the brushwork was exceptionally bold, swift and vigorous, giving the impression that it had been dashed off in a few hours. Alathea stared at it with burgeoning interest. She had found that painting in oils was too stiff and complicated a technique to allow the full freedom, the effortless expression of form and outline that was hers when she worked in pen-and-ink, or chalk. Now, looking at the woman with the lute, she realised that it *was* possible. She might never attain the careful glowing purity of the lady with the letter, but now, with a leap of enthusiasm, she saw that life and movement and bold vigour could also be expressed in paint, and knew that she could do it. Already her imagination raced forward, envisaging a portrait of Oliver, perhaps, he had the necessary outgoing character, flushed with the energy of a boisterous thirteen-year-old, hand on his first real sword . . .

She drew a deep breath. This picture had opened the door, given her new inspiration: who had been the artist? Impulsively, her eagerness showing in her voice, she asked; and received once again an unsatisfactory reply.

'That was sold to my dear wife by a rogue who swore it was painted by the great master Hals,' said Lord Bradfield, with some bitterness. 'She paid a great deal of money for it, more than I could really wish, and then we were told by someone who knows about such things that it was not by Hals at all, but by some female pupil of his.'

Alathea swung back to the painting with renewed excitement. 'It's by a *woman*? What's her name?'

'Leyster,' said Lord Bradfield dismissively. 'Judith Leyster, I believe her name is. How poor Nan can ever have thought that it was by Hals, I cannot imagine. It appears quite mediocre to me.'

Now you know that it's a woman's work, thought Alathea with anger, but held her tongue. She returned to the desk and gathered up the tools for her drawing, that seemed suddenly so inadequate after the limitless possibilities of paint, gave her thanks, made her curtsey, and fled.

It was a lovely morning to stand out even in this succession of lovely May mornings. The sun gave the house, and the grass and water around it, the same clear brilliant purity of colour that distinguished Mijnheer Meer's painting. Even now, scarcely past nine o'clock, it was noticeably warm, and the promise of heat shimmered in the air.

Buoyant with her discovery of Judith Leyster, Alathea was seized with a desire to revert to childhood and race madly across the rough grass of the park, running for pure joy as she had done long ago in the days when Goldhayes was her home: and she could never rid herself of the feeling that it would always be her home, and that it was her uncle and his family who were the intruders.

But her hands were filled with paper, and quills, and precarious jars of ink: she could not run anywhere. So she made her way to the place she had already chosen in her mind's eye, to do the picture she desired, and felt her fingers running, tingling like fire with the urgency to create.

Here, she was facing the eastern wing of the house, that contained the Library and a suite of guest chambers above, at present occupied by her parents. The mellow rose-red brick fell sheer into the moat and continued in reflection, concealing with that magic beauty the fact that the waters of the moat were murky and deep, stained with weed and smelling none too clean when disturbed. But from where Alathea sat, in the warm flowery grass with buttercups dusting her dress with yellow pollen, the effect was enchanting. Carefully, with a skill born of long years of painful practice, she cut the quills with Lord Bradfield's penknife: one with a broad point, another pared finer, a third finer still. For the most detailed work she would have preferred a crow's quill, but for now must make do with the ubiquitous goose. With care she laid the sheets of paper on the board across her knees and considered the scene in front of her. It was impossible, of course, to include all the house from so close: she wanted to concentrate on the moat, on the illicit wallflowers and creeping plants that trailed down the brickwork, on the carved stone window frames and the very slightly irregular octagonal turret that jutted out from the inside edge of each wing. A slow, forgotten smile curling her long mouth, she dipped the finest quill into the jar of ink, and began.

She worked quickly, accurately, feeling the power flowing through her hand as never before. The quill glided over the paper as if it were silk, following the slightest impulse from her fingers, and this small corner of Goldhayes flowered upon the paper in obedience to her command, as if it were enchanted.

A sudden, jeering cat-call rudely interrupted the spell. Involuntarily, Alathea's hand jerked, and the resulting misdirected line all but ruined the picture. Furious, she looked up and beheld the unwelcome figure of her young cousin Rupert, still with the splendidly ostentatious black eye given to him by Mun. He was leaning out of the Library window, not twenty yards away, and as soon as he was sure of her attention produced a grotesquely mocking face for her benefit.

Enraged, Alathea stared for a moment at the child's distended eyes and protruding tongue and waving hands: then she remembered her own, frequently appalling younger brothers, and the best remedy. Gritting her teeth, she bent her head to the drawing, and tried to ignore him.

Rupert, however, was not used to people ignoring him. All his life he had been the centre of attention, and whenever this satisfactory state of affairs appeared to be in danger, he took immediate steps to rectify the situation. Today everyone seemed to be busy: even his sister Mall had told him to go away, and followed it up with one of her twisting, painful pinches. He knew better than to disturb his other sister Anne, who was distant at the best of times and, since their mother's death, had become completely unapproachable. So, bored, he had wandered into the empty Library and seen, temptingly sitting there on the grass on the other side of the moat, his odd cousin. Since she had lost her temper with him the other day, he had become a little wary of Alathea, but he was out of her reach now and yet not, of course, out of earshot. He whistled.

'*I will not look at that insolent little boy*,' Alathea said fiercely to herself. But she had to glance up in order to continue drawing: by which time Rupert, delighted with the success of his stratagem, had rearranged his face into another gargoyle replica and followed it up with a further cat-call, not so loud as to draw the interest of anyone else who might be in the vicinity.

I'm not going to say anything either, and if he won't go away I'll probably end by throwing something at him, thought Alathea, stroking the quill along the sweet rippling black lines of the drawn moat. *I wonder what those frightful teeth would look like blotched with ink? He wouldn't be quite so ugly if it wasn't for those protruding teeth: his mother had them too, but not nearly so bad.*

'Ya – ah! Yar – oo – oo! Look at me – ee!'

'No, I am *not* going to look, you horrible brat,' Alathea muttered. But in the end, of course, she had to, to check the details of the stray yellow wallflower growing from the cracked mortar below the turret. This time, the repellent Rupert had climbed out on to the windowsill and was balancing there, hanging on to the mullion with one hand and thumbing his nose with the other. He looked so ridiculous that Alathea, to her own surprise, burst out laughing.

If it surprised her, that reaction certainly startled Rupert. He lost his balance and his precarious hold, and with a squawk of astonishment fell headfirst into the moat.

The splash was immense. Fountains of water erupted, spraying the walls of the house: Alathea even felt one or two drops on her face. She waited, a satisfied grin lingering, for the inevitable roar of rage and humiliation which would follow when he surfaced.

She waited. There was no sound but the ripples on the moat lapping the brickwork, and the frantic calls of a frightened moorhen. With a sudden, tightening feeling of foreboding in her chest, Alathea got to her feet, laying down her drawing and placing the ink beside it, and walked the few yards to the edge of the moat. She fully expected to see his face leering triumphantly up at her, but below her was nothing, only the boiling, muddy water. She glanced up and down: no sign. Then, she realised that the mollycoddled, spoilt Rupert had probably never learned to swim – and in most places the moat was seven or eight feet deep, mud and weeds and water.

At the full pitch of her lungs, Alathea screamed as loudly as she could: someone, somewhere, would surely hear her. She tore off her shoes and stockings, laid hold of the low stone-capped wall that bordered this side of the moat, and with another yell for help, jumped into the thick evil water.

She had never really learned to swim herself, only paddled long ago in the water with her brothers and Hugh and Jasper and Hen. With terrible fear, she knew full well that her chances of finding him were small, and the risk to herself far greater, but she was the only hope Rupert had. She took a deep frantic sobbing breath and ducked under the water where he had fallen. Desperately, she beat her hands in front of her, blind, terror-struck, feeling only the slimy strands of weed coiling hideously around her fingers. Her ears roared, her chest hurt, she needed air: she kicked upwards, hampered by the heavy clinging folds of her skirts around her legs, and just as she thought she would surely die, her head shot into the blessed daylight and she could breathe. Half-blinded by muddy water, she smeared her hand across her eyes, and looked around at the suddenly towering walls bordering the moat. No one anywhere: no sign, either, of Rupert. Really frightened, she screamed and screamed again, beating her hands and legs against the water to keep herself afloat: her skirts seemed like some dreadful monster from the mud beneath her, pulling her down. But down she must go, hopelessly: and it was the hardest and the bravest thing she had ever done, to leave the air and life, and dive down again into the murky waters that had swallowed her young cousin.

This time, she made herself open her eyes. Jasper had taught her, long ago, and she had never forgotten the knack. It did no good at all, the disturbed water was thick with mud and she could see nothing. She shut them again, quickly, and searched blindly with her hands, kicking her feet through the skirts and weeds that clutched her legs, threatening to pull her down further, to the slimy tentacles that in her childhood she had always imagined to live at the bottom of the moat . . .

Her feet struck something quite hard beneath her, stone probably – she remembered Jasper saying that there were lumps of stone at the foot of the walls . . . and at the same instant her frantic flailing hands met something solid, fleshy feeling: she touched cloth, unmistakeably, and an arm. She clenched her hands around it, and kicked with the last of her strength for the surface.

She thought that she would never get there. The urge to breathe overwhelmed her and she almost let go of her prize. Sparks and flashes dazzled her, the sea sound rushed in her ears: she gasped and drew in a great gulp of foul water and then suddenly, coughing and choking, she was on the surface. Someone shouted her name, but her hair was plastered across her eyes and she could not see anything at all, her last efforts concentrated on the inert weight she had dragged from the depths of the moat. But she could not find any more energy to tread water until help arrived, and despairingly felt herself sinking back, to failure and death.

A splash rocked her: someone grabbed her, painfully, by the hair and pulled her face above the water. Spluttering, still with her fingers clamped on Rupert's arm, she felt herself being dragged efficiently through the water. She tried to speak, coughed instead, tried again and succeeded. 'Rupert – I've got Rupert.'

'Put your hands on the wall,' a familiar voice said in her ear. Not recognising it, she gasped desperately, 'Can't – Rupert – I've got *Rupert*!'

And then he understood. More shouting: she felt the child's body being unceremoniously pulled out of her grasp, and her hands were free to clutch the rough brickwork of the moat. Too exhausted to do anything else, she hung on, feeling the weight of her skirts pulling her down again. She would not be able to resist them for very long . . . she did not even have the strength to drag the hair out of her eyes . . .

'Take this,' the same familiar yet unrecognised voice said beside her, and something thick and rough and round was wound about her wrists and pushed into her hands. 'Take this and *hold on*!'

It was a rope: she had the wits left to realise that. Convulsively she clutched it. More shouting, and then a sudden jerk and pain in her arms and shoulders, as her sodden weight was dragged up from the water, bumping and scraping over the rough brickwork of the wall, over and onto the grass, and safety.

At once, she was copiously and unceremoniously sick, and felt a great deal better for it. Someone, gently, disentangled the hair sticking to her face and air, light, sunshine burst in on her. Despite the heat, she began to shiver uncontrollably.

'What happened?' said a voice, a different voice. She looked round, stupefied with exhaustion, and saw her father kneeling by her side. He, obviously, was not her rescuer, for his clothing was neat and dry. He gave her a reassuring smile and repeated his question. 'Thea – what happened?'

She gathered her wits, painfully. 'It was Rupert – he was fooling about on the Library window – he fell in and I jumped in after him – where is he?'

'Over there,' said Francis, and indicated a group of people crowded around something on the ground. Alathea evaded his restraining arms, struggled to her feet and stumbled the few yards to join them. Hands caught at her but she pushed her way through and saw who her rescuer had been.

Jasper Sewell knelt by the body of her cousin Rupert: his clothes streamed with water, mud plastered his face and hands, and weed draped his hair. He was pumping, squeezing, kneading the child's chest, but under his clenched hands Rupert lay, as inert and lifeless as one of Sophie's dolls. With horror, Alathea stared at the boy's face, the protruding teeth now pathetic, tragic, the half-closed, mud-stained eyes as sightless as glass, and knew that all her desperate efforts had been in vain. Defeated, she turned away, sank exhausted down into the grass, and wept bitterly.

Jasper also knew that his task was futile, but he kept on trying to force air into the dead boy's water-filled lungs. He had seen this done in Holland, where children were always falling into, and being pulled out of, the canals, and he had even seen it work, once or twice, and an apparently drowned child brought back from death. But it must be done quickly, and he knew that it was too late: Rupert had been dead, probably, even before Alathea had found him. Accepting the truth, he stopped at last, and stared down at the still body: then, with a silent, significant gesture, closed the child's eyes and laid his arms by his sides. Rupert Heron, his father's only son and heir, was dead.

Some of the crowd around them, servants, children, began to sob. Jasper, heavy with failure, got wearily to his feet. 'Someone had better go tell his father,' he said, and Francis, with a nod of agreement, set off at a run. And then, obeying the urge which had been filling his heart and soul ever since he had left her on the ground and gone to Rupert, Jasper turned to seek Alathea.

She was close by him, kneeling in the grass, her face blind and streaked with tears and muddy water. Even now, fished out of the moat like a half-drowned puppy, she was beautiful, her fair hair darkened with water and hanging in rats' tails around her face which, bereft of that striking frame, was revealed in all its delicate loveliness, the fine bones and clear lines of a medieval angel. His heart caught for ever, he wanted to fold her in his arms, to offer her his comfort and receive hers in return: but he had heard too much of her pride, and could not bear the risk of a rebuff. He could not prevent himself, though, from kneeling beside her and taking her wet, bleeding hands in his. 'Thea – are you all right?'

Her eyes enormous, she stared at him: then, as if returning from a great distance, she said quietly, 'He's dead, isn't he.'

His hands tightened on hers, and he saw her wince. He withdrew them, and said gently, 'Yes, I am very much afraid so.' He wanted to praise her courage, her determination, but that urge had died as he saw her, still and remote as a statue.

She turned her face away and said slowly, 'Only a day or so ago I was so angry I *wanted* him dead – and now I'd give anything, *anything*, to have found him in time . . . oh God, I tried so hard, I found him, I never thought I would, it doesn't seem fair that it was too late . . . oh, why didn't I realise that something was wrong until it was too late?'

'You couldn't have done anything,' said Jasper, keeping his voice low and level and reassuring.

Alathea jerked round to face him again, her eyes hot and angry with unshed tears. 'Don't be patronising! He wouldn't have been on that windowsill at all if I hadn't been out here drawing: and when he fell in I didn't do anything because I thought he was still playing the fool – and when I *did* realise something was wrong, it was too late.' Her face, bitter with her anger at herself, burned into his. 'And I didn't do anything because I didn't want him to laugh at me – I was angry with him and I laughed when he fell in . . . and in a few minutes he was dead, and I *laughed*!'

'Be reasonable,' Jasper whispered, hardly able to bear the torment he saw in her anguished expression. 'Oh, Thea, you couldn't have done anything more – you have nothing to blame yourself for – *nothing*, do you hear me? You couldn't have known what was to happen, and when you did know, you did your utmost to try and save him – you could have drowned yourself, for you can't swim either, can you? You might very well have drowned yourself for him: could anyone have asked more of you?'

'*I* could,' said Alathea fiercely. 'I *could* have saved him, you know I could, Jasper Sewell, so don't give me platitudes!' Abruptly, with difficulty, she got to her feet and stood, swaying with exhaustion and emotion, her face averted. Jasper, with the feeling that he had hopelessly blundered, rose and put a hand on her arm. She jerked it away and he had a glimpse of her face, the helpless tears pouring down her slender, pale cheeks; then she said, low and furious, 'I said, don't patronise me, Jasper – I don't need your help or anyone else's! Now go *away*!'

He knew his mistake now. This girl was no humble gentle lady to be patted and cossetted like most members of her sex. Instead, Alathea was as proud and fierce and untamed as an eyass hawk, and he realised that she would recognise only those who treated her as an equal, and who did not importune.

He coughed deliberately, and withdrew his hand. 'Forgetting all else, and speaking in my medical capacity, I would strongly advise you to spend the rest of the day tucked up warmly in bed, or you'll contract a fever of the lungs without a doubt. Now are you going to take my advice, or not?'

Alathea stared at him. She was suddenly, weakly filled with the desire to laugh at this abrupt change in tactics: but it would not be seemly, not with Rupert lying dead a few yards away. And her failure to save him still tore at her soul: the urge to withdraw, to hide, to forget was very strong. At that moment, she beheld a familiar, most welcome figure hurrying across the moat bridge, followed by others, her mother amongst them: but it was Rosalind that she needed now, kind, superficial, understanding, undemanding, chattering Ros, and Jasper had to watch, excluded and hurt, as Alathea gave her embrace to her cousin, and received from her the comfort he had thought it his right to offer.

Much later, Jasper walked, tired and unhappy, down the half-mile or so of drive that separated Goldhayes from the Home Farm at its gate. The sun beat down on his back, soaking through the thick black cloth of his borrowed suit, and making him uncomfortably hot, but something inside him could not be warmed. Confused memories of the past few hours warred in his mind: his desperate attempts to revive the dead child, knowing all the while that they were doomed to failure: Alathea's gaunt, lovely face, filled with defeat and anger: and her uncle, struck to stone by the news of his only son's death. Those eyes, grim and haggard and despairing with a double grief he would never share or admit, haunted Jasper still: so did the daughters, especially Anne, her sharp reserve dissolved into tears. Rupert had been a generally obnoxious small boy, but his family at least had loved him, and now Lord Bradfield had no male heir – save his brother Francis, whom he heartily disliked.

And thinking of Francis brought Jasper's thoughts back willy nilly to his elder daughter, lying as he had last seen her in the dim confines of her guest-bed: white-faced, anguished, armoured in defeated pride, rejecting every tacit offer of help or comfort, her whole body shaking with repressed tremors of fear and exhaustion. Looking at her then, he had realised for the first time the compass and depth of his love, and known that, if he was ever to have any hope of winning her, he must somehow rectify his earlier blundering approaches. But, too late it seemed: he doubted now, wearily depressed, whether she would ever look at him with anything other than contempt.

His parents' home was its usual comfortable, shabby self, welcoming everyone. He had been born there, after his Irish mother had married the solid red-haired Suffolk yeoman, Henry Sewell, who had met her during the Low Countries Wars. Jasper's father had been killed early in the Civil War in England, and years later, after long journeying with her dear friend Thomazine Heron, Grainne Sewell had returned to Goldhayes with Jasper and Henrietta, her two surviving children, and married Malise Graham, the Heron cousin she had met in Scotland. Malise, as great a friend to Francis Heron as Grainne was to Thomazine, had taken over the management of the Goldhayes estate when old John Sewell, Jasper's grandfather, died, and had stayed on to work for Lord Bradfield. Jasper had often wondered how Malise could tolerate his autocratic, stern employer: but toleration was one of Malise's great qualities.

He was in the kitchen where, somehow, all the life of the house gathered in the heat of bread-oven and cooking-fire: a big man, tall and gaunt and clumsy, with dark red hair now gently peppered with grey. On his knee, thumb in mouth, his little daughter Bridget curled like a contented kitten. Jasper's half-brothers, Nick and Robin, were elsewhere, and he was glad of the resulting quiet. His mother stood at the big scrubbed table, her hands floury to the elbows, making pastry. She looked up as Jasper closed the door behind him, and smiled her calm, wise smile. 'Hullo. Was it very bad?'

'Yes,' said Jasper, without elaboration. He sat down on the long oak settle opposite his stepfather, and gave Bridget a wan smile. The little girl, who was only five and as shy and timid as a field mouse, looked at her terrifying big brother and then buried her face in her father's chest.

'I still havena got it clear in my heid,' said Malise, his Scots accent still plain, though he had not been in Scotland for many years. 'I've been out in the fields a' day, and I ken only what your mother told me. How did the lad come tae fall in the moat in the first place?'

'He was fooling about, teasing Alathea, who was trying to ignore him: then he fell in from the Library window. She didn't realise something was wrong until he failed to come up, and by then it was too late. She did her very best to save him, though – she nearly drowned herself in the process.'

'Why did the lad no' come up, then?' Malise enquired. 'Surely he could swim, even a little – all o' you bairns used to splash around in yon moat, even Thea and Hen.'

'He couldn't swim at all, apparently,' Jasper told him. 'And he was a bony, skinny boy, and that sort always sink easier than those with a bit more flesh on them. But there's another reason too, that I only discovered when I examined him later: he'd hit his head on something, the house wall or those stones at the bottom of the moat, and that must have knocked him out – and so he drowned.'

There was a small, sad silence. Grainne pulled and twisted the yellow, stretchy dough, her face remote, absorbed, thoughtful. Then she said quietly, 'I never cared much for that child, but it was not his fault, the way he was. He was like Kit, more sinned against than sinning – and now his father must be all but distracted, he was devoted to him.' She sighed, and pushed the tangled dough into a fat creamy ball. 'Poor Rupert, to die so sudden and so young, all his future gone in a few seconds . . . and poor Simon, left to mourn him alone – for I can't imagine those daughters being of much comfort.'

'Aye, the younger one's a silly selfish wee lass, but Anne's none so bad,' Malise said. 'Did ye ken, Jasper, that when her mother was first so ill, while they were in The Hague, she looked after her, ran the house, did everything – and her nae more than nine or ten years old? For a' your years in Leyden, I'd wager she still speaks better Dutch than you do.'

'But I reckon my vocabulary's a good deal wider,' said Jasper drily. He looked at them both, his mother and stepfather comfortable and wise now in calm middle age after their turbulent youth, and came to a difficult decision. He met Malise's gentle considerate eyes and said slowly, 'I know it seems trivial after such a tragedy, but I have a problem which is filling my thoughts to the exclusion of all else – even Rupert's death. And I am not going to be quiet in my mind until it is resolved, one way or the other. May I talk about it?'

'Talk as much as you like,' said Grainne, dusting her rolling-pin with flour. 'It's not as though we're unused to this sort of thing: sooner or later everyone comes to this kitchen to air their difficulties and get advice. I've been telling the Herons what to do for twenty-six years now, so my own son should prove easy to help by comparison. What's wrong?'

'Alathea,' said Jasper, simply.

Malise's eyebrows rose. He had a deceptively fierce face, frowning brows above a big hawk's beak of a nose, softened by a scattering of incongruous freckles. People meeting him for the first time, aware of his martial past under Montrose in Scotland, saw in that face a confirmation of their mental picture of Malise Graham: it generally took a closer acquaintance to ascertain the truth. Malise had fought with Montrose, for love and conviction and adventure, but his nature was really much more suited to the peaceful, rural existence he now enjoyed with his wife and three children. He was the only father Jasper could properly remember, and he valued his opinion highly.

'Alathea?' said Malise. A slow wide smile spread across his face. He glanced across at Grainne, who had stopped her pastry-rolling and was staring at her son in some surprise. 'I know the lass has a mind o' her own and a tongue and a courage tae match it, but she's nae concern o' yours, surely? Unless . . . '

'Lucy hinted as much when we spoke at Nan's funeral,' said Grainne. 'But you tell us – Alathea is your problem. In what way?'

Jasper took a breath, suddenly uncertain. It was going to be a great deal more difficult than he had thought, to bare his soul thus to his parents, but there could be no going back now.

'I've fallen in love with her,' he said at length, simply. 'And the last thing she wants is for anyone to do something as inconvenient as that.'

'I thought that was all a young lass wanted, to have a handsome young man fall in love with her,' said Malise drily. 'Doesn't she like you, then?'

'Not much – I blundered, this morning. I hadn't realised how – how different she is from most girls – you can't protect her or help her, she only thinks you're being patronising,' said Jasper ruefully. 'It's like trying to approach a hedgehog.'

'I've heard that description applied to her mother, long ago,' Grainne told him. 'She's young, and unsure in some things and too sure in others – and it's a condition that usually improves with time. I do admit, nothing would be more pleasing than to have you marry her and link the four of us for ever, after all we've shared: but you can't force her, Jasper, and if I know Thea, the more you push her the more she'll resist. I know what you want, you want to declare yourself and ask for her hand and all the rest – and don't shake your head at me, you've ever been an impetuous soul and you know it – but that's for sure the way to lose her for good. Wait, Jasper, wait until she's grown a little and until your own feelings are sure, and you'll be much more certain of success.'

'The last thing I want to do is to wait,' said Jasper, giving his mother one of his wry, twisted smiles that Grainne thought would probably win Alathea's heart in an instant, were it ever turned her way. 'You're right, I *am* impatient – I want her now, desperately – I only met her, the adult Alathea, two weeks ago but that doesn't mean my feelings are superficial.' He looked from Grainne to Malise and spread his hands in rueful resignation. 'So – you think I should sit like patience on a monument, and never tell my love? Well, if it's the only way to win her – and I have a feeling you are right, there – then I will do it. But I only hope she leaves Goldhayes soon, because it'll be more than I can bear, to have her so close and say nothing, pretend I feel nothing.'

'Thomazine and Francis willna stay any longer here than they must, so you need have nae worries on that score,' Malise said. 'Nor will Lord Bradfield want to see her any more than you, I dinna doot – for though none could ha' done more to save him, it's my guess her face will remind him evermore of how Rupert died. Aye, I ken as well as you that it's unjust, but it's what he'll think nonetheless – it's his nature, to place blame on others when it ought properly to rest on himself. If that bairn hadna been so indulged . . . but it's too late, now. Anyway, Jasper, I'd say you're safe frae seeing too much of Thea for a while – whether you like it or not.'

'I don't like it at all,' said Jasper, with resignation. 'But I can see it's the best course.'

Alathea Heron, the unknowing subject of all that speculation, lay in the bed she shared with Rosalind, in a pleasant upstairs chamber at Goldhayes that once, coincidentally, had been shared by their mothers in childhood. It was strange to think that Lucy and Thomazine had slept in this same bed, held muffled whispered midnight conversations behind these curtains, and kept their clothes in that same clothes-press by the window that looked down into the tiny Courtyard Garden below. It was afternoon now, and full hot sun outside, though none struck the room at this hour, and she was intensely bored. Everyone had been very kind. She had been undressed, washed, dried, her nightdress slipped over her head, a warming pan placed in the bed, extra covers provided, a hot posset on a tray – but nothing could have much effect on the cold hollow emptiness she felt within her at the memory of Rupert's death. Even Ros had retired defeated at the last, and left her to the privacy of her own thoughts. It had occurred to no one to ask if she wanted to be put to bed like a recalcitrant child, and in her exhaustion and grief she had not objected. Now, however, with that splendid day only half over, and the distant sounds of life and movement even in that mourning household so inviting, she was immured in this lonely chamber with no book, no pen, no diversion to keep her mind from plodding over and over again along the morbid track of regret and blame and humiliating failure. Jasper, speaking as a doctor rather than as a lover, had advised her to try and sleep, but although her weary, abused body would have welcomed it, her brain would not rest. Over and over again she heard Rupert's shout of surprise as he fell, and the splash, and the fatal seconds – ten, fifteen, thirty, forty? – before she realised that something was wrong. And if intensity of will could have turned back time and given her and Rupert a second chance, the dead boy would have risen then, triumphant, and her world and Goldhayes made whole again . . .

There was a brisk rap on the door. Even Rosalind, with her cheerful small-talk, would be welcome. Alathea sat up and called, 'Come in!'

It was not Rosalind. It was Anne Heron, Rupert's elder sister. Some of Alathea's surprise and disappointment must have shown on her face, for the girl stood still in the doorway, frowning, and said, 'If you would rather I went away, I will.'

'No, no,' said Alathea hastily, 'come in.' As her tall cousin shut the door behind her, she added, 'To tell you the truth, I'd be glad of company.'

'And I too,' said Anne. Her thin, sharp face with the overlarge nose and narrow mouth would never be pretty, and, obviously, she had been crying.

Again, Alathea found herself feeling sympathy with this rather severe, forbidding girl, the same age as herself. She said, with increased warmth, 'Please, sit down,' and indicated the side of the bed.

Anne crossed the room, her deep black silk skirts rustling gently: somchow the expensive, fashionable gown only served to emphasise her plainness. She sat, and smoothed the creases on her dress, a small frown between the strongly marked black brows. Then she lifted her head to meet Alathea's curious face and said without ceremony, 'I came to thank you. I don't think my father will – he is grateful to you for trying to save Rupert, I am sure, but he cannot face the fact that you failed.'

'Neither can I,' said Alathea softly.

Anne gave her a sharp glance. Her eyes were narrow, long and brown and watchful: altogether, it was not a happy face. She said, 'I know you did your utmost – and yet I am also sure you blame yourself for not doing more, however unreasonable that might seem to an observer. I ought to warn you that I think my father feels the same – and that whereas you have the right, if you wish, to attach blame to yourself, he has none at all. And so I've come to redress the balance a little, and give you the thanks you deserve.' She brushed a hand across her eyes and gave Alathea a small, tight smile. 'You did your best, and if you could have saved him, you would: and on behalf of my family, I thank you.'

Throughout this short speech, delivered in deceptively matter-of-fact tones, Alathea had felt embarrassment and sympathy warring within her, for this humble, grateful Anne was most emphatically not her normal self, and the pain in her eyes was a force from which Alathea, herself raw with anguish, shrank away. But she made herself sound friendly, and offered her desperate regrets for the child's death, and Anne accepted them with this sad, alien grace that became her so ill. But there was more than a note of her old sharpness in her voice as she added, 'I know you didn't much care for him, any of you – he was a tiresome spoilt brat, and no one knew it more than I did. But he could be very loving, and friendly, he was intelligent and showed promise in his studies . . . and we all loved him.' She took a deep breath, suddenly distraught, and Alathea saw she was near the breaking-point. 'Perhaps we loved him too much, especially Father. All his hopes for the future rode on Rupert . . . don't be too hard on him now, for if he is bitter he has good reason.' She got up, abruptly, and produced from her sleeve a folded piece of paper. 'Before I leave . . . I found this, where you had been sitting by the moat. I didn't know you could draw so well . . . it's truly beautiful.'

Alathea took the paper and unfolded it. There, hitting her in the face, was the drawing she had done of that small fateful corner of Goldhayes. The precarious wallflowers blossoming against the bricks, the window from which Rupert had fallen, the calm ripples of the moat, unsullied by death, all combined to provide the turning-back of time she had so passionately desired, and were now unendurable.

With a sudden gesture of despair, she thrust the paper back into Anne's hands, not caring if it crumpled or tore. 'No – I don't want it. Keep it if you like, though it's unfinished – but I don't think I could ever bear to look at it again.'

CHAPTER FIVE

The loving brother

Tetchy and wayward was thy infancy:
Thy school-days frightful, desperate, wild and furious:
Thy prime of manhood daring, bold and venturous.
(Shakespeare, *Richard III*)

Malise Graham and Anne Heron had been alike in their predictions of Lord Bradfield's reaction to Rupert's death, and Alathea's part in the tragedy, and after the child's funeral, his small new-made coffin laid in the family vaults beside his mother's, almost as new, Francis and Thomazine Heron left Goldhayes and returned to Ashcott, taking with them all four of their children. Lucy, however, decided to delay her own departure, the better to offer some further comfort and companionship to her bereaved brother.

Alathea went with her parents reluctantly, knowing there was little choice. She could not stay at Goldhayes, for Lord Bradfield by tone and look had made it plain how little he welcomed her presence there, even if he did not say so, and there was no point, yet, in going back to London, for her painting lessons had finished. And gradually, as Goldhayes receded behind them and the cheerful chatter of the other children, particularly Edmund and Sophie, began to lighten her heart, so did the tragedy of Rupert grow fainter in her mind, and, to the delight of her observant parents, she became more and more like the quick-witted, lively Alathea they knew and loved. By the time, two days after leaving Goldhayes, they all rode down the long hill from the Deddington Road, in and out of the dappled sunshine under the elms, she was laughing and singing with the others, and the shadow seemed lifted.

Ashcott, after five years of Francis Heron's management, was very different from the dilapidated, primitive, neglected place it had been when he first took over. Alathea had been there the previous Christmas, but even since then there had been changes, and she was not prepared for the luxurious growth of Ashcott in summer, the lush green of the water-meadows and the burgeoning, scented garden, confined now within a new, low-built stone wall. There were new stables, too, unpretentious but neat, a little distance from the house, and the few cottages of the hamlet, glimpsed through the trees, looked freshly thatched.

The inside of Ashcott was also very different from the bare bleak place it had been five years ago. The high cold echoing Hall was now a warm panelled parlour, with a new kitchen beyond and bedchambers above. There were new fireplaces, new windows, and hangings and furniture brought from the Oxford house, which had now been leased elsewhere. There was another addition brought from Pennyfarthing Street, and installed with great care, and Alathea was delighted to discover the spry sparse knowing figure of the Widow Gooch, who had lived in the Oxford house and been friend and accomplice to the Herons all through the Civil Wars, seated like a humorous witch in the kitchen chimney-corner as if she had been put there with the mortar. She never changed, and looked now to Thomazine's affectionate eyes exactly as she had done twenty years ago. She must by now be close on eighty, but her mind remained as sharp and well-honed with practical malice as ever, even if, as she put it, 'My legs ain't what they used to be.'

Something in the Widow's acerbic nature had always appealed to Alathea, and during the first weeks after her return to Ashcott, she spent a good deal of time in that lady's shrewd company. They discussed farming and dogs, family history and the greenfly on Thomazine's roses, and gradually, over the weeks, Alathea found herself confiding to this wise and impartial friend her hopes – and fears – for the future.

'So,' said Mistress Gooch, during the course of one of these conversations, 'you want to be an artist, paint pictures, eh? And make a living out of it? Not easy, lass.'

'I do know it won't be,' Alathea said, with some impatience. 'But I *know* I can do it. You said yourself that I had enough will and determination to level a mountain.'

'Yes, maybe,' said the Widow, giving the girl a keen glance. 'But I didn't mean you to take that as truth. And I reckon, lass, you'll find the world a great deal harder on you than you think – however determined you are.' Again, the hooded eyes, still young and perceptive, studied her. 'Because it ain't what a young girl does, earn her living at something like that. You'll need not to mind what they'll call you, what they'll expect from you – you'll need to be as strong as them, lass, and stand up for yourself. And though you might not think it now, the time may come when you'll need help, and protection.'

'Not a husband,' said Alathea, giving the Widow a sidelong suspicious glance that reminded the old woman most strongly of her father. 'Please don't tell me to go out and find myself a nice reliable husband – I swear I'll scream if you do.'

'Been pushed that way already, eh?' the Widow cackled.

Alathea grimaced. 'Yes. Aunt Lucy was most insistent that I should treat Jasper with favour. All he's ever done is look at me, and she as good as married us off.'

'Same old Lucy, I see,' was the Widow's comment, accompanied by a scornful sniff. She added, teasingly, 'Jasper, eh? Jasper Sewell? Taking little lad he was, twenty years ago, an answer for everything and as sharp as a razor. Does he take your fancy?'

By now, Alathea was used to Mistress Gooch's little ways, and words which, from another person, might have angered her now only made her laugh. 'No, but apparently I've taken his, and I can't for the life of me see why.'

'Then you ain't looked in your mirror recently, lass,' the Widow pointed out. 'God knows why, but you've turned into – well, not a beauty exactly, but certainly I'd wager you turn heads everywhere you go. Am I right, eh?'

'I – I can't say I'd noticed,' Alathea told her, with some lack of perfect truth. Somehow the attention she attracted from admiring men was an embarrassment, a nuisance, something that distracted her from her determined path in life.

But Mistress Gooch gave her cynical cackle. 'You're a liar, lass, or I'm dead and buried. You notice, you're annoyed, but you're flattered as well – and who wouldn't be? I never turned heads myself, not the sort, though I always wished I could. And there's your problem, lass – think of yourself, all alone in London, painting, talk of the town I shouldn't wonder, lovely young girl without protection is fair game for the nastier sort, and there'll come a time where neither your wits nor your tongue nor your strength will save you. Face up to it, lass – the men you've known, your father, uncles, cousins, friends, they're gentlemen to the core and would never lay a finger on a girl without her consent: but there's many, many others who ain't. And they'll take advantage of your trust and your friendship and you'll end a bitter old crone like me, croaking advice from a chimney-corner and never listened to.'

'Never,' said Alathea, pretending disbelief. But she had reluctantly to admit that Mistress Gooch had a valid point, much though her desire for independence urged her to make her way through life on her own. Perhaps she would need a protector, a male member of the family who could lurk in the background and give her an aura of . . . not respectability, precisely, but of inviolate chastity.

Chastity! It made her sound like a nun: but she could not envisage any liaison with a man outside love, if not marriage. And her heart and soul were given, exclusively, to her painting.

Despite the lively, stimulating company of Mistress Gooch, the days at Ashcott began sadly to drag. She could draw, but not paint: she had no materials, no canvas or oil or pigment. The memory of Judith Leyster's dashing vigorous picture hung vivid and frustrating in her mind, beckoning and urging her to change and improve her painting style, but for the moment she could do nothing. In London she might have bought what she needed from the merchants and colourmen who had supplied the Beales, but Dan had already informed her parents that the Plague was once more taking its dreadful grip on London. To return would be unthinkable, and Lucy, Rosalind and Oliver were still at Goldhayes. For once, Alathea did not envy them: it would be a long time before she could look at or think of that lovely place again without the grim taint of tragedy to mar the picture.

And to complete her depression, Mab died. It was inevitable, she had already lived far longer than most dogs, and her wiry tireless strength had at last failed her, but Alathea sat up all night with the little black-and-white dog on her lap, feeding her warm milk dribbled into her mouth with her finger, watching the round bright eyes dim and glaze, feeling the once-lively heart faltering under her hands, giving Mab the last comfort of her presence. And as the little dog's life ebbed away with the night, she looked into the future, and felt the last of her childhood flowing away too, the safety and security failing as Mab grew cold, and the bleak challenge of her adult life looming ahead. When at last the dog died with the dawn, she found she could not weep.

Kit arrived the next morning, as they were burying Mab under one of Thomazine's rose bushes. Francis had dug the hole in the red damp earth, and Alathea laid the stiff little corpse into it more gently than if it had been a living animal. Staring down at the body, it did not seem to her like the real Mab any more, but a poor shrunken travesty of the sparkling mischievous dog she had loved so much. Then, as her father began to push the heaped soil back into the grave, Sophie began to sob loudly, and buried her head on Alathea's chest, and only then could she herself give way to her own grief.

In the middle of the hubbub, with Edmund, who had no sensitivity, proclaiming loudly that it was all over now and could he have some dinner free of all these female tears, the distant sound of hooves lurking behind the noise grew louder and stopped with a flourish. A strong lively voice said cheerfully, 'Hello, everyone! What's all this about?'

It was a voice Alathea still heard sometimes in nightmares, charged then with passionate fury and contempt, but there were no such undercurrents now. She turned, wiping her eyes, and beheld her half-brother Kit, for the first time for several years.

He looked very fine on top of his sleek, lovely, well-bred grey mare, and the sun gleamed on the pristine whiteness of his fashionable cravat, and gave fire to the dull crimson riding-suit he wore. His vivid, excited blue eyes swept round his sorrowing family and came to rest on Alathea's face. They widened, just a little, and she felt something, a shock of surprise which sent a tingling shiver across her back: then she looked down quickly, at the tumbled earth, scattered with fallen rose-petals, that hid her dearest Mab. It seemed so strange to be able to walk freely, everywhere, without the little dog forever under her feet or following hopefully at heel. She half-expected to see her now, the appealing eyes and ginger eyebrows and tentatively wagging tail, but she never would again. And as she finally accepted that fact, two hands were placed on her shoulders and her elder brother's voice said in her ear, 'And how's my little sister, eh? Still doodling?'

'Yes,' said Alathea shortly. Kit's hands spun her competently about and she found herself being given a pair of brisk brotherly kisses, one on each cheek.

'You're near as tall as me,' he said, smiling warmly at her. 'Haven't you grown up!' And, as so often before, she felt the deeper, hidden feelings and meanings behind his ordinary words: but before she could interpret it, he had released her and spun away to hug Sophie, and his mother, and Nell, who had mourned Mab with a damp extravagance that had somehow irritated Alathea. Math and Mun were slapped on the back, much to the former's embarrassment and the latter's delight, and with a lordly, flourishing wave of his elegantly gloved hand, Kit indicated the liveried servant patiently sitting on his inferior horse outside the garden wall. 'Jem there has one or two things behind his saddle – go see what he's got, you two young rogues!'

Matthew, who was fully conscious of his fourteen years, increasing height and superior intellect, looked resentful at this bracketing with his ruffianly younger brother, but was still enough of a child to go and investigate the saddlebags.

'What were you doing?' Kit then demanded of his mother. 'You all look as though you've been to a funeral.'

'We have,' said Sophie, raising her huge, tear-drenched, hazel-green eyes to her brother. 'Poor Mab's dead and we've buried her under the roses where she liked to lie best.'

Mab's favourite spot had actually been, illicitly, on one of the sunny windowseats upstairs, but Sophie already had a taste for poetic fiction.

Kit's manner changed immediately: sadness and sympathy came down over his face like a cloud. 'Poor Mab is dead? Oh, I'm so sorry about that. She must have been a good age, though. I can remember you bringing her back from Colchester, Mother, and telling me that she was my present, and she curled up on my bed at Goldhayes – do you remember that?'

'I do indeed,' said Thomazine, smiling warily at her first-born son. Even now, in this expansive, accommodating mood, she somehow did not trust him: too often before she had seen him change with terrifying abruptness from sunshine to storm. And there was something about his greeting of Alathea, and her reaction to it, that made her uneasy. With that old depressingly familiar feeling of guilt, she added, 'To what do we owe this unexpected visit?'

'To boredom,' said Kit. 'To the sheer unadulterated tedium of Upper Denby Hall, where the local hobbledehoys speak a different language and the parson is an uncouth, ignorant old bigot and the only gentleman of any pretensions for miles about has three daughters who've been leading apes in hell for long enough to look and sound like apes themselves, and though I value the place, it's my inheritance after all, I felt like coming and seeing my own dear family – and bringing some life and excitement into their poor lonely lives!'

And over the hot sunny weeks of that summer, while plague cut swathes through the overcrowded fetid slums of London, and far away at Goldhayes Lucy and her two elder children languished in the oppressive, dispiriting heat of a house in mourning, and worried about Dan and Celia who were still in Fleet Street, Kit exerted his abundant vitality and charm to shatter the calm and peaceful life that had been Ashcott before his precipitate arrival. In his invigorating presence Sophie grew insufferable with her studied airs and clever comments, and Edmund's usual rather aggressive behaviour became even more annoying to anyone accustomed to moderation of voice and manner. Math, who had never cared for Kit, retreated wholeheartedly into his books, and Nell became a creeping, sniffling shadow whose only pleasure seemed to be in household tasks. Thomazine and Francis viewed this transformation of their children under Kit's influence with some concern, but had to agree that for some strange reason, the only person truly to blossom in his company was the last one they had expected: Alathea.

It surprised Alathea herself. At that first meeting, she had been wary and suspicious, ready to find again in her half-brother the cruel, jealous tormenter of her childhood. And she had looked in vain. True, there was ever the feeling, lingering unpleasantly at the back of her mind, that Kit's soul ran too deep for her to discern his true nature from everyday conversation, but for her there seemed nothing but smiles, light banter, and a bright rush of excitement after the boredom and frustration of her last weeks at Ashcott.

The first time he asked her to go riding with him, she was reluctant, mistrustful. There were the sheepwalks, all lush grass and sunshine and freedom, and Ashcott an hour or so after dinner seemed as enlivening and stimulating as a tomb. Her father was out inspecting the potential of his harvest, her mother and the maid Martha busy in the kitchen, Math buried in a book as usual, Mun running wild. Alathea's conscience had offered to help with the sewing, and now a big draggled heap of shirts and bands and hose lay sullenly beside her chair in the main parlour, essential, important and threatening to dominate the day completely. To add to her frustration, Nell sat with her, neatly and invisibly mending one of Mun's horrendously mauled hose with tiny patient stitches, the picture of virtuous industry, while Sophie curled on the windowseat with quill and book and paper, passing pert comments on the list of French verbs she had failed to learn the day before, until Alathea had pointed out that since all things currently fashionable in London hailed from France, a knowledge of the language of that country might prove of benefit to her in later life. Sophie, easily diverted from her labours, put down her book and embarked upon a prolonged inquisition of her elder sister. What were the London fashions this year? Where was the best place to shop? Had she seen the King, or the Queen? At Alathea's abstracted reply in the affirmative, Sophie said eagerly, 'Oh, did you? Where? Did you see them at Whitehall? Have you been there? Have you seen the Castlemaine?'

To Sophie's pained surprise, Alathea gave an astonished squawk of laughter which masked Nell's shocked gasp. 'How do you come to know of her, you bad infant?'

'I hear all the gossip,' said the prick-eared Sophie, unrepentant. 'What does she look like? Is she very beautiful?'

'Yes, exceedingly so, and she has fair hair and long eyes and a very languishing look to her,' Alathea told her. 'And all the red-blooded gentlemen at Whitehall find her most attractive, according to the Jermyns.'

'Hmm,' said Sophie, a considering mischief in her eyes. She jumped off the windowseat, smoothed down her skirts and sank into a gracefully roguish curtsey in front of her sister's chair. 'Do you think the gentlemen would ever find me attractive, if I went to Whitehall?'

Alathea put down her sewing and stared solemnly at the child, not yet ten years old, who already possessed enough flirtatious skills to dazzle a bevy of sophisticated courtiers. Laughter and foreboding struggled briefly within her, but serious considerations won the day. She fixed Sophie with as steely a glare as she could muster and said severely, 'For shame to be even thinking of that at your age. Whitehall is no place for a gently reared child like you – and by the way, yes, I think the gentlemen would find you very attractive.'

'Good,' said Sophie, and burst into a stream of giggles. 'I *thought* you weren't going to lecture me. It isn't like you. *Math* lectures.'

'Math lives at a Higher Level,' said Alathea. 'I do not. I just offer the occasional warning. Anyway, I shouldn't emulate the Castlemaine, if you ever do invade Whitehall.'

'Why not?'

'Because she's a thoroughly disagreeable shrew by all accounts, and keeps the King on hanging strings like a baby, and Charles Jermyn said she was appallingly rude to the poor Queen. And if I wouldn't be a good lecturer, you wouldn't make a good shrew.'

'No,' said Sophie consideringly. 'No, I think I'd rather people liked me, really. I shall just be myself, and then they will.' And she favoured Alathea with one of her delightful, dazzling grins, which swung round to include Nell as an afterthought.

Nell wiped her nose with a damp kerchief and laid down the neatly repaired hose with an air of martyred satisfaction. 'I don't know what Mun does to them,' she said, sighing, 'from the look of it he eats them.'

'Knowing Mun, they probably form part of his breakfast,' said

Alathea. 'And I know for sure he eats his cuffs – look at this revolting chewed object! I think I'll make *him* sit down and mend them next time – that'll larn him.'

Nell missed the Suffolk expression entirely, being occupied in picking over the heap of garments for something more to her taste than Edmund's hose. Sophie, humming a dance tune, curled up again in the windowseat and scowled at the book of verbs. Alathea was conscious of an awesome gulf between herself and the two other girls: a gulf in Sophie's case made up of age, experience, a certain knowledge of the world outside Ashcott, however sketchy, and in Nell's case a distance comprised of temperament and intellect. Alathea was visited by a great desire to take her cousin by the shoulders and shake some life and liveliness into her dull personality, and following that urge came a rushing feeling of loneliness. Here in the comfortable circle of her family, who had once been everything to her, she could find no companion, no kindred spirit to share her thoughts, no one on whom she could practise her wit, nobody to laugh with her as Rosalind and Oliver had done. *I wish I were back in London,* she thought unhappily, *or I wish I could find someone to have a joke with, who could see the funny side of things: my parents might, but they're always busy – and there's no one else at all . . .*

The door opened abruptly and, giving her thoughts the lie, her brother Kit came in with a flourish. He was dressed for riding, in the same flamboyant suit of crimson he had worn on his arrival two days previously, and his brilliant blue eyes swept round the quiet little group and came to rest on Alathea. 'You look very solemn, little sister! Won't you come riding, any of you? It's the weather for it, beyond a doubt, and I have a fancy for some company.'

Coming so hard on her depressed feelings, he seemed like a singularly welcome blast of fresh air. Guiltily, Alathea looked down at the heap of undone sewing: she had promised her mother . . .

'Don't worry, I'll do it,' said Nell earnestly. 'You go riding if you want.'

'And you do want, don't you?' said Kit, coming to stand in front of her, his extraordinary eyes so compelling that her body almost moved of its own accord. But there was the sewing, and Nell's readiness to take it over only served to increase her feelings of guilt: and besides, she could not dissociate this handsome, friendly, sophisticated and charming young man with the cruel tormenter of her childhood.

'You can finish it when you return,' he said, and stretched out his hands. 'Come on, little sister – the day's too good to be wasted indoors!'

For a few seconds longer, her conscience battled with temptation, and lost. 'Very well,' said Alathea. 'You've persuaded me – and I shall cite you for an excuse when I'm confronted later by Mother.'

'And I,' said Kit, laughing, 'shall be stout in your justification.'

The wide hill above Ashcott, the sun and the butterflies and the sheepwalks, stretched in front of their horses. Alathea had had certain misgivings about spending such a long time in Kit's exclusive company, fearing an inquisition, once they were alone, on the subject of painting, but Kit's light, joking conversation made no reference to any kind of art. He had a fund of humorous anecdotes – about Oxford friends, Yorkshire neighbours, various relations – which reduced her, frequently, to such helpless laughter that she all but fell off her horse.

'So there was poor Jack Fothergill, stuck fast in his larder window, and no hope of getting him in or out again! Now being more than slightly fuddled, he'd lost all sense of caution and when we all pushed him from behind, he let out a bellow like a raging bull. This would, of course,' Kit added, looking sidelong at his sister, 'be a great deal more amusing if you could only *see* Jack Fothergill, who must weigh near as much as a bullock and carries it all before him. But here's the cream of the jest – his wife, who's some rich man's widow a few years older, and just as heavy save she carries all her weight *behind* her, hears his bellowing from her bed and thinks it's robbers come to murder her in her nightgown. So what does she do?'

'Cries for help?' Alathea suggested, though she could very well guess the probable outcome of the story.

'No, not she – she's made of sterner stuff. No, she creeps downstairs, trying to go lightly, and she carries her warming pan with her, and she tip-toes into the larder and – crash!' said Kit, with all the drama of the practised raconteur. 'She cracks her own husband over the head with the pan, under the mistaken impression that he's a felon trying to force an entry. And the crack even on his thick skull knocks him out, and suddenly we all give another hefty push and through the window he goes!'

'On to Mistress Fothergill,' said Alathea, grinning. 'It's like a tale from Chaucer – have you read Chaucer?'

'I don't read any foreign tongue save French and Italian,' said Kit, solemnly. 'Are you now a very accomplished young lady?'

'I can't sew well,' Alathea told him. 'I play the virginals indifferently, the lute even more so, and I read a little French and less Italian and a smattering of Latin and I dance the coranto and the gavotte and the minuet and even the Brawl when I am pressed, and I can find my way about the London shops and even,' she added with a smile, 'take a clock to pieces!'

'Ah, but can you put it together again?'

'Uncle Dan hasn't taught me that yet.'

'Then remind me not to let you anywhere near my new watch,' said Kit. He halted his horse and turned to study his sister. She smiled at him, rather hesitantly, as his eyes considered her new, graceful maturity, so different from the defensive child he had known before. 'Did you like living in London?'

'Yes, I did,' said Alathea, wondering how she could avoid any mention of Mistress Beale and the painting lessons. 'In fact, I would like to go back. I miss it very much.'

'You can't return just yet – the plague has its grip again, by all accounts. But you enjoyed living in London? The centre of the world, as it were?'

'Well, certainly there was a great deal to do and see,' said Alathea, thinking wryly of Sophie's earlier, more artless inquisition. 'The theatre, for one – Aunt Lucy has a passion for plays and we must have seen almost every one ever performed by the King's Company or the Duke's, though I must say that I agree with her when she says she likes her Shakespeare plain and unadorned and as he originally wrote it!'

'I have a confession to make,' said Kit, patting his horse's glossy dapple-grey neck. 'Do you know, that apart from one or two very tedious student performances, all of them in the most execrable dog Latin, I have never in all my life seen any kind of play? I can see it's a deficiency I shall only be able to remedy in London. Will you be my guide, if I should ever come to visit you there?'

'I might not have the chance to go back,' Alathea told him, unable to keep the mourning note out of her voice: the contemplation of a lifetime of tedious afternoons sewing with Nell was at that moment a most hideous thought. 'The plague may last all year, they may not want me back, Mother and Father may prefer to have me here, helping . . . I shouldn't wager anything on that prospect.'

'Keeping you here,' said Kit, with a force that startled her, 'would be like keeping a singing bird caged . . . or a painting bird. No, don't look at me like that, little sister, I'm not stupid, I know the reason you've been in London all this time . . . I understand you're good.'

'Others are more competent to judge that than I am,' said Alathea carefully.

'Well, I've heard favourable reports, and no, I'm not going to pour scorn on all your efforts, I've quite grown past all that old jealousy . . . Speaking as a musician myself,' said Kit, with an airiness that did not, to his sister's ears, ring entirely true, 'I can hardly desire to limit another's creative urge . . . Why are you laughing?'

'You sound just like Uncle Simon – I beg his pardon, Lord Bradfield – when you say that. He has just the same pompous style.' Alathea grinned, saw Kit's unamused face and hastily changed the subject. 'Do you still play the lute? Do you remember that jig you made up for us all when we were still at Goldhayes? The one we called Mab's jig, because it was so like her?' Involuntarily, she glanced around at the soft sighing grass, and added sadly, 'Poor Mab – I do miss her so. It's a shame you couldn't have seen her before she died – she was part of your childhood, too.'

'Yes,' said Kit, thoughtfully, a far-away note in his voice. 'I remember the night Mother brought her back from Colchester, a little lively scrap who'd get under your feet and then put her paws on your legs to be patted, the terror of the Goldhayes rats . . . and now there isn't any dog at Ashcott, is there? For shame, Alathea, no true Heron is ever without a canine friend at beck and call. You must get another, and soon.'

'Nothing could replace Mab,' said Alathea briefly, the hurt of her bereavement still sore.

But Kit only smiled at the rebuff. 'I'll wager that within a week you'll be swallowing those words whole – just you see, little sister, just you wait and see!'

And, true to his word, Kit rode out the next day, where he never revealed, and returned with a dog – or rather, two dogs, since, he explained candidly, he had been quite unable to choose between them and so had bought both. They were of completely differing types. One was a silky spaniel puppy, brown and white and wriggling, with whom Sophie instantly fell in love and swept it trilling to her girlish breast. The other sat sulking in a corner, an amorphous hairy black shape greatly insulted by the howls of Heron laughter its peculiar appearance had prompted.

'What *is* it?'

'It's not a dog, it's a bear-cub!'

'Which end is its head?'

'Has it *got* a head?'

'That must be its tail,' said Mun, prodding a loose hirsute appendage with his foot. 'Or is it its tongue?'

'I'll settle the argument,' Francis announced, and produced with ceremony a piece of stale meat. The shape instantly resolved itself into a woolly black puppy, with enormous flat paws and a long fringe shrouding bright black eyes, and a tongue of the normal wet red variety which curled hungrily around the meat. Satisfied, it sat down and began to scratch with some dedication.

'I'm sorry,' said Kit, looking at his disreputable gift. 'No one else wanted it, and the farmer threatened to knock it on the head if I didn't take it off his hands . . . '

'Well,' Thomazine observed, studying the animal, 'it certainly has character. What on earth was its parentage?'

'Mother a sheep-dog, father unknown.'

'It *was* a bear,' said Matthew triumphantly. But his father, giving the beast a closer inspection, laughed suddenly. 'I've seen a hound a little like this before, and if I'm right, it might have a more exalted ancestry than you'd think . . . Thomazine, imagine it white, and very much larger – what have you then?'

His wife stared dubiously. 'An arctic bear?'

'No – Boy!'

'Boy?' Kit enquired.

His stepfather enlightened him. 'Prince Rupert's dog, that was with him through the war until he was killed at Marston Fight. A German breed called a poodle, so far as I can remember, and used for pulling down deer – a lusty dog who certainly must have sowed his seed hereabouts . . . we might possibly have a royal dog here,' said Francis, with mock solemnity, and bowed. The royal dog yawned, scratched, and investigated a persistent itch with a black whiskery nose.

'A very common monarch,' was Thomazine's dry observation. 'Kit – is it male or female?'

'Male,' said Kit, 'or so I was assured – I haven't checked. The spaniel, however, is female, and I see that Sophie has already taken her to her heart. What are you going to call her, littlest sister?'

'I think I'll call her Silky,' said the littlest sister at her most arch, 'because she is.'

'Then by that logic, the other one should be Scruffy,' Alathea pointed out. She dropped to her knees beside the dog and offered it a hand for inspection: it was thoroughly washed. 'But he deserves better than that. And he's lovely, or at least *I* think so – how about Lovell?'

Francis began to laugh. Most of his family looked blank, and Alathea, kindly, explained. 'It's an old rhyme – "The Rat, the Cat and Lovell our Dog, Ruled all England under a Hog." It's supposed to be about old King Richard. And Lovell is our dog, and it suits him.'

'Well,' said Thomazine, 'you named him, and you can have him – for I can see he'll be another of your devoted following.'

Lovell the dog spent that night, fleas and all, on Alathea's bed, was thoroughly bathed the next morning, much to his disgust, and became thereafter her inseparable companion. He was so different from Mab that it seemed no disrespect to her shade, to replace her so soon, and Kit, it was obvious, was highly delighted at the success of his impromptu gift. He and his sister found themselves dropping gently into the habit of companionship. Almost every afternoon, that hot and glorious summer, they would be found strolling or riding on the sheepwalks, the clumsy leaping shape of Lovell cavorting around them or lolloping with more enthusiasm than skill after a contemptuously retreating rabbit. They exchanged songs, stories, riddles and wit, read and argued and joked, while the pile of sewing grew larger and a gnawing, fretting anxiety at the back of Thomazine's mind grew also, and would not be subdued.

'Kit worries me,' she said to Francis, one hot summer night. The younger children were in bed, and Nell, Math, Kit and Alathea had gone out for a moonlit walk in the young garden, fragrant with broom and rose and honeysuckle; so they would have a peaceful half-hour, perhaps, to talk about the serious things of life.

Francis looked up from the lute he was stringing. It had succumbed to Sophie's inexpert fingers some time ago, and they had had to wait until a visit to Oxford for a new set of top courses. His hand turning the peg with a sureness born of long practice, he said, 'Kit? He seems the pattern of gentlemanly behaviour.'

'*Seems* being the word I would use,' said Thomazine. She drew her legs up under her on the settle, choosing as always a position unconventional but comfortable. 'Kit has always run so deep, I have never truly known what he was thinking, his real nature – and now I have the sense he is acting.'

'Perhaps you worry about him too much. Yes, he can be difficult, and underneath that charm and poise there's the devil's own temper and a nature as stubborn and wilful as your own – I know whence that side of his character comes! But any other parent would be proud of such a son – why not you, owd gal?'

'I don't trust him. I'm sorry, but I don't – I never have. And he hated Alathea, when she drew. He hated her, you know that.'

'Yes,' said Francis. He plucked the string very gently, and the fragile sound flared briefly in the silence, and faded. He adjusted the peg, and tried again. His head bent over the instrument, he looked to Thomazine's loving eyes exactly as he had twenty, thirty years ago, the boy whose mind and imagination had first enchanted her as a child. And his eyes, when he looked up at her, were the same shadowy, changeable green as always: Alathea's eyes. 'Yes, he hated her – but he loved her too: love is always the other side of the coin. He would not have hated her so much, had she not unwittingly betrayed his love by drawing. He has always had ambivalent feelings towards her, you know that too. And . . . you said he was acting. I have that sense too, and I think you are right. But I think I know also *why* he is acting, and it's something I have only recently suspected – and it may horrify you.'

'What? What do you suspect?' Thomazine sat upright, her great dark eyes, the chief beauty in her pointed brown face, fastened urgently on her husband.

Francis, the lute finished, laid it down gently before answering. The strings shivered and a tiny discord made the room uneasy. 'Kit is acting when he is with Alathea, hiding his feelings; but sometimes he can't help but reveal them. And, my dear owd gal, he does not hate her – what he is hiding is his love.'

Thomazine swallowed convulsively; a dryness had invaded her throat. She said, on a bright, forced note of confidence, 'Well, that's none so bad, surely . . . ' But her words died away into silence, for she knew what kind of love he meant, and she too had seen it in Kit's intense blue eyes, in the changed notes of his voice, and had turned away from the truth.

'It isn't so surprising, in a way,' Francis went on, thoughtfully, as if the situation he had just revealed had not struck at the heart of their own sane, civilised, tolerant private world. 'He hasn't really seen her for five or six years. He comes home bored, ready for diversion, and finds her in like mood, and of course she finds us all tedious company, after London and the Ashleys and the Beales and the Jermyns. She'd be unnatural if she *did* prefer sewing and baking and country peace and quiet.'

'Nell does,' Thomazine could not resist pointing out.

'Nell is, as ever, an exception. How two lively people like Jamie and Meraud ever managed to produce such a dull stick is beyond my ken, as Malise would say; but I digress. Suffice it to say that he came back from Yorkshire and found that the little sister he had despised and feared and loved and hated had grown up, and was a beautiful, witty, amusing companion. Just like you and I, owd gal, long ago at Goldhayes, someone to share your jokes and thoughts and songs, someone to be young with. There's no one else here to be his companion save Thea. But it's my guess that it was her looks snared him. I saw his face that first day, before he'd even got down from his horse.'

'Poor Thea,' said Thomazine. She found that she wanted to cry, but that maligned stubborn pride would not let her. 'She regards her face as her curse, not her fortune. She doesn't think she needs love, not of that sort anyway, and yet everywhere she goes men flock round her. Not for her mind nor her wit nor even for her art, but for sake of her face.' She smiled at Francis. 'Your face, my love: no doubting *her* parentage.'

'For my sins,' said Francis, with a rueful grin. He got to his feet and came to join his wife on the settle. Gratefully Thomazine curled against him, feeling his arm around her, comfort and support and shelter against this new storm.

She said cautiously, 'Perhaps we're both making too much of this. An infatuation to last as long as they are together, and which will die as soon as they are apart, calf-love, no more.' From somewhere, she raised a laugh. 'Do you remember that old play, I can't recall its name? Lucy would know. About a brother who returns from foreign parts and falls in love with his sister. I used to think how ridiculous the plot was, that nothing of the sort could ever happen, and now it has. And to us – or rather, to Alathea and Kit.'

'And I most earnestly hope their tale does not end as the play did – in a welter of gore, as I remember,' Francis said. 'But the sister loved the brother in return, whereas I do not think that Alathea entertains any more feeling for Kit than would any sister for such a brother. She lives forever in his pocket because he's a remedy for boredom, and sewing – which reminds me, I am well aware that our circumstances are not exactly wealthy, but surely our resources could run to some new hose for Mun? Thea and Nell and you have been mending them over and over again, and the pair I saw Nell struggling with today were pretty well footless. I know thrift and industry are generally accredited virtues, but we pay good wages to three maids. I should hand more sewing to them, and allow yourself and the girls more free time. Life's too short to be forever slaving over a needle.'

'I agree,' said Thomazine, 'but Nell swears she enjoys it.'

'She shouldn't – it's unhealthy for a girl her age to be so meek and mim and mouselike. How in God's name did anyone reared in our family come to be such a wan and wittery and winnocking mawther – why are you laughing?'

'Your speaking Suffolk always makes me laugh,' Thomazine told him. 'Why can't you speak plain English and say she droops and whines? Poor Nell, she's a quiet soul and something overwhelmed by us all, I fancy. But she's not our major problem. What *are* we going to do about Thea and Kit?'

'It depends how far you trust him. But for the moment there's little we can do without dragging it all out into the open, and you can guess at the damage *that* would cause. We can't send her to London, and risk the plague. She can't go back to Goldhayes, that would be impossible both for her and for Simon. Apart from sending Kit on his way again, there's no solution but to watch and wait and hope his feelings run their course without mishap.'

'There is something we could try,' Thomazine said slowly. 'Not to separate them, but to make sure she has other company . . . why not write to Lucy at Goldhayes and suggest she brings Ros and Oliver here for a space? They can't go back to London either, and I know Lucy's worried about Celia, and being at Goldhayes must be suffocatingly unhappy at the moment. And if she comes here, with Oliver and Ros, at least Thea won't have to rely on Kit's exclusive company to stimulate her mind. Why are you looking at me so owd-fashioned-like?'

'I'm not the only one who speaks Suffolk, then! Because I am lost in admiration for your brilliant idea, and because when all's said and done, I love you. Very much.' And he kissed her.

So Lucy, immaculate and fashionable in the mourning black she wore for Nan and Rupert, arrived at Ashcott ten days later, with Ros and Oliver irrepressibly in tow, and Kit's nose was thoroughly put out of joint. For Alathea and Ros, though very dissimilar both in looks and character, were close friends and shared the same sense of humour, and Kit found himself excluded from their close, quiet conversations, often punctuated by sounds of mirth. The old worm of jealousy reared its ugly head again, for the deepest, darkest part of him wanted her all for himself: and yet her brightness could not be forced to shine only in his direction.

And the part of him which was still a hurt, rejected child, longing for love and security, heard the laughter and wondered, with unreasoning fear, if it was aimed at him.

It was not, and Kit's unhappy soul would have been greatly heartened if he had been able to pry into Alathea's mind and see her true feelings. But he would also have been obscurely disappointed, for though she had come to feel great liking and affection for her dashing half-brother, yet, like Thomazine, she could never bring herself quite to trust him whole-heartedly. Always, she sensed something hidden, some lurking aura of danger around him, which at once attracted and repelled her. The unpredictable moods, that had hardly been in evidence in his first weeks at Ashcott, returned with a vengeance after the arrival of Lucy and her children. Alathea was hurt and a little frightened at their reappearance, but confident enough of their mutual liking to tackle Kit about his changed behaviour.

'You've hardly said a word to me all day,' she charged him, one evening in the garden, with Lovell-our-dog, even bigger and hairier than on his arrival, if that were possible, curled comfortably around her feet as they sat together on the low wall which bounded Thomazine's infant plants. 'What is it? What's wrong?'

'Nothing,' said Kit, his entire aspect emphatically giving his statement the lie.

'I don't believe you,' Alathea said positively. 'I don't believe you at all! You're sulking because of something I've done, is that it?' She glanced sideways at Kit's pale, immobile profile, the arrogant aquiline nose and repressed mouth, and an awareness of danger crept up her spine. Conscious that she could not retreat with her pride intact, she repeated her question. 'Oh, Kit, stop sulking and tell me! What have I done to upset you?'

'Nothing,' said her half-brother, his stony eyes never leaving the distant wooded slopes above the sheepwalks.

'Well, in that case, why take it out on me? You're lying, you know,' said Alathea, with a bold good humour that inwardly astonished her. 'Is it because I've spent too much time with Ros and Oliver? They're my friends too, you know, you don't have the exclusive rights to me. Ros is my dearest companion – '

'And I can't think why, for she's as empty-headed as a starling,' Kit said unpleasantly. He turned and his fierce blue eyes hooked and caught her before she could look away.

Alathea said angrily, 'That's unfair of you, and you know it! Why don't you like her? Is it because we talk together and exclude you? Is that a crime? Is it? I like your company and I like hers, and there's an end to it, Kit Drakelon – I'll do as I please and if you choose to behave like a sulky child, well, that's your loss as much as mine because we've had fun together over the last few weeks, you and I, and there's no reason to spoil that now, is there?'

Kit said nothing, but those eyes were still fastened on hers, forbidding her to look away. And Alathea, who did not lack for courage, took a deep breath and said with honest exasperation, 'Oh, for Christ's sake, Kit, you won't tell me what's wrong, and I want to know! I want to go riding with you again, and take Lovell, like we used to do, and there's that song you promised to teach me, and some time I want to draw you – '

'No!' Kit said harshly. 'Haven't you given up your scribbling yet, you stupid girl? Even if you are any good, which I doubt, you'll never put it to any use. All you're fit for is marriage to some fat gentleman and breeding a dozen brats – that's all *any* woman is fit for – '

'And it's time you learned,' said Alathea, her voice low and furious, 'that I am not just any woman, to be some man's pawn. I'll *make* something of my life, and you don't own me, you can't rule me, you can't dictate my thoughts or my drawing or my friends. You're behaving as though you're my husband, you're just like a jealous lover – '

With a movement of extreme violence, Kit sprang to his feet. For a moment Alathea thought that he would strike her, so terrifyingly savage was the expression on his face, and then Lovell, with his usual clumsy affection, jumped up to place his dirty paws on Kit's breeches. Her brother hurled him away with vicious force. As the dog cowered yelping in the grass, Kit turned and strode towards the distant hill, every movement of his body eloquent with ungovernable rage.

Alathea sat on the wall for a moment longer, staring after that receding figure, while Lovell, in an agony of self-reproach, fawned around her trying to make amends for whatever transgression had led to his punishment. But he got precious little response from his beloved mistress, for her mind was busy with a whirlpool of thought and speculation and emotion. She had outfaced her brother, once so feared, she had proved the stronger, and yet her victory was a hollow one, for she would much rather have Kit for a friend than an enemy. And running in tandem to that feeling came the wondering as to the cause of his behaviour. True, he had once been thus moody and unpleasant, long ago, but she had thought these last few weeks that he had grown away from that old childish Kit and had become in truth the sophisticated, witty, charming young man who had escorted her so delightfully. And now she saw that she had been mistaken, and the sharpness of her grief surprised her.

A tear somehow escaped down her cheeks. Impatiently she brushed it away, angry with herself and with Kit. His figure, small and remote, was still in sight, beginning to climb the long shallow rise towards the sheep walks, and Deddington. He did not look as if he would soon be returning, and it was starting to grow dark.

Alathea shivered suddenly. She wore only her thin woollen summer dress, a silvery green for once undisguised by paint, and the air around her was stirring and cool. She could still see Kit, tiny and purposeful; even as she watched, he disappeared into the dimness under the trees crowning the hill. An early owl called, a long way off, and was answered by another, and with a feeling of desolation, Alathea got to her feet, cast one more glance at the empty hillside and turned to walk slowly inside the house. Lovell frisked anxiously around her, and even rolled over on his back in her path, so that she almost trod on him, but he received small notice for his pains. Her mind fixed entirely on her errant half-brother, she trailed abstractedly into the house, with the growing thought that she must talk to someone about this.

But who? Her mother was upstairs with her aunt, putting Sophie and Mun and Oliver to bed. She shied away from talking to Ros, or Nell, and Math's interests were largely limited to what could be contained within a book. Pass this tale off as ancient Greek history, thought Alathea wryly, and he'd be quick enough with advice. She pondered a visit to the Widow Gooch, but that lady always went early to bed, saying that a good night's rest made up for the unearthly hour at which she always seemed to wake these days. And besides, the feelings and fears which crowded inside her head, nameless and faceless and threatening, were not phantoms that would be kindly treated by the Widow's bawdy practical cynicism.

So there was only one person at Ashcott she could talk to, and as if she had summoned him, her father came into the West Parlour where she stood irresolute. 'Hello, maw. What are you doing here in the dark?'

'I don't really know,' said Alathea, realising that there was indeed a Stygian gloom around her, and that she must have been standing lost in thought for some time. 'Shall I light the candles?'

'No, don't bother – it would spoil the sky,' said Francis Heron. 'Haven't you seen it? Come and look: it's a feast for your painter's eye.'

Dream-like, she allowed herself to be steered to the window. It faced the glory of the west, and a summer sunset, vivid pink bands of cloud striping the deeply turquoise sky. Against all that explosion of colour, the trees nearby were etched flat and black and still, as though cut from paper. Somewhere beyond them was Kit, probably still striding angrily away from her, and she knew him well enough by now to guess that he would be too absorbed in his own feelings and passions and jealousies to pay any attention to the flowering sky. Out of pity, and regret, and something else she could not name, tears started to spill down her cheeks. Surreptitiously she brushed them away, but Francis had noticed. His hand came gently down on to her shoulder. 'Trouble, maw? Anything I can do to help?'

'I don't think anyone can,' said Alathea. At the quiet, loving concern in his voice, she had almost lost control. She drew in a long shivering breath and added slowly, 'But it would help to talk – do you mind listening?'

'You know I won't,' said her father's dark voice, for once stripped of mockery and laughter. 'Is it Kit?'

'How did you know?'

'I have the devil's perception – and I tend to notice things like that. You've been very friendly with him of late, haven't you? And after your long quarrel, we've been glad of it – make no mistake. You're sister and brother, after all, and therefore should deal together in friendly fashion. Am I sounding too like my own brother, then?'

A reluctant smile had tugged at the corner of his daughter's mouth. 'Yes, a little. You and Lord Bradfield have never dealt together in friendly fashion though, have you?'

'I'll admit to that,' said Francis. 'But everyone makes mistakes, and my chief one was wilfully to disagree with my brother in my youth. Don't you fall into that error, will you?'

'It's he who has disagreed with me,' said Alathea. 'Since Aunt Lucy and Ros and Oliver came, he's been impossible – almost his old self. And I thought he'd changed – he was my *friend*! We had so much fun together, I enjoyed his company so much . . . and now it's just as if the last few weeks had never been.' She sighed, her mind full of Kit's bitter scorn, while at the same time her detached, observant eye noted the strands of cloud, and the rich pink light that still touched them, making them seem with rosy glow and purple shadow almost solid, heavy yet ethereal, drifting in the sky, and the artist part of her was urgent to paint it. And realising this, all in a rush came the knowledge of her true wealth, for she would always be able to marvel at and respond to such beauty, to draw delight from the fascinating world around her. The core of her soul would always, until her death, be a painter: but for Kit, no such fortune.

She turned to her father, seeing his face, so like her own,

watching her, the concerned smile just visible in the afterglow of sunset, and gave him a gallant grin in response. 'But I'm being so stupid, wrapped in my own miseries. Who could be unhappy for long, with that sky to look at?'

'Kit, I fear,' said Francis Heron, whose reading of character was, as ever, startlingly acute. 'Has he gone stamping off into the dark? I thought he'd grown out of that – but doubtless he'll return pretending that nothing has happened, as he always used to do. My advice to you, maw, to take or not as you please, is to treat it lightly. If he values your friendship, he'll come back to you – not exactly humble, if I know Kit, but willing to pick up your companionship where your quarrel left it. And if he doesn't, if he persists in cutting off his nose to spite his face, well, that's Kit, and you'll just have to make the best of it.'

'I suppose so,' said Alathea thoughtfully. 'And I'll have Ros to talk to, now, though he doesn't like her, and that's how we quarrelled. But,' she added honestly, her voice wry, 'it's not really Kit that's making me unhappy. I want to draw, I want to paint. When I see a sky like that or a group of people or even Lovell-our-dog, my hands want to work, they *tingle* with it, so that I can hardly keep them still, and my head is all filled up and jumbled with pictures that I want to do, and I dream at night about painting – did you know, half my dreams are of Goldhayes, even now, and the others have me painting? I can paint in my dreams but I can't in reality and I want to so badly sometimes I feel ill with it. Kit could make me forget that, Ros can for much of the time, but I think I shall run mad if I can't look into the future and see myself painting, soon.'

'And you can't?'

'No. The Beales have gone into Hampshire, and I don't think they'll go back to London for a long time – especially now there's so much plague. And I can't go back either, for the same reason. And London is the only place where I can buy the paints and canvases and oils that I need to start painting again.'

'Well, perhaps there's a painter in Oxford could supply you with what you want,' Francis suggested. 'I have to go there next week – would you like to come too? I can't promise anything for certain, but at least we can make enquiries. What do you say to that?'

For answer, his elder daughter laid her pale glimmering head on his shoulder, and wept. He put his arms around her, feeling the tremors of emotion that shook her thin boyish frame, acknowledging the depth of his love for this desperate, passionatc child, who had her mother's will and stubborn pride, and her father's face and the tight-strung nerves that he had too early learned to control, and she had not. And perhaps because of that acute sensitivity and imagination, she was possessed also of a gift that neither parent had.

But to make full use of it, she would need strength, the strength to withstand the rebuffs and disasters and unpleasantnesses that life would undoubtedly throw at her. He had thought that his brave Alathea would be strong enough to cope, but now, after the events of the last few months, he was not so sure. She seemed very fragile and vulnerable, sobbing her pent-up fears into his old-fashioned black woollen doublet, a child hardly sixteen, confused both by the force of her own compulsive passion for painting, and by the half-sensed power of Kit's incestuous feelings for her. *No wonder she's upset*, he thought with compassion. *She seems so adult usually, that we forget how young she is, and how innocent.*

Under his hands, the sobs lessened and died. Abruptly, Alathea raised her head and dragged the back of her hand roughly across her eyes. Turning to look at the western sky, dead now of colour, she said in a muffled voice, 'I'm sorry – thank you – I'd love to come to Oxford. I didn't mean to cry, only with Kit, and not being able to paint, and Mab dying, and Rupert and Aunt Nan . . . it all seemed too much, somehow. I won't let it happen again,' she added severely, with something like her old irony, and he caught the glitter of a smile and knew suddenly that his fears were unjustified. Fragile, sensitive, vulnerable this most dear child might be, but beneath that innocence was a strength of will that he recognised as the match of his own. She would undoubtedly need it, if she followed her chosen path; and despite his parental fears, he knew that he would find likewise the courage to let her go along that road, to make her own mistakes, to succeed at her chosen task – or to fail.

CHAPTER SIX

The links of blood

Shall, then, for that I am her brother born
My joys be ever banished from her bed?
(Ford, *'Tis Pity She's a Whore*)

There were painters a-plenty in Oxford, for only a day or so after Francis's promise, the King and all his Court came to the town to escape the plague. They had already settled, like a swarm of unwelcome bees, first at Hampton Court and then at Salisbury, where they had annoyed, scandalised and outraged that sleepy little city before a few cases of the plague nearby had spurred them on to Oxford. For the second time in the last twenty-five years, the academic peace of Christchurch and Merton, Magdalen and Balliol was rudely disturbed by riotous young sprigs of the aristocracy, far less controllable as courtiers than they had been as students, and this time untempered by the tensions and disciplines of Civil War. And with the Court came the hangers-on, officials, servants, suppliers, tradesmen, craftsmen, lawyers, actors, musicians – and artists.

They were directed to Master Lely's studio – he had rented a handsome house in St Aldate's, near to the King's lodging in Christchurch – but Alathea was very doubtful. True, Mistress Beale had Lely's friendship, and mention of her name would be sufficient to gain entry, but she was by no means enamoured of his style of painting. Somewhere within her there lurked a shadowy fear, which whispered to her that, once sucked into that frenzied world of fashion, money and portraits signed by an artist who had in fact only painted face and hands, and aristocratic sitters who demanded flattery and enhancement to the detriment of integrity, art, and truth, she would be lost.

And also, she quailed at the thought of presenting herself in that glittering sophisticated studio, and asking like a beggar for paint and canvas. In her present slightly bruised state of mind, she could not tolerate the thought of another rebuff; for Kit, in a fit of pique, or something more, had taken himself back to Yorkshire the day after their quarrel, and nothing had been heard of him since.

Though life at Ashcott was altogether quieter, and less fraught with tension and danger, it also seemed very empty without him, and even the prospect of being able to paint again had not filled her days. Now, looking at the handsome smug frontage of Master Lely's temporary Oxford abode, she could not muster the courage, or the presumption, to go in.

It was warm for late September. Under the folds of her dress, her body was hot and uncomfortably sticky. The people of Oxford brushed past, busy and unheeding, but by her side her father stood, hand on her shoulder in that old loving gesture, waiting for her decision. And she knew, with a clarity and force that would not be denied, what that decision must be. Retreat now, and all her gift, her ambition, would be revealed as a sham, a mockery, a glittering pretence without substance or future. If she was ever to apply herself seriously to her art, she must meet Master Lely on his own terms, one painter to another, and forget the fact that she was a girl of sixteen, for if she was conscious of it then he would be too.

'Going in?' said her father, gently querying. 'He won't be the only painter in Oxford for sure, there'll be others if we look . . . '

'I'm going to see Master Lely,' said Alathea, with a resolution wholly spurious. She knew Francis had offered her a way out of her dilemma, and her pride and ambition refused to take it, despite the inward certainty that it was her pride for certain, and her ambition possibly, that would be the sufferers. So, she set her chin up, gave him a cheerful smile, and walked across the road to the door of the house. Francis, following her purposeful figure between the hurrying crowds, could not resist a smile, and a salute to her courage and spirit. If those qualities were all she would need, she would rise to the heights; but he knew that they would not be enough.

With a hammering that echoed her heart, Alathea pounded the door-knocker, stood back and waited. Francis came to stand by her side, and she was glad of it, especially when the door creaked stately ajar and a resplendent servant, glorious in blue and gold livery, stood superciliously in the gap. She could see him looking at the pair of them, summing them up, doubtless, from the good but shabby clothes as, 'gentlefolk fallen on hard times'. 'Yes, sir?' said the apparition, haughtily.

'My daughter and I wish to speak with Master Lely,' said her father, in the voice which, long ago, had commanded soldiers and directed a siege.

The servant's eyebrows rose still higher, but he inclined his head in acquiescence. 'And what name and business shall I state, sir?'

'You may say that it is upon artist's business. I am Master Heron, of Ashcott in this county, and my daughter has some acquaintance with Mistress Beale,' Francis said courteously.

There was a pause, and then the footman held the door wider. 'If you would care to step this way, sir, madam?'

The chamber into which they were shown was hung with pictures. Alathea's eye, delighted, ran across them, recognising the precise art of Holland and the florid colouring of Venice, but chief amongst them, drawing her attention, a group of Van Dyck portraits, unmistakeable in their effortless grace and delicacy. She had always loved the Van Dyck portrait at Goldhayes, the one of her father and his brothers and sister as children, and especially the fluent dance of the brushwork, the delicate colouring and the fresh innocent beauty of those childish faces, like and yet unlike. For who would have believed that the grave, responsible eldest son would one day become her feared, bigoted uncle, Lord Bradfield? No doubt of it, Van Dyck had been a great master – greater by far, she suspected, than Master Lely. And much greater also than Alathea Heron, who stood looking and lost in the sweep of colour on canvas, and wondering for the hundredth time how she could ever presume to follow in these footsteps, as Lely also had followed.

But perhaps the answer was not to follow, but to carve her own path.

Just as that realisation struck her, the door opened and the footman's pompous tones intruded. 'Master Lely asks that you come into his studio, sir, madam . . . ' And with visible disapproval, he led them above stairs to the improvised painting room which had been planted within that staid Oxford house like an exotic, alien and aromatic flower. The familiar studio reek – linseed oils, primers, nameless chemicals – assailed Alathea's nose at once, bringing back vividly Mary Beale's painting room in Hinde Court, so very much less crowded and industrious than this. Master Lely employed a great number of assistants, each one busy on a canvas: touching in a pair of hands here, there blocking the shadowy shapes of fanciful rocks behind the arrogant figure of some Court gallant, another painting a stone cherub. Everywhere were scurrying apprentices, draped satins and silks of every conceivable colour and tone and texture, statues and busts and helmets and racks of robes and Turkish nightgowns for the less wealthy clients to wear for their fashionably informal sittings: stacks of blank canvases, primed canvases, half-finished canvases, rough sketches of patterns for various poses, tables and boxes and jars full of paints and oils and brushes.

Amidst all the crowded hurly-burly, the prescribed six feet from the window, sat the lord of it all, Peter Lely, working calmly and assuredly upon a large picture set upon an easel, the subject of which was a Court beauty in the fashionable state of undress, with the fashionable ringlets and the long Castlemaine eyes. In fact Alathea, glancing, could not be sure that it was not the Castlemaine herself. The lady, though, was nowhere to be seen; the sleek busy brush was blocking in the details of her careful, careless disarray. When he reached a convenient point, the great artist laid down his brush (it was immediately picked up and cleaned by a small boy no older than Mun) and got to his feet with a languid movement very much at odds with the way he had been painting.

Alathea was familiar with Lely's appearance. The artist's self-portrait, very florid and assured and dramatic, had been amongst Charles Beale's pictures, and she had seen him at Hinde Court once or twice, though never close. She did not think that he would recognise her, but like herself, portrait painter too, he would not readily forget a face.

'I have seen you before somewhere, I think, Mistress Heron?' he said, the proud harsh voice faintly accented even after more than twenty years in England.

Alathea, who had heard the stories of his arrogance and of the great state he kept, curtseyed decorously. She said quietly, as she had spoken to Lord Bradfield, 'You may have done, sir. I was often at Mistress Beale's house, in Hinde Court. She spoke very kindly of you.'

'Ah, yes, Mistress Beale. And you, you were her . . . assistant?'

'Pupil,' said Alathea. The haughty, black-eyed, imperiously handsome face reminded her in tone, if not in looks, of Kit: but, unlike Kit, he could be handled, if she knew the way. She could see that his eyes were appraising her appearance, and was thinking wryly what a sorry picture she would make, when she realised abruptly that it was not a painter's eye . . . and that she had seen that look on Kit's face, too.

'Her pupil . . . yes, I recall her mentioning that she had a young girl to learn from her, and assist her . . . a young lady of some promise, she said, and spoke most highly of you. And since she has now retired into Hampshire, you come to me for your tutoring, hein? Well, as you can see, I am well supplied with assistants, drapery painters, painters of landskips, painters of fruit and flowers and backgrounds . . . I regret I have no place in my studio, even for such a charming young lady as yourself.'

'You mistake, sir,' said Alathea, keeping her courtesy and her dignity alike intact, and feeling the comfort and support and approval of her father's unseen presence behind her. 'I do not wish to become your assistant. I came here to beg entirely another favour of you.' She saw the proud black gaze narrow, and was filled with a quite unaccustomed sense of power. Demurely, she went on. 'The desire has come upon me to paint again, sir – I have touched neither brush nor chalks for too long, but I have nothing at my home with which to work. I was hoping that, for a consideration, you could furnish me with some canvases and oils and paints, so that I may practise my art once more. My father is willing to give you what coin you think they are worth and if you have none to spare, in your present circumstances, I would be grateful if you could direct me to your colourman, or another who could supply me with my needs.' She took a deep breath, aware that this had been the longest and most formal speech of her life, and smiled. 'I pray that you will help me, sir, for I am most desperate to start painting again, and I am sure that is something you will readily understand.'

Peter Lely laughed, the black eyes almost disappearing, and revealed a flashing row of off-white teeth. 'So, the pretty little lady wishes to paint, hein? Then I will supply you, and at no cost to yourself. You may have everything you require – except my ultramarine, even Lely must be careful of his ultramarine, you understand, but everything else you may have. I will order one of my assistants to make a parcel ready immediately – John!' A child hurried over, and was issued with a stream of instructions. 'And wine for the lady and her father, before they go,' Master Lely finished with a flourish, and turned again to his guests. 'And now you must sit and take wine with me, sir, madam, while John is getting your paints and canvas ready: and if there is too much to carry, do not worry, he will help you. Now, sir, you look disapproving – what is wrong? Do you not wish your daughter to paint pictures, eh?'

'I have no objection at all,' said Francis, and there was a note in his voice which warned Alathea that he did not take Master Lely nearly so seriously as Master Lely took himself. 'My only objection, if it may be voiced, is to the fact that you do not wish any payment for your generosity. I beg of you, sir, allow me to give you at least some coin for your paints and canvases.'

'No!' said Peter Lely, with benevolent cheerfulness. 'No, sir, I insist. Your charming daughter – ah, what a picture she would make, are you planning to paint your own portrait, my dear? – if she wishes the materials to paint, it is my great pleasure to give them to her. Then you will have some peace, hein? Ah, the wine – put it down on that table, John, then go pack up the paints for Mistress Heron. And be careful, mind, get the fullest pigs' bladders and the best oil!' He guided Alathea into the empty chair whose previous occupant had been the subject of his portrait, and handed her a cup of wine. Francis, a faintly sardonic smile on his face, stood watching in the background. 'And now, Mistress Heron, tell me what it is you wish to paint so much? A portrait, perhaps, of some sweet little child?'

A vision of her rascally cousin Oliver, painted in the manner of Judith Leyster, rose before her. Alathea shook her head. 'I wish to paint portraits, indeed, but not necessarily of children. My family, friends, servants – anyone whose face interests me.'

'Let us hope, then, that you never become a portrait painter,' said Peter Lely with a condescending smile, 'for I can assure you, my dear, that very few of the faces I paint are interesting at all. But they pay me well, they keep me busy, so I paint them as they wish. Have you other ideas, then? Other fields you wish to plough? Flowers, perhaps – all the young ladies in Holland paint flowers for their pleasure, now.'

'I have no desire to paint flowers,' said Alathea. She did not dare look at her father – if she should catch his eye, she was afraid she would disgrace herself with laughter. 'I paint people, and houses, and things that I like.'

'Then I warn you, do not seek to paint for money,' Lely told her solemnly. 'For if you are besieged with work, with patrons clamouring for portraits of themselves, and their patrons and friends and relations and the King and the Duke of York and everyone else of consequence in the world, then you will never have the opportunity to complete your master work. One day, if I have the time, I will give the world a painting that will open all their eyes . . . but that is of little consequence at the present. Tell me, my dear, do you wish your portrait painted? I can assure you, you need have no fear that you would be outshone, for you are at least the equal in beauty of many Court ladies. What do you think, sir? Would you like a portrait of your daughter to brighten your halls with that hair?'

'I regret that we do not at present have the time for sittings, and you must be very busy,' said Francis. 'Perhaps when we are next in Oxford, we might come to some arrangement. I would certainly be delighted to have a portrait of Alathea, painted by so great a master . . . '

'And quite indistinguishable from the Castlemaine, with my head fitted awkwardly on someone else's body and a nest of rocks behind me and all very fine and handsome and not *me*,' said Alathea to her father as soon as they were out in the street, with armfuls of paints and rolls of canvas and the fulsome, patronising flattery of Master Lely still ringing in their ears. 'And the tragedy of it is, he *can* paint most wonderfully, when he has the time. Master Beale had an excellent self-portrait he painted for them, and a lovely picture of a shepherd boy, and they're both so beautifully and subtly painted, quite different from the things he generally turns out now.' She glanced at her father, negotiating the busy street, and added with a grin,'I don't think he saw me as a serious rival, do you?'

'I don't think he saw you as an artist at all.'

'No, he saw me as a pretty little girl who could be patted on the head and humoured and have her head turned by a great man's flattery. If I had a face like the back of a wagon,' said Alathea ruefully, 'I think my life would be less complicated.'

'But I'll wager you wouldn't have wheedled all these paints out of Master Lely so easy,' her father told her. 'Well, at any rate you're impervious to such wiles, for which I'm most grateful. It does make my paternal duty to guard your virtue so much simpler!'

'You can have no fears for my virtue,' Alathea said thoughtfully. 'But as for my artist's honour, well, that's another matter. I can see, can't you, how easy it would be to go down that slippery slope, to want to be successful, to paint people as they wished rather than as they truly are, to lie and flatter and deceive instead of revealing character and representing a true likeness, and then to find that your success has taken you over, you can't paint truthfully again no matter how much you want to, because you're too busy and you need the clients and the money and all the fame and adulation . . . I feel sorry for Master Lely,' she finished with decision. 'Though he'd think I was mad if he knew – he has all anyone's ambition ever wants, and yet it's such a waste.'

'And you don't intend to go down that road?' Francis queried. 'Stand still, maw – that canvas has slipped.' He pushed the roll more securely under her arm and then heaved the bag of paints, already leaking sluggishly from one corner, back over his shoulder.

'I do not,' said Alathea positively. 'If it ever comes, that I have to choose between truth and fame . . . '

'What will you do?' Francis asked, though the tone in his child's voice had warned him.

Alathea gave him a look of mischief, sideways from the long green eyes. 'Ah . . . I'll forswear my art and find a nice reliable man and marry him, and live happily evermore and create children and pictures for the pleasure of it . . . that's what I'll do if I ever have to choose.'

'Poor man,' said Francis, smiling. 'To be second-best to an easel, for the rest of his days. Which reminds me – what are you going to do for an easel, maw? It seems all artists have them.'

'They're easy to make – we'll ask one of the Deddington carpenters to turn one out for me, and if he makes some frames too then I can stretch and prime the canvas myself,' said Alathea happily. 'Do you know, I feel as if I could dance back to the Blue Boar, it's as if a great . . . *shadow* has lifted, and my way is clear and I can paint . . . oh, thank you, thank you, for all this.'

'Don't try to hug me, or there'll be no paint for you to use. And what – or who – are you going to paint first?'

'Oliver, I think,' Alathea said. 'Oliver, very dashing, and then perhaps Ros, and Ashcott, and even Mistress Gooch if she'll let me, and Lovell . . . Oh, I can't wait to start!'

True to her promise, or threat, next day the luckless Oliver Ashley was hauled protesting into the small north-facing parlour at Ashcott, which Alathea had commandeered as a makeshift painting room. It was uncertain whether it was the unaccustomed scrubbing he had undergone beforehand, or merely his annoyance at having to sit still for upwards of two hours while his cousin committed his likeness to canvas, that was responsible for the truly fearsome scowl that glared from Alathea's easel at the end of the afternoon: but it was undeniably impressive. Oliver, at thirteen years old already well aware of his charm and good looks, admitted that, yes, it did make him look rather fine. After that, there was no problem about the scrubbing, or the sitting still, but Alathea had some difficulty in persuading him to reproduce his original, ferocious expression.

Her blood was up now, and it did not take long to finish. Carefully, scratching her monogram in the tacky crimson paint depicting her subject's best doublet, she signed it with a pride she had never before allowed herself to feel in any of her 'prentice painting at Mistress Beale's, and stood back to admire it. Pride, yes, and a certain feeling of astonishment, that the rushing, tingling magic in her hand and head should have created this, so exactly the portrait she had held in her mind all the months since she had first beheld Judith Leyster's picture in her uncle's study at Goldhayes, and known that the style and dash were right for her, and for Oliver. There he was, captured for all time, the arrogant, black-haired, challenging boy with his hand on his sword (it was in actual fact Francis's), and yet with a suspicion of mischief in the corners of his mouth that suggested the other, more attractive side to him.

Lucy was delighted with Alathea's vivid interpretation of her beloved only son, and her sole lament, the fact that Dan, still in London, would not yet have the opportunity of seeing it. Nor for some time, for though the plague had lessened by the middle of October, when Oliver's portrait was finished, the City of London and its environs were well nigh deserted by all save the poorest, or bravest. Dan had written to his wife urging her strongly to stay at Ashcott with Ros and Oliver until all possible danger was past. Poor Celia was still confined to her bed with a cough that would not leave her, and was not well enough to travel: and all through that autumn, everyone had that small, nagging fear for her at the back of their minds – save for Alathea, totally absorbed in her painting.

She had had three canvases from Master Lely, two of medium size and the third much smaller. The portrait of Oliver occupied one of the former, and for a companion to it she painted Rosalind for the second time, being more careful now to ensure her materials would not change colour or spoil. And the magic did not leave her. At the end of those long, calm, talkative sittings in the little parlour, warmed now by a cheerful fire as the days grew short and cold, there were two Rosalinds in the room, and as Francis commented, with a wonderment his usual casual flippancy could not quite disguise, it was hard to tell which was real, and which her painted counterfeit.

'That's easy enough,' said Oliver, cheerfully insulting. 'The real Ros is the one who moves her mouth – frequently!'

'If I had a cushion to hand . . . ' his sister warned him. 'Little monkey! Oh, Thea, it's beautiful, it really is.'

'I haven't flattered you,' said the artist, staring at the painting as if she could not quite believe in it. Rosalind, plain and well-dressed and lively, had required a rather different treatment to her dashing brother, a more exact and less flamboyant style, but despite her experimentation, it had worked. The girl sat in front of a dull-green mass of drapery (filched from a spare bed), with a dimly-seen landskip in the distance, to her left. She was wearing a loose dress of gold-coloured silk, beautifully suited to her tawny hair and warm complexion, and the expression on her face was one of amusement: light-hearted Ros, to the life.

No, Alathea had not flattered her, but she had shown that a person's essential attractions need not necessarily lie entirely in their face.

Flushed with her success in her first two attempts at portraiture, Alathea decided who her next subject was to be, and with an excess of self-confidence took easel and paints and the last, smaller canvas and, a reluctant Mun and Sophie as her porters, knocked on the door of the little ground-floor chamber, next to the warmth of the new kitchen, that was the Widow's particular lair. The cackle behind the stout oak panelling was her signal, and she marched in with a happy zeal not easily nipped in the bud by Mistress Gooch's opening remarks.

'Oh, it's you, is it? Thought you'd come here sooner or later with all your smelly paints. Can't you leave a poor old body alone in peace?'

'No,' said Alathea, grinning. 'I just have a fancy to paint you – and you're lucky, because in a few years' time you'll have to pay a fortune for the privilege of one of my portraits to immortalise your face.'

'Fortune, eh?' said the Widow, unimpressed. Black-clad and witchlike, she was hunched in a chair by the fire, her crooked ancient hands busy with some sewing, and a pair of spectacles perched perilously on her gnarled nose. There was a curious smell, at once evil and fragrant, which Alathea traced to a long clay tobacco-pipe pushed into the corner of the hearth. 'Fortune? How much d'you reckon you'd charge, lass?'

'Fifteen or twenty pounds for a picture this size, I should reckon,' said Alathea, setting the little canvas on the makeshift easel, improvised from her rough sketch by the mystified Ashcott carpenter.

Mun and Sophie, having deposited their burdens on a convenient table, made their perfunctory courtesies and fled. Mistress Gooch had always taken a perverse and cheerful delight in exaggerating her malevolence, and they were both convinced that she was a witch. She cackled again. 'Fifteen pounds? That's a steep price to pay for immortality, especially at my age when you're too old to enjoy it. Well, lass? Are you going to ask me for the loan of my face for an hour, or, knowing you, for seven or eight?'

'Not all at once: an hour for now will do.' Alathea caught the Widow's eye, still beady at eighty or more, and grinned. 'All right, Mistress Gooch. Will you do me the honour of granting me an hour of your precious time so that I may paint your portrait?'

'Hm. I daresay I can. Should've asked me before. These modern young people, I don't know, forgotten all their manners most of 'em, or never learned them in the first place, more like. Set it all up have you? Right then, let's get on with it. How do you want me to sit?'

She worked on the portrait for more than the prescribed hour, amused by the Widow's mock-irascible talk, and urgent with the need to preserve that unique face with its unrivalled blend of age and shrewd wisdom, malicious humour and youthful vigour. But somehow the very strength of the Widow's crinkled countenance avoided her brush, and all her skills and flair and gifts could not capture it. A travesty of the old woman grinned mockingly up at her from the canvas, and defeated her. She had to pack everything up, cover that misfortune with an old piece of sacking, and carry away all the odoriferous paraphernalia of failure, her pride drastically fallen.

She wondered, later, if there had not been a curse, a sending, an enchantment of malevolent power at work, to stumble her fingers and mar her eye, for that evening, quite unexpected, Kit returned from Yorkshire.

They were having supper, rather cramped in the parlour made out of part of the Great Hall. With seven Herons, three Ashleys, and Mistress Gooch, the alteration was much less spacious than the original, the servants shuffling round the wall to distribute the plates of food. As usual, there was a great deal of chatter, particularly from the younger children, which was occasionally suppressed by their elders when it became too loud or uninhibited. Only Alathea was quiet, her eyes far away, seeing not the long oaken table, spread with damask and plates and bowls and jugs, the candlelight sharp on the apples and more gently diffused over the soft grey pewter, an unplanned still-life, her mind still struggling with the failed portrait of the Widow. The candles and the fire made that face, whose contours she now knew like her own, into a grotesque, humorous gargoyle, all yellow light and deep black shadow, and behind her eyes, Alathea saw her hands obeying the slightest command of muscle and brain, and the mask translated into paint.

And then the door crashed open, and another mask stood there, just as dramatic but much younger and more handsome by far. 'Hullo, everybody,' said Kit, as if he had been for a day's jaunt to Oxford. 'I'm back.'

It was entirely typical of him to make no reference to his unexplained months of absence, and his family were sufficiently mindful of past disturbances to avoid any awkward questions, and to confine themselves to a characteristically overwhelming Heron welcome. If he felt anger at seeing Rosalind, and the Ashleys, still at Ashcott, he gave no sign: nor did he appear to notice Alathea's hands, which despite a thorough scouring were still rimmed with paint on knuckles and under fingernails, and the crimson staining on her old gown. And amidst all the hubbub, the jumping, excited children, his eyes and his smile seemed to be for her alone.

But while he was gone, she had been to Master Lely's house, and had become a painter again.

It was not something she was going to shout aloud to him, and the next morning, very early, she slunk down from her warm bed to the cold stone of the little back parlour, and stealthily packed away her easel and canvases and paints and oils in a chest, covering them with some old pieces of sacking she had intended, copying Mistress Beale, to use instead of canvas. She tried to tell herself, as she replaced the heavy oaken lid, that her creative urge had come to a temporary halt, and the parlour would be needed for some other purpose, and that really she was glad of the respite after the initial failure of Mistress Gooch's portrait: but she knew that Kit was to blame for this concealment – and her fear of him.

Yet she did not want to face him out again. The muddy emotions that their last confrontation had stirred up had upset her too much. And she was glad when he asked her to go riding again, when they played music together, or when Lucy, recalling the long-past days at Goldhayes when she and her four brothers and Thomazine had acted plays and scenes in the Long Gallery, suggested a performance of, appropriately enough, her favourite, *As You Like It*, with Rosalind cast as Rosalind and Oliver as Oliver and Alathea as Celia, and Francis playing the part of Melancholy Jaques, as he had done when a boy, with comical over-statement. Kit claimed the role of Orlando, to bandy words with the disguised princesses in the Forest of Arden. It was all very light-hearted, and there was a great deal of merriment with the costumes, Rosalind borrowing, rather coyly, her brother's best clothes and making a singularly unconvincing boy.

'You would have made a better one,' she said ruefully, straining the doublet over her neat but undeniably feminine chest, and looking with envy at Alathea's tall wiry figure.

Her cousin grinned. 'I don't want to be one, thank you – I'll leave you to look ridiculous! Anyway, how could you *not* be Rosalind? You were named for her, after all. And Celia for the Celia in the play, too.'

'But not Oliver – he gets his name from an uncle.' Rosalind prised the buttons into the loops and peered discontentedly into the mirror. She hated to have any other but her habitual neat, well-groomed appearance. 'And I shall have to pretend I adore Kit, as well.'

'And you don't?'

'Not exactly,' said Rosalind. 'His dislike of me does rather put me off. It stands out around him like spines around a hedgehog.' She giggled nervously. 'I hate making a fool of myself. Still, Mother is so set on this, it's her favourite play, so I suppose we must please her. I know she's worried about Father and Celia in London, and this will take her mind off them.' She looked at Alathea, standing with her usual unselfconscious grace in one of her better gowns, girdled round with a quantity of old bedcurtain and carrying a crook to symbolise her shepherdess disguise. 'You're enjoying all this, aren't you!'

'Yes,' said Alathea, and smiled. 'Oh, yes – perhaps I should have been an actress, and not a painter.'

'Sophie's the actress in your family, and one of her is quite enough,' said Rosalind firmly. 'And much though I like going to the theatre, playing the part myself is another matter. Still, we must grit our teeth, I suppose, and do our duty.'

'Come on, Ros, don't be so pompous – and,' said Alathea, dragging her cousin forcibly into the largest downstairs room, where the play was to take place, 'don't forget – watch out for prickles!'

It was good advice, and a course she followed herself, for the remaining weeks until Christmas. Kit made a very good Orlando, even if he did seem compelled to put his dear love at arm's length with a frosty glare, and Alathea enjoyed herself, then and afterwards, in his company. No uncomfortable references to painting or friendship sullied their talk, and the pigs' bladder containers, hidden in the chest, grew hard with neglect as Alathea discovered anew the delights of sophisticated, witty conversation, and learned to cross swords with a worthy protagonist who had little of Rosalind's warmth, but an abundance of intelligence.

Nothing escaped Mistress Gooch, and as Alathea passed her chimney-corner one chilly day close to Christmas, a wizened claw shot out to detain her. 'Stay a minute, lass – I want a word with you.'

Mildly irritated, Alathea crouched down beside the old woman. The corner was hot and dimly lit, and smelt of the Widow's tobacco. This reprehensible habit seemed to be quite a recent one, and Alathea could never work out where supplies of the noxious weed came from, as it had certainly never featured on any family shopping list for journeys to Oxford. The Widow drew on the long dirty stem of her pipe and exhaled lustily. A cloud of evil-smelling smoke arose from the bowl in sympathy. 'Busy, are you?'

'Not particularly. I was going to get dressed for riding.'

'And in a hurry – I can see, you know, I've got eyes.' The Widow cackled evilly. 'Who are you going riding with, then, this cold and wintry afternoon?'

'I don't mind the cold. I'm going with Kit, over to Barford and back – just for a ride.'

'With Kit, eh?'

'Yes, with Kit,' said Alathea, annoyed at this rather repetitive catechism. Her mind was leaping ahead already to the chamber she shared with Nell and Rosalind, and her riding habit, London-made and by far the finest garment she possessed, being in the natural course of things unsullied by paint, and the wild ride over the grassy sheepwalks to Barford Bridge and back, Lovell-our-dog in enthusiastic and lumbering attendance. But her wandering attention was abruptly wrenched back by the Widow's next words. 'You should be careful, little Thea – remember, he's still your brother.'

Alathea frowned at her. 'Of course he's my brother – like Math and Mun.'

'No, not at all like them, our fine and handsome Kit. Your little brothers are on the one hand too clever and on the other too stupid, to make themselves so dashing.'

'Mun's not stupid!' said Alathea, stung into unwonted loyalty to her ruffianly youngest brother.

'Maybe, but he ain't so wonderful at his books, is he? No, Kit's not like Francis's two – *they* won't lead you astray.'

'Astray? Oh, Mistress Gooch, whatever do you mean?' Alathea put her hands on the rusty greenish black of the Widow's sleeve, feeling the hard and sinewy life below. 'Please don't talk in riddles – *tell* me.'

'You think I've gone soft in the head, don't you? You think it's just a senile old woman's idle chatter? Well, I may be nine-and-seventy, but my wits are what they always were, even if my legs ain't, and I say to you, lass, for your own sake, for you may be bright and young and pretty but you ain't wise in the ways of the world, for all that time you've lived in London. Now your brother Kit, he's a fine and handsome young man, and he has a kind of charm about him, I'm not denying, but then so did his father – and whatever you may think, lass, he ain't *safe*.'

Deep in Alathea's head the warning bells sounded in unison – his early enmity, the jealous nature of his friendship, the lengths to which he would go to gain her exclusive attention, all combined to echo the Widow's words, but her loyalty and her love rose up in his defence. 'What do you think he is – some Court villain from one of Aunt Lucy's plays? He's my *brother*, and I *like* him, and I *like* being with him, he's good fun, and nothing anyone can say will turn me against him.'

'Wasn't trying to turn you against him,' said Mistress Gooch, wryly philosophical. 'Just *warning* you, lass, that's all. Look out for yourself, the Drakelons are a tricky breed.'

'So are Herons – and I can look after myself very well, thank you,' said Alathea, with an indignation that made her feel, afterwards, rather guilty. For Kit *was* dangerous: it was part of his appeal, the moods, the smouldering eyes, the impression he always gave of scarce-contained power and emotion. But she knew how to handle him now, as she had learned to handle restive horses. She had handled the great Lely, after all, she had smiled at him and played him like a fish, hooked by her face, and the ease of it had delighted her. Kit was her servant now, as the London slang had it, her follower, her admirer, played on a line sufficiently long for him to be in ignorance of it.

And then she realised the drift of her thoughts and, rather appalled, had to laugh at herself. As Rosalind had intimated, Sophie was the artful actress of the family: she, Alathea, should be above such things. Stick to your painting, my girl, she told herself sternly, it's what you're best at.

But with Kit in such close attendance, she could neither paint nor draw, and to confuse matters worse, she revelled in the laughter and companionship provided by her brother, who kept her from her easel.

Christmas came upon them as usual, a riotous country festival rather different from the succession of polite dinners and modest junketings that were the rule in London. At Ashcott, as at Goldhayes, the tenants and local people were the happy recipients of Heron hospitality: music, dancing, feasting into all the hours of the night, and in return a visit from the mummers from Deddington, fortunately well-disguised in their tattered costumes. They were a group of elderly grey-heads quavering the ancient ritual words, remembered from happier times before parliaments grew rebellious and kings were killed, and Christmas became a day like any other, at least in public. It had returned, a rather patchwork and motley affair, with the King, but despite the gaps in the mummers' memories, and in their costumes, even the sophisticated Kit could be seen laughing with delight at their antics. Ever after, those twelve days were surrounded by a faint, lustrous radiance in Alathea's memory: a golden glow that gently touched out, like an artist's brush, the holes in the mummers' costumes and the yawns disfiguring Oliver's face and the fight that Mun started with the village boys, and Sophie's shameless ogling of a startled young Adderbury acquaintance of her father's. And the crown of the season was Twelfth Night, which was also Thomazine's birthday.

Much to everyone's (secret) relief, Lucy did not suggest putting on a performance of the play of that name by Master Shakespeare, and the last day of the festival was reserved for the family, the high spot being the supper. Oliver, somewhat supercilious but secretly revelling in it, had been Lord of Misrule for the season, and had revealed a rather fiendish talent for acts of mischief. Rosalind had had to wear a very shabby gown for one day, regardless of patches and stains, and then for another when she complained. Sophie was vowed to silence, with a penny for every noise that escaped her lips, and Alathea forced to go everywhere with Lovell-our-dog roped securely to her wrist. The celebration of Twelfth Night was also a celebration of the end of Oliver's reign, and the big cake that had been many hours cooking in the deep oven would decide his successors: the Twelfth Night Cake.

It was borne in by the cookmaid and her train, rather self-consciously, with a good deal of ceremony and laughter, and Francis, grinning, supervised the cutting while Oliver sat in the corner, his reign ended, sulking, the very image of the boy in Alathea's portrait. And when the pieces of cake were passed around, and probed for their secrets, it was Alathea who found the hidden pea in her portion and became Queen for the last night of Christmas, and Kit who was given the bean, and was therefore her King.

They had music, two fiddles and a drum from Deddington, and

could dictate the dances: desperate country affairs that left everyone gasping for breath, clutching sides bruised by laughter and unplanned encounters with furniture. Alathea, ears ringing with the groans of her subjects as she ordered yet another round of the Brawl, was glad that for tonight at least she would not be involved in that exhausting melee, only to be told, the next instant, that her Royal Consort desired her presence in the dance, along with himself.

'Oh, no!' Alathea said ruefully, but found herself pushed, laughing and protesting, into the centre of the room.

At this stage of the evening, there was no point in trying to remember refinements like footwork or timing: at every twist and turn of the music, Alathea was flung from one male partner to the next, thoroughly kissed, and passed on. Even Mun, scarlet with exertion, joined in the fun with gusto, and planted a particularly smacking, slobbery, eleven-year-old kiss on her cheek, although he refused to do the same to Sophie, simpering behind Alathea, and passed her on to Oliver. In the confusing blur of faces as the dance rushed madly by, Alathea suddenly encountered Kit: flushed face, blue eyes, white teeth flashing in one of his vivid smiles, and his voice laughing, saying, 'Hello, little sister, let's have your kiss.'

Laughing too, the music singing in her ears, Alathea turned her cheek for a brotherly embrace, which Kit gave her, neat and quick, and then, his mouth sliding sideways, touched her briefly on the lips and was gone, pulled away in the riot of the Brawl so fast that she wondered if she had imagined that brief, most unfraternal gesture.

It had not been her imagination. Thomazine, tangled breathlessly in the opposite corner of the dance, had noticed that kiss also, and felt suddenly frightened, as if she had seen that the likeness of Kit was not her eldest son at all, but some changeling of malevolent intent, poised to shatter their comfortable, innocent little world, just as she had always feared he would. She kept watch, as best she could, during the last moments of the dance, but in that noisy heaving mass there was small chance of noticing much, and none at all as the fiddles and drum screeched to a climax and all the younger dancers fell into a sweating, rosy heap, gasping and sobbing with laughter. So Thomazine did not see Kit pull his sister down with the rest: and Alathea, with Oliver across her legs and Nell's hair tangled in hers, had her view of the new white-washed ceiling rudely and abruptly blocked by Kit's face, the eyes and smile for her alone. Warned by something in the quality of that smile, she dodged his descending kiss by sliding sideways, pushing Oliver off her with some difficulty, and struggling to her feet. Without a backward glance, hoping he would think she had not noticed his action and had merely got up at an inopportune moment, she stepped across the heaving bodies of the collapsed dancers, to her mother's side, and safety.

Thomazine did not say anything, but their eyes met, brown and shadow-green, in an understanding that had no need of words. In a rush of exhaustion, and gratitude, Alathea put her arms around her and hugged her mother close. She had rarely talked much to Thomazine. Her father was her confidant, and she had taken her troubles to him, when they grew too much, since childhood. But despite the awkwardness between herself and her mother, despite the gap that had somchow separated them, she was aware, like knowing of the sun's warmth, of Thomazine's great love and affection, and knew that now she could rely on her. For her mother knew Kit, understood him as no other did, felt great sympathy for him, even without the love whose lack had blighted his life. Thomazine would know what to do about Kit.

There was only one solution to that problem simmering underneath their feet like a threatening volcano, and both Thomazine and her husband knew it. Either Kit or Alathea would have to leave, and since Alathea, keeping well out of Kit's way with a sick feeling of apprehension behind her ribs, was deprived both of his company and of her other solace, painting, she would undeniably be better off in the hurly-burly of life in London, free to paint and go to plays and hobnob with Rosalind and Henrietta Jermyn. So to London she must go, and at the first opportunity. Letters were sent to Dan, asking both for news of Celia and for his advice as to whether it was wise to return to London, and on his reply in the affirmative, Lucy decided to set out at once.

It was an unhappy parting, beset with difficulties. Kit, obviously aware that he had gone too far, seemed to have learned some wisdom and attempted to pretend that nothing had happened and that he and his half-sister were no more than the best of friends: but every time his eyes rested on her, Alathea knew that he had not really changed, and was afraid. Suddenly London, even the changed shadow of London described in Dan's letters, seemed a glittering glowing grail where at last she could be free of dissembling and deceit, and be herself again, and she could not wait to go.

Nell, of course, wanted to go with her, living her life through Alathea as she had always done, and Lucy made no objection. But there was the vexed question of Lovell, now a great hairy mat of a dog, large, uncouth and loving, and definitely not the animal for London living, and in need of frequent exercise to curb his enthusiasms. Alathea could not bear to leave him behind, and besides, despite everything, he was still Kit's gift, a reminder of the brother she must now abandon, forever disappointed, and for whom she still felt great affection. Reluctantly, Lucy agreed to take Lovell too, largely because Oliver proved very persuasive, and she had always been swift to grant him whatever he wanted.

'So, goodbye again,' said her father to Alathea, kissing her in the cold January wind, sharp with the threat of snow. 'I don't need to tell you to be careful, do I? And beware of flattery from middle-aged artists!'

'I won't let it turn my head,' said Alathea, grinning to keep back the tears. 'I thought I might try to see Master Cooper – I know he only paints in miniature, but there's no one to touch him for taking a likeness, they say, and I would love to watch him work, and perhaps learn something of him. I don't think there's room in the Ashleys' house for a separate studio for oil painting, but limning in little doesn't take much space and doesn't smell at all!'

'I wish you luck,' her father said. 'And paint your own portrait, if you limn in miniature. Your mother would love to have it, I know.' He held her shoulders, lightly, and looked at her pale, shadowed, cold-bitten face. 'You don't mind? About going back to London?'

'No,' said Alathea, with her usual honesty. 'I want to paint again. And it's too – too complicated here.' She shivered, pulling her thick dark cassock-coat tighter around her. 'I don't . . . I never wanted . . . *you* understand about Kit, don't you? Please be nice to him, he never wanted it either, I'm sure, and if I go now he'll forget me . . . Oh, bother this face,' said Alathea in exasperation, and dragged her leather riding-glove across her watery eyes. 'I *wish* I was ugly – then we could still be friends, we were, and we still are . . . if only he didn't keep looking at me!'

'He can't help it,' said Francis. 'No man could. You draw eyes everywhere, and always will, and that's something you'll have to learn to live with, and handle for yourself. But please, my dearest lass, don't learn to use it to your advantage, for that's a steep and slippery slope, and others have been down before you, and been hated for it. And no loveliness of face lasts for ever, but good nature and the ability to love and be loved will be with you always, whatever the example of Mistress Gooch!' He smiled at her, and gently wiped away a spilt tear. 'Chin up, my brave Alathea – and take care!'

She said goodbye to her mother, with no awkwardness and few words, but with love, and to her brothers and to Sophie, who cried and expressed her urgent desire to come with her and see a play.

'When you've grown a bit,' said Alathea, from the lofty heights of sixteen to the lowly child of nine, and Sophie sniffed heart-breakingly and turned drowned green eyes up to her sister. 'Promise?'

'I promise,' said Alathea, mortgaging her future for a little peace and quiet, and Sophie, easily pleased, was happy again.

Kit was there, too, to receive her farewells, but he avoided her eyes, and was pale and tight-lipped and silent, and she did not know how to make it right again, or if things between them would ever now be mended. She knew how to respond to her family's love, but this was a different kind altogether: deep, and difficult, and dangerous. It frightened her, and repelled her, and yet Kit was still Kit, and part of him was still a friend. So she whispered 'Sorry,' and kissed his cheek, cold and unresponsive, and then turned and walked to her horse, before either of them could break.

CHAPTER SEVEN

Hugh

A friend loveth at all times,
and a brother is born for adversity.

(Proverbs, 17.17)

Master Samuel Cooper stood at the door of his pleasant and prosperous house in Henrietta Street, Covent Garden, enjoying the sunshine, and the gratifyingly rare moment of leisure. A small man, rotund and friendly with a reputation for good company, he was frequently hailed by passers-by, acquaintances, neighbours, friends, exchanging political and less elevated gossip: the high doings at Court, especially of Mistress Stewart, now universally supposed to be the King's mistress, and the Castlemaine's nose thoroughly out of joint: and the latest figures for plague deaths, which had showed an increase over last week's, and the likelihood of the warmer weather bringing back that dreadful scourge to blight the promise of the summer. Master Cooper, who was close on sixty, had attained the philosophical attitude common to most men of his years, and was able to view the prospect with equanimity. He had survived the last appalling summer, and, God willing, would survive another. He had already out-lived his parents, brother and uncle, and he had led a full, varied and highly successful life, the crown of which was to be generally considered, from Italy to Sweden, from London to Heidelberg, the master of all limners. It was a reputation built upon hard work, great gifts and technical skills, and above all upon integrity. There were no crowds of assistants in Master Cooper's studio to paint hands and landskips and draperies, and if a miniature offered to a client was a replica or a copy, he was told so plainly. Each of the tiny, jewel-like, jewel-mounted portraits that left his hands was entirely his own work, painted exclusively from the life, revealing its subject with a clear but compassionate honesty that had no match in England, and hardly in Europe either, whether in limning or in oils. At thirty pounds or so for a work that was no more than two or three inches across, and had taken perhaps ten sittings, it might seem expensive when compared with the grand full-size portraits of Lely or Wright. But Cooper's clients were purchasing rather more than a few oval inches of watercolour and vellum and card, and knew that the quality was reflected in the price. And in London there were plenty of people willing to pay it, as his lengthy and crowded appointments book showed.

And here, by the look of it, came two more: a young lady and gentleman, of some quality to judge by their attire, they were walking slowly up Henrietta Street from the direction of the Piazza, looking closely at each house. They were both dressed in black, the deep mourning for a close relative, but the gloom implied by their garments did not show at all in their faces. The boy said something to the girl and her countenance lit up with laughter all at once, like the unveiling of a candle, whereupon the boy smiled, full of mischief. Master Cooper watched those expressions with a certain professional interest. The boy, darkly handsome though he was, looked to be about fourteen, and really too young to have much character yet in his face, but the girl (sister? cousin?) was another matter. He had painted every one of the celebrated Court beauties, the Castlemaine, Mistress Stewart, the Queen, Jane Myddelton, Mistress Jennings, each one subtly different and yet similar, with the fashionable long-eyed look of languor: and this girl could match any of them. With the pleasure of an artist he noted her silver-fair hair, brilliant in the afternoon sun, the long slender face and shadowy eyes and the look of determination about the mouth, a little wider and more flexible than the pouting rosebud now in fashion. The whole impression she gave was one of brilliant glowing fairness, like the famous Frances Jennings, yet with an innocent grace and spirit that La Belle Jennings most decidedly lacked. But she was not of the Court, and he had never seen her before, and if she and the boy were not looking for his house, he would most like never see her again. For some reason – for he was old, long and happily married – he found that prospect a disappointment. But then he had always been responsive to beauty, of face or soul: it was part of his artist's gift.

They were indeed looking for his house. They stopped on the pavement just by him, and glanced at each other. He saw the boy, with a sensitivity unexpected in such a bold-looking lad, touch her fingers in encouragement. Then he bowed, and she curtseyed, so that a hasty gentleman, following behind, all but fell over them, avoided them with difficulty and a muttered imprecation, and hurried on. The pair did not notice him at all, their eyes and attention being both fixed entirely upon the artist.

'Master Ashley at your service, sir,' said the boy, formally. 'Are you Master Cooper?'

With amusement, and some interest, he said that yes, indeed, he was, and the girl, staring at him hungrily with extraordinary eyes, long and shadowy green, said quickly, 'Then, sir, can we – I – speak with you for a moment? I know you must be busy, but I will not detain you long.'

There was nearly half an hour to his next appointment. Master Cooper smiled, and stood aside to let them pass through his door. 'Of course you may enter, Mistress, uh . . . '

'Heron,' said the girl, and turned on him a smile of such dazzling brilliance that he was startled. 'Oh, thank you, Master Cooper – thank you so much!'

The artist's studio was high up in the garret, lit by a northern skylight to give the cold clear illumination necessary for limning, or indeed for most kinds of art. There was none of the bustle of Lely's studio or the clutter of Mistress Beale's, nor the reek of oils and primers common to both: just a careful orderliness, jars of pigments neatly labelled, containers full of the tiny fat pointed hair brushes needed for such small-scale work, pestles and mortars for grinding, lumps of the yellow gum that bound the colours together and, on a separate table, the little turned ivory boxes in which the prepared paints were kept, ready for the quick sure strokes of the artist's wet brush. Alathea stood and looked, noting the unfamiliar things, known only from the book she had read. She had tracked down a copy of Master Sanderson's treatise on painting from an obliging bookseller who inhabited Paul's churchyard, along with a score of others in the same trade, and who had been recommended to her by Uncle Dan, who, though not a great reader of books himself, was an inexhaustible fountain of information about all aspects of London life. She looked for the miniature easel, quite different from the rough frame that supported an oil-painter's canvases. Master Cooper used a beautiful little wooden box, which stood on a desk by the skylight: it had drawers for paints and brushes and palettes below, and above a sloping, hinged board backed with felt, for the card-backed vellum on which the miniature would be painted. Seeing all the equipment laid out in readiness, Alathea's fingers began to tingle, very slightly, with the familiar urge to create.

'Well, Mistress Heron?' said Master Cooper. 'And how may I help you?'

Looking at him, a round comfortable little man with that humble, ordinary appearance so utterly at odds with his reputation, Alathea, for once in her life, was at a loss. How could he help her? He had no pupils, and few assistants, and they were employed, she knew, in a menial capacity, grinding and preparing colours, cleaning brushes and keeping the studio tidy. Those round dark eyes stared at her expectantly, assessingly, sizing up the proportions of her character and the lines of her face, and she felt as if her tongue had ceased to work.

Eventually, she said hesitantly, 'I – I have some experience in picture drawing, I studied with Mistress Beale, and now she has gone into the country I have no one to school me, and no opportunity to practise in oils, so I wanted to learn something of miniature painting.' She saw Master Cooper's mouth move, and hurried on. 'But I realise that you must be very busy, and you do not take pupils, and I am very sorry for wasting your time.' She smiled guiltily. 'And I haven't even got the money for a sitting.'

'That doesn't matter,' said the artist. He put his head on one side, studying her, in a gesture that reminded her very much of a garden robin. 'A picture drawer, eh? You seem very young for it.'

'I'll be seventeen next month,' said Alathea. 'And I've been studying for nearly five years.'

'And do you have any of your work with you?'

Alathea's hands were empty. She had thought long and hard about this. Her latest work, the paintings of Oliver and Rosalind (the failed portrait of Mistress Gooch had been confined to the very bottom of the chest in which she kept her materials and drawings), had been proudly framed and hung in the Ashleys' upstairs parlour, one either side of the fireplace, and her pride and dignity had not allowed her, or Oliver, to struggle through the crowded streets encumbered with a heavy oil picture. Nor had she really wanted to take a sheaf of drawings, people whom Master Cooper would not recognise, portraits whose accuracy he could not judge. And so she had decided on a ploy which, in its boldness and daring, had astonished her when she had first thought of it, and terrified her now. But Master Cooper was no ogre, nor was he patronising or lecherous. She lifted her eyes to meet his, and said in explanation, 'No, I haven't: but if you have the time to spare, just a little, I have chalk and paper and I will draw my cousin here.'

Master Samuel Cooper looked at this surprising girl intently. Here was courage indeed, to have the confidence to draw in front of one with such a wide reputation. He saw the quiet pride in her face, and smiled. 'Very well, and I'll agree with your thought, Mistress Heron, for I'll be the better judge of your skill this way. Your cousin may sit in that chair, and if you like you can rest your paper on my little painting desk.'

'Thank you, sir, but I have my own board with me,' Alathea told him. 'Or rather, Oliver has it. Noll, you haven't dropped it, have you?'

'What do you think I am?' Oliver demanded indignantly. 'Here it is. I had it over my shoulder in the bag with the chalks.'

The artist watched as Alathea directed Oliver to the chair, brushing his hair smooth with her fingers and firmly turning his head to the desired angle. The boy submitted to these ministrations with a smoulder in his face, but sat still and relaxed as if he were used to such things. Then she slid the old board, lovingly smooth, from the soft cloth bag, along with a little box and a brass chalk holder, settled herself down with unfussy competence, placed the thick brownish paper on the board, pushed a stick of black chalk into the holder and began.

Master Cooper did not know what he had expected. The girl's calm, business-like air had not been that of a novice, but she was obviously very young, and he had no great faith in Mistress Beale's ability to pass even her rather pedestrian talents on to a pupil. He found himself hoping most urgently, as her chalk made its first scratchy smudges over the paper, that she would prove to be good.

Alathea was hoping the same, with rather more desperation, but while the sensitive part of her mind trembled, her hands and eyes seemed to have their own life, their own magic, and the spell was still on them. Swiftly, with each stroke and dash of the chalk, Oliver grew on the paper: the slight curl in his glossy black hair, inherited from his mother and thence from a long-dead Spanish woman who had married a Heron in Queen Elizabeth's time, then the shape of his face, the familiar rounded angles of jaw and brow and the nose that was already lengthening into a true Heron beak. She sketched in the slightly frowning line of his eyebrows, and the round eyes beneath them, blue and vivid in life but so hard to translate into one colour of chalk, then the wide firm mischievous mouth, short upper lip and slightly dimpled chin, with the neat lace band below it. She put in the highlights on hair and eyes, nose and cheekbones and jaw with swift generous smudges of white, sharper along the edges of bone, gave a quick considering glance at the paper and then at the seated boy, and laid the drawing down, finished. Master Cooper glanced at his watch, which he had laid to view on the desk. Ten minutes or a little more, and the skill and the likeness were equally remarkable.

'Is it done?' Oliver asked, and at his cousin's nod leapt to his feet and peered eagerly at his portrait. 'Oh, Thea, that's not bad, is it? Though I think the painting was better, really,' he added, after a serious, critical appraisal.

'So it ought to be,' said Alathea, 'it took ten days, not ten minutes.' She rose and turned to face Master Cooper, the drawing in her hands, and he noticed that although they had been steady and sure whilst working, they were now trembling more than a little. Abruptly, with a gesture that was almost rude, she thrust the paper at him. 'Here it is: my work.'

With a smile of encouragement, Samuel Cooper took it from her. He had hoped it would be worthy of that very mature confidence, and he was not disappointed. There was Oliver Ashley, in black and white on brown, in all the arrogant vividness of youth, and it was a demonstration of her gift more effective by far than a hundred stale sketches from a portfolio. For a long moment he stood looking down at it, and a feeling almost of awe crept over him, for he was at the end of his life, the crown of his career. He had been more than thirty years a limner, he had travelled Europe, kings and queens and lords and ladies, foreign potentates, commoners and gentry had all sat to him and been minutely analysed by the accuracy of his brush and his eye's acute perception of character. But this girl was at the beginning of things, her future stretched before her full of unknown excitements, wonderful prospects. If she had been a man, he could have predicted with confidence a most glittering career, if plague or smallpox did not intervene. But for this striking, self-possessed young girl, the alternatives would be the well-worn path of marriage, childbirth, the inevitable draining away of that bright talent amid the cares and exhaustions of running a gentleman's household, or the struggle to achieve recognition for a largely masculine talent, in an almost exclusively masculine world.

'Well?' said Alathea, hearing with apprehension the old abruptness in her tone. It was not insolence, but nervousness that lent that harsh edge to her voice.

But Master Cooper only smiled again, and tapped the paper. 'The trouble is, Mistress Heron, that I cannot teach you.' He saw the look in her face, and hastened to reassure her. 'I cannot teach you anything of drawing portraits, because from the evidence of my own eyes there is little more for you to learn: form, likeness, line, modelling, you have it already, and I salute you. Mistress Beale was your tutor, you said?'

'Yes – she taught me so much, about technique and drawing and painting – it's all due to her work.'

'Not at all,' said Master Cooper. 'You can *teach* most how to draw. It's fashionable now with some men to pay for lessons for their wives to learn to paint, aye, and some show skill at it – it's only the link between hand and eye, that's all. But what *you* have, Mistress, is something that can never be taught or learned. It's instinct guides your hand, I'd guess. There's no painstaking labour involved, all your drawings flow from your fingers – am I right?'

'Yes,' said Alathea, feeling dazed, numb, overwhelmed at this tribute from such a man, free utterly of patronage or condescension. He spoke to her as an equal, another artist, a fellow-professional. 'How did you know?'

'Because it is the same for me, also,' said Master Cooper simply. 'Do you understand what I am telling you? There is a difference between what is *taught* and what is a *gift*, innate, God-given, and without that gift, no one can be a true artist. You have it, and you should be glad, but sorry too, for it brings penalties as well as delight.' He studied the shining girl before him, with sympathy. 'You live for your art, am I right? You are not truly happy unless you can ponder your work in the past, the present and the future. Everywhere you go you see pictures, your eye discerns the form and the shape of all living things, and your heart frames everything and preserves it in a painting in your mind. Everything you see in terms of paints and chalks. There is room in your life for friends and family, but they take second place, always. If you were locked in a stone cell, bare walls, bare floor, no bed, no food, you would be happy if you had your easel and paints.' He put his head on one side enquiringly. 'Am I right, Mistress Heron?'

'Yes,' Alathea said softly, struck with a sense of wonder and of great kinship with this very ordinary-seeming man. 'Yes, it *is* like that – and it always has been and I think it always will be. Please – please, show me how to paint miniatures. I can't work in oils, there's no room where I live. If I learned limning, I could paint again, at long last. I know you don't have pupils, but all I need is time to watch, to see what you do, and to learn about the materials to use and the techniques.'

'You may not be suited to limning,' Master Cooper observed, studying the drawing of Oliver again. 'Your style may prove too swift and large to adjust to such a tiny discipline. But you may certainly watch me at work, and I will ask one of my colourmen to show you the ways of preparing colours. By the way, do you know Master Gibson, Dwarf Gibson we call him, Little Dickon the limner?'

'I have heard of him,' Alathea said cautiously.

'He has a daughter – he has nine children in fact, and several other daughters as well as this one, Susan Penelope, but it's she who shows some promise of limning. He's taught her much already, and she often comes to watch me work. You'll meet her, I expect. She's a pleasant child, fourteen or so now, and as I said she shows some promise, does Pen: but she does not have such a gift as yours.'

'Thank you, sir,' said Alathea, stumbling over the words.

'I need no thanks,' said Master Cooper cheerfully. 'I merely tell the truth. You deserve my help and encouragement, child, and it would be a most criminal waste of your talents if I did not do my utmost to foster it. Now, that bell means that my next client has arrived – do you wish to watch me now, or would you rather wait awhile?'

'I would like, if I may, to come back tomorrow,' said Alathea. She looked white, dazed, overwhelmed with emotion and excitement. 'Please – don't think I don't want to come – I do, more than anything, and I mean to learn all I possibly can – thank you, sir, for everything, you have been more than kind . . . but I don't think I would learn very much today, if I stayed.'

'I am not surprised,' said Samuel Cooper. 'I will see you tomorrow, then, in morning or afternoon, whichever suits you best: and I will warn you, I prefer silent watchers. Your cousin is welcome, too, if he likes, but if he does not and you have qualms about propriety, I can arrange for my dear wife Christiana to accompany you.'

'I have no qualms,' said Alathea, and took a deep breath. 'Oliver, we must go – goodbye, sir, and thank you – I feel as if I've been given new life!'

'I understand,' Master Cooper told her. 'I understand very well. I will see you tomorrow, Mistress Heron, and thank you for coming to see me. I have enjoyed our talk, and I hope we will have many more such.'

'And so do I, and thank you too, for being so kind,' said Alathea, and curtseyed most deeply, while Oliver bowed, and in a state of huge and rising, joyous excitement, left the house in Henrietta Street and fairly ran the half mile or so back to the Fleet Street house.

During that long, hot summer, when all the talk was of a return of the plague, and the Dutch War, and the City stood still in street and park and by riverside to hear the distant threatening mutter of the ships' guns of Holland and England, battling at the mouth of the Thames, Alathea moved in a world of her own, closed in around the Fleet Street house and the clear cool sky-lit garret that was Samuel Cooper's studio. Days were divided between the good, when she could go to Henrietta Street and watch and listen and learn as the great limner worked, and the indifferent, when she could not. Moreover, the House of the Ash Tree at this time was oppressively gloomy, mourning for Celia, who had died at the end of March, a little wan eleven-year-old ghost sliding unprotestingly out of life with as little fuss as she had lived it. Alathea did not grieve much for herself. She had had little contact with her youngest Ashley cousin, and found it hard to summon up much feeling save for resignation, and a certain relief, that the child's suffering had at last ended, but her Aunt Lucy, stricken, aged ten years by her daughter's death and with those glossy black curls suddenly streaked with grey and an unaccustomed slovenliness in her once immaculate apparel, was a pathetic figure who aroused all Alathea's love and sympathy. The family had had to cope with their own sorrow as well as attempting to lighten Lucy's burden of grief, but at last the pain seemed to be easing, laughter, albeit muted, was heard again in the hushed, solemn household, and

Aunt Lucy was even, once, seen to be reading a play; though it was a lamentable, old-fashioned tragedy about a woman supposedly killed with kindness, and she read it with the tears pouring unchecked down her hollow cheeks. But she finished it at last, and the experience seemed to have exorcised some of her anguish, for thereafter she became much more like the old carefree Lucy, though ever with the shadow of poor frail Celia hovering behind her.

Just as Nell hovered behind Alathea, damp and as doggily devoted as Lovell, but not nearly so entertaining. She followed her to Master Cooper's, to the colourman, to church, to Westminster to see Henrietta Jermyn, to the New Exchange on shopping expeditions, drooping more and more wearily as the days grew hotter, and jumping at every rumble of thunder in case it was Dutch guns heralding invasion. Alathea, intent only on the fascinating and intricate art of limning, had scant time for her, but both Rosalind and Oliver were too lively and sociable to spend long quiet hours in an artist's studio, however eminent the client, and so, usually, Nell was her only companion, and was invariably to be found in a corner of the studio with the inevitable pile of sewing, with an air of silent worthiness that made Alathea at once irritated and guilty. But Nell was there, always, and she accepted it: and besides, to object would have been like kicking the dog.

And once in Master Cooper's studio, a haven of unstuffy, blissful coolness amidst the humid stinking heat of summer London, she was utterly consumed by her involvement with paint and vellum and the other materials of limning, all so different from the clutter and bulk and reek of oil painting. The attic was bare, simple, with none of the elaborate accessories or drapes that Master Lely had thought necessary to adorn his portraits. Master Cooper dealt only in faces, beautifully and minutely drawn, and yet handled with a freedom and boldness Alathea had never seen before in paint, save for Judith Leyster's picture at Goldhayes: and beside Samuel Cooper's wonderful, accurate delicacy, even that would look coarse and clumsy. Over the months she watched, fascinated and enthralled, as the mysteries unfolded through Master Cooper's small, fat, competent hands, so utterly sure of themselves. She witnessed every stage of limning, from the preparation of the stiff ovals of card over which the vellum was stretched, and the grinding and mixing of the paints through the first washes of light colour where the head was to be drawn, the 'dead-colouring' that marked the features and shadows of the face, to the final blurring and blending of the colours to achieve the realistic, accurate subtlety of a typical Cooper miniature. Each client could expect to sit eight or more times, for an hour or so each, to be entertained by Master Cooper's witty and sophisticated talk, and to be put at their ease, before or during the sitting, by a display of his uncommon virtuosity on the lute. This was such that Alathea, who had considered herself quite competent on that instrument, abandoned her initial impulse to offer to play as well. But her singing voice was pleasant, if rather throaty, and often she joined in, where appropriate. Nell, in her corner, said nothing at all, but sewed.

There were a lot of clients, four or five in a day sometimes, and many of them quite ordinary people who were knowledgeable enough to be prepared to pay the artist's considerable fees. Alathea remained unobtrusive in the background, perhaps helping one of the assistants to prepare extra colour or to clean brushes, and she met the child Penelope Gibson, a thoughtful girl, very shy and earnest, who at the tender age of fourteen was already a trained limner, and thus made Alathea feel old. Pen was allowed to copy her mentor's works, and had achieved some skill in that, but Alathea, though she watched, and learned, and practised the strokes of brush and colour when she went home, would not copy. She had her own vision. Why waste it by slavishly following someone else, even someone as exalted as Master Cooper?

The great, nobles like Lauderdale, ladies like the lovely Mistress Stewart, were painted at Whitehall, Master Cooper packing up brush and easel and paint and taking coach to Westminster for the purpose. Alathea, looking at the portraits that resulted, felt that two more different specimens of humanity could hardly have been found. Lauderdale, large and uncouth and Judas-haired, looked as unpleasant on vellum as he was reputed to be in life (she had heard stories from Henrietta Jermyn), and compared most unfavourably with the sweet, if rather vacant, loveliness of Mistress Stewart, dressed in the men's clothes that set off her tall graceful figure and the cloud of curling golden hair that, if artfully combed, could be made to resemble a periwig. But some important clients were energetic enough to journey into the distant wilds of Covent Garden for their portrait, which was how Alathea came to meet a very old friend.

It was, of course, a stiflingly hot day, late in August. By this time, everyone in London from the greatest courtier to the lowliest guttersnipe, would have welcomed the slightest shower or downpour. With no rain to wash it away, the refuse piled in the streets, stinking, alive with flies, and a disgusting impediment to pleasant walking. Dust swirled around the streets and alleyways, accumulating chokingly in the throat and lungs, and adding further gritty discomforts to sweaty clothes. It got everywhere, in food, in drink, a fine sandy film over everything, even in Lucy's pristine parlour that was polished daily by one of the maids, and Alathea felt that she would have given anything for a sight of some good honest mud. Milk went sour within hours of leaving the cow, meat rotted with alarming rapidity, water was invariably tepid, and nothing seemed ever to be *cool*: except, miraculously, for Samuel Cooper's studio.

She escaped thence early that day, a little after eight, when the shadows were still long across Fleet Street, and the burning sun had not yet reached any part of the narrower alleys or courts. Nell was with her, one or two paces behind as always, her mouse brown hair framing a long, rather pasty-complexioned face, still aflower with adolescent spots, and the Heron nose unfortunately prominent. Nell, like Rosalind, was not blessed with good looks,but, unlike Ros, failed totally to make the best of what she had. Her hair was uncombed, her fingers rough and unkempt, and her rounded shoulders made her look as downtrodden as a maid-of-all-work. Alathea, irritated, felt like poking those bony, grey-clad shoulderblades to jolt them upright. The bundle of sewing and the shabby clothes completed the illusion that Nell was some kind of humble maid in attendance upon her cousin, save that few ladies would countenance a servant of such disreputable appearance.

'Why don't you get a new gown?' Alathea demanded, as they approached the Piazza of Covent Garden, busy with fashionable strollers and children and the hawkers of fruit and vegetables who infested the place. A red-faced woman, enormously fat, bawled her wares at them. 'Pippins! Pippins fine! Who'll buy my sweet rosy pippins! Buy my pippins, ladies?' Alathea gave her two pennies, and received two round red apples, the first of the season, firm and sunflushed, from the wide basket she carried on her head.

As they walked on, munching, Alathea repeated her question. 'Why don't you?'

'What?' Nell's reply was rather muffled by the apple.

'Why don't you buy yourself a new gown? You have the same allowance from Father as I do, and you never ever spend it, except on a few books. Why don't you?'

'I don't need one,' said Nell. She twitched the thick, dust-clogged folds of her skirts. 'This one is perfectly good.'

'No, it's not, it looks terrible, and you've had it at least two years and it's been let down twice and mended lots of times and it's about time,' said Alathea, hearing the heat and her irritation get the better of her voice, 'that you started *making* something of your life, Eleanor Heron. You ought to, oh, I don't know, be less of a mouse, less of a shadow – you can't follow me around for ever, can you?'

Nell's reply was inaudible through the apple. Alathea turned to glare at her. 'Oh, you are such a *mouse*! Nell, why don't you *try*? Ros tries to *look* nice, Henrietta tries to *be* nice: you just droop. *Please* try harder.'

'There isn't any point to it,' said Nell, in a voice far stronger than Alathea had ever heard from her before. 'I wish you'd understand, Thea – there isn't any point in me trying to improve myself, I've got nothing to try *with*.'

Something in her strained tones gave Alathea pause. She stopped and stared at her cousin's unlovely face. There were tears in Nell's eyes, and a despair so utter and forlorn that it wrenched her heart. She said gently, 'Oh, Nell, what is it?'

Nell had always been inclined to weep at the slightest opportunity. Now, the floodgates opened, and she put her head in her hands and sobbed and sobbed, regardless of the curious looks of the crowded passers-by. Alathea took her elbow and steered her between the hawkers and the coaches, the pedestrians and the sedan chairs, into the centre of the Piazza where there was a wide area of gravel, separated by small posts from the bustle of traffic and shaded by small trees, with seats and benches for tired strollers. She pushed Nell on to the nearest of these, fortunately unoccupied, and sat down beside her. 'Nell, tell me, please – why are you crying?'

No sound but hiccupping sobs. Alathea ruthlessly repressed her annoyance, for it was obvious that her cousin was most deeply upset, and spoke again, more gently. 'Nell – why? What's wrong?'

'I'm wrong!' said Nell tragically, raising her face: and what with the tears, and the spots, and the nose, it could not be denied that she had a point. Alathea swallowed, torn between compassion and the cruel urge to laugh, for she had never, ever taken Nell seriously, never considered her as a person in her own right, only used her, as maid, seamstress, companion, butt. And Alathea saw all that now, as the bare soul of her cousin stared at her, anguished, from those overlarge, watering eyes, and begged her to listen, and not to ignore her again. She repeated, with urgency, 'Can't you see it? *I'm* wrong, I'm the ugly one, no one ever notices me or speaks to me much except you – and you don't think I'm anything at all, you just get me to do your sewing!'

'Hey, that's not true,' Alathea protested. 'You *wanted* to do it – or you always said you did!'

But Nell, borne on a wave of self-pity, took no notice. 'You've got everything, you've got looks and parents and family and painting, everyone likes you, and it's not *fair*! You have everything, and I have *nothing*, nothing at all, even my own mother didn't want me!'

That was an old family skeleton of which Alathea had only vaguely heard the truth, from dark hints dropped by the Widow Gooch, but she had thought it long dead and buried. How Nell had come to hear of it, she could not imagine. The inference had always been that Nell's mother had been dead for years, and it might very well be true for all they had ever heard of her since the day she had left Goldhayes, and her six-month-old baby daughter, a few days after Alathea's own birth. She had never had the full story, but the little she did know was wrapped in clouds of unpleasantness: betrayal, death, deceit and long-nourished hatred had all played their part.

Floundering in this unexpected quicksand, Alathea said hastily, 'Please, Nell, I'm sure that's not true – your mother's dead, she's been dead for years – oh, Nell, we *do* love you, we all do, we care for you very much, it's just that . . . ' She paused, searching for something tactful to say that would stem the flowing tears, but her cousin filled the gap. 'I'm ugly, that's what you were going to say, isn't it? I'm so ugly nothing will ever set it right, no man will *ever* look at me like they look at you, I'll never marry, I'll be an old maid like those ones in Yorkshire Kit used to laugh at.' And she began to snivel again.

Alathea was not a particularly patient person, and what little she had was already evaporated. She grabbed Nell's thin, spiky shoulders and shook her, as she had so often wanted to do in the past. 'Stop it, Nell, for God's sake! You're just wallowing in it now! Can't you see, it doesn't *matter* what you look like, what your mother did – it's *you* that matters! Look at Ros, she hasn't any more beauty than you, and I should know, I've painted her often enough. But does anyone think of her as ugly? What do they see when they look at her? They see a pleasant smile, laughter in her face, becoming clothes, well-kept hair. They *don't* see the big nose or the round face: they see *Ros*. And it's the same with Hen: she has Judas-red hair and freckles and she looks like a country milkmaid, but she makes the best of herself and everyone likes her. Why don't you? Why *don't* you buy yourself a new gown or two, and take the trouble to wash your hair and get Sarah to do it in ringlets like Rosalind's, and take an interest in something other than sewing, and *smile*? Don't you see? It's up to *you*, no one else. We'll help you, but if you sit like a mouse in the corner that's all you'll ever be – a mouse.'

She paused for breath and stared urgently at Nell. 'Or are you afraid to be anything else?'

'No!' Nell cried, and jumped to her feet, her face distorted with grief. 'No – you're wrong – but I can't – Oh God, I can't bear it!' And with a clumsy abrupt movement that was like a parody of Alathea's gestures, she pushed her cousin away and ran across the Piazza in the direction from which they had just come, a large number of people staring after her.

Alathea was left standing by the bench, feeling at once guilty and infuriated. The impulse to run after her cousin was rejected almost as it was born. It would be undignified and pointless, Nell was already lost to sight amongst the crowds, and would be back at the Fleet Street house within fifteen minutes or so. And, as she had so cogently argued, no man would look at one so plain, and she was therefore safe from molestation. Alathea shook out her skirts of fine sage-green wool, as if shaking off the thought of Nell, and turned to walk the fifty yards or so across the Piazza to Henrietta Street and Master Cooper.

But in that short distance, she discovered emphatically that whereas Nell might be able to walk abroad without unwelcome attention, it was another matter for herself. Before she had gone three yards she was accosted by an over-dressed young gallant who had obviously watched, if not overheard, their altercation and was now moving in with blatant hopes of making a quick killing. She brushed that one aside with a contemptuous comment that showed him quite clearly that she was not one of the harlots who frequented the place; but there were others, more persistent. She had never, she realised with a touch of fear, been alone before in the streets of London. Always there had been some kind of male or female escort, and she had walked freely, attracting some looks but never molested by strangers. Now, alone, her lack of companion meant only one thing to the men who ogled her, despite her plain dress and modest neckerchief and obvious lack of paint and frills and furbelows. Head high, Alathea stalked across the Piazza, ignoring the comments and suggestions and bows and proffered hands as if they came from ants, and revealing none of the rising panic that threatened to overwhelm her. She was not Nell – she would not run.

She entered Henrietta Street. She must be late. Master Cooper's sitter was due at nine, and there, approaching his door from the opposite direction, was a little group of obvious courtiers, colourfully resplendent in falling bands and bright ribbons, periwigged and ruffled, with swords by their sides and one or two much less ornate servants in attendance. She was nearly safe: if they were indeed visiting Master Cooper, she could ask for their help. Then, just as she was thinking all would be well, a hand grasped her shoulder and a wheedling voice insinuated itself in her ear. 'Hallo, my pretty, all alone are you? If you're looking for company, I'll be glad to oblige – how much?' And the hand began pawing at her breast.

Alathea, frightened and furious, pulled herself away, out of his reach, with a rip of her lace kerchief. 'Let go of me, you stinking skellum – I said, let go!' For the groping hand, undeterred, had reached for her again.

This time, she resorted to desperate measures. The lessons learned in the years of freedom at Goldhayes, in the company of rough and ready boys, came tumbling back to her. With all her force, she jabbed him in the ribs with her elbow, following it up with a swift kick to his shins, resisting the temptation to aim much higher. And as he stumbled into the middle of the road, winded and hobbling, she had the satisfaction of seeing him almost run down by a passing hackney.

'Do you require assistance, madam?' said a different voice, dark and deep and humorous, and she looked round, breathing quickly, into a face that was oddly similar to her own. He was one of the courtly gentlemen at Master Cooper's door, but she disregarded the elaborate, golden periwig and dazzlingly expensive clothes, concentrating instead on that face: not so long as hers, nor as pale, and emphatically not angelic, but with the same level eyebrows and far-spaced, greenish eyes, alive with a ruthless yet utterly charming merriment which, more than anything else, told her his identity.

'Hugh!' she cried, and with relief and delight flung her arms around his neck.

Cheerful shouts and whistles indicated that his companions approved wholeheartedly of this action. Hugh Trevelyan, with some reluctance, disentangled her and set her at arm's length. 'Do I know you? You certainly seem to know *me* . . . I'm sure I would have remembered a face like that . . . anyway,' said Alathea's half-uncle, with a sly grin that she recalled only too well, 'since it seems to be my lucky day, why don't you give me a kiss, eh?'

'No, I won't,' said Alathea. 'Since I'm fairly sure it would be incestuous – oh, come, Hugh, *surely* you recognise me? I know it's been – how many years, seven, eight, and I was only a little shrimp, but you must remember me – don't you?'

'Little shrimp,' said Hugh, considering her. 'Seven or eight years ago, so it must have been at Goldhayes – incestuous to kiss her, so must be one of the Herons – and she's in London, so it must be Rosalind or Nell or Alathea.' He gave her another of those knowing grins. 'And my guess is, you're Thea! I think I'll kiss you anyway, it's not every day I discover a beautiful young niece I'd forgotten I had.' And he saluted her soundly on each cheek, and gave her, finally, a very uncourtly bear-hug that recalled their old games.

At this, his companions made their presence known again, and Alathea, laughing with happiness and relief, discovered them to be Charles Jermyn, Henrietta's husband whom she knew well, and his scapegrace brother Henry. They bowed, and she curtseyed, glad to see them, even though both of them had poor reputations, and Charles with his gambling and unreliability was not as good a husband as he might be to Henrietta (though she herself never complained). All three men she knew to be true creatures of the Court, amorous, ruthless, immoral, pleasure-seeking, witty, but there was something rather devious and underhand about the Jermyns, particularly Henry. Hugh had never made any secret of his faults, and indeed, that was a considerable part of his charm.

They could have stood talking at Master Cooper's door for hours, especially Alathea and Hugh. They had seven years' news to exchange, and Hugh in particular was splendidly and amusingly loquacious. She had barely got the gist of why he had spent so much time in France and Italy, and assimilated the fact that the reasons were not very creditable, when Master Cooper's chief assistant put his head around the front door and enquired humbly but pointedly whether or not the gentleman was going to come in today for his sitting, and Hugh began to offer genuinely regretful farewells.

Alathea, grinning, waved them aside. 'No need for that – I'm coming in too!'

'In? To Master Cooper's?' Her half-uncle looked puzzled. 'Are you sitting after Henry, then?'

'No, you sawny fule – I help him!'

'You – help him? Help Master Cooper?' Hugh stared at her as if she were wandering in her wits. 'With the *painting*?'

'Well, in a way, yes – but come in, and I'll tell you while Henry is being painted.'

Master Cooper, once apprised of the reason for the delay in his client's arrival, was delighted and called a servant for celebratory wine and refreshments: and while Henry Jermyn was placed exactly in the chair, and the artist checked that the light was correct and at the last took up his brush for the first wash of pale carnation where the head would be, Alathea and Hugh settled down in a far corner, with the wine and Charles in attendance, for a good gossip.

'But I don't understand,' said Hugh, his greenish eyes shrewdly assessing her, 'why you're here. You said you assist Master Cooper – do you paint?'

'Yes, but only in oils – I'm learning the art of limning from him, but I haven't enough confidence to try it for myself yet,' Alathea told him, with her usual honesty. 'It won't be long, though – would you like to come round to the Ashleys', and be my first client?' As he pulled a mock-worried face, she added, grinning, 'It's all right, it won't cost you anything – and I can promise you won't be bored, we'll have so much to talk about!'

'That's what I'm afraid of,' said Hugh. 'I fear my evil past may not be suited to your tender young ears.'

Calculatingly, Alathea said a word she had learned from Oliver, and watched his eyebrows climb. 'Oh, Hugh, I've lived in London for six years, except for a few months during the plague – I'm no country bumpkin, you know, and there's not a lot could shock me.'

'You looked pretty shocked at that gallant just now,' said Charles.

Hugh laughed. 'Shocked she might have looked – I'll wager she gave *him* a shock, poor wencher. I don't suppose he was expecting quite such a reception as that. Where did you learn that most effective way of dealing with unwanted men?'

'From you, dear uncle,' said Alathea demurely. She added to Charles, 'Don't you remember those fights we all used to have? The lowest and dirtiest tricks were Hugh's, as I recall – and he was quite unrepentant.'

'He always is,' Charles pointed out. 'One word I've never heard him say, out of all the millions of words he spouts, is *sorry*. I think he's constitutionally incapable of saying it.'

Hugh instantly went through a comical pantomime involving his inordinate efforts to utter the disputed word. Alathea found herself almost hysterical with laughter, wiping away tears, her sides aching. Master Cooper, busy on Henry's picture, turned and gave her a tolerant smile. Normally, he preferred a quiet studio, but today was slightly different. Nevertheless, she hastened to calm her riotous companions. 'Shh – we ought to be quieter. Master Cooper doesn't like raucous laughter.'

'It was yours that was raucous,' Hugh complained, leaning back, that amused lazy smile on his face giving him a look of her father, his half-brother. Alathea sighed happily. She had always felt comfortable with Hugh. He made no judgements, no promises, no demands, he was himself, and generous with his laughter and his talent to delight and amuse. He was notorious in his family, and further afield, for being completely untrustworthy, and yet Alathea, even after seven years' separation, knew that she, at least, could trust him utterly. Not to obey conventional laws or morals, not to be careful or provident or sober, but she could trust him to be her friend, always.

The talk strayed from their own concerns to Court gossip, that perennially fruitful source of scandalous conversation, and then on to Hugh's exploits in France and the Low Countries and Italy, where he appeared to have survived on his wits and very little else. Alathea told him something of her own past history and even, knowing he would not mock, of her ambitions to paint, and Hugh was gratifyingly impressed. 'If you're any good, and you must be if Master Cooper takes an interest, then you'll have no problem getting clients if you ever do decide to set yourself up in business. They'd all come just to sit and look at your face while you paint theirs!'

'That's what I'm afraid of,' said Alathea. 'I want to be taken seriously in this, and if I thought my chances of it would be better if I were plain, I'd give thorough consideration to slitting my nose!'

'Oh, I wouldn't do that,' Hugh told her. 'It's much too painful, and very messy . . . What do your parents think about this? Do they mind you being away from them in London, up to all sorts of no good? Or don't they care?'

'They care,' said Alathea. 'That's why I'm here. They understand that for me painting isn't just a genteel occupation to while away a few idle hours while I wait for a husband . . . it's my life, Hugh, I couldn't live if I couldn't paint, if I had no hope of painting, and now I haven't the opportunity to work in oils, so I decided to ask Master Cooper for help – and he lets me watch, and mix his paints, and learn, and without ever really being taught by him, I seem to absorb it – and now I'm ready to tackle limning on my own, and you will be my first sitter, won't you?'

'I might,' said Hugh, and winked.

So it was, a few days later, that Hugh Trevelyan, man of wit and opportunist, with lodgings in Whitehall and a minor post at Court and scant funds to keep him in the style he preferred, strolled down the Strand to Fleet Street and alighted on the Ashleys' honest workmanlike abode like some exotic bird. He was enthusiastically welcomed by all the inhabitants, and if he felt any twinges of Courtly superiority amongst these more down-to-earth people, he never showed it. He had always liked his half-sister Lucy, and her sobersides husband was not the dull stick he appeared. Rosalind and Oliver were an entertainment in themselves and he even noticed Nell, stitching away in her corner, utterly withdrawn after her outburst in the Piazza, and saying not a word in greeting. But it was Alathea he had come to see, and it was Alathea who took him by the hand and towed him into the smaller of the two first-floor parlours, which faced north at the back of the house, and sat him down in a chair six feet from the window. She was surprisingly definite about what she wanted, and Hugh found himself readily deferring to this competent expert who was also, amazingly enough, his niece. She had always been a strong-willed little oddity, but he found it hard to connect the courageous, fair-haired child of his youth, brown and freckled, riding and swimming, running and fighting in the glorious freedom of Goldhayes before Lord Bradfield shattered the idyll, with the tall striking girl who stood before him now, an old shirt of Dan's offering rather inadequate protection against the paint, a frown between her level brows as she mixed the first colours and laid brush to vellum. He asked questions about the technique, and was answered clearly but abstractedly, most of her mind being engaged in manipulating brush and paint. But as she became more involved in the work, so, strangely, her tongue was freed, as if another Alathea was moving her hands and leaving the work of conversation to a subordinate self. He asked about the Ashleys, and Nell, and her family and Lord Bradfield's, and she gave him all the Heron news. Most of it was sad, with the three deaths, Nan, Rupert and Celia, that they had suffered in the past year, and he understood the black that Lucy wore, and Dan's sober clothing. Then the door opened and Rosalind slipped in, eyes sparkling, and informed artist and sitter that dinner was shortly to be served, if they would deign to grace the table with their presence.

'Thank you,' said Hugh. 'I've been suffering from a plaguy stiff neck for the last half-hour.'

'You're doing well,' said Ros, laughing, 'Thea's had one for the last seven years!' And she slipped hastily out again, as her cousin's thrown paintbrush rattled smartly against the closed door.

'I'm sure Master Cooper wouldn't do that,' Hugh told her.

'Master Cooper doesn't have to contend with Ros – nor Oliver, come to that. But it's all right, really,' said Alathea, retrieving the brush and wiping it carefully on a damp rag, 'we always tease each other. Just like you and me.'

'A pleasant girl,' said Hugh thoughtfully. 'And as yet unwed, I take it? How old is she?'

'A year younger than I am, plus a month or two – she was sixteen at the end of June.' Alathea gave him a sideways look from under her eyelashes. 'And no, she hasn't got a husband yet, and before you ask it, neither have I.'

'Good,' Hugh said. 'I can think of several well-connected eligible young men at Court – not the least of which is Henry Jermyn.'

Alathea gave a shout of laughter. '*Henry*? Henry and *Ros*? You can't be serious.' She saw his face, and grinned. 'No, I see you are not. She'd eat him alive, for sure. And I don't think that thoughts of a husband have yet crossed Ros's mind.'

'They have crossed yours, though?'

'Only to be rejected. I am not going to marry,' said Alathea, with a carefree irony that did not quite disguise her earnestness. 'I am already wedded to my brush.'

'Cold company on a winter's night,' said Hugh. He got up and crossed over to look at the vellum, on which only the palest ghost of the carnation head-colour was yet painted. 'Do you mean that, Thea? You don't want to marry?'

'I don't want to marry, not now, not ever,' said Alathea. 'So you can find a husband for Ros, if you want to – though I should think she'd quite like to do her own seeking – but I should forget about me.' Something in the rather quizzical look he gave her made her add hastily, 'I don't dislike men, you know, not like that woman at Court who took a fancy to one of the other maids-of-honour – what was her name?'

'Hobart,' said Hugh. 'Mistress Hobart.'

'Well, I'm not like her, I like talking to men, but I can't ever imagine being married to one,' said Alathea positively. 'I want to do other things with my life than minister to some lazy good-for-nothing with more money than sense, and breed his children. I want to paint, I want to be famous, I want to be better than Lely.'

'You don't want much,' said Hugh drily. He looked at Alathea again, seeing the ambition and pride and certainty shine out of her like a host of candles, and was astonished by the passion contained within that slight and wiry frame. 'I know Lely's not much of a painter, and from what I've heard, he doesn't think he's much of a painter either, but he's fashionable, and people want to look like the portraits he paints – why, I can't imagine, but they do. It'll be a hard task to dislodge him, and you'll need luck, and determination, and a hide like an elephant's, and above all,' said Hugh, suddenly serious, 'you'll need *talent.*' He indicated the ghostly shape on the vellum. 'And that's very pretty, but it's hardly a Cooper, is it?'

'It won't be for another six sittings, you sawny fule, and anyway, you know what they say – fools shouldn't see things unfinished. Nor should children, which is why I try not to let Oliver in here. I *have* got talent,' said Alathea, with pride but no conceit. 'Master Cooper wouldn't trouble with me cluttering up his nice neat well-organised studio if I didn't.' She looked up at her uncle, who was more like an elder brother, and who was not in fact so much taller, and held out her hands to him. 'Hugh – I may not be serious in most things, but I *am* serious in this. I want to succeed, I want it more than anything: and if *you* take that part of me seriously too, if *you* believe in what I want to do, then . . . it would mean a lot to me,' said Alathea, suddenly and uncharacteristically humble. She gave him a wry, apologetic grin. 'I don't know *why* I can talk to you like this – I can be more honest with you than with anyone else, it seems, and yet you only came back into my life a few days ago, after seven years out of it. I feel so easy with you, I can talk so freely – I think it's because I know you're not going to make any judgements or moralistic comments.'

'That's because I haven't got any morals?' Hugh suggested.

'You could be right, you know.' Alathea caught his eye and grinned again. 'Anyway, I'm glad you're back: you might prove very useful, with all your scoundrelly friends at Court to spread the word amongst. And it's nice to have a man of the world to talk to.'

'And you know all about men of the world?' Hugh enquired, gently mocking.

Alathea, laughing, shook her head. 'No – you and Kit are the only ones I know, though Oliver has pretensions to it already. And Kit is still at Ashcott, or he's gone back to Yorkshire perhaps – I don't know. And I couldn't talk to him like I can talk to you,' she added, without giving any indication of the reason for that.

'Kit always was a strange one,' said Hugh. He gave one of his deep chuckles that had been part of his charm, since before he could talk. 'I remember the first time I ever saw him – I couldn't have been more than three or four and he was only a bit older, but

I can see him now, a very pretty little boy and so appallingly naughty that I was shocked!'

'You must have been very young and innocent,' was Alathea's observation.

Hugh laughed again. 'Very – especially since I had no desire to emulate him. Nor have I now, and besides I've no fine estate to look after. My wit is my fortune – what's yours, my pretty lady?'

'Why, my painting, sir,' said Alathea. 'Do you believe it is?'

'Where you are concerned, yes, I do,' said her uncle. 'But any clients you want to impress will have to have more to judge you by than one shadowy piece of painting on vellum.'

'I'll repeat – after six or seven sittings it'll look very different,' Alathea told him. 'So just you make sure you come back tomorrow, or I'll set the dog on you!'

'And that,' said Hugh, looking at the hairy black rug slumbering in the corner, 'is a threat I can't possibly ignore.'

True to his word, he returned the next day, eyeing the vellum, and Alathea, and Lovell-our-dog, with some wariness. And over the next week or so, he was able to watch the first blurred ghostly image of himself take on feature and shadow, background and hair and clothes, until only the highlights were left to delineate brow and nose and jawline in the pale carnation flesh-colour of the original sitting. He did not have a particularly artistic eye, but he knew a good likeness when he saw one, and the charming unscrupulous face that looked back at him was unquestionably his own, and had an affectionate truth that exactly mirrored Alathea's feelings towards him.

'What do you think of it?' she asked him, with some trepidation, for though she had a deal of confidence in her own abilities, she also had a great need for praise and recognition from those she loved best. Ros and the rest of the Ashley family were already convinced, so were her parents. Now Hugh must also join the ranks of her believers.

'Hmm,' Hugh said, thoughtfully. He held the miniature up to the light, seeing the cunning deft brushwork, worked over with infinite patience (Alathea's patience was only immeasurable when applied to her art), and yet giving the illusion of great speed and dash. It was not so fine a piece of work as Master Cooper's, but then he had had thirty years' more practice at it, and the likeness was at least the equal of his best.

And that his little (well, not so little) niece had done this, while he sat there stiff-necked and awkward for far longer than he liked, was nothing short of a miracle. 'You're a very clever shrimp, you know,' he said flippantly, and sent her a grin that told her his true opinion. 'What a clever little Thea.'

'Don't patronise me,' said his clever little Thea, warningly. She came round the table where she had sat to work, and peered assessingly at the fruit of her labours. 'Well, I suppose it's not bad for a beginner.'

'No, indeed, but I can see why Lely flatters his sitters,' said Hugh. 'It's not a pleasant feeling, being brought face to face with the less palatable parts of yourself. You want to be careful, my girl, or you'll find yourself too truthful for your purse's comfort.' He glanced sideways at her, suddenly and uncharacteristically diffident. 'Thea – can I keep this? I know it's the first one, I'm sure you'd hate to part with it – but I would very much like to have it. And,' he added, with a flick of his usual humour, 'the less people who see it and the real me the better, and if I have the charge of it I'll keep it under lock and key so that it can't escape and frighten innocent bystanders.' He put his free arm around her and hugged her, brother-fashion, but not at all like Kit. 'Thank you, Thea. When I need reminding, I'll look at it and remember what I am, and what you are. And we mustn't drift apart again. When will you come and dance at Whitehall?'

'When I have time,' said Alathea, and gave him one of her dazzling, unselfconscious smiles. 'And thank you, for coming back into my life again.' She grinned wider. 'You can be my second-best friend. I'm afraid first place is unquestionably Lovell's, and when I dance at Whitehall, so does he.'

'Yes,' said Hugh drily, 'and if you put him in a periwig and a fancy coat he might not occasion much comment – even if he remained on all four legs!'

CHAPTER EIGHT

No longer a city

A most horrid malicious bloody flame,
not like the fine flame of an ordinary fire.

(Pepys, *Diary*, 2.9.1666)

The night of the first of September was windy. Blowing from the east, it was a hot dry wind to match all the hot dry days that long and droughty summer, and the dust swirled in the thirsty streets and alleys, and all over London people slept with few covers on their beds, gritty and sweating and uncomfortable. Alathea found it hard to sleep at all, with the heat and Nell's snoring and Rosalind, similarly afflicted, tossing and muttering, and at last decided that she would not be able to bear the stifling air behind the bedcurtains any longer. In her shift, she slipped outside them, tiptoed across to the window, and opened it.

London at night was a strange beast, full of impenetrable shadows and lurking danger. Even here in Fleet Street, a busy thoroughfare joining Westminster and the City, the black alleys could hide cutpurses, rogues, thieves of every description, men – and women – who, like rats, only emerged from their lairs after dark. But below her, the alley on whose corner the house stood was deep and dark and silent. Very quietly, Alathea pushed the casement wider, and looked out.

The wind struck her briskly: the air, warm yet cooling, stroked her face and lifted her hair. The smells of summer London, mostly offensive, arose to assail her, river mud, and rubbish, and decay, animal and human. But from further off, and more pleasantly, she could discern grass, and the salty tang of the distant sea.

And something else: another tang, more acrid, that tickled her throat. Smoke. For the first time she looked up, eastwards across the hunched heaped shapes of the roofs of Fleet Street, weird and fantastic in the dark, beyond the huge black bulk of St Paul's, half a mile off on Ludgate Hill, standing against the lightening sky . . .

It was surely too early yet for dawn. The alley below, and Fleet

Street round the corner to her right, were still lost in the silence of night. Alathea, straining her eyes, discerned a source for that light, to the right of St Paul's, further off, and yet definitely not sunrise. Some fire somewhere, she decided sleepily, and yawned. The wind had refreshed her, and suddenly she felt tired. Perhaps, now, she could get to sleep. Nell's snores had dwindled to a rhythmic snuffling sound, and might even cease altogether. Alathea closed the window upon the smoke and breeze and smells of mud in the London dark, and padded back to the soft comfort of the feather mattress and a bed somewhat crowded with Nell, Ros and Lovell-our-dog, and to some much-desired sleep.

The next day was a Sunday, day for leisure and for churchgoing, and Alathea, putting on her best gown and considering, critically, that it was only the best of a most undistinguished collection, and letting her mind drift on to what she might wear when (or if) she danced with Hugh at Whitehall, had forgotten the night-time fire in the east. Then Rosalind came in, flushed and important with news. Like her mother, she relished fresh excitement, interesting events, and gossip. 'There's a friend of Father's downstairs, you know, Master Martin from Lombard Street, and he says there's a big fire in the City, down by London Bridge.'

'A fire?' Alathea's head lifted from contemplation of her bodice lacing, which was woefully crooked and resistant to any attempt to pull it straight. 'Oh, that must be what I saw last night – I couldn't sleep and I opened the window to get some fresh air and I thought I saw something in that direction, but it didn't look very serious – is it?'

'It must be, if Master Martin came all the way over here to tell Father about it. Apparently it's burnt down two or three churches already, and it's taken hold in Thames Street, where all the warehouses are.'

Thames Street, which ran parallel to the river, was full of warehouses storing all manner of combustible goods – oil, tallow, spirits, cloth – brought up from the wharfs along the Thames. The thought of fire, without ever really being discussed, had been in the back of most informed minds that year. Mother Shipton's prophecy, and the plots of the Radicals in the spring that had involved a plan to burn down London, and the dry hot weather, all now seemed to come together with an awful inevitability.

'If I saw it from this window last night,' said Alathea slowly, 'we ought to be able to see it still – let's have a look.'

The two girls jammed themselves together in the window-opening and stared east across the same roofscape as before, but now given form and colour by daylight. The sunrise had also drained the fire's light, so noticeable in the dark: but there was no mistaking the broad plume of smoke, away to their right and probably a mile off or more.

'It *is* quite big,' said Ros, consideringly. As a Londoner, she had some knowledge of fires. In the crowded wooden houses of the City, someone was always being careless with a candle, and it was quite commonplace for a house, or even a row of houses, to be burnt down. This particular conflagration, however, appeared to be of quite a different order. Rosalind giggled. 'Master Martin says it started in a baker's house, in Pudding Lane by Thames Street, and apparently they called the Lord Mayor out of his house to have a look at it, and he said it was nothing, a woman could piss it out, and went back to bed!'

Alathea snorted. 'By the look of it, it'd take rather more than one woman now. Your father's always saying what a fool this Mayor is. I begin to see why.'

'So do I,' said her cousin. She took a deep snuffling breath. 'The wind's in that direction – I can smell it, can't you? A sort of sharp, oily smell.'

Alathea could. She stared out at that distant, sullen smoke, dark against the blue morning sky, and found that, as Samuel Cooper had warned, she was painting and framing it in her mind. Following that, came a vivid dramatic picture of the roaring flames and crashing timbers, the terrified fleeing people, all noise and confusion. She felt abruptly guilty at seeing the fire in that way, and failing to think of the human lives and property inevitably destroyed in such a blaze. Suddenly uncomfortable, she pulled herself away from the window. Rosalind left it slightly open, so that the warm breeze could lend some illusion of freshness to their hot little room, and came to join her. 'Oh, well, it's no concern of ours, though I feel sorry for all those poor people down there. Your laces are crooked, did you know? Come on, or we'll be late for church.'

At the familiar stone porch of St Dunstan's-in-the-West, the fire was the subject of much discussion. Even here, the ominous pall of smoke could be seen, hung above the roof-tops, and Fleet Street was crowded with people pointing, talking, spreading news and rumour. In quick succession Alathea and her cousins learned that it had been maliciously started by the French, by the Dutch, by the Fifth Monarchy men, by disgruntled Papists: that it had begun in a baker's, a smithy, in a heap of hay in an inn-yard: that an invasion force had landed and fired the City in revenge for the burning of a Dutch town and a large number of merchant ships, a month previously. Listening to the increasingly wild talk, Alathea was glad she was no foreigner, for any such would be in danger of rough handling by the enraged, panicky populace.

The parson did his best, but his congregation were a distracted lot, their minds patently elsewhere, and when a great noise of shouting could be heard out in the street, in the middle of his sermon, he did not look greatly surprised when people at the back of the church, already tense and nervous, leapt to their feet and ran outside, to be followed by nine-tenths of the rest. Daniel Ashley, former major in one of Cromwell's crack regiments, was above such undignified panic. He sat solidly in his pew, with every appearance of absorbed attention as the unfortunate minister tried to pick up the thread of his argument. But his wife was as large-eyed and anxiously curious as a frightened deer, and Oliver, sitting between Alathea and Nell, was plainly all of a twitch to find out the cause of the disturbance. Alathea found his fidgetting even more annoying than Nell's quavering mouth and her whispered, terrified prediction that the Dutch had invaded. But eventually the sermon was ended, the service done, and the Ashleys and a score or so of sober, superior citizens emerged from the church into the bright light of a hot late-summer day.

But it was not so bright as it should be, for everyone could see that the pall of smoke, glowering over the city, had all but blotted out the sun. The wind was still blowing strongly from the east, warm and faintly acrid, and, here and there, like gentle black snowflakes, floated and danced the first ashes from the fire.

The cause of the alarm outside the church turned out to be some hothead on horseback, who had ridden madly up the street shouting, 'Arm! Arm!' Naturally, with everyone's heightened state of nerves, this had caused some panic amongst the more fearful citizens, and even now there were people milling in the street, aimless and uneasy, always looking towards that ominous black cloud, blurring and darkening the sun. All of Fleet Street seemed to be standing in the roadway, staring eastwards, and Alathea, filled with a feeling at once of excitement and foreboding, wished she could see what was happening, discover the truth amidst all the wild rumour that was tossed like a shuttlecock back and forth amongst the crowd.

She had her chance when Dan, on their arrival home, announced his intention of taking a boat downriver, to find out the extent and danger of the fire. Oliver instantly begged to come too, and Alathea and Rosalind added their pleas. So they left Lucy and Nell behind, both adamant in their intention to keep well away from the blaze, and walked down through the neat trees and lawns and gravelled paths of Temple Gardens, to the water stairs.

She had not been on the river, she realised with something of a shock, for well over a year. Once, they had often hired a boat to take them up or down, to country spots like Chelsea or the pleasure gardens of Foxhall, to Woolwich to see the ships building and the King's yachts flying down to Chatham all bright and brave with their swooping flags and banners, and she had even, once, at Oliver's instigation, shot the bridge with the ebbing tide, a venture which had cost many Londoners and watermen their lives over the years. But this was different from a pleasure-jaunt, as became apparent from the moment they approached the Temple Stairs and found only a few boats there, instead of the usual score or so. And even as they stepped into the narrow, unstable little craft, two others, laden with people, goods, dogs, furniture and even a cage of linnets, lumbered heavily into land – refugees from the fire.

Out on the river it was cooler, and the breeze buffeted their faces and sent little busy ripples of water chuckling happily under the boat, but as the two oarsmen bent their backs and propelled the long, shallow, sleek little craft into the full downward flow of the ebbing tide, they all had a spectacular view of the burning City. All along the waterfront the buildings were ablaze: not only the squalid hovels and tenements, home to the thousands of wherrymen and dock workers and watermen and their families, but churches, Company Halls, the Steelyard, all furiously alight in the brisk afternoon wind. On the Bankside, away from the inferno, was a scene of peace and beauty, sunlight and warmth, marred only by the jostling crowds of people, sightseers or refugees, along the riverside. Alathea turned away from that, shielding her eyes against the glare of reflected sunlight and the scattering of hot smoky ashes blown from the fire, to stare again at the blaze, and found once more that her painter's eye would not rest. In her mind, her brush moved quickly, loaded with thick vermilion and crimson, yellow ochre and lamp black, describing the bright leaping flames as they fed on the dry wood and inflammable materials stored above the riverside, and the great dirty black shroud of smoke hanging balefully above, threatening the rest of the City. In the middle of the conflagration, a huge blazing torch eclipsing by its size and brilliance all those other flames, the tall church spire of St Lawrence Poultney streamed with wind-whipped fire. At the sight of the burning, even the two oarsmen were silent, staring: and it was not the smoke, nor the sharp bright sunlight, that brought tears to Alathea's eyes.

The ebbing tide was carrying them swiftly downstream. Soon they drew level with the westernmost edge of the flames, that seemed now to be burning inwards towards the heart of London and away from the waterfront. 'Can't they do anything to stop it?' demanded Oliver, speaking after long silence – an indication of how powerfully the fire had affected him. 'Father, they must be able to stop it, surely?'

'Not unless they're ruthless about blowing up buildings to make a gap too wide for the fire to cross,' said Dan. 'And unless our friends in Whitehall take a hand, I don't think anyone will think of aught else but saving themselves and their goods. Certainly the Mayor hasn't got the authority or the presence to risk a few buildings for the sake of saving the whole. He sees it in terms of saving streets and alleyways. We need someone who can save the whole City.'

'And the wind's blowing it on,' said Rosalind. 'Which way is the wind blowing? It's hard to tell, out here on the river.'

Alathea licked a finger and held it up. 'North-east. Just right for blowing the fire into the City.'

'It's as well it *is* blowing from the east,' said Dan, with his usual dry understatement. 'The entire supply of gunpowder for the Navy is stored in the Tower. If that should be fired, there'll be nothing left of London, no Bankside, not even Westminster or Whitehall.'

There was a small, abrupt silence, broken only by the roar of the flames and the impersonal, unceasing, oblivious chuckle of the river underneath the boat. Hot ashes floated around them in greater profusion as they approached the centre of the fire, glowing pieces of what had once been houses, each giving a brief tiny hiss as they entered the water. One landed on Oliver's doublet, and was only with difficulty extinguished, but the fiery rain did not diminish. Nor did the stream of boats, from tiny fishermen's coracles to big wherries and barges, carrying fugitives and their most precious possessions away from the all-consuming flames to the safety of Bankside. Stunned, numbed by the enormity of the spectacle before her, Alathea stared at those laden pathetic craft, heaped with mattresses, prized furniture, pairs of virginals, children, pets, carpets, cooking-pots, all jumbled together in the confusion of panic, and could not help drawing in her mind, those white shocked faces, dazed like herself with the scale of the disaster that had befallen them, a whole world disappeared in one dreadful night of flame. And there was no sign of an end to it.

'Row back,' Dan ordered the watermen, and as they laboriously turned the boat and began the long struggle back to the Temple Stairs against the tide, he said to the three young people, 'I hope you don't mind, but I have seen all I want to, and I must go back and give help. We are not in any danger, so it's our duty – my duty – to give assistance to all those in such need. We may have to give shelter to some people burned out of their houses. There'll be a great deal to do.'

'Can I come with you, and fight the fires?' Oliver demanded. '*Please*, Father – I'll do my best.'

Dan looked at his only son, the bold and handsome lad whose indolent charm had extricated him from many an arduous duty, and found genuine eagerness. 'Yes, yes, I'd be glad of your help,' he said, smiling, and Oliver, in a state of scarce-concealed excitement, spent the rest of the trip staring hungrily back at the flames, as though he could quench them by force of will alone.

True to his word, Dan stayed only long enough with his children and Alathea to see them to the door of his house. Then he vanished off down Fleet Street towards Ludgate Hill and the City in flames, with Oliver, suddenly almost as tall as his father, striding half a pace behind. All the rest of the Ashleys and Herons could do, was to wait.

They watched the fire for a while from the girls' bedroom window. The sky had a reddish, lurid light, evil and malevolent, as the smoke spread to cover the setting sun. Still they could see the tall slender knife of fire that was St Lawrence Poultney, burning all afternoon and long into the night, a beacon of disaster that could be seen all over London. And even when Rosalind and Lucy and Nell had gone downstairs, unable to bear the sight any longer, Alathea sat in the window with Lovell lying heavily and warmly on her feet, propping her board in front of her and resting her water pot and paint-boxes on the windowledge, and painted as furiously as the fire, exorcising with each swift desperate stroke of her brush, the terror and awe and ominous beauty of London, burning.

Dan and Oliver returned at dusk, exhausted, fire-blackened, the boy's adolescent beauty rather spoiled by his singed eyelashes and hair, and a raw red burn-mark on one cheek that drew shocked exclamations from his mother and sister. 'Oh, quit fussing,' Oliver said, in a very off-hand drawl, 'it's nothing at all, just a little singeing.' But he allowed Lucy and Ros to ply him with food and drink and clean clothes and a butter dressing for the burn, which disappeared unaccountably before it could be put on (Lovell was later discovered eating it, probably with Oliver's connivance). And while Dan and his son fell upon their food, they told, in between mouthfuls (or through them, in Oliver's case), of the battle to save the City: a battle which, according to Dan, was far from being won.

'It's too big, and the wind too strong, for the few of us and the Trained Bands to cope with. We tried pulling down houses, but fast as we did it the fire caught up with us. Those same firedrops that were falling on us out on the river, more or less harmlessly, were spreading it across whole streets and alleys, so it leaps from place to place, almost as if set deliberately. And that's half the trouble,' he added, looking round at his family. 'No one can really believe it has spread so swiftly and remorselessly without some human malevolence at work. They see houses burst into flame that are two score yards away from the fire, and assume there are fire-raisers at work – Dutch, of course, or Frenchmen. Any known foreigner is the target for abuse or worse – I saw one poor man, trying to save his goods, beaten to the ground by the mob and kicked half to death before we could save him, and by then the fire had taken his house . . . Oh yes,' said Dan wearily and sadly, 'it's been a bad day's work, and it's not over yet. The King and the

Duke have been helping – I saw your friends the Jermyns, Thea, and Hugh as well, black as coal like their masters – but we are still too few, and until someone is bold enough to use gunpowder in large enough quantities, or until the wind dies, I am afraid we have small chance of putting it out. And most people are concerned only to save their own goods: understandably, since there's no one else to help them.'

'Then will it never burn out?' Nell asked. 'Are we in danger?'

'No,' said Dan consideringly. 'No, not yet . . . but by this time tomorrow, or the next day, if the wind does not abate and the fire continues unchecked, then, yes, we might be. And it would be as well to be in some readiness.' He smiled suddenly, his teeth surprisingly white in his still-grimy face. 'And the best way, always, to prevent a situation is to prepare for it in advance. That's our best insurance – if we go to all the trouble of making ready for flight, then I'll wager long odds we won't have to go.' He grinned wider at his long-suffering wife. 'Better start now, Lucy my love.'

'That's all very well,' said Lucy, her eyes huge and blue in her pale face. 'But where are we to flee *to*? All your friends are in the City, and if the fire is coming westward, where shall we go to escape it? We can hardly all squash into Henrietta's lodgings in Antelope Alley: there's barely room for her and Charles and three children, let alone all of us.'

'There is Covent Garden,' said Alathea slowly. Oliver guffawed rudely. 'Samuel Cooper? Oh, come on, Thea, we can't possibly –'

'No, not Samuel Cooper's house, you brainless worm,' said his cousin briskly. 'Lord Bradfield's house on the Piazza.'

There was a short, surprised silence. Dan whistled. 'That's a good idea, Thea – why didn't I think of that? There's no one living in it at the moment, is there? They used to come to London each spring, until the sickness last summer, and poor Nan's death, and as far as I know it's been shut up and empty for a couple of years.'

'Then we'd have to break in,' said Lucy. 'Do you really think that's wise? Simon can be very unreasonable sometimes, and you never know how he's going to react.'

'You always knew how to get around him,' her husband pointed out, with perfect truth. 'And this would only be done in the direst emergency, Mind you, we may be in as much danger there as here: I don't know.'

'We shouldn't be,' said Rosalind. 'All the houses in Covent

Garden are brick, remember, most of the new houses around it are brick too, and they won't burn so easy.'

'You may well be right there,' her father said. 'Covent Garden it will be, if the flames reach Fleet Street, which may God forbid . . . and now, my love, I think I ought to go back. Not Oliver, though – he's been very helpful and we owe him a lot, but he needs a good rest before tomorrow.'

Oliver protested, but it was half-hearted. He was falling asleep where he sat, and he had had scant energy even to finish the meal so eagerly begun. So Dan, with instructions to servants and journeyman to start packing up the clocks and the more portable valuables, set off into the dark towards the fire, leaving his tearful wife standing anxiously in the doorway, staring after his dim retreating figure and crying farewells of encouragement and urgings to take care, all in the same breath.

Alathea found it incredible that everyone was quite calmly, matter-of-factly taking down pictures and rolling up bed-hangings and packing clocks as if it happened every day. She was filled with a huge unaccountable restlessness, a dreadful urge to run out into the dark, that with the fire was not so dark, and go down to the waterfront at Temple Stairs to watch the progress of the flames, and see again this terrible calamitous monster of fire that threatened the London she loved, even her home. But she and Nell and Rosalind spent the evening taking all their clothes out of the old carved oak clothes-press in their chamber, and packing them carefully away into bags and boxes, Rosalind laying between each garment a fragrant sprig of lavender from the little yard at the back of the house, where Lucy grew herbs and flowers in pots. And every so often, as if drawn by some powerful spell, Alathea found herself going to the little window, and staring out, fascinated, at the fire. In the surrounding dark its extent was hard to determine with certainty, but the flames and the lurid red light glared vividly against the black sky and roofs, like an intimation of Hell.

In the night, the Fire spread, beaten westwards by the wind, defeating all the efforts of the citizens and militia to stop it. Near dawn, Dan came home, escorting a family of his acquaintance who had been burned out of their tavern off Cannon Street with no possessions left save the clothes they stood up in. But his own family knew nothing of it, being utterly exhausted after the alarms and exertions of the previous day. So when the Ashleys woke, they found Master Burgess, who kept the Swan in Dowgate, with his wife and two small children and three servants, huddled together in the parlour, grateful for their shelter but mourning the loss of their tavern and their belongings. The Fire, they learned, had not miraculously abated overnight, and was now devouring even larger areas of the City with greater and greater ferocity. But at last, Court and City alike were rising to the challenge.

They hardly saw Dan that day. He went out, as soon as they had breakfasted, accompanied by Master Burgess, a big red-faced man with exactly the look of a tavern-keeper, Alathea thought, and Oliver, whose energy and enthusiasm had not been in any way diminished by his experiences of the previous day. Despite the work of packing still to be done, the inhabitants of the House of the Ash Tree could not tamely retreat indoors when the three firefighters had left. Fleet Street was a mass of people. A fire-post had been set up on the corner of Fetter Lane, a few yards away, and Justices and the parish constables were organising a motley collection of public-spirited citizens and soldiers into some kind of workforce. There were provisions and beer for their refreshment, and a shilling from the King for the most hard-working, but the numbers did not seem so great in comparison with the enormous scale of the Fire. Soon they were marshalled into some sort of order, with ropes and axes, hooks and chains, and went away down Fleet Street towards Ludgate Hill, Dan and Oliver and Master Burgess amongst them.

It seemed quiet and empty in the street when they had gone, but not for long. All that day Fleet Street, being the chief route on land from Whitehall to the City, was a turmoil of courtiers, citizens, soldiers, going clean and upright and keen to fight the fire, returning defeated, smoke-blackened, bent like old men with weariness. And there were carts, too, of every shape and size and condition, from substantial carriages and wagons, to the humblest wheelbarrow, all being used to transport refugees and their belongings from their blazing houses. From these, as the day progressed and the great cloud of smoke obscured what should have been another glorious hot sunny day, they were able to glean news of the Fire's extent, often simply by asking the fugitives the name of their street: in the morning, refugees from the poorer areas around Queenhithe and the river west of the Steelyard; in the afternoon, rich merchants, the richest in all London, reduced to carrying their worldly goods in whatever passing cart their lavish coin could procure, burned out of their sturdy, beautiful timber houses in Lombard Street and Cornhill, telling of the destruction of the Royal Exchange in Threadneedle Street. And giving weight to their hoarse, desperate voices were the great yellowish-black, boiling clouds of smoke glowering behind them, reddening the sun, darkening the day, scattering ashen debris and black soot everywhere.

There was further panic, too, as those fleeing from the Fire, overwhelmed by the disaster, spun wilder and wilder rumours about its origin. No one with a foreign accent was safe, nor anyone who might conceivably be carrying the materials with which to start any conflagration. The mood of the crowded street changed from despair to menace, and an ugly desire for revenge, and as the day drew to a close the Ashleys retreated to the house, posting one of the maids at the parlour window to report on any new developments cried up from the street below, and continued, with weariness and gloom, to pack up their belongings.

At dusk, Alathea could bear it no longer. All day they had been at the mercy of alarms, hearsay, rumour, trying not to panic, to think sensibly and rationally, to carry on the preparation for flight without thinking of the events and consequences that would surely attend upon it. She was weary of rumour. The Fire drew her like a moth to its flame, and she wanted to see for herself. Knowing that if she told Nell, Rosalind or Lucy of her plans, they would do their best to dissuade her, she left a hasty note propped on the carved newel-post at the foot of the stairs, and while her aunt and cousins were busy in the parlour, rolling up carpets and taking down pictures, she slipped into her chamber and took the little box she had had made to contain her paints and brushes, with a few leaves of paper and a lid that could be detached to form a drawing board, pulled her dark summer cloak about her, and slid unseen and unnoticed out of the house.

As she had expected, everyone in the street was far too busy upon their own or the City's concerns to molest a lone woman. With a quick glance at the distant red glow of the Fire, she turned away from it and walked quickly towards the Strand, turning aside after passing St Dunstan's to go down towards the river along

Middle Temple Lane. It was dark, and narrow, and filled with people carrying their goods up from the river, believing that no fire could reach this far. She dodged between them, feeling strangely detached, unmoved by the distraught faces, the crying children and their weeping mothers. And the magic tingled in her hands that clutched the box of paints tightly beneath her cloak, and raised in her a turmoil of mixed emotions: exultation, excitement, and guilt, that in this dreadful night, she could still be obsessed by painting.

There were boats at Temple Stairs, unloading refugees, preparing to cast off, all lit by the ghastly crimson glare of the Fire behind them. Astonished at her own daring, carried along by the ruthless sweep of the urge to create, to watch, to paint, she commandeered the smallest empty boat. 'Hey, you – there's ten shillings for you if you'll row me out into the stream for half an hour or so.'

The waterman, huge like all his kind with brawny, well-muscled chest and shoulders, stared in astonishment at the tall, well-spoken girl who had thus hailed him. 'Row you out into the river? In God's name why, Mistress?'

'I have a fancy to see the Fire,' said Alathea, hating herself as she spoke. Doubtless he thought her to be some aristocratic lady of the Court who derived some perverted satisfaction from watching as London burned to ashes, but that was his affair, and she would not wait. 'I said – ten shillings.' It was twenty times the normal fare, and all she had. 'For half an hour, no more.'

'Let's see yer money, then,' said the man. He bit each coin expertly, and pocketed them. 'All right, Mistress, I'll take you – though there's better work to be done.'

'Do you think I don't know that?' Alathea snapped. 'Now may we go?'

She stepped into the narrow little boat, just a single scull, and the man pushed off amidst a crowd of others coming in to the Stairs, laden with lamenting people, and pulled strongly into the stream. Tonight, the tide was full and high, briefly at slack water, and the boat swiftly crossed to the centre of the river and began the pull downstream, gently, while Alathea stared in fascinated horror and wonder mixed, at the terrible beauty of the Fire.

Nearest to her, Baynard's Castle was burning on the waterfront, a boiling brilliant mass of flames roaring from the battlements and windows all along the bank, and each flame had its counterpart licking in the water, reflected and doubled below. The light was fierce enough to reveal all the river, the mass of laden boats heading upstream or for Bankside, things floating loose that had been hurled into the Thames by their panic-stricken owners in despair at saving them any other way. And behind the bright flame-streaming pyre of Baynard's Castle, the Fire arced in a huge burning bow from Blackfriars, slanting up the hill to the heart of the City. The flames leapt and sparked with relentless infernal glee in the high wind, and illuminated the great boiling clouds of smoke with an evil blood-red light. It was terrible, powerful, inexpressibly beautiful. Alathea found the tears spilling down her face, blurring that awful picture, and remembered what she had come to do. Surely no one else was mad enough to attempt this, in a precarious little boat wobbling on the windy surface of the Thames, to paint a sight that no person living would ever see again. She took out the box and laid it on her knee, dipped the pot into the black and fiery water over the side of the boat, and feverishly began . . .

'Mistress! Beggin' yer pardon, Mistress, but tide's turning an' yer time's surely up!'

The words came at a great distance. For a long time now, Alathea had been working, totally absorbed, all senses closed except to receive the sight and sound and smell of the fiery monster devouring the City. On the little oblong of rough paper, perhaps nine inches by six, that City lay, black and vermilion, with the scurrying frantic boats sketched in, dark against the blazing reflections in the water, and above, the red infernal smoke and here and there, dagger-sharp, the fire-lit steeples of untouched churches and above it all, crouching miraculously safe as yet, the brooding watchful bulk of St Paul's Cathedral. But such a fire, if not stopped, would reach it in the end. All London would burn, in this terrible wind, and she had a brief feeling of terror. Fleet Street was wooden-built, it would burn like tinder. What if they had indeed to take refuge in Covent Garden? Would the flames reach there too? Suddenly a great weariness struck her, as it always did after a particularly intense spell of painting, but mixed with grief and despair. She looked up at the waterman. His face, watching her in the baleful scarlet light, was a curious combination of respect and pity and fear, as if she were truly mad. 'Mistress, yer time's up,' he repeated. 'Have ye finished?'

'Yes,' said Alathea, from a distance now of exhaustion. 'Yes, I've finished, and thank you. We can go back now.' And as the man turned the boat and began to row for the far-off Stairs, she carefully blew some stray flakes of soot from the precious paper and put it back in the box, replacing the lid and securing the catch, and then sat quite still, turning her head away from the dark, light-pricked mass of the Liberties and Westminster, to look still at the raging fire in the City.

At four o'clock, the following afternoon, a thunderous knocking sounded through the House of the Ash Tree, startling its various inhabitants, and almost frightening Nell out of her wits. They had all been in a state of apprehension that day. Indeed, Alathea's sudden disappearance the previous evening had reduced even the cheerful stoical Rosalind to tears, imagining that all sorts of dreadful things had happened to her cousin, and Alathea herself felt deeply ashamed of her selfish impulse. She did not explain where she had been, or the true reasons why, feeling too guilty and appalled at that callous act, but she had the painting, and when she looked at it secretly, in daylight, she knew that from an artist's point of view her escapade had been entirely justified. But she made no mention of that little, vivid, dramatic picture, having no wish to increase the reproachful looks from Aunt Lucy or the other two girls, and packed it away in a big box with her clothes and books, ready for the unthinkable, impossible moment when they would have to flee.

And as the day passed, the impossible became steadily more probable. Cheapside had burned that morning, London's widest and fairest street and one of the richest, home of the goldsmiths, and all day the wild wind had blown pieces of it, blackened and charred, westward into the City and beyond, starting new fires from sparks and debris still alight. The Duke of York, in charge of the fire-fighters, had ordered men into London from all the surrounding counties, bringing the fire-hooks and axes, ladders and ropes, necessary for pulling down buildings, buckets and brooms for extinguishing the flames: but to little avail. Close to the Fire, the burning seemed to have consumed the very air, so that it was hard to breathe, Dan said, and too hot to work for long, even fifty yards distant. Most of the fire-fighters were stripped to the waist in the heat from flame and sun, for the weather remained warm despite the continuing strong easterly wind. And that wind brought another hardship: the never-ending shower of hot or even glowing ashes, fire-drops, sparks and debris that rained unceasingly down on bare, sweating skin. When Dan and Oliver and Master Burgess had returned late on the previous night, they had been covered, like the freckles on a plover's egg, with raw burns on back and shoulders and face that drew horrified cries of sympathy from their womenfolk, and a copious supply of ointment. They had gone out again, though, at first light, weary but stubborn, unbowed even in the face of such enormous odds. All day there had been no word from them, only the news of further destruction from people in the street, and tidings of the desperate work being done to halt the remorseless wind-driven rush of the flames. The Guildhall was burning, a great beacon glowing as if made of molten brass, high above the City. It could be seen plain even from Alathea's chamber. From the parlour window the frantic bustle of Fleet Street looked like the desperate, aimless scurryings of an overset ants' nest. She felt there must be some pattern to it, but in the confusion it was hardly discernible. Several times that day, they saw the King, as smoke-blackened, perspiring and hot-faced as any of his subjects, ordering their efforts and not afraid to lend a hand with bucket or rope. His brother, the Duke, was also much in evidence, in command of the area between Fleet Street and the river. Alathea caught a glimpse of the plump, grimy figure of Henry Jermyn, his Master of Horse, in close attendance, and wondered with a brief lift of her spirits how that elegant courtier's well-manicured hands had fared after two days of fire-fighting.

And still St Paul's stood, untouched, inviolate, at the crest of the City, while the Fire burned all the crowded, tinder-dry houses about it and charged ever nearer to Fleet Street, with a vanguard of sparks and burning fragments borne on the wind to set even more buildings alight. There was no sign of Dan, and it became more and more obvious that the House of the Ash Tree was doomed . . .

When Alathea heard the knocking, she thought for one dreadful moment that this was the harbinger of tragedy, that something had befallen Dan or Oliver, a falling house, a sudden change of wind cutting off escape. She fairly pelted down the stairs, forestalling the maid Sarah by a whisker, and flung open the door.

Two black grinning masks met her astonished gaze. They both bowed, true courtiers, and she saw that their clothes, now sadly spoiled with soot and fire, dust and water, were richly laced. 'Hallo, Thea,' said the voice of her half-uncle, Hugh. 'Charles and I thought you might need this.'

And 'this' was a miracle: a cart, a real four-wheeled, horse-drawn cart, with admittedly a rather sad-looking decrepit old nag between the shafts, but a cart nonetheless, and worth, at the day's prices for such things, perhaps forty or fifty pounds. 'Oh, thank God,' said Alathea, weakly, with overwhelming relief. 'Oh, Hugh, thank you – wherever did you get it from?'

'I shouldn't hug me if I were you,' said Hugh, removing her arms. 'You'll get that nice gown all sooty. Let us say we . . . acquired it.'

'We haven't come on our own account,' said Charles Jermyn, the other mask. 'Henrietta suggested it – and made our lives a misery till we agreed – *and* found the cart for us.'

'Dear Hen, always so practical,' said Hugh. 'I shall never joke about her good sense again. Now, Thea, listen – where's everyone else? We must load up now. The Fire's across the Fleet, and it's broken out in Salisbury Court, down by the river.'

'But they were clearing the buildings along the Fleet to make a firebreak.'

'Yes, I know they were, and it's the same old story. The wind has blown the sparks right over their heads and set fire to the houses beyond, and unless a miracle happens this whole street will be gone in a couple of hours. Ah, there you are, Lucy,' Hugh added to his half-sister, as she arrived breathless, summoned by Sarah. 'Come on, we've got to load up *now*, before the Fire gets to us or someone steals the cart, even though we've got Henry's servant guarding it with a loaded pistol. Where's Dan? Fire-fighting? So should we be, but Hen thought you were more important, so don't let her down by dallying. Come on everybody, put it all in the cart – now!'

It was as if the people in the house had been wrenched out of a long stupor. Suddenly they came to life and, with Charles and his brother's servant Jack to supervise the loading and guard the cart, everyone, maids, journeyman, 'prentices, ran hither and thither bearing everything that was moveable. Large items of furniture, court-cupboards, beds, tables, could not be moved in time and without more help, but the cart soon filled with smaller Ashley possessions: clothes, books, carpets, cooking implements, food, bedlinen, and hangings, plate and pictures and pottery and, most important of all, the precious clocks and the parts and tools and materials with which they were made. The journeyman, Master Hamilton, and the three 'prentices had long ago packed everything safe in wooden boxes, all bar the two finished long-case clocks that were awaiting collection by customers. They were big and awkward to carry, but no one could contemplate leaving them behind, and into the cart they went, Jack tying a rope around them to make them secure. And that was all there was room for, and a large quantity of goods still to be moved.

Hugh measured the size of the load with his eye, and then pushed out into the crowded street to gaze for a brief moment eastwards, trying to gauge the approach of the Fire. 'We may have time for another journey,' he said to Lucy and Alathea, standing on the doorstep with a heap of belongings in the hallway behind them, and Mistress Byrd, the cook, bearing a huge cheese from the kitchen to add to the pile. 'But it depends on the most important thing of all – where are we going to take it all? St Giles' Fields?'

'Not as far as that,' Alathea told him. 'We thought Lord Bradfield's house in Covent Garden.'

Hugh whistled. 'Well, it's a good idea, so long as my dear eldest brother doesn't mind – and at a hundred miles' distance, what the eye doesn't see . . . won't it be shut up?'

'Yes – we'll have to break in.'

'Then you've called in the experts,' said Hugh, laughing. 'There's no chamber in London, no house anywhere, we couldn't get into if we tried, Henry and Charles and I, and besides, Jack has a dubious past and can pick locks. Lucy – I think you and the girls and the maids had best stay here and bring down all you can, and pile it in the hall and the workroom. We'll be back as soon as we can.'

'What if the Fire comes too close?' Nell asked.

Hugh chucked his niece lightly under the chin. 'Then you bend your backs with whatever you can carry, sweet Nell, and run for it. No sense in frying to a cinder for the sake of a few worldly goods. Make for Lord Bradfield's house in the Piazza. If Dan doesn't return here in time, will he know where you've gone?'

'Yes,' said Lucy. 'We discussed it a day or so ago.' She looked in the smoke-dimmed afternoon light, suddenly very much stronger, and younger, once more the girl who had withstood siege and civil war, and not flinched from gunfire. She kissed Hugh quickly on each smoke-smeared cheek, and stepped back. 'Thank you, little brother – you've been the saving of us. And now you must go – we'll manage here. Goodbye!'

'Come with us?' said Hugh to Alathea. 'I've forgotten where the house is, and you seem to know.'

'I do – I pass it every time I go to Samuel Cooper,' she said. 'Goodbye, Aunt Lucy, Ros, Nell – and take care!'

Amid the turmoil of the street, filled with people escaping from the approaching fire, their cart was one more cumbersome vehicle, jamming the roadway. But at least they had a destination, a roof to shelter beneath, however illicitly, and this gave their efforts a sense of purpose which moved the heavily laden cart and slow old horse far quicker than most of the lamenting, aimless fugitives about them. Charles, good with horses, led the animal, encouraging it softly, and Jack perched on top of the cart, pistol in hand, ready to assail anyone who might consider stealing vehicle or goods. Alathea and her uncle walked beside it, pushing whenever the stumbling animal seemed to strain too much. The main blockage was at Temple Bar, with hundreds of people all trying to force their way under the narrow archway, and it took them fifteen minutes or so of slow walking, shoving, shouting, standing, before they were through and into the Strand, where abruptly the press was much thinner. It was sparser still when they forked right up Wych Street, that ran into Drury Lane, and here they made much faster progress, despite the straining horse. The street was peaceful compared to the chaotic conditions in Fleet Street, and well-surfaced into the bargain, and within another fifteen minutes they had arrived in the Piazza, Covent Garden.

It was plain that others beside themselves had thought this place a good refuge from the flames. The open gravelled square was covered with piles of household goods, watched over by pathetic, dazed-looking people whose sole consideration now was to guard what little they had been able to salvage from the wreck of their homes and their lives. Other refugees had also followed their cart up Drury Lane and down Russell Street, and while Charles halted the horse these citizens, men, women and children, bundles on their backs, pushing handcarts, leading laden horses, trickled past to join the fugitives already in the Piazza. Four boys carried a mattress on which lay a woman, obviously weak from childbirth, her squalling baby in her arms. Another woman, old and bent herself, supported a trembling, aged man barely able to hobble along. They cast no envious eyes at such a capacious cart, but Alathea felt at once guilty, and keenly aware of their own good fortune, at having help, transport and a house to go to, in such a disaster.

'Thea!' Hugh said in her ear, bringing her back to more immediate problems. 'Which one is Simon's?'

'It's on the left-hand corner of James Street, over there,' Alathea told him, and at Charles's shouts of encouragement the cart rolled laboriously forward again, round the gravelled centre of the Piazza to the row of houses on the northern side.

Lord Bradfield's house had been leased by the family for more than thirty years, since its building in fact, although often sublet to other tenants during times of little use: the high rents were a consideration even to a wealthy family like the Herons. Since Lord Bradfield's return to England, he had brought his family to Covent Garden twice a year at least, but not since the plague and his wife's death, and the house had a sad, shut-up appearance in contrast to the activity all about, with people staring out of doors or windows to see the Fire. The white-painted shutters blocking the windows gave it a blind, blank look, and the stout oaken door under the stone arcade was barred by bolt and lock and cobweb.

'Well, there's no one in,' said Charles flippantly, having beaten a tattoo on the knocker that would have wakened the dead, and brought several curious suspicious eyes their way. 'How about the side of the house – or the back?'

Hugh went to the end of the arcade and peered up James Street. 'No – there's probably an alley at the back with an entrance to the stables, but I've no idea how to find it. Jack!' Henry's servant leapt down from the cart and came up with a knowing smile. 'Jack – can you do your worst, without it seeming too obvious what you're about?'

'I'll 'ave a try, sir,' said Jack, a ruffianly young man whose soot-blackened livery only served to heighten the disreputable grin on his face. He fished inside his coat and took out a small hooked piece of metal that hung from a string round his neck.

With a quick glance round that was as furtive as a thief's, he inserted the metal prong into the stout iron lock and began probing, while Charles and Hugh blocked any view of him and tried to look as innocent as they could in the circumstances, and Alathea, left to hold the horse's head, felt herself growing hot with embarrassment and fear, lest anyone should challenge them. But, fortunately, there were few with the leisure or interest to spare for more than a cursory glance in the gloom under the stone arcade, and no one approached them.

Jack, crouched over the lock, was swearing steadily under his breath, a stream of fortunately inaudible curses which changed abruptly to a muted crow of triumph. 'Done it, sir!' And with an anguished groan of unoiled hinges, the door swung stiffly open.

They wasted no time on unnecessary exploration. Alathea, carrying in the smaller bundles, had a brief impression of a very gloomy entrance hall, with a carved wood staircase leading upwards, and doors to other rooms, darkened because of the closed shutters, into which she dumped her burdens. Jack and Hugh, who were sturdier and stronger than the slightly built Charles Jermyn, did most of the heavy work, and the two precious long-case clocks were set upright, with a slight protesting jangle from the works, at the foot of the stairs. For future convenience, they deposited most of the goods in the front room, leaving the entrance hall free for the next load. It was not long before they had finished, but Alathea found her palms sore and blistered from heavy carrying, and she was sweating profusely in the heat.

'That's the lot,' said Charles, meeting her at the front door. 'How long have we taken?'

'Assuming the clocks are still right after all that maltreatment, about an hour or so,' Alathea told him, pushing wisps of pale hair out of her eyes. 'Time for another load? We must go back.'

'We can't leave this here to be plundered,' Hugh pointed out. 'We can't lock the door – you'd best stay, Charles, and guard it. Have Jack's spare pistol.'

'My sword is sufficient,' said Charles with a grin. His reputation with that weapon was widespread. 'I'll amuse myself in exploration. You two go and rescue the others.'

If the journey out of Fleet Street had been bad enough, with so many people and vehicles fighting to get through Temple Bar like wine from a narrow-necked bottle, the struggle to get back into the City again was much worse. There were people screaming, shouting, wailing, horses panicking, carts overset, and all of them intent on going one way and one way only. Even their tired nag threw up its undistinguished head in alarm at the noise and press of humanity around it, and it seemed impossible that a way could be found through the Bar: but while Alathea held the horse, and Jack perched on the cart flourishing a pistol and scowling at all those who so much as looked at it, Hugh pushed his way through to the militiamen on duty under the arch. Coin changed hands discreetly, and then, miraculously, the flow of people and traffic slowed to a trickle, and then stopped. Hugh shouted to her, and Alathea, with relief, walked the horse under the Bar and into Fleet Street while the soldiers with their halberds cleared a temporary passage.

Even in the hour and a half since they had left, the Fire had leapt dramatically forward. There were houses violently aflame a mere two or three hundred yards down the street, and all Ludgate Hill ahead was furiously burning. Yet still, astonishingly, the huge, dim, smoke-wreathed mass of St Paul's remained unscathed in a ring of fire. For how long, Alathea could not guess, and anyway, it did not matter. Already she could feel the heat from the flames, and the dreadful fire-drops showered all around them, wind-borne. They stung the nag's moth-eaten rump, making it dance with weary bewilderment and pain between the shafts, until she dragged it on again, towards the Fire. It was just about level with the water conduit, by Shoe Lane, and at its present state of advance would consume the rest of the street, up to Temple Bar, within the hour.

One of the 'prentice boys was standing in the doorway of the Ashley house, looking at the Fire with awed fascination, when he happened to glance in the other direction and saw the cart pushing its way up the street against the tide, lessening now as the Fire swept nearer, of fleeing citizens. At the fire-station on the corner of Fetter Lane, now all but abandoned, men were gathering with hooks and ladders for a final assault on the last houses still standing between the flames and the Bar: of which the House of the Ash Tree was one.

'Here! Here! They're here!' The boy in the doorway, one Sam Fuller, who was about Mun's age, fairly capered with excitement, shrieking his news back into the house, and then ran up to the horse. 'Quick, oh quick, they're going to pull the house down to make a fire-break – hurry!' And already, pouring out of the house behind him, came Lucy and the rest of her household, carrying their possessions, crying with relief. 'Oh, thank God you're here at last!'

'We couldn't have come any quicker,' Alathea protested.

Ros, coming behind her with a great bundle of clothing, hurled it into the cart and said urgently, 'Come on, there's loads of things yet!' And down the street, the roar and crash of burning houses and a great shower of sparks gave point to her words.

Alathea left the restless horse and ran into the house. There was a great heap of goods piled all higgledy-piggledy, blocking the hallway. She snatched up the first things that came to hand, a bundle of pewter tableware and a couple of bolsters, and dashed outside again to hurl it into the cart. She was glad to see that the child Sam was holding the nag, now thoroughly disturbed by the noise and nearness of the Fire and the red-hot sparks and ashes that fell all around. Then the men from the fire-station approached at a run, ready with hooks and ladders and ropes to pull the houses down. She saw Lucy, white-faced and urgent, arguing with them as she and Hugh and Ros and the Burgess children and the Ashley servants all converged on the doorway for what they knew would be the last chance to salvage what remained. And in that instant, Alathea remembered something of utmost importance, and grabbed Rosalind's sleeve. 'Ros! *Ros*! Where's Lovell?'

Rosalind's startled, horrified face jerked round as she piled her arms high with bedlinen. 'Lovell? Oh, God, we shut him upstairs in the parlour, he was getting under our feet so much – oh, hurry, Thea!'

'I'll see you outside,' Alathea said, and took the stairs at a run; and all the while, a little voice in her head was saying, 'This is the last time you'll ever see this house.'

Lovell, as if aware of the fate that would overtake anything left behind in the path of the Fire, was ecstatically grateful for his rescue. Precious time was wasted while she ordered him, unsuccessfully, to get down and sit, and more when she realised that there was no lead with which to secure him. Desperate, she ran out of the parlour again, up to her little chamber from whose window, only three nights ago, she had watched unknowing the start of the Fire. There, on the floor in the bare deserted room, with only the

voice. Still no sign, urgently though she looked. In despair, she turned with some idea of fighting her way back through the Bar, for perhaps Lovell, lost, had gone back to the only place he knew.

And he would find it in flames. Suppressing a sob, she squared her shoulders for the battle against the tide of fugitives, and was grasped from behind. 'Thea!' said Hugh's deep voice, unwontedly concerned. 'Thea, come on – you can't go back – what in God's name are you doing?'

'It's Lovell!' she cried, the tears suddenly streaking her face. 'Hugh, I've lost Lovell – the cord snapped – oh, I must find him!'

'You can't go back,' Hugh repeated. 'He'll find us, don't worry – he'll follow our scent. There's no sense in risking your life for a dog, is there? If he's this side of the Bar, he'll be all right.'

And if he was not . . . She turned again, vainly seeking that dear familiar hairy shape, praying that she would see it emerging suddenly from the Bar, running towards her with that odd swaying lolloping run, red tongue grinning, eyes shining behind the veiling fringe of disreputable black hair.

But there was no Lovell. Miserably, clinging to the slight hope that he might have run on ahead, she allowed Hugh to lead her in pursuit of the cart, now turning towards Drury Lane, her eyes ceaselessly searching the crowd: all in vain. Lovell-our-dog, Kit's gift and her dear companion, was lost in burning London, and as she followed the cart and her cousins into the Piazza, she found herself wishing with intensity that she had never insisted on bringing him to the town. Then she felt suddenly ashamed of herself, for being so affected by the loss of a mere dog when hundreds of thousands had lost homes and livelihood and all they possessed. She wiped the tears from her face, and made light of her distress when Rosalind noticed, as they stopped outside Lord Bradfield's house, that Lovell was missing. But the guilt and ache and grief of it remained everpresent as they unloaded the cart and piled the motley collection of salvage in the hall, and she resolved that as soon as possible, however futile her quest might be, she would go and look for him.

CHAPTER NINE

Haven

Alcippus:
'Gods, what's a man possest with jealousy?'
Pisaro:
'A strange wild thing, a lover without reason.'
(Aphra Behn, *The Jealous Bridegroom*)

They did not unpack their belongings that night, for no one cared to predict the future course of the Fire, even though they were hundreds of yards away from its western edge, and surrounded by houses made of brick and stone. Being built of stone had not saved the eighty-odd churches from being burned in the conflagration, and nor did it save St Paul's, which finally succumbed an hour or so after their arrival in Covent Garden. From the garret windows of the tall house, it could clearly be seen like a huge beacon, flames streaming from the roof and towers, the windows open on the furnace within, and the light bright enough to read by, even at this distance. Everyone in the house crowded to watch, till late in the night, the vast building exploding with fire as the roof fell in, extinguishing the tombs and monuments, woodwork and carving and even the crypt beneath with tons of calcined stone and red-hot molten lead. Dan, Oliver and Master Burgess had arrived late, utterly exhausted, with reports of the battle to save Fleet Street and the Temple, and Alathea's uncle seemed almost philosophical about the destruction of his house, commenting on their good fortune in escaping with so much. But she noticed that even he had tears in his eyes, as they watched the burning of St Paul's, that everyone had hoped might be miraculously saved.

No one slept very much that night. Though the house itself was large, there was a shortage of beds, and Alathea, Ros and Nell were reduced to lying on a feather mattress, rescued from the House of the Ash Tree, placed on a draughty floor and covered inadequately by a quilt. It was too hot for restful sleep, and she was much troubled by dreams, the most vivid of which had her climbing over the smoking ruins of Fleet Street and seeing Lovell in the distance. She called him again and again, but no sound escaped her lips: she followed him, but he seemed to be always ahead of her, elusive, as if running away. And when at last she got close enough to grab him, strangely once more by the House of the Ash Tree, miraculously restored to its former glory, there was a groan and a crash and the building toppled and fell on them both . . .

Alathea woke gasping, drenched in sweat, and found that the stifling weight across her chest was no roof-beam but Rosalind's arm. The reality of Lovell was so great that she could hardly believe he was not in the room with her; but no effort of will could conjure him up, save in dreams, and she found she could not go to sleep again.

Hugh arrived at the house before eight o'clock that morning. He, Charles and Jack had gone back to help the fire-fighters after unloading the cart the previous night. Alathea, meeting him in the beautiful, dusty, first-floor room that ran the width of the house, was surprised at his grimly weary face, smeared with soot and dirt, marred with burns and blood, his appearance utterly at odds with the lazy, urbane Hugh she had known before, and seeming strangely shorn without his periwig. He looked as if he had been up all night, as indeed he had. 'Good news,' was the first thing he said. 'The wind's dropped.'

'Thank God for that,' said Dan. 'What of all your efforts? Come and have something to break your fast. We only have beer and bread and cheese, but it's good plain fare and it's survived all the jolting in your godsend of a cart. And you can tell us what news while you eat.'

Hugh accepted with alacrity (food was one of his keenest pleasures), pausing only for a much-needed wash of his filthy hands and face before falling with hungry relish upon the bread and beer and pale hard cheese. In between mouthfuls, he told them all how, at last, the Fire seemed to be defeated. 'Your house was one of the last to be burned in Fleet Street – it was the brick one next to yours that checked it first, and by the time the main fire reached the place, they'd managed to pull down yours and the two or three opposite, and the gap was wide enough to stop it. But it was the wind dying down that really did the job. It's as calm as a millpond out there now, which is just as well, because there'd be one hell of a dust-storm if any kind of breeze blew up.'

'Is it all out now?' Lucy asked, as he took a much-needed swig of beer.

Hugh shook his shorn head. A scattering of ash and soot

descended softly to the floor. 'No, not yet by a long way – there are still a few houses smouldering in Fleet Street, on the south side, and up by Holborn and over near Cripplegate, apparently. They're using gunpowder now, to bring down the houses, and make firebreaks. You can probably hear it if you know what you're listening for.' He took a huge bite from the slab of bread and cheese he held, in a hand still very far from clean, and into the sudden silence there came, on the edge of sound, a distant flat thud.

'Gunfire!' Lucy said, running to the window, which, since it faced south across the Piazza, gave no view of any part of London that might be affected by the fire.

'Not gunfire,' Dan said, smiling affectionately at his wife. 'As Hugh said – they're blowing up the houses around the edge of the Fire now. I don't think the Dutch have landed.'

'Twenty different rumours say they have,' Hugh observed drily. 'But the Duke of York has been very concerned to put it about that this Fire was an accident, and not started by malicious intent – and I think he has the right of it. It was sheer bad luck with wind and weather, and that fool of a baker letting his baking fire get out of hand.' He looked round at the ring of silent, drawn faces, suffering from shock and sleeplessness, and saw one paler and more anxious than the rest. It was the first time he had ever seen Alathea looking plain, with hollows under her cheekbones and shadows around her eyes, the spectacular hair lank and uncombed, and the sight wrung his heart. He had thought of little for years but his own survival and pleasure and advancement, but now, with surprise, he realised that his niece's happiness meant a great deal to his ruthless, selfish, unregarding soul. He knew what she wanted. His whole body ached with weariness, he desired nothing more than to lie down and sleep, to forget about his appalling appearance and the pain of his burnt face and hands and the gash on his arm where a falling piece of timber had done some damage, but he would not be happy with his conscience if he deserted her now, even if what she wanted might seem trivial to others. It was not so to her, and if he could help, he would. He smiled at her. 'Thea, I looked for Lovell, but I couldn't see him. Do you want to come back with me now, and try again? He knows your voice, he'll come to you.'

'Hugh!' said his half-sister, shocked. 'You can't go out again –

you need a rest, some sleep, you can't go just to look for Lovell!'

'As well try to find a needle in a haystack,' Dan pointed out. 'Hugh – you've done enough, lad, and there's a bed upstairs you can have and welcome.'

Alathea glanced away, unwilling to put pressure on him. Even if his gaunt exhausted looks had not told her, she knew that he needed a good day's sleep after his labours. Yet she wanted desperately to look for Lovell now, not in a day or so but *now*, while there was a chance he might not have strayed too far from Fleet Street, and she knew that no one else but Hugh would even consider helping her.

'No – I don't suppose it will take long, and I want to do it at once,' he was telling Dan, quiet but firm. 'There'll be no danger – I won't let Thea anywhere near a fire, but I think she has the best chance of finding him. Does anyone else want to come?'

The only volunteer was, not unnaturally, Oliver, whose energy seemed unquenchable, and with a background of rather bewildered, disapproving faces, the three of them set off across the Piazza, still crowded with goods and refugees, towards Fleet Street.

It was trying to be a beautiful day, though early yet, and the blue summer sky was still obscured with the smoke drifting from parts of the City still burning. But as Hugh had said, the wind had dropped from the near gale that had whipped up the Fire, to a flat hot calm. No breeze stirred the low haze that hung above the roof-tops as they walked down Drury Lane. Alathea stopped every so often to produce one of the ear-shattering, unladylike whistles she had learned in her childhood at Goldhayes, and which she had, rather haphazardly, taught Lovell as a summons. But no black hairy dog appeared, and they came to the Strand, and Temple Bar.

In vivid contrast to the screaming crush of people and vehicles that had packed the street the previous evening, the place was almost empty. There were one or two fire-fighters, black and exhausted, stumbling back to their homes, and a trickle of people like themselves, returning to the ruins to seek for what was left, and what was burned. With a mixture of curiosity and apprehension, Oliver and Alathea followed Hugh beneath the ancient beams of Temple Bar and stood, stricken, staring at the view beyond.

Fifteen or so houses on either side of Fleet Street were standing still, with the reassuring, familiar bulk of St Dunstan's-in-the-West prominent on the left. But beyond it there was . . . nothing. Nothing except great heaps of rubble, gently smoking in the still morning air, sending grey wisps to join the soft low cloud that hung still over all the City. Except – there *was* no City. From where they stood, Alathea could see the shallow decline down to the Fleet, and up again, through the haze, past Ludgate, to the ruins of St Paul's, massively dominating the skyline even in defeat. But what shocked her beyond measure was the closer view: of those houses, so familiar from all the years she had lived in London, lining each side of Fleet Street, and then suddenly, abruptly, the desolation, the end of the world, the great white sky unbearably, dreadfully bright where there had once been so many houses, and people. And slowly, painfully, the sun was trying to penetrate the thick foggy smoke, a watery pale disc hovering appalled above the destruction.

For a long time they stood in the middle of the street, unable to believe how complete the devastation had been, and around them, people stood looking, similarly stunned. At last a big man carrying a spade shouldered past them and went stamping down towards the ruins as if nothing at all was different, as if the world did not end at Fetter Lane in a heap of smoking rubble. Alathea found that she had been holding Hugh's arm. She dropped her hand, and received a tired smile in return. 'I'd forgotten it was like this. It looked different in the dark – and there were still fires burning then.'

'I didn't know,' Alathea said, very softly. 'I didn't know it would be so – so huge . . . Do you know, Hugh, what I'd like to do now – now I see it?'

'What?'

'I'd like to paint it,' said his niece, with a wry tone in her voice.

Oliver looked at her and grinned. 'You would,' he said. 'But I'm going to have a closer look.' And he set off towards Fetter Lane with a nonchalant swagger that did not quite disguise his small-boy curiosity. Alathea, feeling very mature in comparison, exchanged an amused, adult glance with Hugh and followed him.

They caught up with him at Fetter Lane, which was only recognisable because St Dunstan's stood, more or less, on its corner. The houses just in front of the church had been blown up, or burnt, but the stone, sooty and blackened, stood unharmed. Peering down the lane, lined now with heaps of timber and smoking rubble, they could see the sharp green of the trees and shrubs in the gardens of Clifford's Inn and the Rolls, now exposed to the street, and further along there was a glimpse of flames still leaping in the packed houses between Fetter Lane and Shoe Lane, and a press of fire-fighters with buckets and ladders and ropes, working to kill the last of the Fire. But in Fleet Street it was all but quenched, the embers still gently smouldering here and there, and no danger. Dazed, they walked on, counting the steps, stumbling over still-hot debris and baulks of charred timber, until Alathea stopped suddenly and said, 'It was here. Wasn't it here?'

The three of them stared at the mound of plaster, beams, charred wood and blackened brick: a heap of rubble like any other in that wilderness, that perhaps had once been the House of the Ash Tree. Oliver leaned forward and set his hand to a black stump sticking out of the pile, and pulled. Like a huge expiring animal, the tumble of debris settled and sighed as the wooden beam moved, and small wistful puffs of smoke and dust arose. Oliver, unable to wield something so large, found a smaller piece, hardly more than a stick, and poked at the rubble. Some of it was still alight, and as the air reached the embers, flames licked up again like wicked scarlet snakes, unsated.

'Leave it,' said Hugh, suddenly and uncharacteristically sharp. 'Do you want to start it all over again?'

As Oliver, with reluctance, backed away from the mound that had once, possibly, been his home, his heel caught on something and he almost fell. Fortunately, since the ashes were hot, he saved himself by grabbing Alathea's arm, and then bent to pick up something in the dust. 'Thea, you were right. This was it.'

In his hand he held the proof: a small fragment of splintered wood, much charred at one edge, but with enough paint left for them to see that it was the top half of a tree, with the letters *e*, *a* and *s* still discernible against the blue painted sky. 'The sign,' said Hugh, tracing the three letters with his finger. 'The *e* at the end of "the", at a guess, then a gap, then the *a* and *s* of "Ash" . . . This was the House of the Ash Tree.'

And not twenty-four hours ago, it had been standing. The thought unspoken in all their minds, they stared at it for a long moment, and Oliver, bold masculine Oliver, wiped his sleeve hastily across his eyes. 'Come on,' he said, gruffly. 'We can't do anything here. Let's look for Lovell.'

Slowly, with difficulty, they clambered over the fallen bricks and timbers, the heaps of smoking spoil that littered the street, so that it was difficult to tell where the way had been. The only things still standing were the brick chimneys, thousands for as far as their eyes could see, like some strange stunted forest of tree-trunks, and the only landmarks left were the spires and towers of the churches that still stood, for the most part, thickly clustered inside the City wall. From a distance they appeared startlingly normal, rising up tall amidst the flattened buildings, but the reality was very different. The church of St Bride's, lying just past the Conduit, had been shielded from Fleet Street by houses. Now it stood tall and proud, the stone calcined white from the Fire, but there was no roof, the delicate windows were blank where the glass had melted and even the stone tracery had disintegrated in the ferocity of the flames. Up on its hill, St Paul's appeared to be still burning. Certainly, it was hung all about with a sullen smoky cloud, in which the occasional flame could be distinguished, licking greedily over the stone and timbers.

It was very hot and airless amidst the ruins of London. Alathea's feet were running with sweat, sore and singed with stumbling over hot stones, and the hem of her dress was caked in thick dirt and dust. Her throat was parched, and it hurt to breathe the stifling smoky air. Whistling was well-nigh impossible through cracked dry lips, but she kept on trying, with growing despair, shouting Lovell's name to the empty dreadful desolation, and receiving only a doleful mocking diminishing echo in reply.

At Fleet Bridge they all halted, as if by tacit consent. Oliver was perspiring heavily, his rosy handsome face dripping and liberally streaked with dirt and soot: as for his once-respectable clothes, the less said the better. Alathea knew she was in like case, and there was a long rent in her skirt, caused by an unseen nail in some beam that had blocked her way. Now, every stride revealed layers of white cambric petticoats, but she was not Rosalind and refused to make a fuss. The only one seemingly unchanged by the last half-mile or so was Hugh, who could hardly have improved on his disreputable state. He took gentle hold of Alathea's arm. 'My dear girl – I think we should go back.'

'I suppose we should,' said his niece, with dreary reluctance.

She knew it was a vain hope, she had known it in her heart all along, but now, in these bleak dead ruins with the Fleet River running choked and sluggish wiht debris below her, she face the fact that she would never see her beloved Lovell again. Gritting her teeth, she turned to walk back the way they had come.

'You're not giving up!' said Oliver indignantly. 'Oh, Thea, we *must* go on.'

'You just want to see St Paul's,' said Alathea, grief and loss making her angry. 'It's no good, he's gone for ever – and I don't think my feet or my heart could stand to go on. So let's go home, Noll, please?'

Oliver stood his ground, red-faced. He also had loved the dog, had taken him for walks in the fields north of the City and gone for muddy romps along the river bank at low tide, which had invariably left boy and animal disgustingly dirty, and foolishly happy. 'No – you can't just give up like that – please, Thea, at least *call* him!'

'All right,' said Alathea, unhappily. She cupped her hands around her mouth, feeling that few things in life could be more ridiculous than to be forever calling a dog who did not respond, and shouted Lovell's name as loudly as her withered throat would allow. The sound bounced away across the Fleet and up the hill towards Ludgate and beyond, a great two-syllabled yell that seemed to mock the deserted ruins. 'Lo – vell! Lovell!'

There was a long silence, broken only by the distant thump of explosions around the Fire's edge, away to their left in Holborn and Cripplegate. The strangeness of it struck Alathea more than anything else that day: silence, quiet, peace, in Fleet Street, in broad daylight. She wiped her nose with the back of her hand and shouted again, and again, punctuated by whistles.

'Ssh!' said Oliver, as she was preparing her aching lungs for one last try. 'Sh! I'm sure I heard something – listen!

A particularly loud explosion intruded on the quiet, and mixed in with it, on the edge of sound, was something that might, or might not, have been a dog's bark, very distant. There was no telling even from which direction it had come, still less any chance of identifying it as Lovell's, but Alathea, with sudden hope, waited until the noise of the gunpowder had rumbled away, and then put two fingers in her mouth, wishing desperately for some liquid to lubricate lips and throat, and whistled that far-carrying, two-part whistle to which Lovell had been taught to respond with the encouragement of scraps of cooked meat. And again, as the shrill sound diminished, they all heard the barking, much louder this time, and coming not from the City but from behind them, towards Temple Bar. Joyfully, Alathea leapt round and saw the apparition of her dreams, the great black dog, hair streaming, eyes glowing, the wet red tongue lolling out of the side of his mouth, come springing down the gentle hill towards them, bounding over the heaps of smoking rubbish and debris as if they were molehills. As the clouds of dust wreathed round his flying body, she had a brief vision of the Ghost Dog, Black Shuck, who had haunted her childhood stories, and then she was hit, solidly, by a very real living, breathing, enthusiastic animal who knocked her over and planted two filthy paws on her chest and licked her face with extravagant joy. And when Hugh and Oliver, delighted themselves, had pulled Lovell off and picked her up, she knew that the wetness of her face was not entirely due to the dog's lavish tongue. But she wiped her eyes, feeling suddenly weak with relief, as if a great weight had gone from her shoulders, and assessed him for hurts. He seemed in remarkably fine fettle, considering the appalling surroundings: the abundant black hair was perhaps a little singed here and there, and of course all caked and revoltingly dirty with dust and soot and worse, but essentially the same old Lovell, dear and ridiculous and her true friend. And she crouched down in the rubble and muck and hugged him, feeling the wiry warmth of the surprisingly small animal beneath all that matted impossible coat, and his hot panting breath in her ear.

'And *now* can we go back?' Hugh enquired, gently.

Alathea, looking up at him against the pale smoke-hazed sun, saw the repressed exhaustion in that grimy, smiling face, and jumped to her feet. 'Oh, yes, *yes*, and thank you – I don't think I can ever thank you enough.'

'I don't need thanks,' said Hugh, even more gruffly than usual. 'Just to see your face, dear girl, is thanks enough. Though I must say your appearance is an entertainment in itself, as well.'

Alathea, grinning, looked down. The little she could see of what was left of her attire confirmed Hugh's opinion. 'It *is* just as well I'm not Rosalind,' she said. 'I need a bath as much as Lovell. We all do,' she added, with a glance at Oliver, who had somehow managed to have ash in his hair and ears, and soot smeared liberally across his nose. 'Let's go home – they'll be waiting for us.'

Despite her own delight in having Lovell back, it was by no means certain that the rest of the household shared Alathea's feelings, but there were no dissenting voices, and since the Covent Garden house had the benefit of a large but overgrown garden, the dog was given the run of it. Unlike Mab, however, he proved to be a decidedly inept rat-catcher, and his quarry dodged his flying paws and wet snapping teeth with cheerfully contemptuous ease. The only one which failed to evade his bumbling enthusiasm proved to be an ancient, half-blind beast with no whiskers, precious little hair and only three legs. It was still up to the servant-boy, Will, to kill it, since Lovell entirely lacked such aggressive feelings towards his fellow-creatures: which led Hugh, regaled with the story, to comment that the dog must have been reared by Quakers. The rat problem was dealt with by a huge, fat, smug, black tom-cat bought for a small fortune from a friend of Dan's, who despatched prey with murderous efficiency and rejoiced in the name of Samson. Hugh wondered if he would be such a good ratter if his whiskers were cut off.

The rats in the garden and stables were but one tiny, faintly amusing strand in the busy weave of days after the end of the Fire. There was a great deal to do in the house in Covent Garden: so much, in fact, that sometimes the prospect horrified Alathea. No time for painting now, with the whole neglected house to clean of dust and dirt and mould, and restore it to its former beauty, to distribute the pathetic two cartloads of Ashley possessions around the gracious rooms, furnished in the heavy oak of thirty years ago, and to bring some order to the chaos of garden and kitchen and outbuilding. And with all this, there were other matters which needed the urgent attention of the head of the household. Dan Ashley had to leave Master Hamilton and the apprentices to set up his workshop in one of the rather dark ground-floor rooms, making workbenches and unpacking the delicate tools and materials saved from the House of the Ash Tree. Dan himself spent most days in the City, Oliver frequently in tow, helping to extinguish minor fires still lingering, to clear rubble from blocked main streets and marking out their line so that some wheeled traffic could pass. The most astonishing thing, that first week, was the speed with which the refugees, some two hundred thousand people or more, camped out in St Giles's Fields, Islington, Moorfields, Tower Hill and on Bankside, were assimilated into houses, hospitals, churches, or inns, wherever shelter might be had. Money and food poured in from the surrounding countryside. The Covent Garden house held, by the day after Lovell's return, not only the Ashley family, fourteen in all with Dan, his wife and two children, Alathea and Nell, three maids and a boy, three 'prentices and the journeyman, but also the Burgesses, four of them and three servants, and an elderly female relative of Dan's who did nothing but wring her hands and lament the loss not only of her own house, but of the half-dozen tenements, all burned, which had supplied her only income. In all, twenty-two people, even in that spacious house, was rather too cramped for comfort, despite Lucy's cheerful reminiscences of war-time Oxford where she and Alathea's mother and sundry others, to the total of a score or more, had shared a house far smaller. There was a shortage of beds, if not of mattresses, and the servants slept head-to-tail in the garret and grumbled, until Dan pointed out their good fortune in having such pleasant surroundings when so many were forced into squalid shelter in tents or boarded over cellars, shacks or huts amidst the ruins of their homes. Dan's aunt also grumbled, or rather whined. A querulous old woman whose life seemed to be one series of disasters, she was rendered almost incoherent by the last and greatest calamity, and the younger members of the family avoided her whenever possible.

And to add to the crowd, there were visitors; friends of Dan's, customers and acquaintances come to find out how he had fared or to enquire after the safety of the clocks they had ordered. Henrietta Jermyn came, round and rosy and capable, at half-past eight two mornings after the Fire, rolled up her sleeves and stayed till dusk, dusting, cleaning, polishing, before departing with her three small children, the five-year-old Beth, Harry who was two and fractious, and the baby Rebecca, named after Charles Jermyn's mother. It was noticeable that Hen had worked far harder than anyone else.

As well as visitors, there were letters written to relatives in the country who would be alarmed by the reports of the Fire, and would need reassurance that the Ashleys and their associates were safe. Epistles in Dan's neat careful hand went out to his sister and nephews and nieces in Cirencester, to Lord Bradfield at Goldhayes to explain about the invasion of his house and to beg continued use of it until the House of the Ash Tree could be rebuilt, and to Alathea's parents at Ashcott. But that letter, at least, was forestalled; for on the Sunday, a week to the day after the start of the Fire, Kit Drakelon rode into London.

They had heard wild horrific rumours at Ashcott, all London burned, Papists to blame, Dutch invasion, hundreds killed, and to give credence to these dreadful tales were the sunsets, blood red and fiery, with an ominous haze blurring the vivid blue of the summer sky. Kit had volunteered to go to the City to find the truth of it, and bring back news of Alathea and the Ashleys to his anxious mother and stepfather. He presented this journey as a duty, gladly undertaken, but still a duty. He gave no indication, when diffidently suggesting that he make the trip, of the turmoil of hope and fear surging within, at the thought of seeing Alathea again, and the terror that harm might have befallen her. He had learned some circumspection of late. He knew that Thomazine and Francis, without desiring to bring matters into the open, were aware to some extent that his feelings for Alathea went beyond the bounds of brotherly affection, and he realised, rationally, that no consummation or even affirmation of his love for her would ever be possible. But that did not lessen his feelings, or alleviate the pain, or make him, yet, inclined to turn to other women. And driven within him, they festered darkly, nourished by an unrequited, unwanted, unassuaged passion which grew and fed upon absence and despair.

So he rode to London, and took no more than a day and a night on the long road from Oxford, riding post, and with every mile he travelled, growing more afraid of what he would find at the end of his journey. He had never been to London in his adult life, though as a child he had visited the Ashleys with the rest of his family, and he knew the location of their house. He knew also, from the talk of the people from whom he asked directions, that it was unlikely to be still standing, since most of Fleet Street had been destroyed: but he was still utterly unprepared for the terrible devastation that burst upon his gaze as he rode under Temple Bar and reined in his hired horse. It was raining, for the first time for many weeks, but he ignored the water dripping gently from his hat-brim, struck still and staring by the fact that surely the house must be burned, and that he had no idea where the Ashleys had gone. For a moment, grief and despair gripped him, and he almost panicked, with somewhere a feeling of astonishment at this, that he, the sophisticated young gentleman, should be so overturned by a relatively minor set-back. But it was a measure of the strength of his desire and love for his sister, and only now was he beginning to acknowledge that strength.

He had to ask four or five people before he could find out anything about where Daniel Ashley had taken his family, and even when he at last met with success, the answer was infuriatingly vague. 'Ooh, Master Ashley? Now I ain't sure where he went – St Giles, was it, Tom? No, not St Giles, sir – Covent Garden, I think it was – leastways, there was a cove yesterday wanted to know where he'd gone so he could get the clock he'd ordered – *if* it hadn't been burnt, mind you – and old Harry Bannister, he said, I'm certain of it, *he* said Covent Garden is where he'd gone, Piazza *he* said, come up a bit in the world has old Dan Ashley if *that's* true, but he's a good old cove for all that, packed all sorts of folk into that house and given 'em a roof over their heads and he's always got an ear to listen to your troubles, has old Dan . . . '

Kit had not, and extricated himself with some difficulty and a generous coin for the information, and directions to Covent Garden. That must surely be right, he could remember now the splendid house, designed by Inigo Jones, that was one of the score or so that graced the elegant Piazza. It took him ten minutes to ride there, leaving behind the void that had been London, that echoed the emptiness deep in his soul, because of Alathea, and another five minutes or so to find someone, emerging from the bare colonnaded church on one side of the Piazza, to tell him which was the house now occupied by Daniel Ashley.

He knocked, and was received and welcomed by his Aunt Lucy and her husband, and Rosalind was there and several people he did not know, and he was made much of and plied with food and drink, but the face he longed to see was not present, though there seemed to be no one else missing. Even Nell was sat mutely in a corner of that delightful first-floor room – 'parlour' was too modest a word – in which the family spent their leisure hours, and he saw that she had the inevitable sewing. He made polite queries and received expansive answers which he scarcely heard, for all the time, beating in his head, was the unspoken question. Alathea. Where is Alathea?

He managed in the end to stop Lucy in her full flood of gossip and news of the Fire (surely, if something tragic had happened, it would show in her face, her clothes, her talk?), and to say, with an attempt at casualness, 'There's someone not here – what have you done with Thea?'

'Thea? Isn't she here?' Lucy turned to peer round the room. As usual, she had forgotten to wear her spectacles. 'Oh – I forgot – when it stopped raining, just before you arrived, she went out in the garden with Lovell. She'll be there now – go and say hallo to her.' And Lucy, with a vague and myopic smile, gestured towards the door.

He needed no urging. He made his excuses, said something mildly amusing – it must have been, for Lucy laughed – and, following her directions, made his way down the plain but elegant staircase and found the door to the garden, off the rear of the entrance-hall. He opened it, with a great feeling of happiness and longing, and stood gazing at the long narrow plot, a wilderness of grass and overgrown shrubs, with the coachhouse and stables forlorn and neglected at the end, and the backs of the houses of Hart Street beyond. But he was not looking at the plants, nor at the bricks and mortar, for there were two people in the garden. One indeed was his half-sister Alathea, standing laughing in the long wet grass, with a quick shaft of sunlight silvering her abundant spectacular hair, just as beautiful as he remembered her. But the other, the ready recipient of her smile and her attention, was a splendid courtier, very fine in his blond periwig, the light flashing on the gold lace of his cuffs and on the fashionable black beaver hat, similarly trimmed, that he held in long pale hands. And Kit, conscious suddenly of the dust on his clothes and lack of a periwig and his country upbringing and provincial experience, was overwhelmed by an explosive surge of jealousy, so intense that his nails bit into the palms of his hands. The sweat broke out on his face and his vision blurred: the two bright oblivious figures wavered and shattered like reflections on water. He blinked, and rubbed a hand across his eyes, feeling sick and dizzy with the power of his emotions. Then a dog barked, loud and sharp, and there were voices, and the next moment he was being attacked by a black hairy animal which, when calmed down and made to sit, proved to be Lovell at his most ingratiating and enthusiastic (it was close to the hour when he was usually fed). And then, at last, dispelling the miasma of destructive jealousy which clouded his mind, came

Alathea, with a smile of welcome that did not quite hide the wariness behind it. Quickly, she gave him the correct sister's kiss, and stepped back, holding his hands. 'Oh, Kit, it's good to see you! Did you come to find out how we all are after the Fire? And look who's here,' she added, turning to the Court gallant. 'Didn't you recognise Hugh?'

Hugh Trevelyan. Hugh, the orphan who was Lucy's young half-brother. Hugh, who had shared his childhood, and Alathea's, at Goldhayes, a happy witty unscrupulous child with too much of a liking for good food, and a completely incompetent rider, transmuted into this sophisticated and attractive young man. He found it hard to believe, but the long green eyes, so very like Alathea's, and Francis Heron's, were unmistakeable in the changed, worldly face. He had no reason to be jealous any more, it was not as though Hugh would ever stand in a lover's place, but the feeling inside him would not die, for it recognised the affectionate trust between uncle and niece – a trust that he himself had forfeited, at Twelfth Night.

They talked at him, and smiled, and said pleasant things, but nothing really made any impression on the emotions boiling within. He found he could hardly bear to watch that easy, instinctive rapport, and after a little while, offered some excuse of making himself presentable after his long ride, and escaped indoors.

Hugh and Alathea stood in the damp garden, a fresh misty rain dewing their clothes unnoticed, and stared after him. 'He's changed,' Hugh said, after a long moment. 'And not for the better . . . those eyes bore right through you. And you especially,' he added, with a shrewd glance at his niece. 'Looked as though he'd have devoured you whole, given half the chance.'

Alathea blushed, a rare occurrence. It washed up scarlet under her fair fine skin, and she lowered her eyes. 'I honestly think he might. He can be very intense, very . . . obsessional, can Kit. And I think I'm his latest obsession.'

There was a small silence, broken by Lovell's cheerful scratching. Hugh took her hand, and turned her face up to his. 'Dear girl . . . is it worrying you?'

'I thought I could handle him,' said Alathea. 'But I know now I was wrong . . . I don't think anyone can, he has something in him which no one can govern, not even himself at the moment. Sometimes . . . I was frightened of what he might be capable of doing, if he let his worse nature get the better of him. And that was why I came back to London, to get away from him.'

'Do your parents know?'

'Yes – but they think separation is the best cure. The trouble is,' said Alathea, with the wry rueful smile with which she made light of her difficulties, 'that separation isn't always possible . . . you look as if you have had an idea.'

'I have,' said Hugh. 'You know I was telling you about a possible trip to France – I am aware that they're allied to the Dutch at the moment, but talk is, Henry says, that there'll be an embassy to Paris in a couple of months, perhaps, to arrange a peace. It's likely I will go, since it's the kind of mission I've been on before, and since I have the collective Jermyn ear, I might be able to take Kit with me. It'll give him something to think about.' He grinned suddenly. 'Talking of Jermyns, have you heard what Henry did on Wednesday night?'

Alathea, slightly bemused, shook her head.

'You remember there was a fire broke out at the Temple, after we'd thought it had all been extinguished? Wednesday night, it was, and the Duke of York got word of it and went down from Whitehall to deal with it, and Henry, being his Master of Horse, was one of those who went with him. Now the Duke knew that the only way to save the Temple was to blow up most of the buildings round Inner Temple Hall, and so he ordered gunpowder to be brought, whereupon along comes some young upstart lawyer who quotes all the Temple rules about not using gunpowder on the premises,' said Hugh, chuckling, 'a typical lawyer, full of fine words and legal phrases, and all the sense of a headless chicken. And Henry, a little hastily I will admit, snatched up a piece of wood and beat the silly fool over the head with it, much to the horror of all the other lawyers standing around like sheep.'

'Was he hurt?'

'Henry? Oh, no, quite unharmed except for an aching arm – oh, you mean the lawyer! Beaten senseless, but afterwards recovered,' said Hugh, with his characteristically cheerful callousness. 'It's said he'll bring an action for assault – well, he wouldn't be a good lawyer if he didn't – but I doubt he'll get very far with it. Too many influential people have been wanting to do exactly that, if not worse, to a lawyer for years.' He chuckled deeply, caught

Alathea's eye, and grinned. 'You think I'm very hard-hearted, don't you. Go on, admit it – you're shocked.'

'Not at all – nothing you do has the power to shock me any more.'

'One day I'll take you up on that,' said Hugh. 'Meanwhile, if you ever find Kit a little . . . difficult . . . then please remember, I'm here to help you. Always.'

'I know.'

'Do you? Good. Now, we must go in – Lucy will be wondering where we are, and so, I should imagine, will your jealous big brother.'

'I hope he doesn't decide to stay,' said Alathea thoughtfully. 'I hope he goes back soon . . . I don't think I could stand to be so . . . watched all the time.' She sighed unhappily. 'And yet we used to be such friends, there was a time last year when we used to do everything together . . . and then it all seemed to go wrong.' She glanced up at Hugh. 'I'm glad you're not the obsessive sort.'

'Far from it,' said Hugh. He gave her a friendly, brotherly hug. 'The only thing I can conceivably be accused of being obsessive about is my dinner.'

'And it's beginning to show,' said Alathea, poking his stomach gently. 'Getting poddy, you are, Hugh bor, not like a Heron at all.'

'Save that I'm not a Heron – I'm a Trevelyan. And remember,' said Hugh, suddenly serious, 'I will be your friend – always – in any difficulty. If Kit is ever a problem – I will help.'

'I hope I'll never need it,' said his niece, with gratitude. 'But – thank you.'

Certainly there was no need of help or support on this occasion. Kit had found, with a mixture of anger and grief and jealousy, that Alathea in London, surrounded by friends, was very different from the bored, lonely girl, eager for any diversion, that he had encountered at Ashcott. She smiled, and talked to him, and asked for news of her parents and Mun and Sophie and Math and the Widow Gooch, but her affection was spread liberally over all her friends, and he still wanted her for himself alone. He tried to hide his disappointment, he did his best not to haunt her with his eyes, but it did not really work: nothing would, save the consummation of his obsession. And even he, in his rational and realistic moments, shrank from that.

So, the day after his arrival, Sir Christopher Drakelon, Baronet, made his farewells to his aunt and uncle, and all his cousins, and took his aching, miserable, jealous heart back to Ashcott. He could not bear to be near his half-sister, to see her so easy and happy with Hugh and Rosalind, Oliver and Nell, but neither could he bear the prospect of life at Ashcott, without her, without any light or shadow to sharpen his existence. And Alathea, too, was troubled by conflicting emotions: pity and grief for this agonised, threatening yet loved spirit, and relief that her days were free of the strain and danger that his presence always seemed to bring to her. Hugh, concerned, saw how Kit's departure seemed to free her from that watchful, wary look of dread that had clouded her expression since his arrival, and was glad that his worst fears seemed to have been allayed. He had never really liked Kit, never felt able to trust him, never, despite their shared childhood, been entirely easy with him, and Alathea's revelations had only endorsed his long-held opinion. He did not feel shock or revulsion at the news of Kit's incestuous desires, he had seen far worse examples of human lechery and greed and cruelty in his years on the fringes of Court, and if Alathea had welcomed her half-brother's advances it would not have been for Hugh to judge the morality of it. But she was repelled, grieved, bewildered by the force of Kit's feelings, and so Hugh was bound by his affection and his promise, to protect her. She was the little sister he had never had, he the elder brother assuming the place Kit had forfeited: and he would do for her what he would do for no other, save himself.

CHAPTER TEN

The offer

> Busy: 'What will you do, madam?'
> Harriet: 'Be carried back and mewed up in the country again, run away here, anything, rather than be married to a man I do not care for.'
>
> (Etherege, *The Man of Mode*)

The third man in Alathea's life, who was neither half-brother nor half-uncle, came to the Covent Garden house in the afternoon of Monday, September the tenth, just a few hours after Kit Drakelon had left. Like Kit, he arrived wearily, after a long, hard-ridden journey, and like Kit, he came with a mixture of hope and trepidation, because of Alathea. But Jasper Sewell, though as passionate in his feeling for her, had not that poisoning streak of guilt and jealousy that twisted Kit's emotions, and at least he had no need to hide his love.

All the long miles from Suffolk, bearing Lord Bradfield's letter to Daniel Ashley which authorised his occupation of the Covent Garden house (at rather more than a peppercorn rent), Jasper had been thinking of Alathea. He had last seen her unhappy, grieving and bewildered after Rupert Heron's death. He wondered, with intense curiosity, how her strong, independent mind would have coped with the aftermath of that terrible day when she had failed to save her young cousin. Her family would have helped her, he knew, but he had no knowledge of the part Kit had played in her mind's recovery, and no suspicion of what she had meant to her half-brother. 'Soon I will see her,' said the voice in his head, with joy. 'Soon I will see her again.'

And see her he did, in that lovely first-floor room above the arcade, light and airy, with restrained plasterwork and a severely classical fireplace, dominated by a massive portrait of Alathea's grandfather, old Sir Simon Heron who had died before the war, presented as a stiff overdressed young man in the slashed silks and starched ruffs of the 1620s. Under his severe painted gaze, the household was engaged in a charming variety of tasks: reading, sewing, writing, and in Alathea's case, drawing.

As he was announced, and the company jumped to their feet with pleasing delight, his eyes went at once to her, assessing changes. She was paler, better dressed, more self-possessed than the sun-flushed, country-loving girl who was the Goldhayes Alathea. And of course there was chalk in her hand and paper on the table, and she had evidently been portraying the little group of Ashleys sitting around the fireplace. He smiled at her, unguarded, with the full warmth of his feelings, and saw, to his distress, the defensive shutters come down over her face. He had wondered if his love would stand the test of time and separation. He had not considered the likelihood that she would not have changed either, and it was a shock to realise that she still regarded him with . . . annoyance, was his rueful conclusion. He was an interference in her life, an obstruction in her path, no more, but he wished with all his heart that he was not so, that he could declare his love, and have it returned, without risk of alienating her for ever. If wishes were horses . . .

'Hullo, Jasper,' she said, quite coolly, and gave him a reserved, reluctant smile which did nothing for his hopes.

Alathea knew that she ought to be more friendly, that it was not fair to Jasper: after all, falling in love with her was not exactly something he could very well have helped. But she could not stop herself being unkind. She shied away from any involvement, any encouragement, and flew instead to the opposite extreme.

'He hasn't altered, then,' said Rosalind, as they were changing before supper. Charles and Henrietta Jermyn had been invited, at exceedingly short notice, and it was possible that Hugh would also be in attendance: he was very fond of Mistress Byrd's excellent cooking. 'Your medical swain.'

'He's not my swain,' said Alathea irritably.

'Well, he'd like to be. Don't you like him, then?' Rosalind asked, gently teasing.

Alathea gave her a glowering stare. 'No.'

'Not just a little bit? I think he's nice. I wish,' Rosalind said wistfully, 'that it was me he looked at like that. *I* wouldn't be rude to him, *I* wouldn't turn away and talk to someone else – don't look like that, Thea, it was very obvious. Why don't you like him?'

'I don't.'

Rosalind frowned at her. Alathea hastened to make herself clear. 'I don't dislike *him* at all. He's pleasant company, he has good manners and good looks and something a bit more, something special . . . a sort of far-away, idealistic look . . . as if he thought further and clearer and deeper than most people. I don't dislike *him*. It's his reaction to me I dislike. If I let him, he'd make me his wife.'

'And where's the harm in that?' Rosalind demanded flippantly. She peered into the mirror, smoothing down one neat, mouse-coloured (or, on Rosalind, dark gold) ringlet, and smiled with satisfaction at the well-cared-for face looking back at her. 'I wouldn't mind being Mistress Sewell, for all he's got no money and few prospects.'

'I would,' said Alathea, well aware that her cousin was teasing her. She was at once irritated and amused. 'You *know* I don't want a husband, Ros.'

'I do know, but I keep on trying. You can't be wed to your paintbrush for ever, you know.'

'You talk as if I was an old maid – and I'm only seventeen.'

'Still less reason to waste yourself on a paintbrush,' said Rosalind tartly. 'And I'll wager that Mother contrives some way to sit you two together, at supper – I saw the beady look in her eyes.'

Alathea hoped that Rosalind's prediction would not be fulfilled, but had little faith; and her cousin was proved right when, a little later, they walked into the main chamber where the supper was to be held. Long tables had been pulled out into the middle of the room, and a succession of Lucy's best snowy white damask tablecloths, saved from the Fire, successfully disguised the fact that what appeared to be one unit of furniture was actually three pieces, all of slightly different heights. There were candles in profusion, yet still the big graceful room remained half in shadow, mercifully concealing the huge filthy cobwebs, in each corner of the ceiling, which no one had yet devised a way to reach. Every member of the household seemed to be there, the servants ready to distribute the food, Dan's Aunt Everitt grumbling about the quality of her wine, Henrietta talking cheerfully to her brother, even the Burgesses, rather embarrassed, huddled together by the fireplace. Alathea, entering with Rosalind, both of them garbed in their best gowns and their hair coiffured with the help of each other and Lucy's senior maid, was very conscious of eyes turning:

in particular, Jasper's. She knew she looked well in that dress, a strong but muted shade of greenish-blue satin which had survived the crumpling and maltreatment of their precipitate flight and had responded well to judicious use of a flat-iron. Rosalind, of course, was immaculate as ever in tawny silk, but it was not at her that Jasper Sewell stared, a forgotten smile on his face and his heart in his eyes. Suddenly afraid, Alathea looked away, aware that she was blushing, and was promptly siezed by Lucy, wearing a blue dress and a coyly knowing smile. 'There you are, Thea – you *do* look nice tonight!'

'Do I?' said her niece, as coolly as she could. 'I hadn't really noticed.'

Lucy's smile broadened, and as the assembled company were directed to their seats at the table, she steered Alathea gently but firmly to her place, and indicated that Jasper should sit next to her: after which, with the suspicion of a wink, she retired to watch the fun from a distance, balancing a pair of small spectacles on her nose for the purpose.

Alathea, with annoyed resignation, sat down with a cool swish of satin and collected her thoughts. She would have to be very careful if she was to extricate herself from this Lucy-made situation with her dignity and integrity intact. She must steer a path between rudely ignoring his presence, and probably thereby casting a blight on the evening, and seeming to be too keen and thus inviting gossip, interest and unwelcome jumping to conclusions, not least by Jasper himself. So when, after they had been served with brimming bowls of fragrant potage (Lucy had at last persuaded the conservative Mistress Byrd to cook a succession of courses in the fashionable French manner), Jasper turned to her with a polite enquiry about her well-being, she answered stiffly, not wishing to encourage any conversation more intimate, and, to keep the talk at a strictly impersonal level, enquired about Lord Bradfield and his daughters. From Jasper's reply, she gathered that her uncle was well in body, if still rather cast down in his mind, more than a year after Rupert's death, and that Anne and Mall were likewise well, though Anne had become very silent after the tragedy, and Mall thought of little but clothes and dancing.

'And you?' said Alathea, sipping her soup and trying not to let too much interest creep into her voice. 'What are you doing now?'

'I lodge in Bury,' Jasper told her, 'and I help Doctor Wright –

who, as you may know, is the man who helped at your birthing. He was young then, and Dr Despotine's assistant – '

'And Dr Despotine was at *your* birthing!' said Alathea.

'Which is why I am saddled with my rather exotic name – for him. Dr Despotine died, Dr Wright took over his patients, and now, being a far-seeing man, I am hoping that Dr Wright will take to me and settle me on the long path to a successful career.'

'No plans to move to London, then?' Alathea enquired casually.

Jasper shook his head positively. 'No: not for me the hectic life of a City physician, ladling out the lies and flattery with his useless medicines, thank you most kindly. There's enough for me to do in Bury. Dr Wright treats many poor people, as well as all the gentry, and I'm making a special study of various afflictions for my own ends. One day, I might put them into a book.'

And Alathea, watching, saw the bright, far-seeing, green eyes lose focus and drift into dreaming, and felt, illogically, a pang of annoyance. She almost wished there was something to dislike in Jasper, some valid reason for so steadfastly refusing to be affected by him: he was so very likeable, and, if not exactly good-looking with that judas-coloured hair and those freckles, at least pleasing to the eye. She controlled her irritation and said politely, 'What afflictions do you plan to study?'

Jasper's eyes flew round to meet hers. He grinned, suddenly very boyish, and said, 'Do you really want to know?'

Alathea, who shared abundant good health with most of her family, quailed inwardly at the prospect of some tedious exposition of other peoples' ills, and, as ever incurably honest, shook her head. 'No. I'm afraid I haven't much interest in the subject. And . . . it frightens me, a little.'

'It frightens me even more,' said Jasper candidly. 'Your average physician – and I, believe me, am exceedingly average – stands defeated before almost every human ailment. If your patient recovers, it's almost certainly a matter of luck, or a strong constitution, and most definitely not the result of the doctor's skills. There's a man in London – you may have heard of him, Sydenham is his name – who believes in interfering with the natural process of recovery as little as possible, and in *observing* diseases and their symptoms, and basing his treatment on that, rather than what Galen said over a thousand years ago. Funnily enough, observation is what Hippocrates advised – but *he's* been dead for two thousand years, so not all the ancients are useless.' He smiled. 'But I don't want to bore you. Tell me about your painting. Lucy said you have been studying with Master Cooper?'

'Not exactly studying,' Alathea told him, and found herself, with increasing animation, describing the progress of her art. And Jasper, far from showing a merely polite interest, revealed himself to be considerably knowledgeable about pigments and oils and the chemical side of painting, and disclosed that he had even, once, visited the studio of Mynheer Van Rijn, and watched the great artist at his work.

'It's as if all his paint is laid on with a shovel, it's so thick,' Jasper said reminiscently, 'and at first, if you stand too close, all you can see is colours mixed together, and very murky colours they tend to be too: but step back a little and suddenly there is a face, a figure, coming out of the dark as if a light has shone on it. And the master himself is a big old man with a peasant's face, very Dutch, very sombre, and yet he is the greatest magician with a brush that ever I saw. Your Lely's best work has never a hope of matching Mynheer Van Rijn even at his very worst.'

'I've heard of him,' Alathea said thoughtfully. 'Samuel Cooper admires him, and for an artist to gain Master Cooper's admiration, he must be great indeed . . . please, tell me more.'

And even if Jasper had not been inclined to do so, the sight of her face, unselfconsciously eager and for once devoid of defensiveness and irony, would have won him over in a moment. He told her about the young mathematics student at Leyden University, Gottfried Kneller, who had decided that he preferred painting and who had had the great good fortune to become Rembrandt Van Rijn's pupil. 'With no discernable effect on his painting, that I could see,' Jasper said drily. 'But he'd only been a few months at the studio when I went there, and I should think being Rembrandt's pupil would blight all but the most confident, to start with at least.' And he went on to talk about the works of various Dutch masters he had seen in Holland, the painters of taverns and low life, of landscapes and seascapes and ships, of gracious wealthy interiors and worthy citizens, stories from the Bible and episodes of ancient history, flowers and still-life. The variety was immense, the quality high and Jasper an enthusiastic critic who knew what he liked and was not afraid to fly in the face of fashion.

'Master Rembrandt's out of favour now, too dark, too unfinished they say. It's as if they're afraid of all that power and emotion in his paintings, they prefer someone like Ruisdael or Steen to put a pretty veil between themselves and reality. Have you seen the Dutch pictures your esteemed uncle brought back from The Hague?'

Alathea, of course, had, and the stewed mutton and roast young pigeons and even the fruit tarts and syllabubs, fresh and lavish and expensive both in time and money, passed her by almost untasted as she discussed those very different pictures in Lord Bradfield's study with a Jasper who was, for the moment, no kind of threat at all, but that rare and wondrous being, a person whose knowledge of and enthusiasm for painting almost equalled her own. She learned that Judith Leyster, painter of the dashing, laughing woman with the lute, had been a pupil of Hals, was his equal in many ways, and like him, and Rembrandt, had gone out of fashion in recent years, so that she was now all but forgotten. 'But a Dutch family I knew in Haarlem were related to her and had a couple of her pictures. Did you like that one?'

'It showed me how to paint,' said Alathea. 'It showed me that an oil painting needn't be stiff or posed or artificial, it can capture an instant of time and look as if it was painted in a moment, even if it took three weeks – and when Uncle Simon told me it was by a woman, that was even better. Though not to him,' she added with a grin. 'The mere fact that the artist was female seemed to devalue it, the bigoted old fool!'

'Don't be irreverent. He's my chief patient, or rather, Mall is – she's one of those people who's never happy unless they're ill, or at least have some interesting condition to complain about, and she's only twelve! God help any husband she manages to hook.' Jasper decided, a little tardily, to steer away from the subject of husbands, and added quickly, 'Did you try any painting in the manner of Judith Leyster?'

He was rewarded by one of Alathea's dazzling swift smiles. 'Oh, yes, I tried – it's the picture of Oliver, behind you.'

Jasper turned to look at it. Hanging up there away from the reach of the candlelight, he had not noticed it, and the details were hard to see, but the vivid reality of Oliver shone through the gloom, as swift and sure a piece of painting as Judith Leyster's. He expressed his pleasure and admiration.

Alathea, with a trace of self-deprecation, pointed out that the light precluded a proper examination and disguised a host of faults in her technique. 'But anyway, though I'm sure that I could match Leyster one day, or even Hals, I could never, ever paint as beautifully as the man who did the picture of the woman by the window.'

'Vermeer? Now that, as you saw, was different from the others – and as high above anything most artists achieve as a mountain towers over a molehill. And yet so simple.'

'Just a few colours, a woman reading a letter, the way the light falls on her face and her dress and the wall behind her, each pearl in her necklace shown with a tiny point of white on grey . . . no story, no moral, no emotion, no sentiment, just an observation of peace, and light, and quiet, and truth . . . I loved it,' said Alathea, 'and if Lord Bradfield ever wants to sell it and I have the money to pay, I will buy it from him for its beauty alone . . . but never in a thousand years could I paint like that. It's not my style.'

'Would a portrait of me be in your style?'

Alathea considered the pale, boyishly freckled face, the orange hair and green wizard's eyes, teasing. 'Perhaps. I could paint you with a skull in one hand and a book of remedies in the other – or should it be spells? – very significant and portentous and solemn, the physician unlocking the secrets of alchemy and medicine. But I don't think it'd be *you*.'

'Then how would you paint me?'

'As you: as Jasper: as yourself. Not looking directly out of the canvas, but at something else, something far away . . . ' She blushed, suddenly aware that she had revealed far more of herself, and her varied feelings towards him, than she had ever intended.

Jasper smiled gently, the dreaming look on his face, and said softly, 'Well, perhaps one day soon you will do it. My mother would like a picture of me, though I have an uneasy feeling that it might completely dominate that little parlour at the Home Farm.'

'Then it will have to be a miniature,' said Alathea, relieved at the changing tone of their talk.

Hugh, sitting opposite, cast a benevolent eye away from contemplation of the delicious plum tart on his plate, swimming in cream, to watch Jasper, who had been their leader by dint of age and personality in that delightful Goldhayes childhood they had all shared, so deep in conversation with his beloved niece. Lucy had been right, Hugh decided. *Despite her plaguey match-making tactics – they do deal well together, even with Thea's prickly distrust of anyone who might want to marry her – and from the look of him Jasper most certainly does. Perhaps*, his mind ran on, thoughtfully, *the reason she and I get on so well is that she sees me as a friend, not as a threat to her maiden status nor to her painting. She's right there. I've no intentions of marrying yet, if at all, and if I do decide to tie the knot at last, it must be some wealthy widow who'll keep me in style and leave me in peace. No penniless young beauty for me!* He took a bite of that exquisitely flavoured pastry, and smiled affectionately at the absorbed pair across the white tablecloth, oblivious even of their portions of plum tart, in their own little world. *She may give him an hour or so's rapt attention, particularly if painting's the subject of the conversation*, Hugh thought, *but if Jasper thinks she'll say yes to him on the strength of it, I fear he's much mistaken*.

But Jasper, the incurable optimist, was of precisely that opinion. He spent the night at his sister's lodgings in Westminster, she having paradoxically more spare room there than had Dan in the big crowded Covent Garden house, and all the way back, in the coach Charles had profligately hired to carry himself, his wife, Hugh and Jasper the mile or so to Antelope Alley, his heart sang within him. All evening, she had forgotten the constraints that had previously stiffened and inhibited her dealings with him, and for close on four hours he had had her almost undivided attention, had experienced the full power and warmth of her personality, that strange and unique combination of pride and diffidence, innocence and worldliness, eagerness and irony, objective judgement and passionate obsession. He had wondered, coming to London, whether he would lay her ghost. Now, aflame in the jolting coach, he knew that his love for her would haunt him for ever.

And he could no longer bear to sit passively by, and never tell that love. He must do something to secure her for himself, and quickly. He slept little that night, the fever of desire had him by the throat so that he could hardly breathe, he felt physically sick with it, and in the morning he barely touched his bread and cheese.

Henrietta, a baby on one hip and the toddling Harry clinging fat-fisted to her skirts, knew at once what was afoot. 'Are you still pining for Alathea?'

'Yes,' said Jasper shortly. The bread and cheese might as well have been hunks of wool for all the taste in his mouth. He took a convulsive draught of cool ale and felt a little better.

Henrietta sighed, sat down on the stool by his side, releasing the children to crawl around under the five-year-old Beth's capable eye, and said, 'Why her? Why couldn't you have picked Ros, who has a fancy for you and will make a very good wife *and* will probably have a sizeable portion when she marries? Dan's a wealthy man, even after the Fire. You couldn't do better than Ros.'

'I don't want Ros. I want Thea. Saying that I'd do better with Ros is like telling you, five years ago, that you'd be better off with Henry Jermyn and not Charles. *You* should understand that, surely.'

'I do,' said his sensible sister. 'But the fact remains that Alathea, as she's been telling all her friends for years, has no intention of marrying. And she's a Heron and you know what that means as well as I do. You've had the misfortune to want as your wife the only girl in London who not only says she'll never marry but has enough determination and stubbornness to keep to it. And how can one evening's chat make a difference? She's too strong to give in; she has a great deal of pride, has Thea.'

'Water can wear away a stone – and I can be very stubborn too.' Jasper took another gulp of ale. 'Hen – I can't just go back to Suffolk and forget her – I *can't*. I have to do something *now*. I can't wait for five years, or ten, until she decides she's had enough of painting and wants to join the real world.'

'You're wrong,' said Hen briskly. 'For Alathea, painting is the real world, and until you understand that, you don't stand a chance, and neither does anyone else. Jasper, it's not a phase she's going through, not something she'll grow out of – painting *is* Alathea, Alathea *is* painting. It's as much a part of her as her hair and her eyes and her hands, and stopping her would be like cutting off a limb, it'd be as good as killing her . . . ' She put a square freckled hand over his. 'If you ever want to have Thea, you must have her painting as well. Otherwise, it would be like caging a butterfly.'

The poetic image sounded incongruous from his practical sister, but the rest of her speech struck him with the force of absolute truth. With surprise, he realised that he had much underestimated

Hen's powers of perception. Grainne, their mother, had this clear-sighted ability to cut to the core of someone's soul, to see the wheels and balances that made them what they were. He had not realised that the gift had been passed on to Henrietta.

He said slowly, 'I will take Thea gladly, with or without her painting. You're right, I'm sure you're right, I will do whatever I can to make her happy, but I want her to marry me.'

'Then you can whistle for the moon,' Hen said roundly. 'Jasper, *think*! She's in London, she has a future here, it could be a wonderful one, she could become a really great artist – and if you marry her and take her back to Bury, then you snuff all that out. She senses that, I'm sure. Unless you're prepared to move to London – and that's something you always swore you'd never do. But you can't hide her away in Bury – that'd be a crime against art – and humanity.'

'I know,' said Jasper, although in fact such practical considerations had never crossed his mind. 'I don't know what I'll do once I have her – I just know that I have to do something *now*!'

'What can you do? You can't go off to Ashcott and ask her parents for her hand in marriage.'

'Why not?' Jasper enquired; for at least, out of all the possibilities that had suggested themselves to his feverish mind, that was the one that promised immediate action. He could not speak to Alathea directly, convention precluded it, but an approach to her parents was the usual first step, and in view of their own past, a tale of lost love at long last fulfilled, he had high hopes that they would regard his suit with sympathy. He got to his feet. 'Clever girl, Henny-Penny – that's exactly what I'll do. I'll go to Ashcott, now, and tell Thomazine and Francis that I want to marry her.' He looked at his sister, and produced one of those disarming grins that would melt stone, given the opportunity. 'I know you're trying to discourage me, I know you're thinking of what's best – but I can't help myself, Hen: I must do *something*. So wish me well, please.'

Henrietta's earnest tawny-brown eyes stared into his. 'Do you mind that I disagree?'

'Yes,' said Jasper, honestly. 'I respect your commonsense, I trust your judgement – and I have a sneaking feeling that you may be right.'

'Then why are you going to Ashcott?'

'Because I'm in love, you sawny fule of a sister! Haven't you ever been in love? Haven't you ever felt so much for someone that even being in the same room with them is a delight, and to talk with them an hour in paradise? To feel ill with it, as if every second away from them drained your blood, drop by drop and little by little? Haven't you ever cast duty and convention, friends and family, propriety and dignity, all out of the window for love? Haven't you, Hen?'

'Yes,' said Henrietta quietly, thinking back to those glorious, golden days when Charles had been so wonderful, and the world seemed made new in their honour: days too soon gone, their brightness diminishing to the muted grey of reality, marriage, London, children. But she had never complained, never betrayed her loyalty to her scapegrace, inconsiderate husband. She had known love, and great happiness, and was the richer for it. How could she, in all honesty, carp at Jasper's urge to snatch the same happiness for himself? Even if, with the clear eye of a bystander, she could see that it would not work?

Jasper, watching her, saw something of those feelings in her face. The expression of soft sadness in her eyes was a revelation to him. He reached out a hand, and she took it, and they hugged each other, something they very rarely did, and then Henrietta said roughly, 'Don't listen to what I'm saying. If you have a chance of happiness, take it. But don't let her hurt you – she won't mean to, but she doesn't understand – not yet, she's never been in love, she doesn't know how it feels.' She grinned at him, the old down-to-earth Henrietta again, her eyes already sliding sideways to check on the baby. 'Good luck.'

'And that is something I may well need,' Jasper said.

'No!' Alathea cried, jumping to her feet. 'No – I don't believe it – he *can't*!'

'Thea!' Rosalind dropped her sewing and stared at her cousin in astonishment. 'Who can't? What's happened?'

'Jasper Sewell, may he be three times cursed, has gone behind my back and sneaked off to Ashcott and asked for my hand! In *marriage*!'

'Has he? Oh, how nice!' Nell's quiet little voice intruded.

Alathea rounded on her, her face scarlet with fury. 'Nice? *Nice*? You *know* I don't want him to pester me! You *know* I don't want him to marry me!' She waved the letter, just arrived from her mother, under Nell's startled nose. 'And rather than ask me direct, he's gone behind my back and asked my parents for "permission to pay his addresses to me".' She spat the prim phrase out savagely.

Ros said mildly, 'He's only trying to go about it the right way. It would hardly be proper to ask you first.'

'Why not? He wants to marry *me*, not my mother! *I* should be the one he asks, *I* should be the one to decide yes or no, not them! Why didn't he come to me?'

'I expect he knew the reception he'd get,' said Rosalind drily. Alathea stalked over to her chair and sat down with a furious thud. 'So? That makes him a coward.'

'I never thought he was a coward,' Nell put in timidly. She had recently had a good deal more to say for herself, and the endless sewing had turned into a new gown, cornflower blue, and surprisingly becoming. She was wearing it now, rather unsuitably for a quiet Tuesday morning at home, and the colour matched her large solemn eyes. Alathea glared at her. 'What do you know? You've hardly spoken to him.'

'He never used to be a coward, at Goldhayes,' Nell insisted doggedly.

Alathea turned away from her with a grunt of impatience. 'The rat! The underhand *rat*!'

'What does the letter say?' Rosalind asked, hastily diverting her cousin before her rage could lead her into more unsuitable language.

Alathea frowned at the heavy paper, covered in her mother's bold thick handwriting. 'It says – he came to Ashcott yesterday – and it was written on Friday, so that must mean he rode straight there when he left here this time last week. And Mother says he didn't waste any time, he came straight to the point and told them what he wanted . . . ' Unable to continue, she screwed the letter up into a tight ball and hurled it into the fire. The flames licked greedily about it and Nell, with uneasy memories, looked away: she dreamed still of burning, and falling buildings. Ros spoke again, quietly reasonable. 'And what have your parents said to Jasper?'

Alathea went a sudden hot shade of red. She leapt up, grabbed a poker and hooked the flaming paper out of the hearth, stamping on it vigorously.

After an astonished silence, Rosalind began to laugh. 'You don't mean to say . . . you haven't read it all? Oh, Thea!'

Alathea, still scowling, picked up the blackened smoky letter and began gingerly to unfold it. Suddenly her frown disappeared. Her long eyes slipped sideways to look at Rosalind, who was choking with amusement, and then she began to laugh herself. Nell, as ever one step behind, joined in last of all.

'Well,' said Rosalind, wiping the tears away from her flushed cheeks, 'what does it say? Is there anything left?'

'A little bit,' said Alathea, still grinning. 'It's charred round the edges, but I can read most of it. Mother says . . . she says that she and Father told Jasper that it must all be discussed with me before it's allowed to go any further – and any decision on the matter is to be mine and mine alone.' She turned the paper over, dislodging a shower of black ashes, and studied the reverse. 'And . . . oh, God, Father is coming here to talk about it, and he's bringing Jasper back with him!'

'When?' Rosalind enquired.

'I can't read it – that bit's burnt!'

Ros snorted. 'Serves you right, then, if they turn up here this afternoon. More to the point, what are you going to say?'

'I'm going to say no, of course.'

Rosalind considered her cousin, still sparkling with laughter and anger. 'Be nice about it, Thea. He can't help feeling that way, or being so – so *rushing*.'

'He always was impetuous.' Alathea smoothed the crumpled letter and folded it carefully. 'All right, Ros, I'll be nice to him – and pass him on to you when I've finished!'

'It's no good,' said Rosalind. 'I'll not play second fiddle to a grand passion for someone else. I'm sure Father will line up some nice rich merchants' sons for me – if there *are* any rich merchants left, after the Fire – and I shall pick the one with the nicest smile, and be very happy.'

Alathea looked at her, very sleek and satisfied in the big carved chair, and thought how feline she was becoming: well-groomed and comfortable, just like a plump spoilt house-cat, all her priorities ordered and arranged. She realised with a pang of regret that the future so casually forecast, the rich merchant's son, was probably quite close for Rosalind: and their teasing, affectionate friendship might not survive her marriage. But that was further ahead. The vexed question of Jasper Sewell lay much nearer, and she must gather her strength and her arguments. Her mother had said that the decision must be hers, but her conscience would not allow her merely to say no, and give no reason. For the sake of that very pleasant evening when she and Jasper had shared an interest in pictures and painting, and he had become a person rather than a threat, she owed him some courtesies.

She did not have very long to marshal her thoughts on the matter, for Francis Heron and Jasper Sewell arrived at the Covent Garden house the next day, quite late in the afternoon. By this time, Alathea's aunt and uncle had of necessity been informed of the reason for their unexpected visit. Lucy, of course, was highly delighted at the success of her match-making, but her husband expressed some reservations. 'He's a nice young man, and he'll go far: but he's not for Thea. Not yet.'

'Oh, come, Dan,' said Lucy, cheerfully oblivious of her niece scowling by the window, 'it's what we always planned – how suitable, Thomazine's daughter and Grainne's son. They were made for each other.'

'Rubbish,' said Dan affectionately. 'You're embarrassing the poor girl. I should keep quiet, or she'll turn you to stone with one of those basilisk glares of hers.'

'You'll get wrinkles,' Rosalind advised. 'Screwing your face up like that, and standing in the sun. And you'll get a headache.'

'I've already got one,' said Alathea irritably.

They had been waiting all day for her father's possible arrival, and her nerves were somewhat frayed. To be the centre of attention, speculation, interest was not what she wanted at all, particularly when the situation was not of her own choosing, and when the pressure was on her, subtly and not so subtly, to let go, to drift with the tide of everyone's opinion rather than strike out on her own, she became liable to outbursts of true Heron temper and obstinacy. The harder Lucy pushed, the stronger she would dig in her toes, and she was glad of Dan's quiet, solid support. It made her feel less isolated, less surrounded by enemy forces. And she knew also that, whatever she might desire, her father would be her ally.

He and Jasper duly arrived, and Alathea and Francis went out into the garden together, just before supper, it being the only place in the crowded house where they could talk privately. The long hot spell had finally broken with a vengeance, there had been rain and high winds earlier in the week, and the grass which the boy Will had scythed down lay thick and wet about them, and stuck to Alathea's skirts. Her father looked as well as ever, lean and long like all Herons, and she was absurdly pleased to see that he wore his own pale hair still and had not succumbed to the fashionable periwig. He gave her brief news of the family, and let fall the information that Kit was going up to Yorkshire for a few weeks to view his estates, and had invited Matthew to go with him.

'Whyever did he do that?' Alathea wondered, for Matthew, remote and studious, had never been very close to his half-brother.

Francis shrugged. 'God knows – probably he wanted some companionship. He's a lonely soul, is Kit.'

They both knew why, but did not speak of it. Her father went on. 'And Matthew, I'm sorry to say, declined to go. Too busy studying, was his excuse – well, I suppose he is going to Oxford soon – and neither your mother nor I could shift him. I think it hurt Kit a great deal: he's been like a bear with a sore head, this last week.'

With a sudden dreadful certainty, Alathea thought of another reason for Kit's mood. As if echoing her train of thought, her father added, 'So, tell me – what do *you* think of Jasper's unexpected offer?'

Alathea took a deep breath. She had always been able to talk to her father: like Hugh, she knew he would always be on her side. But it was still difficult, to drag out all her half-formed, passionate reasons why she should not marry Jasper, and examine them in the cold daylight of commonsense. She said slowly, 'Can I be honest?'

'Of course you can.'

'Then . . . I *like* Jasper. I like him as a person, he has something a little different, a bit special about him. He's very knowledgeable about painting, did you know? He's been to Rembrandt's studio and he knows a lot about pigments and chemicals . . . we talked for hours last week at Aunt Lucy's supper party. But just because I like him, and we have one common interest, that doesn't mean I want to marry him. Anyway, I'm too young.'

'Your mother was married at seventeen,' Francis reminded her gently.

Alathea made an exclamation of annoyance. 'I wish people would stop comparing me to my parents, my cousins – anybody! I'm myself, I'm Alathea, I'm not anyone else, I'm *different*! I don't want to marry anybody, if it means having endless babies and running a household – there'll be no time left for painting, and if there is, I'll be no more than just another fashionable lady dabbling in trivia. I have a gift, *I* know it, you know it, so does Samuel Cooper, and it ought to be used, properly, and not frittered away, year by year until I wake up one day when I'm middle-aged and wonder what I've done with my life.'

'And how do you want to use it?'

Alathea stared at the harsh new brick of the coachhouse, unsoftened by creeper or plant. 'I want to set up a studio: here, if Uncle Dan lets me. There's a room up there, a garret at the top of the house, you can see its window. It faces north, and it has a hearth, it's quite big and it would do very nicely. And it's not as if I don't have contacts, I can paint Henry Jermyn, and perhaps his uncle too, and Hugh, and they can spread the word. There are people who come to the house to see Dan, as well, to buy clocks. If I hung pictures in the hallway and in Dan's workshop, they'd be seen and remarked upon. There might be quite a lot of custom to be gained that way.'

She looked up at her father, seeing his thoughtful face, and prayed that her argument had reached him. He was staring at the window she had indicated, then he turned to face her. 'And what materials would you need? Canvas, paint, oil . . . I shouldn't imagine it will be cheap.'

And her parents were by no means rich, despite their comfortable home and acreage of Oxfordshire land; not at all wealthy compared to Daniel Ashley, whose clock-making had amassed him a small fortune in gold, luckily deposited with a Cheapside goldsmith who had, along with most others of his trade, placed his valuables in the Tower. Dan, therefore, was still rich, unlike those whose wealth lay in the property which had been burnt in the Fire. He could afford to rebuild the House of the Ash Tree on a lavish scale, from materials less combustible than timber and plaster, but she could not possibly ask him for help. Nor, in all conscience could she ask Francis, except that, as she realised it, he was offering. 'Dear maw – if you want some money to help you start, then I'll gladly give you what you need. It may not be very much, but it will be enough to get you started.' He looked at his daughter, and grinned. 'Always assuming you're not too extravagant with the ultramarine.'

'How did you know about the price of ultramarine?' Alathea enquired, her mind still trying to grasp the enormity of what he had said. She was not going to be pressurised into marrying Jasper: instead, her father would give her the essential coin to set herself up as a portrait painter. She felt a great tide of excitement burst within her, an extraordinary emotion compounded of delight and fear. She had talked about this often enough: now she would have to prove herself.

She thanked him profusely, still grappling with that exhilarating, yet terrifying prospect, and had to make an effort to listen when he spoke again. 'I remember Master Lely telling you that he could spare you none of it. He's a neighbour of yours, I understand?'

'Yes – he has one of the houses in this row, but on the other side of James Street.' Alathea grinned. 'Some would say it's a touch pretentious even for Master Lely: it's a bigger house than this.' She grinned wider, feeling all of a sudden ridiculously happy. 'Master Cooper's house is much smaller, and he's twice the artist Lely is. You ought to have him limn you and Mother – he's not cheap, but you'll get a very fine pair of pictures for your money.'

'I'd rather be painted by you, maw,' said Francis, and smiled at her. 'It might be cheaper, but it would be worth far more to us.' He set his hands on her shoulders. 'Well, my Thea? Are you equal to it? Can you take the little we offer you and turn it to gold? Can you be better than Lely, and yet not join his game?'

'I think so,' said Alathea, squaring her stance under his intent gaze. 'I can't promise anything, except that I'll do my best. Always. And I'll try not to let you down – or spend the money on drink or loose men.'

Her father gave one of his snorts of dry laughter. 'Loose men? You'd be decidedly fortunate if you could pay for even half a loose man on the amount I'm going to give you. Mind you, this city is full of 'em: you might not need to pay so high.' He studied her thoughtfully. 'But you may need some friendly male face, to protect you from all those loose men who might want more from you than a smile and a picture. Dan, of course, while you're under his roof, but if you should ever decide to strike out on your own, you'll need someone to look after you. And if only from that point of view, a husband is worth considering . . . no?'

'*No.*'

'You'll have to tell him yourself,' said her father. 'You owe him that, at the least. Thea . . .. there's no harm in him, even if he's a touch hasty in his actions. And he loves you, not a doubt of it. So be kind to him, maw? Don't hurt him too much, he's worth more than that.'

'I'll try not to,' said Alathea. She knew he was right, she knew she had to break the news gently, but she shrank from doing it, from bringing sorrow and disappointment to that pleasant, enthusiastic, idealistic person in whom, despite herself, she had seen something special. It must be done, however. Jasper Sewell would be despatched, grief-stricken, back to Bury and out of her life, to make what he could of his own.

She talked with her father for a while longer, discussing practical matters: the quantities of paint to buy, the quality and size of canvas, colourmen and frame-makers, the charges she might make. They pondered the question of whether Hugh could keep an eye on her, and decided that his Court duties rather precluded it. It seemed, therefore, that Alathea would have to stay with the Ashleys for the present, but the Covent Garden house was ideal, and certainly there would be no trouble with wild courtiers while Dan was in charge. Alathea could see the good sense of this. She had already some inkling, through that walk across the Piazza to Samuel Cooper's, the day when she had met Hugh again, of the perils and pitfalls lurking in wait for a young girl alone in the city. The Ashleys would provide a steady, safe background while she experimented with portraiture, until she felt ready to strike out on her own.

'Now, I've much to discuss with Dan and Lucy,' her father said, at the end of all this. 'And you must go see Jasper: we've kept him waiting an hour or more already. I should do it now, before your courage can fail you: and remember what I said.'

'I will,' said Alathea, resolutely. They walked into the house together, arm in arm, two tall pale-haired figures: and Jasper, who had been watching for a while from the first-floor window of the small, rear parlour, turned away and strove to calm himself. He knew what was to be said, every line in her upright determined carriage spoke of duties to be done and unpleasantness to be endured, and he did not know how he would bear it.

It might not have been any consolation to him, to know that Alathea, also, could not imagine whether or not she was going to cope with the next few minutes or so. It was easy, in his absence, to mock and denigrate and rage against her unwelcome suitor, but far more difficult to face him and tell him of it. It was the hardest thing she had had to do in all her seventeen years and three months of life – harder by far than brazenly walking into Lely's house, or Samuel Cooper's, to ask for help and advice.

But she must get it over and done with, and so she set her shoulders and held her head high and somehow made herself feel remote and detached from it all, because it was only, really, the painting that mattered to her. Then, she knocked briefly at the door and went in.

Jasper stood diffidently in the centre of the room. He looked, like her father, unfashionable but far more human with his own hair, rather than the great artificial heap of curls that was the modish periwig. She still had not grown used to Hugh's. She saw in his face, white and strained so that all his numerous freckles stood out like blemishes against the pale skin, the recognition of defeat. 'I'm sorry,' she said. Somehow, most words seemed awkward, superfluous, when each could tell so clearly what the other was thinking.

'I'm sorry too. Sorry for putting you to this . . . inconvenience.'

'No, no, you needn't apologise . . . if you feel truthfully, strongly enough for something,' said Alathea, her long clear eyes staring straight into his, 'you can't deny it, ever.'

'As you know also . . . is it because of the painting?'

'Yes. I can't . . . I *have* to do it, or I wouldn't be Alathea. You do understand, don't you?'

'I understand . . . I don't like it, or necessarily agree with it, but I understand. So your mind is quite made up?'

'Yes – and it always has been, since I was little. It's not you, I would say no to anyone . . . I wish it hadn't been you because I like you very much – and so I'm sorry.'

'It's your decision,' said Jasper softly, 'and I respect you for it. But if you should ever change your mind . . . I will be there.'

'No!' Alathea cried, stung into anger. 'Don't be such a fool . . . forget all about me and find some nice Suffolk girl and marry her.'

'There aren't any eligible Jermyns left,' said Jasper, with a trace of his old wry humour.

'Well, try some Gages or Herveys, then, there must be someone, but don't for God's sake waste your life moping because I turned you down. Apart from anything else,' said Alathea briskly, to disguise her wrought-up state of nerves, 'it'd make me feel very guilty, and I hardly think that's fair.'

'I would rather be faithful in vain,' said Jasper, with a sad dignity that all at once wrung her heart, 'than indulge in betrayal. Perhaps we can be friends still. And I wish you the best of all possible luck with your painting: from what I've seen, you deserve to do well.' He gave her a brave gallant smile. 'And perhaps one day you will paint me – who knows?'

'Who knows?' Alathea echoed, repeating that hollow smile. With a sudden desire to end the interview now, before it could become yet more painful, she held out her hand abruptly. 'I *am* sorry. Truly. I wish it could have worked, in a way: but I must be true to myself. Goodbye.'

'You are right, now,' Jasper told her softly. 'But one day you may find that you are wrong: till then, goodbye.' He took her hand in his, and raised it gently to his lips in a curiously forlorn, protective gesture. 'God keep you safe, my dear love, and above all, keep you happy.'

And with those parting words, he left her life.

PART TWO

The picture-drawer

1667–74

What vain, unnecessary things are men!
How well we do without 'em!

(Rochester, 'Fragment')

CHAPTER ELEVEN

A court of Jermyns

The desire accomplished is sweet to the soul
(*Proverbs, 13:19*)

Henry Jermyn looked at Henry Jermyn, plump, periwigged, lecherous, sly and just a little ridiculous, and decided abruptly that he did not like himself, or at least, not that particular image of himself. A shame, to be sure, for it was beautifully painted, and very like – too like for his comfort, in fact. Having that unidealised portrait leering down from the wall of his Whitehall lodging would cast a gloom on any amour, and he could imagine only too clearly what Barbara would say if she saw it.

'Well?' asked the clear-eyed, uncomfortably percipient painter of this undoubted work of art. 'What do you think of it?'

'It's not what *I* think of it. It's what Barbara will think of it that worries me.'

'O-ho,' said Alathea, who had long ago lost any awe she might have felt for Hugh's courtier friends, 'are you angling for the Castlemaine again?'

The look which Henry Jermyn gave her was the mirror of the one on his painted face. 'I might be. What business is it of yours, eh?'

'None at all,' said Alathea cheerfully. She wiped her hands and the brush on a piece of rag and came over to stand at his side. Even with his fashionable cork heels, he was aggrieved to see that he was the smaller by some two or three inches. 'But I do like to keep up with the gossip,' she added. 'Otherwise, I might commit some fearful solecism – such as inviting you and John Churchill and that rope-dancer and the Castlemaine to sittings on the same day.'

Not at all pleased by her casual reference to his lady's previous loves, Henry snorted. 'You wouldn't want to paint the rope-dancer. He has legs like hams, and a brain to match. God knows why she ever took up with him.'

'A taste for the high life, perhaps?' Alathea enquired demurely, and Henry, despite himself, laughed. He had agreed to sit for her at Hugh Trevelyan's insistence, and the urgings of his sister-in-law Henrietta, and because his family and hers had been friends and rivals for well over a hundred years in their two lovely moated mansions scarce two miles apart in the depths of Suffolk. And also, there was no denying the attraction of her astonishing beauty, the ashen hair and long eyes and ethereal face, coupled with that mischievous, ironic humour and her unusual and undeniable talent for portrait painting. His own list of previous loves was easily the match of Barbara Castlemaine's, he had an enviable reputation for his prowess and he would dearly have liked to add Alathea Heron to all those languishing maids-of-honour and actresses, but he knew full well that he would incur Hugh Trevelyan's wrath if he so much as laid a finger on her. And due in part to Hugh's protection, and to the plain honest presence of Daniel Ashley and his family, but largely to her own friendly, witty, worldly yet innocent manner, she had remained unpestered, unmolested despite a growing procession of sitters eager to have their likenesses immortalised by this entertaining curiosity.

She had begun with the money lent by her father, and the help of her uncle Dan in displaying the portraits of Rosalind and Oliver in prominent positions in the house. Customers who had come to Covent Garden to order clocks had shown interest, asked questions, and one or two brave souls had climbed the stairs to the wide, bare attic where Alathea had set up her studio. Her first paid commissions had been an honest alderman friend of Dan's, and his overdressed, unrefined wife. The irony with which she had painted his rather piggy eyes and her fussy layers of neckwear had gone unnoticed, and she had received the princely sum of five pounds for the pair, not including the florid gilt frames which the worthy alderman's taste demanded. That five pounds had purchased more canvas and pigment. Nell helped her to prepare oils and grind paints, Oliver lent a reluctant hand with stretching and framing the canvases, and there was enough of the money left over to buy a little, a very little of the valuable ultramarine. But her first flush of triumph soon died. For weeks no other patrons appeared, winter set in, the attic room grew cold despite the fire, and her fingers too numb to wield a brush, until Hugh, coming for a farewell visit before going to France with Henry Jermyn's uncle, Lord St Albans, took one look at her pinched face and decided with uncharacteristic generosity to pay her for making a full-sized portrait of him, in oils.

'I can't take any money from you!' Alathea had exclaimed. She knew that almost all his expenditure went, of necessity, on the trappings of Court life: clothes, entertainments, gaming, wine, women, song. And he had had very little to begin with. But Hugh had insisted, and as usual got his own way. The sittings were accomplished in the week or so until his departure for France, and he had paid her three pounds for a handsome three-quarter-length of himself with olive-wreath and dove, a neat allusion to his peacemaking mission to Paris. It was a portrait which emphasised his charm and humour, and Hugh was delighted with it, even if, as he pointed out, the wreath did make him look like some drunken old Greek philosopher. He kept his other promise, too, and when the Earl of St Albans sailed for France, in January 1667, he carried in his train not only Hugh Trevelyan, whose clear-eyed subtle cynicism he liked and valued on a delicate task such as this, but Hugh's hopeful cousin Sir Christopher Drakelon, eager to see the world and taste the delights of Paris. So, she was safe from Kit, who had been a lurking threatening shadow at the back of her mind for a year and more, and before he left, Hugh had promised to do his best to persuade his aristocratic friends to sit for their portraits as well. But there had been no Court commissions, only a trickle, growing to a steady flow, of City clients, friends and acquaintances of Dan, until now, early in August, when Henry Jermyn had arrived unannounced on the doorstep and requested a portrait. Alathea suspected that Henrietta had been persuasive, but Henry had also had a series of letters from Hugh in France, each one ending with a severe admonition to be sure and go to Alathea for a sitting.

Reminded of them now, she said conversationally, 'Have you any news of Hugh?'

Henry's jovial dark eyes, as bright and mischievous as a goblin's, glanced round at her. 'Why, yes, as a matter of fact I had a letter come this morning. Have you had nothing, then?'

Under his inquisitive gaze, Alathea blushed, very slightly. 'No. My last letter from Hugh arrived a month ago. I've had one from Kit more recently.'

More than ever, Henry Jermyn wondered why Hugh did not take advantage of the obvious affection Alathea had for him: he would in his place, dammit, and ignore the inconvenient fact that she was his niece. He could not for the life of him understand his friend's quite uncharacteristic scruples, but if that was the way Hugh wanted it to be, then good luck to him. He smiled. 'Well, it seems your brother Kit has been up to God knows what.'

'Kit?' Alathea stared at him in bewilderment. 'He – he seemed – well, his letter seemed quite normal. What's he been doing? Has he been rude to the King?'

Henry guffawed. 'No, surprisingly enough – hot-tempered, your brother, ain't he? – but it's near enough as bad. He's half-killed some fine Frenchman in a duel.'

'A *duel*? Kit, fighting a *duel*? He hardly knows one end of a sword from the other – unless he's been practising in secret. I don't believe you,' said Alathea, grinning. 'Give over, Henry, you're making it up.'

'Not at all – you can read Hugh's letter, if you like.' And Henry Jermyn pulled it from his capacious pocket and handed it to her.

It was certainly Hugh's handwriting, full of loops and unnecessary flourishes, and it was dated from Paris, a week previously. Anxiously, Alathea's quick eye skimmed down the page until arrested by sight of her own name. It proved to be contained in a sentence beginning, 'And I beg you, do not tell Alathea anything of this . . . '

'I'm not supposed to know of it!' she said, turning to the unrepentant Henry. 'He told you not to tell me.'

'Well, I thought you should know – you're Kit's sister, after all,' said Henry, who could not have cared less what his own five sisters did. Alathea, feeling his beady eyes fixed upon her, continued to read with a growing sense of astonishment, and anger, and something else she could not – or would not – name.

Kit, according to Hugh, had conceived a passion for some unnamed lady attached to the Court of King Louis, and the lady, apparently, had returned his feelings, her husband being at the time on his country estate in the Loire valley. Such a liaison was not surprising, the lady being an accredited beauty who had the reputation of being most liberal with her favours, and Kit very much the suave English gentleman, with enough manners and intelligence to disguise his lack of experience in such matters, and his astonishing good looks into the bargain. The affair had become the talk of the French Court, with much bawdy comment at the way it mirrored the peace negotiations between England and

France, until, unexpectedly, the lady's husband had returned, and proved unusually obstructive. When Kit had failed to withdraw quietly and conveniently, the incensed and choleric Frenchman had challenged him to a duel. The choice of weapons had been pistols and Kit, far more adept with these than with a sword, had done the Frenchman some considerable damage: so that, Hugh wrote, his life was at present despaired of, the bullet having lodged close to his heart. The affray had not helped the cause of peace one jot, and had Kit not been persuaded to go almost instantly into hiding, serious harm might well have been done to negotiations.

'I know not where Kit is now, save that he is no longer with us in Paris,' Hugh had written. 'Rumour has it that he has gone south towards Italy: rumour may be a lying jade, but on this occasion I feel she is right. To be honest, I am not particularly concerned. He has plenty of money, he is resourceful, he is quite capable of looking to himself. He is after all nearly twenty-four, and a full year older than I! And between you and me, I am sufficiently annoyed and irritated to wish him to the devil. They say Hell lies under Vesuvius; he'd best be careful if Satan is not to claim him for his own. The lady was lovely, but not worth the trouble, and the jeopardy of our mission. I did not think him such a fool.'

Nor did Alathea: and yet she knew, none better, how her half-brother's obsessions could run amok into violence. And she could imagine, with a sudden terrifying clarity, the scenes of seduction, the husband's discovery, and above all the duel, and the contemptuous sneer on Kit's face as he raised the pistol to fire . . .

Had he, she wondered with pain and anger, turned all the thwarted feelings he had had for her, on to some light Frenchwoman who from the sound of it was, in the Widow Gooch's phrase, 'no better than she should be'? Her thoughts ran chaotically back to that Christmas, eighteen months ago, and the burning, devouring, passionate eyes that dominated the face descending to kiss her . . .

For a long time she had extinguished that memory, and now it returned with dreadful force, reminding her of that strange bittersweet time when Kit had been her friend, her chosen companion, and she had tried to ignore what her heart told her. With resolution, she looked back on those days, remembering her own feelings: her delight at the sudden alleviation of her boredom, the pleasure of Kit's flattering attentions, her dismissal of the warnings of the Widow and the fainter, more distant alarms of her instinct. She had encouraged Kit, welcomed him, enjoyed flirting, yes, that was the despicable but entirely apposite word for what she had done. She had flirted with her own brother, and was now aggrieved and dismayed when her feelings had seemed to be returned. For a moment, so great was the torrent of self-hatred, that she could cheerfully have put her fist through the window: but the thought of what Henry Jermyn's bright-eyed gossip would make of that, quickly brought her back to reality. She had seen other girls tease and flirt with their brothers, none more so than Rosalind and Oliver, Sophie and Matthew, but that was entirely harmless. She herself could not possibly have known of Kit's terrible obsession until it was too late: and her own innocence, her own honesty had blinded her to the truth, and her love of danger and excitement had led her on.

And now Kit was disgraced, had forfeited even Hugh's respect and affection, was adrift and friendless in Europe. And she *knew*, she did not think it was fanciful or conceited, but she *knew* that this obsessive, disastrous, passion had sprung from her rejection of him. The thought leapt into her mind: had that lovely Parisian ladybird also been tall and slender, with ash-fair hair?

Abruptly, she turned to Henry, fighting off the demons of anger, or sorrow, or . . . jealousy? She held out the letter to him, steeling every ounce of her flesh to remain still and cool under that greedy gaze. 'Thank you. I expect I'll hear more of it from Hugh, when he writes. Now, I know what I wanted to ask you – how is Beth?'

Henreitta's eldest child, a sturdy, red-haired six-year-old, had recently been struck by some unidentified childish fever. Henry stared at her as if unable to remember who Beth was. *His own niece*, thought Alathea with a certain amount of contempt. Then the pudgy face cleared. 'Ah! Beth! Still abed, I hear, and now little Harry has taken it too. Hen was well-nigh distracted when I spoke to her, but she's sure to be making too much of it. All mothers do, they magnify a cough into a cold and a cold into a fever and a fever into the lung sickness, till the child's at death's door before it's got more than three pimples. They'll all be as fit as fiddles inside a week. And now, what do you want for your splendid picture, my sweet Thea?'

Half an hour later his sweet Thea had persuaded him to part with five pounds in exchange for the portrait, framed, and Henry Jermyn had left the Covent Garden house: and the air felt somehow fresher. At least, thought Alathea, tidying the brushes and scraping her palette carefully of unused paint, that picture might, with a bit of luck, frighten off the Castlemaine. She had a suspicion that Henry Jermyn would be no match for that lady.

And he had given her much to think about. Kit, whether or not the guilty party, forced to flee from France, for reasons which astonished her. And yet . . . were they so strange? He was twenty-four, he could be said to be a young man of estate and culture, a man of the world. Henry Jermyn at the same age had had dozens of lovers, most of them married, and including, so rumour had it, the Princess of Orange before her untimely death. Why should Kit's one affair shock her so much? At least it proved that he could look at other women besides his sister.

I am not going to think of it, said Alathea resolutely to herself. *I will go and see Henrietta in Westminster: It sounds as if she is very anxious about Beth and Harry, and Hen never worries for no reason, however much Henry might denigrate her fears.* And she put on cloak and hood and mask, the better to shield herself against the heat of the August sun, and any leering glances she might attract, and asked Nell if she would like to go with her to Westminster.

For a miracle, Nell was not sewing. She was reading one of the French romances to which, due not a little to Lucy's influence, she had recently become addicted. Increasing maturity had been kind to Nell. Now eighteen and a half, six months older than Alathea, she had lost much of that gaunt bony look, and acquired a more upright carriage, though the slender shoulders were still wont to hunch, especially over a book. Her skin had cleared of spots and had now the fashionable look of pallor, unsullied by freckle or pimple, and she had at last begun regularly curling and washing her hair, so that 'mouse' was no longer a just description of its colour. She had more to say for herself, too, even if sometimes it revealed that, in Hugh's vivid Suffolk phrase, 'she was too green to burn'. But she was still quiet, shy, retiring, too anxious to please even when, as now, it was very plain that she did not really want to leave her book and venture down to Westminster in the heat of the day.

Alathea, as usual, was quite ruthless, and after bespeaking a waterman at the Exchange Stairs, they took a boat up the cool Thames, breezy and ruffled and so much more pleasant than the sweaty packs in the Strand and Charing Cross. In front of them the sun glittered and spun on the rippling water, on their left the dank waste of Lambeth Marsh and on the right, the unglamorous huddle of Whitehall, the coney-warren of a palace that was the Court's lair. But Alathea also looked back, seeing the great sweep of the river as it swung east, and still, abruptly, the huge grey gap where less than a year ago, London had stood. There were buildings going up now, brave outposts in the thief-infested desolation within the City walls, but you could still stand where Cheapside had been, and watch the boats on the river.

They alighted at Westminster Stairs, and went to find Antelope Alley, Alathea looking, as she always did, for the crooked chimney of the house on the corner. One day, after a winter gale perhaps, that chimney would no longer be there, and Antelope Alley would be harder to find, but today her eye located it unerringly, and they entered the London alley gloom and knocked on the door of the lodgings inhabited by Henrietta and Charles Jermyn, and their three children.

No answer. Alathea tried again: still no response. Nell frowned. 'Perhaps they've gone for a stroll in the park.'

'No, they can't have – Henry said Beth had a fever, and Harry was ill too, and Hen was worried. He didn't think much of it, but if Hen's worried, she must have cause.' Alathea belaboured the door-knocker again.

Abruptly the door was swung away from her, leaving her hand ludicrously upraised, and Henrietta herself stood there. She was dreadfully changed from the robust, plump Hen whom Alathea had last seen just over a week previously, almost unrecognisably thin, with a grey and weary face out of which the practical brown eyes stared, unaltered. 'Hullo,' said Henrietta Jermyn hoarsely. 'You shouldn't come in. You'll catch the fever, if it's still contagious.'

'We came to see if you were all right,' said Alathea, shocked to the heart by the change in her friend. 'And you're not, are you? How are the children? Can we help at all?'

'Harry died about an hour ago,' said Henrietta, recording the passing of her only son, just three years old, with the flatness of total exhaustion. 'He had a convulsion and died. Beth's going to die too: she just hasn't any strength left. And the baby's taken it now, and so has Charles, and the maid won't stay, and I can't really blame her,' said Hen. 'Go away, or you'll take it too.'

Just in time, Alathea pushed her foot into the door. As she had suspected, her friend did not have the power to resist. After a token struggle, she stumbled backwards, sweat breaking out amongst the tangled red curls around her forehead, and Alathea, suddenly rather guilty about her own forcefulness, took hold of her by the arm. 'Hen! You look terrible. Are you – you haven't taken it as well, have you?'

'No – I'm all right – but I haven't slept for three days,' Hen said. She looked up at the taller girl, with all her unused health and energy. 'Will – will you stay?'

'Yes, of course I will,' said Alathea, welcoming the challenge. As she had admitted once to Jasper, she had always felt powerless, helpless in the face of disease and death, but she needed something to occupy her mind and body, something to divert her thoughts from running endlessly and futilely around the subject of Kit. But it was not fair to ask her cousin to share the same task, and she told her so. 'Go on, Nell, go back and tell Aunt Lucy where I am. Say I may be a while, and ask her for a loan of Sarah or one of the other maids to help. Please, Nell!'

Her cousin's blank, bewildered face swam pallidly in the gloom of the alley. 'You mean – you'll stay?'

'Well, Hen needs some help,' Alathea said briskly and impatiently. 'Now go on. Go!'

She had been right, Alathea reflected, several sleepless and exhausting days later: there had indeed been no time to spare for pondering the problems posed by her half-brother. She was a stranger to sickbeds, she knew nothing whatsoever of healing, but Henrietta, before she stumbled to her much-needed bed, had given her instructions which she did her best to follow, and the maid, Sarah, arriving with baskets of provisions and a trail of laden hired boys with food and blankets and spare night clothing and all the comforts of life which Lucy deemed to be necessary, proved to be very knowledgeable. Alathea gladly deferred to her instructions, and a treacherous desire crept into her head, for the calm, capable manner of Jasper Sewell.

But she suspected that even Jasper, with his extensive modern training and his fresh ideas, would have quailed before the dark foetid sickrooms, stinking of sweat and vomit and worse, the heat and the flies and the thick clogging air that was a positive discouragement to breathe. Harry's pathetic, wizened little corpse was taken away for burial in a rough wooden box which Alathea could have tucked under her arm: to be followed the next day by a larger one for Beth, whose sturdy strength had not survived the height of the fever. The baby, not two years old, was a little goblin scrap of a child called Rebecca after her Jermyn grandmother. She had always seemed to Alathea to be the most frail of the three children, but proved ironically to have a tenacious hold on life. The fever swept over her, leaving her emaciated and fretful, still more some elf's changeling than a human baby, but at least she seemed likely to recover.

Alathea drew her, lying asleep in her cot with the lank, spiky tufts of hair, cut off during her illness, giving her a hedgehog appearance. She had once seen a very beautiful, moving drawing done by Master Cooper, of someone's dead child, a babe close in age to little Rebecca, lying stiff and stark and still on its deathbed. But this child lived and breathed yet, and she occupied her mind and hand with the chalks that Nell had brought from Covent Garden on one of her innumerable visits, a lost soul, it seemed, without Alathea to follow. Lovell was brought too, and had taken up his usual position on her feet, grunting indignantly whenever she tried to move. She had, greatly daring, opened the window. Sarah had had pronounced views on the conservation of sickroom air, but Alathea, stifling and with sweat running off her almost as if she, too, had the fever, had decided she could bear it no longer. And certainly little Rebecca's quick snuffling breath seemed a little easier, her flushed forehead somewhat cooler.

The child's face and form grew on the paper, careful stroke by careful stroke. She wanted to do it slowly, without her accustomed haste. Apart from anything else, it would take her mind off the next chamber where, quickly and without protest, Charles Jermyn was also dying. Henrietta was with him, so was Sarah and a fashionable physician engaged by Charles's brother, belatedly attacked by pangs of conscience. Henry had come, and a procession of Court friends and acquaintances to bid farewell to their old gambling partner: but at last Henrietta had barred the door to them, and had insisted on her husband's final hours being private.

Alathea's untried emotions shied away from the grief of that deathbed. She could face the loss of the children, for children died with dreadful frequency, and some might say that Henrietta had been fortunate to keep three so long alive past babyhood. But to lose one's husband, the man with whom one had shared joy and sorrow, bed and board, home and children for seven years . . . ah, that was different. Alathea did not think she could cope with Hen's agony, and so had retired, to watch over Rebecca, so soon to be an orphan, and to draw her.

Charles Jermyn duly died, and his fever-wasted body was interred in St Margaret's Church alongside those of his two elder children, and amongst many others who had also died of miscellaneous diseases in the crowded tenements of Westminster that August. And contrary to Alathea's worst forebodings, Henrietta did not weep, nor wail, nor plunge herself into paroxysms of grief, but went about her suddenly empty lodgings tidying, sorting, cooking, as if nothing had happened – save for a certain gaunt, bereft look about her eyes.

It was obvious to all, however, that she could not stay there. Charles's meagre salary had paid for rent and food and little else: now even that was denied her, and there had never been any extra to lay aside for such a time as this. Henry, to give him his due, was generous with his help. He had the Jermyn flair for money-collecting, like his reprobate uncle, the Earl of St Albans. (It was an ability which, unfortunately, had completely passed Charles by.) Henry's casual shower of coin was more than adequate, but could by no means be expected to last for ever.

It was Alathea who thought of the solution to the problem. The Covent Garden house was large, comfortable, even gracious, but had so far defeated Lucy's rather inept efforts to put it in good order. Dust and cobwebs were rampant, the fires could not be made to draw properly, the smoke-jack in the kitchen still did not work, and none of the windows seemed quite clean. Henrietta needed a home for herself and her remaining child, and some outlet for her organising abilities: and the Covent Garden house needed an efficient, energetic and capable housekeeper. Alathea, convinced of the eminent suitability of the arrangement, presented her notion to both parties with some trepidation, lest there be an unseen but obvious flaw in her plans: but there was not. On the first day of September 1667, Henrietta Jermyn and her daughter Rebecca, accompanied by a pathetically small quantity of possessions, moved into a little suite of rooms on the second floor of the house, to the thorough approval of all concerned, and not least Rebecca, who early discovered the view over the Piazza and was usually to be found kneeling on the windowseat, her nose squashed against the glass, murmuring happily and unintelligibly about events outside. From that day on, a certain transformation began to overtake the somewhat haphazard life in the Ashley household. Meals arrived at the appointed hour, well-cooked. The house seemed suddenly lighter, as glass was cleaned, paint-work washed, surfaces dusted. There were flowers in bowls and jugs, herbs in pots in the garden, furniture shining and polished. Henrietta had the gift of home-making, of being able to add just those touches which had made even the squalid Westminster lodging a place to be proud of, and she combined with that, an enviable ability to organise and direct without ever seeming intrusive or overbearing.

And above all, she was a friend, which Alathea felt in some need of, at this time. True, she was busy again with her painting: a friend of Henry's had arranged to sit for her after her return from Westminster, and there were other, unfinished commissions to fulfill. But there was still no news of Kit, and a very uninformative epistle from Hugh spoke of the incident in the vaguest terms. Peace had been signed at last with Dutch and French, in July at Breda, but not before the Dutch, with remarkable daring and initiative, had sailed into the Medway and wreaked havoc amongst the ships there. Lord St Albans, fond of all things French, had lingered in Paris, and Hugh, who knew which side his bread was buttered, was still with him. Alathea missed him greatly. Contrary to Henry Jermyn's sly imaginings, she was not in love with her uncle, never had been and never would be, but he was like a brother, a true friend and confidant, someone to whom she could bare her soul. No one else in London, not even her cousin Rosalind, could take his place, and Ros was now almost entirely taken up with plans for her forthcoming marriage.

It had not altogether been a surprise: if ever anyone was made for comfortable matrimony, it was Rosalind. But she was young, a year younger than Alathea, and seventeen was thought by some to be a very early age to assume the mantle of running a household and ministering to a husband. Lucy, however, had other ideas, and Rosalind, more and more cat-like and smug with every day that passed, seemed to agree. A procession of eligible young men began to parade through the house, in numbers to match Alathea's painting clients: inspected by Dan for their wealth, by Lucy for their charm and personalities, and by Rosalind for their looks. Most passed at least one test, several passed two, but no one matched up to all three sets of requirements, of which Rosalind's were easily the most exacting.

Alathea, perched in her garret, felt rather aloof from these proceedings, which she could not help viewing with a somewhat jaundiced eye. If Ros wanted to be wed to one of those singularly uninspiring young men, then good luck to her: the more she saw of the murky water of the marriage market, the less she liked it. She said as much to Oliver, who now often came up to talk and share purloined food. At fifteen he was a handsome boy, with charm and a winning smile when he cared to use it, but today he was hunched moodily in the window embrasure, blocking out too much light, chewing on an unripe apple.

'Weddings? Huh, don't you dare mention weddings too – that's all that's ever talked about downstairs now.' He glowered out of the window. 'Ros has really gone to the *bad* recently. Marriage, and husbands, and love – boring, boring, *boring*! At least you don't talk about that sort of thing, you're more like a boy, really.'

'For which compliment, much thanks,' said his cousin. 'Get out of the light, will you? I can't see a thing.'

Oliver slouched over to her easel, his hands thrust deep into his pockets and a theatrical scowl on his face that reminded her strongly of her sister Sophie. 'I don't think it's worth seeing, really.'

'How dare you – it's a very good likeness.'

'Oh, I don't quarrel with the likeness – it's the face I'd quarrel with. Look at him – typical mean old City moneybags!'

'Don't let your father hear you saying that – Master Reece is one of his greatest friends.'

'Gives him the best interest on his money, you mean.' Oliver stabbed a finger at the tacky paint on the goldsmith's double chin. 'And to think that the man my sister will marry – my own brother-in-law – is going to look like that!'

'None of the young men Ros has seen have looked anything like Master Reece,' said Alathea, feeling she had to be fair.

'No matter – they all will, given twenty years. And I've made a resolve,' said Oliver, swinging round to face her. 'I am *not* going to end my days with ten thousand pounds in gold, and as many chins. I don't know how I'll spend my life but I'm *not* going to turn into a paunchy Cit. I'd rather be a pirate.'

'You'd make a good one: you've got the right scowl for it.'

'Have I?' said Oliver, sounding pleased. He turned down his mouth and rolled his eyes into a ferocious glare. 'How will that do?'

'Most excellent, and if the wind changes, you're stuck with it. So – you don't want to build clocks?'

'No – I haven't the talent for it,' said Oliver grandly, as if it were beneath him. Nor the application, Alathea added mentally, with a secret smile. Oliver was by nature and upbringing one of the idle rich, and it was fortunate that his father's wealth, and the fact that he was the only son, meant that he would never, bar disasters, be put to the trouble of earning his own living. Perhaps some of Dan's accumulated gold would be used to set Oliver up, with a rich young heiress maybe, on some country estate not too far from London.

As if reading her thoughts, her young cousin went on. 'I'd like to have a house – like Goldhayes, but not so grand as that, unless Father invents some miraculously accurate clock – and some land, and a coach, and to dance at Whitehall and ogle all the maids. Why are you smiling?'

'Because talking about dancing at Whitehall seems to be a metaphor for something long promised that will never actually happen. Hugh was always saying he would take me dancing at Whitehall, and he never has, and I reckon he never will. Anyway,' said Alathea, laughing at herself, 'I'll never, ever be dressed fine enough for it. I'll stay here and paint pictures.'

'And is that *all* you want to do? Paint pictures, for ever and ever? Don't *you* want . . . ?'

'*Don't* say a husband, or I'll bring Master Reece down about your ears.'

'I wasn't going to,' Oliver protested. 'But . . . don't you want to have a fine house? And lots of servants, and jewels, and beautiful clothes, and money to spend on gaming, and a coach and horses? Like Master Lely?'

'Master Lely has all those things, I'll grant you, but he paid for them with his soul. Oh, I do want success, but for its own sake, not for the money it would bring me. I want people to recognise me as an artist, as a good painter – I don't mind much about money, so long as I've got enough to pay for my paints and my food.'

Oliver digested this startling information in silence. Finally, he said thoughtfully, 'But people do think you're a good artist. We all do. And Master Cooper does, and Hugh, and Henry Jermyn.'

'Yes, but that's not a great many, is it?' Alathea, moved urgently by her need to explain, turned and prowled restlessly over to the window and back. 'I want – recognition – from the many, not the few. I want London to know of me, and come to my door to learn the truth, not to look at flattering lies. I don't want to eke out a humble humdrum existence, like Mistress Beale, and I don't want Lely's kind of fame either, all fashion and no substance. I want to tread between them. And I *know* I can, if I'm given the chance. But painting a string of Master Reeces won't bring me the custom I want.'

'But painting Henry Jermyn will?'

'Yes, with a little luck. He didn't like that picture, but he knew it was a good portrait, and he promised to direct his uncle, St Albans, to me, when he returns from France. And if I can paint St Albans, that'll be the biggest fish yet!' Alathea turned abruptly to the window again, and then swung round, her eyes huge and vivid and shining with passion and excitement. 'And *then* I'll show them what I can do – they won't possibly be able to ignore me then – no more patronising chat about being very good for a *woman*, but no, I can't do more because I'm only a girl. I'll *force* them all to take notice, you see if I don't!'

And such was her urgent certainty that Oliver believed it too. But Alathea, deep within her, knew as he did not, how little was her need to be praised by all the world, and how great her desire for the approval, the recognition, the admiration of her half-brother, Kit Drakelon.

The elder Henry Jermyn, Earl of St Albans, returned from France in the autumn, with some reluctance. The country was his second home, and somehow so much more elegant, aristocratic, exotic than England, with its lazy, devious, good-humoured King and slatternly Court, where the passports to eminence were wit, beauty, and impertinence. King Louis, on the other hand, was a very different monarch, who expected, and received, a proper deference and remoteness at his Court.

And besides, the food was so good.

Hugh Trevelyan, who travelled back to England in his train, was glad to leave France in at least one respect. That excellent eating had added unwanted inches to his girth, and he could not afford the expense of a new waistcoat. Alathea had been right, he thought with wry amusement, watching the pale cliffs of England heave and toss ahead of him: he was getting poddy. And it was curious to think that of all the fifty or so people aboard the ship, only he and the Earl of St Albans would appreciate the phrase, being alike Suffolk born and bred.

He was glad to be home. He would see Alathea, and tell her stories of France to make her laugh, and he would have good news for her too. He had persuaded Lord St Albans to sit for his portrait. It was not long since Lely had painted him, but he had not been particularly satisfied with it, and after he had admired Hugh's miniature, that born opportunist had seized his chance, and his mentor had found himself agreeing to sit for some chit of a girl from that upstart family the Herons. Hugh, who had of course not yet seen her interpretation of Lord St Albans' nephew, wondered what picture she would make of this fat, cunning, pleasure-loving man who was yet such a good servant to the Crown. He hoped she would flatter him, just a little, for Lord St Albans, after so many years in politics and on embassies, steering delicate courses between one side and another, had long abandoned any altruistic quest for the truth and was concerned only with outward show. It would be an interesting lesson in diplomacy for Alathea: for her sake, he hoped she would make some compromise. Perhaps her mood would be more relaxed when she had heard his other news.

He went to see her the day after his arrival in London, and was delighted at having to kick his heels in the company of Rosalind and Nell, because Alathea was engaged in painting a client. (Master Reece had been so impressed by her portrayal of his chins and fine lace that he had ordered a companion-piece of his wife.) He heard about Henrietta's bereavement and new home, and of Rosalind's latest and most suitable suitor so far: a quiet, self-contained young man, by the sound of it, and only son and heir of a mercer whose goods and property had mostly been in Bishopsgate, and had therefore escaped the Fire. And he took note of

Rosalind's new sleekness and Nell's pretty dress and curled hair, and wondered what changes he would find in Alathea, in the nine or ten months since he had seen her last.

None at all, was the answer, when Mistress Reece and her maid had taken coach for their temporary home in Holborn, and he could ascend to that light, aromatic room at the top of the house, to speak with his niece. She was just the same Thea, tall and spare, with one of Dan's old shirts thrown over her gown in a rather unsuccessful attempt to ward off the mess, cleaning brushes and coaxing the paint back into pigs' bladder containers. As soon as she saw him, all the business-like professionalism dropped away and she was Thea again. With a cry of delight, she abandoned the brushes and ran to greet him. He took her into one of his rib-squeezing hugs. 'And how's my favourite niece, then? Phew, you smell!'

'Well, that's a fine welcome, I must say. Couldn't you think of anything better, after all this time? Or have you still got French perfumes in your nose?'

'No – I've just forgotten how pungent all your evil substances are. How can you bear it? How can you smell anything else afterwards?'

'I must admit it takes me a while to appreciate roses, after painting. Oh, Hugh,' said Alathea, breathless and grinning with her happiness, 'I *am* glad you've returned. There's few people I can talk *to* as well as I can talk to you. Rosalind and Nell, I tend to talk *at*, and they're both in their own private worlds – as I am in mine,' she added, with disarming honesty. 'Well, what do you think of Mistress Reece?'

Hugh inspected the lady in question. 'I'm glad I didn't bump into her on the stairs – I fear from the look of her I'd have been trampled underfoot.'

'She's a very good and virtuous lady,' Alathea said. 'She just happens to weigh twenty stones. I was kind enough to have her shed five or six of them between my eye and the canvas. Don't sneer at her, Hugh, just because she's a Cit's wife. She's entertaining company, and she's a better gossip than anyone else I know, even Henry Jermyn.'

'I won't sneer,' said Hugh. 'I direct my somewhat limited energies into other paths – such as entertaining My Lord of St Albans. Do you know, he ate them entirely out of beef at the

Dover inn – admittedly they didn't have much to start with, and they had us to contend with as well, but he must have accounted for half a cow.' He grinned at her. 'So you'll need a very big canvas for him, Thea my girl.'

'What? Is he coming to sit for me? Hugh, you're wonderful!'

'Yes, I know. That's partly why I'm here – I've been sent to arrange a convenient time for the first consultation. It'll have to be very grand, Thea – no informal portrait minus wig and robes, and definitely no uncomfortable insights into what passes for his mind.' He added slyly, 'I saw Henry's portrait last night. Up very fine it is, in his Whitehall lodgings. I think he's quite brave, myself: in my place, I'd have turned it against the wall!'

'It wasn't such a bad likeness, was it?'

'No – just an uncommonly penetrating one. Turn the same gaze on Henry's uncle, and you'll not get the price of the paint.'

'I thought he was one of the wealthiest men at Court.'

'He is, which means he's also one of the most careful with his money. How else do you think he conserved and added to it, with only a younger son's portion? I don't much care for the man,' said Hugh, speaking thoughtfully of his employer and mentor, 'but I respect his judgement and example. I don't mean to eke out an irregular Court pension that's so small I'm hard-pressed to catch sight of it. Hugh Trevelyan will end his days in comfort, and he doesn't much care how he goes about it. But you . . . you're too open, too honest, too uncompromising. You expect everyone to be like you, follow your rules, and they won't. If Lord St Albans wants a pretty picture to hang at his splendid new house in St James's, then for the sake of your future I would give him one.'

'I don't know if I can,' said his niece. 'But do you remember what your old nurse Rose used to say? "I'll hev a hack at that," she said when things looked difficult. Don't worry, Hugh, I'll have a hack at painting Lord St Albans in the style to which he has become accustomed, but somehow my hand may not let me.'

Hugh looked at her with fondness. Odd how someone apparently so easy-going should be so utterly uncompromising (save for Mistress Reece's shed stones) in the matter of her art. But she would not be Alathea if she was not, and he had no great hopes of Lord St Albans' satisfaction in this matter. He did not fear for his own position if the artist he recommended should fail to come up to His Lordship's expectations. His mentor was not, with all his faults, a petty man. But this would be the first great chance of Alathea's career, and in her place he would have made any number of compromises in return for the fame and recognition she so greatly desired.

But he was not Alathea, and all he could do was watch, and guide, and support. He said, 'When would be convenient for him to come and sit for you?'

'I'll have to consult my journal,' said Alathea, grinning. 'No, don't worry, I've not reached the point that Lely has, booking 'em in by the hour from dawn to dusk, but my mind's not so organised that I can carry everything in my head.' She opened a drawer in the little desk upon which she executed her miniatures, and brought out a tiny leather-bound book. Hugh, looking over her shoulder, saw that it contained a combination of accounts, payments, expenditure and appointments, marked off daily. Against this date, Tuesday 15 October 1667, was written in her quick scrawl, 'Mrs Reece, ten o'clock': on the day before, details of a payment to Master Norris, the frame-maker in Long Acre. The next two days were blank, and on the Friday one Master Thompson was booked to sit in the afternoon. 'Another friend of Dan's,' she explained, seeing him looking. 'His son was angling for Ros, but she didn't like him. He did like the picture of her that I painted, though, so his father has commissioned me to do the whole family: and don't look so impressed, there's only father and son and daughter. If Lord St Albans can come tomorrow, or better still Thursday, we can discuss the pose and his costume and all the other details.' She looked round at Hugh, her eyes suddenly very wide and dark. 'If I was younger, or more nervous, I think I'd panic. He may once have been plain Harry Jermyn, but he's a great man now, and full of state. What will he think of my little studio, all bare and plain and with no assistants, when he's been used to Lely's? What am I going to say to a man who hobnobs with kings and is supposed to have been married to the Queen Mother? I am *not* going to panic, Hugh, I am *not* – but I can't help feeling a little scared.'

'You'll manage. You'll charm him, as you charmed Cooper, and Lely, and me, and Henry Jermyn. You sawny fule, you'll always charm any man worth his salt: one sort will be snared by your looks, and the other by your mind.'

'And which sort is Lord St Albans? If he's like Henry, I'd best wear my most diaphanous gown and try and cover it with paint.'

'He's over sixty, I doubt he could muster the energy. Be witty and wise, speak of cards and horses and food and you'll not go far astray. Or ask him about France and he'll talk for hours about his years of exile in Paris. Can you speak French?'

'A little. We had a French lady come to us for conversation, Rosalind and I, when I was first in London. Doubtless Lord St Albans is fluent?'

'Indeed he is. He's an easy-going man, at bottom, fond of the good life. I've never found it difficult to get along of him. You're laughing again.'

'No matter how you play the sophisticate, Hugh Trevelyan, your Suffolk origins keep revealing themselves. Odd to think of it, how we all share that, even the Jermyns. I'll wager Lord St Albans doesn't talk like that now.'

'He doesn't.' Hugh watched her write the nobleman's name under Thursday's date, and his suggested time, three o'clock, beside it. She shut the book with a triumphant snap and turned to him, eyes shining. 'I may or may not be frightened of such a big commission – but it's what I've wanted so much, and it's your doing. Thank you, Hugh, and if I can ever repay you, I will.'

'Hold hard with your gratitude, I've another piece of news I was bringing to you, and you may not like it so well.' Hugh saw her eyes narrow and went on quickly. 'It's Kit – before I left France, I had a letter from him. He's in Italy, apparently, seeing all the sights – Florence, Venice, Rome, Padua, he's been to them all. And he didn't mention any plans for coming home. Yet.'

Alathea looked down at the desk: the sharpened quills, the inkstand, the ivory colour-boxes and brass sander seemed suddenly very clear and bright under her intent gaze. She thought of Italy, the name redolent of light and life, warmth and colour, like the lovely vivid pictures that Charles Beale had owned. She envied Kit, and at the same time pitied him, for she knew the emptiness of beauty without the joy of sharing it with a friend.

She said slowly, 'I'm glad he's safe. I'm glad he seems to be enjoying life. All I ever want is for him to find happiness, somehow, somewhere . . . but he has to learn that he will never have it with me.'

'I think he has learned it.'

'I hope to God he has . . . I would like him to be my friend, my brother – like you. Though you've taken his place, really. I feel safe with you, I always felt in danger when I was with Kit. Still . . . ' She shook herself, as if ridding herself of his image, still disturbing after more than a year of absence. 'I hope he's happy in Italy. Will you be with My Lord, on Thursday at least? I shall feel in need of some moral support, and Nell will be completely overawed.'

'I'll be there,' Hugh promised. 'But I may not be his only companion: others may be interested. You'll have to warn Hen that there's likely to be some demand for refreshments. Now, I must go. Goodbye, until Thursday, and take care of yourself!'

'Until Thursday, then,' Alathea repeated, and as she watched him go down the stairs, felt a surge of mixed emotions within her. Exultation at this, her most important commission yet, and also pure terror, lest it be on this occasion that her hand betray her.

When Henry Jermyn, Earl of St Albans, had negotiated his considerable bulk up the stairs on the Thursday afternoon, he brought in his train not only Hugh Trevelyan, his protégé, but four other young courtiers, including his nephew and namesake. He had seen Henry's portrait, and thought that this unknown woman had made a good job of him: a bit too good if anything, the young dog. For himself, he did not want anything grand and imposing, for he had been painted in that manner by Lely, not so long ago. Something more human, this time, was what he had in mind.

He paused for breath at the top (he knew he should not have come out so soon after such a good dinner, but young Hugh had fixed the time and had implied the girl was very busy). Behind him, Henry and Hugh and the rest of them were laughing and making some joke about ascension into Heaven, and the maid, a plain, neat, dark-haired chit at whom no man would look twice, knocked on the door and announced them with a curtsey and bated breath. 'Mistress Heron – the Earl of St Albans!'

And suddenly the bare little attic became very full of people. Alathea, in her best gown but still with an old shirt of Dan's (though a clean one) thrown over the top, curtseyed, and His Lordship bowed deep, and the maid, Sarah, seized her chance and made good her escape. She had already had orders to bring up the wine and cakes which Henrietta had made ready in the kitchen. Alathea, acutely aware of the appraising, curious eyes all fixed upon her, indicated a chair, carried up earlier by Oliver from the great chamber downstairs. 'Will you not sit, my lord, so that we may discuss the type of picture you require?'

With a grunt and a creak of limbs, her noble client sat down. He was a big, broad man with a large belly, well-hidden by his extravagant Court attire, all black velvet and rich white lace, very splendid, and crowned with a luxuriant and improbably blond periwig of which Hugh's was but the shadow. The young men, whispering and ogling, stood behind him or examined the various examples of Alathea's work propped up against the walls: the canvas of Mistress Reece, and young Master Thompson's half-finished, rather sheepish face, and various completed pictures, unframed, of members of the household: Dan, Lucy, their children, Nell and Master Hamilton and, the paint still wet, Henrietta Jermyn and her orphaned daughter Rebecca. She could hear Henry Jermyn explaining her identity and commenting (she hoped favourably) on the likeness. She turned her attention firmly to his uncle, asking him what kind of portrait he wanted, whether full-length, half-length or head and shoulders, what type of dress, formal or informal.

'I'll tell you what I have in mind, Mistress Heron,' said the Earl, when she had explained the choice, and brought out her paper and chalks to do a quick preliminary sketch. 'I saw that picture in little you did last year of young Trevelyan. Very simple, little more than the head, against a dark background. Can ye do that, d'ye think?'

Alathea stared at him, wondering if she was being covertly set down. A lay person might think that was the easiest thing to do, but in a simple picture the head stood alone, unadorned, with no sumptuous detail of drapery or landscape to distract the eye from mistakes or weaknesses. On the scale of a miniature it was essential, necessary, right, but a larger canvas was a different matter. It did remove the problem of costume and background, and she looked at those huge shoulders and the broad bullish strength in his ruddy face and knew that, with such a free hand, she was equal to the task. Quickly, with the speed and facility that people found so impressive, she sketched the heavy lines of his face and upper body, and handed it to him. 'Is that what you have in mind, my lord?'

The Earl's bushy eyebrows climbed as he studied the swift spare chalk lines. 'That's most excellently done . . . I had thought, turned perhaps to one side or the other?'

They spent the next few minutes discussing the details, each variation illustrated by one of those lightning-quick sketches, until they settled upon a pose remarkably similar to that which Alathea had seen in a self-portrait by Lely in the Beales' collection, save that it was shorter. They decided upon a size for the canvas, and parted on most amicable terms, having arranged for the sitting proper to begin the following day. And as the crowd of young hangers-on departed, Hugh caught her eye and gave her a reassuring smile and a wink.

Over the days that followed, she found the Earl a pleasant and undemanding client. He had, being a diplomat and a dabbler in affairs of state, a genial manner which put her at her ease, and she quickly lost any nervousness in his presence. It was the younger men who always seemed to accompany him, who irritated and then infuriated her. Hugh was not always amongst them, and when he was absent, the jesting comments and ogling looks increased tenfold. Inwardly seething, she had to stop her ears to the sly mocking remarks about her dress, her figure, her sex, her face and, most hurtful of all, her painting. Disparagingly, they discussed the pictures of her friends and City clients in the fashionable languid drawl – 'Egad, George, a perfect Cit down to the gold lace.' 'D'ye see that little miss? Hardly worth wasting paint on that face, eh, Jack?' – while Alathea compressed her jaw and her fingers, itching to knock their sneering heads together, and poured that frustration instead on to the canvas. Under her brush, the bulky form of Lord St Albans took shape and grew in character, from the early, flat 'dead-colouring' which sketched in his face and hair, to the detailed working-up of the heavy features, the small shrewd Jermyn eyes and fleshy nose and chins even more prominent than Master Reece's. *It's all very well for them to jeer at Cits with their quivering jowls and fussy lace*, thought Alathea, still indignant. *It's this man who looks as if he made his money selling tallow or shipping coal.*

At the end of the fifth sitting that face was complete, staring with all the arrogance of a prize bull from the canvas, the rest of the figure, cravat and black velvet, sketched in with a lightness that only served to emphasise the strength of the portrait. She could finish the rest in the studio, have it framed and sent round to the house in St James's. Lord St Albans need no longer spend his time in sittings.

He stood and stared for a long while at his painted face, fleshy hand over fleshier chins, while the inevitable crowd of younger men (six this time – word had evidently spread) jostled behind him, waiting to proffer their own comments. Alathea cleaned her brushes, a ritual which served to conceal her shaking hands. She always felt weak, drained by a prolonged bout of painting, especially when, as today, the magic tingled in her hand and every dab of paint seemed to dissolve and cohere with the rest to produce a growing, living counterfeit of her subject. She was still too close to it to be able to judge it dispassionately. She glanced round to catch Hugh's eye, but he was whispering to Henry Jermyn.

'It's a good likeness,' was the Earl's judgement, delivered weightily after prolonged thought. 'A fine portrait, Mistress Heron, and most excellent for a woman.'

If Alathea had been Lovell-our-dog, her hackles would have risen then. She remained silent as the chorus of voices rose from behind her.

'Yes, indeed, my lord, most excellent – a female Lely, to be sure!'

'A remarkable strength of brushwork, one would have thought it done by a man.'

'See how she has rendered the eyes, very perceptive in one so young and tender.'

'Young and tender!' said Alathea later to Hugh, as the wine and cakes were being consumed and she could snatch a moment or so's undisturbed conversation with him. 'It makes me sound like a carrot!'

Hugh choked suddenly over his fashionable glass of sack, and had to be discreetly thumped between the shoulderblades to restore him to normality. When able to speak again, he said, grinning, 'That's the last thing you are, dear girl. Apart from anything else, a carrot has no sensitivity, whereas you, perhaps, are possessed of too much.'

'You mean I mustn't mind what they say?'

'No – because with one or two honourable exceptions, they haven't the brain of a louse between them. His lordship reckons it's good, I could tell from his face, and you must remember, he hasn't encountered a female artist before. Your Mistress Beale doesn't move in quite such exalted circles. He only has Lely and

Cooper for comparison, and you don't quite measure up to them – yet.'

'Thank you for that last word,' said his niece. She had thrown off the old shirt and stood slim and straight beside him in her sage-green gown, the long trailing silk skirt looped back to show the fine cream embroidered petticoat beneath. She glanced down, noticed a small smudge of earth-brown marring the sleek pale folds, and hastily twitched her skirts to conceal it. Hugh, who had also noticed, gave her a swift secret smile.

Then one of the young gallants, wearing a beautiful purple velvet coat almost entirely hidden by gold lace, approached with a flourishing bow. 'My dear Mistress Heron, my compliments! Such a remarkable portrait! I declare, Lely will have to look to his laurels! And from the brush of one so young, and so enchantingly pretty, more marvellous still. When are we to see you at Whitehall, madam?'

'My uncle has promised to take me dancing there,' said Alathea sweetly, with a quick glance at Hugh. He grinned unrepentantly.

The courtier launched into yet another flowery panegyric in praise of her artistic abilities, from which it became patently obvious that he knew nothing whatsoever about painting, and then the questions began, supplemented by queries from others. How long had she practised as a painter? Not for long, surely, or the Court would have heard sooner about such a novel wonder hiding on the fringes of the City. How was such a lovely girl not yet wed? Did she have a prospective husband? Relief was expressed when she said, rather shortly, that she did not. 'For,' commented Purple Coat, 'surely a husband and children would end this exquisite gift, my dear.'

'It might,' said Alathea, determined to take all this as lightly as they intended it, though it touched a raw nerve. 'But I don't intend to put it to the test. I'm afraid I have no intention of marrying, sir – not ever!'

The indrawn gasps of breath could not have been more shocked if she had confessed to murder. Then there was a babble of horrified comment.

'Not marry – such a waste of so much beauty!'

'Then man is to be forever denied a glimpse of your charms, when they flower?'

'You'll break hearts all over London – I vow you have broken mine already!'

'It's unnatural, surely, for a woman not to wed – even if she's more prodigal with her favours than a wife should be!'

'As you should know, eh, Jack?'

'But you cannot live on your own, Mistress Heron – you will need some protection.'

'Aye, from you, you wencher!'

'My uncle is protection enough,' said Alathea, glancing at Hugh. She was very pale, but quite calm, even smiling a little, as if she gained in strength from the extravagant talk swirling about her. 'And I have another uncle, a well-respected man, who lives here – and a brother, *three* brothers in fact. So you see, I do not want for protection.'

'But what can a woman *do*, unwed?' demanded Purple Coat, who was evidently very worried by this problem. 'It's not right – your sex is made to minister to a man and bear his children. You fly in the face of God and nature by denying your birthright. Surely you will have an empty life without such duties.'

'Not at all – for I mean to be a painter, and earn my living at it.'

The astonishment that greeted this statement was, if anything, greater than before. Alathea raised her hand, smiling, and was gratified to see that the hubbub of protest died away almost instantly. 'But I think you'll agree, and you, my lord – I have a certain talent, which should be put to use. How better than to use it thus, to paint portraits? How better to *prove* my worth, than to earn a good living by so doing? I cannot see that my desire is so shocking.'

'It isn't *right*,' Purple Coat repeated, feebly. 'For a woman to earn her living – independent of any man – that's not her place in life, at all.'

'Why not? I am not the first woman to do so, and I'll wager I won't be the last.'

'Right or not, natural or unnatural, you're not lacking in courage or spirit,' said Lord St Albans, from the rear of the babbling group. 'I wish you well, my dear, and I hope I'll one day be proud to point out this portrait on my walls, as being by the great female artist, Alathea Heron. When will it be finished, eh?'

'A few days' work in the studio should suffice, my lord. Then it will have to dry, and be varnished, and then framed, before I can send it round.'

'A fortnight, perhaps? Give me some warning, then, and you may have dinner with me, with your uncle here as your escort, I would suggest. I shall greatly look forward to the charming pleasure of your company, my dear. Until then, I will bid you *au revoir*.'

It had all undoubtedly been very successful, Alathea reflected, as she cleared up after her guests' departure. She had painted one of the best portraits of her life, she had risen well to the occasion of this, her most important commission so far, and she had received the recognition and praise that was owing. She had even been invited to dine with the Earl (for which, she knew, Lucy would insist on the purchase of a new dress in the height of fashion – and she could not really afford it until the Earl paid his bill). But somehow this was not an unalloyed triumph. She had kept calm during that surge of questions, she had even, in retrospect, rather enjoyed their disbelief and discomfiture. Still, however, she resented being treated as some sort of exotic curiosity, an inmate of the Tower menagerie rather than a young woman with views that seemed very sensible to her, however unconventional and alarming they might appear to people whom Oliver, no respecter of persons, afterwards described as 'a lack-witted bunch of silly fops'. *I'll show them*, she thought defiantly, with a glance at the painted Earl of St Albans, shrewd and gross and proud against the muddy canvas. *I'll show them I can be the equal of any man, and surpass most of them in this as well.*

Word was sent to his Lordship that the picture was finished, and the frame was ordered and fixed: and one bright windy morning, early in November, Alathea put on her new gown, a rich dark green that only emphasised the fairness of her hair and the pale, lightly freckled translucence of her skin, and on the arm of her uncle Daniel Ashley, stepped from the front door of the Covent Garden house, to be bowed by her half-uncle Hugh, dressed in his finest, into Lord St Albans' own coach. Dan eschewed such fripperies, and this luxury was most welcome – and very flattering. She admired the splendid equipage, the shining paint, the coat-of-arms, proper to an Earl, on the doors: the familiar Jermyn device of a crescent between two mullets, or five-pointed stars, and greyhounds to support it, and the motto *Nec oriente nec occidente*. Alathea, whose Latin was at best sketchy, had some idea it might be translated as 'neither the east nor the west', but as to its implication, no idea at all: neither could Hugh, whose education at Bury Grammar School had been rather less haphazard, offer any suggestion.

The coach was as fine inside as out, with soft leather upholstery, and glass in the windows, and a multitude of soft velvet cushions upon which to recline, and it was drawn by four beautiful, beribboned Flanders horses, matched dapple-greys. Alathea, with a memory of how often she had been forced against house walls or nearly run down by such carriages in the narrow City streets, grinned to hide her nervousness, and determined to enjoy this unaccustomed taste of luxury. They drove past St Martin-in-the-Fields and so to Piccadilly, and the new Piazza by St James's, which Lord St Albans had recently caused to be laid out in echo of the one at Covent Garden. His own house, in the south-east corner of the square and therefore in deep shadow, was the only one yet finished: a few others rose about it, all abristle with scaffolding.

And inside, despite the smell of new plaster and the tang of fresh wood, it was just as fine as the coach. They were to eat privately, no silly foppish young men to distract their talk, and Alathea could not help noticing the Earl's prodigious appetite. They dined in the French manner, naturally, with silver dishes and forks provided, and a succession of courses: beef, and capon and venison, fricasees and pasties until she could barely force down another mouthful, and then came sweet syllabubs and tansies, rich in cream and eggs and wine. Lord St Albans seemed highly delighted with his portrait, which had been hung with due ceremony above the mantel before the meal, and was full of genial questions about her art, how she had first discovered her gift, and her training. He was, she realised with relief, too polite to make searching enquiry as to her plans for the future, but he left her in no doubt that he considered her in some sort his protégée, and with great pride told her that he had persuaded a young gentleman of his acquaintance to sit for his portrait likewise. 'It's my aim to make you the fashion, my dear,' said the Earl cheerfully, beckoning his servant to replenish his plate. Hugh, opposite Alathea, had said little and eaten a great deal, with evident relish. She hoped that the seams of his waistcoat would prove adequate.

It transpired that the gentleman who was to favour her with his custom was none other than Purple Coat, who rejoiced in the exotic name of Jack Browne, and who was apparently the scion of an ancient family, now somewhat decayed (in their brains as well as in their wealth, thought Alathea caustically: she did not relish the prospect of hours of the young fop's frivolous banter and foolish questions). 'And I am sure,' her host continued expansively, 'that it will be the first of many such that I can put in your way, my dear. We'll have her the toast of Whitehall, eh, Hugh? Such beauty and such talent should not go unnoticed for long, and I'm sure that when my guests see your portrait, there'll be many more requests for sittings. A magnificent piece of work, my dear – quite magnificent.'

'I thank you, my lord,' said Alathea, too honest to behave with womanly humility.

'And what do *you* think of it, eh? D'ye think you could have improved on it?'

'No, my lord – indeed, I can say it's one of my best – so far.'

The Earl roared with laughter, his jowls and chins quivering and his small eyes all but vanishing in creases of fat. 'You don't lack pride, do you, my dear! Still, in this case I reckon it's justified, eh, Hugh? Quite a girl, this niece of yours.'

'I had noticed it,' said Hugh, with a wink in Alathea's direction.

'And so,' his mentor continued, after a comfortable and well-satisfied belch, 'and so, young Hugh, I propose a toast. To Mistress Alathea Heron – the fairest picture-drawer in all London! May she continue to delight our eyes – and may she become not just the toast of Covent Garden or St James's, but of all the town. I give you – Alathea!'

And as the two men rose and drank to her, Alathea felt a wave of heady excitement within her, tightening her throat and bringing with it an extraordinary feeling of power and glory. *I have won*, she thought. *I have won the admiration and interest of St Albans, and once that is done, the rest will be easier. How long, I wonder, before I* will *be the toast of all the town?*

CHAPTER TWELVE

A wilderness of monkeys

Last enter Rochester, of sprightly wit,
Yet not for converse safe, or business fit.
Mean in each action, lewd in every limb,
Manners themselves are mischievous in him.
(Duke of Buckinghamshire, *An Essay on Satyr*)

The fire was dying into a warm comfortable heap of embers, and the candles were burning low: one or two had gone out, and sent a lazy acrid thread of smoke towards the ceiling. It was early September, and the nights already drawing in. The shutters were pulled fast against the lonely, chilly dark, and thick velvet curtains drawn over them. Within, the tall spacious room was hung with warm shadows, amidst which the fire and the candles made a brave but insignificant showing. A table had been pushed against one wall, still laden with dirty plates, empty wine bottles, bowls of half-eaten fruit. The lights sparkled on the silver; Henry Jermyn, in his uncle's absence, was making free with his uncle's plate as well as his uncle's house.

Henry, who had thought to pass a dull evening by inviting a variety of convivial spirits and offering them some of the Earl's best claret, was uneasily watching the activities of one of his guests who, as it happened, had arrived uninvited. The velvet curtains were brocaded and threaded with gold, the hangings were French, new, and impossibly expensive. They depicted the graceful and shameless activities of assorted classical nymphs, stayrs, bacchantes, gods and goddesses, which was why he had chosen this particular room, by no means the grandest, to entertain his friends. They, as it happened, were not studying the lovely human shapes so delicately coloured and elegantly stitched, but the subhuman, grotesque figure that cavorted in mockery by one hand from the cornice, to howls of merriment from the three young men who sat on chairs about the fire, wine-cups in their hands, and who would not have to explain things to the Earl of St Albans on his eventual return from France.

'It's sitting on Aphrodite's lap,' said Hugh Trevelyan, snorting.

He had drunk less than the others, having recently, out of vanity for his increasing waistline, decided to limit his consumption of food and drink.

No such thought, evidently, had crossed the mind of Harry Savile, who like Henry Jermyn was a member of the Duke of York's household. He overflowed his chair and his plump hands rested, comfortably clasping his cup, on a very round belly. 'Sitting on her lap, Hugh? I'll tell you what our Strephon's doing, he's learning that females come in other than monkey-shape, eh, Strephon? That's right, jackanapes, tweak her bubbies for her!'

'He's pulling threads out,' said Henry Jermyn, unable to keep the note of alarm from his voice. It was all very well for Savile to mock, but the tapestries were his uncle's great pride and joy, he did not like to think what they had cost, and he depended utterly upon the Earl's goodwill, favour, partiality and generous distribution of money. 'And he'll do worse in a moment, if he's not got down.'

'He's naturally mischievous,' said the monkey's owner. Taller, fairer, more slender by far than the others, he stood watching the animal's antics from beside the chimney-piece, his dark eyes glittering and amused. 'As I am [illegible] save that his mischief is more naked. Afraid for your dear uncle's tapestries, Henry? Aren't you dying to know just how well I've trained him?'

Henry, who had welcomed his third guest into his uncle's house with the same fascinated reluctance he might have shown to a vivid, unpredictable and lethal leopard, cast a hunted glance sideways. 'You always were a devil . . . how well?'

'Well enough to respond to a special whistle, perhaps. Aphrodite would look very well with monkey-shit decently covering her shamefulness, don't you think? No? Well, it was a very good claret, and I wouldn't like to seem ungrateful,' said John Wilmot, second Earl of Rochester, sweeping his most elegant and courtly bow. 'Strephon – you infamous unmitigated rascal – come down!'

The monkey, chattering insolently, swung itself across the hangings with a beady glance at its owner, and took hold of the intricately carved surround above the chimney-piece, poised dangerously just above Rochester's head. Hugh, grinning, went over to the table and plucked a twig bearing four or five grapes from a bigger bunch. 'Here, Strephon – some grapes, for Aphrodite's rape!'

The monkey swore, and with unerring accuracy spat across six feet of empty space. A roar of laughter went up as Hugh, still grinning, wiped the sticky mess from his sleeve and in quick revenge threw the grapes. Deftly, the monkey caught them in one hand and stuffed them into its wide lipless mouth. Hugh could not help noticing its white and efficient-looking teeth, and spared a feeling of sympathy for Henry Jermyn, particularly since the monkey's greedy inquisitive hands were now probing downwards, to Alathea's splendid portrait hanging amidst the carved foliage above the mantel. He picked up a plum, soft and ripe, from the bowl beside him and threw it, harder than the grapes. With a shriek of outrage the monkey, hit soundly on the head, dropped down past the arrogant painted face of the Earl of St Albans, and on to its master's shoulder where it crouched, rubbing its wound and whimpering dramatically in a way that was absurdly human. Hugh, unrepentant, caught John Wilmot's eye and for a moment was chilled by what he felt within that pale, sensitive, aristocratic face: a danger, a dark wild violence that he had known to lurk there, but had never before seen turned on himself. Then the moment vanished. Rochester smiled, and disentangled the clinging hands and tail. 'Go sleep on that cushion, sinful Strephon, and trouble us no more.' And with a mock-theatrical flourish to accompany the words, tossed the little animal on to one vacant chair and sat down in another. 'Your aim's too true, even with a plum. What will it be, with a stone?'

'Truer,' said Hugh, with a rather uncomfortable and very unfamiliar feeling of being out of his depth. 'But tell us, you hadn't finished – what *did* happen at the Opera?'

'French sots, so drunk they seemed to assume that because our beloved English Navy is undermanned, ill-provisioned and incompetent, so it followed in the fuddled vacancy that passes for a brain in those parts, that if we let the Dutch into the Medway we must also all be cowards, and fair game for their wavering swords.'

'And were you?'

'Indeed, we were more than a match for them – our own blades were like lightning, darting here and there to great effect, the villainous Frenchmen fell back in disarray and were finally trounced and routed, with some blood shed on both sides. And that,' said Rochester, descending abruptly from the mock-heroic style he had assumed as readily as a glove, 'is how the French King himself begged our forgiveness, and threatened all kinds of fearsome tortures for our antagonists, so that we could graciously request mercy – not that they deserved any, a sorrier bunch of rogues I never saw in my life. But it was generally considered that the English came off with honour satisfied. And so, your humble servant was allowed home, and has promised to be a good boy and not box Tom Killigrew's ears ever again, however much he may rail at me.' He looked round at his audience, lazy and amused in the dim light, and smiled. 'Paris was . . . *ennuyant*, but provided me with a plentiful supply of fashionable French phrases. I shall take care to sprinkle my conversation with them, at the most inappropriate moments. Now I'm sure you've heard sufficient of Paris. How has London been?'

London, it appeared, was exactly the same, but different. There was talk of plays put on, new and luscious actresses, maids of honour who behaved with scant regard for maidenhead or honour, Court scandal, royal mistresses. The wine went round again, and the laughter grew louder as John Wilmot's celebrated gift of tongue took flight and soared into an exuberant fantasy beside which Hugh, a wit to his family, felt inadequate and humble, even as he laughed. The Earl was creating now a play, a lewd burlesque of the intricately plotted comedies to be seen every day at the King's house or the Duke's, and each character endowed with a suitably appropriate and obscene name. As the four vied with each other in new masterpieces of invention, the monkey stirred at the shouts of hilarity and sat up, chattering inquisitively. Hugh, suggesting an alternative name for the king of Sodom, saw the movement out of the corner of his eye and groaned inwardly. *God knows why he drags the infernal creature around with him*, he thought. *Surely it's more trouble than it's worth*. But the monkey was licensed mischief, as Rochester himself had intimated, and Hugh suspected that it had been trained with great thoroughness and cunning. Unnoticed by anyone save him, it ducked beneath the chair and slipped, a silent scampering shadow, towards the table laden with tempting fruit. With a gleeful premonition of disaster, Hugh slid down his own chair and tipped his hat forward over his face as the first missile, a distinctly over-ripe plum, sailed overhead and hit Savile's well-covered paunch, splattering the rich velvet and landing soggily on the floor. With a yell of mock-fury, Harry picked it up and flung it back. The next instant, the monkey retaliated in kind and the air was full of erratic and juicy missiles hurtling in all directions as Hugh, Henry Jermyn and Savile joined in the fun. Only Rochester, watching with an expression of lively amusement and savouring his wine, stayed aloof, but offered a soft hilarious commentary that soon had Hugh laughing so much he could no longer see the missiles on the floor to be picked up. His sides aching, he stumbled back to his chair. At the same moment, the monkey tired of its sport and leapt once more on to the much-abused hangings. This time, it was the intricately carved surround to the mantelpiece that proved an irresistable attraction, and once there, swinging by its long crooked hairy fingers from a convenient swag of vegetation, it rediscovered Alathea's painting. Amid yells of rather inebriated delight from its audience, it traced the exuberant curves of paint that described the extravagances of Lord St Albans' periwig, poked an enquiring finger into the little piggy eye, and finally, with smacking deliberation, advanced a wet, pink tongue and explored the delightful taste of paint and varnish. Hugh, reluctantly, felt it was time to intervene. 'I should call it down if I were you – some paints are poisonous.'

'Are they?' John Wilmot's face wore its haughty aristocrat expression, assumed as instantly as a mask. 'Which ones – the flesh tones, perhaps?'

'No – emerald green is generally said to be the most lethal,' said Hugh, grinning. 'But there's white lead, Naples yellow, blue bice, orpiment, all quite sufficient to end a small monkey's life if he's not over-fussy about what he eats. And even the varnish could give him a belly-ache.'

'You seem to know a great deal about it – have you been in Lely's studio of late?'

'No, my niece's. She painted that picture, so I have what you might call a personal interest in the paint if not the Earl – and I really would call that animal off before he makes himself ill. She used a lot of Naples yellow in that periwig, and he seems to be chewing it off.'

John Wilmot glanced up at the portrait and whistled gently. The monkey, with astonishing swiftness and agility, dropped down to the chair and sat in it, legs crossed and arms behind its head for all the world like a shrunken, aged man. 'Your niece painted that portrait? Surely any niece of yours would be a baby.'

'Not so. She's my half-brother's daughter, and just five years younger than I am – which makes her twenty, and all but leading apes in hell.'

'Which is not for want of our trying,' Henry Jermyn put in, with a knowing wink. 'You've seen Mistress Jennings, the Castlemaine, the Stewart – I beg her ladyship's pardon, the Duchess of Richmond – Hugh's little painter niece outshines 'em all, could be the toast of all London and she mews herself up in an attic in Covent Garden with so many jars and bottles the place looks and smells like an alchemist's den, and paints. All day, every day, nothing but paint and varnish – what a waste of a woman, eh? Twenty years old, the beauty of an angel, a tongue to match any of ours – with one exception – and still unwed and what's more, I'll wager, still a virgin.' He subsidèd under Hugh's intense pointed glare, but too late. Rochester's interest had been aroused, and his reputation, however unjustified, was such that no respectable woman could risk being seen to exchange more than three words with him.

'I shall have to visit this paragon,' he was saying now to Henry Jermyn, in the lazy drawl that Hugh was coming to know too well. 'Where in Covent Garden does she reside?'

'On the Piazza,' said Henry, who was drunk enough to ignore Hugh's frown. 'First house on the corner of James Street. Belongs to another of her uncles, Lord Bradfield, he lets her have it, and it's as big as Lely's on the other side of the Piazza. And there she lives all alone bar a maid or two, like some princess in a romance – waiting for her prince to come along and free her, and if he chooses the lucky minute, who knows what he might not achieve?' He laughed lecherously. 'Going to try your chances, John? Don't blame you – she's a fortress well worth the storming.'

'She doesn't live alone,' said Hugh, his voice quiet and deliberate, keeping the discussion as calm as he could. He trusted Alathea, he trusted her wit and sense and humour, he knew she would greet this silver-tongued rake with the caustic honesty he merited: but he thoroughly disliked any idea of a meeting between Rochester, with his evil reputation and the dazzling charm that had enchanted the Court over the past five years, when he had not been banished for his impudence, and Alathea, so wrapped up in her painting that he doubted she had any real idea of the dangers of associating with such a man. He went on, emphasising those aspects of her situation which might deter the Earl. 'There's a cousin lodges with her, and Henry's sister-in-law keeps house for them, and there's her brother as well, to look after them all. Far from a princess of romance, I'm afraid – and Alathea isn't above stabbing you with a paint brush or doctoring your wine with orpiment, if she doesn't care for you.' He found himself wishing, with surprising force, that it was Kit and not the dreamy, absent-minded Matthew, his nose forever in a book and inclined to answer in Greek, who provided the masculine element at the Piazza house. Admittedly Math was now nineteen, studying at the Temple and a responsible and quiet young man, but he was far more unworldly even than Alathea. Kit, with all his difficulties, was quite capable of warding off the most determined courtier, but Kit was in Italy, where he had dallied for the past two years, writing occasionally and revealing little, still less any plan to return home. So, Math was perforce Alathea's protector, and Hugh had little faith in Math's powers of protection.

'Alathea?' Rochester stared at him curiously. 'Is that her name? Alathea . . . what?'

'Heron. Alathea Heron,' said Hugh warily, wondering what had sparked this additional interest.

The fair, slightly arched brows rose a little, the wide mouth smiled gently. 'A lovely name, as beautiful as Henry's report of her. Don't worry,' said John Wilmot, Earl of Rochester. 'I am only . . . curious.'

The evening ended late, with more wine and laughter, and it was early morning, almost dawn, when he came at last to his Whitehall lodgings, the monkey asleep around his shoulders like a grotesque scarf. The bedchamber was silent, shadowy: for once, he was alone. He thought of his wife, the pretty, lively girl he had consigned to live in the country, with their baby daughter, at the house in Adderbury . . .

He opened the box where he kept his letters, notes, scraps of verse. He had it still, after all these years . . . nine years, it must be, since the boy of thirteen had encountered a strange child and her black-and-white dog on the hillside above the house whose name he could not now recall, though it was in the same parish as his own. Nine years on, the memory had faded, grown blurred about the edges, so that he recalled not so much what had been done, or said, but more the strange, enchanted atmosphere of that meeting, the sense of entering a different world: and at the centre of that taste of strangeness, as sharp and bright and tiny as a jewel, or a landscape seen through the wrong end of a telescope, the child stood clear, abrupt and scruffy and honest, with even then the promise of the beauty which Henry Jermyn had lecherously described. Tired, his head reeling with wine and the exhilaration of an evening's talk, his fingers fumbled through the accumulated pages and pulled out the last, the lowest. He stared down at the child he had still been, nine years ago, and who now lay buried so deep he was hardly aware of his existence.

Seen now, with adult eyes, it was not particularly good: the draughtsmanship was faulty, the pen inadequate and uneven, there were confused areas in the hair and an awkwardness in the way head joined neck. But there was also a life, a vivid living likeness in the drawing, that caught him even now. She had promised a beauty and a talent beyond the common run, and he realised, with a remote, weary surprise, that he wanted very much to see what she had become. Not from any lechery, despite what the world and Henry Jermyn would say, but because she had suddenly come to represent in his mind something that he had lost, long ago, and never known he valued until now.

It must be her. He saw the careful neat monogram, *AH*, the childish inscription, and remembered her parting words with sudden, startling clarity. 'One day I'll paint you properly, when I'm a famous artist, and I'll make no charge at all!'

It was a nine-years-old promise, but still binding. He would take her up on it.

The day at the house in Covent Garden began, as every other day before and after, with the chatter of Rebecca Jermyn, talking to the birds. There was a starling who was her special friend, and would perch on the windowsill of her chamber high above the Piazza, and Rebecca had discovered that starlings in general, and hers in particular, were excellent mimics. She fed it breadcrumbs and cheese every morning, and had taught it the whistle with which Alathea attempted to control Lovell-our-dog. That worthy's life had been a misery ever since: each foray into garden or Piazza was accompanied by whistles that might or might not emanate from his beloved mistress, and he had not yet learned to distinguish false from real.

Rebecca's mother, hearing the whistle and the chatter from her adjoining chamber, was next to rise, and once Henrietta was up, the rest of the household lingered at their peril. There was a cook-maid, two maidservants (including Lucy's maid Sarah), and a boy who tended the garden and turned the spit and lit the links: a shockingly small complement for such a grand house, but then they all lived very simply. The Herons being a country family, kept country customs still, and there was always food in the main chamber to break their fast: bread, cheese, beer, cold meat and fish, set out by Betty the cook-maid. Henrietta arrived first, as always, with her black-haired goblin daughter. Then Math came in, still evidently half-asleep, the inevitable book under his arm and his hair, pale as his sister's and unsullied by any periwig, uncombed and matted at the back where he had not bothered to tend it. Food for Matthew was the equivalent of fuel for the fire, a necessary inconvenience and no more. Henrietta, making sure that Rebecca ate properly and did not gobble, saw with wry amusement that he had selected a piece of bread and a chunk of cheese, and was chewing mechanically, his whole attention on his book. She suspected that he could have eaten paper with as much relish. When Alathea and Nell entered, Lovell ambling shaggily behind them, he did not even glance up, but grunted a greeting. His sister, grinning, leaned over him as he hunched above the book and imitated his expressions and movements until he realised what she was about and pushed her away. 'Can't I have a moment's peace? I should have read this yesterday, and I have to discuss a case this morning with George.'

Alathea, helping herself to bread and ale, regarded her younger brother with affectionate amusement. 'Whatever persuaded you to train as a lawyer? You never exactly shine in family arguments.'

'That's because no one can do you down when you join in,' Henrietta told her. 'If women could be lawyers, Thea, you'd be the Temple's leading light.'

'I'll leave that to Math with pleasure – I have other fish to fry. Which reminds me – Becca, do you want to come up this morning, and I'll start your picture? I haven't anyone to paint today.'

'Can I sit with Lovell?' Rebecca asked, after serious deliberation. 'You've never done a picture of Lovell.'

'It's not easy, painting a shapeless mass of hair. Anyway, I doubt he'll sit still.'

'Yes, he will – I'll make him,' said Becca, very firm and solemn. Alathea grinned at her. No child could have been more different, it seemed, in looks and temperament from the round and rosy and practical Hen: Becca with her narrow face and straight black hair and slightly slanted dark eyes had a definite look of Jermyn, but that air of serious serenity was very reminiscent of Hen's own mother, the Irish Grainne, and her love for animals was all her own. A pose with Lovell would be very appealing, and already Alathea was composing it in her mind's eye, the straight-backed, sleek-haired child contrasting very happily with the disreputable ruffianly dog. It would make a pleasant change from the well-fed faces of aldermen and merchants and citizens and their wives, who still, despite Lord St Albans' proud boast, formed almost the whole of her rather small clientele.

Two years ago, she had felt the world at her feet, and somehow that bright moment of infinite promise had never quite been fulfilled. The Earl of St Albans had spent much of his time in France, with other things to occupy his mind besides promoting his protégée's career, and Henry Jermyn had spent some months away from the Court as a consequence of his renewed dalliance with the Castlemaine. In the meantime Dan, whose work on her behalf seemed tireless, had provided her with a steady trickle of clients, augmented at first by members of the family. Purple Coat had proved to be her first and only Court commission. But when Dan's fine new brick residence had arisen on the site of the old House of the Ash Tree, and the Ashley family had prepared to return to Fleet Street, she had taken a deep breath and decided to stay. Dan had written to Lord Bradfield requesting his permission and received a perfunctory and grudging affirmative in return. Henrietta and Rebecca were happy to stay on, as was Nell, and Matthew came up to town from Ashcott to study at the Temple, and lodged with them despite the Inns' official discouragement. And there they had all been for more than nine months, living like church mice in the huge ostentatious house, and able to augment their staff of servants with a second maid and the boy, as Alathea's earnings increased. She could support herself and her friends in a little comfort with her painting, but the fame which she craved had so far eluded her.

After breakfast, she went up to her attic studio to make the final preparations for Becca's portrait. She had stretched and primed the canvas, with Nell's help, but she still missed Oliver's feckless assistance and flippant conversation. He was not even in London any more, having been packed off to Christchurch, Oxford, in an attempt to apply some polish and education to his natural charm, and Rosalind was married, to a young man with shipping interests who lived in Woolwich. Alathea had seen her three times in the last year, and Ros was now pregnant and firmly embedded in wifely domesticity, her status in life assured. The thought made Alathea feel at once very young, still free and irresponsible, and old and wise beyond her years. She had chosen her path, for good or ill, and as she mixed the paints and sketched out the pose on a piece of paper, she felt no touch of envy for Ros at all.

A knock at the door heralded Becca, with Lovell in tow and a large bone clamped firmly between his jaws in the interests of keeping him quiet. With the ease of long practice, Alathea and Nell settled child and dog into the pose, the light falling on them from the left, the little girl seated upon a cast plaster rock in her white voluminous holland shift, arranged to resemble classical drapery, with one hand on Lovell's round hairy head. He was supposed to rest his chin on her knee, but insisted on returning to his bone after no more than a minute or so, and Nell did not stop him: the person who attempted to prise any such item from Lovell's untidy array of white and efficient teeth was either very brave, or extremely foolhardy.

Alathea, sketching in Becca and Lovell with a light liquid brown on her brush, could read Nell's thoughts exactly from her face, and smiled to herself. There was no denying that her mouselike cousin had now, more or less, emerged from her shell of shy plainness. She had acquired a small collection of fashionable dresses, her manner in company was much more easy and relaxed, she contributed somewhat hesitantly to polite conversation. Moreover, her hair was attractive now that it was regularly washed and brushed and curled, and had a definite glint of golden fairness even out of the sunlight. She had grown plumper, too, and lost that round-shouldered, bony, submissive look that had led some visitors to mistake her for a servant. In most company, Nell would have been judged a tolerably pretty woman, properly decorous and mild-mannered: but it was her misfortune ever to be lost within Alathea's brilliant shadow.

The morning wore on peacefully. Outside, it rained in the

Piazza and sent the less persistent fruit-sellers and whores scurrying for shelter. And at eleven o'clock precisely, as one of Dan Ashley's beautiful new repeating clocks struck the hour in the great chamber, John Wilmot's coach entered the square from King Street, and drew up outside the house.

As Court coaches went, it was not particularly ostentatious or luxurious beyond the common run: appearances had to be kept up, though he had little money. He had married an heiress, but not for her estate, and he had tried, so far successfully, to avoid spending her resources. As a result, his equipage was outshone by practically every other Court luminary, including Henry Jermyn. He even took a perverse kind of pride in it. The usual cluster of people selling their wares, and themselves, clustered round the coach. Amid the din, he heard his coachman's stentorian voice and cracking whip, as a way was cleared for His Lordship to leave the conveyance. He found himself wishing, with a stab of regret, that he had dressed plainly and come on foot or in a hackney, plain John Wilmot, unencumbered by trailing clouds of honour and title and privilege. And she was hardly likely, unless informed, to connect the child John Wilmot she had once chance-met on a hillside near Adderbury, with the Earl of Rochester whose doings had horrified, scandalised and delighted all London since his arrival at Court nearly five years ago. The day when he had let Alathea assume that he was an ordinary boy, had been the first of many forays into the world of disguise: it gave him a great sense of freedom to cast away his public self and put on the garb of some humbler person, a tinker or an honest (or dishonest) tradesman. No denying, it would have been very much more pleasurable and amusing to have arrived in Covent Garden incognito, but it was too late for that now, with his coachman announcing in that bullish bellow that the Earl of Rochester wished to see Mistress Heron, so that half the Piazza might know his identity. And then he was ushered within by an awe-struck little maid who might have been pretty if she had not been so frightened, and taken upstairs to the big first-floor chamber that was used by Lely, in his similar house, to entertain his most important guests.

But the young woman who brought in wine and cakes, with the jingling keys of the housekeeper, was assuredly not Alathea, being red-haired, plain and healthy-looking in the manner of a country dairymaid. He had seen her before, he was certain, and she confirmed it by saying briskly, after her curtsey, 'Good morning, my lord. You probably won't recall me, but I have met you at Whitehall. My husband was Charles Jermyn.'

Henry's young brother, who had died untimely: he had gambled away many a night in his company. He expressed his regrets for her husband's death, two years too late, and she accepted them with, evidently, her mind elsewhere, for she said then, a frown between the rather thick, reddish brows, 'My lord . . . to what do we owe the pleasure of this visit?'

'I have come to see Mistress Heron,' he told her, and the eyebrows rose.

'Mistress Heron? Which one? Nell – or Alathea?' The tone of her voice suggested that no gentleman would conceivably wish to see the unknown Nell – sister? cousin? – in preference to Alathea. She went on. 'They're both in the studio. Alathea is painting my little daughter, and Nell – her cousin – is helping. Have you come to have your picture painted, my lord?'

'In a manner of speaking, I suppose I have,' he said, matching her directness. It was simple and refreshing after the convoluted speech of Whitehall wits, himself included. 'Your brother-in-law spoke of her, and I was . . . intrigued.'

'You'd best beware, if she paints your portrait,' was Hen's dry comment. 'Have you seen the one she did of Henry? No, I thought not – he takes care to keep that one in the background. It shows him most plainly for what he is, not what he – and everyone else – thinks he is, and I should imagine it would somewhat discourage any intending lover, if they saw it.' She grinned. 'Henry has a reputation to live up to – as have you, my lord.'

'Unfortunately, yes. You need have no fears for Mistress Heron, though – I was most thoroughly warned off her last night.'

'By Hugh, I expect,' said Henrietta, and smiled. 'I believe she is the only person Hugh gives a jot about, besides himself. I'm afraid we are all very protective of Alathea, and it's something we try to keep from her, for no one could be more scornful of our protection or more fierce for independence. I may do you an injustice by asking you to treat her with courtesy – but you do have a reputation, my lord, and I am sure Henry's report of her was high-coloured in the extreme.'

'I shall behave with the most exact decorum,' Rochester promised, smiling in response to that sudden and infectious grin. He could have taken it as an insult and played the choleric nobleman, but again he was aware, creeping up on him, of a feeling that he had entered a different world from the artificial atmosphere of Court, thick with recriminations, intrigue, secrecy and deviousness, amorous assignations and the politics of the bedchamber. It was as if, somewhere, a window had been opened, and in response to it, he said quickly, 'If you will tell me where the studio is, I shall find it. I would not have myself announced with a lot of ceremony.'

Henrietta looked at him standing in front of her, the picture of a Court gallant in blue velvet and gold lacing, cane and sword and fashionable hat and preposterous periwig, and thought that if he did not want ceremony, he might have dressed a little plainer. But for some strange reason she trusted him here, as she would not have trusted him in other circumstances. 'Go up the stairs, as high as you can, and the studio is the door on the left at the top. Good luck.'

He climbed the stairs alone, slowly and quietly, marvelling at the feeling of apprehension he had – which proved, he supposed, how much that solitary chance encounter had meant to him, both then and now. He went even more softly as he approached the top of the last flight: he could hear women's voices, quiet and indistinct, and the door on the left was open. He paused at the top, debating whether to knock or to wait, just a little, and eavesdrop. With what he considered to be commendable rectitude, he knocked.

The voices stopped abruptly, then someone said, 'Come in!' on a note of interrogation, and he pushed the door wide and walked through.

He had a brief impression of a long low room, lit by two dormer windows set in the sloping roof: a small girl sitting by what he took to be a fur-covered rock, until it leapt up with an enthusiastic bark and he saw that it was in fact a large and hairy mongrel, and a young woman in an old yellow dress stirring something smelly over the hearth. But nearest to him, standing by her easel, her startlingly pale hair loosely knotted out of the way and an old man's shirt shielding her gown, stood the woman that Alathea had become: tall and slim, and still, as she turned towards him, with that abrupt way of moving that caught at his memory. He made her a fine Court bow, and saw as she sank into an equally fine curtsey that she was aware of the irony: and then she laid down her brushes and said over her shoulder, 'I should think you and Lovell can rest now, Becca – take him downstairs and give him a run round the garden. And,' she added with a grin, 'don't forget you're in your shift, or you'll shock the neighbours.'

'I won't,' said Becca Jermyn, and with a slap of bare feet and a scuttering of paws and claws, child and dog were gone. Silently, the other, plainer girl left her noisome business over the hearth and came over: still without a word, she picked up the brushes and began to clean them. Alathea Heron studied her visitor with a look of amused, friendly enquiry which he also, now, remembered. 'And how may I help you, sir? I assume Henrietta sent you up?'

'She did, at my request. I disliked the idea of standing on ceremony, on an informal occasion. I have but come to engage you, Mistress Heron, to paint my portrait.'

'Of course,' said Alathea, and reached for her notebook. 'When would you like the first sitting to be? I am free this afternoon, or tomorrow . . . '

'Tomorrow afternoon will do very well . . . but I regret, Mistress, that I must ask for some rather unusual terms.'

'Oh?' Her tone was cooler. 'And what might they be, sir?'

'Firstly, that I am painted in the company of my monkey. And secondly . . . that you make no charge for the picture.'

'No charge?' Alathea stared at him for a moment, those remarkable smoky green eyes wide with surprise, and then burst into laughter. 'No charge! You must surely be joking! Especially if I'm obliged to allow a monkey in the studio – Becca and Lovell are bad enough,' she added.

'No joke, I assure you. But perhaps this will jog your memory.' And he drew out of the inner pocket of his waistcoat the drawing she had done of him when she was eleven.

Alathea stared down at it. Slowly a tide of warm colour flushed her thin face and receded, leaving the fair skin glowing. Then she looked up, her eyes wide again. 'How – how did you come by this? Are *you* – are *you* John? John Wilmot?'

'At your service, madam.'

'Then you remembered! I never thought you would – after all this time – how long must it be? Nine years, it was the year the King came back, the year we came to Ashcott. Nine years, and you kept it! And it's not very good either, is it?' she added, with rueful honesty. 'I hope I'll do you more justice now. And the monkey.'

'It may not seem so good now, but it was remarkable for one so young,' he reminded her, gallantly refraining from any reference to her present age.

Alathea dismissed that with a sound that was suspiciously close to a snort. 'I was eleven then, just, which makes me now the advanced age of twenty. Much practised in leading apes in hell, if you want me to paint your monkey – and if it causes chaos amongst my paints, I'll be at my last prayers for certain!' She caught his eye, and he laughed, feeling again that sense of kinship, of having always known her. She studied him narrowly, from the top of his head to the ornate buckled shoes, the cane and the periwig and the sword. Then she said slowly, 'How did you come to hear of me? Was it Hugh Trevelyan?'

'Your uncle? He did his best to dissuade me. It was Henry Jermyn who said that you were, to quote him, "A fortress worth storming". And I remembered your name.'

'Henry Jermyn is an incorrigible wencher. If his eyes were hooks, he'd have had all my clothes off me before he'd sat five minutes,' Alathea said.

'Is that why you wear that shirt?'

'It's my brother Matthew's – and I wear it because I only have a few gowns and I can't afford to cover them with paint.'

'I regret to tell you, it hasn't worked: there's green on your hem.'

Alathea looked, swore, and regarded her visitor with a rueful smile. 'Sorry. Though I should imagine you are used to unrefined ladies. I have ruffianly cousins, and brothers, and an even more ruffianly uncle. How did you meet him? I've never heard him mention you.'

'He's but a slight acquaintance – as is Henry Jermyn. One of my closest friends is in the household of the Duke of York, and Jermyn invited us to supper last night – where your name was mentioned. And now . . . ' His eyes met hers, and he felt . . . something, a shiver of feeling, flash between them. 'I am afraid, I have a confession to make. I have to some extent imposed on your good nature, now and in the past: I have misled you as to my identity.'

He saw her eyebrows rise and her eyes widen again. 'Oh? Don't tell me – you're the King!'

'He's black and ugly, whereas I am blond and – '

'Overdressed,' said Alathea, before she could stop herself.

John Wilmot did not, however, seem offended. He laughed, and with a sudden wild gesture sent the cane jumping over the floorboards to clatter against the wall. The decorated velvet coat and waistcoat followed it, and the sword with a tuneful ring of metal. Finally, he snatched off the fluffy pale periwig and tossed it neatly over the top of the easel, perilously close to the wet painted canvas. Then he turned and stood before her, tall and straight and unadorned in white shirt and blue breeches, his close-cropped hair almost as pale as her own.

'*Now*, Alathea Heron, is that more to your liking?'

Critically, she surveyed him, aware of Nell's startled interest in the background. 'Yes. You look more like the John Wilmot I remember, and less like a walking powder-puff. You can't tell me you really like being dressed like that – you don't strike me as a fop, any more than Hugh is.'

'Appearances have to be kept up,' he said wryly. 'Especially when one is not plain John Wilmot, but something more . . . I very much regret, dear lady, that you see standing before you, the Earl of Rochester.'

There was a brief, astonished silence, broken by Nell's gasp of horror. Alathea turned her head slightly on one side. He had the sudden impression that she was trying urgently not to laugh. She said slowly, 'You – are Rochester? *The* Rochester? The man who has a bedding acquaintance with half the whores in London? The man who boxed Tom Killigrew's ears in the King's presence? The one who writes those lampoons I can never persuade Hugh to show me? Well at least,' said Alathea Heron, giving way finally to mirth, 'no one will think me an old maid after *this*.'

'I agree – to have the Earl of Rochester divest himself of at least half his garments before five minutes' acquaintance is a feat any lady should take pride in.'

'You don't like your reputation much, do you?'

The simple, unexpected truth of that struck him with some force. He turned and surveyed the canvas, from which Becca's dead-coloured ghostly face stared eerily. 'No. You're right, I don't. It's something that has grown from an amusement to . . . rather more than a nuisance. I now have to live up to it, a burden which, I freely admit, is more often delightful than irksome. But it may mean that you are compromised – that we cannot enjoy the friendship we would wish, without wagging tongues. And given that, do you still want to paint me? I won't mind, if you would rather not do it.'

'But if I do, the monkey must be in it?'

'The monkey must be in it. I'll crown him with laurel, even as he tears up my poems. Will you paint me?'

'If I gave *that* for wagging tongues,' Alathea said, snapping her fingers contemptuously, 'I would not be here, painting – I would be like my cousin Rosalind, in a snug little house with a snug, smug husband and a smug little baby growing snugly in my belly. I've chosen my life, and not even an earthquake, still less idle tittle-tattle, is going to divert me from it. You may come tomorrow, and bring the monkey – as long as it can be chained up, or I won't answer for the consequences.'

'He's already shown a taste for paint – he tried to kiss the Earl of St Albans' portrait.'

'I wasn't thinking of that. Where interference with my painting is concerned, I'm quite capable of murder, particularly if it's only a monkey.' She looked at him curiously. 'Why a monkey? For myself, I'd much rather have a dog.'

'Dogs I like too – but Strephon is my familiar. I train him to do things even I wouldn't be able to do, and get away with it. He deflates pretension and provides hours of endless and innocent amusement – ah, don't look so sceptical!'

'I'm entitled to look sceptical. Innocence and Rochester are like oil and water, chalk and cheese, Queen and Castlemaine – they definitely do *not* marry together. The more I hear about your monkey, the more I dread tomorrow. How do you want to be painted? Crowning him?'

'With laurel, if it please you, madam picture-drawer.'

'I'd prefer you to crown him with a cudgel, but for you, sir, I shall bow to your every whim – as far as the picture is concerned. What else do you want?'

'Myself, and the monkey, that will suffice: man and animal, rational and irrational, light and dark, savage and civilised – and who's to say which is which? Myself, given the choice between nine-tenths of the Court and the monkey – '

'Would choose the monkey?'

'How did you guess?'

'I know you too well – and I've known you a few hours, and nine years. And already I have decided,' Alathea said, suddenly serious, 'that as far as I'm concerned you are John Wilmot. Any extraneous matters like, say, an earldom are quite insignificant. Here, you are John Wilmot – outside, you are Rochester, with all that entails. A bargain?'

'A bargain – I'll remove my periwig the instant I walk through the door. Tomorrow afternoon, then, Mistress Heron?'

'Tomorrow afternoon – or, if you like, come for dinner first. Henrietta is an excellent cook, and she bullies the cook-maid into a semblance of imitation. I suspect you wouldn't eat better at Whitehall.'

'For dinner, I shall be delighted to accept. Does the invitation extend to Strephon?'

'Strephon? Oh, the monkey. Yes, if I must. Are his table-manners good? Will he set a proper example to Becca?'

'An improper one, I suspect. However, I promise to keep him under as much control as is humanly possible. Of course, accidents may happen despite all that I can do to prevent them – but then it all enhances the entertainment, *n'est-ce-pas*? There, you see, I can practise my French. After five months in Paris I am almost fluent, and in polite company I can utter a few phrases, here and there, to prove I'm quite *à la mode*.' He caught Alathea's eye and they both broke into laughter, while Nell hovered nervously in the background, excluded, bewildered and totally at a loss.

He took his leave then, being careful first to put on his extravagant clothes, his public skin, as Alathea said, smiling. 'And I'll let you go down unescorted, for outside the house you become Rochester again, and I don't think the transformation will suit you.' Once more their eyes met, his dark, watchful, ironic, hers as green and grey and changeable as the sea, and again, both were aware of a spark of contact, communication between them. Then he gave her another mocking, courtly bow, and was gone.

'You must be mad,' said Henrietta, who had shot up to the attic as soon as the front door had closed behind his elegant back. 'Inviting the Earl of Rochester to *dinner*? Good God, in the eyes of half the Court that's tantamount to an invitation to rape for his second course.'

'In this house, he's John Wilmot,' said Alathea. She felt curiously exhilarated, happy, as if nothing mattered at all save those few delightful moments of conversation in which, she knew, she had held her own with the most feared wit in London, and thoroughly enjoyed herself. She added, seeing some further explanation was needed, if only for everyone's peace of mind, 'I met him a long time ago at Ashcott, when we were children. He has a house at Adderbury, about a mile away. And last night he was supping at Henry Jermyn's, and my name was mentioned, and he remembered me. He wants me to paint his portrait.'

'With a monkey,' Nell added, with a certain awed horror. 'Hen, he's bringing the monkey tomorrow!'

'Is he? Well, it and Becca and Lovell will make a rare trio,' Hen said. She turned again to Alathea. 'Are you sure you know what you're doing? He's dangerous, Thea, he really is. Just to invite him to the house will cause gossip – and if he turns against you, he's the worst enemy I know. He used to write lampoons about the maids-of-honour – still does, I expect – and they were completely merciless, he could ruin your career before it's begun, if he wanted. If I were you, I'd become suddenly too busy to paint his portrait.'

'I will do no such thing,' Alathea said. 'I've heard the stories too and I don't believe the half of them, and I don't think he's as black as he's painted. And besides, I have his solemn promise. Inside this house, he is John Wilmot. Outside . . . I must beware!' And to Henrietta's extreme disquiet, she laughed.

No fine coach and four brought the Earl of Rochester to the door of the Covent Garden house the next day. Instead, John Wilmot arrived in a hired chair, wearing a snuff-brown coat and a plainly tied cravat and his third-best periwig. The door was opened by the same maid, who completely failed to recognise the previous day's courtier in this ordinary-seeming young man, and he was announced as Master Wilmot. It was only as she retreated from the room that the maid realised that what she had taken for some kind of greyish-brown muffler around his neck was, in fact, a wizened little grotesque of an ape. She stuffed her fingers in her mouth to stop herself from screaming in astonishment, and ran from the room, away from that beady, curious, disturbing gaze.

Becca was enchanted by the monkey: Alathea could not help noticing that her small bright eyes had the same look. She held out her hands, and the animal swung nimbly down his owner's clothes and jumped on to her. Henrietta made a sudden movement, afraid that it would bite, but no animal had ever bitten Becca. Crooning, the little girl turned and walked slowly away from the adults, towards the windows and into a world of her own, the monkey's arms wrapped round her neck like a baby's.

'Strephon won't harm her, I assure you,' said John, smiling. 'He is like me – his licence for mischief has limits, and he knows what they are.'

'I'm glad you left off your finery,' Alathea said. She herself had on her best gown, though it would have seemed plain at Whitehall. Yet her face seemed to be adorned instead, and with that profound feeling of disquiet, Henrietta realised that she had never seen her beauty shine in that way, as if candles had been lit.

The behaviour of both guests, man and ape, was impeccable. A stool was brought for Strephon, and Becca piled cushions on top of it, and the monkey sat next to her and consumed fruit, daintily, with his long grasping fingers while everyone else did hungry justice to the dinner, which Henrietta had personally produced, with the cook-maid's assistance. John Wilmot talked, entertainingly, of his months in France, his friends at Court, his wife and baby daughter, and managed to keep the conversation on an irreproachably respectable level. After the first few minutes, he had to avoid catching Alathea's eye. She was sitting opposite, with an expression of lively irony on her face which showed her to be as sensitive to what he was not saying as to his actual words. And all through the meal, his awareness of her grew, he became more atuned to the dry, rather low sound of her voice, in contrast to Henrietta's brisk tones and Nell's languor and Becca's soft chattering conversation with his monkey. Words insinuated themselves into his mind, rhyming of their own accord, the wild dancing rhythms that flowed as free as wine: but he was not drunk. Beauty, innocence and wit, she possessed all three in full measure. To have one would be rare in his world, but the gift of them all made this woman a pearl beyond price. His wife Elizabeth had been a little like her, when they were first wed: she was still, when not worrying about his mother, her mother, the baby, his doings in London, his neglect of her. In the country, in the deep silence of Adderbury, he was the devoted husband, but here in the city it was different: he was one of the Merry Gang, as mad and wild and mischievous as the monkey, and not in possession of any such creature as a wife.

There was a tug at his sleeve. Jerked rudely from his thoughts, he turned to behold Rebecca Jermyn, pale and earnest, a look of anxious enquiry on her narrow little face. 'Please, sir, what is your monkey's name?'

'He's called Strephon.'

'And where did you get him? Because,' said Becca, words suddenly tumbling out of her, 'I would like a monkey too. *Very* much. Could you get me a monkey? I have six shillings saved under my mattress. Would a monkey cost more than six shillings?'

'I rather think it would.'

'Oh.' Rebecca seemed suddenly deflated. She toyed absently with an orange, and said in a voice thick with disappointment, 'How long do you think it will take me to save to buy a monkey?'

'A long time, I'm afraid.'

'What's a long time? A week?'

'If you've saved six shillings already, perhaps by the time you're seven . . . '

'Seven! But I'm only four,' said Becca. She looked so woebegone that he was sorely tempted to make her a present, if not of Strephon, then of some other little monkey, but he had a suspicion that it would not endear him to Henrietta. And he liked the child's mother, she reminded him of the country girls of his childhood.

The remains of the meal were cleared away, and the maids brought wine and a thick rich jug of steaming chocolate, fragrant and piping hot – and to everyone's covert surprise, he left the grape untouched and took the chocolate instead. In a sense, he was playing a part, the same part he played when in the company of his mother, or his mother-in-law, being gently, naughtily witty for the entertainment of ladies. But it was with Alathea that his mind fenced, and from her sharp speech that his own wit drew answering sparks. Not all her talents, evidently, were taken up with painting.

Talk, inevitably, turned to the projected portrait, and he was able to describe what he wanted. 'I have it all quite plain in my mind's eye: I stand by a table, so, and I'm holding out a laurel wreath over Strephon's head, while turning to look out of the picture, and Strephon sits on a pile of books on a table, preferably eating them.'

'All highly symbolic. Are you sure you don't want, say, a dwarf or a blind fiddler or any other accessory? Just yourself, and the monkey?'

'We have had this conversation before. Just the monkey, and myself. Will that be sufficient for you to begin?'

'Amply, I should think, with the proviso that if Strephon should chance to sample orpiment or emerald green, I am not held responsible. Would you like to come upstairs and choose the size of canvas you require? And I'll sketch the pose, I have my chalks upstairs.'

'With pleasure . . . Pray excuse me, ladies . . . Becca, may I leave you in charge of Strephon?' And John Wilmot and Alathea Heron rose and went out of the room with some speed, leaving Nell and Henrietta staring helplessly at each other over the still-steaming chocolate pot.

'No good will come of this,' Hen said, her lips compressed. 'I *know* it in my bones . . . oh, I wish Dan were living here still, all that's needed is his presence, and then I wouldn't have to worry. Why did it have to be *Rochester*, of all people? He may seem the charming gentleman, but he's utterly a law unto himself, and if he wants to seduce her, he will. And only someone like Dan in the house would stop him.'

'Or Hugh?' Nell suggested. She stared anxiously at Henrietta, so much more capable and practical, and yet still at a loss. 'Couldn't we ask Hugh?'

'Hugh has duties of his own . . . and besides, Alathea is a woman grown, she's twenty, and I was a wife and mother at that age. Twenty,' Hen repeated with a kind of wonder, 'and I doubt she's ever been properly kissed. And yet . . . she's grown, and she has intelligence and sense . . . but what worries me is . . . oh, it's nothing.'

'What?' Nell asked. 'What worries you?'

'The way she looks at him. She's been in love with her painting for nearly ten years,' said Henrietta grimly. 'God help us, or her, if that changes now.'

She would not have been in the least reassured if she could have seen Alathea at that moment. Standing in the attic studio, she was helpless with laughter as her client went through a brisk series of mock poses, each one more languorous and affected than the last. 'And see here,' John Wilmot said, with the same wild extravagance he had used to remove his Court finery the day before, 'My Lady Castlemaine the Madonna, clasping her beloved infant to her breast, melting with mercenary love.'

'Put my plaster cherub down! It cost me five shillings, and Lovell broke the last one only three weeks ago.'

'And doubtless Strephon will account for this in due course. Never fear, I shall buy you another.' He tossed her the little statue carelessly and Alathea, still laughing, caught it more by luck than anything else. She set it down on the table with exaggerated care and picked up paper and board and chalk. 'It has now undergone a miraculous transformation – from royal bastard to mischievous monkey. There is Strephon, my lord – crown him with laurel.'

'You mistake – I am not your lord. I have not heard your command.'

'John – for God's sake crown that monkey before I throw a varnish-pot at you.'

'Threatened thus, how could I delay?' He took up his pose, standing in front of the table, right hand raised above the cherub's fat white curls, left hand on his hip, staring at her ironically. 'Will that suffice?'

'Exactly. Now hold yourself still for at least an hour, and I will make a sketch.' She set to work with her usual swift dexterity, while he stood still and steady, eyebrows raised with that look of sardonic, rather cynical enquiry, and managed to ignore the growing ache in his right arm. In five minutes she was done. She cast down the board with a conspiratorial, mischievous smile, and said, 'You may now move.'

'I don't think I can. My neck is stiffer than the Duke of York's – why do you painters always insist on such plaguey uncomfortable poses?'

'Because my clients usually make a particular request for them,' said Alathea sweetly. 'Well? Do you like it?'

The pose was just as he had imagined it, unusual and dramatic: the point he wished to make would be quite plain. And she had sketched in his face, but exaggerated it almost to caricature. The long dark eyes leered cynically, the mouth was twisted, the nose too long and haughty: it gave a vivid and astonishing portrayal of an attractive but essentially evil personality.

And he had thought she liked him, he had felt, as surely she had, the bright spark of communication between them. His initial reaction was one of furious, betrayed anger. He thrust the board and paper back at her, and then saw her clear, honest eyes studying him. 'I don't mean it seriously,' she said. 'It's just . . . a warning. To me, too. I'll throw it on the fire, if you like.'

'No – it startled me, that is all. A little idea of how others see you,' said John with some bitterness, 'is very good for the soul.'

'How remarkable – informed report swears that you lack one. You remind me of that long turgid poem by that old Roundhead, what's his name, Milton? Setting out to create the Devil, and falling in love with him despite himself . . . you must beware, Lucifer, or you will become your own creation.'

'I will bear your warning in mind,' he said, with portentous solemnity, and had the satisfaction of making her laugh again.

CHAPTER THIRTEEN

Portraits à la mode

Wild, witty, lovesome, beautiful and young.
(Etherege, *The Man of Mode*)

It did not, in the nature of things, escape the attention of his friends that the Earl of Rochester had a new interest in Covent Garden. He might tell Buckhurst or Sedley that he was merely sitting for his portrait, but after Henry Jermyn's assiduous scandalmongering, the entire population of Whitehall, from the King down to the washerwomen, knew that the painter of that portrait was young, female and delectably pretty.

Hugh heard it, and his skin crawled. In vain he wrestled with his conscience: for what, after all, did he want for Alathea? A humble obscurity quite at odds with her gift? He could not condemn her to such a fate, and yet the recognition that was her due brought also the dangers that any young, relatively unprotected and inexperienced girl would face, drawn into the greedy, lustful clutches of the Court.

And Alathea was essentially honest: her name itself meant 'truth'. How would she fare, amongst all those lecherous, devious, stifling intrigues? He could only guide, advise, warn, and there was a fierce independence in Alathea that spurned such protectiveness, as Henrietta had seen.

He met Rochester one evening, at a Whitehall supper given by Mistress Gwynn, newly and highly in the King's favour. It was a bawdy, drunken, riotous occasion, taking its tone very much from the cheerful, lusty vulgarity of its hostess. Hugh had only to think of the absurd contrast between this earthy beauty, reared in a bawdy-house, who had entertained more men in her bed even than the Castlemaine, and the other Nell he knew, pale and wan and anxious, in Covent Garden, to laugh aloud. On the whole, it was an excellent evening, save that at one point, the wine mastered his better judgement, and he found himself doing that most ill-advised thing, dispensing veiled warnings to the Earl of Rochester.

It was a grievous mistake. Those dark, inimical eyes, glittering with drink and a wilderness of malice, stared coldly back. 'Mistress Heron? I have done nothing, I recall, save sit to her for my portrait. And besides, what concern have you in the matter? Unless, of course, you want to bed her yourself.'

Fortunately, no one else had heard, and Hugh was not sufficiently far gone in drink to yield to his first impulse, to strike him. With a great effort, he kept calm and said briskly, 'Of course not – I'm merely concerned for her welfare. She's young, and unused to the ways of the world.'

'She's older than Nelly Gwynn,' said Rochester, drawling lazily in a way that Hugh recognised to be a danger signal. 'And I don't see much evidence of any concern for *her* welfare.'

'Thea wasn't raised in a bawdy-house. Nor does she have a drunken drab for a mother.'

'No? You surprise me.'

By some miracle, Hugh kept his temper still. Aware that he was being goaded, he said deliberately, 'No matter. But I stand in a brother's place, and I have a care for her. I pray you, remember it.'

'Perhaps. But I'll wager she'll be in my bed – *willingly* – before the year's out. You hear that, Charles?' Sedley's flushed face, blearily and stupidly drunk, leered into view. 'I'll wager this gentleman twenty guineas I'll seduce his niece before Christmas. Done?'

'Done,' said Hugh, between his teeth, his hands itching to kill.

'You *what*?' Alathea stared at her client in astonished disbelief. 'You wagered *that* – with *Hugh*? Why are you still alive?'

'Because your Hugh in his cups has some sense still. I have less and less, and grow as undisciplined as a monkey – hence that rather ungentlemanly wager. In mitigation, I plead that it was the Earl of Rochester made it, m'lud – honest John Wilmot stands innocent.'

'As innocent as Lucifer,' said Alathea. Mechanically, her brush dabbed at the florid, orange-tawny satin classically draping that slender, arrogant body, immortalised on her canvas. She wondered, with a certain bemused detachment, whether he would notice that her hands were shaking and that her face was unusually flushed. 'I shall endeavour to keep my honour intact – Hugh would be glad of twenty guineas.'

'A shame,' he said, lightly. Over the last few weeks, as the portrait and their friendship had grown together, he had come to value her wit and humour and intelligence. The fashionable world outside this house expected him to bed her as a matter of course, but true friendship seemed more important.

And yet . . . the attraction was there, growing stronger each time he met her: and to be unmoved by that face, that hair, even if they had adorned a statue, would have been impossible for a saint. That he most assuredly was not, and when beauty combined with other, less tangible assets, far stronger men than he had been lost. Once more, words were forming their patterns inside his head: verses praising her beauty, wit and innocence, yet begging her to surrender the last of those qualities at least to his lust. The absurd irony of it struck him with some force, and he began to laugh.

'Don't do that,' said the artist, severely. 'Or I'll laugh too, and spoil something. And that would be a shame, after all my work.'

'Your work? I thought an army of assistants crawled out of the woodwork at dusk and touched up the unimportant bits until dawn broke over Covent Garden.'

'You mistake, sir – I am not Lely. All of this has been done with my own fair hands.' She glanced round at the hour-glass on the table. 'Your time is almost up, I regret to say. One more sitting should do it – and then it will be finished.'

'A shame – I look forward to our meetings, and now I will no longer have an excuse that will satisfy the gossips. May I move? More to the point, may I look?'

'You may not, until next time. I want it to be a surprise.'

'That doesn't exactly inspire me with confidence. What have

you done?'

'Nothing very horrific – the horns are very small, and the tail amost invisible unless you hunt for it.' Alathea turned back to the picture, and his next move took her completely by surprise. With startling speed, he dropped the laurels and whipped round to the front of the easel, which was placed quite close to where he had been standing. With a yell of indignation, Alathea lunged to stop him. She was strong and wiry, and for a moment she succeeded. They struggled together, paint-laden brushes dropping to the floor, and then his superior strength told. He pinioned her flailing arms to her sides, ignoring her breathless, laughing protests, and peered past her at the picture. After a moment, as her movements ceased, he said, his voice puzzled, 'But it's finished.'

Alathea had made herself small and still in his imprisoning grasp. She knew a way, taught long ago by Hugh, of escaping, but hesitated to be quite so ruthless, for inflicting grievous harm on a Peer of the Realm might not be a particularly good idea. But she would not have to use such methods against John Wilmot. Relaxing, she grinned. 'You're quite right, it is.'

'Then why did you pretend it was not?'

'For the same reason as you regretted that there would be only one more sitting.'

'I was under the impression that you had been aptly named. Now, I'm not so sure. Do you promise not to struggle or scream or behave in an unladylike way?'

'Yes – if I can.'

'Good. Now, I'm going to do something that I've been wanting to do since I first came here.' And gently, with mischief, John bent his head and kissed her: then, he let her go.

Alathea stood quite still, a riot of emotions churning within her head, staring at him. He found he wanted to do it again. Instead, he said roughly, 'Dear Christ, you look as if no one has ever tried to do that to you before . . . have they?'

'No . . . ' said Alathea, and her voice died away as she remembered suddenly, like a bad dream best forgotten, the moment when her brother Kit had tried to kiss her at the Twelfth Night celebrations at Ashcott, nearly four years ago. He made a most inauspicious, ill-timed revenant.

She shivered abruptly, and John, watching her closely, said at once, with an irony that scarcely disguised his concern, 'Do you find me so repellent?'

'No – no, a ghost walked over my grave, that's all.'

'A past lover?'

'No, I haven't had any – but one who might have been, given the chance.' She resisted the impulse to confide in him, for one day, his path and Kit's might cross again, and instinct told her that disaster might follow if the truth were known. And besides, she was still loyal, to Kit's previous, happier self.

His next question took her completely by surprise. 'Was it Hugh?'

'*Hugh*?' Alathea stared at him, and then began to laugh. '*Hugh*? No, of course not. Oh, he's dear to me, and I to him, and he's like another brother to add to the three I have already. But no – he has no desire to be my lover, and I have no desire for him.' Suddenly confused by this frank conversation, she turned away to stand by the window, feeling her skin flushed, her heart hurrying. He had kissed her, and brief though it was, she had enjoyed it . . . enjoyed it, and wanted more. And this was a man already married, a man, however charming a companion, who had an appalling reputation as a rake, a drunkard, a wencher with a taste for whores and actresses. To accept his attentions was to place herself, in the eyes of the world, on that lowest level: to become a creature as depraved and dishonoured as they.

And yet, what was a woman's honour? Alathea asked herself savagely. A concept designed by men for men's benefit, to protect their goods on offer before marriage, to gain the highest price, and after marriage, to ensure the legitimacy of their children and their own standing amongst their friends and relations. Since she had no intention of marrying, neither argument could possibly influence her. What did weigh heaviest in the balance was the opinion of those she valued. She had no intention of reducing herself in the eyes of her family and friends, for the sake of one kiss from a practised and reportedly unscrupulous seducer.

'Have I upset you?' he was saying, suddenly very close behind her. She stiffened, still staring out of the window. 'I meant it only in friendship.' It was a lie: friendship was no longer enough for him. But he was not dealing with a cheap and easy strumpet, and he was aware that, in a sense, he had betrayed her trust. He put his hands on those thin, straight, stiff shoulders, and felt the sudden tension beneath his fingers. 'Forget it, if you would prefer.'

'But I can't!' Alathea jerked round to face him. 'You may have meant one kiss in friendship, but I can't help but think it was more.'

'And if it was?'

'Then it was a kiss from Rochester, not John Wilmot. And I don't want that Earl's kisses, or anything else he may offer, for in the world's eyes it's tainted coin. It's honest John Wilmot I would rather have for my friend – and he would not take advantage.' She drew a rather shaky breath, and managed a grin from somewhere. 'And besides, the monkey would be jealous.'

'Strephon, jealous of Celadon and Alathea – your name fits too well into a pastoral poem. Don't worry, dear girl, I will importune you no more, if you are disturbed by it.'

'I've enjoyed our friendship,' said Alathea slowly. 'I am honoured by it, for I know that you do not show it to everyone, and those who count themselves your friends must have earned the privilege. And it's not one I would want to lose. But more . . . more I am not ready for. Not yet.'

'Not yet . . . ' he repeated. 'Then you give me hope, fair nymph – ouch!'

'That was to remind you that I am no nymph. They don't make a habit of treading heavily on the toes of their importuning swains. Do you know an old sonnet by Shakespeare? "I grant I never saw a goddess go: my mistress, when she walks, treads on the ground." I'll be wooed by no fine phrases, sir, no talk of shepherdesses and sighing rustics.'

'Then what will win you, if not praise and sweet talk?'

'Laughter,' said Alathea, smiling.

Jóhn stood quite still, his curious dark eyes searching her face. He said at last, 'If one day you change your mind, if you decide to enter the lists of love, and can throw honour to the winds . . . I have already discarded mine. And you have rare beauty, and a rarer wit, and a gift you should not hide away under a Covent Garden bushel: "Small is the worth of beauty from the light retired." '

'Waller,' said Alathea immediately. 'A song which begins, "Go lovely rose" . . . it was always one of my favourites. If I ever emerge from my garret into the merciless light of Court, may I count on your favour, if not your protection? And remember, that if I should chance to read a scurrilous lampoon about myself, I shall know the author – and I can reply to your words with paint.'

'I've already seen what you can do. May I come back, next week, to finish the picture?'

'It is finished.'

'No – I'm not satisfied with the monkey. And may I bring a friend or two? I have spread word of my portrait, and they are with child to see it – you may have some custom there. Sedley is particularly keen for some dramatic likeness, full of symbols and signs.'

'And what do I paint him crowning? A dildo?'

'I don't know why all your friends seem so concerned to protect you from me and my Merry Gang,' he said when he had done laughing. 'You are more than capable of protecting yourself. Next Thursday, at two?'

'I will see you then, and I won't tell Hen about your friends, or she'll probably hire a trio of bully-boys with cudgels to guard my virtue. Goodbye,' said Alathea, escorting her distinguished client to the door. 'And thank you, for settling for friendship.'

Thursday was a week away, and that week dragged sorely. Alathea, by nature prone to analysing herself, had plenty of time to ponder her last conversation with John Wilmot, and came reluctantly to a conclusion that appalled her. She, who had so stoutly defended her right to enter a man's world on masculine terms, and rejected the more 'natural' role of woman as slave and helpmeet to man, was in grave danger. Danger not so much from Rochester, though that she knew, and found that it added a delicious spice to her emotions to arouse the interest of such a notorious man, but from that proverbial enemy of honour and reputation and maidenhead, Love. It was as if she had been long a-drowning, and had only now realised her peril. She made stern resolutions, and forgot them all when, on the Monday, a boy brought a note to the door.

Fortunately, she managed to seize upon it before Henrietta could become aware of its delivery. The writing was jagged, individual, spiky: she did not recognise it. There was no letter within, no explanation, no signature, only a poem. And as she read, in growing wonderment, she knew who thus addressed her. True, she was fancifully named ('Olinda', indeed: she crackled the paper scornfully). But it was the second verse that caught her attention, and led her on, helpless, ensnared by the words he had dedicated to her:

When innocence, beauty and wit do conspire
To betray, and engage, and inflame my desire,
Why should I decline what I cannot avoid,
And let pleasing hope by base fear be destroyed?

Her innocence cannot contrive to undo me:
Her beauty's inclined, or why should it pursue me?
And wit has to pleasure been ever a friend:
Then what room for despair, since delight is love's end?

There can be no danger in sweetness and youth
Where love is secured by good nature and truth.
On her beauty I'll gaze, and of pleasure complain
While every kind look adds a link to my chain.

'Tis more to maintain than it was to surprise
But her wit leads in triumph the slave of her eyes,
I beheld with the loss of my freedom before,
But, hearing, forever must serve and adore.

Alathea, reading, felt an extraordinary mixture of emotions tumbling within her. Wonder, that this graceful, accomplished poem was addressed to her: astonishment, and joy, at the feelings it expressed – *if* they were true, a little cynical voice added. But she was also afraid, frightened of the power she had unleashed, the feelings she appeared to be able to command in this strange, complex, disturbing man, the deep waters she was fast running into. She had been able to deal with Jasper, but she was not at all sure of her ability to cope with this, and her first instinct was to flee from it.

But she could not, would not run away. *He promised friendship,* she remembered firmly. *and friendship he shall have, till I decide, or he does, that we shall have more, or less. And if he thinks that a pretty poem will change my mind so easy, well, it's plain to see he's had no acquaintance with Herons.*

On Thursday, at a little past two, My Lord Rochester's coach drew up outside the Covent Garden house, attended by the usual rabble of whores, onlookers, street sellers and urchins, and belched forth three members of the Merry Gang, all of whom had dined rather too well at Chatelin's, the highly fashionable, and highly expensive, eating-house in Drury Lane. The jostling, curious crowds were vastly amused by Harry Savile, who misjudged the step and fell heavily on his face in a puddle, and by Sir Charles Sedley, who picked him up, solicitously wiped off the worst of the mud and attempted to dance with him. The Earl of Rochester, apparently oblivious to these unseemly goings-on, was addressing a verse, extempore, to the nearest horse, and his monkey, sporting a neat little tailored jacket of the same cloth and style as his own, sat on the astonished animal's crupper and scratched itself in a shockingly intimate place. One of the whores called out an obscene suggestion, pertaining to himself and the monkey, and windows began to open. Belatedly, he remembered the value of discretion in this particular place, gave orders to the coachman, retrieved Savile and Sedley, and sought admittance to Alathea's house.

The door was opened by Henrietta Jermyn, with a face like rock. She cast her eyes stonily over the unedifying spectacle of the three Wits, variously the worse for drink, supporting each other in the arcaded walkway outside, and seemed inclined to turn them away. Rochester, grinning, cast about in his mind for a suitable couplet, but was forestalled. Alathea came into view down the staircase behind her housekeeper, and quoted happily, ' "Knock, knock, knock, who's there 'i' the name of Beelzebub?" '

' "The three things that drink prooked," ' said John Wilmot, who had a nodding acquaintance with *Macbeth*, having seen it many a time at the Duke's playhouse in Lincoln's Inn Fields. 'Mistress Jermyn – may we enter?'

'If you must,' said Henrietta. She opened the door wider, and the three things that drink provoked came, or rather fell, across the threshold.

Alathea, standing with hands on hips at the foot of the stairs, did not seem to be in the least shocked or angry. In fact, the main emotion seething behind her bland, slightly ironic expression was an urgent desire to laugh. 'Will we need a bowl, do you think?'

'I'll get the shovel from the bread-oven,' Henrietta added. She was still annoyed and uneasy at this uncouth invasion, but had decided, for Alathea's sake, to behave in a light-hearted manner, just as she had once behaved to her husband Charles, late home from some Whitehall carouse. 'You might need to shovel them out of doors again.'

'I might at that,' said Alathea, consideringly. 'I take it, gentlemen, that you have already adequately dined?'

'We have indeed – and it was ambrosia – nectar – the gods could not have feasted with more pleasure!' cried Harry Savile. 'Monsieur Chatelin's cuisine is exquisite, and the wine . . . '

'I take it, then, that your pockets are all to let as well as your brains?' Alathea enquired caustically.

'I shall make a gallon or two of coffee,' Henrietta said. 'I always found it an excellent remedy for too good a dinner.' She vanished purposefully in the direction of the basement kitchen, leaving Alathea alone with her disreputable guests in the hall.

'Mistress Heron . . . ' John, for once, seemed more sober than his companions, from which she had deduced that he possessed some shreds of a conscience still. 'Alathea, may I humbly present Sir Charles Sedley . . . '

'Forever and most abasedly yours, madam!'

'Most honoured, sir . . . you are the friend of Oxford Kate's, I take it? I shall *not* offer you a glass of wine, and I wouldn't advise you to do what you did on that balcony in Hen's coffee. She heats it almost to boiling!'

Sedley's plump, red-nosed face was a picture, a mixture of the imagined pain her words had implied, and amusement at her boldness. 'I would not have thought a virtuous, modest young maiden like yourself would have known of that exploit, Mistress. You cannot have been more than a young child – it was seven or eight years ago.'

'I heard of it from my cousin, who I fear is rather a ruffian,' said Alathea, the picture of demureness, eyes cast down, and inwardly boiling with wild and astonished laughter at her daring. Sedley, overcome with delighted mirth, was roaring with rather inebriated laughter: one of the acknowledged Wits of the town, the man whose running commentary on bad plays was heeded more avidly by the audience than the words of the actors, and she had genuinely amused him. Intoxicated at her success with this incongruous gift for humorous, oblique bawdry, she turned, suddenly sparkling, to Harry Savile with a smile that stopped his breath for a moment. 'And who is this, John? Pray present me.'

'My fat friend is Master Harry Savile, who lays claim to a love of wine, women and songs almost as great as my own. Make your bow, Harry, and stop gawping – you've surely seen a woman before?'

'But never one of such beauty,' said Savile gallantly, making a modish bow rather spoiled by a certain unsteadiness of stance. 'I am most deeply honoured, and most humbly your servant. And has this lovely lady also painted your portrait, John? It seems too good to be true, such loveliness, such wit, such a gift!' He belched, and Sedley slapped him exuberantly between the shoulders.

Above their corpulent figures, the eyes of Alathea and John, grey-green and brown, met with amusement. 'Do you think they will manage to negotiate the stairs?'

'I doubt it,' John said. He gave her the vivid, sudden smile that was part of his abundant charm. 'I am sorry for this . . . for them. I am afraid the wine was too good, and it tempted us.'

'That's no matter,' Alathea told him. 'You have no idea how my days are enlivened, even by a pack of drunken Wits – and a monkey.' She held out her hand, clucking softly, and Strephon, eyes bright, sat upright on his master's shoulder and clucked back.

'They came to see the picture, as well,' he reminded her. 'Perhaps, the coffee will flatten the stairs for them.'

The coffee was hot, strong, and a sovereign remedy, as Hen had long ago discovered, for the effects of over-indulgence in alcohol. Under its sobering influence, Savile and Sedley became rather less prone to bouts of riotous and unexplained mirth, and their wit flew less hectically. Even Henrietta, still suspicious, could find little to which she might object, and Becca, drawn by the lure of Strephon the monkey, crept through the door of the downstairs chamber like a little dark ghost, and curled up unnoticed in the corner to play with him. Only Alathea, rising to escort her guests to the studio, saw them, and smiled to herself, and left them in peace.

Three increasingly steep flights of stairs above them, the portrait of John Wilmot, second Earl of Rochester, and Strephon his monkey, stood alone, propped on its easel, drying tackily. Alathea, very conscious of the fact that she had made a considerable impression on these courtly men of mode, ushered them into its presence with a certain amount of trepidation. She might have been admired for her looks and her wit, but her painting was still the criterion by which she desired to be judged.

Even John, who had seen it before, was struck by the graceful, fluid lines with which her brush had described him, and the likeness both to himself and to Strephon was very convincing. Sedley, seeing it, gave a bray of laughter. 'Rochester, you devil, that's you to the life – and that damned monkey, too! I'll wager you decided upon that pose, eh? Crowning that ill-mannered creature with laurel, that's a fine joke!'

Harry Savile, whom Alathea already preferred to his more boisterous companion, stood thoughtfully staring at it, arms folded across his neatly rounded stomach. 'I agree – the likeness is quite remarkable. Who's to have it, John? Your wife? God forbid, your mother?'

'If I gave it to one, the other would be jealous. My dear wife and my dear mother have been vying for my undivided heart for nearly three years now, and neither know that they cannot have it – for I'm no more capable of loving one person exclusively than of flying. Never acquire a wife, Harry – of all the banes of a man's existence, they are the worst. You may love 'em dearly, but they always manage to make you feel guilty for sins of omission – or commission!'

Over Sedley's laughter, Alathea said wryly, 'It seems, then, that I've been born the wrong sex.'

'Never, fair Alathea!' Sedley cried, sweeping her a perfect flourish of a bow.

John watched her, the clear serene face at odds with the mischievous irony around her eyes and mouth, and smiled. 'Explain yourself, dear girl.'

'It seems that it's the fashion for a man to deplore ever taking a wife. Of all impediments to a modish life, a wife is the worst, you say. Are you all agreed on that?'

The answer came in triplicate. Alathea, grinning, went on. 'But I also have no intention of marrying. I do not desire a husband. I have no protector, save my young brother, who lives here, and my father and mother who live in the country. I can survive on my wits, and on my painting. And yet I declare my life's philosophy, which isn't too dissimilar to yours, and I'm howled out of court. Why am I not allowed to be as independent as a man? Why is it so shocking for me to abjure marriage? And you *are* shocked, Master Savile, I can see it in your face.'

'Not he,' John Wilmot pointed out. 'Only a direct strike of a lightning bolt could ever shock Master Harry. There's sense in what you say, I'll admit, but it's agreed by all the world that a woman's place is under a man's thumb. And before you throw something at me, may I remind you that the *world* may think that, but I do not necessarily agree with them. You should meet a friend of mine – Mistress Behn. She is somewhat older than you, and she's led a wild life, but she has many ideas that echo yours. She doesn't paint, though – or not in your style – but she writes poetry, plays one day perhaps, and she wants to earn her bread from it too.'

'Bring her with you when you come here next,' Alathea said innocently.

John glanced at her, and grinned. 'Why should I need to come back? My portrait is finished. I do not require another.'

'You'll require another sight of Mistress Heron, I'll wager,' said Sedley, sotto voce. 'And so will I,' he added, more loudly. 'Will you paint my portrait, Mistress Heron?'

It seemed to Alathea that the next few weeks were the most hectic of her life, for suddenly, with dazzling speed, fame had embraced her after the years of neglect, and she found herself feted by the Merry Gang, and deluged with requests to paint them. Sedley, Savile, Lord Buckhurst – all arrived on her doorstep to make appointments, closely followed by other Court luminaries, of more or less savoury reputation, driven by curiosity or whim. Astonishingly, she discovered that she was the fashion. She scarcely heeded Christmas as it passed wanly amidst the whirlwind of activity around her, and her abstracted appearances at the handsome, new-built House of the Ash Tree alarmed her aunt. But Alathea was not ill, nor over-worked. Like Math, she had the capacity to absorb herself utterly in whatever consumed her interest at the time, and if forced to pay a social call during a particularly intense bout of painting, was apt to be still planning her picture and making polite but abstracted conversation at the same time. Henrietta, ever practical, made sure she received regular meals and an early bedtime, Nell mixed paints and taught a boy, Jonathan Carter, who had been taken on to assist in the rush of commissions. Matthew took a mild interest, and did not know whether to be amused or insulted when shown a series of his sister's quick sketches in the new soft grey plumbago, depicting varied and riotous activity all around while he remained the constant, unchanging centre in each one, nose in book. She sketched her new friends, too, for they had taken up the habit of visiting her studio for an afternoon's witty talk over pots of hot coffee while she worked, and as a break from the task of painting Alathea would amuse herself, and them, with little quick vivid pictures, catching them all in a moment: Savile's rotundity, Sedley's extravagant gestures, John Wilmot's sardonic gaze, the wild antics of Strephon the monkey and his teasing of poor Lovell, whom he rode like a jockey on a racehorse. Lovell had nearly wrecked the studio the first time that Strephon had crouched on his back, completely overset by this devilish, inaccessible creature: now he just grunted and tried to roll over. All of it went down on paper, and the corner of the studio was filled with overflowing boxes containing Alathea's drawings. It was as if a great and glorious enchantment had gripped her, as if she moved in a heady, exciting and intoxicating new world where everything she did and said had the touch of inspiration and the spark of sorcery. She had never encountered these powerful, exalted and very dangerous young men outside her own door, and she had a superstitious fear that, if she did, the tables would be turned and she would become just another well-born virgin, ripe for the plucking. But in the Covent Garden house, she reigned supreme, mistress of paint and wit, coffee-pot and wine and racy double entendre, the property of no man and the equal of all. For the first time she discovered that her intellect, as well as her gifts, was the match of theirs, and met them on the same level, mind to mind, eye to eye, joke to laughter.

Yet all the time, as she painted Sedley and Buckhurst and a string of foppish hangers-on, it was to John Wilmot that she silently dedicated her wit, John Wilmot's admiration and approval that she looked for, John Wilmot's eye that she sought in secret, joyous understanding of a jest or an inspired flight of verbal fancy. She tried to deny it, to suppress it, to forget it, but was forever betrayed by the movement of her heart when he looked at her. She did not mention the poem, and for the time being there were no more, but she kept it in a little box by her bed, with her most precious possessions.

The year turned, and spring grew slowly, and her circle widened still more. Maids-of-honour, dripping with jewels and giggles, escorted by poker-faced maidservants, came to the fashionable female painter from whom they need fear no assault on their, mostly, rather dubious virtue, and one very meek and pious young girl, grave and quiet, who turned out to be related to her by marriage. Margaret Blagge's father had been the brother of Nan, Lord Bradfield's wife, and in the eyes of both girls that made them cousins. It was all they proved to have in common, however. Margaret wished to have herself painted demurely, eyes downcast to a book of devotions, and in a very concealing dark dress, and regarded this shocking female artist with a rather appalled wariness. Court gossip, Alathea suspected, had already made her the mistress of half the Merry Gang. She tried to be friendly to Margaret, but never progressed beyond stilted family enquiries. Other Suffolk courtiers came to be painted: the brothers John and Tom Hervey, contemporaries of her parents, and the infamous Bab May, Sir Tom Hervey's brother-in-law, who turned out to be a fat, merry, middle-aged man with a leering eye and a roving hand. She would not have scrupled to kick him in the shins, or worse, but avoided embarrassment by making sure that the boy assistant Jonathan was always obtrusively present when Bab May sat for her. It was part of the price she must pay for her new-found and glorious fame.

CHAPTER FOURTEEN

A dragon in the heart

. . . In his soul
He feels the torment of his raging lust.

(Ford, *'Tis Pity She's a Whore*)

One cold raw winter's afternoon late in February, the attic studio was warm and crowded with people and tobacco smoke. The two fires, one at each end, had been burning cheerfully all day, tended by Jonathan. He was crouched over the lesser blaze now, coaxing it into new life in preparation for boiling varnish. By the other, Alathea sat in her everyday winter gown, a rich sea-green velvet with a warm lacy scarf around her shoulders, board and sketch-paper and chalks and plumbago on her knee. A coffee-pot stood on a trivet in the warm ashes, keeping hot, and Nell, her pale face intent, was attempting to toast bread over the glowing embers at the heart of the fire. Around it sat or sprawled the afternoon's visitors: Sedley, Lord Buckhurst, Savile, John Wilmot, and Buckhurst's companion Fleetwood Shepherd. There was a bottle or two of wine, empty now, but the talk was theatrical, of the new play written by the actor Betterton, the sensation of the week and still playing to packed houses, and of how it compared with the various dramatic works produced by the Merry Gang, when they could muster the energy and self-organisation to set aside a week or two for the transformation of their sparkling wit into written plays and comedies. Alathea drew, and kept her counsel with a small amused smile lingering at the corners of her mouth. She had seen Sedley's contribution, *The Mulberry Garden*, a year or so previously, and been singularly unimpressed. Sir Charles's famous wit and banter had not, it seemed, translated well to the stage, and the King had not laughed once. She sketched Nell, hunched over the fire with a smoking slice of bread impaled on a clean paint-brush, and then Lovell, who was putting everyone else to some inconvenience, being squashed as near to the flames as he could and blocking out a large part of the heat, the target of lazy, amiable abuse at regular intervals.

Faintly, she became aware of some kind of distant commotion. A disturbance in the Piazza, perhaps – save that the studio's two windows looked over the garden, and were firmly shut against the cold. The noise grew louder: she could distinguish Hen's voice, intermingled with some man's. Then feet ran heavily up the stairs outside, and the door was hurled open, almost taking it off the hinges. And there in its place stood a tall, extravagantly dressed figure, sporting an exuberant dark periwig curled in an unmistakeably French style, silver lace, crimson velvet and a hat almost hidden beneath its burden of red-dyed plumes. For one mad instant, she did not recognise the sun-tanned, handsome face, and then the very blue eyes and the wild smile told her his identity, and with genuine gladness, she jumped to her feet, scattering chalk and paper.

'Kit! Oh, Kit, you've come back!' Spurred by impulsive delight, she ran to welcome him. The long arms caught at her, and she was kissed with respectable enthusiasm on both cheeks, as befitted brother and sister, but one quick glance at his face, at the devouring passionate eyes, told her that after three years in foreign parts, nothing had really changed. As if stung, Alathea dropped her hands and turned back towards her guests, her heart cold within her.

'A long-lost lover?' drawled Buckhurst, completing her discomfiture, and Alathea's skin crawled.

Kit's laugh was loud, jovial and entirely false. 'Lover, eh? Long-gone brother, sir – to my regret.'

Thinking it time to set things in some order, Alathea said quickly, 'May I present my brother, Kit – and pray excuse my welcome, he's been three years in Italy. My Lord Buckhurst – My Lord Rochester – Sir Charles Sedley – Master Savile – Master Shepherd. My brother, Kit Drakelon.'

There followed the usual exchange of courtly bows and rituals, during which Kit's polite mask never cracked to reveal the terrible maelstrom of emotions beneath. He had heard, as who had not, of these men, had laughed at their obscener exploits, knew them for thoroughly debauched rakes – Sedley and Buckhurst were widely reputed to be the wickedest men of the age and Rochester, though much younger, was fast catching up. But to laugh at their exploits was one matter: to find his adored sister in their exclusive company (as usual, he had not noticed Nell), was quite another. She obviously knew them well, they addressed her by her given name, they made free with her coffee and her time and her talk. What else had they made free with?

Hungrily, but also with dread, he searched her face, her talk and gestures, for any sign that she was more than friendly with her aristocratic and unruly guests. They themselves seemed to accept him on his own terms, and he found that he could acquit himself tolerably well in such fashionable company, particularly since he was able to regale them with the latest gossip, news and fashions from Paris, which he had left only a few days previously. Alathea sat on her stool by the fire, poured him coffee, offered him wine before discovering that the bottles were all empty. He noticed the tumbled pile of paper and chalk at her feet, and saw the stacked canvases and the fat jovial face of Sedley peering down from the easel, all the signs of a busy studio. She had achieved her ambition, it seemed, she was a successful painter, the height of fashion judging by the presence of the Wits. But what price had she paid for it? demanded his jealous, fevered mind, tormenting him with scenes of her seduction by any or all of these wild, lecherous young men who sat in her studio with as much ease as if they lived there. And he could not help noticing that of all of them, it was Rochester to whom her eyes turned most often, the devil with the angel's face, and tongue, the man who could lure any woman into his bed and discard her like a rotten apple once the prize was won.

As darkness drew close, the Wits uttered their farewells and departed, after making an appointment for Sedley's next sitting in a few days' time. Despite all that amicable exchange of French gossip, there was no doubt in Alathea's mind that Kit's arrival had cast something of a blight over the spirited banter of the afternoon, and so much was she now a part of their company that Kit's entry had seemed like an intrusion, an invasion of their privacy. His eyes were an invasion of hers. Sitting by the fire, ignoring Nell and the boy Jonathan, he stared at her as she moved about the studio, tidying and cleaning, never moving from her face. At length, as she came to sit beside him, the wary smile back around her mouth, he said angrily, 'Why in God's name do you invite those men here? They're rogues and wenchers, every one. Have you no thought for your virtue, at all?'

'A little,' said Alathea, who had just decided that light-heartedness was the best answer to this sort of attack. 'But they are my friends, and have been for a few months now, and I can assure you that no harm has come to me. Nell and Hen will vouch for them,' she added cheerfully. 'And I don't think they're as black as their reputations have painted them. Perhaps their conversation might not be acceptable to elderly ladies of prudish disposition, but none of them has ever behaved in any disrespectful way towards me – and I don't think they'd dare,' she finished, with a grin.

Kit did not echo it; he sat glowering at her. 'You shouldn't let them past the door,' he said. 'And if I had any say in the matter, you wouldn't.'

'But you have no say in the matter,' Alathea pointed out, more coldly. Her initial pleasure at his return had quite disappeared, and she found herself wishing, with some force, for the presence of Hugh. But he had not been to Covent Garden for several days, and she was not even sure whether or not he was in London. 'The house is Lord Bradfield's, and I have rented it from him, with his permission. I am mistress here, and I will welcome my friends as I please. If it doesn't please you, Kit, then I am sorry – but I run my life to suit myself, not anyone else.'

'As I can see,' Kit said unpleasantly. 'But it might be wise to run your life more to Lord Bradfield's taste. What would he think if he'd walked through that door this afternoon?'

'He didn't, so it's immaterial,' Alathea pointed out, the anger growing inside her like a cold hard fist within her ribs. If he was not threatening her, his words certainly seemed to imply some sort of warning, and she knew that if any word of the disreputable company she kept was ever to reach Lord Bradfield's bigoted ears, her comfortable, successful life at Covent Garden would become very precarious indeed.

And Kit was quite capable of sending that word. She knew how his passionate jealousy could transcend all standards of fairness and reason. Life in the company of the Merry Gang had honed her wit and vastly increased her confidence, she had proved herself capable of handling their diverse and unstable natures, and with a little cool-headedness and cunning and perception, she could surely handle Kit.

So, she hid her anger and added, with her most dazzling smile, 'But let's not quarrel, the instant you come home . . . you look very fine, Italy must have suited you. Come on, Kit, let me get you some chocolate, with cream and cinnamon just as you like it, and we'll have a quiet cose and you can tell me all your travels – you've three years' news to give me, don't you dare try to get away with the little you've said so far. Do tell me more of Venice – they say it's the most ravishingly lovely place in all the world.'

And it worked. If her tone sounded false to her own ears, it did not to Kit, to whose desperate tormented mind such evidence of her care and affection and interest came as the finest healing balm. The chocolate was brought, made indeed as he liked it, and they sat by the studio fire long after dark, long after Nell and Jonathan, moving as silently as people who fear to provoke an earthquake, had crept from the room. And Alathea felt again the old pull of Kit's attraction, the danger and the charm together. In this mood, free for the moment of doubts and suspicion and corroding jealousies, he was a most entertaining companion, his stories delightful and his descriptions of the beauties of Italy, France, the Alps, most lyrical. She listened spellbound, seeing in her mind's eye the blue hills and tall dark cypresses, shimmering and dancing in the heat like a Titian painting brought to life, and felt great envy for Kit, who with a man's freedom and a man's money had seen all those things. And as if to heighten his own superiority, he sent for one of his travelling boxes, which had been left downstairs, and brought triumphantly forth from its packed depths two fat sketchbooks, crammed and crinkly and crackling with water-coloured painting of Italian prospects and Alpine vistas.

He had never had her gift. The scenes laid before her were painstaking, laboriously composed replicas of what he had seen, without any dash or flair or even any particular skill. But they breathed Italy, the bright heat and vibrant hazy air of Tuscany or Florence, and she was still more deeply envious of the opportunity he had so negligently grasped, taken for granted as part of his birthright, an opportunity which, her honesty told her, she would have turned to far greater advantage than he. She had always loved drawing views, prospects, places, like Ashcott and Goldhayes, almost as much as her painting of portraits. What could she not do, in Italy?

She sat rapt, dazed with dreams and visions, grief and envy, as his paintings followed one after the other through her fingers, and Kit saw the wonder in her face and the power of the emotions that had made her eyes fill with tears, and utterly misinterpreted her expression. *She admires them*, he thought, with fierce exultation. *I drew them all for her, and she loves them – my paintings!*

'They're beautiful,' Alathea whispered. 'Oh, Italy must be a wonderful place – so lovely – oh, how I wish I could go too!'

'Why don't you?' Kit demanded. 'Well, why not? I would take you, show you everything, teach you Italian – we could see the paintings and the churches, go to Rome and Venice and Padua and Florence . . . the Grand Tour for Alathea! Why don't we, Thea? There's no reason why we shouldn't.'

But there is, thought his sister, looking at those hungry blue eyes staring intently at her. *I could never support a week, let alone a year, two years, gallivanting round Europe in his exclusive company. I would be mad to go, and driven mad if I did. The world might think there was no harm in brother taking sister on such a journey, if a little strange. It's not a womanly thing to do, after all. But I would never be able to lower my guard, all that time, for he would slip through any chink in my defences, and . . .* She turned her mind away from that prospect with a shiver of fear. Hugh loved her, Oliver did, and in their diverse ways so did Math and Mun, but they were rational, sensible people, there was some inbuilt restraint on their affection for her, some barrier that prevented any progression from brotherly love into something more. But Kit, she knew, lacked that barrier, and she was beginning to wonder, remembering Hugh's story of his duel in Paris, how many other restrictions of civilised, sane behaviour were also missing from her half-brother's mind.

He is dangerous, said the voice inside her head, chiming the old warning bell. *He is beautiful and charming . . . and dangerous. Far more perilous than those wild rakehells you entertain so daringly in your studio, crossing mental swords and walking the balance between virgin and whore like a rope-dancer, and never falling from grace. With them, all you have to lose is your reputation. With Kit . . . the stakes are higher.*

But she enjoyed it, this feeling of being able to control and contain such power, as she enjoyed those elaborate games of wit and bawdry and double entendre with Rochester and Sedley and Buckhurst. For the moment, Kit was hers, her brother and her servant, and she had with her own skill calmed the whirlwind.

But she had to say that she could not go to Italy, diplomatically and tactfully, leaving the door open for future discussion. 'I can't, Kit – oh how I would love to go with you . . . but I haven't any money, and neither has Father. And I'll wager, after three years of high life on the Grand Tour, neither have you. Have you?'

Kit, with a slightly shamefaced smile, had to admit he could not afford to send himself on a second jaunt, much less take his sister along as well. 'But in a year or so, then we can go, eh, Thea?'

'And in a year, I should have saved some money from all this,' Alathea told him, with some pride, waving a hand around her studio. 'It may have escaped your notice, but of late I've been doing rather well. I have commissions from about a dozen courtiers at present, and as many again finished during the last few weeks, and they pay a good deal better than Dan's friends, as well.' She smiled. 'It appears I'm the latest fashion – although I won't be utterly in the mode until I receive a Royal Command from Whitehall. Or so says Hugh.'

'I still dislike the thought of you letting those rogues into the house,' said Kit, abruptly returning to his first theme. 'And still less the prospect of you painting the King.'

Alathea made a rude noise before she could stop herself, and it was perhaps fortunate that Hen chose that particular moment to announce that supper had been ten minutes on the table, and would they kindly favour everyone with their presence before the pigeon pie grew cold? And with, undeniably, a certain feeling of

relief, Alathea was able to break off the conversation
less fraught surroundings.

It was a very pleasant evening. Kit repeated his Italia
an enthralled supper table, and afterwards, round the
smaller back parlour (the great chamber being too big
these February days for informal gatherings), he was pers
display his virtuoso skill on lute and guitar, for everyone's
Alathea had a good true voice, and so did her brother Math
was surprisingly strong and pure, and by contrast, Hen
pitch was almost as low as a man's, throaty but accurate. They
and Kit played, to the great joy and satisfaction of all, and no
found their way to bed until past midnight. Kit, who had assu
his right to stay with an off-hand certainty that had even anno
Hen, had to share Matthew's chamber.

The next morning was cold, raw and damp. Alathea, castin
gloomy eye over the dripping Piazza from the great cham
windows, was of the opinion that the weather reflected her mo
She wondered unhappily how long Kit was going to stay. It rat
seemed as if he wanted to take up permanent residence with the
and she found that the prospect displeased her not a little. K
with his hungry frustrated eyes on her at every turn, was n
helpful to her calm or her art. Sooner or later her nerves wou
snap, and she would say or do something that might cause irrepa
able damage. And his attitude to her friends was also liable
prove exceedingly awkward. Neither of them seemed likely to gi
way on that point, and her heart sank at the thought of endle
arguments, tantrums, storms and crises within their once-quie
household. She had been greatly honoured, she knew, by he
acceptance into the circle of the Wits, and she was not going to cas
aside those friendships so lightly on the jealous whim of her
brother.

Kit went out early, having business to attend to in the City. Alathea suspected strongly that it was both urgent and financial. Once he had gone, she sat down at her studio desk and scribbled a hasty note, then sent for the household boy and bade him take it to Hugh Trevelyan at Whitehall. Young Tom, who had been on many similar errands and enjoyed the chance to gawp at the fine ladies and gentlemen of the Court, accepted it with alacrity and trotted down the stairs, his day made. She had an hour till her morning sitting, which was Margaret Blagge, not a particularly

thralling prospect. She and Jonathan placed the canvas on the sel and set up the chair and draperies for the pose: then she took n steps backwards down the studio and surveyed her handiwork. ler cousin-by-marriage sat demurely on the chair, open book in er lap, eyes cast down, her coiffure simple and her draped silk gown covering rather more of her pale sloping shoulders than was the fashion. *Not the style in which I'd paint myself*, thought Alathea with an inward grin, and realised with something akin to shock that she must be unique amongst portrait painters, having never depicted herself. *I shall have to sit to Master Cooper*, she decided. *If I can afford it.*

'There's a letter for you,' said Henrietta, coming in with her usual brisk jangle of keys and tap of heels on the echoing polished floorboards. 'A boy brought it just now. From the palace.'

She watched with a certain interest as Alathea, after a cursory glance at the superscription, tucked it into the pocket of her skirts and continued to study the portrait. 'It should be finished today,' she said casually.

Henrietta was not deceived, but kept her own counsel. 'It looks finished already,' she said dubiously.

Alathea gave her a quick grin. 'No, the face is done, but I want to put the last glazes on her dress. That blue is ultramarine – I've had to charge her extra for it.'

'She's a pleasant enough girl,' Hen observed after a pause. 'And it's a good likeness. Doesn't she have a strong look of poor Lady Bradfield?'

'You mean the turned-up nose and the prominent teeth? Yes,' said Alathea, 'today's my day for being cruel. I know she's a miracle of virtue at Whitehall, famous for her gravity and devotions – but she doesn't make for sparkling company. I have to keep remembering not to be witty, or speak profanely, or make a rude joke.' She grinned again. 'And Buckhurst is sitting this afternoon – he'll think I've been converted!'

'Unlikely,' said Henrietta drily. She added, with a change of tone, 'Thea, have you any idea of what Kit's plans are?'

Alathea turned away from the portrait to give her friend her full attention. 'No – he hasn't told me anything directly. He does seem to assume a lengthy sojourn in London, though. I rather think he wants to set himself up as my chaperon.'

'I was afraid that was in his mind,' said Henrietta, her shrewd

gaze once more bent upon the younger girl. Alathea remembered, belatedly, that she could have no knowledge at all of the long-standing problem of Kit and herself. But Hen had always been a good guesser: she looked as if she were guessing now. All she said, however, was, 'I wonder how long he does plan to stay here . . . he seemed very cheerful last night, didn't he? I haven't seen him for so long, and the chief thing I remember him for is his moods: sun one moment, storm the next.'

'He hasn't changed a great deal,' Alathea said slowly. 'Save that his time in Italy seems to have made the sun sunnier, if you take my meaning, and the storm stormier. I rather hope he goes off to Yorkshire soon – my nerves can never stand too much of his company.'

'Which makes two of us,' said Hen. 'I feel very sorry for Kit – I always have. Even when I was a little maw, I wanted to mother him – and I still do, to some extent.'

'He doesn't need it,' said Alathea, beginning to laugh, but Henrietta was still quite serious. 'He may not need mothering now,' she said. 'But he needs a lot of love, I think. What he really wants is a wife.'

This time Alathea could not contain her mirth. She snorted with laughter. 'A *wife*? *Kit*? I don't think anything can be further from his mind.'

'Well, it ought to be,' said Henrietta, looking, as ever, on the practical side. 'He's . . . well, he's eight months younger than me, so he must be twenty-six. He's the last of his name, and it's an ancient one – he ought to be thinking to continue it. If he died tomorrow, who would have his lands in Yorkshire?'

'I've no idea. Lord Bradfield, probably – all things seem to end in his possession. You shall have to find him an heiress, Hen – what of Margaret Blagge?'

'Charles used to call her the Blessed Margaret – she's cousin to all the Jermyns as well. Very in-bred, we Suffolkers – so not a good idea. It's a shame,' said Henrietta carefully, 'that he can't marry the one person he might want to marry, isn't it?' And she gave Alathea a smile of understanding, and went out, leaving her to make what she would of that last remark.

Hen was a shrewd guesser . . . and, seemingly, had guessed right. Kit's feelings must be more transparent than even she, Alathea, had thought. Then she remembered Buckhurst, due to sit that afternoon, and possessed under his lazy exterior of a dagger's wit second only to Rochester's, and quarrelsome into the bargain. She doubted that she could keep the peace, should Kit prove pugnacious, and her soul blenched at the possibility of his involvement in another duel.

Thought of John Wilmot brought to mind the letter. She had recognised the writing instantly, distinctive and spiky, its quick jagged changeable rhythms the echo of his mind. Alone now, she could read it: slowly, she drew it from her pocket, and slipped her fingernail under the seal.

It was another poem, shorter than the last, and in a different metre. It was also a good deal more cryptic. She frowned over the light, dancing works, and the relaxed, letting the insistent, lively rhythm lie inside her head like a song. The second verse was more plain:

But if this murder you'd forgo,
Your slave from Death removing:
Let me your art of charming know,
Or learn you mine of loving.
But whether life, or Death, betide,
In Love 'tis equal measure:
The Victor lives with empty pride
The Vanquish'd die with pleasure.

In the first verse he had spoken of his heart, broken 'with a load of love'. *It cannot really be me*, thought Alathea in bewilderment. *Not me, the subject of a poem like this, not me, surely, that he claims he loves. It's all an elaborate game, they all do to – if Margaret Blagge wasn't so prim she'd have hundreds of poems addressed to her, all begging her to surrender her virtue. He cannot possibly* mean *it – and if he doesn't, then I am certainly not interested.*

But there was no doubt that she was tempted. It was extraordinary, too, that she felt so safe, so sure and confident with a man widely acknowledged to be a deadly enemy to virtue. But it was as if she had always known him, as if the essential Alathea, the child she had been, had met John Wilmot soul to soul that long ago day at Ashcott, and so now could draw on that kinship.

But he did not want kinship, friendship. He wanted more, and more she did not desire to give. She knew why: pride, honour, the wish not to cheapen herself in the eyes of her family and friends.

Those were the expected reasons, reasons any woman in her position would give, but underlying them all, sleeping at the bottom of her mind, was the greatest fear of all. Her love of painting dominated her life, she regarded her skill almost superstitiously. It was magical: what harm might it not do, to transfer her power of love to something more human?

A knock at the door announced the arrival downstairs of Margaret Blagge, with her maid in attendance, and Alathea folded up the paper with care, put it back in her pocket, and went to greet her client. She knew she could not go on for ever, pretending that the poems did not come. Sooner or later, something would have to be said to him by way of answer, for the quality of the questions deserved that respect. But she had other things to think about just at this moment, and pushed the whole problem successfully to the back of her mind.

As if to ensure that it stayed there, Margaret Blagge brought with her some surprising and disturbing news, which she imparted as she sat on the draped chair, eyes on book, while Alathea put the finishing touches to her portrait, and thought that Strephon the monkey would have been a more congenial companion – at least he could make her laugh. The Blessed Margaret sat and made polite conversation, rather limited by the fact that Alathea was not a regular churchgoer, did not make a habit of listening to sermons and rarely picked up a Bible unless to check a literary allusion, and Alathea in her turn hampered by her client's total lack of interest in music, poetry, painting or the theatre. She was curious, however, about Margaret's life at Court, her duties and diversions as Maid-of-Honour to the Duchess of York, and it was in the course of this conversation that Margaret said suddenly, 'Oh, I had almost forgot. I have some news for you, cousin.'

'News?' Alathea, brush in hand, was engaged in mixing up a little ultramarine and concentrating on getting the quantity just right – not too stiff and unworkable, not too thin and liquid. 'What news is that?'

'Your uncle and mine, Lord Bradfield, has written to me desiring to know if there are any places at Court for his daughters, as he wishes them to acquire some sophistication to round off their education. And a husband, I should think,' she added.

Alathea grinned. Just once or twice, Margaret had revealed a rather more lively and worldly personality underneath all that daunting self-discipline and piety. 'And are there any places? And have you any influence in the matter?'

'Well, one of the Queen's maids may leave soon to be married, and I may be able to influence a decision upon her replacement. But I have never met either of them,' Margaret added gravely. 'Can you tell me a little of their characters? I pray you, be honest.'

'I'm rarely anything else, alas,' said Alathea. She applied the paint carefully, thinking about that and her answer at the same time. At last, her task completed, she laid down the brush and stared thoughtfully at her client. 'I scarcely know them myself. I prefer the elder one – Anne. She is honest and sharp and speaks very plain – but she *is* very plain, I fear.'

'An undistinguished countenance may disguise a pure and devout heart,' said Margaret, with a note of solemn reproof that Alathea, for her sake, was glad John Wilmot had not heard. 'And the other girl – Mary, is that her name? She is younger.'

'Yes – she'd be no more than fifteen or sixteen, whereas Anne is a little younger than I am. Mary – Mall – is much prettier than Anne, and knows it only too well. I fear her father has spoilt her somewhat.'

'And he has no son?'

'No – not now. Rupert . . . died.'

'Then they will be heiresses,' Margaret said slowly. 'I care nothing for such things myself, but it will greatly enhance their prospects of finding husbands, plain or not. Who will have Goldhayes, then?'

Alathea stared at her, her mind leaping to the obvious conclusion, which somehow had previously escaped her. 'Why . . . neither of Lord Bradfield's daughters . . . I'd never thought of this before, but of course the house and Suffolk lands are entailed and must go in the male line. Anne and Mall will have large estates elsewhere, but it must be my father who is Lord Bradfield's heir to Goldhayes.'

'Unless Lord Bradfield marries again,' Margaret pointed out.

Alathea laughed in disbelief. 'Marry again? But he's elderly! He must be well past fifty!'

'But that kind of marriage happens frequently,' said Margaret. 'I am sure your acquaintance will furnish you with examples. He has mourned my aunt for five years now, and in his letter he seemed to indicate that he wished to enter the world again. He talks of taking this house next autumn – '

'Taking *this* house?' Alathea dropped the paintbrush, leaving a scattering of jewel-like blue paint all down her fourth-best gown, the one she used for painting less fashionable clients. '*This* house? Here? Are you sure? He's never informed me of it.'

'I am sure,' said Margaret calmly. 'He told me of it most definitely – unless he has *two* Covent Garden houses?'

'No,' said Alathea gloomily. 'Just this one.' She pushed a stray wisp of pale hair out of her eyes. 'And he's not the kind of person who can exist comfortably with others – his principles are too prickly for comfort. He disapproves of my painting, but he can forget about it at a distance. If he wants to move in, he will undoubtedly want it to stop – and in any case, I shall have to move out. It *is* his house, after all.'

'If he is a good Christian at heart, he will not turn out his own niece when she has no other home,' Margaret said. 'And it will not just be you – there will be your brother, and your cousin Nell, and Mistress Jermyn and her little girl. He cannot evict you all with a snap of the fingers.'

'I have a sneaking feeling that he may,' said Alathea. She bent and picked up the paintbrush. 'He ought to have told me, though – that's not fair, to leave me in the dark about his intentions, when they'll affect my whole life. Anyway,' she added, with philosophical cheerfulness, 'the autumn is half a year away. He may change his mind, Anne or Mall may marry, there's a lot could happen in half a year. But thank you for the warning, Margaret. If you have any further news, could you tell me? My uncle, Hugh Trevelyan, will take any message.'

'I will send it by him,' Margaret promised, and the talk turned to other matters. But all through the remainder of the sitting, Alathea's mind was seething with fury and anxiety: fury at Lord Bradfield's casual intention, however justified, to evict her from her lovely Covent Garden studio, and anxiety about that eviction. Where could they find any place so fashionable, so suitable and yet so very cheap?

She wrestled with the problem while painting, while having dinner and while exercising an energetic Lovell in the garden. Hugh, who had taken up tennis in a bid to reduce his waistline, had given her an old racquet and a split leather ball, and she had devised the perfect way of exercising her dog – standing by the back door, using the racquet to hit the ball for Lovell to chase. Math had worked out that if this process was gone through twenty-five times, the dog had run about half a mile at top speed: more than enough to exhaust him, temporarily at any rate. There was no sign of Kit, and no message either from Hugh, and with a feeling that her secure, safe world had suddenly been revealed to be poised over a pit of uncertainty, she went in to prepare for Buckhurst's sitting.

She had barely got beyond the dead-colouring of Nell Gwynn's erstwhile lover, her Charles the Second – the actor Hart having been the first, and the King the third – and she was not especially pleased with it. She had found it difficult to paint those features in repose without making them seem heavy and coarse. In his presence it was different, the drooping eyes sparkling with laughter and the over-large mouth unnoticed in the flow of wit. She could not flatter: she could only hope he would not wish her to do so. It would be a difficult afternoon's work, and only the prospect of being once more in John Wilmot's company could make her regard it with anything other than apprehension.

The coffee was keeping hot on the trivet, the wine and cakes set out, cups ready, everything was arranged. She changed into one of her better gowns, knotted up her hair more tightly, pulled on the customary old shirt and climbed the steep stairs to the studio in a mood of some gloom. If they were forced to leave Covent Garden, where could they go? She could not imagine her new and lordly friends, full of ease and bonhomie though they were, coming to visit her so readily in a squalid Westminster garret, but even now she did not think she could afford anything else. Lord Bradfield had at least been generous. He had let her have the use of the house for far less than the usual rent for such a place. Her new position in the fashionable world demanded a residence in St James's or Pall Mall, locations which she could not possibly afford.

She was still frowning over this when Buckhurst and Sedley and Rochester arrived, and their usual noisy eruption into her thoughts succeeded, as usual, in banishing all worries from her mind. The quips and jokes and innuendo flew thick and fast as Charles Sackville, Lord Buckhurst, took up his pose and Alathea, trying not to laugh, applied herself to her brush and paint while the wild talk flashed around her like a whirlwind. And this time, as it had not done before with this particular painting, the magic tingled in her hands and her brushwork was inspired. The solid, magnificent face of My Lord Buckhurst gathered animation. She gave him a wicked, characteristic twinkle in those small eyes, and a sardonic curl on that rather ugly mouth. Halfway through the afternoon, Fleetwood Shepherd came in, delayed by some errand, and expressed his opinion, which was highly favourable. There was a pause while the subject of the portrait came over with idle joviality to inspect himself and decided, to Alathea's relief, that it was indeed a startling likeness.

'It looks,' said John Wilmot, 'as if he's about to step down from the canvas and assault the ladies. You'd best be careful, Alathea, up here alone with that.'

'Rape by a picture doesn't figure high on my list of fears,' said the artist, drily. She turned again to the portrait. 'Perhaps, my lord, if you would return to the pose?'

The hour was quickly over: she felt pleased and satisfied. Jonathan built up the fire and cleaned the brushes, Nell poured coffee and distributed cakes. Sedley was talking to Buckhurst, discussing the merits of their respective portraits. Alathea hoped that their opinions were still favourable.

'Hallo,' said John Wilmot, very quietly and suddenly at her side. 'You have no coffee.'

'I'll have some in a moment. I always need something strong after painting. It seems to drain something from me, especially when it goes well.'

'And it did?'

'Today, yes. I was becoming a trifle worried. There's something about Lord Buckhurst which makes him very difficult to paint. But today – no problems. Or at least, not in the painting.' She glanced sideways at him, seeing the dark eyes watching back at her, the angelic face stripped of artifice and wit and mockery, reduced to the essence of himself, as always seemed to happen when they were alone.

He said, with a smile, 'Did you receive a letter today?'

One of Alathea's rare blushes swept over her face, but she held his gaze steadily. 'Yes, I did.'

'And have you an answer?'

'It deserves one, truly – but I cannot reply in kind. My talents do not lie that way. And besides, I come from a breed famed for their obstinacy. The more you importune a Heron, the less likely you are to succeed – and so my correspondent may be wasting his ink and paper, not to mention his time.' Their eyes were still locked, and for one mad moment she knew that he had only to move closer to win, and she would be lost for ever: and she had a wild impulse to move herself, to surrender. But something – fear? Superstition? Surely not honour, it was more like that old stiff-necked Heron pride – held her still.

Then he turned away, saying casually over his shoulder, 'No matter. It's said that water will eventually wear away even stone, and you are flesh and blood and bone, I think, and not alabaster – though you may look like it, fair nymph.' And his wide grin was one of friendship again. She was out of danger.

'It shapes well – you have made a fine likeness,' Buckhurst told her in that lazy, soft drawl of his, as if he were too idle to give sufficient volume and emphasis to his words. 'We shall have to see if we cannot arrange for a more exalted client to sit for you, eh, Rochester?'

'Beware – she knows too little of flattery. Can't you hear him? "Oddsfish, my dear lady, but I fear you have made me even uglier than I already am." '

Alathea had never spoken with the King, only seen him from a distance in the park or at the theatre, but she had heard enough from Hugh to know that John's imitation of his talk must be tolerably exact. Sedley, his plump red face beaming, laughed and said, 'That's His Majesty to the life, I'll swear it! And it'll be true too, Alathea – you should flatter a little, if you want more success. You can catch a better likeness than Lely, you know – you can afford to paint your sitters in a more kindly light.'

'Smarting at the accuracy of your portrait, Little Sid?' Buckhurst enquired, grinning in his sleepy, cat-like way.

Sedley shook his head impatiently (his periwig slipped a little), and stared earnestly at her. 'Just a little compromise, a little honesty – make the ladies look lovelier, the men more handsome – why not, eh? Won't do you any harm, and it'll do your reputation the world of good. Heard the Sainted Blagge telling some chit she was sitting to you, and the chit, very la-di-da, said, "That's all very well for you, my dear – you are too good and honest to sit to Lely or Cooper. Nothing less than the bitter truth will suit you!" And the Blagge said, quick as lightning, "Let those who need false flattery go to other painters. I can value truth and honesty." '

'If I know her, she atoned for that remark with five hours on her knees,' said Rochester. '*What* a waste of a pretty, witty girl!'

'You won't turn to devotions, will you, Alathea? I beg of you, on my knees, do not turn to religion!' Sedley cried, plummetting with a thump to the floor and gazing up at her in a parody of adoring prayer. She had to laugh, but he went on, more seriously. 'Naked truth is out of fashion – why adhere to it?'

'I can't do anything else,' Alathea told him, spreading her hands. 'I can't. You may feel it's stupid, foolish, naive, but I have a gift, a knack for catching a likeness, for seeing people as they truly are. That's what makes me different, makes my pictures individual rather than indistinguishable dummies without life or personality. Do you *really* want me to paint like Lely? I would rather paint like Cooper – he doesn't flatter, he tells the truth, and because he works in miniature and he's famous, people can accept his honesty. Why can't you accept mine?'

'I can,' said John thoughtfully. 'But many would not – and though we have made you the fashion, it might not be for long. The truth always hurts.'

'Only those who deceive themselves,' said Alathea.

'Then you must count nine-tenths of the Court under that heading. The King, however, is not of that majority, which is why Buckhurst suggested you paint him. We will do our best, eh, Charles?'

'Yours to command,' said the Earl of Dorset's scapegrace son, lazily. 'Flattery would be your best policy, though, my dear – Sid's right.'

'It's a matter of honour,' said Alathea quietly. 'If you were abused and challenged by some upstart rogue, would you refuse the fight? I thought not – nor have you, any of you. It's your honour requires you to duel – certainly not commonsense or any practical consideration. And so it is with my painting, my lord – sense and sanity may tell me to compromise my art, but I cannot in all honour do it. *Now* do you understand, all of you?'

'Girl's mad,' said Little Sid, downing a brimming wine cup. 'Lovely as a summer's day, and mad as a March Hare. Still, I give you her honesty, in all honour – Alathea!'

They drank her health uproariously, in coffee and wine, and as the cups were quaffed with much flourishing, the door opened and Kit walked into the room.

It was evidently raining outside. His periwig was wet, and his clothes ran streaky dark with water. It was also unfortunate that at the instant of his entry, Sedley had chosen to give her a rather wine-fumed embrace on her mouth, something which Kit, from the look on his face, had misinterpreted entirely. Compounding the blunder, Alathea blushed, and Kit said, his voice deep and furious behind the stilted words, 'I beg your pardon. I had not known you had company – I will withdraw.' And the door slammed behind him, a little louder than normal.

I shall pay for this, later, Alathea thought, with a profound feeling of fear and disquiet. *I hope he takes it out on me, and not on anyone else: I can stand his anger, but Nell can't.* And she made light conversation and indulged in friendly banter and gave every sign that she desired that her guests should stay, for the longer she could keep them there, the more courage could she gather.

But they left at dusk, as usual, and if any had thought Kit's behaviour unusual, they did not say. She bade them farewell at the top of the stairs. John, who missed nothing, saw the trouble in her eyes and guessed its cause. He knew that now was not the time or place to mention it, but he had a sudden uncomfortable memory of the way Kit had burst into that parlour at Ashcott, long ago, and with some surprise found himself deciding to try to contact Hugh Trevelyan.

When they had gone, the studio seemed very quiet and dark, the candles and firelight small soft oases of light in the gloom. With Jonathan's help, she lifted the canvas of Lord Buckhurst from the easel and stacked it carefully against the wall, consulted her appointments book, noted there was a new sitter in the morning, a friend of Hugh's, and arranged a selection of fresh stretched and primed canvases for him to choose size and pose. Then she told Jonathan to go and have his supper. Henrietta came up to say that the meal would be in an hour or so, and Nell went down with her, saying something about sewing. Alone at last with her thoughts, she sat down by the fire and poured herself a last, bitter cup of coffee from the dregs of the pot on the trivet. It had boiled, and tasted terrible. She put it down and stared into the glowing heart of the flames. She had meant to wrestle with the problems of Kit and Lord Bradfield, but the day's work had left her drained, weary yet peaceful, and her mind drifted back to Goldhayes, to the lovely house that might, one day, if her uncle did not marry again and produce his desperately wanted heir, become her father's . . . it seemed like all their dreams come to flower, and much too good ever to be true.

She must have dozed off in the warmth and comfort of that chair by the fire, for suddenly, without, it seemed, any break after her daydreams of Goldhayes, she woke to find her wrists clutched fast in someone's agonising grip, and a dark shape looming over her, hideous and formless in the dim light. Gasping and bewildered, she was being shaken viciously by a brute strength which had no concern for her pain, and Kit's voice hissed savagely into her face. 'You whore! You *whore*! I *told* you not to let them into your company – I *told* you!' And his hand left her wrist and came up to strike her, hard, across the mouth. 'Take *that*, you whoring trollop! Perhaps that'll teach you not to go whining after them like a bitch in heat!' And he raised his hand to strike her again. Alathea, with an immense rage surging through her, dispelling her initial shock, found her own right hand free, and lunged. He caught it, and pulled her up out of the chair until their heads were almost touching. She saw his face, distorted by closeness and fury, and with impotent rage, knew herself utterly in his physical power. It sobered her own fierce anger, but at least she might be able to talk her way out of his grasp.

'Whore!' he said again, and drops of spittle fell on her face. 'Whore! Why did you, Thea! Why did you let them come?'

'I told you. They are my friends, and I choose my friends, not you.'

'Friends! You let that foul rogue kiss you – have you heard all the stories? You let him kiss you, *Sedley*, the most evil man in London, and if he isn't then the other two assuredly are. What else have you let them do? Have they climbed into your bed, eh? Have they?' He shook her again.

Far away within her mind, behind the rage and terror, Alathea found a still clear space of reason, and sanity, and drew on it as a drowning person draws in air. 'No! No, they have not!'

He did not seem to hear her. With horror, she saw flecks of foam gather at the corners of his mouth as he ranted, his dreadful imagination spouting more and more obscene suggestions about her activities with the Wits. Words that she did not understand, deeds of which she had no knowledge, fouled the air around her until at last she could bear it no longer. 'Stop it! *Stop it*, I say!'

The strength of her voice surprised her: it also surprised Kit. The vicious stream of words abruptly ceased. He stared at her with something like bewilderment, and beneath all her other emotions she began to feel a different kind of fear – fear for him, and the state of his mind. But she had an advantage now, and leapt into speech. 'Kit – what in God's name are you talking about? How *dare* you accuse me of – of all those things? Dear God, I don't know what half of them are, or mean! Kit, for Christ's sake calm down, and think, and *listen*, just *listen*, do me that honour, will you? I have done no more than let Sedley kiss me, and that I won't do again – he stinks most abominably of wine, and stale perfume. And I won't let any of the others so much as lay a finger on me. What do you take me for? I'm no whore, no Castlemaine or Betty Foster – and they *know* it, Kit, they *know* it and *accept* it and *understand* it! Do *you* understand it?'

His face, slowly, pitifully, was changing, the terrible power and madness leaving it, draining away until only the pale haunted husk of the features was left, grey and pinched like a dead man's. 'Is that true? Are you virgin still?' At her simple nod, his hands slid up her arms to grip her shoulders. 'Are you, Thea? Are you really? Swear it!'

'I swear it,' she said quietly, and to her horror he drew a deep, racking, quavering breath like a sob, and then another, and the tears stood suddenly in his eyes. 'You are indeed? You've never lain with a man? Oh thank God, thank God for that!' And the clutching hands slid around her, to crush her body against his, while he shook and trembled with the force of his emotion. 'My Thea – *my* Thea – mine for ever – you are mine always, do you hear me? Never anyone else, never, never, never!' And with that dreadful force, at once implacable and curiously gentle, he turned her face up to his, and kissed her.

It was like being devoured. His mouth and tongue seemed to plunge into her very soul, to suck out her life's blood, her strength, her individuality, and above all her gift, and leave her withered. Desperately, aware too late of the danger she was in, she struggled for air, for freedom, but to no avail. He was so much stronger, so much in the possession of his terrible love, or lust, that she could do nothing. She could not see, hear, breathe, only feel the dreadful invasion of his kiss, and the rough greedy pawing of one hand at her breasts. She heard her dress rip, felt the pain as his fingers scratched and tore her skin in his haste to reach his target, and the sudden agony as a nipple was squeezed too hard. She had no air to scream, no strength to cry out: she was doomed, for ever.

Let yourself go limp, said a faint desperate voice to the last of her sanity. *Let yourself go limp, suddenly*. And she had just enough wit to obey it. She allowed her legs to buckle beneath her, taking him completely by surprise. Her mouth was abruptly free, and she gulped air as she fell through his clutching hands and arrived in a crumpled, gasping heap on the hard, wooden floor. But she could not so easily escape him. As if in a nightmare the great black bulk of him followed her, crouching over her, ripping, touching, mauling. Then his full weight descended upon her, and she knew that she could do no more.

And then, the miracle happened – a man's voice, that was not his, the tone one of horror and fury, the slam of a door, running feet across the floor, and suddenly the weight crushing her was torn away, and she saw her saviour.

Hugh stood there, possessed with a terrifying rage and repugnance, his two hands grasping Kit round the neck, and despite his inferior height and fitness, he looked ready to kill. His hands tightened on the other's windpipe. Kit's mouth opened and closed, gasping for air like a fish.

'No!' Alathea cried. With a tremendous effort, using limbs that felt like wet rags, she tried wildly to sit up. 'Hugh! No, don't!'

'Give me one good reason why not,' said Hugh – easy-going, tolerant, cynical, sophisticated Hugh – and prepared to choke the life from his cousin's throat.

Alathea struggled up, fell, and crawled the brief distance towards them. 'Hugh! No, you can't – Hugh, I think he's mad, please, *no*!'

For a moment longer, her uncle's hands clenched still, and then, with a gesture of total contempt, he flung Kit away from him. Her brother stumbled back, crashing into the carefully stacked canvases and sending stools and chairs flying. He staggered upright and stood swaying, his face purple and his eyes glazed. With his dishevelled clothing, and the spittle around his mouth, he looked mad indeed.

'It's her you have to thank for your life,' said Hugh. His voice, low and terrible in its rage, was barely above a whisper. 'But if I ever see you look at her – touch her – defame her – molest her –

before all the gods of earth I will kill you then and there. Do you understand me, you disgusting, incestuous rapist?'

Kit shook his head, as if to clear it. His voice came so strained and hoarse that at first Alathea did not recognise it. 'Yes.'

'Then go now, before I do to you what you richly deserve, you slimy reptile, and if you ever breathe a word of this to anyone, I'll make sure it's the last breath you ever take. Understand? I don't want to see you again for a long, long time, or my hands may start to itch – so I suggest you go back to Yorkshire and stay there until all the poison gets out of your blood, you venomous little snake. Go on, now, go!'

For one moment longer Kit stared at him, and something of Hugh's own horror began, eerily, to be reflected on his face. His mouth worked desperately: then he said, still in that terribly altered voice, 'I must – I must have been mad. Thea – '

'Go, I said!'

'Thea, Thea, oh God I'm sorry, forgive me – '

'*Go*!' Hugh's voice was louder, and Kit, with one last despairing glance at his sister, crouched on the floor by Hugh's feet, turned and fled from the room. She heard his descending, hurrying footsteps down those break-neck stairs: and then, no more.

'Thea!' Hugh was by her side, his hands pulling her against him. Confused and still repelled by any touch, she jerked away from him with a sob of fear. He had to quieten his own anger before he could begin to quieten her, stroking and soothing and muttering soft words of gentleness and small meaning. 'Thea . . . it's all right, dear girl, he's gone and gone for good, he won't ever hurt you again, it's all right, it's all right, don't cry.'

'I'm not crying,' said Alathea after a while, anxious to set the record straight. She struggled up to a sitting position, and Hugh had a good look, for the first time, at her bruised and battered state. 'Dear God, did he do that?'

'Do what?' Alathea looked down. Her dress was gaping to the waist, ripped apart, and great red and blue marks and lines of drying blood disfigured her breasts where Kit's hands and nails had torn her fine pale skin. She blushed, fierily, and crossed her arms over the wreckage.

Hugh's hand came up to touch her mouth, gently, and she winced. 'God, if I'd seen that, he'd not have got off so lightly – dear girl, did he hit you?'

Alathea nodded. Despite all her care, a tear escaped her, and slid shinily down the side of her nose. She drew in a shaky breath. 'I think – I think he was mad. Is mad. I don't think he really knew what he'd done – or wanted to do. He didn't rape me – you arrived in the nick of time.'

'You have your note, and your friend Rochester to thank for that – he sought me out, warned me that there might be trouble from that quarter. Though how he knew . . . and to think that I feared *he* would rape you!'

'He wouldn't. He's my friend.' Alathea's voice wobbled, as she remembered that Kit had once been that to her, and then went on with waxing strength. 'We met once as children, and remembered it – I trust him. And he met Kit too, at a bad time, so he knows what he can be like.' She found she could muster quite a successful smile. 'Anyway, you needn't fear for my virtue – it'll be a long time before I can ever steel myself to let a man near me again!'

Hugh stared at her, with love and admiration for the spirit that could make a joke, so soon, out of something so utterly appalling. He said, his voice rough with emotion, 'I wish I had killed him.'

'And gone to Tyburn for him? He's not worth that, poor tormented soul that he is . . . Hugh, can I ask you a favour?'

'I will do anything for you, you know that. What do you want?'

'Two things. That piece of blue drapery on the table, for one – thank you. And for the other . . . Hugh . . . please, I would rather . . . I don't want anyone to know about this. About Kit, and what he tried to do tonight. It'll be no secret that we've quarrelled, and people can make what they will of it, but as to *why* – let them think he played the prude about the company I keep. It'll keep his reputation intact.'

'Does he deserve it?'

'Perhaps not – but it'll keep *my* reputation intact, too. I don't want that sort of notoriety . . . and think of my parents, and Math, and Aunt Lucy, and Hen . . . we *must* keep quiet, Hugh, you can surely see that we must.' She smiled wanly. 'And besides, I still have my pride, my honour: I'd rather not admit to the humiliation of an attempted rape by my own brother. I'll wager it doesn't come even into the Castlemaine's experience.' And to Hugh's disquiet, she began to laugh rather wildly, and then, at last, her control broke and she wept.

He held her, like the brother Kit could never be, for a long time, feeling his rage trickle slowly away into a tenderness and compassion for this girl who was so much stronger than she needed to be. Such spirit was wasted in a woman, who was born to man's rule and direction, and had no reason for independence or pride, as opposed to honour: and yet Alathea had enough for twenty men. But for all her strength of spirit, she had been powerless against the evil tainted force of Kit's lust, and the thought reared up ugly in his mind. How many more times would her honour be thus forcibly besieged, whether by Kit or by some other of the men she daringly, rashly called her friends?

He loved her more than any other person in the world, he realised wryly: more even than himself. But his love was that of a dear friend, and unlike Kit's, owed nothing to passion. He would protect and defend her always, to the best of his ability, and he had only to think of what her brother, whose duty it was to protect her, had done and so nearly done to her, to feel physically sick.

'Thank you,' said Alathea, after a long time. She had control of herself now, and the horror that had overtaken her was receding at last. If she concentrated her mind, she could rid herself of the terrible reality of the past hour. It seemed to have happened to someone else, like a scene in a play. 'Oh, Hugh, what would I ever do without you?'

'A great deal,' said Hugh. 'But let's think of practical matters. It must be nearly supper-time – and you cannot possibly appear in that state. At the very least, you will have to change your dress.'

'Can you get one for me?' Alathea asked: a hint of shyness had crept into her voice. She described the location of her chamber, and the garments she wanted, and Hugh, with a conspirator's smile, softly left the room.

Alone again, she began involuntarily to shiver. She stumbled over to the fire and sat down in the same chair from which Kit had so violently wrenched her, not long before. The appalling reality of it began to intrude again, the contorted mask of his face loomed once more above her. Steadily, with determination, she drew several deep, slow breaths, calming herself, and thinking deliberately of the part she must play at the supper-table. She hoped she could carry it off successfully, and her bruised and swollen mouth could be explained away, truthfully, by saying that Kit had struck out at her. How much more he had done, must ever be her deep and deadly secret: and Hugh's, and Kit's.

Hugh returned then, with a fresh gown and a chemise, and she slipped behind the light screen in the far corner of the studio to put them on. Her wrecked clothes, torn, bloodstained and defiled, she kicked into a crumpled heap well away from her. Perhaps she could claim to have spilt varnish on them? A sudden hatred for all the complications of such a tissue of lies came upon her. How much simpler it would be, just to tell the truth.

But the ramifications of such a course stretched out in front of her, a web of such horrendous complexity that she quailed. Better by far to lie now, and leave the matter buried, than to bring all that poisonous scandal into the open.

Newly clothed, her bruised flesh hidden and her hair deftly knotted up by Hugh, she felt almost normal. But deep inside her soul a leaden weight had settled, a burden of guilt and humiliation and betrayed friendship. For she could not rid herself of the feeling that she had in a sense encouraged this, that her blindness to the nature of his feelings for her had led him on to this last, fatal error. They had been friends, once: now, she did not think she would ever be able to bear the sight of him again without thinking of the fate she had only just escaped. *Why did his love have to light on me?* she wondered with desperate sadness. *Of all the women in the world, why the one he could never wed?* And though, as yet, her understanding of love, and passion, and lust, was imperfect and lacking in experience, her imagination was sufficiently powerful to see, with clarity, the full hopelessness of Kit's position. What must he be feeling, now?

In a squalid tavern in Drury Lane, her brother Kit sat, attempting to numb the agony in his mind with strong waters. It was the fool's way out, he knew, to follow such an undignified path to oblivion. *But dear God,* he thought, *I have reason. An hour ago I tried to rape my own sister, and not even a gallon of geneva will ever erase that evil from my soul.*

He took another gulp, and stared into the poor apologetic fire. He had lost control completely. He could not tell why, save that she had allowed that debauched swine Sedley to kiss her, a favour she had denied to himself. And he had been jealous of her other companions, he had seen the way she looked at Rochester, and he at her, as though they shared a private world which no other could penetrate, and he, excluded again, could only watch helplessly as his beloved, pure, innocent sister behaved with the scum of Whitehall like any Court whore . . .

And there was the painting, too. What had he to show for the last three years? A vast expenditure, a few beggarly sketches for mementoes, a clutch of failed love affairs . . . a hole of three years in his life. And with those years, evidently, Alathea had transformed hers. She was talented, successful, fashionable, her company sought after and her beauty famed. *The toast of the town*, he thought with grief and fury. *She is only a woman, meant for some man's wife, she should not brazenly enter a man's world, her gift is wasted on a woman, she should not be so good at what she does*, I *should be the artist . . . it is not* fair!

He hurled the glass into the fire: the remaining spirits flared briefly and died. The landlord, coming to investigate the noise, found him sobbing into his arms, hunched over the table. Used to the maudlin drunk, he poured enough liquor down his throat to send him unconscious, and then with a tapster rolled him into a corner to sleep it off. It was fortunate that no one thought to rob him, an unaccountable lapse on the part of those within the tavern at the time.

In the morning, with a bleak, agonised soul and a savagely aching head, Sir Christopher Drakelon, third Baronet, took horse and rode back to Yorkshire, to the neglected empty home that he had not seen for years, and took, too, the burden of pain and grief and lust that could never, ever, now be assuaged. He was forbidden Alathea, by his own actions, for all time to come, and most bitterly he regretted the madness that had prompted him to such a terrible impulse. He could not be her friend now; he had denied himself even that.

He was twenty-six years old, and all meaning, all reason, all purpose to his life had been ended by one hour when his self-control had broken. All he had left now were his estates, the legacy of six centuries of Drakelons, and the empty, lonely, pointless hours and days, weeks and months and years stretching out ahead of him, without Alathea.

CHAPTER FIFTEEN

The revenant

This thing of malice, this woman . . .
(Ford, *'Tis Pity She's a Whore*)

'That dress is a disgrace!' said Lucy Ashley, with shocked severity, and her daughter echoed it. 'Thea, is that *really* the best you have?'

Alathea glanced down at the gown she had always considered to be her best. True, there were one or two spots of paint on it, but mercifully they had blended in fairly well, being green: the hem was shrunk and stained a little after that unexpected downpour that had caught her in Long Acre a few weeks ago, and the place on the sleeve where the smoothing-iron had burnt it was cleverly concealed by a few scraps of silver lace. 'It's quite good enough for me,' she said defensively.

'Well, it isn't for me,' said Rosalind. 'If we're to go to the theatre, I want to be seen with the fashionable and shocking female artist, not some dowdy scarecrow in a five-years-old gown. *Surely* you can afford another?'

'I suppose I could,' said her cousin, cautiously. Since the news of Lord Bradfield's possible move to London, she had been careful to put by as much money from her painting as she could spare, and since her practice seemed to expand daily, Dan Ashley's goldsmith had secured an appreciable sum in her name.

'That's settled then,' said Lucy, beaming at the thought of another shopping expedition. 'The New Exchange, I think. Shall we go this afternoon? You can surely spare one afternoon, Thea!'

'I have the whole day free. My afternoon sitters both cancelled their appointments.'

'And you look as though you could do with a rest,' her aunt went on relentlessly. 'We've hardly seen you for months – '

'I haven't seen you for nearly a year!' Rosalind put in.

' – and you look quite peaky. Doesn't Hen feed you enough? Do you have time to eat, even? You can't surely be *that* busy!'

'No, but I nearly am,' said Alathea, resisting the temptation to say to her well-meaning aunt, 'Don't *fuss*!' She really did not want to go shopping. It was a hot August morning, and there had been some talk earlier of going up the river to Chelsea, or driving out to Islington or Highgate, away from the stifling atmosphere of the City.

'We can go for a drive when it's cooler,' said Rosalind, stretching like a cat. 'And I shall stay here, while you're at the shops. I don't want to lose this baby as well.'

Her first pregnancy had ended in a still-born child, the second had miscarried very early, and she had been advised to rest as much as possible for the third. Seven months had been completed successfully, and Ros, sleek and round and lazy, appeared more feline than ever. By contrast, Alathea looked and felt like a gawky straw-haired hoyden, and Nell was a little pink-faced mouse. This was an injustice to Nell, whose manner and appearance had been steadily improving over the last few months. Today, in silver-blue silk and white lace, her hair done *à la mode* and her skin pale and clear, she looked very pretty in a meek, demure sort of way. This final transformation owed, or so Alathea suspected, a great deal to their fashionable friends. Sedley in particular had taken a jovial interest in her, laughed at her laborious jokes, and encouraged her to shine.

'I think I need a new gown too,' Nell said now, thoughtfully. 'And a fan – I broke my nice ivory one last week.'

'You got that in the New Exchange – perhaps you can get another the same,' Alathea said, resigning herself to the inevitable. Lucy was right, however irritating her constant misplaced concern might be. She did, desperately, need smarter clothes: her new-found status demanded it. Sooner or later, she would be invited to dinner, to Whitehall or to places only a little less grand, and besides, she had begun to feel a little uneasy about playing host to the wide and sophisticated circle of the Wits in such dowdy garments. She thought of John Wilmot's face when he saw her tricked out in the first stare of fashion, and grinned. 'You've persuaded me – shall we go directly after dinner?'

Two hours later, the three of them, Lucy, Alathea and Nell, left Dan's handsome, new, brick house that had risen like a phoenix on the ashes of Fleet Street, and made their way on foot up towards Temple Bar and the Strand, where the New Exchange stood on the left-hand side, opposite Half-Moon Street. It was strange, still, to walk along the new part of Fleet Street, in raw red brick, sharp-edged and bare, and then to pass under Temple Bar, itself newly and handsomely rebuilding in honey-coloured stone, and find the same London that had always been, unchanged and old, the wooden houses piled storey upon storey and jostling the street. It was like stepping back to her life before the Fire, before she had ever lived at the Covent Garden house. With a slight sense of shock, Alathea realised that she had been four years, all but a week or so, in that lovely mansion – for house was too ordinary a word. She had grown to love it, ill though its grace and beauty and elegance suited her forthright style, and it seemed that soon she would lose it. Lord Bradfield had at last warned her directly of his impending visit, and she knew, even if he civilly professed the opposite, that her continued presence would not be welcome for very long. And *then* where would they go?

'You're looking very thoughtful,' said Aunt Lucy, cheerfully. 'Thinking about what you'll buy?'

'Yes,' Alathea improvised hastily. 'I think I'd like a change of colour – I always seem to wear green, or grey. I've taken a fancy to crimson – or ivory, perhaps.' She glanced sideways at her aunt, and was gratified to see that Lucy was shocked. '*Crimson*? Oh, no, Thea, I really don't think that's quite suitable.'

'I reckon it will do very well,' said Alathea, trying not to smile. They really would think her a scarlet woman, she decided, if she appeared in that. What would Lord Bradfield think? What would John Wilmot say? She could imagine only too clearly – should she encourage him?

And what, oh what would it do to Kit, if he ever should see her in Court finery, like the high-class whore he had, so insultingly, presumed her to be. In the six months since his assault on her, she had heard nothing, seen nothing of him: and still every thought of him brought pain, and rage, and pity. She had even dashed off a quick impulsive note, a week later when the agony of guilt and grief had reached a crescendo inside her mind, and sent it, unbeknownst to anyone, to his estates at Upper Denby in Yorkshire. It had contained just two brief lines. 'I am sorry, I still value your friendship. I will forget everything.' And she had signed it, 'Your affectionate sister.'

Remembering it now, those three bare sentences seemed to imply that she, and not Kit, had been the transgressor. And there had never been any reply.

Sternly, Alathea whipped her errant mind back from this fruitless, endless treadmill. *I will not think of Kit*, she told herself. *Here we are at the Exchange, and I have money to spend and ideas in my head, and I am going to enjoy myself.*

And of course, once inside the building, she did. The place was packed with the fashionable, the rich, and those neither rich nor fashionable but who wanted to be seen in their company in the hope that the gilt would rub off. And since the Fire had driven many shopkeepers westwards to the more aristocratic areas on the fringes of Whitehall, it had received a new lease of life, and each tiny booth was bursting with all manner of goods and chattels: fans, gloves, books, trinkets, laces, ribbons, cloth, all spilled out into the narrow walks. The noise of voices bargaining, calling wares, making assignations, gossiping, and the smell of a hundred mixed perfumes and essences and ten times that number of unclean bodies, gave its thick heady atmosphere a unique flavour. The heat was stifling, and Nell quickly began to droop. Alathea, suspecting she might shortly complain of a headache, ruthlessly ignored her. They bought gloves and a fan, laces and ribbons and a little book of Waller's poems for Alathea, who wanted to cap John Wilmot's quotations, and came to a halt by an overflowing mercer's booth. By this time Lucy's maid and Alathea's boy Tom were both laden with parcels: every conceivable kind of knick-knack had been bought, every possible trimming and accessory for the most fashionable gowns, but no material for the gowns themselves. And here, squashed into a space no bigger than a closet at the Covent Garden house, were bolts of cloth enough to make a thousand modish gowns, in all the colours and materials at present in fashion. The shopgirl, seeing them looking, squeezed past the tottering bales and accosted them with beady eyes. What were they looking for? A fine satin? The moire, so fashionable just now? What of this lovely watered silk?

It all reminded Alathea of her first shopping expedition in London, but then, she had only been eleven, and she did not recollect having had much say in such matters as colour or weave. Now, however, she was in control, despite Lucy's half-shocked, half-laughing protests. It was her money, her dress, her looks she would be enhancing. She bought a deep, rich, crimson velvet for the coming winter, unmaidenly though it was, and then decided on a lovely heavy cream silk that Lucy's tailor could make up in a hurry before what remained of the summer could slip into autumn. The purchases measured and made, she edged her way out of the cubbyhole of a shop to wait for Nell to make her choice. There seemed to be fewer people here, in one of the upstairs passages, and she could indulge in her pastime of watching the faces.

Her eye was caught, amid the jostling crowd, by two figures examining some gloves at a stall on the other side of the way, some yards distant. One was a most elegantly dressed lady of, she guessed, mature years but still possessing considerable beauty: tiny, with fragile delicate features and pale blonde hair, artfully curled. If the ravages of time had been cleverly concealed with paint or colour, at this distance Alathea could not tell, but she admired the faultless garments and the still-lovely profile, with its charmingly tilted nose and small chin. Beside her was a young girl who must surely be her daughter. She had the same sleek cream-and-silver hair, immaculately coiffured, and the same beautifully drawn profile. Then she turned, with a rustle of silk and lace, and for a moment looked directly at Alathea, across the shifting pattern of passers-by. There was something oddly familiar about that face, about its proportions, about the slight, modish pout and droop of the full little mouth. Their eyes met casually, hers blue and artless, and then the girl turned coolly away, to talk with her mother.

'She's taking the blue,' said Lucy, emerging breathless from the booth. 'I know she always wears that colour, but you can see why – it suits her very well, and she needs all the help her clothes can give her . . . what were you looking at?'

'That girl over there – very pretty in a rather babyish way, and her mother – I suppose it must be her mother – I was thinking how well she carries her age, she must be well over forty.'

Lucy's rather myopic blue eyes peered idly in the general direction of the two ladies whom Alathea had indicated. Abruptly, shockingly, the expression of mild curiosity on her face changed to horrified, total disbelief, and then all the colour ebbed from her skin. Painfully, she grabbed Alathea's arm and fairly dragged her back into the crowded gloom of the booth, almost knocking Nell over as she did so. 'Dear God,' Lucy gasped, 'It's her! I thought she was dead!'

'Who?' demanded Alathea, with curiosity and a little annoyance (the grip on her arm had been somewhat painful). 'What *are* you talking about? Was it that woman?'

'Which woman?' Nell's voice intruded plaintively. 'What's happened? Who's dead?'

'I thought *she* was,' said Lucy, and there was a grim hardness on her face that Alathea had never seen in her life before. It sat alien upon her round, still-pretty features, and her niece found it deeply disturbing. 'And she should have been dead – she should have died years ago – *why* isn't she *dead*?'

'Who?' Nell and Alathea cried desperately.

And Lucy, her eyes filling with tears of distress and futile anger, said savagely, 'Meraud, Meraud Trevelyan, her name is – and she's your mother, Nell.'

There was a dreadful silence in the hot, stuffy little booth. For a moment Alathea, struggling herself with the shock, thought that Nell was going to faint. She stood utterly still, her face ghostlike, the pale blue eyes enormous and haunted. *And that's where you'd seen that other girl's face before*, a corner of Alathea's magpie mind whispered. *She was familiar because she had a look of Nell.*

'My mother?' Her cousin's voice was hardly bigger than a whisper. 'My mother? My mother . . . she's not dead? She's out there? *Now*? Oh, let me past, I must *see* her!'

'It's better you don't,' Lucy said urgently. 'Oh, Nell, no . . . she didn't want you when you were born and I doubt she'll want you now. *We* love you, *we* want you – *she* won't – don't meddle with her, Nell, please, she can bring you nothing but pain and heartache and trouble.'

'I want to *see* her,' said Nell, still in that hoarse whisper. 'Please, Aunt, please, I just want to *see* her! Let me *past*!' Tears of desperation glittered in her eyes, and her mouth trembled. 'Oh, Aunt Lucy, I just want to see her . . . my mother . . . you all said she was dead . . . oh, please, let me *see* her!'

Lucy's eyes sought Alathea, pleading for help, and she, being nearest the entrance, slid backwards cautiously until she had a clear view of the passage-way outside. She had her father's face, after all, and the woman who was, so incredibly, Nell's mother might recognise her. She glanced up and down, but to no avail. Meraud Trevelyan and the girl who must be her daughter had both disappeared.

'She's gone,' she said over her shoulder. Nell gave a little sob and pushed roughly past her, as if she did not believe her. She stood staring wildly up and down the crowded walk, as if the power of her wish alone could bring the cool elegant figure of Meraud Trevelyan, so improbably her mother, back to her, and then she began, noisily, to weep.

The shopgirl was standing at the back of the booth, her hands full of soft blue silk, staring at her customers in bewilderment. Alathea, feeling she could do no other, put comforting arms round her sobbing cousin. Over Nell's glossy, mouse-gold curls, her eyes sought her aunt's. 'You'll have to explain. She's never known what happened to her mother – I don't know, either. What did she do? Why would she have been better dead?'

'I can't explain *here*,' Lucy pointed out with some force. 'Let's go home and we'll have some chocolate and I'll tell you in good time – but not here. Come on, I'll pay her and we'll go – but for God's sake keep a look out for that woman and if you see her, keep out of her sight!'

But they did not see Meraud Trevelyan or her lovely daughter again, and after escorting a tearful Nell the quarter-mile or so back to the House of the Ash Tree, the laden servants following curiously behind, Lucy called for chocolate and installed her two nieces in the smaller and more private of the two first-floor parlours. Beautifully panelled and hung with prints and pictures, it was cool in summer because of its northern aspect, looking over the tiny square of paved yard that was graced with the name of back garden. On this hot day, after the fraught stifling atmosphere of the Exchange, it was very refreshing, and by the time they had placed her in a comfortable upholstered chair, and the fragrance of chocolate had permeated the room, Nell seemed a great deal better. Very pale, but calm, she stared at her aunt over the top of her steaming cup, like a solemn little mouse looking over a nut, thought Alathea whimsically. Lucy poured out two more, passed Alathea's to her, and settled herself down in another chair, near the empty hearth.

'You were going to explain,' said Nell, wan but determined. 'About my mother.'

Lucy, now that the reckoning was due, could be seen to be balking at it. She took a small cautious sip of the chocolate – which must still have been almost boiling – and deliberated. 'Do you really want the whole truth?' she enquired at length. 'It's not very pleasant.'

'Yes,' said Nell. 'I want the whole story, none left out, I want the *truth*. Tell me, Aunt Lucy – please tell me. What did my mother do?'

'It's a long time ago,' said Lucy slowly, reluctantly. 'A very long time ago – before you were born, most of it happened. Your mother . . . do you *really* want to hear it?'

'*Yes*!' Nell cried, with more force than Alathea had ever seen in her. 'Yes, yes, *yes*! Now *tell* me!'

'Very well,' said Lucy. She sighed heavily. 'Your mother was . . . is, by the look of her today, very beautiful – the sort of woman men easily believe, easily fall in love with. She looks helpless, fragile, feminine, and she isn't at all.' There was a movement, a noise from Nell. Lucy held up her hand. 'As you'll find out if you listen. Now, it's all to do with Goldhayes, the inheritance of the Herons. It's entailed, so it can only pass in the male line. During the War, more than twenty years ago, it should have been Lord Bradfield's – Simon Heron, as he was then. He was married to Nan, but she was sickly, and unlikely to have children – so it was thought. The estate was in the hands of trustees – our mother, her second husband Richard Trevelyan, who was Meraud's uncle and Hugh's father, John Sewell, that's Jasper's and Hen's grandfather, and one or two others who weren't much concerned. But when Simon went into exile in Holland with Prince Rupert, it seemed very unlikely that he would ever return. So – who was the next heir? The eldest surviving brother after Simon was your father, Thea – Francis. And no one knew where he was at that time; for all the news we had to the contrary he might have been dead. So it was our youngest brother, Jamie, who looked to be the one to have Goldhayes, by default. Now before all this became clear, your mother, Nell, had had some sort of understanding with a friend of ours – Charles Lawrence, who'd been in the Royalist army, and had a little manor or two in Warwickshire, near Stratford I think it was. But as soon as it became possible that Jamie Heron might inherit Goldhayes, she switched her affections to him, and poor Charles's letters went unanswered. And she and Jamie were married.' An uncharacteristically bitter smile twisted Lucy's pretty little mouth. 'You may ask – why were so many deceived? I thought, right until the last, that she was a nice, pleasant, virtuous girl. Jamie was infatuated, just as poor Charles had been. She . . . she had such a candid, open, truthful look about her, you never thought it might be false. But still . . . '

'Go on,' said Nell. 'Please go on.'

'Well, she married Jamie, as I said. And very soon, you were conceived, at about the same time as rebellion was hatched in Suffolk, against the rule of Cromwell and the army. Jamie was very young, and rather headstrong – he was a dear lad, Jamie, we were all very fond of him, but he was like all of us, you couldn't dissuade him from anything, once he was set on it. He ended up with the rebels at Colchester, and was killed there. And by a dreadful coincidence, killed by Francis, who was in Fairfax's army.'

Alathea's stomach seemed to have turned to cold stone within her. This, this was the deep-buried horror she had always sensed, lurking, behind her parents' stories of those troubled times. Her father had killed his own brother – Nell's father! She glanced at her cousin, and saw that the pale resolute eyes were full of unshed tears. 'Go on,' Nell repeated.

Lucy seemed to find this retelling of an old but tragic tale still very upsetting. She had paused to dab at her own eyes, and her voice shook a little as she went on. 'Jamie had brought Malise Graham with him to Colchester, but Malise wasn't killed. He was very ill, though, when the siege ended, and Thomazine and the Widow Gooch – with Mab, of course, whom they'd just rescued – went back to Goldhayes to get the ransom for him, and the next day, the next morning in fact, Francis brought Malise to Goldhayes himself. He'd deserted, and rescued Malise from prison – and if they were found, Francis would be shot, and Malise sent to the Indies, and in his state of health he'd surely die on the journey.

'So – Malise was hidden, and nursed by the Widow. And somehow, eaves-dropping, Meraud discovered exactly how Jamie had been killed, which had been a secret between Thomazine and Francis and Malise and the Widow.

'Then, soldiers came looking for Malise. They didn't find him, he was too well-hidden for that, and Francis fooled them. And besides, the officer in charge of the search was my own dear Dan, and he had an old debt to repay: he would not betray one of us, even if he was on the other side. So Malise and Francis were safe – or so we thought. But they weren't – because Meraud had put two and two together. She could see that Francis and Thomazine would be married, have children – and the children would inherit

Goldhayes instead of her own unborn child, Jamie's son. And she had a thirst for revenge too, for Jamie's death, even though it had been an accident of war. So – she sought out Thomazine and Francis, and told them that if he did not leave Goldhayes instantly, without Thomazine, she would betray him, and Malise, *and* Dan, to the Parliament.'

There was a short appalled silence. Nell sniffed noisily, and rubbed her eyes.

'What else could Francis do? He left,' said Lucy sadly. 'He left Thomazine, to whom he had promised marriage, and he left her carrying his child, that was you, Thea, and she had to bear all the taunts and sneers and the gossip – because no one knew the real reason he had gone. She had to keep quiet, or Meraud would have proclaimed him a murderer, even after the danger from the army had gone.

'But . . . the best-made plans are often flawed, and Meraud's was too – for she had counted on one thing. She counted on her unborn child being a boy.'

'But it wasn't,' said Nell, in a strained whisper. 'It was me.'

'Yes, it was you – and a girl couldn't inherit Goldhayes, unfair as it may seem. All her plans had gone for nothing: no wonder she didn't want you. And Thomazine looked after you, when she had Thea.'

'You haven't finished, though,' Alathea reminded her. 'You haven't told what happened to Meraud – why she left Goldhayes.'

'Yes – why did she go?'

'Because she was told to go,' said Lucy. 'The whole story came out eventually – over poor Richard Trevelyan's deathbed, incidentally – and it was a terrible shock. We had all thought her such a sweet, gentle girl, and she was just like a cornered tigress. Oh, it was all true, I've no doubt of it, you had only to see her then: she was eaten up with spite and hatred and greed. She was desperate for Goldhayes, you see. But she had no cards left to play, and John Sewell told her to go. And she did.'

'And that other girl, the one who looked so like her? Could she be Meraud's daughter too? Nell's sister?' Alathea said thoughtfully.

Lucy spread her hands. 'She could well be. Meraud may have married Charles Lawrence, you see – he had always loved her, and he wasn't there when the illusion was shattered. If she was careful, he'd never know the real Meraud. And we've never heard anything of what happened to her: I thought she must surely be dead. And you can see, can't you, Nell, it was best to tell you she *was* dead. It might well have been truth, and what really happened . . . might have upset you too much.'

Nell said nothing. Tears were pouring down her face, but she was quite still and silent, looking into a past, a self, a future that no one could guess. Alathea found she was shaking and sweaty: the parlour no longer seemed so cool. She took a gulp of chocolate, which was almost cold, and felt a little better. But how must Nell feel, to learn in one short half-hour that her mother, of whom she must always have had a rather idealised picture, was a liar, a deceiver, a greedy and spiteful betrayer of friends?

But Nell said nothing, and the silence stretched out interminably. Alathea caught Lucy's eye. Her aunt blew her nose with a briskness reminiscent of Hen, and said brightly, 'Well, don't be too unhappy, Nell my love. It was all a very long time ago, twenty years and more, and your mother's probably a very pleasant, respectable woman now. We may have hated each other then, but it's an old quarrel, and it'd be stupid to take it up again now. Best not to try and meet her.'

'But I want to,' said Nell, still in that scarcely audible voice. 'I want to meet her. Now I know she's alive – whatever she did – it doesn't matter now. I want to meet her. She is my mother, after all.'

Lucy, remembering the savage, beautiful girl who had faced Thomazine over Richard Trevelyan's deathbed all those years ago, thought sadly that Meraud, brought face to face with the plain little mouse that she and the vivid, handsome Jamie had so improbably produced between them, would most likely dismiss her out of hand, and she doubted Nell's ability to cope with such a situation. Where had gone Meraud's cold steel, Jamie's headstrong impulsive courage? All her parents' qualities had ebbed quietly away from this wan little ghost, pleating her blue satin skirts with anxious fingers, desperate for the mother's care she had never truly had: for Thomazine's love, always, had been given first to her husband, then to her own children, and Nell, however affectionately treated, however petted and indulged, had always since babyhood been something of an outsider. Lucy felt a surge of sympathy and guilt for Nell, perennially the cuckoo in the nest, and now determined upon a quest that seemed doomed from the start. For however could she track her mother down, amongst all the crowded London houses, when they were not even sure of her surname?

Nell was determined, implacably, obsessively so, with a look in her eyes that disturbed Alathea as well as Lucy. And so, on their return to Covent Garden, the boy Tom was despatched to make enquiries for a lady of forty-four years, fair and lovely still, with a young daughter, whose name might possibly be Lawrence . . .

As well look for one pebble on the beach, four leaves amongst the clover. Tom thought it a fool's errand, and his sharp, foxy Londoner's face said so, obviously, when he set out: it said so even more plainly on his return. But there was something in Nell's expression that sent him out again the next day, and the next, for they were all fond of her, with all her spinelessness she was gentle and kind and considerate, and to see her in that curious condition of terrified obsession was upsetting to everyone. Even Hugh, on one of his regular visits, was driven to ask Alathea what was the matter with Nell, and she, setting down her chalks from a sketch of her uncle's knowing, slyly humorous face, gave way to the impulse to tell him the whole story. With some trepidation, remembering that this mysterious Meraud was Hugh's first cousin, she unfolded the whole sordid tangled skein of hate and spite, greed and betrayal: and Hugh snorted. 'I'd always thought the tale must have been something like that. We Trevelyans are an unchancy breed at the best, and I fear she's a typical example. Wonder what the daughter's like?'

'Very pretty. Very, very pretty. Quite Lely's type, I reckon. You should keep your eyes peeled at Whitehall. I should imagine they're on the catch for a husband. Would you recognise her, do you think?'

'My cousin Meraud? Gods, no, I haven't seen her since I was about four. I can remember someone who must have been her, playing ball with me and Kit, but I'd never know her face again. Unless . . . can you draw her?'

Alathea snapped her fingers. 'Yes! I looked at her for a long time, before I even knew who she was . . . she is very lovely, still. I can't promise an exact likeness, but I can give you a look of her.'

And a look was what she caught: a good look, a rather smug touch to that child-like, flower-like face, the hair still silver-gilt, the china fragility still so attractive, for two days later, Hugh saw her amongst the crowds in Hyde Park, at the most fashionable hour of the evening, strolling on the arm of some stout gentleman in a periwig who might, or might not, be her husband. And with her, turning heads and collecting glances all along the tree-lined walks, was the girl who must be her daughter.

And Hugh looked at her, a child, hardly more, little and lithe and laughing and demure, with her mother's flaxen hair curling about her face, heart-shaped and perfect, the nose a little tilted at the tip, the delicious rosebud mouth and small, rounded chin, and those lovely, languishing eyes . . . and something happened to him, something that he could not explain, as though his hard and worldly heart had suddenly surrendered without ever being under siege. He did not even know her name; for all he knew, she might be as hard and mercenary and false as her mother had been, but for the first and only time in his life, he fell in love with a face.

He could not possibly let her go by. She had paused, a little behind her mother, to look at the parading coaches (of which the finest was Henry Jermyn's), and he stepped up to her with a bow and a flourish, wondering at himself, and still more wondering what Alathea would say to this, if she could see him now.

'Mistress Lawrence, I believe?'

The girl stared at him, her slim arched eyebrows wrinkled in surprise. 'Why, yes, sir, that is my name – but I do not know you, sir. How then do you come to know me?'

Her voice was just as lovely as the rest of her, soft and sibilant, with a suspicion of a lisp. His gamble had paid off. He had not even known her name for sure, but now he was certain of her identity. His heart in his eyes, he smiled at her. 'My name is Hugh Trevelyan, and I believe, Mistress, that we are cousins.'

'Cousins?' The blue eyes turned so innocently up to his had an almost roguish look. He had a most uncomfortable picture of Alathea, commenting on all this in her mischievous, ironic style. He repressed it ruthlessly as the girl continued. 'Cousins? I have cousins in plenty on my father's side, but I did not think there were any relations of my mother's left alive.'

Little does she know that there is a whole tribe of us, thought Hugh, wondering whether the reaction of the rest of the Herons to Meraud's resurrection would be as horrified as his sister Lucy's. He said, with practised ease, 'I can assure you that I at least am one. Your dear mother's uncle was my father, and to my mind that makes us close kin.'

'It may,' said the girl, considering him. 'But it does not explain how you know who I am.'

'A friend of mine, who knows your mother, pointed you out to me,' said Hugh expertly, pleased, but also a little perturbed, to find even in conversation with this radiant beauty, that his courtly skills had not deserted him. 'But pray introduce me to your mother. She will remember me, although she has not seen me since I was a small child.'

'I will indeed,' said Mistress Lawrence, eyeing him somewhat dubiously. He guessed that many gallants, attracted as he had been by that surpassingly lovely face, had tried to force their presence upon her. One with genuine credentials must be something of a rarity.

She turned and hastened to catch up her mother. He saw her touch her arm, saw Meraud's head turn, and then mother and daughter conversed briefly. Suddenly, he began to regret most bitterly what he had done. Meraud, whatever her past transgressions, had made a new life for herself, and most successfully by the look of it. She must have thought her early history forgotten, decently dead and buried, and now he had appeared, a most unwelcome reminder of people and places and events that must have unpleasant memories. The daughter obviously knew nothing of this, and explanations would evidently have to be given. He knew her to be a most formidable lady, and it was with a great deal of trepidation that he watched her approach, her daughter on one arm and the ponderous escort on the other.

But she was smiling, very cool and gracious, a smile that somewhere, in the recesses of his memory, struck a chord. Close to, her age showed in the fine lines around eyes and mouth, but the carefully coiled hair was as bright as her daughter's, and her figure as young and trim. 'Why, Hugh! What a marvellous surprise, after all these years! What a very small world it is indeed, Sir Robert, for this is my dear dead uncle's son.'

In the middle of the gravelled walk, with the fashionable strolling by, they were all introduced. The escort proved to be a Sir Robert Manners, of whom Hugh had vaguely heard rumours, none of them good, and the girl, all demure dimples, was presented as 'My dear and only daughter, Susannah.'

But Nell was also Meraud's daughter. Had she been so easily erased from her life, Hugh wondered. His cousin was all smiles, very assured and affable and friendly, but somehow all her fine words struck a false, jarring note. He did not know how much his reaction to her had been coloured by the report he had had from Alathea, but he, who could be so smooth and hypocritical when occasion demanded it, could always recognise similar insincerity in others. She was being pleasant to him because it suited her to do so: there was no warmth in her, at all.

The girl Susannah was different, despite her flirtatious glances and smiles, which were probably just part of an enjoyable game to her, never meant to be taken seriously. He learned quickly enough that Meraud had indeed married Charles Lawrence, but that he had died the previous year, leaving just the one child, Susannah, as his heiress, and that they were in London to give the girl a taste of the fashionable life, now that she was seventeen. Catching a husband was not mentioned, but it was obvious that it was the end in view, and Hugh, looking at the fat, leering Sir Robert, making his excuses to leave, wondered with a sudden unease whether he was the intended spouse.

It was very pleasant casually chatting there, after bidding farewell to Sir Robert, but Hugh was determined to discover where they lodged, and how long they planned to stay in London. He also wanted some chance to give Meraud at least some hint of Nell's existence, perhaps arrange a meeting, and he needed time for such an exercise of all his diplomatic skills.

'If I may be so bold as to make a suggestion,' he said politely to Meraud, 'would you care for some refreshments? The keeper's lodge sells excellent cheesecakes, syllabubs and milk: just the thing for a warm evening.'

He escorted them to the lodge, a little building surrounded by trees and benches and tables, and bought a cheesecake and foaming warm tankards of new milk, fresh from the cow. They sat on the wooden benches in the red evening sun, not so warm now on the first day of September, and talked until Susannah, in her happy ignorance, gave Hugh the opening he needed.

'But do tell me,' she said, turning wide eyes upon her mother, 'why have I never heard of Hugh before today? I never even knew I *had* a Trevelyan cousin! You have never spoken about him.'

'I have always had other matters to talk about,' said Meraud, sipping her milk elegantly. Hugh, watching her closely for any signs of stress, could detect none whatsoever. 'I have many other cousins as well, and I have never talked about them either. It is not in my nature to be nostalgic about the past: the present and future are my sole concern, Susannah.'

'Other cousins?' The girl seized on that scrap of information and turned those devastating eyes upon Hugh. 'Oh, have I? Are there more of you? Do tell me!'

'I have an assortment of nephews and nieces,' Hugh said. 'Two of them – Alathea and Matthew Heron – are living in London. You must meet them. Thea is a painter, and if you are very nice to her she might paint your portrait. And Math is at the Inns of Court. Then there is my half-sister Lucy Ashley, and her husband Dan, who live in Fleet Street. Their son Oliver studies at Oxford and their daughter Rosalind is married and lives in Woolwich. So you see, there are quite a lot of us, even here in the City. And Thea and Math's parents, my half-brother Francis and his wife, are in Oxfordshire with their other two children; and of course the head of the family is Lord Bradfield, at Goldhayes in Suffolk.'

'Lord Bradfield?' Meraud's voice cut in quickly, with just a shade of genuine interest. 'Has Simon been made Lord Bradfield, then?'

'Yes – it was a reward for his services in exile. He received the title on his return with the King. He's a widower, he lives at Goldhayes with his two daughters, but I believe he plans to come to London this autumn.'

Meraud's face had sharpened perceptibly. Something he had said, clearly, had really grasped her attention. 'A widower, did you say? Then his wife – Nan Blagge, was it? – then his wife died?'

'Yes, about five years ago. And his only son was drowned, a terrible accident, at about the same time, and since then he's been something of a recluse. But he's supposed to be bringing his daughters here soon. He has a house in Covent Garden, which Alathea uses as a studio. If you are still in London when he arrives, you must call upon him. I am sure he will be glad to see you once more.'

'I am sure he will,' said Meraud, smiling charmingly in the kindly, fading sunlight. 'As I shall be so pleased to see him, for I was always very fond of Simon – a most upright, principled and godly man, Susannah my dear, an example to us all. I am so glad he received his due reward for his years of devoted service to the King.' There was no word of sorrow, Hugh noted, for the loss of Lord Bradfield's wife and son.

Susannah was eating her rich, crumbly cheesecake with the elegant greed of a little cat. She dabbed at the crumbs with a finger and sat back with a sigh of satisfaction. 'Hugh – can I call you Hugh? That was delicious. Thank you *so* much.'

'My pleasure,' said Hugh gallantly.

'And all these cousins!' Susannah went on, artlessly. 'Cousins here, and in Oxfordshire, and in Suffolk – have I any more? Do tell me.'

Hugh glanced meaningfully at Meraud, who was watching him with cool assurance, and decided that this was the moment to broach the most difficult question. He said casually, 'There's Nell, of course – but she is not your cousin, though.'

There was a pause that somehow became loaded with significance. Susannah glanced at her mother. Meraud was sitting quite still, gazing at Hugh, and he stared back, sending the message that his words had already implied. You have to tell your own daughter about Nell, about the half-sister she doesn't know she has: because if you don't, I will.

'Not my cousin?' said Susannah: and Meraud, so casually that Hugh at first did not realise what she had said, answered her. 'No, Nell Heron is not your cousin. She is your sister.'

This time, there was no pause at all. Susannah jerked round to face her mother. She knocked the table as she did so, and all the plates jumped and rattled. 'My sister? My *sister*? I have a *sister* as well? Why didn't you tell me? Who is she? Why doesn't she live with us? Why didn't you ever *say* anything about her?'

'She is a Heron, and stayed with the Herons,' said Meraud, as if poor Nell had had some say in the matter. Hugh, much though he was coming to dislike her, had to admire her coolness: nothing seemed to ruffle that graceful, elegant poise, as lovely and hollow as a shell. 'Before I married your father, Susannah, I was wed for a time to Jamie Heron, who was Hugh's half-brother. He was killed during the War, leaving me with his child – your half-sister. I trust she is well?' she added, turning to Hugh.

'Very well,' he said, noticing the look of angry astonishment on Susannah's face. He was beginning to get the measure of young Mistress Lawrence. There was a decided and forceful personality under all that guileless, artful, naive fluff, and he had received the distinct impression that she did not care much for Meraud either.

'Do you mean to say,' Susannah demanded with rather less than dutiful politeness, 'that I have a sister, here in London, and you never told me about her?'

'No, I chose not to,' said Meraud, sipping the last of her milk. 'It was a part of my life gone by, and I did not think it necessary to inform you. And now, Hugh, it grows late, and I think Susannah and I should leave before darkness falls: we have a little way to go to our lodgings. Thank you so much for the refreshments. It was most kind of you, and quite delicious.'

'Allow me to call you a hackney,' Hugh said, rising to his feet as she did, but Meraud declined graciously. 'No need, there is one waiting for us by the gate. It was most pleasant to see you again after all this time, Hugh. You must call on us some time. We lodge in Pall Mall, near to Charing Cross. Come, Susannah, we must be away.'

There were bows and curtseys and farewells, and with a mixture of emotions he watched them make their elegant way through the thinning crowds, towards the park gates. Once or twice Susannah looked back at him, and in the dimming light he thought he saw her smile. But he did not envy her that evening, alone with her mother and the sordid details of Meraud's past. Now, he believed all the stories. He could sense, within that most assured, calm, gracious and spurious shell, the callous selfish steel that was Meraud's core. He was angry for Susannah's sake, but for Nell, doomed to most bitter disillusion, he had profound compassion. He had never felt much beyond irritation when in her presence, and had tended to forget her entirely when he was not. But he knew that any meeting between her and the mother who had carelessly flung her aside, an inconvenient obstacle to her long-laid plans, must assuredly be a disaster. Somehow, Nell had to be dissuaded from such a course: but he remembered her white desperate face, and doubted it.

He called upon Alathea the next morning, and had to kick his heels while she completed two sittings, both of fashionable people. Nell was not in evidence and neither, unfortunately, was Hen, apparently dealing with some crisis in the kitchen department. He was entertained by young Becca, grave and shining in a new, rustly, ivory silk dress, soon to be five and carrying her years with a very wise look on that goblin face, and an earnest style of conversation that he found quite enchanting. They discussed the weather, and the servant who had just been caught pilfering sugar to sell elsewhere, and life at Whitehall, and her tame starling, with a total solemnity rather spoilt by the presence of Lovell-our-dog, who seemed to choose to mask their most important utterances with a noisy yawn or a good rattling scratch. He then pushed his nose and paws at Rebecca, asking for a walk, and left a quantity of long black hairs all over the cream satin.

'Go away, you horrid dog!' Becca cried, brushing the hairs off with frantic hands. 'This is my new, *best* dress – do you like it?' she enquired anxiously of Hugh, who said that he did indeed.

'Thea had some left over from *her* new dress, and so Mother had this made for me out of it. I do like it, it feels so smooth when you stroke it,' said Becca, with happy satisfaction. 'And I mustn't wear it too often or it'll get dirty.'

'And covered in dog hairs.'

'Yes. But I'll tell Lovell to stay away. He will, you know. He always does what I tell him.'

'I don't doubt it,' said Hugh, and at that moment, the door opened and Alathea walked in. There was no sign of any ivory silk. She wore her usual grubby green, with the man's shirt flung over it to take the worst of the paint. Lovell towed Rebecca outside, and Hugh embarked on an account of his meeting with Meraud.

It took some time, and he found himself trying to diminish the dislike he had taken to her, but in vain. When Alathea asked him what she was like, his response came without hesitation. 'She's an artful, selfish, scheming, callous woman. I didn't believe it when you told me the story, but now I've met her, I most certainly do. I can quite understand how she came to abandon her own baby, and she shows not the slightest interest in her. Thea, I don't think Nell would survive a meeting with her. That woman's . . . malicious, deadly, like a spider.'

'Then we must make sure they never do meet,' Alathea said. 'Well, that should be easy. I haven't the slightest desire to invite her here, and I don't suppose she wants to renew her acquaintance with any of us. We must just try to keep Nell away from Pall Mall till she leaves London.'

'The trouble is,' Hugh said slowly, remembering, 'I have a

feeling that she *does* want to renew her acquaintance with at least one member of our family. She seemed remarkably interested in Lord Bradfield's movements, and when he comes here, you may well find her on the doorstep. When *is* he coming here, by the way?'

'Early next month,' said Alathea gloomily. 'He's written to inform me of the date, given instructions to make the house ready – and he's assured me that I can stay, but I can't possibly. What am I to do? I can't afford to rent anywhere else as fashionable, and I need to be well-placed near Whitehall if I'm to continue to be so successful. And even if Lord Bradfield is prepared to tolerate my painting, I doubt he'd be so welcoming of the company I keep.'

Hugh had a swift vision of Lord Bradfield encountering Buckhurst, Sedley and Rochester at their drunken worst. His imagination quailed before the prospect. 'I'll try to find somewhere,' he said, wondering if, in his busy life, it was a promise to which he could hold. 'Surely your noble friends would help?'

'Perhaps, but I don't feel I can ask them. They come here to relax, for civilised talk and pleasant afternoons free of the pressures and strains of life in London *à la mode*,' said Alathea drily. 'If I start importuning them, they'll vanish like snow in summer, and I do enjoy their company.'

'Some more than others?' Hugh suggested slyly.

His niece's green eyes, so like his own, slid sideways to look at him: then she smiled, a secret smile that told him all he needed to know. 'Not especially. And, speaking of enjoying company, you seem to have relished young Mistress Susannah's. Poor girl, it must be difficult living with such a mother. And is she so very lovely?'

'Perhaps,' said Hugh guardedly.

Alathea grinned. 'You're smitten, Hugh Trevelyan! You've seen a pretty face and you've fallen head over ears in love! And I thought you of all people were immune!'

'No – I mean yes – yes I am immune, no I am not in love,' said Hugh, with a force his heart belied. 'She is very pretty, I grant you, and she's a taking girl: very young and innocent, of course, and yet she has a spirit that is most diverting – '

'What did I say? I'm right, aren't I? I should be careful, old lad,' said Alathea, suddenly serious. 'You know what they say: to find out what a girl will be in thirty years' time, look at her mother.

Susannah Lawrence may be all she appears to be – but on the other hand she may not. *And* you said she was an heiress.'

'Not to very much, I gather.'

'But still to something. And heiresses, very unfairly, tend to marry heirs. And what are you heir to?'

'Precisely nothing,' Hugh said. ' "My face is my fortune, sir, she said." I take your point. I am no longer in love – if, indeed, I ever was. But if I should see her again, with that neat little vixen's face and blue eyes a man could drown in, and a waist I could span in my hands – then I may well find I am wrong there. You've never loved, have you, Thea? People have fallen in love with you, Jasper has, even Kit in his poor perverted way was in love with you – but have you ever loved in return?'

'I don't think so,' said Alathea seriously. 'I think I would know if I had, don't you? A state people fondly imagine they're in, like a game – and then they really do fall in love, and there is no doubt any more. No, I am not in love, and not like to be, despite all John Wilmot can do.' She saw Hugh's look, and smiled. 'Don't worry. We have a pact merely of friendship between us, and if it is broken it is I who will do the breaking. But he has been sending me poems.'

'Love poems?'

'Oh, yes, calling me Clorinda or Phyllis – it's all part of the game. And that's all it is – a game, no more. Don't *worry*, Hugh. I can look after myself.'

But she had not been able to save herself from Kit. The same thought hovered in both their minds, so dissimilar and yet in some ways so alike.

'If I find you lodgings near to Whitehall,' Hugh heard himself saying, 'would you let me move in? Math's a broken reed as far as protection's concerned, and anyway he's hardly ever here. And you do need somebody – and don't look at me like that, Thea, you *do*. Even if Rochester and Sedley and the rest respect you, sooner or later there'll come along someone less scrupulous, who'll think you fair game. Whereas if I share the house, they'll assume you're under my protection.'

'But you're my uncle!'

'Half-uncle. And that'll make little difference in the eyes of the world – or at any rate the gossip-mongers. Would you mind that?'

'No, of course not. I'd be grateful. But Hugh – please understand about John – he is my friend. A *good* friend. If it hadn't been for his warning you, you know what Kit would have done. He may write me stupid poems – well, that's doing them an injustice, they're really rather good – but that's only a game. Truly. Friendship is all I want, just as you are my friend. Do understand, Hugh – he means me no harm.'

'I'll accept that,' said Hugh, hiding his unhappiness at the situation. 'But if it should ever come to pass that you are wrong – well, God help him. You know, I think I could easily have killed Kit, that night, and I might kill anyone else who tries to do what he did.'

'Unless I consent, of course.'

'There is that, yes.'

'I have my own life to lead, Hugh – let me do it, please. I don't mind you watching over me – but don't feel tempted to interfere. And I won't interfere in yours,' said Alathea, smiling to take the sting from her words. 'I would like to meet your Susannah, without her mother, if possible. Why not try to keep in touch with her yourself, and I'll invite her to supper here one evening. I'm already planning one final farewell before Lord Bradfield arrives and spoils it all. Bring her to that, if you can prise her away from her dreadful Medusa of a mother. Is that a bargain?'

'A bargain,' said Hugh, and they struck hands on it like the country people they still were, for all their London gloss, and parted, as ever, the best of friends.

CHAPTER SIXTEEN

The unlucky moment

'But if you're fond of baubles, be, and starve:
Your gew-gaw reputation still preserve:
Live upon modesty and empty fame
Forgoing sense for a fantastic name.'

(Rochester, *The Advice*)

Lord Bradfield, with his two daughters, was expected to arrive in Covent Garden in the middle of September, and Alathea accordingly planned her farewell supper for Thursday, the fifteenth of the month. It was not really a farewell to Covent Garden. She knew she would have to stay, for a little while at least, as no suitable alternative had yet been found, despite Hugh's efforts on her behalf. But it was a wake for her present, carefree life: no more would her raffish, rakish friends be able to visit her on long afternoons, drinking coffee and wine and displaying their wit and songs and bawdry for her laughter and delight. So she had invited Sedley and Savile and Buckhurst and Fleetwood Shepherd, all recently returned from Paris, whence they had gone in July to attend the funeral of Madame, the King's beloved sister. The summer had seemed quiet without them, but John Wilmot had continued to visit her, to make her laugh and bring her small, well-chosen gifts, such as might be passed between good friends: a book of poems, a pair of perfumed gloves, the lyrics of the latest sensational ballad. No poems of his own had come for some time, and Alathea found, with a mixture of annoyance and regret, that she missed them. He had taken lodgings in Lincoln's Inn Fields, only a brief walk from Covent Garden, and Henrietta was always suggesting, only part in joke, that he stayed with them instead, since it would shorten his journey to Whitehall. Alathea knew that he had not moved to be near her. She suspected that the streets around Drury Lane and Lincoln's Inn Fields, packed with theatres, coffee shops, alehouses, ordinaries, taverns and brothels, were sufficient lure in themselves. She could not help feeling anxious about her uncle's imminent arrival, and also, quite naturally, concerned with the preparations for the supper, and so the significance of the ivory silk dress quite escaped her.

Lucy's tailor, who shared with Lucy a secret despair over the sheer waste caused by Alathea's lack of interest in her attire, had received the lovely folds of material and the vague instructions to make a gown in the height of fashion, with professional delight. At last, here was his chance to dress this obstinate and frankly dowdy young woman in the style which her beauty deserved. He had cut it low even for Whitehall, and trimmed it with green ribbon as a concession to his peculiar client's favourite colour, and made also a deeper yellow petticoat, flounced and frilled and trimmed with the same ribbon. Alathea had hardly looked at it since its delivery, a week ago. She had not even tried it on until now, an hour or so before the appointed time for the supper.

All was ready in the lovely room below: the long shining table, covered with snowy damask and laid with plates and knives and spoons, the beautiful silver wine-cups, chased with the Heron coat of arms, glinting sharply in the light of the honey-smelling candles, made of finest beeswax. Down in the kitchen, lurking below ground level, the meats were baking, the sauces simmering over the fire, while the cook-maid laboured to carry out Henrietta's competent instructions.

Henrietta herself was elsewhere. She was standing in Alathea's chamber, exerting her not inconsiderable strength in tightening the other girl's laces, the ivory silk gown having proved too narrow even for Alathea's slender figure. When at last the corset had been pulled in and the soft folds of the dress slithered down over her head, Alathea felt as exhausted as if she had just run from the Piazza to Whitehall and back. Deftly, Hen laced the gown up the back, arranged the frill of the chemise around her neckline and cascading from her sleeves, and stepped back critically to view her handiwork. Alathea squinted doubtfully down at the expanse of swelling flesh thus revealed. 'I still think it's too low.'

'Nonsense. The Castlemaine wore dresses cut far lower than this, all the time. Still does, as far as I know.'

'Then all the gentlemen must have great fun when she curtseys,' was Alathea's tart comment. 'Show me, in the mirror.'

'Not until Sarah's done your hair. To look now would be to spoil the effect.'

Mutinously, with a sudden sick feeling of panic beginning somewhere below her ribs, Alathea sat on the tapestry-covered squab stool and submitted to Sarah's ministrations. The maid, previously in Lucy's employ, had a good touch for hair and combed, wound, curled and pinned with efficiency, despite her mistress's occasional squawks of pain. It was a long time before Henrietta, satisfied at last, whipped the big mirror out from its hiding-place behind the bed and propped it on the table before her. 'There you are. Not so bad, is it?'

Alathea looked at this languid, elegant Court beauty, pale and magnificent, and said, 'That's not me.'

'It is, you know,' said a dearly familiar voice behind her. 'I saw your lips move in the mirror.'

'Hugh! You should know better than to come into a lady's chamber unannounced. We could all have been discussing your qualities – or lack of them.'

'Well, you weren't,' said Hugh, grinning. 'Anyway, I'd much rather discuss yours. Stand up and turn round, there's a good girl.'

'If you take that tone with me, Hugh Trevelyan, you may find a syllabub down the back of your neck, later,' Alathea warned him. But she obeyed, stiffly yet with her usual grace, and stood with a soft rustle of silk before delicately turning to display her new self. 'Do you like it?'

'You'll have all the men's eyes out on stalks. A good thing I'm here to look after you. Which reminds me – your first guest has arrived. Mistress Susannah Lawrence awaits you below, and is being entertained by Becca and Lovell. I did warn her that this would not be a typical London supper, but she seems equal to anything. Her mother doesn't know she's here, by the way. She's supposed to be enjoying a quiet supper with Margaret Blagge, who's taken an interest in her.'

'I wonder whose idea that was,' his niece murmured demurely at the floor.

Hugh grinned. 'Whose do you think? Anyway, the appalling Meraud is supping tête-à-tête with the equally odious Sir Robert Manners, who has none, and the Blessed Margaret is under the impression that Susannah is resting at her lodgings with a sick headache. I am nothing if not devious, and Susannah is here, and awaits you. I warn you, she won't be expecting a goddess.'

'She won't meet one,' Alathea retorted. She swept him a mocking curtsey. 'Will you present her to me, dear Hugh? And you'd best start planning now how best to keep Sedley's paws off her. He has a predeliction for innocent-looking blondes.'

'Hence his interest in Nell? I should imagine Susannah will eclipse her entirely: fortunately for Nell, unfortunately for Susannah. Though,' said Hugh thoughtfully, 'I should imagine he'll meet his match there. She's one of your metal, dear girl, and more Heron than Trevelyan I should reckon. But come and see her and judge for yourself.'

Susannah Lawrence was certainly not in the least discomposed by her unorthodox welcome. She sat by the gentle fire, a halo of light cast around her head by the candles, sipping chocolate and stroking Lovell, who had pressed himself up against her pristine skirts, of a delicate shade of pale blue. Also sipping chocolate was Becca, her little monkey face, in the strongly shadowed light, bearing a marked resemblance to Strephon with those piercing beady eyes. As Hugh entered and stood aside for Alathea, Susannah jumped to her feet, nearly spilling the chocolate. She hastily put the cup down on the hearth and turned towards them with a delightful expression of eagerness on the lovely face Alathea had seen across the crowded arcade in the Exchange.

'Oh, Hugh!'

'Alathea – may I present Mistress Susannah Lawrence,' said Hugh, at his most pompously formal.

Alathea, very conscious suddenly of her new plumage, put extra effort into her curtsey. If Hugh really had fixed his eye on this unknown quantity, she must take the same care of him as he had of her, and she had heard enough of Meraud to be more than a little suspicious of the character of her daughter. Should Susannah turn out to be of the same base metal, impressing her now with a display of elegance and sophistication could do no harm.

But as she rose from her curtsey, and Susannah swept into hers, she saw that this was no country bumpkin, despite the fact that she had been immured in Warwickshire all her life. Whatever else she had received from Meraud, a thorough training in manners and formal behaviour had evidently been given, but it could not quite subdue the girl's natural, vivacious eagerness. 'So you are my cousin Alathea,' said the quick, light young voice. 'Hugh has told me *so* much about you!'

Alathea found herself abandoning her pedestal with undignified speed. Without thinking, her retort came immediately. 'Oh, he has, has he? Well, I'm surprised you've dared to meet me – most respectable people find me rather shocking.'

'But I don't,' Susannah said, coming closer. She had such short swift steps that she seemed almost to glide under those full, bell-shaped satin skirts. She was very small and finely-made, her immaculate silver-gilt curls hardly reaching Alathea's chin, and her cousin began to have the disagreeable sensation of being an unwieldy giant beside this petite and exquisite creature. 'I don't think you're shocking,' said Susannah. 'If *I* had such a gift as yours, I'd do what you have done – whatever Mother might say!' She produced a friendly, appealing grin which rather spoilt the doll-like effect. 'And I'm so glad I could come this evening. Mother would be furious if she found out I was here, but I'll make sure she doesn't. Hugh says all *sorts* of people are going to be here – he says you count half Whitehall as your friend!'

'I wouldn't say that – and I'm afraid that it's the disreputable part,' said Alathea, disarmed by this flattering enthusiasm. 'I ought to warn you now – they generally behave themselves in my presence, but I wouldn't swear my life on it. They may drink rather a lot of wine, and one or two may pay you some court.'

'Don't worry, I'm used to that,' said Susannah, making a little moue of wry distaste whose charming effect, Alathea noticed, was not lost on Hugh. 'After Father died last year, and I became his heiress, there were *always* people queuing at the door to look me over – as if I were a prize cow! And some of them were quite horrid. There was one man awfully scarred with the smallpox who *slobbered* all over me – but I trod very hard on his foot, *and* put my finger in his eye, and he never came back again,' she concluded with artless satisfaction. 'I've told Mother I'll marry someone *I* want to!'

'And what did your mother say to that?' Hugh enquired.

Susannah's delightful little face turned dazzlingly in his direction. 'She gave me to understand that it'd be *her* choice, not mine. It doesn't matter anyway – if I can't marry the man I want, I shall elope with him.'

Alathea took a deep breath at this confidence, and was careful not to catch Hugh's eye.

'I haven't met anyone yet, though,' the girl went on guilelessly. 'That's why Mother's brought me to London – to find me a husband, a fine rich husband. But that's enough of me – do tell me, when am I to meet my sister? Do you know, I didn't even know until last week that I even *had* a sister? I had three little brothers but they all died when they were babies and I never had anyone to play with when I was a child and I can't wait to meet her. Where is she?'

'She's making herself ready,' Alathea told her, thinking of Nell, green-faced with nerves and apprehension, upstairs having the mousy hair curled and the insignificant figure fitted into a dress of very much the same colour and style as her radiant half-sister's. Poor Nell: yet again, she would inevitably be eclipsed.

But she had reckoned without Susannah. The girl had an impulsive generosity that seemed quite genuine, and when the door opened hesitantly a few moments later, and Nell stood tense on the threshold, her fingers pleating the folds of her skirt, the younger girl gave a cry of delight and rushed to embrace her. 'Oh, at last, my *sister*! How pretty you look! And your gown – it's the same colour as mine but so much finer – I shall have to get all the details of fashion from you, I can see – oh, we shall have *so* much to talk about!' And the bemused but happy Nell, tears of joy and relief in her eyes, was led away for a quiet cose by the fire, leaving Alathea and Hugh standing by the open doorway. With a certain quiet and joyous satisfaction, they shook hands and Alathea, reverting to her childhood, gave him the old 'thumbs-up' signal of success.

Very shortly after that, the first of the evening's Court guests arrived, in the disparate shapes of Sedley, short and fat, and Buckhurst, long and lean. They ascended the stairs quoting Racine at each other and pretending to execrable French accents. Fleetwood Shepherd came next, bearing their presents for their hostess: Alathea found herself in receipt, in quick succession, of a very large bottle of exotic scent – 'Why? Am I not sweet-smelling enough already?' To which Buckhurst retorted that it was intended to drown the aroma of varnish in the studio, and she must splash it around liberally – a lovely pair of gloves, kidskin and minutely embroidered with pearls and silver thread, which Sedley adjured her solemnly never to sully with paint, and a fat flower-vase of Venetian glass, very slightly green, with bubbles of air trapped here and there within the twisted shining bowl.

'There was a pair to it,' Shepherd informed her sadly. 'Alas, my lord here was taken in extremity, and decency forbids me to tell you what then befell the vase (though I am sure you can guess), save that it now lies at the bottom of the Seine.'

There were gifts for Nell too: another pair of gloves, not quite so fine, and a bottle of similar scent, not so large or expensive, and, from Sedley, four solid-looking volumes of the very latest French romance. Alathea hoped that Nell's command of the language would be equal to the task. She had only previously read romances in translation. But her delight was very real, and she thanked her benefactors profusely. Then Susannah had to be introduced, with a brief and expurgated account of her relationship to the other Herons, and Sedley, basely forsaking Nell, at once declared himself to be dying of love.

'I doubt it, Sir Charles,' said the damsel, her eyes demurely cast down. 'For you look in the best of health to me.'

There was much laughter, and Buckhurst, grinning, said, 'Admit it, Little Sid – you've met your match here.'

'Mind you,' Shepherd added, 'it might very well be true, Mistress Lawrence, for he is looking somewhat paler than his usual self.'

'That can only be because he's had no wine at all today,' Buckhurst said.

'And that was because he'd had too much the night before, and was feeling too ill to consider it – until now,' Shepherd finished. 'I trust there is wine, Alathea?'

'There is, and if you come into the Dining Chamber you'll have it – if Sid wants it, of course,' she added, with a grin in the fat Wit's direction. 'After all, if he's been so ill . . . '

Sedley announced hastily that he was now, thank you, quite recovered, and they made their way from the smaller parlour to the lovely room where the supper was to be held. Susannah proved herself quite unaffected by the merry banter that was tossed around her head by the four men, Hugh included, and even joined in, demurely but tellingly. Nell tried to follow her example, with rather less success, but it was noticeable that Sedley gave her encouragement. It looks fatherly and pleasant enough, thought Alathea, watching warily: but I'll wager long odds that it isn't!

She herself was also the centre of attention, and everyone had remarked on the beauty of her gown and her looks with an astonishment that spoke volumes for the way she had previously dressed. Buckhurst in particular seemed in favour, and his hot dark eyes were always turned in her direction – but to no avail, as

Alathea had no intention of adding herself to a very long list which had included a shopgirl at the New Exchange, a variety of ladies of very dubious repute, a notorious whore called Black Bess, and Nell Gwynn, who had dubbed him her Charles the Second.

Then Henrietta entered, having just put Becca safely to bed. She wore her best gown, a deep and unfashionable russet-red that served to emphasise her flaming autumn hair and her wholesome, shining country face. She had never entirely lost her suspicion of the ulterior motives of these exotically plumaged birds of Whitehall, but now, after a year in their company, could be as free with her deflating commonsense as could Alathea with her wit. She also was the recipient of gifts far-fetched from France, gloves and scent and a fan of exquisite ivory, to her astonishment and delight, which, being Hen, she concealed very well behind a flow of down-to-earth advice.

'I should go easily with the wine,' she warned Buckhurst, pouring with a free hand. 'Or all my good cooking will go to waste.'

'And that would indeed be a tragedy,' Sedley informed Susannah. 'Mistress Jermyn's suppers are famous, have been for years, ever since you used to do wonders with rabbit and Rhenish in that little Westminster garret – oh, yes, I heard all about 'em from your rogue of a brother-in-law. What delights have you in store for us tonight, sweet Hen?'

'Humble pie and vipers' tongues in aspic, washed down with a quantity of cock ale,' said Alathea. 'She's vowed to give you the worst meal you've ever tasted.'

'Rubbish – would I be so ungrateful, after such splendid gifts?' Henrietta demanded. She looked around the company. 'Are we all here now? I have the suspicion that someone is missing.'

'Someone certainly is,' said Sedley, with a keen glance at his hostess. Then, on cue, the door was flung open, and the boy Tom, cheerfully familiar, made his announcement in his high Cockney voice, redolent with inappropriate authority. 'Master John Wilmot, and Master Henry Savile!'

So the party was complete. Alathea turned to greet her favourite Wit, an affectionate and delighted smile on her face, and something more than affection, unacknowledged, in her eyes, very wide and dark in the candlelight. John Wilmot – Tom had called him that, deliberately, as he had done for the past year – had not dressed magnificently for the occasion. He wore a plain suit of silver-grey satin, laced with silver, and a grey plume in his hat, a picture of under-stated elegance that somehow managed to make every other man in the room look showy and ostentatious. He bowed with a flourish, as did fat Harry Savile, as ever by his side, and as he straightened up, looked directly at Alathea. Across the width of the room, she saw his eyes widen, the sudden smile on his face, and knew with something akin to irritation that his reaction was not to her, so much as her attire.

Typically, the first words he spoke to her were someone else's. ' "In heaven itself thou sure wert dressed, With that angel-like disguise." '

'Waller,' said Alathea, knowing full well his habit of quoting that poet, and making a shrewd guess.

As usual, he was not impressed. 'One day I'll quote Spenser at you, or Crashaw, and you'll still look at me with those ironic eyes and say, "Waller".'

'Credit me with a little intelligence – I should think Becca could tell Crashaw and Waller apart, never mind Spenser. You like my dress, then?'

'It becomes you very well – which means, my dear and only Alathea, that you've at last appeared in a garment that does you justice. You'd outshine them all in Whitehall, from Castlemaine to Stewart, if you wore that. Come to Whitehall and dance with me, next week – and don't laugh.'

'That's what Hugh always says. In this house, "When I dance at Whitehall" means never.'

'Hugh may not keep his promises. I do – sometimes. And here is Harry, and he has a gift for you, from France.'

Harry Savile's plump face came into view, beaming. 'You're wrong there, John – it's from Italy. I went to Florence, with Colonel Hamilton, to offer our condolences to the Grand Duke on the death of his father. And I happened to see this, and I thought of our fair Alathea, and how she would love it – and I mortgaged all our allowance and beggared us both to bring it to you. So I trust you will show a proper gratitude, eh?' And he brought from behind his back a small flat package, perhaps twelve inches in each direction, neatly wrapped in stout cloth and tied firmly with string.

'I'll get Strephon to open it,' said John mischievously, and Alathea realised with rueful amusement that the little monkey had been sitting at his feet all the time.

'Oh, no, you don't,' she said hastily, and turned her mind to the unwrapping of her parcel, for something in the pleased eagerness of Harry Savile's face had informed her that this was a truly splendid gift.

She undid the knots with care, and gently drew the string and wrappings aside, and found that it was indeed something to marvel at. As she had suspected, he had brought her a picture: a very old picture, a little cracked here and there, and dark with varnish, yet still the colours glowed through, fresh and warm. It was a young girl's face, framed in serpentine locks of very fair hair, a face of sad and pensive delicacy, the eyes beautifully outlined to catch their lovely, dreamy melancholy, the long, slender fingers holding a rose whose fragile petals were falling, one by one, on to the shelf which formed the base of the picture. She had never seen anything so lovely. Even the jewel-like picture in Lord Bradfield's study could not equal this in its gentle, exquisite purity of line and colour, and the symbolism implicit in that rose, the fading of youth and life and beauty.

'Do you like it?' Harry was asking, a note of anxiety in his voice.

He must have paid a great deal of money for it, Alathea thought, *a fortune, it's so old and so lovely* . . . and she was aware, suddenly, that a large tear was trickling down the side of her nose. Fiercely she brushed it away, and lifted her head reluctantly from the painting. 'Harry – I can't possibly accept this. It must be very valuable.'

'It is indeed, and I brought it all the way from Florence for you, and I refuse utterly to take it back there,' said Harry. 'So you'll have to keep it, won't you! Do you like it?'

'Do I like it . . . . Harry, you don't have to ask, do you . . . I think it's the most beautiful painting I have ever seen in my life.'

By now everyone else was crowding round, craning their necks to see.

'It looks like you, a little,' Nell observed hesitantly, and her comment was enlarged by others, Susannah's light breathy little voice amongst them. In the middle of it all, Alathea stood with her soul in her eyes, staring at the portrait as if she could not look away, and yet as aware as she was of the sun's direction, or the wind's, of John Wilmot by her side, his hand resting gently on her shoulder.

'Do you know who painted it, Harry?' she said at last, hating the wobble in her voice.

'I was told it was by Sandro Botticelli, and it's certainly in his style, but not signed nor dated.'

'It needs neither,' said John, very quietly beside her. 'Like a great poem, or a great song – you need no name nor provenance to understand and admire. You did well to get that, Harry – I wish I'd thought of it.' The seriousness vanished like snow in summer, and he added with mock solemnity, 'Alas! It seems I'm the only one here who has not brought our lovely Alathea a gift!'

'You are not,' said Hugh. 'If I brought her one every time I visited, I'd be beggared within a week.'

'And John in a month,' Harry pointed out. 'I ought to warn you, Thea: Strephon is looking most inquisitively at your lovely picture, and I haven't brought it all the way from Florence, from the grand Duke's own palace (or at any rate a shop very close by), at vast expense, my coach positively *groaning* under the load, for it to be eaten by a monkey within five minutes of its delivery. I should lock it away at once.'

'I'll put it in the studio for you,' Nell offered, and since Alathea could not with courtesy leave her guests, she had to entrust the precious little painting to her cousin's tender hands. Then Henrietta, a little tartly, broke into the conversation to point out that suppers were not generally enhanced by being kept waiting for forty minutes, and would they therefore take their places at the table.

It was not a grand dinner, but an informal supper party of old friends, so there were no elaborate rules of precedence. Alathea took her place at the end of the long table, with John Wilmot on one side and Lord Buckhurst on the other. The rest distributed themselves down the length of it, admiring the silver (mostly borrowed from Dan), and the fine damask tablecloth and the astonishing number of forks (also borrowed from Dan) – one for each guest, and no fingerbowls needed. Henrietta, with a certain satisfaction, saw that everyone was suitably impressed, and rang her bell to summon the meal.

It was a simple supper, and of two courses only, but Henrietta had done her exalted diners justice, and the food, borne in by a stream of perspiring servants (most borrowed from Dan), was superb. There was the rabbit stewed in Rhenish that had made her name as a cook amongst her husband's hungry companions, roast mutton with a spearmint sauce, a dish of anchovies, a chicken fricassee, some lobsters and a pigeon pie, and of course there was wine, Alathea having taken the precaution of ordering a cask of sack from a neighbouring tavern. It was not long before the party grew something riotous, a state of affairs helped along by Strephon, who retired to the mantel with a bunch of grapes which he methodically picked to pieces and ate, spitting the pips all around the room. For a while these were heroically ignored, until Fleetwood Shepherd, incensed by one well-aimed missile landing with a plop in his wine cup just as he was raising it to his lips, reached across to the fruit-bowl decorating the centre of the table, selected a plum, and hurled it with accuracy at Strephon's head. The creature screeched, gibbered and jumped up and down for some time, while everyone laughed at it: then it picked up the last of the grapes and began an indiscriminate bombardment. Fruits flew through the air, to land where Strephon's erratic aim had taken them, in hair, in clothing, in food and once, spectacularly, right down the neckline of Alathea's immodest ivory gown. Feeling that she had best remove it before someone else made the attempt, she hastily delved into the depths. John got up and went to retrieve his errant other self, and Susannah, who was sitting beyond him, leaned across and said earnestly, 'Are your suppers always like this?'

John heard her. With Strephon wound round his neck like a scarf, having just received the kind of spanking a naughty two-year-old child might earn, he turned back to the table. 'No, they are not, Mistress Lawrence – save when Strephon is of the company.'

'Then I must be glad he will not usually be amongst us,' said Alathea, and spoilt the stern effect by laughing. 'Why you and that impossible creature have managed to escape a hanging, I shall never know.'

'The Devil looks to his own,' Buckhurst commented, and Rochester smiled.

'He does indeed – did you not know that I am Lucifer? The Bringer of Light – and of Chaos.'

It stuck in Alathea's mind, that name, as being peculiarly apt, and lingered all through the evening. They finished the meal at last, and retired to sit around the fire, where two silver pots of chocolate (one belonging to Dan) sat steaming gently on trivets in the hearth, and the cups and cream and sugar had been set out ready. Save that the numbers of people crowded around were greater than was usual, it might almost have been one of Alathea's convivial studio afternoons, but there were ten of them now, she saw with surprise: it had not seemed so many, seated at the table. Outside, she had noticed that it was raining, but the shutters were drawn against the dark and the drops beat harmlessly and impotently against the glass. Hen poured and distributed chocolate, and the Wits talked about France, and compared the grandeur of the new palace of Versailles with what Buckhurst contemptuously referred to as the King's Royal Rabbit-Warren of Whitehall, and the splendours of the Paris Opera with the more down-to-earth delights at the Theatre Royal or Lincoln's Inn Fields. That, of course, led on to discussion of the latest plays, and one soon to be performed by the Duke's Company at the Lincoln's Inn Fields Theatre, came in for particular discussion.

'I tried to bring the lady here with me tonight,' John said to Alathea, 'but she was otherwise engaged with work on the rehearsal. Do you remember me telling you of the shocking female writer, and saying that you must meet her? Well, it's Mistress Behn's play to be performed next week, her first, and sure to be a success.'

'I don't doubt it,' Alathea said, rather cynically. 'Half of London will come to see if a woman can string two words together and make a sentence. I know *exactly* how it'll be, for I've had it all myself. Don't deny it, the only reason most of you came here in the first place was to see if I knew white lead from vermilion.'

'That may once have been true,' Little Sid cried from his recumbent position at her feet. 'But rest assured, dearest Alathea, we come now for your beauty, virtue and wit.'

'And your delicious chocolate,' said Buckhurst, grinning lazily. 'I've never met this remarkable woman, John – is she as lovely as our artist here?'

'I learned long ago from Paris, never to compare one woman's beauty with another – especially if one of the ladies is present when you do it. Aphra is not to be judged by ordinary standards of beauty: she is herself, as Alathea is herself. And like Alathea, she believes in her gift, and she sees no reason why she should not be allowed to exercise it to the full, even if she is a woman. You will like her, Thea – she has a very pungent wit, and great spirit.'

'Perhaps I can paint her,' Alathea suggested.

Savile laughed. 'I doubt she'd be able to afford even your prices, Thea. But this time next week, when her name's been cried all over town, and people are flocking to see her play – then she'll have some coin to spare, I'll warrant.'

'What is her play called?' asked Susannah, her lovely, flower-like face turned towards John.

Hugh, watching, saw in her a strong resemblance to her mother, but also something more, a generosity and warmth which must have come from her dead father. The more he saw of her, the more his heart ached to have her, and yet, despite her apparent openness and sincerity, he had no idea at all of her opinion of him. Rochester might have been answering a child. It had been obvious all evening, painfully evident to Hugh, that his attention was given wholly to Alathea. *No good will come of that dress*, Hugh thought with clear-eyed desperation. *It's shown him she's a woman, not a companion, and now he'll pursue her in earnest.*

John Wilmot's light, quick voice was telling Susannah that Aphra's play was called *The Forc'd Marriage*, or, *The Jealous Bridegroom*, and the great Betterton had the chief role in it. 'Like Alathea, beginning her career with the Earl of St Albans, Aphra has aimed high from the start.'

'Have you read the play?' Alathea enquired.

'Naturally I have. It was partly my word that persuaded Betterton to take it on. She'd offered it to the King's Company first, but they were wary of it, being writ by a woman. More fool them, for it's good, for a first attempt, and she's certain to improve with each play she writes. I won't bore you all with a résumé of the plot: I shall expect you all to come and see it next week, or Strephon will be instructed to plague you all to death.' He turned to his hostess, who was sitting in a cane chair, very pale in her ivory silk and flaxen hair, and gave her one of his rare, genuine smiles. 'So – will you come with me on Tuesday, and see the play, and meet Aphra too? We can make up a party, monopolise the boxes, eat oranges and give her our support, for she'll need it. She told me that bringing this into the glaring eyes of the world was like giving birth, and quite as painful. *The Forc'd Marriage* is her first child, and we must be midwife and gossip to it, or it'll surely fail. Will you be there?'

'Of course I will, dear Lucifer,' said Alathea, smiling in return: and more than one person in that group crowded sitting and sprawling around the fire, saw their eyes meet and felt excluded, as if they had unawares stepped into a private conversation.

It was Susannah, who noticed such things, who realised, a few moments later, that Strephon had disappeared. Being Susannah, she did not wait until a suitable break in the talk, but jumped up with a cry of alarm. 'The monkey – where's the monkey?'

Buckhurst, who had been interrupted in the full flood of a long and scurrilous story about the supposed parentage of the French King, only laughed – she was, after all, a remarkably pretty girl, if a trifle ingénue for his tastes. 'Don't bother your sweet little head about it, my dear. As far as I'm concerned, if he's disappeared it can only be for the good.'

'He was sitting on the mantel,' said Susannah. 'I was watching him just now – and he's gone and I keep thinking he might come up behind me . . . ' She gave a shiver that made most of the men there long to protect her. 'Can someone find him? Please? I don't feel easy unless I know where he is.'

'Well, somewhere in this room, surely,' said Shepherd robustly. 'After all, the creature can't open doors . . . ' His voice died away as something in the controlled set of John Wilmot's face warned him that Strephon could, in fact, open doors.

Still, the door to the stairs was firmly shut. Wielding candles, more or less steadily, the male section of the party undertook a search, while Nell, Hen, Susannah and Alathea watched the fun from their fireside seats. Strephon was not on the mantel, nor hanging by his feet like some distorted goblin from the plaster-work. He was not hidden in the curtains (Harry Savile gave each one a thorough shaking which, gratifyingly for Hen, released only a very little dust). He was not on the table, under the table (Sedley checked that, accompanied by much ribald comment), nor crouched on the sideboard amongst the dirty dishes and uneaten remains of the supper. The fruit bowl was as they had left it, and the number of grape pips adhering to floor and walls was no greater than before. He was not on or beneath the chairs, either, nor hiding in the hearth, and Sedley, whose wine-flown enthusiasm had by now rather got the better of his judgement, had to be forcibly dissuaded from braving the flames to look up the chimney.

It was only when they had to admit defeat and apologise most humbly to the anxious Susannah, that John Wilmot let slip the information that, as well as training Strephon to open doors, he had taught him to shut them behind him. 'Without a sound,' he added, with disingenuous pride, and was promptly the target for a torrent of good-natured abuse from his friends, which ended with him snatching Buckhurst's wig from his head and hurling it accurately over one of the curtain poles, well out of reach. 'I'm afraid you'll have to ask Strephon nicely to get it down for you.'

'I'll be damned if I will,' Buckhurst growled. He looked quite different, and very much less imposing, without the black bulk of his periwig to lend consequence to his rather florid face. 'You put it up there, you rogue – and you can get it down.'

'Not without Strephon,' Rochester said, his dark eyes alight with mischief and the effects of a couple of bottles of best sack. 'And we shall have to find him. I can see Henrietta is desperate for her furnishings.'

'And my kitchen,' said Henrietta. 'And the poor dog.'

'And my studio!' Alathea cried, with sudden and awful foreboding. Strephon knew where it was, had been fascinated by paints and brushes and bottles, and she had a dreadful vision of the chaos that might result from half-an-hour of the monkey's uninhibited activities, and in the centre of the room, the stiff little corpse of Strephon, John Wilmot's alter ego, dead of orpiment or blue bice. 'It's no good you sitting there making mischief like some pagan god, John – you must help me find him before he tears the house to pieces.'

'We'll all help!' Sedley added with alacrity. 'Come on, Buckhurst, take that scowl from your face, it becomes you ill, and join in the search.'

'Does that great hairy dog of yours hunt apes?' Savile enquired of his hostess as she was halfway to the door.

Alathea glared at him with mock severity. 'On the contrary, he runs as if Lucifer were after him whenever Strephon's approaching, and I don't think you could have a hunt in reverse. Come on, Harry, you can do the kitchens, and I'll trust you not to sample any food that's been laid out.'

'I'm forever at your command, my dear!' Harry Savile cried with a flourish, and the wild hunt for Strephon began, as the Wits, the charmers and terrors of Whitehall, poured out of the Great

Chamber in search of the errant monkey like a horde of overgrown schoolboys.

She herself would go up to the studio: no one else could be trusted with that task. She took the stairs at a run, her ivory skirts bunched in one hand, and halfway up became aware that someone was following her. She stopped and turned, to come face to face with Rochester, eyes glittering, on the step below hers.

'You *are* the very devil!' she said, with reluctant amusement. 'I'll lay long odds you *told* that cursed monkey to make good his escape.'

'How? My command of languages may include Latin, Greek, French and Italian – but not African Ape.'

'From what I've seen of you and Strephon, you call mind to mind, like to like, warlock to familiar. Anyway, now you're here you can help me look, and if he's wreaked havoc in my studio, then God help you both.' And she turned and ran up the last flight of stairs, leaving him to follow her flying skirts and rapping heels.

The studio was quiet, aromatic, seemingly untouched. The light from their two candles cast huge wavering shadows on the ceiling, shadows of themselves, of the two easels with their burden of canvas and frame, the shapes of pots and brushes and, grotesquely vast, the plaster cherub that had once stood in for John Wilmot's monkey, to be crowned with laurel. Of Strephon himself, there was no sign. Alathea put the candlestick down on a table and began a quick search of the stacked canvases, but with no result. It did not take long to satisfy her that the ape had not sullied her sacrosanct studio. Then she turned to John Wilmot, who was standing by the door, his arms folded and his face bright with amusement.

'Lucifer! You did it on purpose, didn't you! Where have you hidden him?'

'I am not my monkey's keeper. What he chooses to do is his own affair – for my part, I'll guess only that he has beaten Harry to the food in the kitchen. But it's turned out for the best, after all. How else could I make sure I was alone with you?'

Alathea stood very still, tall and ghostly in the fitful candlelight, no colour anywhere on her save for the cream-and-ivory of her skin, hair, gown, and the green of her eyes. She found suddenly that breathing within the narrow confines of the corset had become very difficult, and a less innocent lady would have been very aware of the quick provocative rise and fall of her breasts above the low-cut gown. 'Not for long,' she said, trying to recapture the light-heartedness that had been in her voice only an instant before. 'It won't be long before someone else comes up here.'

'They won't for a while – they're mad with the hue and cry for Strephon. You don't know it, do you?'

'Know what?'

'How beautiful you are. You wear old clothes, you dress in paint, you knot that wonderful hair back out of the way, you never give a thought to your appearance, and yet it's like trying to disguise a rose amongst weeds. And now . . . tonight . . . you have your true colours at last, and *still* you don't know . . . Alathea, my dearest lady, you cannot remain a virgin for ever.'

He had been coming closer all the time as he spoke, until he was so near she could have put out a hand to touch him, the elegant, sleek, grey satin that hid, as his Court cynicism and his Court manners and his wild Whitehall ways hid, the young, real warmth of the man beneath. She said, her voice trembling between laughter and fright, 'You've had too much sack. Come on, let's go back downstairs.'

'Not yet,' said John softly. 'Oh, you're right, I *am* drunk, a little, though not much by my usual standards – how else do you think I can stand here and say what I've been wanting to say to you for a year or more? We have been playing games, you and I, games of friendship and flirtation, and we have danced around the edge of love – and now it is too late for games, for I have fallen in too deep. I think of you always, damn it, I even dream of you . . . standing before me in your shabby green dress with the paint on it and Math's old shirt . . . and you laugh and smile and I can see your soul in your eyes as it was tonight, when we looked at Harry's picture, and I reach for you and you turn away . . . Can't you see? I am obsessed by you, I have written a hundred poems to you, and fifty songs, and torn them all up because none of them do justice to you, save those I sent you. I look at every tall girl with fair hair that passes in the street because it might be you, and my heart lifts at the thought – and yet I have never seen you outside this house.'

'You might turn into Rochester,' said Alathea, in a voice that did not seem to be her own.

'But I am Rochester too, to my misfortune, and I want you.'

'You have a wife, and a daughter,' said Alathea, with increasing desperation, for she, too, had fallen in too deep for games, and was only now recognising what her heart had long told her to be true.

'I have Elizabeth, yes – and she was once a little like you, before marriage to me changed her, and it's not her fault, poor girl, she thought she could change me and no one told her how wrong she was. I'm not made for constancy in love, I can promise no happiness, no eternal bliss – only my soul, yours in perpetuity, for at least a week.'

' "Out upon it, I have loved Three whole days together: And am like to love three more If it prove fair weather," ' said Alathea, laughing rather wildly.

'And don't quote Suckling at me either, or I shall quote Shakespeare. "Oh, she doth teach the torches to burn bright . . . " I am deep in love, besotted, quite as besotted as Romeo, and with far greater cause. Can you do anything other than laugh, and look at me as if I were Lucifer in truth? Will you not kiss me?'

Unexpectedly, a tear made its hesitant way down the side of her nose. Alathea, mute, helpless, bewildered by the wild strength of the feelings within her, stared at him, anguished, and shook her head.

'Not even one kiss, no more than that? I did not think you were so cruel.'

'I can't,' said Alathea despairingly. 'I want to – but I'm afraid.'

'Of losing your virtue?' His words had a sting in them that reminded her of all those lampoons of supposedly virtuous Court ladies, exposing their hypocrisy. 'The world thinks you lost that to me a year ago.'

'The world can think what it likes. The people whose opinions matter are mostly in this house at this moment. I *am* afraid,' said Alathea, knowing that honesty was the only course. 'I'm afraid of losing something – but not my virtue.'

'What then?' His long finger came up, gently, to caress her cheek, and her skin burned and tingled as if a flame had touched her. 'What are you afraid of losing, oh most rare and lovely Alathea, if it is not your virtue, or your honour?'

'It's . . . ' Alathea, for once at a loss for words, stared down at the floor, found it lacking in inspiration, and raised her head to look straight at John Wilmot's waiting face. 'I have a belief – a silly superstitious belief – in a kind of magic to do with my painting. It's as if my gift were something I was *given*, but not necessarily for ever. You see, what makes me paint is skill, partly, and that will always be with me: but the power, the power that makes me paint till dusk, the power that makes me see pictures in everything around me, the power that drove me out on to the Thames when London was burning, to draw the flames . . . I too have my obsessions. And I am most afraid that if I . . . did what you wanted, that power . . . would leave me, somehow.'

There. She had said it – the belief that stood at the core of her heart and soul. She had laid aside the cloak of wit and laughter she had always used to mask herself, and set herself as naked to that merciless gaze as if she had divested herself of gown and corset and petticoat. *Do not laugh at me*, her eyes pleaded. *For love of me, do not laugh – it is my soul I am showing you.*

There was a long, long silence. One of the candles, near the window, dived and waved and flickered wildly in a sudden draught. John's eyes held hers, very dark and deep and strange, and she realised suddenly that she did not know him at all, had never known him. The John Wilmot who amused himself in her studio was but one facet of a personality as many-sided and brilliant as a diamond.

And he was dangerous, too – as dangerous as ever Kit could be, and with far greater power to hurt, should they come to grief.

Yet he cast his own spell, and she had fallen under it long ago, without knowing, so that he only had to crook that long finger for her to cast all her scruples to the winds, and abjure her magic and her art, and follow him for glory and happiness and heartbreak, to the world's end if necessary.

Something in her eyes, her lost and wondering face, told him that he had won, despite her words, and he understood, for he too had known the power of creation, when the poetry flowed from his fingers as if he were possessed by some divine sorcerer: and it was wine, most often, that unlocked his heart to release the glorious flood of words and wit for which he was famous. Elizabeth, once, had turned the key too, and now it was Alathea, with that ethereal beauty and ironic mind, who was his inspiration. She was his, he had only to touch her. Yet still something, something he defined wryly as respect, held him back. There were, after all, several degrees of rape, and when she became his, it must be with a glad and whole heart.

'Is there not room in your heart for both of us?' he asked softly. 'Isn't it possible to have two obsessions?'

Alathea looked at him, and her expression became more down-to-earth. 'I don't know,' she said. 'I've only ever been in possession of one at a time.'

'Then there's only one way to discover it,' he told her, his voice gentle and persuasive still. 'Is it then only because you believe your painting will suffer? Is it just that which stops you?'

'*Just*? *Only*?' Alathea's face took on a look of outrage. 'I'll have you know I *am* my painting. That is me, no more, no less. If I surrender to you I surrender my honour, which in some eyes is still untainted coin, and my virtue, which you may think is worth nothing, and I surrender myself, as well. Are 'just' and 'only' the words to use, think you, Master Wilmot?' And suddenly, appallingly she felt the urge to weep, to run, to hide from this situation where, whatever she did, she would lose one of her dearest friends. Defiantly, she lifted her chin and stared intently at him, willing herself not to shed tears.

'Don't worry,' he said, and smiled suddenly, and she knew that he spoke the truth when he said he loved her. 'I will not force you, if you do not wish it. I like my pleasure shared, for then it is greater. But remember only this, my love: youth and beauty and the power to captivate will not last for ever. "Had we but world enough and time, This coyness, lady, were no crime." Do you know that? It's Marvell's, and I will copy it and send it to you perhaps, if words of my own will not suffice. I will woo you, Alathea Heron, with love and poetry and songs, until your honour seems empty and your painting falters, and you realise that love is not a game nor a romance, and that passion is real. You feel it too, I know you do – so why resist? You have more courage and spirit than twenty women – why fear this?'

'I've told you,' Alathea said. She felt suddenly drained, exhausted, incapable of further effort. 'But you are right – I know you are – whatever you feel, I feel too, the power of it . . . please, give me time.'

'And time is not as unlimited as you might think . . . but at least you now know my feelings, and you have admitted the strength of yours. Starting with honesty is not such a bad way to begin . . . will you not kiss me, sweet and twenty? Youth's a stuff will not endure.' And he smiled again, and Alathea knew that this time, as he drew her towards him, she had no power left.

And at that moment the most terrible hammering erupted from downstairs. The windows shook, the candleflames jumped, and Alathea sprang out of his grasp as if stung. Below, a confused hubbub of noise replaced the hammering. Alathea, her hands crossed over her bodice, stared at her unlucky would-be lover, her eyes wide. 'What in God's name was that?'

'It sounds as if the King's Messengers have come to arrest someone,' he said, his face wry. 'Doubtless we shall soon discover what has happened, and meanwhile, I think the lucky moment has disappeared.'

'I think so too,' Alathea agreed, her voice back to dry normality. 'Someone's coming up the stairs.'

Someone was indeed. The hurrying steps grew louder and louder and then the door burst open and Nell stood on the threshold, an expression of total panic on her face, her eyes distended and her breath rasping in her throat. 'Oh, Thea – Thea, come quickly – Lord Bradfield's here!'

CHAPTER SEVENTEEN

Hang love

My heart at home in my own breast did dwell
Like humble hermit in a peaceful cell:
Unknown and undisturbed it rested there,
Stranger alike to hope and to despair.
But love's tumultuous train does now invade
The sacred quiet of this hallowed shade.

(Rochester, 'The Discovery')

Alathea supposed, afterwards, that her uncle could have chosen worse times to arrive unannounced, but at that particular moment, she could not think of any. Breathless as Nell, she followed her cousin back down the stairs, pausing only to hiss desperately to John, strolling unconcerned in her wake, some details of the exceedingly awkward situation that might arise if the Merry Gang behaved with anything other than the utmost decorum. And then, head high and her spine quailing, she walked quietly and soberly into the Great Chamber where, from Nell's urgent jerks of the thumb, Lord Bradfield must be awaiting her.

The Wits were all there, looking as if butter would not melt in their mouths. *And cheese wouldn't choke them either*, thought Alathea ruefully, lapsing into the Suffolk idiom of her childhood. But dominating the younger men, standing in front of the fire like a great black stork, tall and gaunt and frightening in his sombre clothes, stood Simon Heron, first and probably last Lord Bradfield, an expression of severity on his face. The lovely stately room looked as if an animal had run riot in it, and the unspeakable Strephon, she noticed with panic, was hunched on the long table, his feet imprinting the damask cloth with something brown and unidentifiable, chattering softly to himself and thoughtfully dismembering a pigeon carcass. Praying that Lord Bradfield had not yet looked that way, Alathea sank into her deepest and most reverent curtsey

Her uncle bowed politely, and the grim lines on his face did not alter. Playing the gracious hostess with a feeling of increasing desperation, she began the formal introductions. As she spoke each name, bows were exchanged with chilly correctness, and out of the corner of her eye she saw Strephon, alone on the table, mimic each bend and flourish to a nicety. Smothering a rising and insane desire to give way to hysterical laughter, Alathea turned to the only other stranger in the room. 'And may I also present Mistress Susannah Lawrence, who is our long-lost cousin.'

Susannah stepped forward and with pointed foot and sweeping bluebell skirts, sank gracefully to the floor. Lord Bradfield's face softened suddenly into warm and genuine feeling. He raised the diminutive girl to her feet, with an awkward, unpractised movement. 'Mistress Lawrence? But you are surely Meraud's daughter?'

'That is my mother's name, sir,' said Susannah, very demurely. 'I am Nell's half-sister – and you are my cousin, my lord?'

'I believe I must be, if you are Meraud's child,' said Lord Bradfield. He had not let go of the girl's hand, and his face was of a sudden relaxed, open, as Alathea had never seen him before. For the first time, she could distinguish a strong resemblance to her father. 'And you are surely that – you are exactly like her when she was a girl – is she well?'

'Very well, sir, and in London also. She was supping elsewhere tonight, and Hugh invited me here,' said Susannah, with one of her characteristic lapses into informality.

'Is that so? We must undoubtedly meet again,' said Lord Bradfield, as Susannah withdrew her hand with artless grace. 'She was married to my young brother, you know, while I was in exile, and Eleanor was born . . . and after his death, I presume married your father? Lawrence? I seem to remember a Charles Lawrence amongst our Oxford friends during the War.'

'He was indeed my father, my lord, but alas, he died last year, and my brothers are dead too, and there is only my mother and me,' said Susannah simply. 'I never knew I had any cousins on my mother's side at all till I met Hugh last week – and now I find I have so many I cannot count them, and a sister as well!'

'That must give you great pleasure,' said Simon Heron gravely.

Alathea snatched a moment to indicate to John, with a forceful jerk of her head, that he find some way of capturing Strephon, now investigating the fruit bowl again, without attracting too mucn notice. Her uncle addressed his next words to her unexpectedly, and she whirled round guiltily to face him.

'I apologise for my unexpected arrival, my dear niece. Our journey from Suffolk did not take so long as we had planned, and when we had reached Whitechapel and it was not yet dark, I left Anne and Mary with my man and the maids, they being tired from the travelling, and rode on ahead. I see you have been entertaining your friends, niece. I trust my arrival will not interrupt your party. Perhaps we might all take a glass of wine together?'

The next few minutes were hectic in the extreme. Henrietta, acting with her usual efficiency, disappeared in search of the servants, who had understandably expected a peaceful evening after the bustle of preparation for the supper, and within a surprisingly short time the remains of the meal were cleared away, wine and cakes and cold meats brought, and orders given for Matthew's chamber, empty at present since he was spending the latter part of his vacation with a friend from the Temple, to be aired and made ready for His Lordship's occupation. Lord Bradfield sat like a granite statue in the best chair, closest to the fire, and proved to have a remarkably stilting effect on the conversation. Alathea, praying that he had spent sufficient time in the seclusion of Suffolk never to have heard of the notoriety of the five Wits who lounged about the fireside on stool or chair, tried to direct it into decorous channels: and Buckhurst, who had a reputation for wit and malice almost the equal of Rochester's or Sedley's, had none of their concern for her and with insistent devilry kept steering it back. Somehow, a discussion of German wines turned into a review by Buckhurst of some long-gone drinking bout at a Drury Lane tavern, and Susannah's naively enthusiastic description of fashionable Hyde Park was capped by an equally vivid account of the fine variety of vizard-masks and doxies to be found parading there. John Wilmot, seeing Alathea's increasingly desperate expression and Lord Bradfield's increasingly stern one, took pity on her and turned the talk to the theatre. This, it rapidly became evident, was a mistake. Lord Bradfield disapproved of the theatre, and still more of the disgraceful modern practice of putting women on the stage in defiance of all decent morality, whereupon Buckhurst, seeing his chance, took the opportunity to launch into a defence of actresses in general and his erstwhile mistress, Nell Gwynn, in particular.

'And if you think female actors are immodest,' he finished, with a swift malicious glance at John – the periwig, now rescued, had evidently not been forgotten – 'here is worse to come – for next week, a woman writer is to present her first play at the Duke's Theatre. What think you of that for impudence, my lord?'

'It seems no more impudent than Mistress Heron's painting of portraits,' said Savile unwisely, as Lord Bradfield frowned.

And Susannah, her enchanting face turned up to his, added her voice. 'And do you not think it the bravest thing, for a woman to write a play and have it acted by Betterton? We are all going to see it next week. Do come with us, and bring Anne and Mary – I do so want to meet them!'

It was already apparent that Susannah Lawrence, whether for her mother's sake or her own, had had some effect on Lord Bradfield's stern and flinty heart. His face, grim and severe in repose, with that great eagle's beak dominating the sombre dark eyes and long compressed mouth, softened noticeably when she spoke. 'I do not think I will go to the play, cousin, but there is no reason why Anne and Mary should not accompany you. I have brought them to London to give them some taste of society, after all, and I know that Mall in particular is all afire to see a play.'

'Then let us hope Mistress Behn's first foray is as good as it's cried up to be,' Buckhurst commented lazily. 'Not every aspiring author makes a success of their first efforts, eh, Little Sid?'

Sedley, reminded of the sorry fate of *The Mulberry Garden*, hastened to change the subject, asking Lord Bradfield if he had ever been in France. Alathea's uncle, once more stone-faced, replied that he had, during his years of exile. Savile flippantly compared the country, not to its detriment, with the stolidity and dull morals of Holland, whereupon Lord Bradfield, with some force, embarked upon a lecture in praise of solid Dutch worth and decent virtues, as opposed to the frivolous decadence of France. Alathea, seeing that the evening was likely to end in blows if this was allowed to continue, plunged in gallantly with a monologue on the beauties of Dutch art, and single-handedly brought the talk around to painting. The Botticelli picture was carried down from her studio, and much admired, as were the portraits of Henrietta and Rebecca, hanging on either side of the mantelpiece: and at last, after the longest half-hour she had ever experienced, John rose with belated tact and announced that in view of the lateness of the hour, he felt it time to leave. The rest of the company rose also. Hugh offered to escort Susannah back to her Pall Mall lodgings, and the boy Tom was summoned and told to light their way with a link. Farewells were spoken with exact correctness, as if the conversation had not teetered on the edge of disaster for the past half-hour, and Alathea, standing trembling with fatigue both emotional and physical, could at last feel some relief. No sooner had she allowed herself to think that all was safely over, however, when fate, in the form of Strephon, took a hand. The little jackanapes had assumed his usual position on John's shoulder and had sat there quietly for some time, evidently plotting mischief, for when his owner bowed to Lord Bradfield, Strephon suddenly leapt from his perch and swung gleefully up the panelling, chattering with delight.

'Oh, *no*!' Alathea cried, seeing her uncle's look of outraged astonishment as Strephon swung by one hand from Sir Simon Heron's portrait and gibbered at his audience below. 'Call him down, John – *please*.'

John Wilmot, seeing her look of despair, abandoned any plans for mischief, and whistled a command. The monkey shrieked rudely back and began, with intense concentration, an obscene ritual of intimate hygiene. Nell giggled and blushed, Susannah turned modestly away. Henrietta, sizing up the situation with her customary briskness, took up a pole used to close the shutters and prodded Strephon severely in the ribs. With a squawk of angry surprise, the ape swung into action. It ran down the pole, pulled Hen's hair, and leapt from shoulder to shoulder, dodging all the grasping hands, before taking a flying leap through the door to the glorious freedom of the house. And after it, suddenly and exuberantly released from the constraints of polite convention, poured the Merry Gang, uttering alchoholic tally-hoes and whoops of pursuit.

'I'll go see they don't wreck the house,' said Henrietta, with ominous grimness, and followed them. Alathea was left helplessly with Nell and Susannah, to face her uncle's wrath.

Astonishingly, it did not descend, for Susannah began to laugh. She had a delightful laugh, light and merry and infectious, and after a moment Nell joined in: and then, like a miracle, Lord Bradfield's forbidding face relaxed, his mouth twitched and something approaching a smile appeared in the lines around his ferocious nose. Incredulous, Alathea at last gave way to the rising hysteria that had threatened to engulf her ever since Lord Bradfield's arrival, and joined in the mirth.

'I trust that creature is not a regular visitor,' said Lord Bradfield, as their laughter died away at last. Alathea hastened, gasping, to assure him that it was not, and apologised for her friends' behaviour, only to receive, instead of the expected diatribe, a mild comment on the wild ways of modern young men. He *cannot* have heard of them, Alathea realised with incredulous relief. If he'd had any whisper of what they usually do in London, he'd have barred them from the house as soon as he heard their names.

But, of course, the longer he stayed in London, the more likely he was to hear tell of the profane Wits and their drunken exploits: hardly fit company for his brother's unwed twenty-one-year-old daughter.

Strephon was soon captured, not without hurt to a few pieces of crockery and a pie (he had once more made for the kitchen), and the Merry Gang took their breathless leave, alive with drink and repartee which made Susannah laugh again: and so long as she laughed, Lord Bradfield did not seem to mind.

The house seemed as empty and hollow as the grave without them, and when Hugh and Susannah had also left for Pall Mall, the reckoning came. Lord Bradfield did not, upon reflection, think it suitable that his niece entertain such a party in the house. It was not seemly for a young girl to carry on in such a way, and allow such men to be so familiar.

'They are my friends, and have been so for some time,' Alathea said, clenching her hands together, aware that this was a battle she might not be able to win. 'I have painted them all, and we do no more than sit and talk around the fire in the studio. I have done nothing improper in this, my lord.'

'You may not have done, indeed, but I am sure the eyes of the world see things differently. I do not know what my brother can be thinking of, to allow such a state of affairs.'

'I think he trusts me,' Alathea said.

Her uncle frowned, and continued regardless. 'To expose a young girl to the temptations of London society, without protection, to allow her to entertain all manner of dubious company with complete licence, and above all, to allow her to earn a living by *painting* . . . ' He shook his head severely. 'I had not understood the true situation, and neither, I am sure, does your father. Even he cannot condone this. I shall write to him tomorrow.'

'Are you planning to turn me out of doors?' Alathea asked, as calmly as she could. One part of her mind was wondering what would happen, were she to faint. She was certainly feeling remarkably dizzy and exhausted. But she could not, would not lose control now – she must, for all her friends' sake, continue her fight. 'I am sorry if my conduct displeases you, my lord, and I can only say that if you do not wish me to remain any longer beneath your roof, I will make every effort to find somewhere else to set up my studio.'

'There is no need for that,' said her uncle. 'Indeed, I positively forbid it. At the least, if you remain here I am able to ensure that neither you nor your reputation are harmed by such unseemly goings-on. I am not telling you to stop your painting, although I disapprove of that most strongly. I am not your parent, after all, and your father appears to see no harm in it. But I shall be most concerned to protect you from those extremely wild young men who have made so free with your hospitality. I shall not bar them the house, but I am sure that my presence will greatly restrict their activities.'

And that was that. She was too exhausted to argue. At least she could still paint, still live in the house she had grown to love, still see her friends, albeit under much quieter circumstances. *John's missed his lucky moment*, she thought wryly, climbing the stairs to her bed with all the energy and spirit of a wrung-out dishcloth. *There's small chance of my ever becoming his mistress, under Lord Bradfield's eagle eye.*

The next morning, his two daughters arrived, surrounded by bag and baggage and servants, and the household was doubled in an instant. There was Lord Bradfield's cook, a tiny Frenchman with impressive moustachios and little English, who struck terror in the kitchen and insisted on only the very best and freshest ingredients. The maids complained despairingly of the ungodly hours they were forced to keep in order to be up to have the pick of the City markets. Henrietta was confirmed in her position of housekeeper, and to her offended astonishment was offered a wage, which she indignantly declined. The relaxed, happy household, Herons and Jermyns and servants, who had muddled cheerfully along together for nearly two years in varied circumstances, found itself dragged abruptly and reluctantly into formality. Lord Bradfield had a position to keep up, a style to maintain. He insisted on proper dress, proper decorum, punctuality and, most horrendously, household prayers at six o'clock, morning and evening. There werę two footmen, a coach, a valet, two grooms, a laundrymaid, as well as the cook. A gardener was engaged, and Lovell's and Becca's overgrown paradise, refuge for rats and mice and birds and local cats, was tortured into an ordered travesty of its former self, with clipped hedges and regimented herbs.

But all of this unwelcome change, Alathea at least could have borne. She was after all able to escape to the sanctuary of her studio, immune by tacit consent to the stifling formality of Lord Bradfield's daily ritual. For everyone else, no such joy, and no one suffered more than poor Lovell, at best barely tolerated, and unable to raise a bark or even a whine under pain of banishment to a chained-up existence in the garden, away from the comfort of bed and floor and fire.

Lord Bradfield's daughters, however, were altogether different, and much more difficult to avoid.

Five years ago, after the tragedy of Rupert Heron's death at Goldhayes, Alathea had felt some sympathy with Anne. She had seen that, however much her cousin tried to hide it, she had truly loved Rupert, obnoxious child though he was, and grieved deeply for his death. But she had not had much contact with Anne at all, and little idea of the abrasiveness of her personality.

Anne, unfortunately, took after her father in looks and, it seemed, in temperament as well. She had been plain five years ago, at the age of sixteen, and maturity had not been kind to her. It was just as well she was an heiress, for her dowry was most assuredly not in that thin, narrow face, with the over-large nose and undistinguished dark eyes and thin mouth, set in a dead-white skin that had neither life nor colour. Mall, in contrast, took after her dead mother and had the Blagge nose, turned up at the tip, a much rounder face, paler and more curly hair and the fashionably languishing eyes. She had a look of her Aunt Lucy about her, but without any of Lucy's good nature. Mall was intensely curious, and like her unfortunate brother, thoroughly spoilt. She spent an excruciating hour in Alathea's studio on the afternoon of her arrival, poking, prying, complaining of the smell but refusing all tactfully worded hints that her departure might be welcomed, and only the entry of her elder sister brought that about.

The two, it appeared, thoroughly disliked each other, and Alathea could see why. Whereas Mall was lazy, provoking, spiteful, shallow and really interested only in the latest fashions, and men, Anne had claws, and did not scruple to use them. She told Mall in no uncertain terms to leave her cousin alone if she was busy, and then subjected Alathea to a fifteen-minute inquisition on the art of painting. Nor did she suffer fools gladly, and poor Nell, who at least had been treated, on the whole, with kindness and consideration all her life, found her short-comings mercilessly upbraided in Anne's sharp staccato voice. She seemed to be forever in tears, which, of course, earned her short shrift from Anne. Alathea, coming upon the end of one such exchange, was prompted to take her cousin to task for it.

'Poor Nell, she can't help it if she's not so quick as you – and she takes criticism very much to heart.'

'She should learn not to,' said Anne, her black eyebrows raised. 'Really, not to be able to do a simple stitch like that – it's ridiculous, she's not in the nursery any longer.'

'She was probably flustered by you breathing down her neck,' Alathea pointed out, with rising annoyance. 'I don't think you're very fair to her. She can sew beautifully, as a matter of fact, when she doesn't think every move of her needle is going to be unjustly criticised.'

'I don't consider it unjust,' said Anne, looking down her long nose in a way that Alathea found intensely irritating. 'I was only speaking the truth, that's all.' And she swept grandly from the room, leaving Alathea seething in the middle of the floor, and Nell sobbing quietly in a corner.

There were only two good things to result from Lord Bradfield's unwelcome and unwanted invasion of their lives. One was that Alathea was at least no longer charged rent. Admittedly, it had not been a very large amount, but its absence would make some difference to her savings. More than ever, she wanted to set up her own establishment, free of her uncle's imprisoning conventions. And for the other, the quiet Covent Garden house, that had only seen the company of the Merry Gang and Alathea's sitters, became suddenly awash with visitors. It seemed as if half of fashionable society had beaten a path to their door during the first week after Lord Bradfield's arrival. There were old Suffolk acquaintances, relatives like the Jermyns or Herveys, fellow peers come to pay their respects, impecunious young men who had heard of a pair of heiresses in the offing. There was a constant stream of callers, only a few of whom had come to sit for their portrait, and not infrequently some confusion resulted, so that Alathea's clients found themselves ushered into the forbidding presence of Lord Bradfield, while bewildered gentlemen and ladies from Whitehall were asked to climb the steep stairs to the studio. Since at least three extra commissions came as a direct result of such errors, Alathea did not mind very much.

And on the Monday, Mistress Meraud Lawrence and her daughter Susannah came to pay their respects.

Alathea had had a busy morning. She had cancelled the sitter for the following afternoon, because of Mistress Behn's play, and had had perforce to fit him in at an inconvenient time between two others. Working on three different pictures in the space of one morning had proved exhausting, and there were another two booked for the afternoon. Young Jonathan Carter was proving himself an increasingly able and useful assistant, but he could not do everything, and, more to the point, he could not paint. For the first time in her life, Alathea was beginning to see the need for Lely's army of apprentices.

Nell was helping too: it was a refuge from Anne. She looked terrible, like the old Nell, bony and round-shouldered, her hair lank and her skin lumpy with spots. All her new-found confidence seemed to have ebbed away from her since the twin blows of her mother's return and Lord Bradfield's arrival. Alathea felt the old mix of pity, guilt and annoyance as she looked at her cousin cleaning brushes. Why could she not make more of herself?

And then Henrietta came hurrying up the stairs, panting, and burst into the studio without her usual brisk rat-tat on the door. 'You'd better come down, both of you, if you can. Meraud's just arrived.'

Nell gave a tiny gasp and turned quite white. She put the brushes down and turned to Alathea with a hunted, desperate expression on her face. 'My mother – my mother's come to see me – and look at me!'

'You'll have to change,' said Hen practically. 'You can't possibly see her wearing that old thing. Put on the blue you wore the other day, that's a lovely dress.' She took Nell by a limp, unresisting hand and shepherded her down the stairs. Alathea, who needed no such help, stayed only to finish making ready for the next sitter before running hastily down to change her own clothes.

Ivory silk was too elaborate: it must be the green velvet, if the moth had not got to it first. She had not worn it since last winter, but today was cold and it would not be inappropriate. When she reached their chamber, Nell was already laced firmly into her blue silk, and Henrietta was doing her best with mousey uncurled hair that had not been washed for too long. Beneath the older girl's firm freckled hands, brushing and winding and pinning, Nell's face had taken on a greenish tinge which Hen's cheerfully brisk chat was doing nothing to dispel. Alathea, rather nervous herself, changed quickly into the green, knotted her hair back afresh and helped Hen to put the finishing touches to her cousin's toilette. She remembered the cold loveliness of the woman she had seen in the New Exchange, and the callous mother of Hugh's description, and her heart quailed, for Nell's sake. What could such a poised, elegant, fashionable widow possibly find to inspire maternal love in this gaunt pathetic scarecrow of a daughter?

Meraud Lawrence, once Meraud Heron, née Meraud Trevelyan, sat in the Great Chamber, drinking coffee and nibbling sweetmeats with daintiness, her daughter Susannah beside her. In the clear September daylight, it was possible to guess her true age from the fine lines about her rosebud mouth and wide blue eyes, but her silvery hair was as fine and glittering as Simon Heron remembered it on the child Meraud he had brought newly orphaned from Cornwall to Goldhayes to be his ward. He had always had a soft corner of his heart for her, the sweet, demure, kittenish girl with that fascinating combination of beauty, fashionable elegance and piety, and had never been able to understand the dislike felt by some other members of his family, especially Francis and Thomazine: for, having been in exile in Holland between 1646 and 1660, he had no knowledge of the events at Goldhayes after the end of the Siege of Colchester, and Meraud's treachery. He had never even thought about Nell, and the reason why she had been brought up by Francis and Thomazine instead of by her real mother: for Simon, like certain other Herons, could take a very blinkered view of inconvenient facts when his own preconceptions demanded it.

If he had not already been promised to Nan Blagge, he might well have been tempted to make this still lovely woman his bride, long ago, and perhaps it was not too late.

But there was also Susannah, sitting demurely on a stool beside her mother's chair, the image of Meraud in her captivating youth: the same kitten's face, vast blue eyes, lovely silver-fair hair and perfectly tailored clothes. Yet Susannah, he must admit, seemed to have more. Meraud, fond though he was of her, had never in his memory had that quality of warm laughter, of spontaneous generosity that marked her daughter. The only thing he remembered about Charles Lawrence was his habit of making excruciating jokes: that jollity seemed to have been passed on, albeit in a properly gentle and feminine form, to Susannah.

Anne Heron sat poker-backed by her father's side and saw only too clearly what was happening. Silly Mall would not notice, her head was too full of Hyde Park this evening and the play tomorrow. Anyway, she was obviously fixing the details of Susannah's attire in her head for future reference, and could not conceivably be aware that her father was in danger of making a fool of himself over this fluffy little chit who was probably younger than his own daughter.

There was a hesitant tap on the door, and in response to her father's barked command it opened slowly, and Nell and Alathea stood on the threshold. Anne, who did not of course know the full story, saw Nell's terror-struck face and felt only contemptuous annoyance. Then the girl advanced further into the room (in response to an unseen prod from Alathea), and curtseyed deeply. 'Good morning, Mother.'

Alathea was watching Meraud closely, her hands locked together. With a sinking heart she saw the arched, carefully tended eyebrows rise, and the lovely face took on an appraising look. 'Well – so this is what my daughter and Jamie's has become, it it? Rise, girl, and let me look at you.'

Beside her, Susannah was making faces of encouragement. Alathea's heart warmed to her. Meraud got to her feet and glided over to Nell. She was significantly smaller than her elder daughter, and beside her the poor girl looked like a half-starved ploughboy. She walked all around, tweaking the dress, examining her features, giving a brief dismissive twitch to a stray lock of dull straight hair, which made Nell start like a restive horse. 'And what name were you given? I forget, it is so long ago now.'

'Eleanor, Mother,' said Nell, in a voice that Alathea, two yards away, could scarcely hear.

'Eleanor? How very droll. I do not think I chose it. And you must be . . . let me see, it was Christmas, forty-eight as I recall . . . you must be close on twenty-two. And not wed yet? Well, that is no surprise.'

'I have no dowry, Mother,' said Nell, still in that faint despairing whisper.

'I did not mean your lack of dowry, girl. There are other qualities looked for in a woman, and you appear to have avoided all of them. Your hair . . . your face . . . have you never been taught to stand upright? And your dress . . . really, one would have thought that living in London would have had some effect on your garb. Still, since you obviously have no care for your appearance, I will not take the matter in hand. I presume you can read?'

'Yes, Mother.'

'And write?'

'Yes, Mother.'

'And cast accounts?'

'Not very well, Mother.'

'What instruments do you play?'

'A little on the guitar and the harpsichord.'

'And do you sing?'

'Not very well, Mother.'

'She is being modest, Mistress Lawrence,' said Alathea, feeling she ought to speak up for Nell even if her cousin would not speak up for herself. 'She sings most beautifully, and her guitar-playing is not at all bad.'

'Indeed?' said Meraud coolly. 'Well, I myself have never had much time for music. Do you speak any languages, Eleanor?'

'I read French a little, Mother.'

'No Latin or Greek, I trust. Your mother, Alathea, was always avid to learn those languages: so unseemly for a female. French is much more suitable. And your sewing? Do you sew well?'

The remorseless inquisition went on, while Alathea stood rigid, torn between compassion and a towering anger that made her long to leap to Nell's defence. But that would not do any good: it would only make Nell seem more of a pathetic waif than she already appeared. And at last it ended, with Meraud staring at her elder daughter, mouth pursed with disdainful disapproval.

'Well, I suppose a husband might be found for you, though with no looks and no dowry it will be well-nigh impossible. Really, I cannot imagine how Jamie and I came to produce such a sad mope. I see I did the right thing, to leave you to Francis and Thomazine to rear, though a sorry job they seem to have made of it.'

Nell's drooping head raised to look her mother in the face. Her wan blue-grey eyes were heavy with unshed tears. 'Well, at least they were kind to me!' she cried, far louder than her previous whispers. 'Which is more than you have ever been to me, *Mother*!' And with a strangled sob, turned and fled the room.

Alathea, remembering their quarrel long ago in Covent Garden, when Nell had at last in despair turned on her persecutor in much the same way, was not surprised, but Meraud laughed in astonishment. 'Really – what an odd girl, to be sure. Is she as feeble-minded as she appears?'

'No,' said Alathea between shut teeth. 'She just reacts badly to unfair treatment – as I would do in her place. If you will excuse me, madam, I will go look to her.' And still choking with rage, she sketched a furious curtsey that just stopped short of an insult, and abruptly left before she could say something she might afterwards regret.

Nell was sitting on their bed. She was not crying. Her hands were clenched in her lap and her bleak eyes stared hopelessly yet defiantly into space. A great shaking sob tore through her as Alathea entered, but her face was tearless. For once unsure, her cousin hovered by the door, watching anxiously. Then Nell said, with frightening intensity, 'I wish she *was* dead!'

'So do I,' said Alathea. She crossed to the bed and put her arms around Nell.

The older girl went rigid and twisted out of the embrace. 'I don't need your pity. I've had enough of that, over the years. I don't need *her* either, to tell me all that's lacking in me! I wish she'd never come back! She's . . . she's . . . she's *evil*, Thea, she's *evil*, she's cold and calculating, she's everything Aunt Lucy said she was, she's cruel – she said not one *word* of welcome, not one *word* and I'm her *daughter* – she must be a *monster*!'

'I agree there's not much to endear her to me,' said Alathea drily, aware as she spoke that it was the wrong response to such deep and soul-shattering distress.

Nell got to her feet and walked to the window, and back again, driven by the agony of her emotions. 'She's discarded me as useless, hasn't she? No looks, no dowry – even Anne has a dowry. She'll never lack a husband, though she's far plainer than I am – and you could be ten men's mistress if you chose – and no one will ever want me, I have nothing, no beauty, no money – I'll be an old maid all my life! You can see why she washed her hands of me – she's got Susannah to take pride in, Susannah's the heiress, Susannah has her beauty, and what have I got? Nothing! That's what *she* thinks. Well, I'll show her,' Nell cried, turning on Alathea with her face a white mask of grief. 'I'll show her I'm *not* useless, I'll show her I can look good – you just wait, *Mother*, and I'll prove it to you!'

The play began, as most did, at half-past three on the following afternoon. Bills had been posted, and word had flown around the town. A play by a woman was a rare curiosity, worth going to see if only for the pleasure of booing it to extinction: and there was always the risk that it might be some good. Rochester, anticipating a large crowd for the first performance at least, had taken the precaution of hiring a box and positioning his own servants and his friends' footmen to hold their places until his party arrived, just before the start of the play.

He sent his own coach to the Covent Garden house, and since he lodged in Lincoln's Inn Fields, next door to the playhouse, there was an invitation to refreshments afterwards, and Mistress Behn would be there. Alathea found she was looking forward to the play, and to meeting a woman apparently forged from similar metal to her own. But she also longed to see John Wilmot again, and yet dreaded it, for the memory of those moments in the studio, when she had all but surrendered to him, was still vivid. She could not recall it without a mixture of shame – for surrender went against all her instincts of pride and independence – and longing. She did not yet know whether or not she loved him, but she supposed she must, for this confused feeling of desire and joy and kinship seemed to be the poets' idea of love. Common sense dictated that she could not go on for ever like this, her heart warring with her head and her soul, but she could see no way out that would not bring hurt.

And he loved her: she knew that he did. He would not love her for ever, it was not his way, and that she could accept. It was enough for her to have enchained him, even if it was by reason of her beauty, which she would rather disregard.

She put on the ivory silk again, against her better judgement. Anne was wearing pink, a girlish colour lamentably unsuited to her face and her skinny figure. Mall was in the same shade, which gave her face a rosy glow it had robbed from Anne, and only served to heighten the painful contrast between the sisters. *No wonder Anne's got such a shrew's tongue, poor girl*, Alathea thought when she saw them together, plain and fancy. *I think I would, in her circumstances*.

But the biggest surprise was Nell. No one seemed to have noticed her distress at her mother's callous treatment – indeed, no one, apart from Alathea, Hen and Nell herself, seemed to think it *was* callous. But it had certainly had a remarkable effect. The Nell who presented herself in the hall, awaiting my lord Rochester's coach, seemed a different species entirely from the down-trodden girl who had wilted under her mother's contemptuous gaze. She wore the blue, admittedly, but she had borrowed Alathea's best corsets, rather smaller than her own, and used the tighter lacing to make her figure trim and neat, with straight back and graceful walk. The modest lacy kerchief which previously covered her shoulders was gone, her hair was clean, shining and curled, with some of Mall's camomile water to lighten it, and artfully arranged by Sarah to cover the worst of the spots around her hairline. Two on her face had been cleverly concealed by patches, a tiny black star and a black heart. Her cheeks were lightly rouged, and her eyes sparkled defiantly behind the little black mask which it was customary to wear for the theatre.

'Well? How do I look?'

'Superb,' said Alathea generously, and for once it was not too much of a lie. Lord Bradfield, coming down the stairs, curtly agreed that they all looked very fine: and where was that young rascal Hugh, who was to escort them?

Hugh, as if summoned, chose that exact moment to hammer on the door, and very soon after, Rochester's coach arrived. It was obvious that Lord Bradfield was divided between pride in his daughters' finery, and disapproval of their destination. And in the background, Becca hopped from one foot to the other and urgently desired to go too.

'You can't, you'd be much too little to see anything over all those gentlemen's heads,' her mother told her.

'But I'm big! I'm *five* now!'

'When you're seven, or come up to my shoulder, whichever is the sooner,' Hen promised, and the five ladies left the house, Hugh following them, to squash into a coach which was rather less roomy and comfortable than its outward appearance would imply.

They arrived at the playhouse with fifteen minutes to spare, and found the expected crowds thronging the entrance. Their tickets had come with the coachman: Hugh presented them to the door-keeper, and they pushed their way through the press to the box that had been reserved for them. Alathea had a pang of conscience about the price of the tickets: twenty-four shillings was not an inconsiderable sum, and she knew John did not have a great deal of money. But there was no way to pay her share without offending his masculine and aristocratic pride, so she would have to keep silent.

The box was the best in the theatre, directly facing the stage, and was already crowded with her friends. She saw Buckhurst, Savile of course, and Little Sid, but her eyes went straight to the Earl of Rochester, for once dressed according to his rank, with a great knot of ribbon on his right shoulder and agleam with gold lace. It was the first time she had ever met him outside her own ground. Now she beheld his public face, stately and magnificent, and saw how he outshone all the other men there. Beside him, Sedley and Savile were fat nonentities, Buckhurst coarse and crude. This glittering, splendid young man, tall and graceful and angel-faced, was the pattern of the handsome, witty, rakish hero of the fashionable comedies.

It frightened her, a little. Everyone bowed or curtseyed, compliments were exchanged, greetings offered to acquaintances elsewhere in the theatre. Susannah and her mother were in the next box, accompanied by Sir Robert Manners, and Alathea felt some satisfaction in seeing Meraud's raised eyebrows behind her black velvet mask, as she beheld her transformed daughter. Nell, seating herself on the bench, sent a cool nod in her mother's direction, and then Sir Charles Sedley, eyes twinkling with friendly lechery, sat down next to her and engaged her in animated conversation, which soon had her laughing.

Thank God for Little Sid, Alathea thought. *If anyone can restore her confidence, he can*. She then promptly forgot all about her cousin's woes, as John Wilmot, Earl of Rochester, came to stand beside her. 'So those are the fabled Heron heiresses! Are they as grim as they look?'

'Even more so,' said Alathea, keeping her voice low in the hubbub around her. 'One's a shrew and the other's an empty-headed jade – take your pick.'

'You sound very ill-tempered – has it been difficult, then, Lord Bradfield's descent on your happy household? My mother has much the same effect on mine.'

'You could say it has somewhat transformed our lives,' Alathea told him drily. 'Where is Mistress Behn?'

'She said she would join us later. At this moment, she is probably behind the scenes, trying to coax some life into the poor fool she wanted to play the King – last I heard, he'd threatened to cut his throat rather than face a hostile crowd. Still, that's typical of Aphra – generous to a fault. Will you present your two charming cousins to me?'

Ignoring his sarcasm, she obeyed, drawing Anne and Mall to her side and performing the introductions. A gleam in Mall's eye revealed her to be not uninterested in this splendidly dressed and aristocratic courtier: an interest that, from John's lazily ironic expression, was noted but in no way returned. Feeling in a somewhat better humour, Alathea relaxed and gave herself up to the heady atmosphere of a crowded, expectant theatre. She did not like this one – a converted tennis-court that was cramped and ill-suited to its new use – so much as the King's Company's theatre in Bridges Street that had been built for the purpose, and on the whole she preferred the other company's actors and choice of plays. But despite these drawbacks, any theatre, any new play, was an occasion for excitement: the babble of the gallants and doxies in the pit, the harsh cries of the orange-women, the smoke of candles and the sharp fragrance of oranges overpowering the underlying aroma of sweat and dirt and stale perfume. It was a mixture of which she could never be tired.

There was no sign of Mistress Behn, the bold Astrea as she called herself in her writings: and the curtain was raised up, the noise in the theatre subsided somewhat, and the occupants of John Wilmot's box squashed on to the benches and prepared themselves for two or three hours' entertainment – or not, dependent upon the unknown Mistress Behn's abilities as a playwright.

An actor spoke the Prologue, in words that gradually became more audible as the audience settled down, and it became apparent that the author, far from apologising for her sex, was declaring herself in martial terms to be the equal of male writers. When an actress joined him to finish it, a murmur went through the crowd as she pointed to the ladies amongst them:

'Can any see that glorious sight and say
A woman shall not victor prove today?
Who is't that to their Beauty would submit
And yet refuse the fetters of their Wit?'

Mistress Behn was evidently a kindred spirit, and Alathea, a forgotten grin on her face, settled herself comfortably on the hard bench, John Wilmot on one side of her and Hen on the other, and prepared to enjoy the play.

It was not, in fact, she decided afterwards, particularly good in comparison with others she had seen, being neither a comedy nor a tragedy, but something in between. There was not much at which to laugh, and there were coincidences and events which strained the credulity of even the most gullible, but all the same, it was a most creditable first attempt. Even the lamentable performance of Master Otway, in the small but important role of the King, could not disguise the promise of the play: its theme, marriage for love rather than for policy, was one which Alathea thoroughly approved, and everywhere, in word and song, were sentiments that struck echoes in her own heart:

'Hang love, for I will never pine
For any man alive:
Nor shall this jolly heart of mine
The thoughts of it receive:
I will not purchase slavery
At such a dangerous rate,
But glory in my liberty
And laugh at Love and Fate.'

If only she could.

It all ended happily, which was greatly to the audience's satisfaction, and when the course of true love had run smooth at last, and the star-crossed lovers were joined by the stuttering, stage-frightened King, an actress came on to speak the Epilogue, still concerned with the war between the sexes:

'But we are upon equal treatment yet,
For neither conquer, since we both submit:
You to our Beauty bow, we to your Wit.'

The applause was long, loud and led by the box containing the Earl of Rochester, Lord Buckhurst and sundry ladies and gentlemen. Since fashion tended to follow the Wits, and since their approval was so marked, *The Forc'd Marriage* was ensured of success despite, or perhaps because of, the sex of its author, and Alathea felt that it deserved its acclamation.

They all repaired to Rochester's lodgings when the play was done, waiting until the mass of the audience had gone before attempting to leave. Alathea was intensely curious to see the house he inhabited. Seeing him in all his Court finery, she expected a mansion tricked out in the most fashionable taste, and was somewhat astonished to discover that, like the coach, it was nowhere so grand as she had supposed, being far less fine than the house in Covent Garden. He was not rich, of course, and presumably kept up little state, but even so, she was surprised at the shabbiness of the hangings, the aged furniture, and the scarcity of ornament.

'It's a poor place,' said Rochester, seeing her look as they crowded through the front door. 'But at least I have no fear lest Strephon do irreparable damage to it!'

In the main chamber, on the first floor, there were wine and refreshments set out, and servants waiting. And there was also Strephon the ape, chattering happily on a perch by the window, chained to it to prevent mischief.

'Hallo, you rogue jackanapes. Shall I let you off that infernal rattling chain, you old ghost?'

'No!' said Hugh, Harry Savile and Sedley in unison, and Rochester smiled. 'I bow to the opinion of my guests.'

There were, just, sufficient chairs and stools for the company. Wine was distributed, sweetmeats and cakes handed round by impassive, liveried footmen, inured to their master's cheerful, chiding tones. Alathea wondered wryly what drunken carouses they usually attended in this room, with its dark, old-fashioned panelling and bare wooden floor, covered here and there with a Turkey rug of decidedly threadbare appearance. Dominating everything, she was pleased to see, was her portrait of John Wilmot crowning Strephon, the destroyer and mischief-maker, with the Bays of Poetry. Coming to it fresh, some nine or ten months after she had last seen it, she was gratified to find that she still found it good.

'Still like it, eh?' Buckhurst said, seeing her studying it. 'Damned good likeness, that picture, eh, Sid?'

'Damned is the word,' Sedley commented. He was still at Nell's side, and now she had taken off the mask the difference in her was quite startling. *She looks almost brazen*, Alathea thought with surprise. Then Anne appeared at her elbow with her usual abrupt questions. Was that portrait her work in truth? It was remarkably fine: she had not appreciated Alathea's talent so fully.

'I am sure that there is more to most people than at first meets the eye,' said Alathea, pointedly, and somewhat to her surprise, saw Anne Heron blush unbecomingly.

There was a stir at the door, a hush in the conversation, and into the room walked a plainly dressed woman, with a round, merry, attractive face and an abundance of curling dark brown hair.

'Congratulations!' Little Sid cried, leaping bombastically to his feet and hastening over. 'My heartiest felicitations, my dearest Astrea – a veritable triumph!'

Then the floodgates of praise and compliment were released, while Mistress Behn stood in the middle of it all, smiling, waiting for them to finish. She was not at all how Alathea had imagined her, but there was a firmness about her mouth and chin that suggested a character more than strong enough to enter a man's world on equal terms.

When the noise had abated somewhat, Rochester performed the usual ritual, introducing those she did not know: Anne and Mall, Hen and Hugh, Nell and Alathea. And at mention of the last name, Mistress Behn's face broke into a cheerful smile. 'So you are the artist! We meet at last! I have heard a great deal about you from my friends, and I have long admired your magnificent portrait.'

'As I have admired your play,' said Alathea, with sincerity. 'I'm very glad to meet you, for you give me hope that I am not such a strange creature as some think.'

'Strange?'

'Strange for a woman to be a picture-drawer to earn her living – and stranger still, for her to abjure matrimony.'

'Yes, Strephon did mention something of your views to me,' said Mistress Behn. She saw Alathea's look of surprise, and laughed loud and merry. 'I don't mean the monkey, though I'm sure it is intelligent enough for such thoughts, if it could only speak honest English instead of that vile chattering, like nails rattling in a box – but I digress. My Lord of Rochester is Strephon, as I am Astrea – and you are in truth Alathea!' She grinned, obviously pleased with the aptness of her pun, and Alathea, finding herself liking this forthright, witty woman very much indeed, found herself smiling in return.

'You mistake my history a little, though,' said Aphra, a little more seriously. 'I have already fallen into the quicksands of wedlock, even if I was able almost immediately to clamber out again: but I had enough taste of it to be as confirmed in my opinion as you are in yours. There's nothing wrong with men as lovers or as friends, and I count less for the former, and more for the latter, than many might think. But as husbands, they change overnight from companions to tyrants, and I will have no more of it. And nor, if you want to continue being an artist, will you.'

'You're preaching to the converted,' Alathea said. 'I've vowed to devote my life to my art – and entered the nunnery of the paintbrush.'

'And yet you have known Strephon for some little while?'

'For a year – but we met long ago as children, and so he is an old friend. As he is still my friend,' said Alathea, meaningfully.

The playwright laughed. 'Which is less, I think, than he would like to be. Still, that is his affair – and yours. Now, I must ask a favour of you – will you paint my portrait? I do not have a great deal of money – indeed, that was one reason why I decided to turn what small gift I have to plays, for if they please they will make me enough to live – but I am assured, they tell me, of a full house on my benefit night, so in two days' time I shall have some coin at your disposal. Would you be agreeable?'

'Of course,' said Alathea, mentally scaling down her charges for a small portrait. She enjoyed Mistress Behn's talk, and the prospect of a succession of hours spent painting her and indulging in congenial conversation was a pleasant one. They arranged a time and day, Alathea having a fairly good idea of the location of the blank spaces in her appointment book, and promising to send a message if she proved to have made a mistake. 'For I'm not naturally an organised person: I have to make myself so, or run mad.'

'I have the same problem,' said Mistress Behn. 'When I give myself over to my writing, all else pales – and if I did not have an admirable maid to take me in hand, and make sure I eat and sleep, I do not think I would do either. I even find that I can write in a room full of people. Hello, my lord – did you enjoy the play as much as your praise would indicate?'

'Are you setting me up for a hypocrite?' Rochester teased her, his mouth twisted in one of his more wicked smiles. 'Of course I enjoyed your play, dear Astrea – and I hope I'll enjoy the next one even better. You'd best go soothe Buckhurst, he swears he's seen your play before under another guise, and denies you ever wrote it.'

'The idea is not my own, that I'll acknowledge – I had some of it from a sad, dull thing by Fletcher. But the words, the characters, the plots and scenes – that is entirely Astrea, and I shall tell him so most plainly.' And she marched off to carry out her intention.

'What think you of our Astrea? Is she not a brave lady?'

'Braver than I would be, I know,' Alathea told him. 'After that poor young man who played the King did so badly, I think I would have died of mortification if I were her.'

'At least he didn't entirely ruin the play – and I should imagine a great many who were there today will be back tomorrow, if only to find out what his lines were. Astrea tells me young Otway is quite cured of any desire to act again, and the part is to be given to a professional. But on the whole – a good beginning, I think.'

'Yes, a good beginning.' Alathea glanced up at him, saw the dark watchful eyes studying her face, and found herself blushing. Annoyed at her weakness, she added, 'And I must thank you for your kindness.'

'What kindness? I have done you no kindness.'

'In arranging for us all to see the play. It was most generous.'

'Generous be damned – I wanted as many as possible to make sure that Astrea's first child wasn't hissed to oblivion. But why so stilted, my lovely Alathea? You're as distant as if you had never met me before.'

'I'm no longer on my own ground, and I cannot help but think of you as Rochester, and John Wilmot no longer.'

'And has what happened the other night upset you?'

Under his penetrating gaze her blush, infuriatingly, deepened. 'No. Not in the slightest.'

'You lie, my lovely Thea. "Can you forgive the rashness of a Man, That knows no other laws but those of Passion?" '

He was quoting from the play they had just seen,and Alathea capped it with a wry smile. ' "You are unkind to think I do not, Sir; Yes, and am grown so softened by my pity, That I'm afraid I shall neglect my Vows, And to return your Passion, grow ingrate." '

'I shan't continue, or we shall have half the play spoken – and besides,' said Rochester with disarming honesty, 'I can't remember the rest of that particular exchange. But I do recall that Alcippus would not, after all, achieve his desires with Erminia – so I hope it is not an omen. And when you return to your own ground, or Lord Bradfield's, perhaps you might care to read this over.'

It was a piece of paper, folded and sealed. She knew what it must contain. And sure enough, when she was at last in the quiet privacy of her studio, and could take it from her pocket and unfold it by the dimming light from the windows, it proved to be another poem, of thirty lines or so, entitled 'The Discovery'. Like the others, it urged her to take pity on her 'faithful servant' – the irony of it made her smile. His heart, he claimed, had dwelt quietly, 'stranger alike to hope and to despair', until her arrival: now it had been invaded by Love's tumultuous train. And he called her cruel, and asked only her leave to love her, 'and glory in my chain'.

In addition, he called her Celia. She grinned at the extravagance of the emotions he claimed – as if he could ever be anyone's slave! And she did not, on reading it again, like it so well as the other two. Those had been original, surprising and sincere, whereas this was the sort of poem Sedley or Buckhurst might write, true to the conventions of fashion, and applicable to anyone – another courtly salvo in the wargame of Love.

But she added it to the first two, in her private casket, and wished she were as skilled with words as he, so that she might contrive a fitting answer.

CHAPTER EIGHTEEN

An ancient lover

'That you languish, that you die
Alas, is but too true
Yet tax us not with cruelty
Who daily pity you.'
(Sedley, 'Advice to the Old Beaux')

That autumn dragged drearily towards Christmas, wet and windy and raw, with fogs and storms, and Alathea's mood reflected the weather. True, there were the visits of Mistress Behn, come to sit for her portrait, cheerful and talkative, witty and wise and far more adept at bawdy repartee than most of the Wits could ever hope to be, and they became bright oases in the greyness of the days. Her play had been a roaring success, performed for six days until replaced by *The Tempest*, and she was engaged in writing another. Alathea often found herself being asked for her opinion on the latest scenes. It was to be called *The Amorous Prince*, and Betterton had already agreed to put it on as soon as it was ready. Mistress Behn was a rising star, and knew it.

She was also the only one of the Wits whom Alathea saw with any regularity, that autumn. Rochester was often engaged at Court, where he was a Gentleman of the King's Bedchamber, and before November was out he had gone into the country, where his wife was about to give birth to their second child. Buckhurst also had business in the country, and since she cared for him least of all the Merry Gang, she was not sorry for his absence. Even Sedley, whom she could never take seriously, called only occasionally, and his attentions were paid to Nell.

Alathea did not know whether or not to discourage this. Sedley was a notorious rake, who kept his unfortunate wife (report said she was lunatic) in country seclusion while he worked his way with jovial lechery through a string of complaisant ladies of the Court and town. Yet she herself liked him. He made her laugh, he was good-natured and sometimes surprisingly kind, and he was a good and affectionate friend. He praised her beauty and wit and art with typical extravagance, but it was all part of the conventional game, and she did not think his treatment of Nell was a game.

Nell, disturbingly, obviously did not think it either. She bloomed in his company: her eyes sparkled, her face glowed, she even laughed and made her own modest jokes. On days when he was expected she positively danced about the house. At all other times she became once more the sad mope her mother had dismissed with such contempt. Alathea thought that Meraud had, by her callous indifference, brought about this behaviour in her rejected daughter, and yet the more desperately Nell tried to attract her attention by her dress and manner, the more her mother ignored her.

Meraud Lawrence was perhaps the most frequent caller at the house during those months. Hardly a day seemed to go by without her cool elegant presence in the Great Chamber, very much the lady of fashion despite her advanced years, sipping chocolate and showing off her younger daughter to best advantage. Somehow, in spite of this blatant parading of a highly saleable commodity, Susannah seemed to keep her integrity intact, to treat everyone with a friendly smile, and to display that endearing naivety which even jaded rakes like Sedley could not help but find refreshing.

She got on very well with Alathea, with Nell and with the frivolous Mall, who spent long hours discussing the exact motions of a fan or the latest dictates of fashionable dress, but Anne remained aloof, unreachable, armoured with her sharp tongue and forbidding aspect. Alathea, watching Lord Bradfield's increasingly obvious affection for Meraud's daughter, wondered whether Anne's resolute unfriendliness to Susannah stemmed from her concern for her father.

It was certainly becoming embarrassing. Here was a Peer of the Realm, a highly respected and respectable man of over fifty, friend and contemporary and fellow-soldier of the great Prince Rupert (who had twice dined with them), almost the puritan in his tastes, a widower with two adult daughters, becoming besotted with a fluffy little ingénue of no great intelligence and only her beauty and good nature to recommend her – and only just eighteen years old. Alathea found the idea of marrying this lively, likeable girl to her elderly, repressive uncle peculiarly repugnant, and yet Susannah's own mother seemed to be doing her utmost to further her daughter's prospects.

She was not the only one who was disturbed by the turn matters were taking. Her Aunt Lucy did not need many encounters over the dinner-table at Covent Garden to form her own opinions, and it was not long before she invited Alathea to the Fleet Street house for a cosy chat over a cup of chocolate, ostensibly to celebrate her becoming a grandmother, for Ros's child, a boy, had been safely born at the end of October. But Lucy made the real purpose of her invitation quite clear the moment the chocolate had been poured. 'Simon must be turned in his wits!'

Alathea looked at her aunt quizzically and said, deliberately obtuse, 'Lord Bradfield? Insane?'

'You know very well what I'm talking of,' said Lucy, leaning forward and giving a vigorous poke to the already fervent fire. 'He's the wrong side of fifty, father to two grown girls, and he's mooning over that little kitten like a lad of eighteen, and her mother encourages it. I do believe it would have been better for all of us,' said Lucy, with bitterness, 'if she'd died bearing Nell – as she so nearly did. Ever since she came into our lives she's brought trouble and discord, and we thought we were rid of her once when she went off to marry poor Charles – and a fine dance she led him! And now she's come back with her honey voice and sweet face, to meddle and make mischief again. It's all I can do to be civil to her, knowing what I know – and of course Simon doesn't, nor could I tell him without seeming a spiteful gossip. He's always taken Meraud's part, always been blind to her faults. Mind you,' Lucy added honestly, staring into the fire, 'I myself thought Thomazine's hate for her was unreasonable – until I saw Meraud cornered at her uncle's deathbed, when her treachery was revealed. After that, none who were there could ever believe in her again. But Simon didn't see it, of course – he was in The Hague. And he still thinks she is sweet and innocent, just as he always did, despite her treating poor Nell worse than the dirt beneath her feet. She wanted him for herself once, you know – and now she's throwing her daughter at him.'

'But why? Why does she even consider it? He must be thirty years older than Susannah, and a blind fool could see he wouldn't make her happy.'

'Susannah's happiness isn't even considered,' said Lucy. 'Meraud has an eye to the future, as she has always had. Why did she want Simon for herself in the first place? He was rich, certainly, but there are richer, and he had no title then. No, it was Goldhayes she wanted. It must have seemed very fine and splendid to her after the draughty old Cornish mansion where she'd been reared. It was for Goldhayes she married poor Jamie, for Simon was in exile, remember, unlikely to return for years if at all, and it didn't seem at that time as if Nan would ever have children. Francis hadn't been heard of for some while, and besides, he was in love with Thomazine, who was already married to Kit's father. With a bit of luck, Jamie would inherit Goldhayes, and his sons after him; save that he died, and Nell was the wrong sex. And look at the situation now. The heir to Goldhayes was Rupert, but he's dead. The girls can't inherit, so when Lord Bradfield dies your father will have the house and the Suffolk lands that are entailed, and Anne and Mall will have the rest. But if Simon were to marry again – a young girl, likely to produce children – sons who would inherit Goldhayes, *and* the title – then all would be very different.'

'But why doesn't she marry him herself, if she wanted him, and he's always been fond of her?'

'Too old,' said Lucy concisely. 'She must be . . . let me see, she must be close on forty-five. Too old to be sure of having children. I know my mother was forty-three when Hugh was born, but that's a rarity. But he could beget a string of heirs on poor Susannah, die in a few years' time, and leave Meraud to run Goldhayes in the name of her daughter and her grandsons. She takes a long-term view, does Meraud Trevelyan,' said Lucy with a weary bitterness that sat ill upon her. 'I've seen her do it before.'

And in furtherance of her dynastic ambitions, her elder daughter was trampled underfoot and her younger sacrificed to an ageing grouch almost old enough to be her grandfather. Alathea felt sick and angry at the prospect, and her instinctive dislike of Meraud suddenly concentrated into hatred. 'Someone ought to have killed her, long since,' she said.

'If the thought had been enough, Thomazine would have done it,' Lucy told her. 'There's one thing Meraud might have forgotten, though, in all her plotting. What are Susannah's thoughts on the matter?'

Alathea pondered the problem. It was most improbable that the girl was ignorant of Lord Bradfield's interest – or of her mother's plans for her. She was no sparkling wit, but she seemed to have a certain shrewd commonsense. Surely by now she must have guessed, particularly as she appeared to have few illusions about her mother. And she remembered that conversation the first time she had met Susannah, when she had announced her intention of marrying where she pleased, rather than where her mother wanted – and, if prevented, would elope.

'If she wants to marry Lord Bradfield, then she will,' Alathea said at last, thoughtfully. 'I must say I would die rather than do it myself – the whole idea revolts me, it puts women on the same level as brood-mares – but she may like the idea of living in the grand style and being Lady Bradfield. It would certainly be a triumphant match for a girl with small fortune. And her mother's very cunning, she may have been persuasive enough to fill her head with thoughts of a glittering future. But . . . if she doesn't want to, it's my bet there'll be trouble. She doesn't look mulish, I'll grant you, but I think she's got a lot of strength under all that sweetness. She said once she'd elope rather than be forced to marry where she did not love, and she meant it.'

'Well, we might help her, if it should ever come to it,' said Lucy, whose ideal of romantic true love had remained undimmed since her girlhood. 'I'd never force anyone to marry from policy. Ros was different, she was quite happy to marry for comfort rather than love – but I wed where my heart dictated, and so did your mother, and I'm sure no one could have been happier.' She cast an assessing glance at her niece. 'Have you ever heard from Jasper?'

'No, never – though he often writes to Hen. Aunt, you're incorrigible – you *know* I don't want to marry anyone, least of all Jasper.'

'There's no harm in trying,' said Lucy, sighing. 'I'd jump at him, were I you – and he was such a dear little boy, quite delightful, and so intelligent. I'm sure he could do better for himself than a mean little country doctor's practice in Bury. Still, that's his affair – what he needs is an ambitious wife to push him upwards. In London, perhaps his talents would be recognised.'

'Aunt Lucy!'

'All right – I promise not to mention the subject again. For a while, at least. And now do tell me – what is the shocking female playwright like?'

'Very pleasant – and not very shocking,' said Alathea, and the conversation turned to other matters. But her new understanding of Meraud's motives and plans had left a very unsavoury taste in her mouth: more than ever, she felt sorry for the exploited Susannah, and hatred for her designing mother.

Christmas came and went, and at Adderbury the Earl of Rochester's son was born, and christened Charles. Buckhurst and Sedley stood godparents, and attended the ceremony, and the town was even quieter than before. Nell moped, and even Hugh seemed an abstracted shadow of his usual self. She had thought it unwise to tell him of Lucy's speculations about Susannah's fate, for his interest had seemed transient and light-hearted, but he was quite acute and intelligent enough to size up the situation from his visits to Covent Garden, and she wondered if in fact his feelings ran deeper than she had thought at first. By most people's lights, Hugh Trevelyan and Susannah Lawrence might seem an unsuitable match – more unsuitable, certainly, than Lord Bradfield and Susannah Lawrence. But judged by the standards of humanity, it did not seem so odd. *She would give him friendship and kindness at the least*, Alathea thought, *and for my dearest Hugh nothing less will do*.

It was the dead time of year, slack and dull after the festivities of Christmas, if such muted celebrations could be dignified by such a description. Nell and Hugh were miserable companions, Matthew his usual absent self, Anne as sour and shrewish as ever: no sign of a glittering match for her. Only Mall seemed to be cheerful, even persuading her father to take them all to the play, which was the second part of *The Conquest of Granada*, newly acted, and since a saint would not have found fault with the heroic plot and stately dialogue and high-flown ideals, it was an excellent choice. But Mall had several servants, hopeful young men who had an eye to her face, or her fortune, or both. It would not be long before someone offered for her. Alathea would have felt sorry for Anne, had not her cousin's manner precluded any display of sympathy.

And then something happened to drive everyone else's problems entirely from her mind: for Kit returned to London.

Alathea had heard nothing of him since that terrible day, nearly a year previously when he had tried to rape her. Her letter had gone unanswered, though he had apparently sent various brief notes to her parents, advising them only that he was in Yorkshire, and offering no further explanation. Usually she had contrived to shut him out of her mind. In daylight, that was easy enough, but she still sometimes woke in terror from a nightmare that was appallingly real, in which Hugh had not after all come to her rescue, and Kit had won. And the horror was compounded, on waking, for so convincing and vivid were the scenes inside her head, that her mind always took some moments to realise that it had in fact all been a dream.

She had been visiting the Beales when he returned. Mary Beale and her husband had been back in London for some months, and had taken up residence in Pall Mall, one of the most fashionable streets in the town, a position which Alathea, noting the fine new building and the spacious accommodation, deeply envied. But it was also a very expensive area, and Mistress Beale confided that only the benevolence of a distant relative, who had leased them the house at advantageous rates, had enabled them to afford such a prestigious place. She had set herself up in some style, with a fine studio on the top floor of the house, and false ceilings made to carry canvases. Her appointment book was full already, and she was evidently the breadwinner of the family. Her husband, who still, to her disgust, called Alathea 'Puss', worked in the studio, preparing canvases and paints. He had grown to be quite expert in this field, and they spent a long time discussing the relative merits of various yellow pigments, which faded the most, which were easiest to use, while Mistress Beale worked at her easel on the background to a portrait, and put forward her own opinions from time to time. Alathea had brought along, cluttering up her hired hackney, two or three of her smaller pictures to show to her former teacher, and a little book she and Nell had made up of her best drawings and sketches. Mistress Beale seemed genuinely impressed and appreciative, and her younger son Charles, who was ten and already showing much talent, took the book afterwards into a corner of the studio, where he pored over it, turning the stiff pages with reverent delight. His mother was also lavish in her praise.

'I see Master Lely will have to look to his laurels – he cannot relish having so promising a rival with the impudence to set up a studio almost on his doorstep!'

'I had little choice in my residence in the Piazza,' said Alathea, and explained about the Fire and about Lord Bradfield. 'But you may find me in my impudence moving to this part of the town – I am keen to find somewhere closer to Whitehall. Will you tell me, if you hear of a place?'

Mary Beale assured her that she would with all speed, if only to relieve Lely of the burden of such a rising star in such close proximity. 'He has always been a very good friend to my husband and myself – has he been so to you?'

'No, I regret to say he hasn't,' said Alathea, honestly. 'He has taken no interest, nor have I asked him to, save for some moments of advice several years ago. It is Master Cooper, the limner, who's been of more help to me – I often go to visit him, and I've asked him to paint me. It will be a present for my parents.'

'The greatest limner in the world,' was Charles Beale's judgement on the miniaturist – and Alathea, knowing he was right, could not help wondering how that shrewd, wise little man would interpret her own face.

She could have spent far longer in discussion, for it was very pleasant for a change to talk as artist to artist, without feeling the need to display her wit or repartee. But at the same time, she was well aware that she and Mistress Beale moved now in very different circles. She herself drew her clientele largely from the Court, and to a much lesser degree, these days, from Dan Ashley's City friends. She was the fashion, with the success and the penalties that such a position implied. Mary Beale's customers were less exalted figures, country gentlemen and their families, divines and bishops, people of solid worth like herself, very different from the erratic brilliance of Alathea's Merry Gang. She sensed that the older woman, despite her friendly talk, mildly disapproved of her ex-pupil's companions.

But, on the whole, it was a very pleasant afternoon, and it was almost dusk when the hackney was called and Alathea, Nell and the pictures, along with some recipes for varnish, written out on a scrap of paper in Charles Beale's clerkly hand, left to return to the Piazza, supper, and the uncomfortable company of Lord Bradfield and his two uncongenial daughters.

And, had they known it, of Kit.

The fact that Henrietta was lying in wait for them in the hall warned Alathea that something unusual must have happened, even if she had not seen her worried face. 'What is it, Hen? What's wrong?'

'I thought I'd better warn you,' said the older girl, her voice lowered. 'Kit's here.'

Alathea stood very still, her mind churning and her heart cold within her. She had often wondered what she would do, what she would say, when their paths should cross again, and her imagination had always shrunk away from the prospect. How, in the name of God, to pretend that nothing had happened when the events of that February evening had shattered so many illusions and torn down the barriers of convention and decency and normality? How was she to touch him, when the very thought of it revolted her and brought back the stench of nightmare?

And yet, at the same time she could not help but remember the vivid charming companion, the first of her Wits, the man who had given her Lovell and shown her such kindness, even if he had been revealed afterwards to have had an ulterior motive. He had been her friend, and was her brother still. She had succeeded very well in making that dreadful incident a thing of the past, shutting it from her waking mind even if it surfaced, like some terrible sea-serpent, into her undisciplined dreams. She, after all, had been able to pick up the threads of her life, to carry on as if nothing had happened, to keep her mind busy, and she had other, less malevolent men to give her companionship. But Kit had had eleven months in the remote tedium of Yorkshire in which to brood. How had his mind coped with the agony of guilt and self-recrimination which she knew instinctively he must have felt, after the first madness of lust had diminished?

By the time Sarah had taken their cloaks and Jonathan and the boy Tom were puffing up the stairs to the studio, bearing her pictures, her imagination had constructed a very different Kit from the handsome, supremely confident young man she had always known, and she did not think she could face the broken-down wreck of her brother with any less difficulty than the jealous, would-be incestuous rapist he had been at their last encounter. She walked up the first flight of stairs with sticky hands and pounding heart, and entered the chilly fastness of the Great Chamber with something approaching panic.

'Why, there you are,' said her uncle, rising from his comfortably upholstered chair, very close to the great and roaring fire. 'Look who is come to visit us – such a pleasant surprise, eh, to have your brother here!'

And she faced Kit.

He had stood also, and there was a slender Venetian glass of wine in his hand. But there was no sign of any weakness, no madness, nor distraction, no grief and no guilt: and no devouring flame in the blue eyes, slightly more hooded than before, that met hers with frank and brotherly warmth. 'Hello, Thea,' said Kit. 'You're looking very flushed – is it cold outside? Come and kiss your brother, then.'

He must have forgotten, thought Alathea wildly, *but he* can't *have forgotten what happened the last time we met – he* can't. Disbelieving, like a sleepwalker, she crossed the miles of polished floor between them, and her steps seemed to go on for ever, until at last she reached him, and was given the obligatory fraternal kiss on both cheeks. His hands were touching hers: they felt warm and life-filled, in contrast to her limp cold paws, but there was, incredibly, no tremor in the contact, no spark of emotion in the kind, concerned regard of those very blue eyes. 'You don't look very well – have you a touch of fever?'

'No,' said Alathea, disengaging herself. 'No – it was cold outside – I am just a little hot by the fire, that is all.' She stood while Kit, very much the courteous gallant, drew up a chair for her and went on to greet Nell with many compliments on her appearance. Then she sat down, suddenly weak-kneed, with thoughts jostling madly in her head. Not only was he behaving as if nothing at all had ever happened between them, but somehow, he had quenched that look in his eyes, the look she had interpreted too late as lust, the look that had once followed every move she made, every word she spoke. What had happened? Had that poisonous night cauterised all the unnatural love from his soul, leaving only a properly fraternal affection? Were his feelings unchanged, but now successfully disguised for reasons of prudence, or decency? Or, most disturbingly of all, had that attempted rape been completely erased from his mind in the torment that followed it?

She could not guess – and she could hardly ask him, either now in company, or later in private. She could only look at him intently, as he had once always looked at her, for some clue as to what he was truly thinking. But he was speaking to Nell, and then to Anne and Mall, then to Lord Bradfield, the model of correct and polite behaviour, and for once her judgement had failed her: she could not tell if he were false, or no.

She was included in the conversation, and managed to overcome her feelings so far as to address seemingly light-hearted enquiries to him. Why had they not seen him for so long? Had he not been bored to a distraction in Yorkshire? And Kit smiled that polite, empty smile and told her that he had had much to do on his estates, which had been too long neglected, and had only recently managed to put his house into a civilised condition at last. 'There were even hens in the parlour – and hardly an unrotted rafter in the roof! But I wouldn't be ashamed if the King himself were to see it now,' he added, with a satisfaction and pride that sat strangely with the Kit she had known before. 'And I have news of Ashcott – indeed, I spent Christmas there.'

So she asked him about her parents. Yes, they were both well, and exactly the same as ever, save that their mother's hair was almost grey now, and Francis would keep teasing her about it, and calling her pepper-pot – to which Thomazine had replied in kind. Mun, now sixteen and very much at a loose end, seemed to be presenting something of a problem. 'It's obvious he is not suited to an academic life at Oxford,' Kit explained, 'but it's hard to say what life he is suited to, save a soldier's or a sailor's – still the same old rough-and-ready Mun, always spoiling for a fight. Best not allow him near London, or he'd be duelling every week – and I don't think his swordsmanship is equal to the task!' Sophie was flourishing, though, a taking little minx, 'So pretty all the ploughboys sigh after her,' said Kit, grinning, 'and by Heaven she knows it, does Sophie! And by the way, it was all I could do to stop her coming with me – she said you'd promised to take her to a play.'

'Did I? Well, I haven't seen her for so long – I suppose I ought to go home once in a while,' said Alathea guiltily. 'But I have been very busy of late.'

'Your painting? How is your work going along?'

It was the sort of question a maiden aunt might have asked. Alathea, who had her mother's sense of the absurd, was tempted to laugh. Instead, she drew a breath and gave a brief résumé of her career over the last few months – it did not take very long, as there were so many people she did not want to mention. But she went on to speak at some length of her visit to Mistress Beale, feeling that a reminder that there were other, highly respectable female artists in London would not come amiss either to Kit or to Lord Bradfield.

The rest of the evening passed in a blur of unreality. She remembered, vaguely, eating her supper with little relish, and the cheerful games of cards that followed it, ombre and piquet and whist, while Lord Bradfield and Math sat gravely together over a dignified game of chess. She remembered being Nell's partner in the whist, and that they won, and that Kit beat her at piquet, but no more than that, for the bewilderment at her brother's behaviour filled her mind to the exclusion of all else. He could not have forgotten – he could *not* – and yet it seemed that he had.

The result of that tension and the tumultuous, endless treadmill of her thoughts was an agonising headache, something so rare for her that everyone showed an astonishing and most gratifying concern. She was put to bed, given compresses and infusions, and somehow, at last, fell asleep despite the red-hot band of iron that seemed to be gripped across her temple: and fortunately, her dreams were small and harmless.

But Kit was still there in the morning, even if the headache was not, and she must face the unpleasant fact that his stay in London would be a long one, and she must accept his presence in her life, for good or ill. She could tell no one of her problem, least of all Kit, for at least he seemed to be no overt threat to her now, and she shied away from probing too deeply lest she open that dreadful Pandora's box again, to worse effect. She would have to cope alone, and she did not think she could, but there was one other person who knew the truth, and as soon as she was dressed she sat down at the table in her chamber and dashed off a hasty scribbled note to Hugh, to be taken to Whitehall by young Tom.

Hugh, trying to force his tired and aching eyes – there had been a very late-night carouse with Henry Jermyn – into deciphering the wild handwriting, idiosyncratic even by Alathea's standards, could not make head nor tail of it at first. Then, he saw Kit's name, and guessed. Weary anger seeped into his mind. *Dear God*, he thought, *if that misbegotten swine is threatening her again, I'll kill him –scandal or no scandal.* And then, his eyes clearing a little, he saw the sense of what she had written.

'Hugh – please come as soon as you can. Kit is back. He behaves as if nothing had happened. What can I do? Please come – please.' And she had signed her monogram, such had been her haste.

He had never had such an appeal before, from anyone, let alone the fiercely independent Alathea. It was an indication of her trouble. He called his manservant, and dressed, and sent the man to find a hackney, and in the space of an hour from receiving the note, he was knocking on the door of the Covent Garden house.

One of the footmen answered it, and directed him to the studio. Pausing only to exchange polite greetings with Mall, whom he passed on the stairs, he hurried up as quickly as he could, knocked, and went in.

Problems or no, life must go on, and she had a sitter due that afternoon. There were draperies and a background to work on, and Alathea was standing frowning at her canvas, brushes and palette in hand. He was shocked at the change in her, although he had only seen her two days previously: her face was white, her eyes dark-ringed, the hollows under her cheekbones very pronounced.

'Is that you, Nell?' Alathea asked, glancing round the canvas, saw her uncle and, most upsetting of all, made neither sound nor movement but began to weep, the tears suddenly flooding her eyes. Blindly, anguished, she tried to wipe them, left a streak of blue paint across her face, laid her brushes and palette down on a table (the brushes promptly rolling on to the floor), and struggled with the old shirt.

Hugh, in almost as much distress himself, hastened to help her. He pulled it over her head, dislodging the pins in her hair and sending it tumbling haphazardly down her back, and drew her close to him. 'Oh, my dear girl – has it been so bad?'

The slender body under his hands was shaken by sobs, and his waistcoat began to feel damp. 'No – I don't know what's wrong – what can I *do*?' Her voice was muffled, but her agony was plain. He escorted her over to the fire, a half-hearted flicker of flame in the grate, and gently pressed her into the chair. He had never seen her so upset, the tears poured down her face, and she seemed unable to stop. Suddenly, he wondered if she were ill: certainly, the change in her looks suggested it. The idea alarmed him. Apart from the occasional cold, soon thrown off, she had always enjoyed robust Heron health even in London's foetid air.

'Thea – my dear girl – tell me what's wrong? Are you unwell?' An awful possibility crossed his mind, only to be dismissed. He could not imagine the tough, unconventional Alathea being so overturned by a small matter of pregnancy, not in an age when maids-of-honour seemed to drop little bastards like piglets.

She shook her head, and then blew her nose firmly on his proffered handkerchief, before taking several deep breaths to calm herself. Then her voice, strained and hoarse, came quietly. 'Oh, Hugh, I'm sorry. What a silly weakling you must think me!'

'Not in the least. I know you, you're not like Nell to cry for nothing. Is it Kit?'

'Yes – he came last night, and oh, Hugh, it's horrible – he behaves just as if nothing had ever happened! I can't believe it – I can't forget – and yet he seems to have wiped it out from his memory.'

'What did you expect him to do – go down on bended knee in front of Lord Bradfield and apologise for trying to rape you? Anyway,' said Hugh, gently persuasive, 'you know he's always been like that, it's the pattern of his behaviour: the rage, the outbursts, the words or deeds that everyone else takes to heart, then he stamps off, cools down, whether it takes six hours or six weeks or six months, and returns as if nothing had happened. You *know* he's like that – it's Kit.'

'How *could* he forget?'

'He probably hasn't – he's probably just pushed it to the back of his mind. Why is he here?'

'I don't know – I went to see Mistress Beale yesterday, and when I returned, there he was, just the same Kit as ever – except his eyes don't follow me any more.'

'*Surely* you don't regret that!'

A rather watery grin was his reward. 'No,' said Alathea, after a moment. 'No, of course I don't – but it's still disconcerting. Do you think that what – what he tried to do has somehow exorcised his feelings?'

'I don't know – and I wouldn't attempt to ask him.'

'I wasn't intending to!'

'It could be that he's come to his senses at last,' Hugh told her. 'You never know – even he must have a grain of reason, somewhere. Perhaps he's realised at last that he can never have you. He might even have come to London to look for a wife!'

That made his niece laugh in earnest, albeit rather wildly. She wiped her eyes again with the kerchief, and grinned. 'Now I come to think of it, he has spent the last year putting his estate in Yorkshire to rights – and making his house "civilised", he said. Perhaps he *does* want to marry, and settle down?'

'The best thing he could do,' said Hugh. 'So the chances are, he won't be here very long – and there'll be celebrations at the end of it, and then he'll take his poor bride off to the wilds of Yorkshire, and won't trouble us or you again for a very long time. So cheer up, my dear girl – all your problems are over!'

'No, they're not – *he* may be able to behave normally, but I can't. Every time I see him I think of what – of what he tried to do, because I don't trust him and I never have trusted him, I think he still wants me, and he runs too deep for anyone to see him clearly.'

'Yes – but you knew before that there was something strange about him, about his feelings, about the way he looked at you. Didn't you?'

'Yes – yes, I did, very strongly.'

'And now that feeling has gone?'

'Yes – he seems almost as harmless as Math!'

'Well then, he may have changed in truth. And you're not alone – you have Nell and Hen and Math on your side, and Lord Bradfield's presence doesn't exactly make rape easier, and above all there's me, always at your beck and call, for ever and ever – that is, if I'm not to be at someone else's,' said Hugh, smiling broadly.

Alathea, gradually emerging from her depression, took notice of him for the first time that morning, and saw the grin and the air of suppressed excitement, and pushed her own concerns away. 'I can tell you've something to tell me. What is it?'

'Well,' said Hugh, moving closer and casting a comically conspiratorial look about the empty studio, as if spies were hiding behind the furniture, 'don't noise this abroad just yet, for it's not certain for a day or two yet – but there's a good chance of my becoming Groom of the Bedchamber to the Duke of York.'

'Hugh!' Alathea jumped up from her chair to hug him, all her sorrows gone. 'Oh, *Hugh*! How wonderful! Groom of the Bedchamber – the Duke of York! Oh, Hugh, now you've really succeeded – you're a real courtier!'

'What was I before, then? And I haven't got the position yet,' Hugh warned. 'And it's only a very small step on the ladder of preferment. But Lord St Albans owes me many favours, and Henry Jermyn has the attentive ear of our Jemmy.'

Alathea thought that his use of Whitehall's slighting nickname for the Duke of York boded ill for his future in that prince's service, but Hugh was enough of a survivor to be irreverent only in private. 'So Henry Jermyn has been speaking for you?'

'He has indeed, and so has St Albans. There's a place in the Bedchamber vacant, and my name has been put forward – and if I succeed, or rather if Henry succeeds, then at last I will have some substance to live on!' His smile could not have been broader or happier, and Alathea suddenly knew why.

'To hell with Kit's search for a wife – you've got your eye on one, haven't you?'

'I won't deny it,' said Hugh, with satisfaction. 'I've been a man of the world too long – high time I settled down.'

'Being at Court won't settle you down. And you're only twenty-six.'

'Nearly twenty-seven, and still unwed – the last of my name. Pity those Cornish estates weren't entailed like Goldhayes, or I'd have those – as it is, I suspect they'll form part of Susannah's dowry.' The smug look increased. 'Well?' said Hugh Trevelyan, cunning scion of a very cunning breed. 'Do you think I stand a greater chance, now?'

For a moment, Alathea was silent, thoughts jumbling in her head – Meraud, Susannah, Lord Bradfield, Hugh – a potent combination of raw and disparate ingredients which, she suspected with sudden foreboding, might prove very explosive indeed. 'Oh, dear,' she said wryly. 'Oh dear, oh dear, oh dear.'

Hugh looked at her with quizzical amusement. 'Am I such a bad prospect as a husband? I may be a rogue and a rascal, but I'm not a hopeless rakehell – yet.'

'You yourself may not be such a bad catch now in the marriage market,' said Alathea, feeling with some desperation that honesty was the best policy – *surely* he must have guessed? – 'but set against Lord Bradfield, you haven't the slightest hope.'

There was total silence. *Oh God*, thought Alathea, looking at the sudden taut set of Hugh's normally relaxed and cheerful countenance. *He didn't know – it's just as well I told him, though I ought to have done it more gently*.

'Lord Bradfield?' Her half-uncle's voice had altered, subtly, in the same manner as his face. 'Susannah is going to marry my brother Simon?'

'I don't know,' said Alathea, already regretting her words – why could she not think for once, before blundering in with leaden feet and a lamentable lack of tact? 'I shouldn't have said it – I thought you knew – and it's no more than speculation, truly, there's been no announcement, no talk, nothing to give any indication of it save Meraud's tactics and Lord Bradfield's regard – and that's no secret, for Aunt Lucy has noticed it as well, and it was she who thought Meraud might have that marriage in mind.'

'And Lucy has always put two and two together and made a countless number,' said Hugh. Something of his usual manner had returned. 'But why in God's name didn't you *tell* me what you suspected?'

'Because I didn't think your interest was serious, because I thought you'd guessed already, and because I didn't want to trouble you with trivia,' said Alathea, on the defensive despite herself.

'Trivia?' Hugh's rich dark voice was thick with disbelief. '*Trivia*? The girl I want to marry is going to be promised to my brother, who must be old enough to be her grandfather, the whole idea's repellent, and you call it trivia? Oh, Thea, if you had any knowledge of love you wouldn't think it trivial.'

'I didn't think you loved her.'

'Didn't think I was capable of it – I know your opinion of me,' said Hugh ruefully. 'Well, here we have a pretty pickle – for Susannah has said nothing of Lord Bradfield to me, nor of any schemes for imminent marriage, and indeed has given me to understand that life under my protection, with the sanction of a parson of course, would not come amiss.'

'Then have you been *meeting* her? In secret?'

'Don't act the prude – it ill becomes you. Yes, dear girl, I've been meeting her: not too difficult, when you think of it, for her mother has concerns of her own, and it is quite often possible to extract Andromeda from the dragon's den without the said dragon being aware of it. I have consumed more fruit tarts, syllabubs and glasses of cold milk – and cold milk, believe me, however refreshing, can never measure up to a brimmer of Rhenish – in that pretty little lodge in Hyde Park over the last few months, than I ever have in my life before.'

'Months? You've been meeting Susannah in secret for *months*?' Alathea stared at him in astonishment.

Hugh, quite unabashed, grinned. 'Since October. October the twelfth, to be precise. Don't laugh.'

'I didn't. Oh, Hugh, that's nearly four months. Are you *sure* Meraud doesn't suspect?'

'Quite sure. She dines regularly with Sir Robert Manners – and if she marries him it's no more than she deserves – and various other cronies around Whitehall. Susannah has made friends with a girl who lodges at the same house, and she helps us, covers up for Sue, says she's dined with her, or goes walking in the park with her – so we can meet. She's very accommodating, is Mistress Judith Prescott. It's a shame she hasn't a beau to meet in secret, for then we could help her in her turn. Why are you looking so serious?'

'Because I'd like it if *you* were, for once. The trouble is, I can't, still, quite believe it. I like Susannah, I like her very much, and I think you and she will deal very well together, if only because each of you seems to be as devious as the other – but do you really want to make that rapacious harpy your unwilling mother-in-law?'

'No, but for Sue I'll risk it,' said Hugh. He took her chin and turned her sober face towards him. 'Listen to me, my dear girl. You may or may not believe me, but this is what I have to say. I love Susannah Lawrence. I have good reason to believe she loves me. She is an heiress, I admit, and has a small estate or two due to her – but I also have some prospects to offer, now. A Groom of the Bedchamber has five hundred pounds a year, lodgings in St James's Palace if he wants them, and meals paid for – not a small item. Duties are not exactly onerous, the company's congenial, and the prospects singularly good. Lord St Albans began with no more – and now he owns half of the new building in London.'

'Yes, and how did he come by it?'

'Favour, care, bribery and prudence,' said Hugh briefly. 'I don't aim so high – a comfortable life with the woman I love is all my desire, and I mean to get it. They may offer me wealth, a peerage, lands – I don't want 'em. I do want Sue, and I mean to have her, rapacious harpy or not. There you have my position, dear girl – do you disapprove?'

'How could I, knowing my parents' story? But Lord Bradfield did his best to prevent their love, and nearly succeeded. You may find him an implacable opponent.'

'I don't even intend him to discover my plans until it's too late for him to do anything about it,' said Hugh. 'If he does want to marry her – and I suppose I can't blame him, I want to marry her myself – then we'll elope before he can have the chance. And I hardly need tell you, Thea, to keep all this information very securely inside your sleek yellow head, and on no account to let any of it slip to Lucy, or it'll be the talk of London inside an hour.'

'I'm insulted that you think it necessary to warn me,' said Alathea. She sat back in the chair and studied her half-uncle, thoughtfully. 'I suppose this *is* all true, and not just some ploy to divert me from my own problems?'

'It's all true – every sack-soaked word of it.' Suddenly serious, he took her hands in his and kissed them, gently and courteously. 'Thea? Wish me happy?'

'I wish you happy,' she said, thinking that he had made it all sound so easy, so simple, so disdainful of the consequences. Meraud's spiteful capacity for revenge, Lord Bradfield's thwarted fury, the scandal that was bound to follow any elopement, the inevitable split in the family, she saw it all with clarity, and wondered that Hugh, worldly, cynical Hugh, could not. Cupid was blind, so said the poets: probably he made you blind, as well.

But she would not say any of that to Hugh, so certain of success. She would give him her love, her approval, her hope, as he had given her his, and keep her doubts to herself.

CHAPTER NINETEEN

The betrothal

All heiresses are beautiful.

(Dryden, *King Arthur*)

There were daffodils in pots along her windowsill, and a pile of books, paper, paints, pens, drawingboards beside her bed. A low fever, had said the doctor, summoned by an anxious Hen when it became obvious, the day after her talk with Hugh, that Alathea was genuinely ill, and the indignant patient, protesting the length of her appointment book, had been hustled reluctantly into bed.

Once there, of course, she had realised the unpleasant truth: she was really sick, for the first time since childhood. The doctor had named it accurately – she felt low, depressed, lethargic, remote from the busy world outside, without even the enthusiasm to draw. She heard the doctor mentioning 'rest', and talking disapprovingly about 'strain' and 'over-work', and it roused no urge to refute the claim. She had painted day in, day out for well over a year, without a break or a holiday beyond the Sabbath and an occasional jaunt to the countryside. She had not been to Ashcott, to the deep peace of Oxfordshire, for five years, she realised with distant surprise, and had not seen either of her parents since their summer visit. And now, as never before even in a lifetime of dreaming of it, Goldhayes filled her feverish sleep. Her heart lay there, and would always do so, in the home of her childhood, and she had the strange feeling that one day, when she was long, long, dead, she would haunt that house, as it now haunted her.

The fever lasted ten days, off and on, and she slept for most of it, hardly knowing what went on outside that high, rather draughty chamber which faced out on to the garden on the second floor. People came to visit her: she would wake up from some doze to find someone, Hen, or Nell, or Becca, sitting by the bed. But she could hardly keep her eyes open for long enough to hold a conversation, and soon they would tiptoe out again, leaving her in peace to work through the illness and build up her strength again.

Somewhat to her surprise, the doctor's infusions and potions seemed to work. The fever disappeared at last, but the lethargy was left, a weakness and lassitude that she could not shake off. She felt perfectly well, sitting up in bed in the February sunlight, looking at books or daffodils, but if she set one foot outside the bed, her feeble muscles refused to obey her. And she was quite happy to lie there, being waited on hand and foot, free of problems and pressures, with nothing more to worry about than the choice of delicacies from the kitchen.

She was fed also with gossip, daily by Hen and Becca and Mall: all the household news came to her door. The French cook had quarrelled, loudly and passionately, with the gardener, who had proved obstinate in the matter of planting exotic herbs: everyone's vocabulary of that language had been dramatically increased. Lovell, taken for exercise in St Giles' Fields, had also quarrelled, this time with a pugnacious little spaniel belonging to a lady of quality, and Lovell, to judge by the rakish bandage that inadequately covered a ripped ear, had not come off best despite his superior size. There had been a variety of pleasure trips. Hugh had taken everyone by boat across the river to the gardens at Foxhall, in celebration of his new position at St James', and had hardly been seen since in his enthusiasm for his duties, or so Lord Bradfield chose to interpret it. Buckhurst and Sedley had called frequently, bearing extravagant gifts – fruit, French sweetmeats, diverting romances – and making her laugh. They also had escorted various members of the household to Hyde Park, the theatre, and sundry other pleasant places of popular resort. There was no direct word of Rochester. From what Sedley and Buckhurst let slip, she gathered that he was in London with his wife and, obscurely, found the thought distressed her.

She did not, to her relief, see very much at first of Kit. He had always distrusted illness and shied away from sickrooms. Supremely healthy himself, he had no patience with those who were not. But as she grew better, he came quite often to sit with her, and fell into the habit of reading various books aloud to her, plays, poetry, romances, each declaimed in a style suited to its subject. She began to welcome his visits, after her initial wariness. He was so kind, so cheerful, so much the attentive brother, as if that other, darker, dangerous Kit had never been.

It was as well that she did not know that it slumbered still, repressed but not forgotten, behind his smile and his charm. He had suffered great agony of mind, those long tedious months in

Yorkshire. He had attempted, with a certain success that seemed also like a betrayal, to submerge his love and lust and guilt in a frenzy of repair and renewal of his neglected estate. He had learned that his feelings were hopeless, wrong, doomed to despair, but he had also realised that if he could control his passion, hide it away within the tortuous passages of his mind, pretend it had never been, he could at least make contact with her again. She could not ever reveal that he had once aspired to be more than a brother. She would keep his terrible secret, and suffer him to be near her.

It had not occurred to him that it was a secret almost too dreadful for her to bear alone, and even looking at her gaunt, changed, pale face on the scarcely paler pillows, he did not realise it. But he sensed, in the middle of his self-absorption, that he was not really welcome, that however much he smiled and joked and laughed, her answers were a pale, stilted shadow of the sparkling, instant wit that she had always delighted in. She could not escape his attentions, she was in a sense his captive, but she was withholding her friendship.

Well, she would see how much she meant to him. He had news for her which would surely wrench her out of her wan indifference. He had kept it to himself for some days now, since the rest of the household did not know, but they were soon to be informed, and he wanted to be first with the news, to see the shock and horror on her face, to see her jealousy aroused at last. In his way, he truly loved her, and always would, but, perversely, he also wanted to see her suffer, because she would not love him, and never would.

She was drawing: she must be better today. There was a little colour in her face and she was out of bed, warmly wrapped in a fur-lined robe and her abundant, astonishing hair loose and curling down her back. He was conscious of a stab of anger at seeing her with pen and ink, and some of her shells of watercolour for limning were on the table beside her. There was a pot of daffodils, yellow in the pale light of early March, and it was these that she was drawing, with her usual deftness and speed, each delicate petal and triumphant trumpet swiftly noted on the paper. He preferred her ill in bed and at his mercy, without any reminder of that unconventional artist who had been such a threat to him, but he said politely, 'Daffodils? I did not know you were interested in such things.'

'I didn't either, but the urge to draw something came over me this morning, and I thought I had better take advantage of it before it left me. I feel almost my old self again – now I want to draw, I must be almost well.' She bent her head over the paper. He watched with grudging admiration as the skilful strokes of the quill delineated the rough edges of the fat earthenware pot in which the bulbs had been planted. At last she was finished, with quick hatching, crossing and recrossing the paper, to indicate the shadows, and suddenly, miraculously, the flat drawing sprang to life. She laid her pen down, studied her work thoughtfully, and then turned to him. 'How are you keeping today? You look very cheerful.'

'I have some news,' said Kit. He turned, and drew up the other chair to face her at the table, across the daffodils. 'Some most splendid news, Thea. I am to be married!'

He was gratified to see that she became suddenly quite still, her face frozen in surprise. Then she said, her voice careful, 'Married? Oh, that is good news, Kit – my felicitations. But who's the lady? Who have you been courting in such secrecy?'

'Anne Heron,' he said.

Anne. Plain, sharp, shrewish, unsympathetic Anne. Her first thought was: *But she's plain – so dreadfully, terribly plain, she has no beauty, no wit, no generosity, no kindness: she is my utter opposite*. And the next thought followed hard on its heels: *But she is an heiress, a great heiress, she has a magnificent dowry, she will bring him a vast amount of money*.

'How nice,' she heard herself saying, remotely. 'I am glad for Anne – and for you, of course. Do you love her very much?'

And Kit, smiling, played his trump card. 'Love? What has love to do with it? No one could marry for love of her – her dowry's her chief attraction, and it's a most splendid and appropriate match for both of us. A business arrangement, no more, no less.'

Utterly appalled, Alathea stared at him, her mouth slightly open. 'Marriage? A *business* arrangement? Kit, she's going to be your *wife* – surely you should be thinking of her happiness, and yours?'

'I dare say we shall deal well enough together – though I must try to curb that scold's tongue. Perhaps the purchase of a bridle would do the trick. No, I jest – if she runs my house efficiently, gives me children to carry on the name, and keeps that very long nose out of my affairs, that will suit me admirably.'

'But do you not feel any affection for her *at all*?'

'Not at present, I confess – though of course wedded life may change that, in time,' said Kit cheerfully. He saw the repugnance on her face, and misinterpreted it. *She* is *jealous*, he thought. *At last, I have pierced her indifference, I have made her suffer! She* does *care, she does, she does*!

But Alathea's thoughts were quite different, and chief amongst them, the revulsion she felt at his whole conduct. His slighting references to Anne's looks – and she could hardly help those, whatever the shrewishness of her tongue – the callous way in which he had emphasised the mercenary nature of the betrothal, his complete disregard for his bride's feelings and interests, crystallised into two sad words. 'Poor Anne,' she said.

'She's hardly likely to be that,' said Kit, insensitively. 'With the revenue from my lands and all hers, poverty won't come into it. What more could she wish for? She'll have wealth, a fine house in Yorkshire, this house as well – it's part of her dowry, the lease on this house, so it will be mine after the wedding. And she'll be Lady Drakelon, and live in state. What more could she want?'

'Love,' said Alathea bleakly.

Kit laughed, triumph and anguish both in the sound of it. 'Love? Love? You don't know what the word means – you don't know what it is!'

She tried to speak to Anne, but the other girl, secure behind the armour of her tongue, refused to respond to Alathea's tactful probing and would say only that her father thought it an excellent match and, since she agreed with him, would behave obediently and gladly, as a dutiful daughter should. Alathea gave up. After all, Anne might even, within that forbidding exterior, harbour some kinder feelings for Kit and his vivid handsome face. And although he had spoken so contemptuously of her behind her back, in her presence he was smiling, charming and attentive, the perfect betrothed.

The hypocrisy of it all disgusted Alathea. She knew she was too idealistic, even too romantic, in these practical mercenary times, but she was appalled at this treatment of women as a commodity, bought and sold for the value of their lands and their dowries, or their potential fertility. She could put no warmth into her congratulations, the night of Lord Bradfield's announcement of the happy arrangement, and did not know that Kit, secretly exultant, took her strained face and stilted words to mean another emotion entirely.

But there was worse to come. Lord Bradfield had invited all his London relatives to hear of his elder daughter's betrothal, and the Great Chamber was crowded with Heron connections: Lucy and Dan Ashley, Rosalind and Master Thomas Wootton (her kind, comfortable and uninspiring husband), Hugh, who was still almost a stranger to his eldest half-brother, and who looked a stranger even to Alathea in his new, luxuriantly curled periwig and a Court suit frothing with lace and ribbons, and Mistress Meraud Lawrence and her daughter Susannah, very quiet and pink and demure in a new and exquisite gown of sky-coloured velvet. They all drank the toast to the happy pair, and Alathea saw Anne's sideways, almost proprietorial glance at her intended husband and realised with misgivings that it might not just be a daughter's obedience that had led her so willingly to this betrothal.

Lord Bradfield was still on his feet: wine-glass in hand, it looked as if he had not yet finished. Seeing the softening of his grim face, his glance down the table to where Meraud Trevelyan sat next to her daughter, her lovely face folded in a smug smile like a cat's, Alathea knew with sudden dread what he must be about to say.

'But that announcement, happy though it makes me to see my dear Anne settled so favourably, is not the only one I have to make this evening. I have wished my daughter and her groom well, and we have all toasted their future together. Now I am asking for your blessings for myself.'

Opposite Alathea, Hugh's clever, humorous face had suddenly become very still and tense. She wanted to reach out, to hold his hand, to give comfort and support and hope, but could not without giving him away. She willed him intensely to look towards her, but he would not: his eyes, she saw, were staring at Susannah. The object of his affections, and of Lord Bradfield's, was oblivious: she was flushed a rosy and maidenly pink, and examining her plate.

'It is my pleasure,' said Simon Heron, Lord Bradfield, in that abrupt harsh voice, 'and my joyful duty to inform you all that this morning Mistress Susannah Lawrence did me the great honour of consenting to become my wife. I may confidently say that her answer has made me the happiest man in this room, with the possible exception of my dear future son-in-law: and so I give you, Susannah!'

It had been expected, or worked for, by almost everyone present, and yet the faces around the table, showed varying degrees of silent, stunned disapproval. Dutifully, the glasses were raised, the health drunk. Dan rose and proposed another, in rather less glowing phrases, to his brother-in-law and host. Lucy, sitting beside him, looked appalled. Further down the table, Anne Heron's intimidating face would have turned lesser men than her father to stone. By contrast, Meraud Lawrence was all smiles, her triumph, albeit at second hand, assured, her grand plotting on her younger daughter's behalf brought to a successful conclusion. And Alathea, with a wave of loathing, knew that, whatever the consequences, she must in all conscience do her utmost to oppose and prevent this marriage.

And yet the worm of doubt nagged her. She only had Hugh's word for it, that Susannah preferred him and his modest prospects to a splendid future as Lady Bradfield. What if the girl had accepted the betrothal in earnest?

There was a council of war a few days later at the House of the Ash Tree, convened by the irrepressible Lucy, who might have been thought by some to be old enough to know better. Messages had been sent, word passed, and all those who might have reason to support her were in attendance. Alathea, arriving with Nell – Hen was concerned in some domestic upset, Math at the Temple – found Ros there already, and Dan nowhere to be seen: presumably he had more important things to do than settle family disputes. Then, hard on her heels, came Hugh, his face showing quite untypical signs of strain, so that Alathea's heart went out to him. The last arrivals, however, were more of a surprise, for just as they had sat down around the table, and coffee had been poured, Sir Christopher Drakelon and his intended bride entered the room.

Lucy had obviously expected them. She ushered them to their seats, and gave them coffee in the two remaining cups. Kit glanced around the company with a broad smile of greeting; Anne, more coolly, gave a brief nod. They had earlier announced their intention of going for a drive in Hyde Park: evidently the hackney had brought them to Fleet Street instead. With a certain feeling of disquiet, Alathea wondered how much more deception and subterfuge would be employed before this business was done.

'We are gathered here today,' said Lucy Ashley, in a probably unconscious imitation of religious solemnity, 'for the purpose of preventing my brother Simon's marriage to Susannah Lawrence. Are we, first of all, agreed that this marriage is, for various reasons, undesirable?'

There was unanimous assent. Alathea, looking round the assembled faces, thought of all the different reasons behind their agreement: desire to follow the dictates of true love, revulsion at the difference in age between bride and groom, feeling for the wishes of Susannah, so blatantly ignored, and above all, hatred for Meraud, whose dynastic strategy would be crowned by her daughter's espousal to one of the greatest landowners in Suffolk. And of course Hugh, whose motive was love.

'Well,' her half-uncle said now, with a smile round his relatives which did not quite ring true, 'at least I have some support – although I need help of a more practical nature, at present. Who can find me a complaisant parson?'

There was a brief silence. Then Anne said, her harsh, abrupt voice a curious echo of her father's, 'What about Susannah? We have heard nothing of her thoughts in the matter. She agreed to marry my father, did she not?'

'Only to allay suspicion,' said Hugh. 'She told me so herself. If she presents herself as a willing bride, it will make it all the easier for her to elope with me – we decided on it some time ago. She has thus allayed any suspicions her mother might have. At the same time, she's assured me that she would not marry Lord Bradfield if he were the last man on earth, lands and title notwithstanding. And in truth, even if I did not love her, even if I didn't want to marry her myself, I would still oppose her marriage to my brother. The idea of it . . . I find it appalling.'

'And anything that thwarts Meraud has my wholehearted support,' Lucy said, with a force that was surprising to anyone who did not know the strength of her feelings. 'I won't tell the story now, it's too long: suffice it to say that by this, she hopes to gain control of Goldhayes, and cheat Francis and Thomazine out of what would otherwise be theirs, settling a few old scores in the process, I don't doubt. And she won't succeed if I can help it!'

'I agree,' said Kit. 'I can remember her, vaguely, when I was a small child – and I know now what happened then. But what do you say, Nell? She is your mother too, even if she seems to ignore that fact. Do you oppose her too?'

'Yes,' said Nell, in a voice hardly above a whisper. 'Yes, I oppose her. She is cruel, heartless, devious – and I like Susannah, I know she loves Hugh, and I want to see them happy.' She faded into silence, and brushed her hand across her eyes.

'So – a parson,' said Lucy, looking at her young half-brother with affection. 'You plan to marry her instead, then? No dishonourable intentions?'

'How could you think it of me?' said Hugh, smiling. 'The weddings are set for the end of April or the beginning of May. There's lawyers' business to sort out, apparently. But the sooner we can organise our escape, the more chance we have of success. We need a parson to marry us, and a haven safe from pursuit. There will need to be a licence, too.'

'I am sure someone from my raffish acquaintance will be able to supply me with the name of an unscrupulous parson,' said Alathea, thinking of Sedley and Buckhurst – doubtless one of them would oblige with the information. 'I would not entirely trust them to keep a still tongue, though.'

'And secrecy is all,' Lucy pointed out. 'Simon has important connections, friends in high places. If he got wind of any attempt to elope, matters could become very unpleasant. He had one brother thrown into prison once, for daring to aspire to marry Thomazine – how much more ruthless will he be when it's his own bride being stolen from under his nose? For Hugh's sake, we must preserve utter secrecy. None of this must go beyond the seven of us – not even to people like Dan or Hen or Matthew, who are all on our side. You must all swear yourselves to say nothing at all, to anyone, no matter how close. Will you swear that?'

Rather embarrassed by her insistence, they did. Lucy sat back, beaming, and took a gulp of coffee. Romantic intrigue had always been the breath of life to her, and she thrived on it. 'Now, I think the details of the elopement are best left to Hugh – he knows Susannah's movements, after all, and the best moments for escape – but I am sure that all of us will help him, if desired: finding parsons, laying false trails, that sort of thing.'

'You will understand,' said Kit, with a glance at Hugh, whom he had never liked, 'that I have no wish to fall out with my father-in-law, however much I may approve your plans. But it has occurred to me that my house at Denby may prove a safe refuge for you and

Susannah while the hue-and-cry is in full swing. It is a considerable distance from London, and I doubt if anyone would think of searching for you there.'

Hugh looked at his cousin, the boy with whom he had been reared, the man he had never trusted, the man he had loathed for his attack on Alathea. Watching him, she could sense his suspicion. Then Hugh, who could be as devious as anyone given the chance, smiled. 'That's a most generous offer. I thank you most heartily.'

'My pleasure,' said Kit, and glanced at his betrothed. 'We will stay in London for some little time, I think, after our own marriage – and by then you will be safe, the *fait accompli* will have been accepted, and you will both be free to return. But first, of course, you must be wed . . . and your enquiries for a parson must be very circumspect, to avoid suspicion.'

'You don't need to find a parson,' said Nell's reedy voice. 'All you need do is go to a church like Pancras, or St James' in Duke Place in the City, and you'll be wed with no questions asked.'

There was a startled silence. How on earth had Nell, of all people, come by such information? Alathea had her suspicions, and Nell's answer, in reply to Ros's astonished query, confirmed them. 'Where did I have it from? I overheard some talk in the lodge in Hyde Park, when we were there last. It may not even be true,' added poor Nell, blushing at all this unwonted attention. 'It was just gossip I overheard.'

'I'll find out,' said Hugh. He looked of a sudden very much more cheerful. 'Pancras, did you say? St James', Duke Place?'

'Yes – and apparently all you have to do is appear with bride and witnesses, and wait in the queue,' said Nell, becoming nearly as scarlet as a cherry.

'And what could be easier than that?' Lucy queried. 'Well, Hugh my lad, there you are – the means, the opportunity, the hiding-place all supplied. Have you your resolution still? Or is it vanishing by the minute as matrimony looms nearer?'

'I know it's the fashion to decry marriage,' said Hugh. 'I know that at Whitehall the only wife permissible is an heiress, and Sue's hardly that. But I love her – and I'm not ashamed to have the courage of my convictions. I'm not denying I might not go so all-out for a wedding-ring if she wasn't betrothed to someone else; but if marriage is the only way to save her from my brother's clutches, then marry her I certainly will, and gladly.'

April was warm, amongst the sheltered roofs of London. There were daffodils and early tulips, Dutch and exotic, in the transformed garden behind the Piazza house. It was not a particularly happy time for Alathea. Although to all intents and purposes quite recovered from her illness, she still suffered from bouts of lethargy, depression and doubt quite alien to her character. She had resumed her painting, but sometimes had little enthusiasm for it, and found on these occasions that it was all she could do to be polite to her unfortunate sitter. She did not know what was wrong with her, only that the world had lost its savour, and she missed her friends: missed John Wilmot, too.

In addition, she was worried about Hugh. She had seen him perhaps once since that brief meeting at Lucy's house. She had gathered that all was well, and plans proceeding smoothly, but he had given no details, and she thought it best not to know any. She could not help feeling considerable disquiet at the carefully woven web of deceit and underhand manoeuvring that had been constructed over the past few weeks. She did not feel any regret on behalf of Meraud: that lady's conduct towards poor Nell had for ever damned her in Alathea's eyes. But for Lord Bradfield, so endearingly transformed in Susannah's demure deceptive presence, the gulled and unsuspecting victim of the rest of his family's plots, she felt pity and guilt, for if Hugh's plan succeeded, he would be the chief sufferer. His feelings for the girl might be described as pathetic, ludicrous, undignified, but she did not think they were any less genuine for that – even if, as Kit had remarked maliciously to her last week, he was the old fool there was no fool like.

She did not trust Kit, either. She would not put it past him to betray Hugh's plan, at just the right moment. But Anne did not want her father to marry a chit younger than herself, and of course her dowry and eventual wealth might well be reduced substantially, should her father produce more children – especially a son. Kit might want to ingratiate himself with his bride-to-be's father, but he was marrying her for her considerable inheritance, and would not like to see it reduced.

The real puzzle was Susannah. How could she be so sweet, so naive and innocent, as open and sunny as a June morning, and yet give no sign at all that she was plotting to elope with someone else? Either Hugh had read her wrong and she had no intention of running away with him, thought Alathea, put quite at a loss: or she was just as devious and cunning as her mother, despite that warm generosity, and Hugh had met his match in more senses than one.

Still, she reflected wryly, *if the latter conclusion is correct she must really love him, to give up all that money, that title, to marry an impecunious courtier with very precarious hopes of advancement: so I sincerely pray that she is a true, Machiavellian Trevelyan.*

The most Machiavellian Trevelyan of them all came unduly late to the Covent Garden house, one showery evening in the middle of April. She had visited them earlier in the day, without Susannah who had been confined to bed with a headache, and when Alathea saw the familiar, disliked, immaculate figure enter the Great Chamber where they were all having a light supper, she thought at first that some possession must have been mislaid.

And so it had, but not a fan nor a glove.

'Have any of you seen Susannah today?' Meraud demanded. Her face was white with rage, her expression grim, and Alathea's stomach clenched suddenly. *She's gone*, she thought, with a strange mixture of happiness and dread. *She's gone with Hugh at last*!

'Susannah?' Lord Bradfield had risen, an expression of the liveliest concern on his long, dark face. 'No, she has not been here all day, my dear Meraud – what has happened?'

'I have just discovered,' said Meraud Lawrence, between shut teeth, 'that as soon as I left the house to visit you for dinner, leaving madam ill in bed as I thought, the hussy packs a bag and leaves by the back door, and no one has seen her since. There's an odious little minx in our lodgings seems to have put her up to it – it's taken me half an hour to wring the truth from her, and the instant I had it I came here.' She looked at her host, her intended son-in-law, and said savagely, 'I have the sad duty to inform you, sir, that your betrothed has eloped with another!'

Alathea could not look at Simon Heron's face after that first moment of truth, so terrible were the naked emotions revealed upon it. She found her hands were shaking, and clenched them in her lap.

'Eloped?' Lord Bradfield's voice was thick with astonishment.

'Susannah? My little Susannah, eloped? It cannot be true – it cannot!'

'I regret that it is undoubtedly true,' said Meraud. Her furious, ice-cold gaze swept around the faces at the table: Henrietta, Becca, Matthew, Kit, Mall, Anne, Nell, Alathea. 'And someone here must know of it – they must! Good God, that Prescott jade told me she'd been meeting him in secret for months – you can't tell me none of you knew!'

'Who?' Lord Bradfield's voice cut in sharply. 'Who is she said to have run off with – if indeed she has, I cannot believe it of her – who is he?'

'Your precious half-brother,' said Meraud, 'and my uncle's child – Hugh Trevelyan is the man, it's he she's betrayed you with! And they knew, I'd swear to it, look at them all around the table – they put them up to it, they've done it to spite us – who knew of this, I say?' Again the chill blast of her eyes cast around the faces of her cousins. 'Answer me – where have they gone?'

Silence. Lord Bradfield broke it. Hesitantly, in the voice of a man dealt a mortal blow, he said, 'Hugh? You tell me she has run off with Hugh? Who says this? Have you any proof? Could she not be shopping, or gone to the theatre?'

'At this time in the evening? And there is no play today at either house,' said Meraud. 'Had you forgot? They are closed because of the Duchess of York's death. No – there is no doubt of it, she has gone to meet her lover, and I doubt very much if marriage is in that filthy rakehell's mind.'

'He *is* going to marry her!' cried Nell. Every face swivelled towards her. Pale and furious, she had risen to her feet, quivering with a passion quite alien to her retiring nature. For the first time, Alathea saw some resemblance to her mother in the white, angry stare. 'He *is* going to marry her, he loves her and she loves him!'

'Love?' All the scorn and contempt in the world was present in Meraud's eyes and voice. 'Love? You silly little simpleton, love doesn't enter into it.'

'It didn't enter into your arrangements either,' Nell said. 'And you've never cared a toss for anything but your own ends, ever – and I'm the living proof of it!'

Her eyes glittering, her mouth a slash in her savage face, Meraud walked round the table and with one vicious blow on the side of her head, hurled her elder daughter to the floor. Lord Bradfield uttered an exclamation of dismay, but Meraud, utterly transformed with fury, did not heed him. She stood over Nell, quailing on the floor with a hand pressed to her face, and repeated her question. 'Answer me – where have they gone?'

'Where you won't find them!' Nell sobbed, the tears running between her fingers.

'Answer me, you pathetic little half-wit – you've ruined my plans once in your life and you won't do it again, do you hear me? *Answer me*!'

'Leave her alone!' Alathea said, her hands on the older woman's arm. 'For God's sake, you've done her enough harm – we're all of us just as guilty, so why pick on poor Nell?'

'All?' Lord Bradfield's deep voice broke in. Meraud turned, distracted, and Alathea seized the chance to pull Nell to her feet and push her, still sobbing, towards Hen. 'All?' her uncle repeated, and Alathea moved round to face him, her expression a stubborn, insolent echo of her father, who had also defied Simon Heron, long ago. 'Did you know of this also, niece?'

'I knew,' she said, keeping the tremor from her voice quite successfully. 'Others knew as well, but they are not here.' She did not send a betraying glance at Kit. If he wanted to reveal his own knowledge he would, but she was prepared to face the storm alone, so long as Nell was sheltered thereby. She was strong enough. Her cousin, sobbing quietly in Hen's maternal arms, was not, despite her earlier defiance.

'Others? What others?' Meraud's sibilant voice, hissing like a serpent, came from behind her. Alathea's arm was grasped, painfully. 'Who else knew? What do you know? *Where have they gone*?'

'You won't catch them now,' said Alathea, putting all the contempt she felt for Nell's mother into her face and voice. 'All your scheming has gone for nothing – by this time they will be married, and gone – and there is not one jot you can do about it, so you may as well accept the fact.'

Meraud's eyes were distended with rage, her mouth shaking. For a moment Alathea thought she would be struck, but she was no mouselike Nell, and the older woman obviously thought better of it. She whipped round to face Lord Bradfield, still standing at the head of the table with a face grey-white under the swarthiness. 'She defies me! The hell-spawned bitch defies me! Dear God, her father should have died after Colchester! Simon, she knows where they've gone – force her to tell!'

'How?' Alathea demanded, keeping her tone level and calm as Meraud's climbed remorselessly to screeching hysteria. 'I do not think torture would be appropriate, and I cannot see myself letting slip such information under lesser persuasion. You've lost them, your plotting is in ruins – why not admit it?'

'May I remind you, niece,' said Lord Bradfield, his voice grievously distorted with the power of his emotions, 'may I remind you that you are under my roof only on sufferance? And if you do not tell all that you know, immediately, you will be on the streets where you belong in five minutes – and all the other mischief-makers as well! By God, niece, you presume too much – how dare you meddle in my affairs? What right have you to rob me of my bride? What right have you to play the whore in my own house with scum such as Sedley – yes, I am not the ignorant country bumpkin you seem to think me, I have heard the stories, I know now what manner of man you have been entertaining in your studio. Your father's tainted blood shows in you too plain! Well? Will you speak, hussy? Or you'll be turned out now, and your snivelling cousin with you – aye, and your brother as well!'

'Math is innocent,' said Alathea. 'He knew nothing of any plot.'

'Since I have only your word for that, I do not choose to rely on it! Will you tell?' His voice rose to a shout. Becca, white-faced and frightened, put her hands over her ears.

'Math?' Alathea glanced round at her brother, who had been sitting silent all this while, his face showing a bewilderment now changing to anger as Lord Bradfield's language grew more intemperate. 'Math – I can't tell him – partly because I don't know for sure where they've gone, partly because I will not spoil their happiness to escape a brow-beating bully.' She heard her uncle's savage exclamation, and went on hardily. 'I'm sorry, Math.'

'That's all right,' said Matthew. His pale face, very similar to her own, reflected a like defiance. 'After the insults you've received, I wouldn't want to stay here anyway. Shall we go?' With astonishing aplomb, he rose to his feet and bowed to Lord Bradfield. 'I may also have reservations about Hugh's actions, my lord, but that does not excuse your base slurs on my sister's virtue and honour – and if I believed in such things, you would soon be receiving my challenge. Will you retract those insults?'

'By God, I will not!' Simon Heron said through clenched teeth.

'You insolent puppy, you're as bad as she is – tainted, both of you, ungodly creatures delighting in evil and deception – we are well rid of you, and your corrupting influence. Now go – get out – before I forget myself and do you some violence!'

'I trust we may send a cart for our possessions?' Math said, as if he were discussing a shopping arrangement.

Lord Bradfield spluttered, his voice incoherent with rage. At last, the words struggled out. 'Yes – so long as I do not have to clap eyes on the three of you – ever again, do you hear me, and anyone else concerned in this – I do not want you in my house, or consorting with any of my children – never again!' He turned, seeing a movement further down the table. Hen had taken Becca's hand and was ushering her from her stool. 'And where do you think you're going, Mistress?'

'With Thea,' said Hen. 'I don't intend to expose my daughter to such scenes again – and I certainly have no wish to remain here and listen to your insults. Goodbye, my lord – goodbye, Kit, Anne, Mary. Come on, Becca – we must go rescue poor Lovell.'

'But what about my starling?' Becca's high indignant voice carried back as she followed her mother through the door.

Alathea took Matthew's proffered hand and dropped a brief curtsey. She met Kit's vivid eyes, and could not blame him for remaining quiet. He had more to lose, after all.

'We will be gone in five minutes,' said Math, still in that calm, reasonable voice. 'You will not deny us five minutes to pack a few necessities? Someone will be sent tomorrow to collect the rest. Goodbye, my lord.'

'Wait!' It was Meraud's voice, taut with astonished rage. 'You are going – you are leaving, rather than tell? You fools, you have nowhere to go!'

'I'm sure we can find somewhere easily,' said Matthew, and sketched her a perfunctory bow. 'We do not lack for money or friends, after all. You need not worry about us, Cousin Lawrence – we will be quite all right.' And leaving her speechless and spluttering at his insolence, conducted his sister and Nell through the door in Hen's wake.

Meraud, robbed alike of her dignity and of her cold hollow mask, stood staring savagely after them, and knew the bitter truth: Francis Heron's family had defeated her once more.

CHAPTER TWENTY

An ill-starred wench

When weeping, sighing, fainting, down she fell
Whilst Knavery, laughing, rang her Passing Bell.
(Rochester (?), 'Plain Dealing's Downfall')

'A letter for you,' said Nell, coming into Alathea's studio one warm June afternoon. 'I think it's from Hugh.'

'Hugh?' Her cousin left the table, where she had been grinding vermilion – no colourman had ever supplied the colour sufficiently finely ground, and she always did it herself – and took the proffered epistle. 'At last – he's remembered us!'

'One of Dan's 'prentices brought it round, he had sent it to Fleet Street,' said Nell, sitting on the windowseat and staring anxiously at Alathea. 'Oh, I do hope it's good news!'

They had heard nothing of their errant half-uncle since his disappearance with Susannah, over two months previously. Those months had been a hectic, worrying time, fraught with recriminations, revenge, guilt and a family dispute that was better described as a war than a quarrel. Ejected from the Covent Garden house, Alathea and her supporters had gone to Fleet Street, and Lucy, jubilant at the success of her plans and dismissive of the consequences, had swept Dan's mild strictures aside and welcomed them with open arms, a course of action which called her eldest brother's wrath down on her head. Quite unabashed, Lucy had roundly informed him that he was a fool to become besotted with a girl less than half his age, and Meraud's daughter into the bargain, and then took him to task for his words to Alathea, which had lost nothing in Nell's recounting. The upshot had been her own forcible ejection from the Covent Garden house, with the melodramatic but terrifying command never to darken the door again. The rift was complete.

Dan, an essentially peaceable man, ignored his wife's tearful protests (for Lucy could be as stubborn in her quarrels as the rest of her family, given the chance), and bore his olive-branch to the Piazza, only to find it rudely spurned with an unpleasantness that ensured Lucy and Alathea and Hugh of his whole-hearted support from that hour onwards.

'Let him stew in his own bile,' said the normally calm, reasonable Dan, with a fervour that shocked his family. 'I want nothing more to do with the man. He may feel justly wronged, but there's no call at all for such offensiveness and insults.'

Only Kit and Anne, unknown to Lord Bradfield, had a foot still in both camps, and a series of messages arrived at the Fleet Street house advising its occupants of their wedding (to which, naturally, no resident of the House of the Ash Tree was invited), of Mall's betrothal to an effete young sprig of the aristocracy with a title, a great deal of money, an exquisite taste in dress, beautiful manners and no brains whatsoever (it was Kit's description), and of Lord Bradfield's intention to remove himself, as soon as his younger daughter was married, to Goldhayes to lick his wounds, leaving Kit and Anne in possession of the Covent Garden house. It was clear what Alathea's brother wanted her to do, but she had no wish to move back there. She did not want to compromise Kit with his father-in-law, and still less did she want to intrude on his new marriage and the awesome complications that might ensue. She did not know whether or not he still harboured some feeling for her, but she felt almost as much distaste for his match with Anne as she had for Lord Bradfield's with Susannah. She would leave them well alone, and make her life independently of anyone's charity.

Her search for new lodgings, a place self-contained and free of intrusive landlord, where she could paint and entertain her friends in peace and freedom, had led her here, to a tall house in Jermyn Street. It was the property of the Earl of St Albans, who owned pretty well every brick for some distance around, and had so far forgone his usual interest in gathering money as to rent it to her for half the usual sum. Even that was almost more than she could afford, but the house itself was splendid: of three storeys, it had a basement kitchen, a small garden for Lovell, a big first-floor room that would be adequate for dinner and supper parties, bedchambers enough for them all, and a long attic room that would suffice for a studio, and had a fireplace.

And above all, she was in the most fashionable and select part of town. She could number more Peers of the Realm amongst her neighbours than could Lord Bradfield in Covent Garden. To her delight, one of the residents in Jermyn Street proved to be Harry

Savile, Rochester's fat jovial friend and drinking companion, and though his duties at St James's Palace and at Whitehall, not to mention his giddy town life, meant that he was infrequently at home, he still seemed to find time to make regular visits. She had tidings of John Wilmot, who was in Bath and would shortly be at Adderbury, and pleaded for Harry's help in restoring Hugh to favour.

It had not, of course, endeared him to his new, royal master that Hugh had run off with someone else's bride not three months after his appointment as Groom of the Bedchamber, and there had been talk of imprisonment and dismissal when the errant courtier should return to London – probably fuelled by Lord Bradfield, whose rage knew no bounds and who had friends in Whitehall. But Hugh was a Jermyn protégé, and St Albans had just been made Lord Chamberlain of the King's household, and was high in favour. In consequence, protest was muted – for Hugh had not, after all, run off with an heiress of importance, and what were a manor or two in Warwickshire and a few neglected acres in Cornwall, compared to the vast dominions of most Court brides? Harry was able to report that on his eventual return, Hugh would face no more than a severe reprimand; his position was secure.

But, not knowing his whereabouts, it had not been possible to inform Hugh that he was safe from retribution, and this letter would doubtless give the vital information. Alathea ripped open the seal and her eyes flicked rapidly over the contents before she gave a laugh of relief. 'The insolent swine! Would you like to guess where he is?'

'Denby?' Nell suggested, naming Kit's Yorkshire estate. Alathea shook her head. 'No – much worse than that. He's at Goldhayes!'

Nell gave a gasp. Her cousin studied the letter again. 'Not staying at the house, you understand, but at the Home Farm with Hen's mother and stepfather – and if Lord Bradfield returns unexpectedly, he'd best look to his head! But it seems from what he says that he wanted Sue to see it – to see what stakes her mother was playing for.'

'Do they seem happy?'

'They seem happy,' said Alathea, looking down at Hugh's quick exuberant handwriting and wondering at the transformation of her cynical sophisticated uncle. It was obvious she no longer occupied her exclusive place in his heart – but she did not grudge Susannah her superiority.

'I wish we could go back to Goldhayes,' said Nell on a sigh. This exactly echoed Alathea's own feelings. She sent her a quick smile and then saw, with a stab of irritation, a single tear wend its way down her cousin's pale cheek. There was no denying, Nell looked ill, even more pinched and wan than usual. Perhaps she had caught the same fever as had laid Alathea low earlier in the year.

'What's the matter, Nell? Don't you feel very well?' She tried dutifully to put a note of gentle concern into her voice, and was rewarded by Nell's hunched shoulder and curt tones. 'I'm quite all right, thank you. Don't bother about me.'

Every line of her thin body spoke eloquently of martyrdom, and Alathea, with an inward sigh, decided to ignore it. 'Sir Cyril Wyche is coming in half an hour – we must make the canvas ready. Has Jonathan come back from the Beales' yet?'

'Not yet,' said Nell. The assistant had gone to collect a parcel of pink and lake made up by his cousin Carter, Mary Beale's colourman. 'Which canvas?'

'The larger – he wants a half-length.' Sir Cyril was Lord St Albans' brother-in-law, and a well-respected and rising man at Court. She had already painted his wife, a lively chatterbox little older than herself, for Lord St Albans' father had married again, late in life, and Elizabeth Wyche, née Jermyn, was forty years younger than her august half-brother. 'Help me put it on the easel.'

The two girls selected the appropriate canvas from the stack against the wall. It was heavy, stretched on a stout wooden frame, and over four feet high. Without Jonathan to lend his adolescent muscles to the task, they had to struggle to lift it on to the easel. At the critical moment, Nell gave a sob of pain and let go. Alathea, caught off balance, was left to carry the weight on her own and, not surprisingly, dropped it. The corner of the heavy canvas narrowly missed her foot. She jumped back, swearing under her breath, and stared at Nell, who was grey-white and sobbing in a confused huddle on the floor. 'Oh, Nell, what's *wrong* with you?'

'Nothing,' said Nell, plainly lying. Alathea sighed. 'You're ill for sure – have you a touch of fever? Why don't you go to bed, and Hen will make you up one of her possets, and you'll be as right as rain in a day or so – go on!'

'I'm *not* ill, nothing's wrong, leave me alone!' said Nell fiercely. She struggled to her feet, revealing a face blotched and uncomely with tears, and glared at Alathea. 'Stop nagging, will you – I'll be fine in a moment. I just want to sit down for a space, that's all.'

Fortunately, at that moment Jonathan returned, breathless, having run from Pall Mall with the precious pigments and an invitation to dine at the Beales' the next week. He helped Alathea to place the canvas on the easel and prepared the palette, by which time Nell had recovered herself and without a word was busy about her tasks. Puzzled and exasperated, Alathea greeted her client, and immersed herself in a discussion of pose and costume, trying gently to dissuade the flamboyant Sir Cyril from his wish to be painted in the attire of a Roman Emperor. If Nell chose to be awkward, that was her own affair.

Late that afternoon, in the warm sunshine, she took Lovell-our-dog and, with Hen and Becca for company, went for a stroll in St James's Park. Lovell was in ecstacies at the prospect. In contrast to his somewhat limited exercise in the garden at Lord Bradfield's house, the royal park, thronged with fashionable walkers, offered boundless opportunities for communion with other dogs, pursuit of the King's precious water fowl, and even a longing look or two at the deer, safely fenced away from potential harm. Alathea, aware that the penalties for molesting royal stags were high, always took a stout leash and a recurring vision of their ignominious ejection from the park with an unrepentant Lovell, some prized duck clenched between his jaws. It had not yet come to pass, but not from Lovell's want of trying.

They were a long time in the park, greeting acquaintances, skipping stones on Rosamund's pond, and throwing sticks for Lovell. It was close to supper-time when the four of them returned, Becca leading a panting Lovell and Alathea and Hen walking behind, indulging in cheerful gossip. The maid Sarah, who had loyally followed them from Covent Garden, opened the door and stared in surprise. 'Why, is Mistress Nell not with you?'

Something, some premonition of disaster, seized Alathea's stomach with icy fingers. Hen, briskly stepping within and wiping her feet quite unnecessarily, said, 'No, she's not – why, did she come out to meet us, then?'

'Yes – she said she felt a great deal better, and would go find you in the park,' said Sarah, her pleasant face anxious. 'And I nearly stopped her – I thought she looked so strangely – and she was wearing her cloak.'

A heavy cloak would be entirely superfluous on such a sunny June day. Alathea and Hen exchanged glances. 'You don't suppose she's gone to meet a lover, do you?' said the younger girl, forcing a joke.

'Nell? Be serious,' said Hen. 'Where would Nell find a lover?'

'She's been behaving very oddly of late, but I thought she was ill. Sarah – was she carrying anything under her cloak?'

The maid stood deep in thought, her finger to her mouth and her brow furrowed. Then she said slowly, 'She *may* have been – I couldn't see that she wasn't, if you take my meaning, you could carry half a trunk under a cloak and not have it noticed.'

'And how long ago did she leave?'

'Oh, not long after you'd all gone, Mistress Alathea – not long at all, five minutes or so, she said she'd catch you up. I *thought* it was odd,' said poor Sarah. 'I should have said something to her – that I should – I'm sorry!'

'Don't worry – she's probably hunting for us in the park at this very minute,' said Alathea with a confidence that she did not feel at all. 'But before we go back to find her, let's just go upstairs to our chamber.'

The note lay, white and forlorn, on the table by the window in the bedchamber which Nell shared with her cousin. It was addressed to her in Nell's round, childish, painstaking hand, and Alathea picked it up with fingers that were not quite steady. Nell must have run off – but in God's name why? And where would she go?

Alathea unfolded the paper, her heart hammering suddenly, and stared down at the two or three mis-spelt lines contained within.

'Deer cousin, I cannot stay heer any longer with my shame. I do not want to be the butt of all the town, so I am going back to Ashcott, and if I should die on the jerney you will be spared all further trubble from your cousin, Eleanor Heron.'

She gazed down at the pathetic note, her mind refusing to acknowledge the truth.

'What does it say?' Henrietta demanded, at her side, and with a sudden gesture of irritation, Alathea thrust it into her hands and walked to the window. From here, she could see the rooftops of St

James's Square and, more distant, the trees of the park and the towers of Whitehall and Westminster. Out there, perhaps, Nell had met her fate, and had suffered and fled for it.

'The sawny little fool!' Hen's round, country scorn burst into her reverie. 'She must have gone and got herself with child!'

'That's what I understand it to mean,' Alathea said, turning away from the window. 'But in God's name when? And who? And where?'

'I can make a guess at who,' said Henrietta grimly. 'Sir Charles Sedley, perhaps?'

'I don't believe it – not little Sid! He was *kind* to her . . . ' Her voice trailed away, remembering how Nell had blossomed under Sedley's attentions – and how 'kind' had more than one meaning to a Court gallant.

'*When* . . . ' Henrietta continued thoughtfully. 'She doesn't show yet, and since it's her first child, she may not show as much anyway – so not later than six months gone at the outside. And two months for her to be certain of it – round about February or March it happened, I'll wager. When you were ill.' She stared at Alathea, frowning. 'We used to go to Foxhall, or St James's, or Hyde Park – and I suppose to a practised seducer there would be plenty of opportunity. We often split up – I was with Becca, or Lovell, Anne and Mall were usually there, Sedley took her for strolls – and dear God, I never suspected, never thought – not *Nell*!'

'I suppose she couldn't be mistaken?'

'Even if she was mistaken – and your courses *do* stop, if you're ill or haven't been eating enough – even if she was mistaken in that, surely not even Nell could think she was pregnant, yet still be a virgin?'

'I think I'd believe anything of her,' said Alathea despairingly. 'Of all the witless, stupid, self-pitying little *fools* – why run away? What did she think we were going to do, have her paraded through the streets as a fornicator? Good God, these days there's little enough shame attached to the odd by-blow or two – maids-of-honour pup with monotonous regularity, half the lords in England aren't their father's sons, and how many girls at Goldhayes or Ashcott go to their wedding already carrying a child? If the highest in the land sets such an example,' said Alathea with some bitterness, 'who is Nell to speak of shame and being the butt of all the Town Wits? They never noticed her, except for Sid.'

'I think lack of sympathy may have been her greatest fear,' said Hen quietly. Alathea caught the different note in her voice, and met her eyes. There had indeed been little sympathy in her outburst, she had received the news of Nell's plight with anger and irritation. Yet it had quite possibly, she realised, thinking back over her words that morning, been her reaction to Nell's silent pleas for help that had driven her to flight.

Poor Nell, she thought, for once without any annoyance. Poor Nell, always drawing the short straw: abandoned at birth by her mother, reared in a family who despite their kindness could not give her equal affection with their own children, growing up plain and shy, feeling unloved and unwanted, forever in Alathea's brilliant shadow, without the courage to make the best of her limited gifts, until, rejected by her mother for the second time, in terms which carried the utmost humiliation and contempt, she had been driven into the arms of the one person who had been kind to her, and taken an interest in her for her own sake – and in so doing, perhaps, had thought to experience a joy which Alathea had spurned. *She didn't have a chance*, thought Alathea, with sadness. *We none of us ever gave her a chance*.

'I think some of the blame is attached to me,' she said.

Henrietta, never one to mince her words, nodded in agreement. 'Yes, you should have been kinder – we all should. But to my mind, two people above all share the guilt for this: Sedley, if he is the father, and Meraud. But,' said Hen, practical Hen, 'it's not much use apportioning blame and beating our breasts. What are we going to do?'

'Do? What can we do?'

'Well, for a beginning we can't let her make her own way to Ashcott. She's ill, pregnant, ignorant – anyone of evil intent would find her easy meat. It's my guess she's taken a coach, or a carrier – how much money does she have?'

'Very little,' said Alathea, thinking of Nell, alone, virtually penniless, in desperate case, trudging to Oxford or taking her chance on the public stage-coach or in some smelly carrier's wagon all in amongst the goods. The thought was heartbreaking, and her duty plain.

'We must find her,' she said. 'I know there's not much hope of it, she has three hours start and we've half the inn-yards of London to search – but we *must* find her!'

But find her they did not, though she and Hen and Jonathan and Sarah went desperately from inn to inn, from St Giles to Holborn, until the sun set and it was obvious that Nell must be long gone. She had not taken the Flying Coach, because that would reach Oxford in a day and had left very early that morning: nor did any remember seeing a young woman of Nell's description boarding the ordinary Oxford stage. There was a stable lad at a Holborn inn who thought she might have been in a carrier's wagon, bound for Oxford, which had left some while before, but at this time of day the traffic was all in to London, and not outward bound. Despondently, they made their way back to the house in Jermyn Street, to be met by an anxious Matthew, who had come in after a hard day's disputation at the Temple and found only Becca, Lovell, the boy Tom, the cookmaid and two kitchen girls in residence, and none of them able to give a satisfactory explanation of the whereabouts of everyone else. He had it, in full measure, from his sister when she returned with the others from their failed trip to Holborn, and his decision, for Math, was quick and decisive.

'Well, if she's gone to Ashcott, I suppose someone must follow her in case she comes to grief. I'll go, if you like, as long as someone can tell them I'm in bed with a purple fever.'

'You should be careful,' was Alathea's comment. 'That's not the first time you've used that excuse.'

'I'm not very concerned,' said Math, with a careless shrug that would have reminded Lord Bradfield very much of his father Francis Heron as an insolent boy with too many ideas and not enough inclination. 'If Father does inherit Goldhayes, then I've no need to be a lawyer, have I?'

Alathea looked at her tall, fair, vague younger brother with mildly irritated affection. 'Don't count your chickens before they're hatched,' she said warningly. 'What's to say Lord Bradfield won't marry some other more willing young bride and produce a quiverful of male heirs?'

'His Friday face,' said Math, and grinned. 'Will you come with me to Oxford tomorrow? We can ride post, if your riding is equal to it, and if we start first light tomorrow morning, we might even overtake the coach – if she's on it.'

In the end, though, they hired two horses from a Holborn inn, for riding post was expensive and would be awkward should they miss Nell on the way. They wasted precious time making further enquiries in one or two inns that had not been checked the previous evening, and then the brother and sister set off, a little after nine o'clock of another warm June morning, along the Oxford road, past Tyburn and out into the country.

It was over fifty miles to Oxford, more than could be done in a day: certainly more than Alathea, who had not sat a horse in earnest for several years, cared to ride, Nell or no Nell. In addition, the blue skies rapidly clouded over and it began to rain a little after eleven, turning the dusty rutted road into a quagmire. Matthew, who had never had much patience with Nell and who had privately decided that he would put himself out no more than was necessary, proposed a stop at Uxbridge. They dined there, in a less than passable inn, the subjects of some curious glances from other travellers who admired them, so obviously brother and sister, a handsome pair despite their thorough soaking from the rain.

Alathea asked about coaches and carriers, but there was no information of any help. She wondered how much money Nell had really had – would she have had enough to hire a horse?

But jolting about on a side-saddle was not the way to travel if you were pregnant, and unwell into the bargain. She must be mad, thought Alathea, bleakly staring into her beer (the inn did not aspire to fashionable luxuries such as coffee or chocolate): mad, or driven by despair.

They pushed on after the rain had stopped, and spent an uncomfortable night at High Wycombe before making an early start the next morning. With luck, they would be at Ashcott before the sun set, and perhaps, Nell would be there before them.

It was a pity that Alathea's mind was so entirely taken up with her worries about her cousin that she failed utterly to appreciate the fresh, burgeoning beauties of the countryside around her. Oxford passed by in a blur of tiredness and anxiety, a snatched late meal at the Blue Boar which had been her parents' favourite inn from Civil War days, and then on: aching bones, weary muscles, and a level of physical discomfort that Alathea, lapped in London luxury, had not experienced for years.

And at last, beyond sunset, the familiar yellow stone of Deddington, and the valley of the river Swere – and the other side of it, Adderbury, where John Wilmot lived. She wondered briefly if he were there now, with his unknown wife and two children, and then Ashcott came into view, down the long avenue of elms towards the river, surrounded by green grass and willow trees. A nightingale sang, gloriously sweet, in the trees, and Math sent her an encouraging smile. 'Come on, Thea – we've done it!'

They had been seen. There were lanterns bobbing in the garden, and her father came out to take their horses. Even in the dimming light, she could see his face, long and serious, and foreboding seized her. 'Nell – is Nell here?'

'Yes,' said Francis Heron, briefly, and helped her down from the horse. All her joints were stiff and sore, and she found she could hardly walk, but she heard his next words clearly enough. 'She's here, and very ill.'

'Well, at least she's safe,' said Matthew, with weary relief. 'I hope there's some supper left – I could eat a horse.'

'You don't understand,' said Francis, his voice quiet and sombre. 'The doctor is with her now, and has given her over. Unless a miracle happens, which I doubt, Nell is going to die.'

That silenced Matthew. He glanced apologetically at his father and turned to go inside. Alathea, despite her exhaustion and the shock of the news, grasped Francis's arm. 'Is she really dying? The baby – did she lose the baby?'

'She lost the child, yes. She was brought here this afternoon by a carrier. She'd tried to ride here – she may have ridden all the way from London – and the carrier found her fallen from her horse on that lonely stretch of road near Steeple Aston, about five miles from here. She told him where she was going, and he very kindly went out of his way to deliver her, and the horse. But by that time she was in agonies. The doctor says it was already too late, the damage had been done. We sent Mun to Banbury for him, and he did what he could, but I don't think there's any hope.'

Alathea found she was crying. She brushed the tears from her eyes. 'Can I see her? Will she know me?'

'You may see her, certainly – but she has been in and out of unconsciousness for some time now. Your mother is with her. I don't think it will be long.' He paused, his eyes on her drained, exhausted face, and then said quietly, 'Thea – what happened?'

'To Nell? We knew nothing, none of us, till she'd gone . . . can I tell you another time?' said his daughter, doggedly. 'I don't want to be too late.'

Nell was lying in the bedchamber she had once shared with Sophie and Alathea. Her slight, wasted body hardly disturbed the blankets, and her thin face was as pale as the sheet. Her eyes were closed, and it took Alathea a little while to realise that she was, in fact, still breathing, so slight was the movement. The doctor was there, with all the paraphernalia of modern medicine, potions and bleeding bowls and knives and cloths, and in the middle of it lay Nell, her life quietly and gently draining away towards death, unheeding of any assistance.

Alathea met her mother's eyes across the bed. Their reunion would come later, but Nell, who had so little time left, must be first. She knelt down and took one limp hand in hers: so cold it was, on such a warm evening. Nell's eyelids flickered and then opened. Her voice, so faint that Alathea had to struggle to make sense of it, came with a note of recognition. 'Thea?'

'Yes – yes, it's me,' said Alathea. She had never presided over a deathbed, save Mab's, had never had this terrible feeling of powerlessness and grief. 'Nell, you sawny fule, why in God's name did you run away?'

'I didn't . . . want to . . . be nagged,' came the slow, halting reply.

There was no possible answer to that, save the one that Alathea gave. 'Nell – oh, Nell, I'm sorry – so sorry.'

Nell said something so feebly that she could hardly hear it. It sounded like, 'Don't bother about me.' Someone else perhaps might have struggled against fate, might have made an effort to escape such a death, but all her days Nell had made no resistance, and now was too late to make amends for the years of dismissive affection and kindly neglect. Too late, to mend a wasted life.

She did not speak again, but died some ten minutes after Alathea's arrival, so quietly that no one noticed it at first, despite their intent watch. The doctor pronounced life extinct, and began to gather up his remedies, and Alathea sat, mute and drained by the bed, unable to believe that Nell, who like the dog Mab had been under her feet all her life, was gone for ever.

And it was her fault.

That thought stayed with her, like the evil black dog of Suffolk legend which followed the footsteps of the doomed, and nothing could dispel it. She talked to her parents honestly, omitting nothing – her neglect of Nell's welfare, the attentions of Sir

Charles Sedley, her drastic misinterpretation of the course of those attentions, her brusque dismissal of the girl's distress – and not sparing herself in the process. She did not like having to explain herself thus, but her feelings of guilt drove her on. They remained with her during the funeral, a brief bleak service held at Adderbury Church, with few mourners outside the residents of Ashcott. She stood at the graveside with Sophie clutching her arm and weeping easy dramatic tears, and found that the only water on her own face was from the rain.

It took the powers of the Widow Gooch to bring her out of her depression. The ancient cornered her after supper, on the day of the funeral, and employed her usual mode of attack, without preamble or verbal niceties. 'Still moping, lass?'

Alathea stared at her with annoyance. It did not seem credible that Mistress Gooch could still be alive, yet she lingered toughly on, growing more and more dried-up and shrunken and withered, like a winter leaf, but preserving still a semblance of her youthful self, her eyes as sharp and her brain as shrewd and wise as it had always been. Dressed in deepest rusty, rustling black, she barely came up to Alathea's shoulder now, and it would not, it seemed, be long before her nose bent down to meet the chin jutting up.

'Well?' came the remembered cackle. 'Trailing around like a rainy day won't bring your cousin back – so why not try and forget her for a while, eh?'

'I can't,' said Alathea. It was no use attempting to deceive the Widow, and she did not even try. 'I can't forget her – I feel it was my fault – I failed her.'

'Rubbish – she failed herself,' said the Widow concisely. 'Oh, aye, I grant you she hadn't got much to offer – but we can't all be beauties or artists or heiresses, can we? We make the best of what God's given us, and if He's given you a plain face but a kind sweet nature, you should make that a virtue – not an excuse for thinking the world's agin you. You never had much patience with her when she was alive – why change now she's dead?'

'Because she *is* dead – and it's too late – and I feel I could have been more – more sympathetic.'

'But she'd been a moaning martyr all her life,' the Widow pointed out. 'There's an old story I heard once, you may know it – boy looks after sheep, gets bored, thinks he'll amuse himself – runs up to the shepherd crying "Wolf! Wolf! There's a wolf!" Shepherd goes to look – no wolf. Brat goes back to the sheep, and the next day same thing happens – after a while, bored with it, raises hue and cry after a wolf. No wolf. If *I'd* been that shepherd,' said the Widow with malicious glee, 'I'd have thrashed him then. Would've saved the bother of getting another boy. Anyway, to cut a long story short, the day after that there *was* a wolf.'

'Let me guess,' said Alathea, with something approaching a smile. 'The shepherd didn't take any notice – and the wolf in consequence dined very well!'

'You spoilt the ending!' Mistress Gooch complained, prodding Alathea's black-clad middle with the crooked stick she always used now to help her get about. 'Too quick for your own good, you are, lass – just like your father. You're right, of course – wolf gets brat, and probably half the flock as well!' She cackled, and then sobered suddenly. The stick came up again, to poke Alathea's ribs. 'But you see what I'm trying to say, lass? Eh? Nell, all her life, cries, weeps, moans – no one really believes her because little things upset her – things that you or I would shrug off like water off a duck's back. Then the time comes when she really *has* got something to weep about – and no one takes her seriously, and who can blame them, eh? I certainly don't – so don't blame yourself. Blame the man who seduced her, blame that hell-cat unnatural mother, blame Nell for not having the courage to make more of her life – but don't blame yourself.' Another prod. 'Understand? It's an order, from one a deal older and wiser than you. I'll be eighty-five next birthday, and I've seen more or less everything this wicked world has to offer, and nothing surprises me any more – I've seen it all. Nell was doomed, lass, she never had much of a chance in life – and it was because she never gave herself one! Understand? So don't you go fretting about something that wasn't your fault, that you couldn't have foreseen or avoided. If you still feel you made mistakes, errors of judgement, then learn from them, girl, don't brood on 'em and make your life and everyone else's a misery too. Grieve for her, that's fine – but don't put the blame where it don't belong.' Her bright beady eyes scanned Alathea's face, and a witchlike smile appeared. 'That's better! Feel more cheerful now?'

Alathea nodded, smiling in return. The old woman cackled. 'So – London suits you, eh? Painting all the lords and ladies? Found yourself a nice young man yet?'

'Several young men – though "nice" might not be the word to apply to them.'

'Like that, is it? Not in love? You look a little peaky to me,' said the Widow assessingly, 'though mind you, all your breed run to paleness and lots of lean. Except for Lucy, of course – still as plump and pretty as ever, your Aunt Lucy?'

And Alathea, laughing a little weakly, embarked upon a juicy and entertaining exchange of London scandal and gossip, and found after a while, with some sadness and a little guilt, that Nell dead was even easier to forget than Nell alive.

She spent two weeks at Ashcott, revelling in the fresh country air, the silence and the sunshine, the grass and freedom and emptiness, and found the rest better than any tonic. All the lethargy and depression seemed to be sloughed away from her like old skin, leaving her fresh and invigorated. She drew her parents, the Widow, her brothers and sister, the servants, the dogs, the house and gardens. No sooner had she put a piece of blank paper under her hands than it seemed to be filled, her fingers tingled with bursting and exuberant life. The days flew past until the reckoning came: a letter from Hen, offering sorrow and sympathy for Nell's death (the news had been sent to her immediately), and hinting tactfully at a queue of frustrated clients enquiring after their unfinished pictures, chief amongst them being Sir Cyril Wyche. 'I have told them of your bereavement, and most were satisfied with my explanation – but that will not last for ever, and probably not beyond the end of the month,' Hen wrote in her thick positive handwriting. 'And besides, your paints grow dry, so Jonathan says.'

So, with a heavy heart, Alathea packed her scanty baggage and bid farewell to her family. She was truly grateful for her parents' support and tact over the past weeks. They had listened to what she had to say, made no judgements, attached no blame. They knew, however much it might secretly grieve them, that she was her own self now, a child no longer but a woman grown, strong and independent, making her own life. Not for her the fate of Nell, crushed by circumstance: her path lay ahead of her, shining and beckoning, leading to fame.

She kissed Mun, who was seventeen, tall and surlily handsome, smelling of the stables and rough with his new beard, and he blushed. Sophie, clutching her spaniel Silky, cried enchantingly and said earnestly, 'Can't I come with you? When *can* I? I want to see a play!'

'Next year, perhaps,' said Alathea, glancing at her mother. Their eyes met with perfect understanding. Sophie, lovely and flirtatious, with that ruthless, innocent, yet knowing charm, would wreak far more havoc amongst her masculine rakehell friends than any Castlemaine or Gwynn, and Alathea did not intend to give her the opportunity to try.

So she and Math rode away from Ashcott towards London, at a much more leisurely pace than their outward journey. It took them three cheerful days, until at last they rode into Holborn in the afternoon sun, on the last-but-one day of June, and hired a hackney to carry them the last little distance to Jermyn Street.

Henrietta met them at the door, Becca and Lovell hopping with joy and excitement behind her, and her face heavy with news. 'I defy you to guess what has happened,' she said, as Sarah and Tom took their bags and cloaks.

'Bad news?' Math queried, his eyes roving round the familiar, sparsely furnished hall. Seeing it unburned, apparently unrobbed, he relaxed. 'What's happened, Hen?'

'Yes, don't keep us in suspense,' said his sister. 'Come on, Hen, what's happened?'

Henrietta looked from Math to Alathea and back again, and her smile was grim. 'She's won in the end,' she said. 'That woman's won after all.

'Meraud married Lord Bradfield yesterday.'

CHAPTER TWENTY-ONE

Woman's honour

Had we but world enough, and time
This coyness, lady, were no crime.

(Marvell, 'To His Coy Mistress')

Summer was always a quiet time in London. Those with country estates went home to look to the harvest, and escape the stifling, airless heat trapped between the tall buildings and in the narrow streets and alleys. Even St James's, new and spacious and fashionable, was not at its best in August, and most of the houses were shuttered and blank, empty of all but a handful of servants left behind for security.

Alathea was loth to admit it, but she was bored. There was another war with the Dutch, and a great sea battle at Sole Bay which, according to Harry Savile who had been present, had been nowhere near the great English victory it had been cried up to be. Savile was now back at Whitehall, but busy machinating for a new position: John Wilmot was in Somerset with his wife, and she had scarcely seen him over the past year, for he had been ill, and much in the country. She had had several letters, though: joking, fantastical, every one a different parody, one mocking the Bible, another aping a Royal Proclamation, a third in the style of a medical treatise, lugubriously lamenting his symptoms. And she treasured them with his poems, and did not think to wonder how this strange friendship might end, or be transformed.

A year and more since Nell's death, and sometimes still she missed her, as one might miss a shadow, a coloration in the air without form or substance, hardly noticed when present, and yet its absence leaving a lack, a sense of something lost which could not be replaced.

Yes, she grieved for Nell, with sad resignation, and had vowed, after her death, never to follow that same slippery path. John Wilmot's letters would be kept in her little box with his poems, to gladden her heart, but she, like Gloriana, would remain smiling and impervious to his blandishments, a player in the game of Love. It was a pleasant fantasy, and she indulged it sometimes, in her less realistic moments of daydream. The brutality of all the other games she had seen staged around her, the Wits who talked so coarsely about their conquests and seemed, however much they might pay court to her in particular, to have no regard whatsoever for women in general, also served to discourage her from entering the lists herself. And there were the legal matches she had viewed with such abhorrence: Kit and Anne, their marriage begun so inauspiciously in clouds of filial obedience and mercenary gain, stayed but a few months more in London, before leaving abruptly for Yorkshire after, the talk had it, quarrelling monumentally with Anne's father over his unexpected wedding. Nor, so town rumour whispered, did Lord Bradfield's younger daughter take any more kindly to her new stepmother. She was leading a life of merry luxury at Whitehall with her bridegroom, and since news of his marriage had not spoken to her father at all. It was hardly surprising that, given the complete animosity of the entire Heron family to his bride, Lord Bradfield had lingered only a few weeks in London after the wedding before leaving for Goldhayes. Alathea had since heard through an acquaintance in the Piazza that the lease on the Covent Garden house had been assigned elsewhere by Kit, so presumably, he and Anne did not intend to visit London in the future. She was glad for the sake of her own peace of mind, but sorry for Anne, immured in the wilds of Yorkshire with her moody, unpredictable husband.

Free of interference from the less benevolent of her relations, Alathea was happy in Jermyn Street. She was free of financial worries, too: despite the Dutch war, she had a waiting list of clients eager to be made immortal by her brush, and in addition, much to her delight, two lodgers swelled her income, for Hugh and Susannah, on their return to London, asked if they could share the house.

So there they all were, Alathea, Matthew, Hen and Becca, Hugh and Susannah, with their servants to tend to their needs, successful and happy in their various ways, and peaceful, despite the distant war.

A pity, that it was all to change so soon.

The very pretty girl walking purposefully along Jermyn Street drew all eyes, and not a few comments and whistles. The tall, scowling, fair-haired boy tramping beside her, fingering his sword, was all too evidently a country bumpkin, although the pickpocket who assumed him to be, therefore, an easy touch was sent sprawling to the gutter with a kick to follow him and a few well-chosen epithets that made his delicious companion giggle and blush.

'Mun! You shouldn't say such things!'

'What would you have me do? Call him a sweet deserving angel and give him a guinea?' Edmund Heron, harassed, uneasy and wishing with great fervour that he had never agreed to accompany his little minx of a sister on this harebrained escapade, glared at her. Sophie smiled enchantingly back and an overdressed gallant on the other side of the road, his eyes hooked and almost starting from his head, walked slap into one of the bollards put up to stop coaches encroaching on the pavement. His yell of pain passed quite unnoticed by the cause of it: Sophie was looking around at the tall, handsome, brickbuilt houses on either side of her, with interest and admiration.

'Which is Thea's, do you think? Perhaps that gentleman there will tell us.'

The gentleman, still clutching his injured foot, recovered miraculously at the approach of this fair vision, and bowed with a stupendous flourish. Asked the whereabouts of Mistress Heron's house, he proved quite ignorant, but when the words 'female artist' were mentioned, recognition swept across the smooth, immaculate face (by God, he's *painted*! thought Edmund, with horror), and the gallant offered to escort the lady to the door.

'That won't be necessary,' said Mun hastily. 'Which one is it?'

The gentleman, seeing the fearsome scowl and the practical-looking sword, decided that discretion was the better part of gallantry and pointed out the artist's residence. Sophie, charming with her thanks, might have lingered, but her brother hauled her ruthlessly away before she could display her most graceful curtsey.

'Ow!' she cried indignantly, rubbing her wrist. 'You were very rude – and he was such a nice helpful gentleman.'

'That prinked-up, painted powder-puff? Gentleman be damned,' said Mun. 'If you take everyone at their face value you won't last five minutes in London – and don't sulk,' he added warningly.

'I'm *not* sulking,' said Sophie, hunching a shoulder. 'But I'm sure you could have been more polite. You were rude to that gentleman in Holborn too, and he was only offering to drive me round Hyde Park and I would *so* much like to do that!'

'And drive wouldn't be all he'd want to do,' said Mun, mopping his brow. The sooner he delivered this explosive charge to his elder sister and escaped back to the uncomplicated life of Oxfordshire, the better. He had embarked on this journey at Sophie's insistence, finally decided by her threat to go on her own if he was going to be so boringly strait-laced, but he had not bargained for the havoc caused by her looks and her uninhibited behaviour. What made it worse was that he had a strong suspicion that she was very well aware of the effect she had on every red-blooded male between the ages of thirteen and eighty: indeed, one very aged gentleman on the public coach had almost had an apoplectic fit when in receipt of the full force of one of his sister's dazzling smiles. The family nickname for the child Sophie had been Mischief: all too apt, he felt, to describe both cause and effect.

They came to the door that the gallant had indicated. The porter, engaged to carry their baggage from the inn where the coach had stopped, deposited his burden (one small bag for Edmund, a stout box and two much bigger bags belonging to Sophie), and wiped his red and perspiring face: it was warm for September. Edmund, with considerable relief and some trepidation, hammered on the knocker and stood back. He knew that Alathea might well disapprove of this, and she was not one to mince her words.

He was right. His tall, fair elder sister, in her painting clothes, came whisking down the stairs to the entrance hall, summoned by a flustered Sarah, took one look at Mun and Sophie and demanded in astonishment, 'What in God's name are you doing here?'

Mun gave his little sister a prod in the ribs. Sophie turned and glared at him before saying, a note of petulance in her voice, 'You *promised* me I could come and stay with you in London! You said I could come when I was older, and I'm sixteen now, and I want to see a play!'

Alathea looked at her. There was little resemblance between them. Sophie took after their mother, and was small and light-boned with dark glossy hair and a heart-shaped face, but she had Francis's eyes, long and smoky green, framed by the longest lashes Alathea had ever seen. It was not, in repose, a face to break hearts, but the life and sparkle of Sophie's merry, selfish, heedless personality gave it great beauty. Alathea thought of her raffish friends, of Henry Jermyn and Harry Savile, John Wilmot and Lord Buckhurst and gentle George Etherege, who had not ceased to enjoy the pleasures of London to the full since his return from Turkey the previous year, and her heart sank. At least Sir Charles Sedley had somewhat retired from the society of the Wits. He had packed his insane wife off to a convent in Flanders, and was now living in domestic bliss out at Bloomsbury Square with a strong-minded Yorkshire woman who claimed to have married him. To do him justice, he had been genuinely sorry for Nell's tragic fate, and Alathea had often wondered whether her death had been in some part responsible for his new-found respectability. No, Little Sid was a danger no longer, but she could not vouch for anyone else, and there was a blatant yet innocent quality in Sophie's manner that boded ill for her future in wicked London.

'You did promise,' said the imp of mischief, on a quieter and more pleading note. 'And I was tired of waiting, so I persuaded Mun to bring me here.'

'Only because she said she'd go alone if I didn't,' Mun growled.

An awful possibility insinuated itself into Alathea's mind. She glanced at her brother and sister, still in their dusty travelling clothes, and said warily, 'Do tell me . . . do Mother and Father *know* you've come to London?'

'They do now,' said Sophie carelessly. 'I left a note, after all, and they should have found it – I put it on the table by my bed.'

'You mean to say you didn't even *tell* them?'

'Yes, I did – in the note!'

Mun looked uneasy, shifting his weight from one stoutly shod foot to the other. 'She said they wouldn't let her go, and she was determined. So we crept out yesterday morning, very early, and rode to Oxford and got seats on the stage.' He looked despairingly at Alathea. 'I know it was wrong – but you don't know what she's like, she'll get her own way in everything – and I couldn't let her go alone, could I?'

'No, you came with me, and it was very sweet of you,' Sophie told him gratefully. 'Though I still think you could have been more polite to people who were only trying to be kind.'

'Kind!' Mun all but choked. He turned to Alathea, his hands spread. 'You've lived here for years, you must know the sort of thing that happens – it was like putting jam out for wasps, bringing her here, and she *encourages* them!' And he proceeded to illustrate his point with several graphic anecdotes of their short walk from the inn to Jermyn Street, in terms which did everything to confirm Alathea's worst fears. It was no good – Sophie would have to be sent home.

But she was wise enough not to insist upon it happening immediately. Best to let the little minx have some taste of London life before packing her back to Ashcott; she would surely be less eager to repeat the experience. Alathea, feeling something of a hypocrite, gave Sophie a serious lecture on her behaviour, stood over her while she wrote an apologetic letter to their parents, doubtless waiting anxiously for news, and extracted from her a promise that she would return to Oxfordshire when told, on the understanding that any further jaunts to London would be strictly controlled. She rounded it off with a brief explanation of the dangers and pitfalls lurking in wait for an unwary and innocent girl let loose in London, and pointed to the sad example of Nell.

Sophie, to her annoyance, tossed her head. 'I'm not a silly simpleton to be gulled by the first man who pays me compliments!'

Alathea pointed out with some force that she had already been gulled by all those 'gentlemen' Mun had described so heatedly, and Sophie had the grace to look a little abashed.

Fortunately, the family took a hand. Lucy, with glee, treated her youngest niece to a prolonged and expensive shopping expedition, for, as she pointed out, if the child was to see a play, she should be tricked out in clothes that did not shout 'country'. Hugh showed her the sights of Whitehall and the park at St James's, and there was a splendid drive in Hyde Park, in Henry Jermyn's magnificent coach, which even Alathea secretly enjoyed, and which left Sophie dazzled with excitement and pride at the exalted circles in which her sister moved. They went to the Foxhall gardens, took boats upriver and down, saw the King's yachts and the countryside at Chelsea, hired a coach, rather less ostentatious than Henry Jermyn's, and drove out to Highgate for the day. Sophie was given no time at all to dally with any of the young men who seemed to appear as if by magic, bowing and complimentary, whenever her pretty foot was set outside the door of the Jermyn Street house. And at the end of the first, hectic week, Lucy's tailor had finished her new dress, and they could go to the play.

It was a pity, said Lucy, that Sophie had not come earlier to London. The Dutch wars had meant that the King and Court had stayed at Whitehall all summer, and in consequence the new Dorset Gardens Theatre had put plays on in July and August – including *Sir Martin Mar-all*, a perennial favourite. Now, as September drew to a close, there was little to see at either playhouse: a revival of *Henry VIII* at Dorset Gardens, with the much-mocked dancing angels, or a new play by Dryden at the Lincoln's Inn Theatre, Hart and Kynaston playing the chief roles. Lucy, who had had the misfortune to see an earlier performance of *Henry VIII*, declared that there was no choice at all, and after a fine dinner at the House of the Ash Tree, they repaired to Lincoln's

Inn Fields, to see the King's Company perform *Love's Assignation: or, Love in a Nunnery*.

It was a promising title, not fulfilled either in the play or in the acting. Admittedly, the King's Company were labouring under great disadvantages. Only nine months before, their fine theatre in Drury Lane had burned down, and they had been forced to cramp their style in the old theatre in Lincoln's Inn Fields, recently vacated by the Duke's Company who had gone to their new and splendid building in Dorset Gardens and were putting on spectacular shows with great success. But, as Lucy pointed out, it was quite possible to act well in a barn or a hayloft, and nothing could excuse the wooden voices or the forgotten lines. Sophie, however, was spellbound throughout, her eyes shiny, lips parted, her whole being lost in the spectacle before her. Not even the loud, derogatory comments from the pit could sever the enchantment, but Alathea, who had recognised the voices, paid very little heed to the play from then on.

There, below her, sure enough, she could see various very familiar figures: the rotund shape of Henry Savile, the tall dark Buckhurst, the cheerful shambling profile of Gentle George Etherege, famed for his idleness in all but the pursuit of women. Sitting in the middle of the group, his height unmistakeable, was John Wilmot, his voice louder than all of them in witty condemnation. Alathea wondered if he had seen her, and as if in response to her thought, he turned. She caught a glimpse of a smile, a brief wave of his hand and a face that even in the ruddy, flickering light of the candles looked ill, and then his attention was once more upon the stage. It was unfortunate that shortly afterwards a song was sung, easily the most accomplished item in the entire performance, and the words seemed to mirror exactly the confused state of her emotions.

Long betwixt love and fear Phyllis tormented,
Shunned her own wish yet at last she consented:
But loath that day should her blushes discover
Come gentle Night, she said
Come quickly to my aid,
And a poor shamefaced Maid
Hide from her lover.

Now cold as Ice I am, now hot as fire,
I dare not tell myself my own desire:

But let Day fly away, and let Night haste her:
Grant ye kind Powers above
Slow hours to parting love,
But when to Bliss we move
Bid 'em fly faster.

And again Rochester turned, as the actress sang, and his eyes met hers across the jostling, untamed crowds in the pit, and she knew what he was thinking, as clearly as if a window had been placed for her to look into his heart. Her own hammering suddenly, she looked away, trying to pretend that she had not seen; but she could not.

Three days later, a poem came, delivered to her door by a boy in street livery, rags and tatters. There was no letter, as usual, just that jagged writing, more distorted and hasty than normal, as if the writer had not been well, and her face burned like fire when she read it, though she had taken care to be alone.

Love bade me hope, and I obeyed:
Phyllis continued still unkind.
'Then you may e'en despair,' he said,
'In vain I strive to change her mind.

Honour's got in and keeps her heart:
Durst he but venture once abroad,
In my own right I'd take your part
And show myself the mightier god.

This huffing Honour domineers
In breasts alone where he has place:
But if true generous Love appears
The hector does not show his face.'

Let me still languish and complain
Be most inhumanly denied.
I have some pleasure in my pain:
She can have none with all her pride.

I fall a sacrifice to Love
She lives a wretch for Honour's sake:
Whose Tyrant does most cruel prove,
The difference is not hard to make.

Consider real Honour, then:
You'll find hers cannot be the same.
'Tis noble confidence in men:
In women, mean mistrustful shame.

'Mistrustful shame!' Alathea, for once apparently really angry, hurled her words at her unrepentant visitor.

John Wilmot, smiling ironically, sat on her chair, by her studio fire, drinking her wine, and said mildly, 'If words were brickbats, we'd both be dead by now.'

'Sometimes I wish they were,' said his hostess, with some venom. 'You know full well why I haven't given in to all your blandishments – and honour is only one reason for it. Mistrustful shame, indeed! Are men so much more to your taste, then?'

'What talk have you been hearing, sweet Alathea?'

'None,' said Alathea, looking at him more narrowly. 'However, the aroma of rat is suddenly overpowering. Nor do you look well, despite a summer in the country.'

'No other woman I know could go from abuse to concern in so short a space – my felicitations!' He tossed down the wine and stretched his long legs comfortably towards the fire. 'So – is that delightful creature with the curls and dimples really your naughty little sister? How old is she?'

'Sixteen – and much too young for a confirmed old rake like you.'

'And you are twenty-three – be careful, my Thea, the bloom of youth does not last long.' His eyes, dark-ringed in his pale, sensitive face with its overtones of irony and humour, humanity and cruelty, acquired a far-away look which boded no good. Alathea surreptitiously took up paper and chalk and began to sketch him. He was not so abstracted as she had supposed. 'How dare you presume to record me in the Act of Creation!'

'How dare you presume to such pomposity!' She laid down the paper, seeing that she would have no peace if she did not, and clasped her hands around her knees. 'To be serious, though, Sophie is not to be touched. I haven't forgotten what happened to poor Nell, and I've no intention of letting Sophie go down the same road. The trouble is, she's a born flirt and makes a habit of fluttering her eyelashes and giving come-hither looks: then she complains when gallants assume she's no better than she appears. And to cap it all, she's besotted with the stage!'

John gave a shout of laughter. 'Better and better! Are we to see a new ornament at Dorset Gardens, then?'

'Absolutely not,' said Alathea, laughing despite herself. 'She's impossible, the little minx – she'll drive me to the bottle if I don't take her back to Ashcott soon. Do you know, we have been to that tedious play of Dryden's four times this week – I notice you only went the once – and a stupid play called *The Citizen Turned Gentleman* which no one likes and everyone goes to see, and she has all the lines by heart and quotes from them incessantly – *and* we had to go behind the scenes at Dorset Gardens and speak to the actresses and she kept poor Mistress Betterton occupied fully an hour with her questions, until I was ready to sink through the floor. And as if that wasn't enough, your lecherous friend Etherege came in with some cronies and I damned nearly had to prise him off her with a chisel. But that hasn't put her off – not a bit of it, she's convinced she'll make a magnificent actress.'

'Then why not let her do as she wants? You followed your own path – why can't your sister do the same?'

'Because the word "artist" is not synonomous with "whore"! Oh, I know there are some virtuous women on the stage – Mistress Betterton, for one – but I'm sure you know better than I, how rare they are. Girls become actresses because they hope for advancement – it's more exciting and better paid than a servant's job, and if they're noticed by gentlemen who will take them under their protection, so much the better. Nell Gwynn, Moll Davies, Peg Hughes, Roxalana – all gone the same way, and many more besides. And what happens when the gentlemen tire of them? Cast off to become common whores, most often. Even you,' said Alathea, with a wry glance at her guest, 'even you have to admit that Sophie deserves a better fate than that. She's very pretty, she'll have some small portion and perhaps a greater one – she could make a reasonable match for herself. And besides,' she added honestly, 'I don't think I could face Mother with the news that I'd let her become an actress.'

'And what if she has a gift, as you have? What if, with a little coaching, she could become a brilliant player? Or is there one law for Alathea, and another one for Sophie?'

Under his mocking, teasing gaze she was silent, knowing the truth of it, and yet still utterly determined not to give Sophie the chance to prove herself. At last, more gently, he said, 'Nell haunts you still, doesn't she? Why cannot you forget her? She directed her own fate.'

'I know – I have been told that before, by a splendid old harridan who would soon put you firmly in your place, but she's another story. You are right, I can't forget what happened to her. I think I would be stronger metal in the same circumstances – and perhaps Sophie too, though I don't know her well enough to say for certain.'

'She's your own sister.'

'Yes, and I've seen her perhaps three or four times in the last ten years. Mun likewise. And you know what *he* wants to do? Join the fleet!'

'A very laudable wish for a young gentleman of warlike disposition,' was John's dry comment. He had met Edmund Heron briefly, and had not been particularly impressed. 'I served on the *Revenge* at Bergen, with poor Sandwich who was killed at Solebay – and Harry Savile was at Solebay too, so why not your martial Mun? It keeps him from mischief, and there might even be prizes to be won. One glimpse of that fearsome scowl, and the Dutch will crowd on all sail and run back to Holland with their tails between their legs.'

Alathea laughed, but had to admit that he was right, and certainly, if her brother's glowering surliness was the same at Ashcott, she could not imagine her parents objecting. She came to a decision and smiled. 'It's an excellent idea, in which case, Mun may go to the fleet – can Harry speak for him, do you think? – and I shall have to escort young madam home to her country retreat.'

'You may yet find that all the ploughboys have committed suicide for love of her!'

'Better that than all the Wits – who die for love in quite another sense.'

'Oh incomparable Alathea – the unique, the nonpareil, the matchless – a wit, a beauty, an artist, twenty-three and the oldest virgin in London! You see patience on a monument,' said John Wilmot severely. 'What other man would have stayed constant for so long?'

'Inconstant, you mean – yes, I heard all about that doxy Foster from Harry Savile – he seems to think I need protecting from you. And there is also the little matter of your wife.'

'My wife? Ah, yes, Elizabeth. Which reminds me – if you are going to Ashcott soon, will you take the children some presents from me? I have been casting about in my mind for some poor, trusting fool to oblige, but you will do as well – no, don't please throw that, it will do damage if it hits me, and your aim is too true for comfort.'

'Very well,' said Alathea, putting the wine-cup down again. 'What presents are you sending?'

'A dog – a King's dog, no less, for my son: that should bring a smile to his face, he's like Hen's little girl, he loves all animals, even Strephon. He hasn't been well recently, and he's only a baby, just walking, babbling: an engaging brat, given his parentage. And for my Nan there's a doll, one of those French ones tricked out in the latest Paris gown, the image of Mademoiselle de la Vallière. Well? Are you equal to the burden of conveyance? Will you be my ambassador to my neglected, put-upon, mother-hounded wife, and bear these valuable gifts?'

So it was that, some ten days later, having deposited her unruly sister at Ashcott, and greeted her parents, Alathea took one of her father's grooms as escort and his favourite horse to ride, and travelled the two miles or so to Adderbury, the place of Nell's burial and also, after some Civil War skirmish, of Hen's and Jasper's father. It was also the home of John Wilmot, Earl of Rochester, and of his wife, his mother and his two children.

The groom carried the puppy, which was one of the King's silken spaniels, probably whelped in the Royal Bedchamber or even, if rumour spoke correctly, on the Royal Bed. She had commented wittily on the animal's connection thereby with certain exalted young humans, and made John laugh. The doll, secure within layers of soft paper and cloth, was a magnificently clad creature some eighteen inches high, with a haughty expression. She could not imagine it lasting very long as the plaything of a three-year-old girl, unless the Lady Anne Wilmot were exceptionally gentle.

The house was a little distance beyond the church and the rest of the village. A pleasant place in the local golden stone, it had evidently been enlarged quite recently, and stood amidst wide, well-tended gardens, bounded by a high stone wall. Alathea, with a mixture of nervousness and curiosity, dismounted at the steps leading up to the front door, and asked politely if the Countess of Rochester was at home. She was shown into a large airy chamber on the first floor of the house. Behind her, the footman had the doll, and Alathea, using all her experience of dogs, held the puppy in her arms and prayed that it would not disgrace itself.

The girl who greeted her was, to her surprise, probably almost as young as herself, and pretty, with dark eyes and fair hair and a plump figure, well-dressed in yellow satin. Looking slightly askance at the dog, she said, after an exchange of courtesies, 'Mistress Heron? I have met your father and mother several times, and they speak well of you – and you are the picture-drawer, are you not?'

Alathea admitted that she was indeed, and the girl who had once been Elizabeth Malet, the heiress of Somerset, pursued by half-a-dozen rich and titled suitors, gave a conspiratorial smile. 'Please, don't call me "my lady". I am Betty to my friends, and I would like you to be one of them too – especially since you painted that picture of my husband.' She smiled. 'How on earth did you persuade that monkey to sit still?'

'I glued him to the table, and painted very quickly,' said Alathea with solemnity. She caught the other girl's eye, and they burst out laughing.

'Perhaps you could paint me for a companion piece,' said Elizabeth, when her mirth had ceased. 'When I next come to London, perhaps . . . but then I don't often have the chance of it,' she added a little wistfully. 'But do tell me – why have you that wriggling little dog? Why is poor Ned standing there with a parcel bowing him down? Has my husband been importuning you?'

He had indeed but not quite in the way Elizabeth had in mind. Alathea, with some uneasiness, produced the letter that John Wilmot had written, and handed it to his lady. 'I think this will explain it.'

'I have my doubts about that,' said the Countess, with a rueful smile. She broke the seal, scanned the brief lines within, and laughed in delight. 'Oh, how very like him – do listen! "Madam, This illustrious person is my ambassador to my son and daughter. The presents she brings are great and glorious and I hope will gain her an equal reception." Which reminds me, would you like some refreshments? Ned, do put that down and go bring us some tea – would you like tea?'

Alathea said that she would, very much. The footman disappeared. Elizabeth continued with the letter.

' "To my son she will deliver a dog of the last litter of lap-dogs so much reverenced at Indostan for the honour they have to lie on cushions of cloth of gold at the feet of the Great Mogul. The dog's name is Omrah. To my daughter I have sent the very person of the Duchess la Vallière, late mistress to the King of France, dried up and pined away to a very small proportion by fasting.' And the wretch doesn't even sign it! But how kind – the children will love them, though I do not think my mother-in-law will care very much for poor Omrah, somehow. But isn't he delightful!'

The footman, entering a few moments later with tea and cakes, was entertained to find his titled mistress sitting on the floor with her guest, playing with the puppy and a screwed-up piece of paper. He retired, bowing, with orders to tell the nurse to bring the children, and shortly, John Wilmot's son and daughter were ushered in.

The girl, Nan, was very like her mother, big for her age and chubby. She made a wobbling curtsey and gazed curiously at Alathea without the least trace of shyness. Given the doll to unwrap, her podgy fingers fumbled with the cloth and paper and Louise de la Vallière fell to the floor with a thump. 'Oh dear, she's fallened,' said Nan anxiously. 'Are you hurted, lady? Are you hurted?' And the august and shrunken person of the French King's former mistress was taken up and lovingly hugged.

'Thank Mistress Heron for bringing her to you,' her mother instructed.

The little girl obeyed with solemn politeness, before demanding urgently, 'Can I show her to Jane, can I?' And the doll was thrust into the nurse's hands for her approval.

The little boy meanwhile, with the unsteady, purposeful stagger of the very young or the very drunk, had made his determined way to Omrah and was now clasping the unfortunate animal to his bosom. Undoubtedly the gifts were a great success, and over the next hour or so, Alathea conceived a great liking for Elizabeth, Countess of Rochester, and her children. It was hard to believe that John, by his own admission, could be so neglectful and unfaithful to so pleasant a lady, but she suspected that he would be unfaithful to any wife, however beautiful, witty and wise. Elizabeth belonged to the country, and in the country he was hers: in the town, or at Newmarket or Windsor, it was another matter. Alathea could understand it, a little, for the difference between the two worlds was so vast, and she herself had felt the gulf, had experienced the change in character and behaviour in herself at Ashcott and at Jermyn Street. But it was evident that Elizabeth did not: she had married hastily, for love, and wanted love, constancy and faithful attentiveness in return. Unfortunately, she had picked the wrong man.

They parted in friendship, with promises to meet again if opportunity demanded it, and Alathea made her thoughtful way back to Ashcott and a hearty supper. Seeing Elizabeth, so open and friendly yet so obviously loving her scapegrace, ungrateful husband, had increased her determination to resist all attempts at seduction. She would not fall into the same trap as Nell, and all the other countless young women of more or less good family who had gone to the bad in London. *There's one set of morals for men, and another for women,* thought Alathea with some grimness, *but if it could be arranged that men produced the infants that are the women's badge of shame, I'd wager long odds that the situation would change soon enough. I'll be left with no one's love-child, and respectable fingers pointing at me. I shall live independently, and paint, and be damned to stupid taunts about woman's honour.*

There was another poem waiting for her at Jermyn Street, when she returned from Ashcott: no gentle persuasion this, no polished compliment, but brickbats in earnest, and as she read it, she found herself weeping.

Phyllis, be gentler, I advise
Make up for time misspent:
When beauty on its deathbed lies,
'Tis high time to repent.

Such is the malice of your fate
That makes you old so soon,
Your pleasure ever comes too late
How early e'er begun.

Think what a wretched thing is she
Whose stars contrive, in spite,
The morning of her love should be
Her fading beauty's night.

Then, if to make your ruin more,
You'll peevishly be coy,
Die with the scandal of a whore
And never know the joy.

It was too much. He had gone too far and, as Hen had once

predicted, he could be terrifyingly cruel. Honesty compelled her to keep the poem, one more plot on the chart of their friendship, and one which had run her on to rocks. She knew he showed his poems to his friends. She herself had inspected one or two, addressed to other ladies, or mock pastoral pieces to make her smile, and she grew hot to think that Buckhurst or Etherege had seen this – even if they did not guess (and they surely would) the identity of 'Phyllis'.

Age: she was not so old – more than two years younger than the poet, in fact. But compared with Sophie, with the fashionable actresses (and Nell Gwynn had been a King's mistress at eighteen), she was losing the bloom of youth. It did not matter – it was ridiculous – her face was not her fortune, she had other gifts. But deep within her, only just beginning to be acknowledged, was the truth: that she had never cared about her appearance because she had never had to – she could have looked strikingly beautiful in rags. And despite her contempt for people who judged her by her looks, it was undeniable that her ostensibly despised beauty had brought her fame and friendships that she might otherwise not have had.

And Nell, poor, down-trodden Nell, had never had any beauty to start with, and never any self-confidence, either.

She did what she had never done before, and examined her face closely in the mirror. It seemed exactly the same as it had always been, as Samuel Cooper had depicted it in his miniature of her, left unfinished at his sad death early that year. She pulled a grimace at it, and forced a smile, thinking what the Widow Gooch, or Hen, would have to say to such foolishness. But the worm of doubt remained, nagging: she had been hit in an unsuspected and vulnerable place, and it hurt.

When he was announced, a few days later, she sent down a curt message to say that she would not receive him, and got a childish satisfaction from it, even if she did then tip-toe stealthily up to the window of her parlour to see him walk away with, possibly, a slightly disconsolate look about the set of his shoulders. It was typical of the confusion and conflict within her that she should then regret her action most bitterly, and found herself looking for him in the park, in the Ring at Hyde Park, in Spring Gardens, at the theatre.

In vain. She assumed he had returned to Adderbury, and tried to be glad, for Elizabeth's sake. Harry Savile had gone to Paris as Envoy Extraordinary: there would be no news from him. Henry Jermyn, unasked, volunteered the information, one day late in November when she encountered him at the theatre, that Rochester was ill, with the stone or, more like, something less respectable, and confined to his lodgings. He then uttered a scandalous aside which showed that his view of her relationship with the wickedest rogue in London was very much exaggerated. Alathea snapped at him, while the last lines of that poem clattered mockingly inside her head:

Die with the scandal of a whore
And never know the joy.

It was quite true – all London thought her his mistress already, so why not live up to the rumours?

Why not, indeed? She knew enough about herself, now, to realise that she was hovering on the brink of love, of a passion so strong that she did not know if she could cope with such a force. She had few illusions about the man all his friends declared to be three-quarters devil with an angel's tongue, Lucifer indeed, whose words could tempt angels, not to mention Alathea Heron, to a second fall. She was in love with his face, his voice, his laughter and strangeness and the wild fantastical shores of his mind. Even the cruelty of that last poem had hurt her mainly because it had shown her the truth. The only reason she was, in his taunting words, the oldest virgin in London was her fear – fear of the unknown, of dishonour, of a lowering of her esteem in her own eyes and those of her friends. And in the long dark days approaching Christmas, she knew at last what she would do, if he ever gave her another chance: but she would not, never, ever, go importuning to Portugal Row.

CHAPTER TWENTY-TWO

Something of the sea

Joy ruled the day, and love the night.
(Dryden, 'A Secular Masque')

'There's a fearsome rogue below,' said Henrietta. 'He says you must see him, and I can't get rid of him – he swears he'll stay there till Doomsday if necessary.' She stared at Alathea, a frown between her thick reddish brows. 'What can he want with you?'

'I don't know – I have several people among my acquaintance who might be described as "fearsome rogues". Did he give a name?'

'Henry Lee, he said,' Henrietta told her. Alathea frowned, turning to look out of the window. It was past four o'clock of a cold, windy January day, and few people were abroad: snatches of fine snow swirled down between the houses and were swept madly up again on a gust of wind, seemingly destined never to fall to earth. She was bored: Mun was with the fleet, and Matthew and Oliver, having more or less completed their education, had gone on a jaunt to Paris at the invitation, very kindly, of Harry Savile. Hugh was occupied at Whitehall and Susannah in bed with a heavy cold. She had just completed her only sitting of the day, a young and silly maid-of-honour with a good deal of conversation and no discernable wit, and she wanted some relief from tedium. 'I don't know any Henry Lee – perhaps he's a colourman, or a frame-maker. Did he say what his business was?'

'Not at all – he said only that it was most important he see you.' Henrietta's disapproval increased as she saw Alathea's curiosity. 'Shall I get Tom to see him off?'

'No – perhaps he has a message for me.' Alathea gave her friend a quizzical look, head on one side. 'Fearsome, did you say? Do tell me, Hen, what on earth does he look like?'

'Dressed in rags, probably crawling with lice – filthy face, villainous eyes, a great black periwig which looks as if it's a cast-off from Dorset Gardens, and a huge, old-fashioned cassock-coat that probably belonged to Henry the Eighth,' said Hen. 'You *can't* want to see him, Thea – the floor will never recover.'

'Well, I do – and I will. I'll see him in the studio, and then the fleas will be poisoned by the paint,' said Alathea, and hurried from the room before Hen could make any more objections.

There was still a fire in the long room at the top of the house. She lit candles, wishing for warmer weather, and sent Jonathan, who had all but finished his duties, downstairs. Shortly afterwards, she heard footsteps, and the boy's voice, breaking now and hilariously poised between gruff and squeak, giving directions. And then the mysterious Henry Lee entered her studio.

He was quite as villainous as Henrietta, not given to exaggeration, had described. He stood hunched and surly in the doorway, twisting in his hands an ancient beaver that had seen better days some thirty years since, and glowering at her. 'Mistress 'Eron?'

'Yes?' said Alathea politely, checking that the varnish pot was within reach if necessary – he did have a most ferocious appearance. 'Have you some message for me?'

'Yur, reckon I 'ave.' And a grimy hand fumbled in the disgusting rags and brought forth a tattered, scruffy piece of paper, which he thrust ungraciously at her. Alathea took it, knowing already what it must be, and broke the seal.

Yes, it was a poem, but not his. She recognised the two verses, in his distinctive hand, as being the first and last of an old song by Waller, written before either of them were born, and not a plea for her forgiveness.

It is not that I love you less,
Than when before your feet I lay
But to prevent the sad increase
Of hopeless love, I keep away.

But vow'd I have, and never must
Your banish'd servant trouble you:
For if I break, you may mistrust,
The vow I made to love you too.

She smiled as she read it – no apology, and a pretence that it had been he who had banished himself: but he would have an answer, after all.

'Will you take a reply?'

'Yur, might.' The rogue looked hopeful: she added, 'You'll have a shilling for your trouble if you will deliver it soon. Wait, while I write.' She went over to the desk, uncorked the ink, chose a quill and after a moment's thought, a forgotten smile on her face, began to write in the same metre.

Dear fool, when I sent you away
And vow'd I'd never see you more
'Twas angry pride ruled me that day,
And bade my heart declare this war.

But now my heart lays down its arms
And bids the truth be known to you
My pride is vanquished by your charms,
I hereby vow to love you too.

She read her handiwork over, quite pleased. It did not say exactly what she wished, she was not skilful enough for that, but it was tolerable doggerel, for a complete beginner. She reached for the sand. It was whisked out of her grasp by some incredibly grimy fingers, and a well-remembered voice said behind her, 'You show some promise as a poet – although I object most strongly to being dubbed a fool.'

Alathea whipped round, to behold the offensive presence of 'Henry Lee', smiling John Wilmot's smile and speaking with John Wilmot's voice. She stared at him in total confusion and astonishment, and then began to laugh. 'It's I who's the fool – you gulled me completely! Henry Lee, indeed – who's Henry Lee, apart from being what Hen described as a "fearsome rogue"?'

'He was my lamented half-brother, lately deceased. I didn't think he'd mind my theft of his name, but I fear he would be most insulted to find himself described thus.' He bowed ironically. 'You were convinced, then?'

'Yes, oh yes – I could see the lice crawling. What in God's name possessed you, to disguise yourself like that? What did you do, roll in the gutter?'

'No – should you ever feel tempted to try the same, soot is most effective. And I promise you, no lice – or at any rate, not many, I took care to smoke these over the fire before I put them on.' He gave her his brilliant, dazzling smile, hilarious with exuberant mockery. 'Well? I make a good rogue, it seems.'

'Most excellent, sir – and your garments only heighten the effect.'

'Pest! You'll insult me too often, one day.'

'I didn't think it *was* possible to insult you.'

'But I insulted you.' Suddenly serious, his dark eyes held hers. 'I was desperate to use any weapon I could – and that was the last in my arsenal. I know it was cruel – but as in my lampoons, I tend to use whatever fits the sense, the rhyme, the metre, and ignore such unimportant matters as truth, or kindness to a friend!'

'But it hurt precisely because it *was* the truth.' Alathea stared at him, the lovely planes of her face emphasised by the contrasting light and shadow from the candles, her eyes very wide and dark. 'All the town thinks me your whore already – why cling to virtue from fear, when all my instincts run the other way? Why dwindle into middle age, wedded to my brush and paints, never having known love, or joy, or passion – and incomplete? So – my answer is true.' She touched the paper, and smiled. 'I have changed my mind, dear Lucifer. Like you, I shall swear no constancy, make no vows or contracts, impose no chains or conditions – I shall only promise to love you, as I have loved you for years and never admitted it.' She added, with a hint of her usual irony, 'And if you think I am making too much of this, pray remember that for me this is a huge leap into the dark, and for you, just another conquest to be added to your list.'

'You misjudge me,' he said quietly. 'I am not made to love one woman exclusively, and for ever – I don't think any man is. And so, like you, I make no promises save that the limits of my passion are bounded by joy, and where pleasure ceases, so do we. But I would have you for my friend, always, whatever should happen between us as lovers, for no one else has quite your eye for my faults, and can insult me so wittily, and I do not want to be wafted up to Heaven puffed up with my own conceit and other people's flattery.'

'Heaven? You assume greatly – or have you blackmailed St Peter?'

'No blackmail of anyone – I was just tempting you to further brickbats,' said John Wilmot, and smiled, and held out his hands. 'So – will you seal our bargain, my dearest Alathea?'

'Not until you've washed,' said his mistress, severely. 'I have no wish for unexplained handprints in stretegic places all over my dress. I've only a hazy idea of what I desire in a lover, but one thing I do know is that he ought at least to be *clean*. Dirty sheets are so difficult to wash in London.'

'Oh, you are unique indeed,' he said, smiling wider. 'And how I love you, to madness and beyond, how you have haunted my thoughts for three years – and have you really changed your mind?

Are all my dreams really about to come true?'

Their eyes locked: she could not look away. As if drawn by his power, she found herself drifting towards him, trapped in a spell of passion that cast out all memory and thought and rational logic, and left only this moment, these feelings, this man and herself the only beings in all the world, alone in the small light of the candles amidst an ocean of dark. Then she was in his embrace, heedless now of mundane matters like rags and soot, and his mouth came down to meet hers. And everything was forgotten, her fear for her self-respect and her power to paint, her fear of what everyone would think, her fear of unknown experience and undreamed-of emotions, the fear implanted long ago by Kit, all obliterated in the torrential force that swept through her, a hunger that had never been acknowledged or assuaged.

The kiss ended. She stared at him blindly, dizzy still with the power of her emotions and his, wanting it never to stop. He said softly, 'Come sup with me in my lodgings at Portugal Row. I have a cook almost as good as your dear Hen, and some excellent wine, and a bed as soft and wide as any in London – will you, my dear love? Can you wait, just a little while, until I'm clean?'

Alathea laughed, breathless, feeling his arms tight around her, and a sense of wonders and miracles inside her head. Nothing mattered now except the two of them – everything else was blotted out in the gathering dark. 'Yes – oh, yes.'

'Then I will send my coach for you. Don't worry – you're not very dirty. Shall I brush you down?'

She laughed again, and twisted out of his arms to turn this way and that in front of him. 'Where am I marked?'

'Here – and here – oh, sorry – here as well. Perhaps Hen won't notice.'

'Hen will – and will look on, and worry, and say nothing. I shan't mind her, they can all go to the devil as far as I'm concerned,' said Alathea, a wild note in her voice to match his own. 'For who would dare fly in the face of such passion?'

And for once, she was not being ironical.

He sent his coach for her, and it arrived a little after seven, in a swirl of powdery snow. She had told Hen quite openly where she was going, and left her friend to draw her own conclusions, which Hen, not liking them, did. For old times' sake, she put on the ivory silk, taking care to practise what she preached where cleanliness was concerned. There was no paint or powder, but the heady mixture of fear and anticipation made her eyes brilliant and her cheeks flushed, so that her face had no need of enhancement. Hugh was still at Whitehall, so she did not have to explain to him yet: of all her friends, his disapproval was what she most dreaded. She wrapped a thick cloak around her, muffling her from head to toe, and ran from the house to the coach, her feet and skirts making new patterns in the powdery snow.

It was bitterly cold. She had no companion in the chill darkness of the carriage, its blinds drawn against the winter, save her own thoughts. She had committed herself now, irrevocably, and she was glad despite her trepidation, for she was just beginning to realise that she had been incomplete.

She was ushered within the dark hallway at his house by an imperturbable footman, bowing as if unescorted young women came to his master's lodgings every day of the week – which they probably did, thought Alathea wryly. She was conducted upstairs, not to the big room she remembered from that day they had gone to Mistress Behn's first play, but to a smaller, more comfortable parlour with a roaring fire, curtained against the wind and cosy with tapestries which, she saw with interest, were uninhibited and evidently French. And there to greet her was her host.

The footman had taken her cloak. She curtseyed low, with laughter inside her head and a wild reckless joy, and saw as she rose the same emotions on his face. They came together and kissed, a long tender exploration and greeting, and then he said softly, 'You look very beautiful. Love becomes you, sweet Alathea, it does indeed. Do I satisfy your standards of cleanliness?'

'Let me look at you.' Obediently, he stepped back, smiling. He was wearing informal clothes, a shirt and breeches and one of the loose Indian nightgowns over them in soft, trailing grey satin. His head was bare of cap or periwig, and he looked younger, and somehow more vulnerable. Alathea smiled. 'I suppose you will pass muster.'

'I sincerely hope I do – my poor valet has worked hard these two hours and more, to remove all that soot, and has earnestly begged me never to attempt such a disguise again. I threatened to dismiss him for his impertinence: he threatened to leave my employ because of mine. He is French, so suffers from crises of temperament, but we deal well enough together – he knows to a nicety where is the line between good taste and foppery, which is useful.' He grinned. 'Which is more than My Lord Buckhurst's new valet, I fear. Would you like some wine? This claret is very good, and as you might expect, I have a great deal of it.'

'I must take it in moderation,' said Alathea. 'I'd like to be able to remember this night.' But she accepted the brimming, delicate glass he handed her, grateful for its warming and encouraging effect. She did not want to lose her virtue in cold blood.

The food was excellent and simple – pasties, oysters, a fricassee of chicken and a dish of anchovies, salty and flavoursome and chased down with fresh bread and cheeses and the wine – and they talked, exchanging anecdotes and gossip and bad jokes and laughter. Often their eyes met across the candlelight, and his hand would touch hers as if he could not keep away.

The servants came to clear away the remains of the meal, and their master bandied cheerful words with them as if they were his equals, a practice that surprised and delighted Alathea. When they had gone, leaving them to the fire and the wine, she said, 'I wonder you can get anyone to serve you at all, you're so rude to them.'

'Perhaps – but they give as good as they get. It may astonish you to learn that Alcock, for instance, has been in my service some years. He obviously thrives on brickbats. Did you know, by the way, that he has a drawing of himself by Samuel Cooper? It was done years ago when he was eighteen, and in the service of the Earl of Westmorland. Cooper was your tutor, was he not?'

'In some sense, yes, since I learned the art of limning from him, but only by watching him and observing his methods. I had him paint me,' said Alathea sadly, 'but he died before he could quite finish it, just before the battle of Solebay last year . . . such a shame, he was not so very old, sixty or so, no more – and the greatest painter of a face in all London, and probably in Europe.'

'Don't let Master Lely hear you say that.'

'If he wasn't so puffed up with his own importance, he would acknowledge the truth of it – Cooper was a far greater artist than any of us, and a very kind, good-hearted man into the bargain. I admired him a great deal – and I *wish* he'd lived long enough to finish my portrait!'

'You must paint yourself, sweet Thea.'

'No – I shall not even wear patches,' said Alathea, laughing. Her hands, relaxed at last, played idly with the slim stem of the wine glass, and her eyes were only for him: and he knew that the lucky moment, so often described in those pastoral poems, full of Chloes and Strephons, was upon them now. He rose, and came round the table to stand behind her, his hands on her pale, slender shoulders, so much more graceful than the plumpness of fashionable beauties, and yet still feminine, infinitely desirable. He slid his hand down over the warmth of her breast, gently exploring, feeling the quick rise and fall of her breathing. Then she rose and turned to face him, a smile surprisingly shy on her lips and her eyes vast with the power of her emotions, and he took her in his arms as if she belonged there, and they kissed again, with increasing fervour. His hands roved, touching, raising the passion within her to match his own, and after three years of waiting, suddenly neither of them could wait any longer. There was a rug before the fire. He guided her there, their mouths still locked, and laid her down on it, his hands caressing, unlacing, exploring. And on the Turkey carpet, soft and yielding under her body, Alathea Heron at last ceased to be the oldest virgin in London, and gave up her virtue gladly, with a passion that ignored any pain, and a wild and exclusive joy that she had never experienced in all her life before. At the end, she was dazed, breathless, aware only of the great wash of delirious pleasure that had flooded all through her body and soul and then receded, leaving a glow of utter peace and delight, and mixed in with that the wry thought: *How stupid I was, to be so afraid of this, all these years*!

Gradually her senses acknowledged the continued presence of the outer world: the warmth of the fire heating one side of her, and the other sheltered from the cold by her lover's long body, pressed against her, his head on her shoulder and his arm heavily across her breasts, the tickle of the rug against her naked skin, and the gentle, crimson, flickering light of the fire and the last guttering candles. She lay there drowsily, thinking of nothing at all but this extraordinary feeling of peace and contentment, and then the fire crackled spitefully and spat a little shower of sparks. Several landed on her skin. She sat up with a yell of pain and indignation, slapping at the offending places.

'At least give me the pleasure of doing that,' said John, captur ing her flailing hands. 'What happened? Sparks?'

'You hid a grenado in your coal-bucket,' said Alathea, with mock outrage. 'And for that, I'll demand a forfeit.'

'And what will that be, sweet Alathea?'

'Oh, a kiss at the least,' she said, grinning, and he leaned over and did as she asked. 'Well? Was it such a terrible experience, to lose your maidenhood at such an advanced age?'

'Tolerable only, sir,' said Alathea, casting her eyes down in mock humility. 'And I do not think that my rheumatics will ever be the same again – and as for my grey hairs, they must have been doubled!'

'Wretched girl! Tell me in truth – for I'm anxious to know if you want to repeat the experience.'

'I didn't know it was possible to be deflowered twice,' Alathea told him with wide-eyed and spurious innocence, but she took pity on his need for reassurance, suddenly apparent behind all that rakish confidence and bravado. 'I did not know it could be so good,' she added simply. 'And if I had – I don't think you would have needed to write all those poems. I'd have fallen joyfully into your arms as soon as you asked.'

'That's excellent news,' John Wilmot observed, taking her in his arms. 'And now, we can do it again.'

CHAPTER TWENTY-THREE

Run away like a rascal

It is not that I love you less
Than when before your feet I lay,
But to prevent the sad increase
Of hopeless love, I keep away.

(Waller, 'The Self-Banished')

The fire was as bright this night as it had been on that first, momentous occasion, and just as sparkish. The Turkey rug was pockmarked with small brown charred holes, but no one had thought to move it out of the way. They kept themselves well clear of it, however, and chaffed their host on the poor quality of his sea-coal: to which he replied carelessly, from the depths of his chair, with a wine-glass in one hand and a lock of his mistress's pale hair in the other, that his damnable poverty would not allow him to buy any better. 'I've been pestering Clifford for my money from the Treasury – and small chance I'll have of seeing it before Christmas.'

'You behold the result of marrying an heiress,' said Buckhurst. 'Lifelong penury invariably ensues.' He spoke lazily, like the smug cat he so much resembled, full of the confidence and security of the heir to vast estates, a house more fit to be a palace than Whitehall, and an earldom well over a century old. In comparison, Rochester was a parvenu, and the other occupants of the room barely emerged from obscurity – save one.

Alathea had had few meetings with the Duke of Buckingham, who the disaffected whispered to be the highest power in the land – higher even than the King, whose ear he had. A man of astonishingly varied accomplishments, he was still basking in the glow of his successful play, *The Rehearsal*, a hilarious parody of all the worst heroic plays, and which hit out at various actors and playwrights along the way, notably Master Dryden. The actor playing the author had been coached by Buckingham in the appropriate mannerisms and habits of speech, and had acquitted himself most convincingly, to the rich delight of all the town and the humiliation of poor Dryden.

The compiler of this theatrical lampoon – for *The Rehearsal* was a glorious mixture of quips, comments, suggestions, jokes and ideas from most of the Wits here tonight, tidied up and given form and substance by the noble Duke – was a big man, florid and still handsome although much older than his friends. Alathea, sitting on the floor with her hands around her knees and her head propped against her lover's thigh, found herself studying that bold powerful face, younger and less gross than Lord St Albans, but still with that look of authority and confident magnificence, a man at the centre of his world, assured of his enormous power. She would like to paint him, she was sure that she could do that impressive face and figure due justice. Perhaps she would drop a word in John's ear.

John. She had known many people of that name. Only one man came to mind, quick and vivid and malicious, when she spoke the word inside her head. She had been his mistress for ten months now, deciding not to desert her profession, nor her house, nor her friends, but to carry on her life as it had been before. That, of course, had proved impossible. She was in love, and love demanded that she see the man she loved as often as she could. So they met: at Whitehall (she had danced there at last, and been presented to the King), at eating-houses, at his lodgings, even at Will's, the famous Bow Street coffee-house where she sat with him and drew, and listened to the talk of the Wits tossing back and forth in discussion or dispute, and ignored the pointed, indignant stares of lesser customers who resented the presence of a woman in their sanctum. And always there was the fire of his touch, and the promise in his eyes, and every meeting, whether in daylight or in dark, ended with the two of them withdrawn into the dim, warm world within the bedcurtains, alone to slake their passion.

Everything else was the dream: this alone was reality. Her whole existence circled around the hours they spent making love, with invention, with a frenzy of pleasure, and with mutual delight and tenderness. When she left his lodgings, her thoughts were full of what they had just done, and as the hours passed and one memory merged into the glow of many others, she would turn her mind forwards to the next night, the next day to be shared in love.

Her head told her that this was madness: madness to throw her whole soul, every part of her self, into such an affair with a man who was a notorious lecher, a rake who would have a woman, any woman, as easily as he would gulp a glass of wine. Her head told her that she would be replaced before long, in his bed if not in his friendship, by some other compliant lady more desired in the wooing than the winning. Her head knew that he would inevitably tire of her, that friendship was the best she could hope for, that his passion would not continue for ever. She knew already, from remarks his friends had let slip, that she had lasted longer than any other mistress yet. And above all, her head noted the lengthening waiting-list of people who wanted her to paint their portraits, and the fact that those portraits were no longer painted with her whole heart, for that heart was John Wilmot's, irrevocably. What she had always feared had come to pass: her magic had left her, and she did not care.

She lived only for the day, the hour, the moment, she did not dare look ahead. She was his now, at this instant, and that was all that mattered, to feel his hand gently twining her hair through her fingers, and bask in the tender affection the gesture implied.

They were talking of the sensation of the month, the arrival in England of the shy, sheltered fifteen-year-old virgin who had been married by proxy to the ageing, humourless, plodding rake that was the King's brother, the Duke of York. Harry Savile, who had no love for the Duke, had at last achieved his ambition of a place as Gentleman of the King's Bedchamber. He was telling now a series of scurrilous, obscene and extremely funny stories intended to illustrate the appalling horror the poor Italian Princess would have faced on her wedding night, whether from her groom's excess of zeal or his total failure was not decided. The company's opinion inclined to the latter, and there were a good many suggestions as to what the unfortunate Duke might do to arouse his jaded appetites in order to perform his marital duties. Then Mistress Behn, her round bright eyes dancing with amusement, entered the fray.

'Your talk is all of the Duke. If he's blunted his ardour so much with all his plain-as-a-pikestaff mistresses that he can't deal with his own pretty little wife, that's his blame. What about her, eh? Trust you, Savile, not to think about the poor girl – expecting a handsome prince, and gets a ruddled old duke who like as not can't do what's needed. What's she to do, then?'

'Get his brother to do the job,' Wycherly suggested. A big man with a look of brooding savagery, he was a fairly recent admission to their circle by virtue of his success as a writer of plays, as well as his mordant wit. Alathea was wary of him. He was the only one of her friends who could not be witty with a light and careless heart, and she had the uncomfortable feeling that his eyes saw too much and too deep. Who would he pilloried, if he ever got around to writing another play?

'That won't answer,' said John, and proceeded to explain, in elaborate detail, exactly why it would not. There was general merriment, and the wine went round again, from hand to hand and with a lot of spillage. Buckhurst leaned back lazily in his chair (typically, he had chosen the most comfortable), and said that there was only one remedy: the poor bereft Princess would need a dildo. 'Got any left, Harry?'

'None, alas – all given away long ago,' said Savile, heaving a monumental sigh.

'Then another supply must be got – where did you have 'em

from last time? The ones that were confiscated by the Customs Farmers? France, was it?' Buckingham demanded.

'Italy,' said Savile, grinning. 'Signor Dildo came from Florence, I believe – or was it Venice?'

'Perhaps the little Duchess has one already,' Aphra Behn pointed out. 'Doubtless every lady in her train has one – and if they pass 'em round Whitehall, where will all you fine gallants be then, eh? Signor Dildo is never late, never unfaithful, never too drunk to do his duty, never poxed, ever present when required – what more could a lady ask for, eh, Thea?'

'A subject for a lampoon,' said Alathea, smiling broadly. She twisted round to glance up at her lover. 'There you are – I challenge you. A lampoon on Signor Dildo – now, and no huddling in the closet to think!'

The cries of agreement rose on all sides. Buckingham's delighted voice dominated the noise. 'An excellent idea, sweet Thea! And I'll impose another condition – at least twenty verses.'

'And every verse about a different lady of the Court – and we suggest 'em!' Buckhurst added. 'Come on, Rochester – down another brimmer and show us what you can do!' He filled a glass to overflowing and passed it over.

John drank it down in one gulp and looked around the company, his eyes glittering with wild invention. 'I'm not casting my pearls of libel before such a pack of roguish babbling swine: be silent, all of you, or Strephon won't dance.'

The monkey, hearing its name, lifted its head from contemplation of its wine-cup (it had recently taken to drink, and Alathea thought it a considerable improvement), and chattered blearily at its master before sinking back into somnolence. John Wilmot cast a quelling glance at the jackanapes and at his hardly more exalted or sober company, and began, the slight hesitation in his speech rather more marked than usual.

'You ladies all of Merry England
Who have been to kiss the Duchess's hand,
Pray, did you lately observe in the show,
A noble Italian called Signor Dildo?'

There was a burst of applause. Pausing only to acknowledge it, with an ironic bow, he supplied the next three verses in quick succession, the absence of his fingers in Alathea's hair the only sign of his increased thought. Then Buckingham interrupted with an objection: where were the ladies of the Court he must mention?

'Suggest one,' said Rochester: and Savile, with a wicked and knowing grin, said, 'Lady Southesk.'

The lady concerned was exceptionally promiscuous, even by Whitehall's generous standards. John paused only a moment before supplying the required verse.

'My lady Southesk, heavens prosper her for't!
First clothed him in satin, then brought him to Court:
But his head in the circle he scarcely durst show,
So modest a youth was Signor Dildo.'

'My turn,' said Buckhurst, before the laughter had died down. 'Put Lady Suffolk *and* her daughter Betty – in the one verse. Twenty guineas says you can't do it!'

'Then hand over your money, my dear lord: I win, I think.' And he declaimed in that quick, light voice, stumbling sometimes with the speed of his thought:

'The good Lady Suffolk, thinking no harm,
Had got this poor stranger hid under her arm,
Lady Betty by chance came the secret to know,
And from her own mother stole Signor Dildo.'

'Lady Falmouth next,' suggested Wycherley, naming a woman of exceedingly unsavoury reputation who had worked her way, so it was rumoured, through most of the inhabitants of Whitehall, of every rank. The catholic nature of her tastes was reflected in the next verse.

'The Countess of Falmouth, of whom people tell
Her footmen wear shirts of a guinea an ell
Might save the expense if she did but know
How lusty a swinger is Signor Dildo!'

The laughter at that one was prolonged, and Alathea, prompted by an imp of mischief, said, 'Lady Montagu.' Harry Savile groaned and put his head in his hands. Two years ago, when the lady concerned had been the recently widowed and fabulously wealthy Countess of Northumberland, he had made an ill-advised and loquacious attempt to woo her, late at night in her bedchamber. She had rung her bell in a panic, and the thwarted swain had fled to France, hotly pursued by irate relatives. The Wits had never let him forget it, and when the lady had recently married Ralph Montagu, some wag at Garroway's coffee-house had posed the question: 'How came Montagu to gain the widow from Savile?' To which the answer had been, that one was witty in going to bed: the other wiser, in cutting the bell-rope.

'Come on, Harry, take your medicine,' someone was saying, and John's voice above her head began again, rich with malicious laughter.

'By the help of this gallant the Countess of Ralph
Against the fierce Harrys preserved herself safe:
She stifled him almost beneath her pillow
So closely she embraced Signor Dildo.'

'There was only one Harry, surely?' Aphra queried.

John grinned. 'Yes – but he was so ardent he did the work of two!'

And so it went on amidst increasingly riotous laughter: names tossed into the circle, wrapped round a rhyme and a scandalous idea with John's fantastic, swift and inventive mind, and flung back again, immortalised in a lampoon. Alathea saw Fleetwood Shepherd writing busily in a corner, and guessed that it would not be long before all Whitehall was laughing at it too. Weak and aching with mirth, she listened as the story of Signor Dildo was brought to a triumphant conclusion after more than twenty verses, with no flagging of invention and a soaring and exuberant flight of bawdy, extempore fantasy. It was the climax of the evening. After that, and Shepherd's re-reading of the poem, everything else seemed as flat and stale as a morning's old wine. The Wits departed, Buckingham in much splendour, Buckhurst less so, the rest more quietly, calling for link-boy or, in the impoverished Wycherley's case, walking unlit to his lodgings. The servants withdrew discreetly, chivvied by their master's cheerfully hectoring tones, and Alathea and John Wilmot were alone again, free to retreat into their own private world.

He stood by the dying fire, looking at the paper, covered on both sides in Fleetwood Shepherd's neat secretary's hand with the twenty-three verses of the night's lampoon. There was a smile on his face as he read it, and Alathea relaxed. He might have the reputation for instant, witty, well-honed verses, but she knew from past experience how frequently such extempore offerings were re-written and teased into perfection, late into the night, before braving the cold light of day and Court assessment. There would be no burning of candles into the small hours tonight, and she came across the room to stand beside him, feeling the swift, unthinking movement of his arm encircling her waist to pull her closer, so that her head rested against his.

'The King will enjoy this,' he said with a tired amused smile. 'It will be something of a novelty for him, to read a lampoon that derides neither himself nor his ministers. Your hair tickles.'

'So does your periwig – do I complain?' Alathea reached behind her head and began pulling out the pins that held her fashionable coiffure. It had taken her maid Sarah an hour to coax her pale heavy hair into the required curls and ringlets: now with two shakes of her head it was down, streaming untidily over her shoulders, down her back, covering the low neckline of her dress. 'Are you coming to bed, my lord?

'A merry monarch, scandalous and poor – restless he rolls about from whore to whore,' said John Wilmot, Earl of Rochester, as if she had not spoken. 'Shall I add another verse, d'you think?'

'It won't fit the metre,' said his mistress. 'It needs another poem. Come to bed?'

But he did not, and she slipped back into the room some twenty minutes later, barefoot and dressed only in her chemise and her hair, to see what he was doing, and found him bent over his writing desk, quill in one hand and a bottle of wine at his elbow, while the words poured from his pen. One glance was enough to convince her that beheading would be a comparatively mild punishment for the liberties taken by this particular work with good taste and loyalty to the throne, the couplet that he had quoted earlier, reversed and slid into the middle of the poem, being one of the least offensive.

'Do you plan to *show* that to the King?' she said, amusement struggling with disbelief in her voice and face.

'Show it? Oh, God, no,' he said without turning round. 'Doubtless he'll see it eventually, but by that time it will have passed through many hands and my name may well no longer be attached to it. My dear love, I have more respect for His Majesty than that.'

'More respect for your liberty, you mean,' said Alathea, hearing the derisive note in his voice. 'Not even the most easy-going monarch alive could let that one by without punishment. Is it finished?'

'No – I'll read it tomorrow, and polish it then, but I had to put it on paper tonight, before the wine and you made me forget it.' He rose, clumsy with fatigue and too much to drink, and set his hands on her shoulders, looking earnestly into her face with eyes that did not seem to focus properly. 'Alathea, my most lovely Alathea – will you always be my friend, whatever should happen?'

'Yes,' she said quietly. 'Even if you lampoon me as terribly as your King: for I know what lies in your heart.'

'I don't deserve you,' he said, and his hands tightened painfully. 'Not you, nor Elizabeth, waiting patiently at Adderbury for the two weeks out of six months when I deign to force my company on her, and fending off my mother and hers. That's why I want the Rangership at Woodstock. There's a hunting-lodge goes with it, and she and I can be alone there. Have I hurt you?'

'No,' said Alathea, lying.

'Despite your name, you are not always honest. Dear lady, would you scream and throw tantrums and hurl china at my head, if I were to take another mistress?'

Her breathing seemed to stop, her heart faltered and then went on, too fast: but under his grip she stood perfectly still, her eyes enormous, filling her face. 'You know me better than that,' she said at last, in a voice that did not seem to be hers. 'We made a bargain, after all. Would you write lampoons that burned the paper and charred the quill, if I took another lover?'

'No – but I would kill him.' He laughed, and the sound was a little off-key. 'Have you another lover, then?'

'No – have you?'

'I stand innocent, my lady fair. There is no other woman in my life – except my wife, of course.'

'Except your wife. I feel sorry for Elizabeth,' said Alathea thoughtfully.

'Sorry for her? Oh, Christ, not you too!' He released her and swung away, knocking into the desk. The wine-bottle toppled over and a few dregs trickled out, staining the paper and the stamped, gilded leather. 'Everyone feels sorry for Elizabeth – everyone! Does she feel sorry for herself? You've met her – does she mope and whine?'

'No – but I think she must be lonely sometimes.'

'Perhaps. But does that give you any right to interfere in my marriage?'

'I thought I already was,' said Alathea, drily. There was a pause: then he laughed, and took her hands, and the moment of danger was over. But later, after their lovemaking, she lay quiet and wakeful in the big warm bed, with his arm around her and his soft sleeping breath stirring in her ear, and pondered the instant when they had trembled on the brink of their first quarrel, and then drawn back. He had been half-drunk, of course, and wine sometimes made him touchy and argumentative as well as wild and brilliant. She knew his many moods by now, knew that he drank not for the reasons that most men would have, but for the inspiration it gave him, the flood of words and wit and ideas that somehow could only be fully released under the influence of the grape. All his friends drank hard, but because it was the fashion: only he drank to give full rein to his genius.

She had had nearly a year: a year of ecstatic happiness such as she had never known, in a life that had held more than its share of delight and satisfaction and fulfilment. She had been admitted to his heart and his soul, she had inspired his love and his poetry. No other woman, out of those who had voraciously pursued him, or been pursued by him, had been so blessed – save for his wife Elizabeth.

The thought brought old feelings of guilt to the surface. She had liked Elizabeth. She knew that he must have been unfaithful to her a hundred times, five hundred times, but she could not erase that nagging guilty sense of personal betrayal. If she ever met the Countess of Rochester again, she doubted she could look her in the eye, much less hold a conversation with her.

She realised with disquiet that she was looking into the future, for the first time since she had become his mistress: and the future was empty of him. She had known it, ever since that moment when she weighed up love and virtue in the balance, and chose love: she had known that it would not be for ever. She knew also that she had never dreamed that she would still be his mistress at the end of the year. It was November, the last week of the month. Soon it would be Christmas, and she had almost promised herself that she would go home, to Ashcott. All the Heron family would be there, those that were speaking to each other, of course. Dan and Lucy were to spend the season there, with Oliver: from Lucy's bright-eyed hints, Alathea had gathered that her irrepressible aunt had hopes of a match with Sophie. The prospect of two such volatile temperaments joined in holy matrimony was one to make a lesser spirit quail: to Lucy, once more stirring life's brew with vigour, it was the most appropriate union possible.

The thought of a merry, cheerful Christmas at Ashcott was very tempting, and since the Widow had not been in the best of health recently, she knew she ought to go. Guilt reared its head again, and she thrust it down with annoyance and grief. Her instinct told her, no matter what her heart said, that her days as the mistress of this strange, fantastic, basically unhappy man sleeping uncharacteristically peacefully beside her, were numbered. Soon, his eye would wander, if it had not done so already: another woman would slide honoured into this bed, and she would no longer be needed. And she realised that if she was still to keep his friendship, the parting must be made with pride, with dignity, with affection and acceptance. One day soon, she would need all her strength.

She did not go to Ashcott. If her time with John was limited, she must make the uttermost of what she had left. So she danced at Whitehall that Christmas, and was ogled by the King and, less flatteringly, by the Duke of York – of whom his brother had claimed that his mistresses were so ugly that they must have been foisted on him as penance by his priest. She made His Majesty laugh, and was taken into his private closet to inspect his collection of miniatures, many of which had been painted by Samuel Cooper. She fended off the royal hands with an adroitness born of long practice with less exalted Wits, and was rewarded, much to her amazement, with a request to add a work from her own brush to the royal cabinet. Accordingly, an appointment was made with an official for the week after Twelfth Night, and for the first time for nearly a year, Alathea's mind and heart were totally, if temporarily, taken up with her painting.

It lasted until her next visit to the house in Portugal Row. Her friends, who had been looking on with increasing disquiet over the last few months, could do nothing. As Hugh, unhappy but resigned, pointed out, she was an adult, and had gone into this with open eyes as well as open arms. She was happy, no denying, but her painting had suffered, her affairs were neglected, and Rebecca and Lovell had almost forgotten what she looked like. Hugh, despite his delightful marriage, missed his niece's company, her conversation and her dry ironic wit. He hardly seemed to see her, for when she was not painting, she was invariably to be found at Portugal Row. And he could not understand the attraction:

could she not see, with that clear, calm, intelligent eye that gave her portraits such a telling observance of character, that the man was a ruthless, unprincipled rogue?

But he himself was hardly a shining angel, as he well knew. He had risen to his present position as a trusted member of the Duke of York's household by the relentless application of selfishness and cunning. Now he was assured and successful, of course, and with the prettiest wife in London into the bargain, he could allow his better nature to assert itself, but his sense of humour would not permit him to pontificate on another's somewhat similar shortcomings. *He makes her happy, he makes her laugh*, thought Hugh wryly. *Who am I to deny her that? After all those jokes about being wedded to a paintbrush, how can I be churlish when she loves a man who'd tear anyone in half in a lampoon, even the King, when it appealed to his whim?*

Four days after Twelfth Night, my lord of Rochester, being drunk at Whitehall, was asked by the King for a copy of his hilarious verses about the ladies of the Court and a certain Signor Dildo: and took the wrong paper from his pocket.

The Merry Monarch, scandalous and poor, was famed throughout the land for his wit, his sense of humour, his easy lack of pretension: but a poem which described his sceptre as being of a length with a certain well-used part of his anatomy, and which went on to attribute to that part a far greater share in ruling the country, was more even than he could tolerate. My lord's presence was no longer permitted at Whitehall, the Rangership of Woodstock was in doubt, and he disappeared from the town, leaving no word for his mistress.

And exactly a week later, on the seventeenth of January, 1674, Alathea Heron was forced at last to the realisation that she was pregnant.

It was the day she had gathered up her vellum and her brushes, her ivory boxes and her pigments, and put on her new dress of rich dark green velvet, taking care to fill in the low neckline with a lacy scarf, and gone to Whitehall in the King's own coach to paint his portrait in miniature. The King, contrary to her apprehensions, had been in jovial mood. He had teased her about her wayward lover, and confirmed her suspicion that he had been banished more for form's sake than for any actual royal displeasure.

'Rumour has it I send him to the Tower every year,' said His

Majesty, surveying the female artist with dark eyes that saw, disconcertingly, far too much. 'Oddsfish, where do these libels spring from?'

'Perhaps from my Lord Rochester, Your Majesty,' said the female artist, demurely, from behind her brush, and the King laughed. 'Miss him, do you, Mistress Heron? You look pale and peaky – are you pining?'

'Not as far as I know, Your Majesty – I don't think I am the pining sort.'

'Breeding, then? I know the look,' said the King cheerfully. He met Alathea's wide, horrified eyes over the top of her paintbrush, and laughed again. 'I beg your pardon, Mistress. Pray forget what I said – it was shockingly improper.' There was a glint in his eye that implied that he was enjoying every moment of this, and the female artist, dead-colouring the royal face in a rather darker shade than she normally used, forgot her awe and alarm so far as to give way to the bubble of amusement welling up within her, and laugh.

For the rest of the hour-long sitting, they talked as amicably as if they had known each other for years, and Alathea found it increasingly hard to remember that this was her Sovereign Lord the King, so free and unassuming were his conversation and his manner. But later, going home splendidly in that magnificent royal coach, redolent with the aroma of new leather and fresh paint and wet dog, she remembered what he had said – about breeding – and a growing dreadful certainty took hold of her mind.

She had not thought of it. Even with poor Nell's tragic history in her memory, she had not given it a thought, so utterly consumed had she been in the torrent of their love. And even when the signs that now seemed so obvious had first made their appearance, she had been too absorbed with John Wilmot to pay them any heed at all. It was almost as if she had willed herself to ignore them, knowing that a child must surely portend the death of their affair.

But she could ignore them no longer: no use any more to force herself not to feel sick when she rose in the mornings, or faced the cheesecakes that she had once found so delicious: no use to make light of the weight and tenderness of her breasts, or attribute the absence of her courses to a heavy cold, emotional upheaval or any number of trivial reasons, while wilfully ignoring the most obvious cause of all, staring her full in the face.

You stupid fool, she told herself savagely. *For ten months you've blithely assumed that it will never happen to you – that what has happened to every other woman in the land (except the poor Queen), will never blight your life. After all your speech-making about Nell and her fall from grace, it's not three years before you go the same way yourself – and you never even thought!*

Scowling harder, she forced herself to count back through the missed dates she had somehow never noticed, and then to count forward. It seemed the baby would be born in May, or possibly June. *Dear God, you half-wit,* thought Alathea with humiliated fury, *you've been with child for more than three months and never realised it – Nell knew far earlier, and she'd miscarried and died, for God's sake, before she'd been four months pregnant. But I'm not going to share her fate: I'm not going to slip feebly out of life on a moan and a groan. Whatever happens, I will* not *let this ruin my future.*

The coach turned into Jermyn Street: she was nearly home. She would have to tell Hugh, and Hen, and Susannah. She had a vision of their faces, reproachfully and silently saying, 'I told you so.' The only way out of that was to hold her head high and behave, even if it was not true, as if the child within her was as desired and wanted a love-child as she herself had been.

There was an alternative, though: to seek out some obliging woman who would rid her of the child. Easy enough to do, and with only a slight risk to herself, but even now, in the middle of her self-recrimination, something in her quailed at the slaughter of his child. She did not know much about children, and the only one with whom she had had much contact was the intense and solitary Becca, but she remembered his legitimate offspring, and of a sudden the prospect of a baby, a love token to cherish for John's sake as well as its own, was not so terrible.

I will manage, she told herself, as the royal footman opened the door for her. I will bear his child without any furtiveness or shame, I will bear his loss as best I can. My life will go on – and even if it holds no such happiness again, I have had my glory, to hold forever alive in my memory, and to live again in our child.

The first person she told was Hugh, after supper that evening, and there was an air of defiance about the way she held her head high and stared at him, daring him to apportion blame or regret. But to her surprise he smiled, and offered his congratulations. 'It will be good for Becca to have a small human to think of, instead of that smelly dog.'

'I know, I must bath him – he rolled in some water-fowl dung in the park today,' said Alathea. She caught Hugh's sardonic eye and grinned suddenly. 'Aren't you going to call me slut?'

'You don't think yourself one, do you? Then I have no right to describe you thus,' said Hugh. 'I was thinking of the irony of life, that Sue and I have been wed more than two years now, and no sign of any child, and you are Rochester's mistress for less than half that time and breed already!' They laughed, a rather forced sound, and then Hugh came to stand close to her, and put his hands on her shoulders. 'Dear girl – tell the truth. Are you putting a brave face on this? Do you really want to have the child? Or do you want me to demand revenge of your honour at swordpoint?'

'Don't look so apprehensive – I wouldn't dream of asking,' Alathea told him. Her eyes roved over his face, seeking his reaction to her words, praying she had won his true support. 'Hugh – I went into this with open eyes. I accept the consequences joyfully – well, this consequence, anyway. I am glad and proud to have his child, even if it means the end of our affair – oh, yes, I knew from the start it wouldn't last for ever.'

'And you can stand so calm and tell me that?' Hugh's eyes narrowed. 'I thought you were in love, dear girl.'

'I am!' Alathea's cry was full of desperation. 'I am, you fool, of course I am – but what else can I do? If I scream and shout he'll still leave me – but there'll be half-a-dozen vicious lampoons within a week, and I'll have lost his friendship for ever. And in a way, that is more valuable to me than a place in his bed. So, I have decided on it. I shall have the child, and leave him his freedom, and with luck and judgement I'll still have him for a friend.' And she gave Hugh her brave, gallant smile, her eyes heavy with tears she would not release.

He was not deceived by her show of courage. He said softly, 'Why so brave for me, dear girl? I can see it's more than you can bear – why bear it alone?'

And that, as he had calculated, opened the floodgates, for he was, as usual, quite right. Alathea had stood looking at him, feeling her heart and soul crumbling with grief, and yet too proud to give way: and the knowledge that Hugh understood, and would give her the support and love she needed, broke her down. She wept for a long time against his broad, compassionate shoulder and then, her sorrow spent for a while, mastered herself and wiped her eyes and face and blew her nose on the kerchief he offered. She did not apologise. Instead, she said, 'Thank you. Thank you so much. Why is it that you always listen, and understand, and never pass judgement?'

'I am not without sin, and therefore unable to cast any stones. Do you feel better now?'

'Yes,' Alathea said. She turned to face him, her eyes suddenly calm and the despair vanished. 'I *knew* it would not be for ever: I didn't expect it to last as long as this, even in my wildest dreams. The baby just brings it to a quicker conclusion. But at least I'll have something to remember it by,' she added, with something like her usual dryness. 'And if I brazen it out, expect no sympathy, and no brickbats either – ' she smiled briefly, remembering an old joke ' – then I can take anything, even brickbats. Why shouldn't I have a love-child? I'm one myself. What difference did it make to me?'

Hugh felt constrained to point out that, since Alathea's parents had married when she was but a month old, bastardy had hardly had an effect on her life. 'This child will have no father to care for it. How will you manage?'

'Oh, Hugh – I am not some drab off the streets, some beggar faced with the choice of starving my child or abandoning it! I have money of my own, a house, a profession which supports me in comfort and more – of *course* I can manage! I'm just as independent as any man, dammit! The question is,' said Alathea, suddenly bleak, 'I have grown so accustomed to him – grown to need and want him so much that I even miss him now, when he has only been gone from me for a week, and I love him so much – how can I do without him now?'

'You did without him before.'

'Yes – but I didn't know what I was missing, and besides, I had him for a friend. Now – it would be like amputating a limb, casting aside a part of myself . . . oh, I shall miss him, Hugh, I shall miss him so much!'

'But you'll manage,' said Hugh, knowing he spoke the truth. 'You'll accept it, and be philosophical, and hide your breaking heart, and one day you'll wake up and find that it's healed – or at any rate, doesn't hurt so much.' He kissed her, gently, on the forehead. 'I speak, of course, from my vast experience in such matters. The only woman I have ever loved – apart from you – I have never lost, God willing. But I think one day you will find that the agony becomes mere pain, and then diminishes to an ache, and disappears. Does that make it any easier?'

'No,' said Alathea, and smiled bravely. 'Not much. But I do, faintly, begin to see a future for myself, instead of lonely darkness. Thank you, Hugh – I don't think I can ever repay you – for always being here, when I need you.'

'But you have,' said Hugh. 'You put me always in your debt, when you helped me win Susannah.'

Telling Hugh had been difficult, imparting the news to Henrietta and Susannah was somewhat harder. Hen in particular she did not find easy to face. Her friend was too kind to say 'I told you so,' and too sensible and practical not to show it in her face. She could not inform John Wilmot that he was to become a father for the third time. He had gone into temporary hiding, and would not be seen again at Whitehall for a few weeks yet. She hoped that he had not gone to Adderbury, for she knew she must visit Ashcott, and break the news to her father and mother, that they would soon become grandparents.

So, like Nell, she left London in a coach (though this one was hired, and she and Sarah and Lovell-our-dog had it to themselves), to flee pregnant to Ashcott: but unlike Nell, she did not go in shame or terror, but in a mood of slightly defiant optimism. She might have fallen down the same slippery slope as had her unfortunate cousin, but she would not let it blight her life nor crush her spirit.

Ashcott in winter was quiet, damp, raw, the flood waters from the River Swere making the ground soggy and lending an unseasonably lush green colour to the grass. She had sent a letter warning of her arrival, and found roaring fires, a celebratory pot of chocolate, and the delighted welcome of her family. Her father, now past fifty, kept the lean and hungry look that was characteristically Heron, and if his face was lined with weather and his hair liberally peppered with silver amongst the fair, his eyes, keen and ironical and perceptive, were just the same. Her mother, small and brownly grizzled like a badger, had also changed little, and her indomitable energy was if anything greater. There was new furniture, new hangings to be admired, her father's plans for taming the errant river, drawn up in conjunction with Matthew, to study, and a seemingly endless stream of Sophie's pert questions to answer. Alathea, looking at her very pretty little sister's animated face, wondered if Aunt Lucy's machinations had borne fruit, but knew better than to ask. She diverted the conversation to family gossip. Mun's new-found love of the sea-faring life was discussed with some astonishment, and a letter to his parents passed round. To Alathea's amusement, it proved to be a most graphic description of the hardships and pleasures of the daily round on board his ship, coupled with a series of requests for essential items of warm clothing, food, weaponry and obscure books on seamanship, all in a thick black aggressive hand that was unmistakeably Mun's. Perhaps he'll be the pirate, not Oliver, thought Alathea, with an inward smile.

In amongst all the items of news and tit-bits of gossip, two names were conspicuous by their absence. No one had seen anything of Kit and Anne since their withdrawal to Yorkshire more than two years previously: apparently Anne had been expecting a child, but there was no news of the baby's safe arrival, although it must by now be about a year old, and Thomazine's last three letters to her eldest son had gone unanswered. Alathea, listening to the discussion, viewed her emotions with a certain astonishment. Her love affair with Rochester seemed to have cauterised her ambiguous, agonised feelings for her half-brother: she could hear his name mentioned, discuss his marriage, that had once seemed like a slap in her own face, with an equanimity that was quite genuine. He had left her life for good: nothing he could do now would ever touch her again, for she had known a genuine love, a true passion that transcended all the other, muddier emotions that Kit had inspired in her. *He means nothing to me at all now*, she thought with relief and a great sense of freedom. *Why was I ever so bound to him?*

'I had a letter from Grainne,' said Thomazine, turning the talk to Henrietta's mother, and Jasper's. 'She is well, and all her family, but there has been a great deal of upset over Lord Bradfield's marriage, and she says he has become almost a recluse. It is Meraud who is seen in all the local mansions, Meraud who queens it over everyone, and Grainne writes that she is becoming very popular with all the wrong people, and very unpopular with all the right ones. She treated poor Jasper like a menial when he came to see the butler, who'd fallen down the stairs, but she's quite ingratiating with Grainne and Malise.'

'Because they know the truth about her,' said Francis. 'Neither of them would reveal it unless grievously provoked, but Meraud thinks everyone follows her own very amoral code, and sees betrayal everywhere. She has what she wants now, she has Goldhayes, but I wonder if she is happy?'

'I wouldn't want to be married to Simon,' Thomazine commented. 'He was prickly company at the best of times: how much worse must he be now? And they've alienated themselves from all their children, and many of their friends. Poor Simon – how he has brought it all upon himself, and how little he sees that it's his own fault! *He's* the one at odds with the world, but from his viewpoint I fancy it's the other way about.'

'I felt sorry for him, about Susannah,' said Alathea, acknowledging her guilt. 'But the whole idea of him marrying her – the difference in age, in character, *and* the fact that she loves Hugh, and Hugh loves her – made the thought of it completely repellent. Women treated as brood-mares, as commodities, as stakes in a game of estates and fortunes – I hate it all!'

'You do right to,' said her father. He gave her a long, penetrating look. 'And how is life in the London fleshpots? Give us all the most spicy gossip.'

And she did: but saved the spiciest for the next day, when at her suggestion he went with her and Lovell along the path towards Barford, the path where, more than ten years before, the child Alathea had met the young John Wilmot, and set her feet on the road to London, and fame, and love, and the baby curled tiny and growing within her, token of a passion that had been doomed, yet utterly delightful, from the beginning. It was cold and crisp, there was little wind, and the grass was brittle with frost under their feet. Lovell, exuberant at the country air and country freedom, raced ahead of them, tail waving wildly, uttering his deep barks of excitement and thereby warning off every rabbit for miles.

'You seem thoughtful,' said her father, as they turned their footsteps up the hill towards the path. He glanced sideways at the fine-drawn face of his eldest, and dearest, child, seeing the rosy flush of cold glowing under her skin, and the taut slender figure under the heavy winter cloak. 'Did you by any chance want to tell me something?'

There was a pause while Alathea sidestepped a tussock and stopped to pluck a long dried stem of grass. She slid the stalk into her mouth and chewed it, absently, like a country yokel. Then she said, 'Yes. Yes, I did, as a matter of fact.'

Another silence. They reached the path and began a leisurely stroll towards Barford St John. Ahead, to the west, the sky was grey and heavy with the threat of snow. Alathea, seeing it, knew that they must soon turn back and that the moment of truth was upon her. She said, so quietly that Francis thought at first that he had misheard, 'You're going to be a grandfather.'

That stopped him in his tracks. She turned and faced him, and he saw an unspoken appeal in her eyes as she went on, elaborating. 'I am expecting a baby. It should be born in May or June. I love its father very much, but the affair is ended, and I cannot marry him.' She smiled wryly. 'Just in case you were contemplating forcing him to it at the point of a pistol.'

'You know me better than that,' said her father. 'I must say, I'm not sure I like the thought of being a grandfather. I haven't nearly enough grey hairs, and I can still walk without a stick. But tell me – the most important thing of all, you haven't said – do you *want* this child?'

'Yes,' said Alathea. 'Yes, I do – very much indeed. When I first realised it, though,' she added with honesty, 'for a little while I saw it as the thing that would end the affair for ever – but it was ending anyway. Yes, I *do* want it – but at the moment, I think, more as a keepsake than anything else. But when it's born, I think he or she will come to be much more than that.'

'And will you keep the baby, and look after it yourself?'

'I've seen too much of the disadvantages of being an abandoned child,' said Alathea drily. 'Oh, yes, I'll care for it myself, and rear it myself, and take full responsibility for the consequences of my affair. It – it does frighten me, though,' she added thoughtfully. 'I'm afraid of the whole business of giving birth – too many people die – and I want to do so much *more* with my life! I want to travel in Europe, and continue my painting of course – perhaps trying out other things than portraits. I don't know exactly what I will do: but I do know that my life won't be ruined or changed or blighted simply by the proof that I've become a fallen woman.' She grinned. 'I wonder what Lord Bradfield would say?'

' "I told you so," without a doubt,' her father said, a faint smile on his face. They stared at each other for a long moment: then Alathea gathered all her courage and said, 'Do you mind?'

'Mind? About the baby? No, of course not,' said Francis Heron, and spoke the perfect truth. 'You did what you did for love's sake – and you have accepted the consequences gladly. You'll have to put up, as your mother did, with pointing fingers and wagging tongues, but I shouldn't imagine they're very common in London nowadays, and besides, you are not the sort to let it upset you, are you? If you welcome it, if you are glad you are pregnant, then I am glad with you – and that, I would wager, will go for your mother as well. You know the story of our past – how could we not love you and support you, whatever you might do?'

'You haven't asked the other question,' said Alathea. 'Don't you want to know who is the baby's father?'

There was a silence. Francis studied her face, seeing in the pale loveliness the subtle signs of strain and tension. 'Yes,' he said at last. 'I don't deny I would like to know who the father of my grandchild is – but you don't have to tell me if you don't want to. I trust your judgement enough to believe that whoever he is, he is worthy of you.'

'Oh, he is, he is,' said Alathea, and despite all her hard-won strength, tears sprang suddenly to her eyes in her grief for what she had lost. 'He's a man of words and genius, an artist with his pen as I am with my brush, and he could enchant the devil with his talk, and he was my friend – and I would like to keep his friendship if I can.' She drew a long unsteady breath. 'But he is married, and my child is not his first, and his reputation trails fire and brimstone, the lewdest rake in London – the Earl of Rochester was my lover.' She gave him a wry, despairing, defiant grin. 'And I don't desire to make apologies for it.'

He had suspected something of the sort, from the heavy hints in Lucy's letters. His first impulse was anger, at such a practised lecher's exploitation of his daughter's honest love. But then he realised that she had evidently gone into this with the clear and open eyes of a mature young woman, who had known the risks and accepted them, and was not going to whine at the unfortunate consequences. He said slowly, 'Apologies are not needed – nor are any self-justifications. Love strikes at random, and we none of us can help whom we love. Did he ever love you?'

'Yes,' said Alathea, and her eyes were glowing suddenly with remembered passion. 'Oh, yes, undoubtedly he did – and I think he does still, and in his strange way always will. He was not made for fidelity, and I knew it would not last for ever – and if I can break off the affair quietly, and with grace, I think I can keep his friendship.' Her voice, playing traitor, wobbled suddenly. 'But oh, I shall miss him so much!'

'Does he know about the child?'

'No – he is, er, temporarily absent from Whitehall,' said Alathea, and told the story of the mistaken lampoon. It made her father laugh: then he said thoughtfully, 'Are you sure you have read him aright? Was he about to leave you in any case?'

'Yes, I'm almost sure of it. And I don't know for certain, but I hardly think he'll be long faithful to me when I'm so swollen up I can't see my own feet. He's like everyone else,' said Alathea ruefully. 'He's partly in love with my repartee and almost entirely in love with my looks. And besides, there's the question of Elizabeth.'

'His wife?'

'His wife. I met her once – do you remember when I brought Sophie back, and I had presents for their children? It was before I became his mistress. I liked her,' said Alathea sadly. 'And I keep thinking of her at awkward moments. She had enough to bear, poor girl, without the knowledge that someone she treated warmly and with friendship has gone behind her back and been her husband's lover for nearly a year. The trouble with me,' she finished wryly, 'is that I'm too scrupulous by half.'

'You fall between two stools,' her father told her. 'By my dear brother's standards you're totally immoral – and by Whitehall's, much too honest. You take after me, in fact.' He looked into her tired face. 'Did you know that the Countess is also expecting a baby?'

To his distress, all the colour drained from her skin, leaving those great smokey eyes fastened on his. 'When?' she said at last.

'Some time in the summer, I understand from your mother. She is sometimes invited there, you know – we move in exalted circles now.' He added, with concern, 'Does it upset you? I'm sorry – I wouldn't have told you so abruptly if I had thought.'

'It doesn't matter,' said Alathea, trying, and failing, to disguise the fact that it evidently did. 'He went to Adderbury last autumn – in the middle of October, it was. Don't worry – please – I can hardly accuse him of being faithless to me with his own wife!' She wiped her eyes with the back of her hand and stared at the rapidly approaching storm. After a while, she went on. 'It's hard for me to understand how you can love two people at the same time: when I love him I love exclusively, there is no room for anyone else, nor anything else, not even my painting. Yet he loves me – and he loves Elizabeth too, despite the way he neglects her.' She shook her head in bewilderment. 'I can't understand it – and how can I bear it, being in London and watching as he takes another mistress, some actress or a maid-of-honour? How can I bear it without making the kind of scene that would drive him away from me for ever?'

'Then don't stay in London.'

'But where can I go? If I come back here, it's not two miles from his house, and I would go mad if I had neither him nor my painting – I must *do* something, occupy my mind, or go insane. How I wish I could go to Holland, or Italy – I might not forget him, but it would make the pain so much more bearable.'

'Then go.'

Alathea's head jerked up. She stared at her father. 'Go? Go to Italy? I can't – what about the baby?'

'Go now – or wait till it's born and take it with you.'

'But supposing it died, or I miscarried?'

'You didn't miscarry on your journey here, did you? Take care, take it gently, slowly, relax . . . you're as strong as an ox. Nell died because she was a weak, insubstantial spirit – you're made of sterner stuff, and I don't doubt the baby will be too. It's up to you to decide,' said Francis. 'It's your choice, and yours alone. There is a risk, you're right – but I think with care you could avoid it. Anyway, you could lose the baby falling out of your own bed, or have it die from something boringly English like the measles – a child is at risk anywhere. And if Italy will make you happier, I would consider it a journey well worth the taking.'

'I have some money put by – but it won't be enough.'

'I also – between us, there should be sufficient.' He smiled. 'Kit went, and had so little to show for it. I always thought how unfair it was, that you should not be given the opportunity too. So – now is your chance. You have my offer of money – and why not take Matthew? I know he's a trifle vague, but he'd be quite an adequate escort – and he'd leap at the prospect.'

'Kit offered to take me, once,' said Alathea. 'And I declined.'

'Most wisely, I feel. Kit is uncomfortable company at the best of times. Well, maw?' He smiled encouragingly. 'You can consider it all day, if you like – but I think we ought to be turning back, the snow's starting.' His smile grew wider. 'I believe snow is very rare, in Italy.'

And it was.

PART THREE

The Artist

1674-1677

Not Heav'n itself upon the past has pow'r;
But what has been has been, and I have had my hour.

(Dryden, *Translations of Horace*)

CHAPTER TWENTY-FOUR

Advice to a painter

All my past life is mine no more,
The flying hours are gone:
Like transitory Dreams given o'er
Whose images are kept in store
By Memory alone.

(Rochester, 'Love and Life: a Song')

Once the idea of going to Italy had been planted in her mind, it grew and flourished with astonishing speed. She returned to London, taking Matthew and a quantity of money from her father, added her own savings to the funds and found, to her delight, Dan Ashley contributing as well. And Oliver, twenty-one, handsome, lazy and bored, and also keen to escape from his mother's matrimonial plans, expressed a desire to come too. She was relieved, for Matthew, intelligent and knowledgeable though he was, would not be of much practical use on a long and difficult journey. Oliver, on the other hand, had a command of gutter French, the devil's insolence and an efficient grounding in the use of the sword and his fists. Passes were obtained, bills of exchange arranged, an itinerary worked out: Holland first (Alathea would not be dissuaded from this: she wanted to see the work of the great Dutch artists), then by easy stages down through France to Italy. As peace was now being negotiated with the Dutch, there seemed to be no obstacle to such a route. Maps were bought and studied, advice obtained from experienced friends, purchases made of guidebooks and works on the Italian language. Matthew, whose lawyer's education had made him rather pedantic and painstaking, proved so obstructive that Alathea, riven with impatience to be off on this, her greatest adventure, threatened to go alone. She did not say, though certainly Hugh guessed it, that she was also desperate to leave London before her lover returned from his disgrace, for then all her desperate resolve would crumble, and she would be reduced to begging for what he could not give her.

None of her friends objected, although Hen, characteristically, filled a notebook with instructions on the proper care of herself and the coming baby. She had the profound mistrust of most Suffolkers for customs strange and foreign. Hugh, a seasoned traveller, wished her well and gave her much useful advice. Susannah hugged her and declared how much she would miss her. Lucy mixed orders to write frequently with rather muddled warnings about Italian behaviour, apparently based on the wilder works of William Shakespeare and John Webster. At last, however, all was packed and arranged, and there was nothing left to do, but to go.

Rochester was still not returned, and she had no idea of his whereabouts, but she had given a cryptic note for him to Harry Savile, with tears that he, perceptive soul, had understood, though she had mentioned no child. And her scrawled words were blotched with her weeping, and spoke only of her love, and her pain, and the hope that he would understand. It had been her farewell to John Wilmot, and to their affair, and writing it had been the most difficult thing she had had to do during those two weeks of decision and making ready. By the time she stood on the rail of her ship, docked by the Tower, waving to the Ashleys who had come to see her off, she had passed through the first terrible sharpness of grief, to a kind of acceptance. She had chosen her fate, all along the paths of her life, and she had chosen this. Excitement mixed with her sorrow, she watched the familiar reeking bulk of London recede as the ship made sail up the shining waters of the Thames, and then turned to face the approaching sea, and this, her greatest adventure.

It was more than two years before she saw England again, two years filled with incident and experience, packed with colour and warmth and glorious freedom: the paintings in Holland, the sights of Paris, the russet-faded roofs of Florence where they took a villa and where, in June, 1674, Alathea's son was born. It was an easy birth, and he was a delightful, smiling child who rarely cried and learned early to laugh and to gurgle. His eyes were dark and his hair pale, and he already resembled Rochester, who possibly did not even know of his existence. She prayed with more earnestness than she had ever prayed before, that he would not be burdened with his father's glittering, spectacular, unhappy genius. His name was Alexander, for no particular reason save that his mother liked it, but the kind, voluble Italian woman engaged to look after him insisted on calling him Alessandro, invariably shortened to Sandro, and thus he was known by everyone in the Villa Alba.

From his first day, he was universally beloved: even Oliver could be seen dandling him on his knee, and Matthew spent long hours studying him and trying, unsuccessfully, to instil in the infant the rudiments of Latin and Greek. Alathea was content to enjoy him, to forget the love that had conceived him in this new, unlooked-for delight. And of course, she drew him incessantly, and discovered that the inhabitants of Florence were rather more tolerant of female painters than had been their counterparts in London. Visitors remarked upon the picture she had painted of her son, dressed in the style of his illustrious namesake, and suddenly she found herself once more in demand as an artist.

By this time Sandro was a crawling, babbling baby, with sun-flushed skin and sunbleached hair, and although she had not planned to stay more than a year in Italy, suddenly it became very much easier to linger than to go. Here there was the warmth, the friendliness of the people, her growing command of Italian, the obvious happiness of her brother and cousin – fast friends and very good for each other, absent, intellectual Matthew, wild Oliver – while the news from London was of cold weather, Hugh and Susannah, Hen and Becca all flourishing, no need to return for them. And above all, there were the tidings, couched in one of Harry Savile's expert, gossipy letters, that Rochester had replaced her in his bed with a seventeen-year-old actress called Elizabeth Barry, who had a goddess's face and the devil's own temper. Even after eleven months in Florence, that news made her weep, for what she had lost, but she knew, in her soul, that she had been right – right to leave him when she did, before love turned to jealousy, bitterness and hate, and above all right to come here, to drown her sorrow in the sleepy, warm, colourful sensuality of Italy, and to discover again the joys of seeing, of painting, of simply being, and to explore the unknown wonders of motherhood. As she had suspected, Sandro became, very quickly, much more than a mere token of her love affair: every pale, silky curl of hair, the soft curves of his face, the long-lashed dark eyes, his chuckling smile and waving hands, caught her heart as she watched, and held, and spoke to him, and she discovered adoration.

She painted, and was paid for it despite some grumbling from other local artists; visited Bologna, where there was, to her astonished delight, a long and venerable tradition of female painters; went to Venice and fell in love with a place for the first time since Goldhayes; and filled her life with work, talk, excitement. The seasons, so less sharply differentiated than in cold England, blended one into the other. Money from home had run out, but her painting supported them all in their simple but comfortable existence, and she was, to her bemused surprise, almost completely happy, for two years and more.

They would have to go home eventually, of course, and in August, 1676, the summons arrived. Dan Ashley, who was past sixty, had fallen ill. It had not been very serious, and he had soon recovered most of his strength, but Lucy wanted her son's presence once more, and there were tearstains on the letter. Oliver grumbled, and bid a passionate farewell to the young madonna he had been courting light-heartedly for months, and was heard to mutter dark words about his mother's predeliction for arranging marriages. Matthew ended his sessions with an ancient, self-styled philosopher and studier of languages, who in his youth had known an old man who had known the great Leonardo, and Sandro, who could speak and understand Italian as well as English, and who frequently mingled the two languages in one sentence, bid a tearful goodbye to his nurse and all the neighbours who had welcomed his expeditions to their houses, for as soon as he had mastered walking, the little boy had treated all homes as his own and was such an intrepid explorer that Matthew had dubbed him Sandro Polo. They gathered their belongings and purchases (Lucy had sent a detailed request for Venetian lace and fragile glass), and on a hot September day, left Florence, and started on the long journey back to England.

Hugh did not recognise his favourite half-niece for a moment, in her new Italian gown and her hair dressed in a shorter style, and her skin lamentably brown and freckled, but once he realised, his welcome was joyous. 'Thea! You look superb!'

'Do I?' said Alathea, studying him. 'You look very fine yourself – if you get a periwig any larger, even you will be lost under it.' She turned to the small, beaming figure being carried on the shoulders of a rather bashful Oliver, who was just remembering that English ways with children were rather different from Italian ones. 'May I present your half-great-nephew, sir – Master Alexander Heron!'

'Let down!' Sandro commanded. Oliver obeyed, and to Hugh's delight the scrap went into a formal flourishing bow which would not have been out of place at Whitehall. The effect was somewhat spoiled when he overbalanced and fell forward on to his nose. Not even Sandro's sunny nature was proof against such an assault, and the first sight and sound that Hen, Becca and Susannah had of the newest addition to the Heron family was of a rather smothered wailing and a quantity of bright red blood. Sandro was cleaned up, and soothed with sweetmeats, and Becca, now a pale, solemn ten-year-old, took charge. She capably fended off the delighted attentions of Lovell, still as black and hairy as ever (the Italian heat had sorely tried his endurance), and who was insisting on celebrating their reunion. The adults gathered for a welcome pot of chocolate, and news was eagerly exchanged.

Oliver's father was much better, and the only person who still worried for him was Aunt Lucy, but it was evident that their only son's presence would be required at least to take some part in the running of the business, even if he did not soil his gentlemanly hands with making clocks. All was well with Rosalind, who now had three children, a boy and two girls, and at Ashcott, where from all accounts the Widow Gooch still put her robust oar into everyone's affairs despite being now virtually confined to her chair. No one had heard anything of Kit and Anne for a long, long time. Anne's younger sister, the flighty Mall, was leading Whitehall a merry dance, not to mention her husband, and was rumoured to have added the Duke of York to her list of conquests. And Lord Bradfield, to judge from the letters of Hen's mother Grainne, had no contact with either of his children and lived in seclusion at Goldhayes. His wife, Meraud, had abruptly withdrawn from her dizzy round of Suffolk society after an illness that summer, and was apparently not very much missed. Susannah, of course, was not now on the list of people to whom her mother spoke, and from her comments, did not greatly care.

'And there'll be more recent news of Goldhayes soon,' Henrietta added, and her eyes went to Alathea, sipping good strong English chocolate by an unfortunately necessary English fire. 'Jasper wrote last week, and asked to come and stay for a while. He's a great admirer of Doctor Sydenham, who lives in Pall Mall. They've corresponded for some time, apparently, and now the doctor has invited him to dine and talk with him.' She regarded Alathea thoughtfully. 'I haven't seen Jasper for some months now – though he's been to stay several times, while you were in Florence.'

Unwillingly, Alathea thought of Jasper Sewell, his pale freckled face and his idealism and his hopeless, endearing, infuriating love for her that had at last, she prayed now, received its *coup-de-grâce* when she had refused his offer of marriage. With a shock, counting back, she realised that it had been just after the Fire – and almost exactly ten years ago.

'He's never married,' said Hen, answering her next, unspoken thought. 'And not likely to, either, he's devoted to his work. He's something of an authority on fevers and diseases, from what I understand – let's hope we won't need his services.'

So that was one unwelcome visitor she must expect, and a week or so after her return, there was another.

He arrived quite without warning. Harry Savile was in Paris, so Hugh had told her, and the Court was largely at Newmarket, watching its racehorses. She had heard no news of him, though he had never been far from her thoughts. No one had told her anything, and she had been reluctant to ask. That wound, she thought, had almost healed over: no sense in picking at the scars.

And yet, she had also been afraid of re-awakening those emotions that once, astonishingly, had dominated her whole existence for one enchanted year. She had shied away from thinking of him, even though so many small things – a song, a phrase, a place – could bring him vividly into her mind. But she forced herself to pretend that their affair was ended, over, in the past for ever, and in the bustle of her return, the adjustment to the cold English weather, Sandro's first, pouring English cold, she succeeded very well.

Until this afternoon, when she was in the parlour with Sandro, who was feverish and sneezing and would not be parted from her. Hen and Becca and Susannah had gone shopping, Hugh had taken Matthew to Whitehall, Oliver was long since restored to the stifling bosom of his family. When the door opened, she was kneeling in front of the fire, rolling a ball to her son while Lovell lurched about from one to the other, trying to snatch it and making enough noise, barking and whining, to carry to Piccadilly. It was not surprising that she heard nothing until Sandro pointed, his mouth wide in his 'welcome stranger' smile, and then she turned, and saw him.

She did not remember getting up. Lovell, whose memory was failing, let loose a fusillade of threatening barks and Sandro added his yells to the pandemonium. So in quieting them and retrieving the ball, which had run into the hearth and begun to smoulder, she was able to gain control of her shattered heart, and to face him at last with some rags and tatters of calm about her, and her face only a little flushed.

'I'm sorry, the cold makes Lovell fierce.'

'In October?' said John Wilmot, Earl of Rochester.

'It's colder here than in Florence,' Alathea told him, her eyes searching his face. He had changed: he looked ill, older, harder, and there was a narrow, bitter set to his mouth and a brooding, piercing look in his eyes. Long ago, she had drawn a caricature of him that had looked a little like this, but the reality was alarming and disturbing. 'As you already know, I think.'

'I remember Florence, indeed.' His eyes were sombre, accusing. 'Why did you go, Thea?'

'I had to,' she said, and her eyes turned to Sandro.

He stood between them by the hearth, a small elfin child with heavy, blond hair and dark brown eyes the image of John Wilmot's, his face made pale and shadowed by his illness. The small nose was red, and running: regrettably, he wiped it with his hand and, obviously aware of the sudden tension, produced a rather watery, tentative smile. 'This is Alexander,' she said, wishing that the first meeting between father and son could have been in other circumstances. 'Make your *best* bow, Sandro.'

The child did so, rather wobbly, and then, overcome, retreated behind her skirts. A loud sneeze emerged. Alathea suspected that he was using her dress as a kerchief.

'My son,' she said, using all her strength and purpose to keep her voice calm and her eyes unaverted. 'And yours. I'm afraid he's not himself at the moment – he's not used to English weather, and he has a terrible cold.'

Another sneeze gave point to her words. A weary smile touched Rochester's lips. 'Can you not send him out of the room for a space?'

She had no intention of it. 'Why? Are you afraid of catching it too?'

'Because I want to shake you to pieces,' he said angrily. 'You went away – while I was in disgrace – one very inadequate note left with Savile and no clear idea of where you'd gone, save that it was where I could not find you – and, for God's sake, no mention of – of – what did you call him?'

'Sandro. He speaks Italian much better than I do.'

'My second son.' The wild, harsh voice softened suddenly. He gave her the ghost of his old smile. 'I have two more daughters, you know. Betty must be about the same age as this one, and Malet is just a baby. But to find that you have a son – that *we* have a son – I did not know for certain.'

'For certain?'

'Oh, Harry had a good idea of why you'd gone. He heard some talk, too. But why, Thea? *Why*? You weren't afraid of talk – what were you afraid of? Why run to Italy? Why leave with no proper word? I loved you – why leave?'

Alathea took a deep breath, praying she would not weep. 'Because – because I knew that one way or the other, our affair was ending. You must have felt it too: we were too close to quarrelling, too many times. Sooner or later we'd have destroyed love, friendship – especially friendship. And I wanted to keep that. So it had to be on my terms. Sandro . . . was another reason.'

Hearing his name mentioned, the child tugged at her skirts. She turned, seeing the white, curious little face. 'What is it, shrimp?'

'Who's that?'

There was a long silence, during which the eyes of the two adults who had made him, met and held, and without words, decided on the truth. She bent and scooped the little boy up, noting with wry amusement the unsavoury state of his nose, and spoke gently. 'Who's that? That's your father, Sandro – that's your papa.'

'Papa?' Sandro's observant brown eyes travelled up the glorious garments of a courtier, and came to rest on the preposterous periwig. 'That my papa?'

'Hello,' said John Wilmot, gravely. He had evidently had much practice in speaking to small children. 'So you are Sandro? How are you today?'

'Godda co'd,' said poor Sandro. 'K'chief?'

With a grin that grew more and more like the old, light-hearted Rochester, he brought one with a flourish from his coat pocket and presented it. 'I trust you know how to blow your nose?'

His son proved the point loudly. Alathea, fearing for her dress, put him down on a chair and bade him sit still for a while. Uncharacteristically, Sandro obviously found it easy to obey: clutching the already sodden kerchief in his fingers, he stared at his father with wan interest. John Wilmot smiled at him, and then turned to Alathea. 'But I would have helped you,' he said, as if there had been no interruption. 'Helped you to care for the child – damn it, he's mine too, I had the right! Oh, Thea, why did you go?'

And she gave the real reason, the one which lay under everything she had done for the past three and a half years. 'Because I love you too much. Too much for your peace of mind: too much for our happiness. I knew it had to end soon, and I wanted to do it as painlessly as I could.'

'Painless for you, perhaps,' he said bitterly, and she realised that her chickens were coming home to roost, two years late. 'For you, perhaps. Did you not think how I might feel?'

'Yes!' Alathea cried, knowing that she had not thought of it enough, had run away, cowardly, from his grief and anger, only to face it now. 'And how long did it last? Only until the next actress in your bed!'

There was a long and terrible silence. For a moment she thought he would strike her, or fling himself out of the room. Then he said at last, very quietly, 'You were right. You did the wrong thing, but for the right reasons. Understand me – I loved you then, I love you now, though not perhaps in the same way, but I love Mistress Barry too, and my poor wife. I could never be yours exclusively, and I think that is what your heart wanted. But I wish, how I wish you had not run away.'

'I wish it too,' Alathea whispered. 'But it's too late – and all I can say is that I made a terrible mistake – and that I am more sorry than I can possibly say. I'm not asking for us to be lovers again – don't think that, I know it is well and truly over – but could – could we possibly be friends?'

Another silence, broken by Sandro's miserable sneeze. Several tears wended their way, tickling, down the side of Alathea's nose. He noticed them and said, smiling, suddenly, 'I'm afraid I only had the one kerchief, and I don't think you would want that now.'

'No – I wouldn't.' Alathea wiped her face vigorously with a corner of the lace-edged scarf she wore around her shoulders, and stared desperately at her former lover. 'You haven't answered my question.'

'No, I haven't, have I. I suppose that if you were the usual lady of my acquaintance, and thus a promiscuous, greedy, callous bitch, I would say no, and write a dozen lampoons, and blacken your name over all the town for the thinly disguised whore you are. But that description does not fit the Alathea I knew – and it does not fit you now. You are different – and we began as friends, and though we may once have been lovers, I see no reason why we should not continue our friendship. I need you to laugh, to insult me – during these last years, it was not Alathea the lover I missed so much, as Alathea the friend.' He gave her that strangely vivid, affectionate smile he used so rarely. 'And so I agree to friendship – can you bear that? Mistress Barry is a jealous woman, and I am jealous of her friends too.'

'I have never had any reason to be jealous.'

'Then will you kiss me, for old times' sake, and part friends? I would like to come and see my son – do you mind that?'

'I think it would be an excellent idea,' she said, and was kissed, for old times' sake, and found that she could bear it very well, this last token of a strange and fantastic love affair, that now, with good fortune, would hold only happy memories for them both.

And the next day a poem came, the last that she would ever receive from him, and unlike all the others, it was accompanied by a brief explanatory note.

'This is not new, and comes sullied by music, but you were the seed of it, long ago, and deserve to see it now. I trust it will meet with your approval.' And below, he had signed, 'Your most affectionate and humble servant, Rochester.'

And the poem made all the others she had seen sound like feeble, rattling doggerel: beauty, grace and felicity were its hallmarks, and she knew as she read it, wiping the tears away, that this was his token of their love, as Sandro was hers.

All my past life is mine no more,
The flying hours are gone:
Like transitory dreams given o'er
Whose images are kept in store
By memory alone.

Whatever is to come is not:
How can it then be mine?

The present moment's all my lot,
And that, as fast as it is got,
Phyllis, is wholly thine.

Then talk not of inconstancy,
False hearts, and broken vows:
If I, by miracle can be
This livelong minute true to thee
'Tis all that heaven allows.

After the trauma of her reunion with the Earl of Rochester, the arrival of Jasper Sewell, who had once so troubled her with his importunate, inopportune love, came almost as an anti-climax: indeed, she was at the theatre with Lucy and Oliver when he arrived, taken to see the play referred to by everyone in town as *Sir Fopling*. Lucy had been loud in her praise, saying that it was the most amusing play she had ever seen, but Alathea knew that the real reason she had been haled along to the Dorset Gardens theatre on a cold and foggy October day, was that the play's author was George Etherege, Gentle George with his genial idleness and wandering hands and eyes, who had been a habitué of Rochester's lodgings in Portugal Row. And Lucy, having seen it at its first performance, evidently knew what else to expect. Alathea did not, and was not prepared for the delightful, painful echoes of her former lover in the character of Dorimant – his wit, his habit of chiding his servants, the quotations from Waller: he even spoke the very poem that had been used to woo her, 'The Self-Banished'. Nor had she realised, until Lucy told her with a sly nudge, that the queenly, fiery actress playing Mrs Loveit was Elizabeth Barry, Rochester's present mistress. She stared at her with keen interest, noting the beautiful voice, the brilliant impersonation of character, and hoped very much, but rather against her judgement, that this superb young woman would be worthy of his love, and make him happy.

On the way back to Jermyn Street, where they were to have supper, Lucy kept up her usual flow of gossip, amongst which was the tit-bit that Rochester had taken Mistress Barry to his Lodge at Woodstock (it had evidently never become the love-nest for himself and his wife that he had hoped) and there tutored her in the dramatic arts – both in and out of bed, supposed Alathea – for she had been the worst actress in the world, and the other members of the company had despaired of ever making her even tolerable, let alone as magnificent as the performer they had seen today. 'And they say she's a termagant,' Alathea's aunt added, 'she has a terrible temper and she's as jealous as the devil – and yet he's supposed to be deep in love with her.'

She looked meaningfully at Alathea, who said mildly, 'They're two of a kind, if that description is true. I only ever saw his better side, and I went to Italy before we could have any bitter quarrels: so I was lucky. But he can be merciless to anyone who crosses his path.'

Lucy, who was after all rather more than just an idle gossip, looked earnestly at her niece for a long moment, in the shadowy gloom of the jolting coach. Then she said gently, 'Do you regret what you did?'

Alathea glanced at Oliver, but he was gazing abstractedly out of the window and pretending aloofness. She shook her head, honestly. 'No, on reflection, no, I don't. And there's Sandro, you see. I didn't think there could ever be anything more valuable to me than painting, and I've discovered now that there is.'

Lucy, the romantic, smiled in satisfaction, and Alathea was left with the wry thought that perhaps her satisfaction would have been somewhat less if she could have seen into her niece's mind.

They arrived at Jermyn Street, and found a beaming, happy Hen, and a very cheerful Hugh, and Susannah unwontedly shy, and in the middle of them, tall and unfashionably red-haired, the once-familiar, once-dreaded figure of Jasper Sewell.

Alathea had had no time to prepare herself, no warning at all. She knew that the shock must show on her face as she stopped in the doorway of the parlour, and stared at the man who had once offered to marry her. He did not look ten years older: his face had sharpened, perhaps, grown keener and at the same time more thoughtful, but it retained its endearing, boyish enthusiasm, the freckles and the bright red hair, undisguised by any periwig. She knew, as soon as she saw his face, that he, too, had not expected to see her – but surely Hugh had said? – and also, more tellingly, that ten years of absence had not made his heart less fond.

'Look who's here!' Hugh said, and out of the corner of her eye, Alathea saw her Aunt Lucy's delighted, conspiratorial grin, and felt a rush of infuriated anger. It was all turning out too pat. Who had suggested to Jasper that he come to London, now of all times? She could just see Lucy, dropping her veiled hints, gently pushing her niece and the son of Thomazine's dearest friend together again, thinking this a most opportune moment: Sandro would need a father, Alathea a husband, and who better than Jasper?

I will not be pushed again, Alathea thought fiercely. *I shall have a long and forceful talk with dear Aunt Lucy, when I next find her alone.* But despite her resentment and indignation, she was no longer a tactless seventeen-year-old. She found it quite possible, even pleasant, to sit next to him at the supper-table and talk of Holland, where she had spent some time on her way to Italy, and which of course he knew so well from his student days at Leyden. She wondered how much he had been told of her recent past: surely the infallible grapevine of family gossip would have filled in the more scandalous details? But she kept the conversation on a relatively impersonal level, and he made no reference to her reason for going to Italy, nor to the child sitting under Becca's capable wing at the end of the table, fussing about English food but now blessedly free of English cold. Once or twice she saw his eyes stray to the child, and then back to her face, as if checking the resemblance, but save in colouring, and that was also his father's, there was little. Sandro had her hair, silver-fair and curling, and Rochester's dark eyes, but the rest was himself, and his sunny, wilful, solid personality all his own as well. Her dearest wish for him was that he should escape his father's strange, fantastic, tormented mind, and grow up unsullied by genius or wild high spirits.

After supper, the little boy was taken off to bed, drooping, by Becca, and they gathered round the fire and the pot of coffee in the hearth. So strong was her feeling of nostalgia, as she poured the black, fragrant, steaming liquid, that she could almost imagine that her companions were not her family, permanent and reassuring and somehow a little stifling, but Etherege and Buckhurst, Shepherd and Little Sid, and that if she looked up she would see not the dark-panelled parlour at Jermyn Street, but the bare plaster walls and long low ceiling of her studio in Covent Garden, and John Wilmot's amused dark eyes, bright with appreciation of her beauty and her wit.

Tears sprang to her eyes. Bending over the coffee-pot, she upbraided herself for her foolishness, but deeper came the knowledge that her tears were not so much for that glorious year of love, that had excluded and eclipsed everything else around her. The time in her life for which she felt most regret was that time at Covent Garden, when she had pitted her wits and her painting against the keenest minds in London, and won their friendship, affection, and respect. She had been accepted on their terms, as a companion rather than a woman – and women, to them, were delightful creatures to be bedded, or wedded, or lusted after, or lampooned, but never to be met mind to mind, wit to wit, poetry to painting. Once she had become Rochester's mistress, inevitable though that step had been, everything had changed, and now, if she invited them again to her studio, she would be fair game like all the other lovely frailties they courted so assiduously. Those days were gone for ever, and she must face the fact: what she could not face, yet, was her other fear – that she would not be able to resume her painting successfully.

Italy had helped her to cope with the end of her love affair. She had been surrounded by warmth, colour, light, excitement, new experiences, different sensations, so that the pain and bitter regret had been gently eased from her mind, and Sandro had been an additional and even more potent delight and distraction. Seeing Rochester in London had brought all the old feelings back, and for a little while she had been miserable with longing and grief, but now she was increasingly able to put it all into perspective. It had never been intended to last: it had lasted longer and given her more pleasure and joy than she had ever dared to hope, and she had been left with little hurt and a store of delightful memories. She felt guilty still about her treatment of him, running away with no word, but she knew with certainty that whatever the hurt she had done him, her action had saved them both much greater agony. For he was not really like Dorimant, who next to the coming to a good understanding with a new mistress, loved a quarrel with an old one.

And though, to the upright, she had been left with the infant badge of her shame, neither she nor her friends would ever think of Sandro in those terms, and she had, with great good fortune, escaped another common and less pleasant hazard of such an affair. She had been lucky. She had emerged almost unscathed, she had her beauty and her painting and her beloved child, money, a little, and family and friends, and she was only twenty-seven. She could not, would not pine for past phases of the moon.

Resolutely, her eyes bright and her mouth set, she looked up and straight into Jasper's freckled face, raw and painful with love. Confused, she glanced away immediately, overwhelmed with feelings of anger and embarrassment. *For God's sake*, she thought with annoyance, *who can possibly love unrequited for ten long years?*

Someone, the inconvenient conscience inside her said, *who is more constant than either yourself or your former lover – who professed such pain at your desertion, and was so quick to find his consolation.*

He was asking her a question. She snapped at him bad-temperedly, losing ten years' hard-won maturity in an instant. She saw her aunt's frown, but Jasper seemed unaffected by her rebuff, and some moments later seized his chance to move near to her. 'Have I offended you in some way?'

Only by existing, her foul mood wanted to say, but he was very hard to hurt. She said, in the same quiet tones, 'No – no, I'm sorry. I did not mean to be unkind.' She forced an empty smile. 'This chill weather disagrees with me.'

'Then you would wish yourself back in Italy?'

Alethea looked at him. He had now stripped all emotion from his face, but could not hide it in his eyes, and from her irritation and grief and uncertainty, came a new feeling of compassion. She gave him her first truly honest answer. 'No – despite the cold in my bones, and the cold in Sandro's nose – it's good to be back in a country I know, with a language I can speak without prompting all the natives into fits of laughter.' She grinned, remembering her first faltering attempts to make herself understood in Italian, and the misunderstandings and hilarity that had resulted. 'But I haven't wasted my time there: I have two boxes of sketches upstairs, and several paintings of my own, and some others that I bought while I was in Amsterdam and Florence.' She thought with a pang of Harry Savile's gift, the girl with the rose, its peace and beauty and melancholy acceptance of fate. She had not found anything half so fine, and would not have been able to afford it if she had.

'I would very much like to see them some time, if you would be so kind as to show me?' he said quietly, and something, whether it was pity, or the desire to make amends, a desire for friendship and an end to petty squabbles over a situation that neither of them could help, something made her say, 'Yes, of course: why not now?'

The attic room that had been her studio before she went to Italy was still, faintly, aromatic with the smells of paint and varnish and size. Unused canvases were still stacked against the walls, her limning table was pushed into a corner, the squab couch on which, so many times, she and John Wilmot had made such passionate love, on which, quite possibly, Sandro had been conceived, stood forlorn, dusty, neglected. But the stout wooden boxes that had travelled with her down more than a thousand miles of road, to Florence and back, were travel-stained and battered with much use. She knelt by them, heedless of the dusty floor, and opened the first.

Jasper Sewell, crouching beside her, his head filled with the wonder and the glory of being so close, alone, after so long, stared intently as she brought out four fat sketchbooks, sewn together and bound in plain dark red leather: though Alathea, with a simple pride, had had her monogram, AH, stamped in gold in the lower right-hand corner of each. And inside, painted in watercolours swift and flashing and true on the thick paper, was her response to Italian warmth and life and landscape: picturesque antique ruins decorated with sheep and trees; studies of the people of Florence, servants and friends who had sat for an afternoon and been made immortal; flowers bursting with profuse, colourful vitality from a bowl or jug or urn; the pale hair and baby curves of her son. So potent was the spell, the breath and enchantment of Italy, that he forgot the physical presence of the artist by his side, and saw through her eyes and with her vision, and into her soul.

There was another book of paintings, and two of drawings. These last were much quicker, sketchier and yet still abundant with life. People captured in the street, at their daily tasks, cypress trees tossing in the wind, a skittish horse, an Italian fop, a mother pulling a reluctant child, Lovell scratching, Oliver in an uncharacteristic moment of repose, Matthew caught playing exuberantly with his nephew, and Sandro, above all Sandro, from a tiny baby like any other, to the little boy Jasper had seen at the supper-table, elfin-faced and smiling, his personality fully and delightfully delineated, with great love. A sharp pang of sadness smote him: would she ever bear his children? And his imagination supplied a string of infants, variously red and blond, that would be depicted in some similar, future sketchbook.

'I take it you have heard about Alexander?' Alathea's voice, its usual ironic tone very marked, broke in on his dreams. 'Given the efficiency of family gossip, you can't have *failed* to have heard about him.'

'I have,' said Jasper carefully. 'Your aunt gave me some details.'

'Oh, has Lucy been talking to you? Then I don't need to explain any more,' said Alathea, with a wry grin. 'Everyone has been very silent with their disapproval.'

'Except Lord Bradfield – I heard him on the subject. The gist of it seemed to be that he was amply confirmed in his opinion of you. I came close to knocking him down,' said Jasper. 'But unfortunately he was my patient at the time, and that sort of behaviour is not expected in a physician.'

'Hardly.' He had at least brought a proper smile to her face. 'Or you'd have no practice left.' She turned to face him fully. 'Does my uncle keep well?'

'Do you require the truth?' he countered, his expression serious. As she nodded, surprised, he went on. 'I give him six months, perhaps a year of life – no more. He has a wasting sickness, a growth in his belly: he is in pain even now, and it will grow worse. He is not a particularly old man – what is he, fifty-five? – but he looks withered and ancient, so that you would not recognise him, and he is not reconciled to anything – illness, his family, his wife – he rails against them all.'

There was a silence. Alathea thought of the proud, intimidating man who had spoken to her so terrifyingly, now approaching death and refusing to accept his fate, and she thought also of her father, his brother and only three years younger, who did not now seem so immortal. Something of her distress must have shown in her face, for he said with concern, 'Is the news a shock? I did not think – I should have broken it more gently – have I upset you?'

'No – I was surprised, more than anything,' said Alathea sadly. 'I won't be a hypocrite, I'd be the first to admit I have no love for the man – but pity, that's another matter.'

'He'll have none of any pity,' Jasper said, grimly. 'He has dismissed me – told me I was a rogue and a liar, and he's shut himself away and sees nobody save Malise, who brings him the estate business and has the devil's own job to wrest any money out of him. He refuses to be helped, or pitied, or even to take something to dull the pain – you know as well as I do how stiff-necked a breed Herons are, and he's the worst.'

She could well imagine it, but she still pitied that lonely, embittered, despairing man. 'And what of his wife? What does Meraud do?' She glanced at Jasper. 'Do you know the story?'

'About Susannah? Of course. And about what she tried to do before poor Nell was born. But she has her just deserts now, I suppose, for somehow, God knows how, he has seen her in her true colours. She lives in Goldhayes still, but she has separate apartments, and few favours, and no friends.' He shook his head thoughtfully and his eyes were bleak. Alathea guessed that she was not being told the whole story. 'But the talk's gone morbid – let's speak of something more cheerful. Your pictures are truly beautiful – are you going to resume your painting, here in London?'

To his surprise, she did not answer at once. Then she said slowly, 'I don't know. If I want to continue my independent life, to provide for myself, and Sandro, then, yes, I must. But there are difficulties.'

'Difficulties?' he said in disbelief, for her talent shone so clear, he could not imagine why there was not already a shining path beaten to her door.

She nodded. 'Yes, difficulties. I have been two and a half, nearly three years away, and I have been forgotten. I offended several clients when I went to Italy so abruptly – and I never finished the King's miniature, that might well have established me as a Court painter.'

'Then why did you go?'

'Because I was in love,' said Alathea, bleakly. 'I was in love, and ran away from the pain of its ending: and I was pregnant. Italy seemed like a wonderful solution to all my problems – and it exceeded all my wildest dreams.' She flicked a finger along the pages. 'As you have just seen. But more than any of those, I know now what it is to paint the truth. I learned things in Italy that make all that I did before seem shallow, of little worth, and I learned above all that my soul will only be satisfied with the truth: no more, no less. I want to paint life, all life – I want to observe everything that goes on around me, as the Dutch do, I want to put the colour of Italy into my painting. And,' she finished sadly, 'the prospect of doing portraits of fat, overdressed courtiers and fat, underdressed maids-of-honour for money no longer appeals.'

'I can imagine,' he said. He saw the answer so clearly – it screamed at him, why was it not so obvious to her? – but he had learned a little wisdom and patience in ten years, and he knew what she was like. Push her now, and he would lose her for ever: but stay here, pretending some indifference, gradually winning her trust and friendship, and he stood perhaps some small chance of success.

So, he kept his counsel, and helped her put the books back in the boxes, and when he saw Lucy Ashley's keen and expectant face on their return downstairs, determined to have a quiet word with her. It would be just like Lucy to leap in tactlessly with broad hints about the marvellous suitability of a match between Alathea and himself – and then she would turn against him for good.

Gently will do it, he thought, and hoped, and prayed, and trusted that the multitudinous sick of Bury St Edmunds would survive without his care for a month or so.

CHAPTER TWENTY-FIVE

A harbinger of death

. . . But never yet
Incest and Murder have so strangely met.
(Ford, *'Tis Pity She's a Whore*)

It was a very cold November day. Alathea had spent most of it in the attic studio, trying to put it in order for painting. She had been to see the Beales and their colourman, and had come away somewhat poorer but well-supplied once more with good quality oils and pigments and varnishes. Now the bottles and containers stood unused on a table while she struggled with canvases and primer and wished wholeheartedly for the efficient services of the boy Jonathan – but Jonathan was long since apprenticed to Norris, the Covent Garden frame-maker, and she thought wearily of the difficulties involved in training up another young assistant.

The unwelcome truth slid into her mind: she had lost the heart for painting portraits as a profession. She would never lose her fascination for faces, she would always love painting those whose features interested her, but she had a hideous vision of the procession of unlovely countenances, male and female, that would present themselves down the marching years, the endless demands for flattery, concealment, lies, disguise, the elimination of character in favour of fashion, the sneers at her sex, her style, her ageing face, her bastard son by London's most notorious rake, the inevitable assumptions that she was therefore ripe for the plucking, over and over again . . .

I'm too old and wise for this, she thought wryly, *and Sandro and John Wilmot between them have given me a new perspective on life. I am a painter, I always will be a painter, that will never change, but I can no longer please anyone but myself. My pride tells me I must try again, build up the clientèle I had before, behave as if John and Sandro and Italy had never been: but I don't know if I can.*

Dispirited, she finished the last canvas, cleaned the big priming brush, took off her old shirt (one of Hugh's, these days), made sure the fire was safe, and left the room. How to go about re-establishing herself in the eyes of fashionable London? She could hardly go to Whitehall and ask the King nicely to sit for her again, she thought ruefully, and then wondered – why not? It was just the sort of action that would appeal to the King. *And if he can pardon Colonel Blood for stealing the Crown Jewels*, said Alathea to herself, grinning, *he can certainly forgive me for failing to finish his portrait.*

Somewhat cheered by that more positive reflection, she ran down the stairs with more lightness of heart and foot than she had felt since her return, and nearly bumped headlong into Sarah, trotting up with an anxious frown. 'Oh, Mistress, there's a woman wants to see you, but I'm not sure if . . . she seems a little distracted,' said Sarah, disapprovingly.

'What kind of a woman?'

'Oh, poor, I think, her cloak's shabby and patched – but she speaks like a lady of quality,' said Sarah, who had never been afraid of offering her own opinions. 'Asking for money, most like – *and* she's got some squalling brat. Shall I turn her away?'

'No,' said Alathea, although she had just then been thinking of it: mention of a child had changed her mind. And in the wake of

Sarah's uneasy disapproval, she descended the last flight of stairs to the hall.

The woman was there, standing close to the fire, muffled up in her cloak: save that she was quite tall, nothing further could be distinguished about her. There was a child, similarly wrapped and bundled, clutching her skirts. As Alathea's feet tapped smartly down the polished wooden steps, she turned to face her, and put back her hood.

Revealed thus, her eyes huge and dark in the gaunt plain face, was Anne, Lady Drakelon.

Alathea's first emotion was one of total astonishment. She stood utterly still, as if she had taken root, and stared at her cousin. Anne had never been beautiful: now, she looked painfully ugly, thin to the point of emaciation and totally exhausted. A sudden fear struck Alathea, an old and long dormant emotion. Had something happened to Kit?

'I hope you don't mind,' said Anne, with a flat, harsh note in her voice that implied that if Alathea did mind, she herself did not particularly care, 'but I could not think of anyone else to whom I could go. I have left my husband.'

The uncompromising words fell like stones into the echoing air. Alathea stared at her, foolishly open-mouthed. 'Left? You've left Kit? But why?'

'I'm sure you can guess why,' said Anne, bleakly. 'May I stay?'

There was only one answer she could possibly give, and give it she did, despite the tumbling rush of misgivings that suddenly overwhelmed her. 'Yes – of course you may stay.'

It did not seem to penetrate: those dreadful, sombre eyes, so like Lord Bradfield's, and with that extra dimension of exhaustion that seemed to drain them of every vestige of light, stared lifelessly at Alathea. Then all of a sudden the tension went out of Anne's stiff, upright figure, as if pride had been the only thing keeping her erect, and she bent down to the child and pulled it against her, hugging it.

Such a human reaction touched Alathea – surely Anne had not been afraid that she would not let her in? She said tentatively, 'You must want something to eat – and the child, too – come up and sit by the fire and warm yourselves.'

With a visible effort, her cousin turned towards her. Sarah, smooth and efficient, moved quickly over and helped her to take off her cloak, and Alathea could not suppress an indrawn breath of shock. The gown that Anne wore underneath was appallingly ancient and threadbare, more suited to a beggar: and disappearing under her sleeves, in great streaks of purple and yellow, bruises marred her arms.

She saw Alathea's horrified expression, mirrored by Sarah's, and flushed painfully. The maid, covering the moment of embarrassment, knelt down and briskly divested the infant of its outer garments. It was about Sandro's age, perhaps, but much too thin, with a white, frightened expression and sexlessly clad in petticoats, and its face, clearly visible for the first time, was disfigured by a great, new, jagged gash that ran from eye to jaw.

'Sweet Jesus Christ,' Alathea said, and her eyes shot to Anne with the unspoken, horrified question.

'A thrown wine-bottle,' said Anne. 'I can bear it for myself, but not for her. So I left.'

Alathea, seeing the maid's face as appalled as her own, said quickly, 'Sarah, can you ask Mistress Lewis for some hot food, a posset for the little girl, some mulled wine, a nourishing broth – and bring some more coal up to the parlour?'

'And I'll make up the spare bed in Master Matthew's old room, and put a warming pan in it,' said Sarah, who like Hen responded to distress with action, and disappeared in the direction of the basement kitchen.

'Come upstairs,' said Alathea, gently, and like a sleepwalker Anne Drakelon followed her, the child clinging to her skirts and hampering her progress. Alathea turned once, offering to carry her, but the child in sudden panic shook her head wildly and hid behind her mother. Unlike the talkative Sandro, she had not spoken at all in the five minutes or so that she had been in the house.

She waited until Sarah had come in with her steaming tray, until Anne and her daughter had ceased to huddle quite so close to the fire, and until the hot food had restored some colour to their cheeks. The little girl bore small resemblance to her father, poor child: she had Anne's straight, black hair, and grey-blue eyes that flinched away from every movement save her mother's. And that dreadful gash, that had obviously missed the eye only by the smallest of margins, would almost certainly scar her for life. *If Kit did this*, thought Alathea with grief and anger, *he's run mad in earnest.*

Anne put down her posset cup, and turned those dead eyes to her hostess. 'Are you alone here?'

'Oh, no – Hugh and Susannah and Hen live here too, but Hugh is at the Palace, and will be tonight, he's on duty in the Duke's bedchamber. And Jasper Sewell is here too, Hen and Sue have taken him to the theatre. And there are Becca and Alexander as well.'

'Good – I am glad. He may pursue me, you see,' said Anne, and she shivered, as if she had spoken of something immeasurably evil.

Alathea felt the first pangs of emotion – grief, pity, terror – begin to spring up in her heart. She said quietly, 'Can you tell me what happened?'

Anne turned to look at the raging fire: one bruised arm crept out to hug the silent, waif-like child closer. After a long while she said, her voice low and taut with feeling, 'It was all right at first. I did love him, I think – I knew he did not love me, but so many marriages start with less, and end in great affection on each side. I thought it didn't matter – I thought that his love would grow. And there was so much to do, at Danby, you cannot imagine – he thought he had made it so fine and comfortable and it was like setting up home in a leaking barn. Then I found I was with child, and he was so pleased – a son to carry on the family name, you have never seen such delight – and I was so happy.' She glanced down at the huddled child beside her. 'But it was Isabella.'

Hearing her name, the little girl looked up and said something in a high treble. Her mother smiled, and spoke softly. 'Yes, we will go to bed soon, but I must tell your cousin a story first. Do you want to sit on my lap?'

There was a nod of assent. Anne lifted the frail-looking infant on to her knee, and held her close. Isabella buried her scarred face in her mother's appalling gown, and seemed to fall asleep. Her thin, bruised hand stroking the child's head, Anne went on.

'He was very disappointed when he found his heir was a girl – the first in his family for three generations, he said. He got very drunk, and accused me . . . ' Her voice faltered and another painful flush stained her cheeks. 'He said all kinds of dreadful things, but he did not touch me. Not then. I put it down to the drink, the disappointment – I still loved him, I did not think he was really like that.'

Alathea, remembering that terrible rage directed against herself, said nothing, and Anne continued, her voice growing more and more strained as the dreadful tale was told.

'For a while it seemed as if I was right. I had hopes of another child, and this time I was sure it would be a boy. And then he had – we had – a letter from Aunt Lucy. It was in January, nearly three years ago – there was snow on the ground, I can remember the light in all the rooms, and the fires crackling, and sitting in a chair by the hearth in the parlour, stitching, and Bella in her cradle – so peaceful, the last time that I was happy. And then a boy came in with the letter, and Kit sounded pleased, and opened it, and began reading . . .'

Her voice tailed away, and her eyes stared at remembered horror. Alathea, a cold and terrible fear inside her, knew what was to come, even as her cousin continued, her speech labouring.

'Aunt Lucy wrote that you had gone to Italy, and she said also that you had been the mistress of the Earl of Rochester, and you were going to have his child. It was family gossip, like all Aunt Lucy writes – but he crumpled it up, and threw it in the fire before he had finished reading it to me, and shouted when I protested.' She swallowed convulsively, and took a gulp of the mulled wine, still tepid by the hearth. 'He got drunk again within the hour. He shouted and railed against you – he said things – things I could not believe. He said you were a slut, any man's whore, I had never heard such words, such obscenities.' Her voice acquired a wry, self-mocking tone. 'I was innocent – then. I remonstrated with him. He hit me. Then he raped me. He was weeping as he did it – as if I were someone else. And that night I lost the child I was carrying. And it would have been a boy.'

The brief, sparse words carried their own burden of unbearable tragedy: the flat sound of her voice was quite without drama or self-pity. Alathea had disliked her, once, but the agonies Anne had endured at the hands of her husband transcended such petty emotions as dislike or irritation. The other girl continued, bleakly. 'I think I knew the truth then, but for a while I could not accept it. But he had married me because I was everything you were not: I was plain, dark, wealthy, not gifted with any talent. And he turned against me because I am plain, and dark, and an heiress, and ungifted. He taunted me with it, endlessly, he railed against you –

and yet he did not hate you.' For the first time her eyes turned to stare fully into Alathea's face, and the words came with difficulty, as if she still found the thought appalling. 'He is in love with you – his own sister.'

'I know,' said Alathea unhappily. 'But I thought – I thought he had suppressed – I thought his marriage would be the end of it.'

'You were wrong,' said Anne. Her breathing came fast: she tried to speak, failed, and tried again. 'You – forgive me, I must know, I must, he seemed to imply – did – did you ever do anything to encourage him?'

The silence was broken only by the crackle of the fire, and the ragged, gasping breaths of her cousin. Alathea swallowed, and knew she must tell the truth: and did so. 'I did not know I was doing it – I enjoyed his company, I did not think – how could I think he intended more? And by the time I realised, it was too late.' She fell silent for a moment, remembering that terrible night when Kit had at last made the true nature of his feelings clear, and then finished honestly, as she must. 'He tried to rape me, but Hugh stopped him. And I suppose it could be said that I encouraged him . . . certainly he did not think he would be rebuffed . . . yet I did not realise what he wanted of me, it was so utterly alien to all I knew . . . ' She looked at Anne sitting like a statue, marble and ebony by the fire, and added quietly, 'I am so sorry, so very sorry.'

'You are not to blame. Nor am I, nor Isabella, nor Kit himself – for he is a victim of the past, like everyone else in this benighted family,' said her cousin, and real, passionate anger informed her voice for the first time. 'All of them, our parents, still bound in chains of guilt and remorse and love and hatred that were forged thirty years ago. And we suffer the consequences, and none more so than my husband. I hate him now, for what he has done to me, and above all for turning Isabella from a happy child into this little ghost: but I loved him once, and I can understand why he is so violent, and grieve for what might have been if his stars were kinder.' She sighed, her eyes gazing unblinking into the ebbing fire. 'I hope he will not come here. But if he does . . . he loves you so much, you can reach him if anyone can. Will you help? I cannot go back to him, I cannot – and I have nowhere else to go.'

Alathea knew that she could not reject this desperate plea from her once-proud cousin, now so tragically humbled. She must give her refuge, and try to support these extra mouths on the scanty income from her painting. Her heart still was not in it, however imperative it became to reconstruct her career, but she knew where her duty lay, regardless of the trap that seemed to be closing in upon her, and she determined grimly to succeed.

The arrival of Anne Drakelon and her small daughter at the Jermyn Street house was not at first entirely welcomed by the rest of the inhabitants: Hugh, for one, found the prospect of Kit, avenging angel and drunken brute, descending on them to reclaim his wife a profoundly disturbing one. But the days went by and there was no sign of him, and gradually the tension trickled out of the household. Sandro was delighted to have a companion near in age to himself, Becca revelled in her new charge, and all Henrietta's maternal instincts were aroused by the tiny Isabella, so wan and silent, so hideously scarred. Jasper, giving his professional opinion, pronounced that the gash was not so bad as it appeared, and stood a good chance of mending with very little mark. 'Children heal much faster than adults – perhaps it's because they're younger, and fresher!'

He had been with them for three weeks, and showed no signs of leaving. And Alathea's resentment and annoyance at his visit had faded, over those weeks, into a friendly acceptance of his presence in the household. She could talk with him about Holland, and the Dutch painters, converse about matters chemical, connected with metals and poisons and pigments, or just enjoy his talk, which was amusing without making a conscious effort, unlike so many Wits, and which had a thread of fantasy woven into it which reminded her, with a pang of nostalgic regret, of Rochester.

But she would not, would never, take the easy way out of her problem.

The winter would be hard, the portents were all there: heavy crops of berries in the scrubby trees left in Pall Mall or St James's Park, frost-laden fogs that rimed every branch and twig and blade of grass in glittering white, and robbed the warm breath from the lungs. There were chaldrons of coal in the cellar, and the boy Tom, no longer such a boy, joked that his arms would be as long as an ape's after heaving buckets of it upstairs all winter. Sandro was enchanted by the white whorls of frost on every window, and his health improved in the crisp dry air. Alathea had had several warm winter suits, coats and petticoats in blue and green and dark red, made up for him, but he seemed in a fair way to outgrowing them already. Lacking any other infant with whom to make a close comparison, she had never thought him to be a particularly large child, but Isabella, more than a year older, was like a little doll, tiny and fragile-looking, beside her cousin. He was the only male of whom she had shown no fear at all, for such was the scar that her father's violence had left upon her mind as well as her face, that at first she had shrunk away from the friendly approaches of Hugh and Jasper and Tom, and had buried her head in her mother's skirts. Gradually, however, she had become a little more confident, and she had even submitted, albeit reluctantly, to Jasper's gentle investigation of her face.

Looking now at the two heads, one dark and sleek, one bright and riotously curling, bent together over some crude chapbook, Alathea thought with amusement that Lucy, beholding the same scene, would immediately begin to plan a marriage, twenty years in the future. It was another cold evening, and she had finished her work early: in November, the painting hours were short. She had managed to glean a trickle of clients, old friends, acquaintances from the past: Henry Guy, who was on the fringe of the Wits, had sat to her today, and she had enjoyed talking to him, teasing him about his ambition to go to Heaven (or a hotter place) as much encumbered by wealth as possible. It had almost been like old times, if she had been able to ignore his leering hints, and once that little misunderstanding had been cleared up, they had got on famously. The portrait would be a good one, she had felt the tingling magic in her fingers for the first time since leaving Italy: and for the moment, she was satisfied and content with the day's work.

She glanced round at the other occupants of the parlour. Anne stitched away, with a neat patience that Alathea would never emulate in a hundred years of practice, at a new gown to replace the one in which she had arrived, for Kit, in addition to all his other crimes, had refused his wife any new clothes at all for the last two years. Alathea had lent her cousin two of her own, since they were of similar height and build, tall and slender, but Anne was thin, gawky and bony-looking, entirely lacking her more fortunate cousin's grace and unconscious elegance, even when dressed in paint.

How we are slaves to our looks, Alathea thought ruefully, gazing at Lady Drakelon's large, uncompromising nose and thick brows. *Anne, Nell, myself, Susannah: our beauty, or the lack of it, has shaped our lives, and yet we cannot choose our features nor rearrange them at our will. The only person I know well who has risen above the handicap of her face is Rosaling – she has always made the best of what she has.*

And Hen, of course. Henrietta Jermyn, now in her thirties, still looked like the popular ideal of a country milkmaid, with that round face and freckles and red hair. But Hen had never asked much from life, and life in return had been generous to her. Alathea had wondered recently if Hen were truly happy at Jermyn Street. But she gave no sign of misery, no indication of a yearning for pastures new, no desire for a new husband, and seemed perfectly content with her daughter, her organising talents occupied in running the house, her friends around her, all the diversions of fashionable London within her grasp. She was sitting at one end of the table by the tightly drawn curtains, instructing Becca in the mysteries of reckoning, and her daughter, ten and serious with long straight hair swinging round her face, pored over her page, quill in hand. Beyond, at the other end, Jasper and Susannah hunched intently over a chessboard: it had come as no surprise at all to Alathea to discover that Hugh's fluffy wife was a demon chess-player with a fine command of devious tactics. She had penned Jasper into a corner, taken his queen, and was now constructing a masterly trap from which there would be no escape. Alathea, whose talents lay elsewhere, got up to take a closer look: chess had always defeated her, and Math had tried several times, and failed utterly, to teach her more than the basic moves.

Jasper, a thin, freckled hand running through his hair, was conceding defeat. 'I thought I had some competence, but beside you I'm a beginner! What fiend taught you to play like that?'

'Hugh,' said Susannah. 'I'd never played before I met him. He taught me everything.'

'Do you beat him?'

'Most times, yes, I do,' Susannah said artlessly, lowering her long lashes.

Jasper, with a groan, began to put the pieces away in their carved box. 'And he's the best player I know. How about cards, now? Are piquet or whist amongst your accomplishments?'

'A little,' said Susannah, and gave him her wide, friendly,

dazzling smile. 'I'm not very good at those, though. I'm glad you can play chess – no one but Hugh will give me a game now, and I do so like to win!'

A knocking sound came faintly up above the hiss and crackle of the fire. It could not be Hugh: he was on duty at St James's Palace and would not be back until the morning, and besides, he had a key. Probably Oliver, Alathea decided. He was a frequent visitor, fretting under the restrictions of life at the House of the Ash Tree, and nostalgic for Italy. Whoever it was, Sarah or Tom or the new maid, Jane, would answer it.

There was a sharp tug at her skirt. She turned to see Sandro, finger at the corner of a mischievous grin, staring up at her. 'Mama? When's supper?'

'Not yet, piglet,' Alathea said, and scooped him up. The long arms linked round her neck, and the golden head was pressed against her own. 'I'm *so* hungry,' he complained persuasively.

'It'll be ready when the cook has finished it. Here's Sarah now – let's ask her, shall we?'

But Sarah stood in the doorway, her dark, pleasant face set in lines of stiff disapproval, and made her announcement. 'Sir Christopher Drakelow.'

It was as if a spell had been cast. No one moved, except for the maid. She stood aside to let the intruder pass. Alathea glanced involuntarily past Sandro's fly-away curls to where Anne was sitting, as if turned to stone, her eyes dark holes in the stark white of her face, and below, in reflection, the smaller countenance of her daughter.

And then Kit walked into the room, and Alathea, mindful of Anne's earlier plea, turned to confront him.

It was as much as she could do not to gasp at the change in him. The once-handsome face had grown bloated and puffy with drink, the aristocratic nose was reddened and swollen, there were grim lines on his face and bags under his eyes. Those eyes, alone unchanged, stared out from the travesty of his face with an unbearable agony emblazoned within. They locked on Alathea's, and she saw his eyes dilate with shock. Then he mastered himself, and the well-remembered voice, that she had heard laughing and joking, and ranting with insane rage, said savagely, 'I've come for my wife – is she here?'

'She is,' said Alathea, guessing that she was blocking his view.

'However, I'm afraid she has no intention of committing herself to your custody – not now, and not ever.'

There was a brief silence. No one moved save for Sandro, who twisted round in her arms to stare at the stranger. Then he said, his voice curious, 'Who's that?'

'That's your Uncle Kit,' said Alathea, her throat constricted with the effort of keeping her voice normal. 'Say hello to your Uncle Kit.'

'Hello,' said Sandro, with interest, and gave his uncle an exploratory smile. Kit's face underwent an extraordinary struggle, terrifying in the strength of the passions it revealed. Then, with a single explosive movement, he thrust past her, almost knocking her flying, and stood over Anne. With a gesture more eloquent than any words or cries, the child Isabella's pale face crumpled with fear, and she turned and buried her head in her mother's lap.

'You are coming back,' said Kit, his voice low and desperate. 'You are coming back – and the child, too. I have a room at an inn in Holborn. Leave this house and come back now, and we will go to Yorkshire in the morning.'

'No,' said Anne bleakly, and her hands, free of bruises now, tightened around the thin, trembling body of her daughter.

'You will come back.' Kit stepped forward: his bulk loomed over the fragile figure of his wife. 'Leave. *Now*.'

Alathea glanced round. Sarah was still standing in the doorway, an expression of lively concern on her face. Swiftly and soundlessly, she moved towards her maid, and when she was within hearing distance, mouthed desperately to her. 'Sarah! Send a message to Hugh!'

Sarah was not stupid. She gave a nod of understanding and vanished: doubtless Tom, who knew the ways of palaces, would be routed out of the warm kitchen and sent on his chilly errand. Feeling a good deal safer for her action, Alathea turned back in time to see Kit's hands shoot out to grasp Anne's thin shoulders.

'You will come back, do you hear me? You're my wife, you *will* come back!'

'No, I won't,' said Anne, her voice level and seemingly calm, in sharp contrast to the wild rage in her husbands's. 'You must be mad to think I'd go back to you – after what you did to Isabella – she's terrified of you.'

'It won't happen again,' said Kit, with a note in his words that gave that statement the lie, and his wife, still with that deceptive calm, repeated her reply. 'No – understand me, Kit, I will not go. I will stay here, with Isabella. Our marriage is ended, Kit, understand? It is over, finished, dead – if it had ever lived. You will have no more of me, and if you want your precious heir, think you on the one you killed!'

There was a dreadful silence. Sandro, who was a sensitive child, had picked up the undercurrents of emotion in the adults' words, and Alathea could feel tremors running through his solid little body. 'Why they fighting?' said his small, unhappy voice into the quiet. 'Mama, why they fighting? Please make them stop.'

Kit turned at that, his face distorted and convulsed with rage. Alathea stared at his eyes, the blue, vivid eyes that had had such terrible power over her, all her life. She had deceived herself when she had thought his interest in her had died – for now that look, the devouring lust and engulfing, insane passion was back in full measure. Appalled, she stood transfixed by his malevolent stare, like a rabbit before a snake, or like the child Alathea, who had once stood powerless as her terrible elder brother ripped up the drawings that were her life.

Only this time, it was not her art that was in danger.

'You put her up to this, didn't you,' said his voice, savage with grief and fury. 'You told her to say it – you told her not to come back to me!'

'It was her decision alone,' said Alathea. She had read his eyes, she saw the killing intent in them, but there seemed to be nothing she could do: her limbs would not obey her, and the child, rigid and heavy in her arms, seemed to weigh her down. 'Kit, it seems you have made some mistakes. Why not leave us now, and come back tomorrow when you're in a better frame of mind?' Looking at his wild face and swaying figure, she was fairly sure he was drunk. 'We can discuss it more calmly then – '

'No!' Kit shouted. 'No, you whore, you brazen slut – you dare to stand there with your bastard in your arms and preach morality at me? Where's your morality, eh? Where's your precious virtue? You didn't want me, oh no, you didn't want me even though you led me on to believe that you did, you led me into loving you, with your angel's face and devil's heart, and turned all your contempt on me – and then you go behind my back to become Rochester's whore! That evil reptile! Did you catch anything else from him, besides his bastard? Are you rotten from within, like a Sodom drab? I wouldn't touch you now, you scum, you filth . . . ' And he took refuge in shouting obscenities at her, advancing step by step, and she saw the glare in those terrible eyes, and the flecks of spittle around his mouth, and recognised his madness. Desperately she clutched Sandro tightly to her: he had begun to cry, and his sobs added to the endless, mindless stream of sewer language emanating from her brother's distorted mouth.

'Stop!' she cried: it had succeeded once before, but this time he was gone too far. She shouted it again and again, and someone else's voice joined in, masculine, it must be Jasper, and Susannah yelled something and then she realised that his words had changed, they made sense now and she knew with horror what he was saying.

'I love you Thea, why did you have to do this to me, you deserve to die, you hurt me so much, you whore, you're better dead, I'd be better off without you, and your brat as well, he comes of foul stock, kill two evils with one blade . . . '

And with a harsh metallic rasp that cut through all the noise, he drew his sword, and lunged at her.

She saw the bright blade coming, and screamed, flinging herself aside. The tip caught in her skirts, and was ripped free, and Hen was shouting something at Kit and he, his face terribly contorted with grief, and madness, and rage, and twisted love, drew back his hand and lunged again.

And this time, he could not miss.

The point stabbed at her, aiming for the heart through Sandro's small body. She was pressed hard against the door, she could not possibly escape. And then something, someone, came between them, there was a scuffle, a gasp and grunt of pain as the sword went home. Hen appeared at her side and pushed her away as Jasper, his waistcoat suddenly pouring scarlet, fell face downwards at her feet.

'My God, you've killed him!' The cry was Susannah's.

Kit stood staring at the body on the floor, the growing puddle of blood, and the rank red stain on his sword, and then, with a great wordless cry of anguish, turned the blade against his sister for the third and final time.

It never reached her, for Anne Drakelon, her face as impassive as stone, had risen from her chair by the fire, and picked up the heavy iron poker from its stand by the hearth: and with all her force struck her husband across the back of the head.

It felled him as an axe fells a forest tree. He stood swaying for an instant, all the terrible life suddenly fled from his face and an appalling vacancy in its place, and then he crashed forward on to the body of the man who had, once, been his childhood friend.

There was silence in the room, though there were confused noises from downstairs, where some commotion had evidently been heard. Anne stood above her husband, the poker still in her hands like a two-handed sword, her breath coming suddenly in great gasps: then she turned abruptly and thrust the weapon into the heart of the fire. Alathea stared blankly at the two men lying on the floor, the blood, her sobbing son, arms clutching her neck and his hair in her face, Becca's distraught, tearstained expression as she comforted Isabella, who was also crying, and above all, the look on Hen's face as she stared at the body of her beloved brother.

'Are they dead?' It was Susannah who spoke. Less emotionally involved than any of them, she walked round the table, knelt by the huddled shapes of Kit and Jasper, and took one outstretched hand. It was Kit's. The moment seemed to stretch for aeons as she sought for a pulse, only to lay it down again with a shake of her head. 'I think he's dead.'

Hen seemed to rouse herself from her shock. She knelt also, and turned Kit over with two blunt, capable hands. There was no doubt of it, life had left that flaccid, empty face with the staring, half-closed eyes and slack mouth. Alathea could bear only a brief glimpse: then she turned abruptly and buried her face in her son's fair hair, and wept bitterly and helplessly for a tormented, useless life and a fate that was so futile and so tragic.

'Jasper's alive,' someone said behind her. 'Quick, what can we use for bandages?' And a hand tugged at her sleeve and Becca's voice, serious and kind, said, 'It's all right, Jasper's alive, he's alive!'

But it was not Jasper she wept for, not Jasper's life wasted, despatched at the end as a herdsman would destroy a mad bull: and she wept also for herself, and for the guilt she felt for her part in that waste, and the agonising feeling – if only she had acted differently just now, perhaps he would be living still?

And she might be dead, not him, said the still small voice of reason within her, and if it had not been for Jasper and for Anne, both she and Sandro would undoubtedly have been killed.

So her conscience made her master herself. She gave the weeping Sandro to Becca, and turned reluctantly back to the appalling scene behind her. Someone had cast a table-rug over Kit's dead face, so that she did not have to see him. Hen was kneeling by her brother's side, supporting him while Susannah's tiny deft fingers swiftly undid buttons and ripped apart his shirt, to expose the wound that Kit's sword had made. It was a long, ragged and evil-looking gash, deep and heavily bleeding, running along his right side. Jasper had regained consciousness: his face grey-white under the freckles, he peered down at the damage and offered his professional opinion. 'It's not so serious. But get something to stop the bleeding, for Christ's sake!'

Three petticoats were simultaneously ripped, folded and placed over the wound. Jasper flinched with the pain, and his eyes closed briefly. He opened them upon his sister's face, pinched and taut with shock, and said on a gasp, 'Kit! What of Kit?'

'Dead. Anne hit him too hard with a poker.'

'Then you're safe – Thea's safe – he must have been mad . . . ' Jasper closed his eyes again, feeling himself dazed and floating, suddenly remote. He had seen this often enough in patients suffering from injury, and knew that it could kill quicker than any mere wound. 'Hen – a rug – cold – cover me.'

Another table-carpet was brought: voices hovered above him, exclaiming, explaining: the servants had appeared on the scene. A hand touched his arm and he opened his eyes briefly, to see Alathea's face, running with tears. She wiped them away with the back of her hand and said haltingly, 'Thank you – you saved my life, you saved Sandro too – how can I ever thank you?'

It was typical of Jasper that even in this extremity he was capable of a joke. A smile of mischief appeared suddenly, and lingered on his mouth. 'I think . . . you know very well how you can thank me best!'

CHAPTER TWENTY-SIX

Love in a snowdrift

I yield upon great persuasion.
(Shakespeare, *Much Ado About Nothing*)

When Hugh Trevelyan, summoned by an urgent and garbled message from his house, finally managed to extricate himself from the coils of Court life and return to Jermyn Street, he found the house strangely quiet. He stood in the panelled hall, with its Dutch pictures and tiled floor, and listened. There were voices, and they came from upstairs. With a terrible premonition of disaster, he ran up to the first floor and opened the door of the chamber from which the voices had emanated.

It was Jasper's room, and his boyhood companion, the other member of that long-vanished, unholy triumvirate, lay in the bed, evidently ill, with Susannah bathing his brow and Henrietta, an unaccustomed frown between her eyes, talking to him quietly and administering something from a spoon. Bewildered, Hugh stared at the little scene, unnoticed by the others until he spoke. 'What in God's name has happened?'

'Hugh!' Susannah flung down the damp napkin and hurled herself at her husband. Once in his arms, she did not weep, but he could feel her slight body trembling violently.

He looked over at Henrietta, and repeated his question. 'Will one of you please tell me what has happened?'

Henrietta put the spoon down by a nameless, small glass bottle on a cabinet by the bedside, laid a gentle hand against her drowsy brother's cheek, and turned to face him. Quietly, she said, 'There's been an accident – no, a murder would describe it better.'

'A murder!' Hugh took a step forward, dislodged Susannah, and stopped. 'A *murder*? Who, for Christ's sake?'

'Kit,' said Susannah, and briefly, without embellishment, the two of them told him what had happened.

The silence when they had finished was broken only by Jasper's sleeping, slow breathing. Hugh said at last, his composure shaken for once, 'Anne? *Anne* killed him? With a *poker*?'

'Why not? It worked,' said Hen wearily. She rubbed her hand

across her tired eyes and glanced around at her slumbering brother. 'He tried to kill Thea: he would have done, too, in that small space. Jasper put himself between them, though he was quite unarmed, and saved her then, and Anne saved her life afterwards. She hit him from behind with the poker before he could strike again.' She glanced once more at Jasper's still, pale figure.

Hugh said quickly, 'Was he badly hurt?'

'Since he was able to diagnose the extent of his injury, I don't think so,' said Henrietta, with a faint, tired smile.

'And Thea? Did – is she hurt?'

'No, she's not harmed,' Susannah told him.

Hen elaborated. 'There's no mark on her, no – nor on Sandro, she had him in her arms, Kit fully meant to kill him too. But,' said Hen, prosaic practical Hen, 'I think the damage to her mind is much greater.'

'Where is she?'

'She is watching over him in the little parlour: we put him there, afterwards. Anne is there too. Becca has put Isabella and Sandro to bed, and pray God they all forget what they have seen and heard tonight,' said Hen soberly. 'Do you want to go see her? Sue and I will stay here for a while, until Jasper is properly asleep.'

'Yes, I want to see her,' said Hugh, with a mixture of relief, that she had escaped unscathed, and anxiety both for his beloved niece and for the other witnesses of the tragedy.

As he reached the door, Hen added, 'Hugh – before the night's out we must make plans. I don't think public revelation of the truth would do anyone any good – least of all Anne and Alathea. Shall we talk later?'

'Later,' said Hugh, smiling bleakly at those steady, amber eyes. 'But first, I must see Thea.'

He found her, as Hen had told him, in the smaller parlour, seldom used and facing on to the backs of the houses in St James's Square. There had been no fire lit, and the little room was icy cold and smelled of stale air, despite Henrietta's care. A small half-tester bed dominated one half of the room, and on that bed lay all that remained of Sir Christopher Drakelon, the last male bearer of a name that had dominated Yorkshire for six hundred years.

His wife sat on one side of the bed, her face white and impassive, withdrawn so utterly into her own thoughts that she did not look round when Hugh entered. Since the act of murder with which she had put an end to his life, she had said nothing, although she had helped to lay the body out with a business-like and practical lack of emotion that had appalled Hen. No grief, no remorse, no pity or regret appeared on that plain, awkward face, only a bleak and chilly remoteness from reality. Hugh, who could have done that deed in rage, in the heat of the moment, found himself recoiling from such cold callousness. His eyes sought and found Alathea. She sat on the floor by the other side of the bed, her thin, pale cheek resting against the counterpane, as if she could not bear to look at the body of her brother, and yet could not be parted from him: and unheeded tears were trickling down her face.

She had all but forgotten the reason for his death, the insane and murderous rage which had been the last emotion on his face: her one thought was that she had failed him. For only now, when it was irrevocably too late, could she acknowledge her feelings for him, could she say, from her full heart silently to his empty shell, *I love you*. Not, perhaps, in the way that he had wanted, but still she had loved him, and that love, that took note also of what might have been, and of the Kit who had too soon disappeared behind his obsession, had stayed true and constant through the years, had somehow survived his actions and his words, and now at last was resurrected and accepted.

His tragedy had been that the fierceness of his feelings had prevented her from revealing her own love, knowing it would be misinterpreted and twisted into something more akin to his: and so, for Kit, it would always have been too late.

It was this, and her regret and sorrow, that had caused her tears. She sought back through her memories, seeing the moments when, perhaps, some word from her might have turned the tide a little, averted some of the pain and torment for them both. But also, in a way she was glad that his life had ended so suddenly, in such a dreadfully fitting manner, for he had seemed truly insane, and she knew that death was preferable to the agonies he faced with a mind disintegrating into violence and drink, obsession and fantasy. Perhaps, if Jasper and Anne had not acted, if he had succeeded in killing the sister he both loved and hated, he would then have killed himself. She thought it very likely: and if it had indeed been so, Anne had saved him from two great sins, and lessened the burden on his soul.

Then, she looked up, and saw Hugh standing in the doorway with that look of affectionate concern on his face, and felt suddenly safe, and protected, and shielded from further harm. She got up, stumbling as pins and needles tingled up her stiff legs, and came towards him, but her control was not as great as Susannah's, for when she reached Hugh's arms she wept.

She did not, however, cry for very long. Hugh's presence had reminded her that what had happened might be tragic to herself, to Anne perhaps, for she had loved him once, or possibly to Thomazine, but no one else had cared for him, no one else would mourn. And most would say, as she knew that Hugh would, that his death removed many problems, and was no more than a relief to all who knew him.

Oh, Kit, what a waste, she thought on a sob: but she knew that, despite her own guilt and remorse, like Nell he had been his own worst enemy, and like Nell, his fate had at last overtaken him.

'Are you all right?' Hugh demanded quietly, and Alathea nodded briefly.

'Yes – I'm quite unharmed. And I have a great deal to thank Jasper for – and Anne.' Her eyes slid sideways to glance at the still figure of her cousin, silent and grim by the bed. 'It's terrible – how she – she killed him – as if it were her duty, and shows no feelings at all – it's unnatural.'

'Perhaps she hides them,' said Hugh. Anne's behaviour had indeed been unnatural, but the quickness and boldness of her action had saved two lives, perhaps more, and she deserved respect for that, even if she had thereby committed one of the greatest of all crimes.

That thought reminded him of what must be done to shield Anne, Lady Drakelon, from the penalties inflicted on women who had murdered their husbands – even if under some provocation, or to save the life of another.

So he took Alathea's arm and guided her gently back into the main parlour. There, Henrietta and Susannah were sitting by the fire, supping chocolate and talking quietly. For once, their free consumption of a beverage so expensive that Alathea had had to ration it, went unnoticed.

'Like it or not,' said Hugh to his wife, his niece and his friend, 'we must talk. Now. Anne's life may depend upon it.'

'She wouldn't be the first lady of quality to get away with

murder,' said Hen. 'Look at that Carr woman, in King James's time. There are witnesses aplenty to testify that Anne acted in Alathea's defence – that Kit had lost his reason, as well as being drunk – it would be rank injustice if she was not acquitted.'

'And if she was not?' Hugh pulled up a stool and stared grimly at them. 'That girl in the next room is half-way to madness herself. You must have seen it, you must have. What she's endured, these last few years, would be enough to unhinge most women. She's stronger than most women, it seems – but if you push her any further, she'll break.'

As she certainly would, under the burden of a trial, scandal, notoriety, possible imprisonment. Alathea thought suddenly of Lord Bradfield, lonely and ailing at Goldhayes, and of what such news would do to him; of Isabella, known the rest of her life as the daughter of a murderess; the whole family, tainted with suspicion. There were times, she acknowledged, when the truth was best hidden.

'Do you have a plan, then?' she asked Hugh, and Hugh, the devious and cunning courtier, of course had one ready.

'We give out that he and Jasper have a fever: Anne too, perhaps. Sarah can spread the news round about. And then, no surprise, in a day or two he dies. No coroner, no doctor, no problem. Sounds too easy, doesn't it? But I think it the best and simplest solution.'

And that was what they did. Since Jasper had developed a fever in truth, Sarah did not have to lie about her purchases of Peruvian Bark and other medicines in the apothecary's shop at Charing Cross, and the boy Tom, after some diligent search, found Kit's inn at Holborn and collected his baggage, spinning his tale as he did so. The Ashleys were informed of the illness at Jermyn Street, and warned not to come by for fear of infection, and Alathea wrote briefly with the news to Kit's steward at Denby, and also to her parents. Sooner or later, she would have to tell her father and mother the terrible truth, but for Anne's sake, for the moment she must lie.

She had, in any case, little chance to brood. Jasper's infected wound meant that he was for a while quite ill, tossing in delirium and needing constant care. The Peruvian Bark, which she could ill afford, brought the fever down, but she wished that he was well enough to advise her on his own treatment. Hen, who had nursed her husband in his fatal illness, was a tower of strength: Susannah helped stalwartly and Sarah was invaluable. Anne, however, had retreated into her own grim, silent world, and not even Isabella's fretful cries could bring her back.

Alathea sat with Jasper often, watching in case he harmed himself in his delirious tossing and turning. She listened, wishing that she did not have to, as he talked incessantly to people who were not there: patients, his mother, students in Holland, people in Bury, speaking in English, sometimes in Latin and very often in a hard, guttural-sounding language which she took to be Dutch. And once, in the soft dark of the early hours of morning, she was dozing by the bed, a book on her knee, and was jerked abruptly awake by the sound of her own name.

'I'm here,' she said quietly, and went swiftly to the bedside. By the light of the candle she had left burning on the table, she could see his overbright eyes shining, and his hand stretching out for her.

'Thea! Are you there?'

'I'm here,' she said again. His hot, dry hand touched hers and held it, so tightly she felt she must hear the bones crack.

'Thea – my love – I love you, do you know that?'

'I know,' she said sadly.

He went on, rambling inconsequentially. 'Your hair – the sun on it when I saw you – so beautiful – I love you so much, for ever, never to have or to hold, never to have, you won't marry me, might as well cage the wing – but think on me kindly, once in a while, will you?'

She found she was crying. What a waste, she had thought of Kit's tragically brief existence, and now she pondered Jasper's ten years, immured in Bury, lonely, bereft, while she filled her own days with all she could grab from life. A tear dropped from her nose on to Jasper's hand. He did not notice, but went on, his voice rising and falling, snatches of poetry and fragments of song, parts of conversations they had had together in the past, subtly distorted by time and fever; until suddenly, out of the shadows of the bed, his words rose, challenging. 'I love you – will you marry me, Thea? Will you marry me?'

And she was silent, filled with an extraordinary feeling, a sensation she had never dreamed that she would ever experience when faced with such a question, from anyone.

It was temptation.

For she did not want to return to the treadmill of a professional painter's life, and yet she would have to do so in order to support herself and maintain her independent existence in London. *If I marry Jasper*, she thought, *if I marry him* . . . and for the first time, allowed her mind to dwell on the possibilities.

He loved her very much. He was kind, considerate. He had something, that spark of difference, of mischief, that was very endearing. Already, in the three weeks he had been at Jermyn Street, she had come to admire his professional dedication, enjoy his sense of humour, and to respond to him with affection. He had saved her life, at great risk to his own, he had run unarmed between herself and Kit's sword, an act which must have taken enormous courage even if he had been spurred by his usual impetuous nature. He would tolerate her painting, even take an interest. He had a little house in Bury, she knew, and her imagination ran on to envisage them living there, with Sandro of course, supported by Jasper's earnings and her sale of a few paintings, leaving her time to 'study and improve', as Mary Beale put it. She cared no more for fame: she had seen now what it did, and what price it demanded. She wanted to tell the truth, and to satisfy her soul, and those desires were wholly at odds with the demands of fashion.

Oh, yes, she was tempted, sorely tempted: and she thought also of Lord Bradfield's deteriorating health and, hating herself, leaped ahead in her mind to the obvious conclusion. Soon, her family might once more be in possession of goldhayes, and they could go home.

Home. Home to Suffolk: home to Goldhayes. 'London is like being inside a drum,' Rochester had said to her once, 'you cannot think there.' The deep, slow peace of the countryside was a balm to her soul which she had applied too rarely. She thought of Goldhayes, of rose-red brick and green grass and walled gardens, sunshine and bees and plaster ceilings carved and lanced with light, reflected from the moat, the gracious, ancient tranquillity of the house where she had been born.

But you can't marry Jasper because you want to go home, said her conscience severely. *You do not love him: you might come to love him one day, I suppose, but you will never love anyone with the passion you had for John Wilmot. You have stuck out against marriage for so long, so stoutly, it'd be a blow to your pride to give in now. How would the mighty be fallen*!

'Thea?' Jasper's light quick voice, curiously altered and slurred by his delirium, intruded upon her dilemma. 'Thea, are you there? When will you answer? Will you ever answer?'

And Alathea, knowing that her own fate might overtake her yet, touched his other hand with affection, and sorrow, and respect. 'Yes – yes. I'll give you an answer, one way or the other – I'll give you an answer at Christmas!'

News of Sir Christopher Drakelon's sad demise was given out, two days after the tidings of his illness: and the next day, very quietly, his troubled spirit was at last laid to rest in the church of St Martin-in-the-Fields, in whose parish Jermyn Street lay until such time as the new church as St James's was finished. Alathea did not go, nor did any of the female members of the household. It was cold, and rained, and Hugh Trevelyan, standing at the graveside at the unfashionable hour of three in the afternoon, looked around at Dan Ashley and Oliver, who were the only other mourners, and reflected sadly on Kit's unhappy life, which had ended so abruptly and tragically, unmourned by any – save one – and unloved by any – save one.

And ironically, it was his attempt to kill that one that had brought about his death.

No questions were asked, even by the undertaker, who might properly have enquired why the body seemed to have been dead for longer than a day: but Hugh had not chosen him for his sobriety, nor for his powers of observation. The house was draped in black, and the news was sent out to the far-flung members of the family. Anne herself wrote to her father, and Alathea, who saw the letter, marvelled that her cousin, without apparently the slightest trace of humour or irony, had mentioned only that she was with her husband when he died.

Gradually, the inhabitants of the Jermyn Street house emerged from the shock of that terrible night, and began hesitantly to resume something like their normal life, despite the inhibiting necessity of mourning. Jasper's fever lasted for three days before it broke, and he slept the clock round and woke cool and well, demanding breakfast. Alathea often sat with him during his convalescence, talking and drawing and reading, but that strange conversation in the dark early hours of morning was never mentioned, and she doubted if he remembered it at all.

So she did not have to give an answer by Christmas, but her own sense of honesty, and fair play, demanded that she must. Yet she still could not decide, still could not make that last leap of commitment to one side or the other that an answer must demand. And time was running out.

All the signs had predicted a severe winter, and it duly arrived, with ferocity, in the second week of December. The fall of snow on the Sunday was so thick and heavy that there was no hope of stirring abroad until it had stopped, and the Jermyn Street household, unanimously and without a great deal of grief, decided that they would not grace the church with their presence that day. Sandro spent hours on the windowseats, rushing from place to place, squealing with glee, utterly enchanted: he had never seen snow before. Isabella, still quiet and subdued, drifted behind him, and knelt, chin on hands, nose pressed against the glass, and stared at the falling flakes as if she would devour them.

'When can we go out?' Sandro demanded over and over again. 'When can we go, Mama, when? *Please* can we go outside?' And Alathea, plagued, was driven in the end to say, with mounting exasperation, 'If you ask me just once more, we won't go at all.'

Sandro obeyed her, to her relief, for she was just as eager to go out in the snow as her son. It was ten years since she had seen such snow, and it brought out the child in her. She loved the thick bed of it in the street, muffling all sound, the peculiar walk adopted by those forced out in it, the slivers of fragile flakes so delicately balanced on each twig and branch, turning the back garden, or rather yard, into a well of pure and crystalline beauty. She found chalks, and some of her tinted paper – grey, dull pale blue, fawn – and spent the afternoon curled up in windowseats on both sides of the house, drawing exactly what she saw, in the Dutch manner. Jasper, by now almost recovered, came quietly once to watch, and found her quite oblivious to anyone's presence, her whole being intent upon the paper in her hand and the scene outside. On the floor around the window of the smaller parlour were drawings, scattered with more care than at first appeared, so that one would not fall on top of the other and smudge the delicate outlines, black and brown and purest, finest white, that described in fragile perfection the roofs and chimneys of the backs of the houses in St James's Square.

He had never watched her at work before, and found it utterly fascinating to see the swift flight of the chalk over the paper, and the transformation in just one or two strokes from a jumble of unrelated marks to a brilliant, evocative representation that took his breath away.

She dropped the paper with casual care on to an uncovered section of floor and said, without turning round, 'Do come in properly and sit down. I've finished for the while.'

'How long have you known I was there?' enquired Jasper, obeying. He skirted the drawings and sat down on a free chair. Lovell, occupying all the space by the fire, grunted a welcome and stretched luxuriously in the warmth.

'How long? Oh, ever since you came in,' said Alathea. She drew her knees up in front of her and wrapped her arms round them: with her hair coming down from the simple knot she put it in during the day, and the Italian freckles scattered still across the bridge of her nose, she might have been the sixteen-year-old he had fallen in love with ten – no, eleven years ago. He wanted to reach out, to touch her. The urge was so strong that he had to clench his hands on the carved walnut arms of her fashionable chair.

'They're beautiful,' he said, indicating the drawings.

'Some of them I'm pleased with – some haven't worked at all.' She pushed a stray wisp of hair out of her eyes and glanced out of the window, at the chimneys and roofs, snow and smoke and surly, grey sky, free for the moment of falling flakes. 'Strange as it may seem, that's one thing I missed in Italy – real cold! No snow, no crisp frosts, no autumn – just more or less warmth. Would you like to come to the park tomorrow? It should be cold enough to freeze the canal and there'll be skating – can you skate?'

'I lived five years in Holland – of course I can skate! I have proper skates, too, metal ones I brought back from Leyden – but I left them at Bury, alas. Perhaps we can buy some, although where I have no idea, or polish up some bones and bind them to the soles of your shoes.'

'I think I'll restrict myself to sliding, just as we used to on the moat at Goldhayes,' said Alathea, and gave him a smile of pure, reminiscent happiness. 'Do you remember when we all held each other in a long line – you must have been about sixteen or seventeen, it was just before you went to Holland – and we went down in size, you, Hen, Kit, Hugh, me – I suppose I was seven – and Math and Mun and Nick and Robin hanging on behind, and Father said we were like a centipede and Mab fell through a hole in the ice? Do you remember?'

Her eyes were shining with amusement and nostalgic joy, her defences were all down, and for the first time he was subjected to the full force of her personality, her unconscious charm. He could barely speak. He said something banal, caught the faint ironic lift of her brows in return and somehow, getting a grip on his errant emotions, steered the conversation into less personal and evocative areas. He loved to see her thus, all alight with happiness, but he could not easily bear to be so close, and still not touch.

A search through the snow-covered streets of London Town failed to provide any skates, and Jasper of course did not have his to give to a blacksmith for a pattern: but they went to St James's Park anyway, setting off after dinner the following day. The house was left locked and empty, for Sarah and Jane and Tom and Mistress Lewis, the cook, were of the party, all well wrapped up in mufflers and coats and hoods and hats against the bitter cold. All that could be seen of Sandro, carried in his mother's arms, was a small red nose and two very bright dark eyes within the thick woollen scarf wound around his head and crowned with an old felt hat. Fashion had played no part in anyone's choice of clothes.

The park was surprisingly crowded: ladies, some not so wise, in their flimsy finery and blue with cold, gentlemen parading, children running hither and thither, freed from convention by the unusual severity of the weather. Alathea let Lovell off his leash and the great, black, hairy dog, barking joyously, raced over the smooth, white, boundless surface of the snow, running in circles, wheeling, leaping, scooping up mouthfuls of it as he ran. Behind, her skirt hems sodden and crusted with snow and ice, Becca leaped in hilarious pursuit. That brought a faint smile even to Anne's wintry face: a smile which increased when they reached the canal and beheld the skaters. There were at least two dozen, swooping, calling, gracefully pirouetting on their metal-bladed boots, showing off their prowess. One of them, Alathea was mildly astonished to see, was the Duke of York, who had, like Jasper and Anne, spent some time in Holland. Hugh was recognised, and invited to join the royal party: Alathea saw several she knew amongst them, and Buckhurst and Shepherd gave her a friendly wave. But

Sandro, still in her arms, was desperate to get down and run in the snow, and on the ice. She bent, and set his small feet on the crisp white stuff, and watched in delight as he sat down in it, rolled in it, picked it up and threw it totally at random, shrieking the while at the top of his voice. Isabella, also released, stood still, bewildered, and then crouched down and fingered the snow through her stiff little leather mittens.

'Let's go on the ice,' said Becca, damp, laughing, her normally serious little goblin face split by a huge grin. 'Come on, everyone, let's go on the ice!' And before anyone could object, she whistled to Lovell and ran on to the white rippled surface of the canal, sliding until her shoes hit an obstruction and she went down in a flurry of skirts, Lovell jumping around her with joyful barks. Alathea wondered what the Duke would say to Hugh about this indecorous behaviour, but at that moment one of the royal party also fell, and was greeted by whistles, laughter and a shower of snowballs.

'Come slide with me?' said Jasper, laughing at her, his face flushed and boyish in the cold and his breath in great plumes like dragon's smoke. 'Come on, let's make a line – as many as possible!'

So they formed up one behind the other, Jasper in front, Alathea clinging on to his waist, Susannah holding hers. Somewhere behind were Hen, Becca and Sarah, Jane and Tom and Peg Lewis the cookmaid: Anne stood watching on the bank. The ice was not very slippery where they were standing, but as they moved out into the middle of the canal it became smoother, and sliding first one foot and then the other was much easier, and suddenly they were travelling with a little speed. 'Turn!' Jasper cried over his shoulder. 'Turn left!' And the line of nine swung with ponderous grace in the required direction. People were looking, a series of bumps from the rear indicated that some complete strangers had joined in: then two glowing young courtiers in proper skates swooped towards them and asked to lead the line. With this added power the speed increased dramatically. Alathea, helpless with laughter and keeping her balance by instinct alone, was pulled along effortlessly, swung from side to side and finally, with a flourish and the rest of the line for company, deposited gracefully in a pile of swept snow on the side of the canal. Then a snowball fight began in earnest, and she looked for Sandro, finding his small figure leading Isabella, literally, a merry dance on the edge of the ice. It was a delightful sight, the two tiny children, so enveloped in winter clothes that they looked like round bundles of cloth, pulling each other around the ice, and Isabella, her small face glowing with the chill and a new, unaccustomed happiness, was smiling at last.

A snowball hit Alathea in the back. She turned, saw Hugh's grinning face, and hurled one in reply. Then a giggle behind her announced Susannah, also armed. Alathea whipped round, snowball in hand, only to find that her cousin had dodged behind a bush. Snowballs flew fast and thick: Jasper joined in, rescued her with a few well-aimed missiles, and took her hands. 'Look – I've borrowed some skates from a friend of Hugh's. Slide on the ice again?'

'If you promise faithfully not to desposit me in a snowdrift,' said Alathea, breathless with exertion and laughter, and was whisked out on to the ice and steered by an expert hand. She wobbled more than once, was saved, and whirled around the ice by the respected, dedicated physician of Bury, shouting and laughing and behaving like a mischievous schoolboy. Sandro, yelling with delight, rushed around them, falling incessantly and picking himself up and pulling Isabella along in imitation. Then the inevitable happened: Jasper took one turn too many, and slid too far. Alathea was pulled along in his wake, and saw the snowdrift just before she fell into it, on top of Jasper.

It was wet, and cold, and obviously a hilarious spectacle: roars of laughter came from all around them. Jasper, grinning, stared up at her bright, laughing face, very close to his, and framed in a sudden cloud of pale hair – presumably the pins had come out again. And because it seemed the right and proper thing to do, and he would not have the chance again, he pulled her head gently down towards his, and kissed her.

She did not struggle or scream or kick: indeed, from the way she responded, he received the distinct impression that she liked it. And when it ended, he stared into her eyes, very wide and smokey and dark, and saw from the look on her face that something of significance had happened. With love, he kissed her mouth briefly. Then she said, her voice coming oddly in gasps, 'Do you remember anything of when you were ill?'

'Not a great deal,' said Jasper, his mind on other things: one kiss was certainly not enough, even if it was in full public view in the middle of a snowdrift.

'Do you remember in the night – waking up – and talking to me?' Alathea's voice sounded strange even to herself. Already, her caution was trying to overrule her conscience, and sundry other emotions had entered the fray: that kiss had awakened feelings which she had thought long extinct, and she could hardly control her breathing. At his shake of the head, she went on, with increasing sureness. 'You said a lot of things I won't embarrass you with, now: and at the end of it, you asked me to marry you.'

Jasper became suddenly very still. She noticed his eyes for the first time, she had never looked fully into them before. They were clear, a bright grass-green, wizard's eyes, and they looked at her with love, and hope, and apprehension. She said slowly, 'You asked me to marry you, and I said I'd give my answer at Christmas.'

'It's not Christmas yet.'

'Perhaps not – but my answer is decided on, so you may have it early – unless, of course, you would rather wait until Christmas.'

'It depends what the answer is,' said Jasper, but he knew already, he could see it in her face, the mixture of daring and fright and self-mockery and hope.

She took a deep breath and said in a low voice, 'Please, understand – it's only if you can tolerate me, *and* my painting. I couldn't live without that. And Sandro, what about Sandro, he's another man's child . . . '

'I don't care,' said Jasper. 'I don't care about any of the difficulties other people might put in our way – and as for Sandro, I don't mind, I don't mind at all. Just to – to hear your answer is all I want – so before I throttle you, what is it?'

Another deep breath: the dark, smoky-green eyes stared intently at his face. 'That's no way to speak to your future wife, is it?'

A great springing feeling of joy rose up inside him, threatening to choke him, but he said, his voice deceptively calm, 'Then the answer is yes?'

'The answer is yes,' said Alathea, and suddenly it was as if a great load, a burden of indecision, had been lifted from her heart. She gave him her brilliant smile. 'There are things I can't give you, yet – you may know, perhaps. But I'll do my best to be a good wife.'

'I don't want a good wife,' said Jasper. He sat up, and took her narrow, pale face in his hands. 'Understand, my dear love – I want you. You as you are. I don't want you to change in any way, you're unique, I would not have you forced into a mould of anyone's making, least of all my own. I take the rough with the smooth, the bad with the good, I take you and your painting, I will love Sandro as if he were my own – it's *you* I want, and not some conventional little shadow to cook and clean and sew. Understand?'

'Understood,' said Alathea.

'Then it's a bargain?'

'A bargain, husband.' And like farmers they spat on their hands and struck palms, smiling. And Jasper, his voice and face suddenly charged with an emotion that astonished her with its power and longing, said, 'There's another way to celebrate a betrothal – will you kiss me, my dearest, dearest love?'

And in the snowdrift, the cold and wet quite forgotten, they kissed again: and Alathea was not prepared for the sweetness of it, the melting of her armoured heart, the sudden awakening of desire. When it was ended she stared at Jasper's face, wondering, shaken by her feelings, and experiencing a sudden wild upsurge of joy. It would be all right; she had made the right choice after all; and love was a distinct possibility.

Their chilly idyll was rudely disrupted by a snowball, landing soggily and squarely on Jasper's shoulder. They looked round, to see Hugh, his face wreathed in smiles, and another missile in his hands. 'Hadn't you best come out of there before you both catch your deaths of cold?'

'I'm not sure that I can,' Alathea said. Hugh dropped his snowball and offered her his hands. Laughing, suddenly weak-kneed, she took them and was pulled with some difficulty from the snow-drift, Jasper scrambling after her.

Hugh regarded them both with a look described in Suffolk as 'old-fashioned'. 'You look as though you share some secret.'

Jasper's hand found hers. Alathea turned, and saw him smiling at her. Something of his own joy communicated itself to her. She said, 'Shall we tell him?'

'Why not? He has a right to know, being both your uncle and your protector-in-residence.'

'For my sins,' said Hugh.

Alathea, grinning, made the inevitable addition. 'Which are

many and manifold. Hugh, my dearest Hugh, would you like to sit down?'

'No, thank you – it's too cold and wet. I'm sure I'm man enough to survive any shock – even the one I suspect you are about to inflict on me. Go on, Jasper my old friend, let's hear it.'

'We have agreed to be married,' said Jasper, simply, and Hugh, by way of celebration, retrieved his snowball, halved it, and hurled a piece joyfully at each of them.

CHAPTER TWENTY-SEVEN

A passing bell

The wheel is come full circle: I am here.
(Shakespeare, *King Lear*)

It was a strange beginning to a marriage – a betrothal in a snow-drift, honoured with snowballs – and Alathea began to suffer from a sense of unreality. Had she really given him that answer? Or had it all been some fantastic, unexpectedly pleasant dream, one into which Jasper seemed to have strayed as well? She became increasingly bewildered as the momentum of it all began to gather apace. There would be a Twelfth-Night wedding, at St Martin's because Hugh could not leave London over the festive season, and letters went out to friends and family, apologising for the short notice and the inclement weather, inviting them to the ceremony. Jasper's epistle to his parents was short and overflowing with happiness: Alathea's to Ashcott was also brief, and began with the immortal words, 'I know you will not believe this, but it is true: I am to be married to Jasper in three weeks' time.'

Her mother, reading it by the fireside in her parlour, some five or six days later (the post had been much delayed by the weather), felt an absurd impulse to cry. Suddenly, a memory returned to her, of something she had not recalled for years. She was back in Oxford, in the house in Pennyfarthing Street, dark and panelled and cosy: she could not remember when it had been, save that it was in the earliest days of her ill-fated marriage to Kit's father, Sir

Dominic Drakelon. She could remember a conversation between herself, and Lucy, and Grainne, into which the young Jasper, aged three, had broken with the news that he wanted to marry his mother. When it had been pointed out that this was impossible, he had announced that Lucy would do instead, but Lucy, laughing, had declined, adding, 'If Thomazine has a daughter, you can marry her.'

Well, Thomazine had had that daughter, that unpredictable, beautiful, independent and gifted child, who had grown up into fame, fortune and the dubious delights of the Earl of Rochester's bed. Thomazine, always well aware of her own history, and the love which had shaped her life and surrounded her still, had taken the view that happiness was everything, and obedience to other people's morality came a long way in the rear, if indeed it was to be considered at all. But she was aware that not every man would wish to marry the cast-off mistress of such a notorious rake, nor take on the bastard child of the liaison. It was, perhaps, a measure of Jasper's love that these considerations seemed unimportant, and he had waited, uncharacteristically patient, for more than ten years for the obstinate object of his desire to change her mind.

Thomazine wondered why she had altered her stance so radically: the fiercely independent female artist would never have contemplated retreating into matrimony. She suspected that it had something to do with Italy, and more to do with Alexander, the grandchild she had never seen.

And she had never seen Isabella either, and now she would never see Kit again. The news had come in a brief note, terse to the point of suspicion, hard on the heels of a letter informing them of a mysterious fever that had laid both Kit and Jasper low, and Thomazine and her husband had both been aware that they were not being told the whole truth.

She had tried to feel grief for Kit's death. She had shed a few tears, remembering the handsome, passionate little boy whose allegiance she had won with such difficulty, only to supplant him with a sister. But it was hard not to feel some sense of relief, as if a burden had lifted from them all, and particularly from Alathea: hard also, not to deny her own guilt in forming the fate of that unhappy, unloved, wasted life. If she had not abandoned him as a baby, if his embittered father had not indulged him in every way, if Kit's own nature had been more placid, less jealous and stormy –

then things might have been very different.

But they were not, and there was no use, as the Widow was fond of saying, a-crying over spilt milk. Francis was out, feeding snow-bound sheep, so the first person whom Thomazine told of Alathea's betrothal was the old, old woman who had stood in a mother's place to her for more than thirty years. The Widow Gooch admitted to being ninety-one: Thomazine suspected that it might well be more. She no longer went about the house, but sat in state in the parlour, stick in hand, and rug over knee, missing nothing and commenting sharply and maliciously on everything. Her response to Thomazine's news was completely characteristic.

'He always was a brave little lad, that one – hasn't changed, has he?'

'Brave?' Thomazine queried, head slightly tilted, amusement deepening the smile lines on each side of her rather aquiline nose. 'How so, brave?'

'Taking your Thea on – and her little brat, what's its name, Alexander? Hope he likes paint,' said the Widow, cackling. 'Well, at least you've been invited to the wedding – more than you were to young Kit's. I shan't come, of course – too much to do here, someone's got to keep an eye on things. You go and have yourself a London holiday,' said Mistress Gooch, grinning evilly. 'And for God's sake take that other daughter of yours and give me some peace in the last days of my life.' She coughed lugubriously.

Thomazine was unconvinced. 'Last days of your life? I'll lay long odds you'll see a hundred. But we will take Math, and Sophie – apart from anything else, if we leave her behind, I think she'll follow on her own!'

So the Ashcott contingent packed their bags and struggled through the winter weather towards London, leaving the Widow in gleeful charge of half-a-dozen apprehensive servants, most of whom were convinced that she was a witch. And a hundred miles away in Suffolk, Grainne Sewell and her younger son, Robin, and her daughter Bridget, left Goldhayes and her husband Malise behind. She had not particularly wanted to go without him, and Malise had intended to come, but his employer, Lord Bradfield, was increasingly unwell and needed his assistance in running the estate. And since everyone around Lord Bradfield but himself, knew that he was dying, Malise, a generous man, had stayed.

The house in Jermyn Street was packed, every available bed

occupied and servants nose-to-tail in the garret. Thomazine and Francis, Sophie and Matthew, Anne and Isabella, Hugh and Susannah, Grainne and Robin and Bridget, Hen and Becca, and of course, Jasper himself. Alathea, counting the heads at the supper-table, two days before the wedding, arrived at a total of sixteen. She had had to buy an additional set of chairs, and eating was only possible, said Jasper, if elbows were firmly clenched against sides, and spoons and forks raised in unison. As the day drew closer, he shed years of responsibility, of dedication, of quiet and sober living, and became again the mischievous, enthusiastic boy she remembered from her childhood. Often she found herself staring at the face, oval, fair-skinned and freckled, with those brilliant green eyes, that had haunted her for so long, and wondered that he was ten years older than herself – it did not seem as if he were more than twenty-five or so. And she wondered also, with a mixture of fear and delight and expectation, what it would be like to share her life so closely with this man, as she had not been able to share her life with John Wilmot. She had told her former lover of her coming marriage, and to do him credit, he had wished her joy with sincerity, and expressed his pleasure that Sandro would have a permanent father. It was obvious that he was very fond of the child, though he saw him but seldom. He gave Sandro a dog, a little silky spaniel like the royal dog, Omrah, that Alathea had carried to his other, legitimate son, years ago. It was a mistake, for Lovell took umbrage and grew exasperatingly jealous. Becca was the only one who could calm him and persuade him to accept this yappy young upstart into his empire.

But she did not, tactfully, mention this to Rochester. He was, obviously, quite ill, as short-fused as a petard and as liable to explode when provoked – she had heard the stories, seen the lampoons and libels and satires that had poured from his pen over the last years, full of bitterness and hate. The light-hearted, fantastic, brilliant boy had burnt himself out too early in the search for pleasure, the new philosophy of life, and she beheld his altered, cynical face and could have wept for the blazing promise, a comet of genius amongst the Wits, that had dribbled away unseen, leaving a handful of poems. The flying hours were gone: she had memories in store, to treasure, for she had known the force of passion and the ecstasy it could bring. And she was glad that she was returning to Bury with Jasper, for she would not have to witness the gradual disintegration of the man she had loved so much.

She spoke of that year to Jasper, feeling he should know, but he took her hands in his and stopped her mouth with a kiss. 'Whatever happened, I do not need you to tell me. I know you loved him very much, and I shall count myself lucky if you should ever come to love me. Oh, Thea, I have no illusions, I never have had – just an unreasonable fund of hope. I can't offer you much – a home without fashionable frills and furbelows, a husband who's often tired and busy, called out at all hours to people who wait until early morning to fall desperately ill, and not a great deal of money. There's only one wealth I can offer you, and you cannot touch it nor see it.'

'I can see it,' said Alathea. 'I can see it in your eyes. You've been patient for ten years – can you be so for a little while longer?' And she smiled, shyly. 'I don't think, somehow, that you will have to wait very long.'

The Ashleys, of course, took a hand in the proceedings. Dan, ever generous, gave the bride and groom a substantial gift of money, quite enough to pay for a royal feast for the large numbers of guests expected (Alathea, with some misgivings, had invited a quantity of people for old times' sake). Lucy, calculating the cramped sleeping arrangements and adamant that the groom should not share the bride's house just before the wedding, insisted that he, and the younger guests, should stay at the House of the Ash Tree and relieve the pressure at Jermyn Street. So Math, Sophie, Jasper, Robin and Bridget were whisked off to Fleet Street, leaving Alathea in comparative peace for her last few days as an unmarried, independent woman.

It was a time for preparations, quiet talking, for memories and a certain feeling of nostalgia. She did not regret her decision: indeed, she welcomed the chance to leave London and the hurly-burly of fashionable life. But she was uneasily aware that people who did not know of her artistic dilemma would think that she had chosen the easy way out and abandoned her proud stance, and it was one of the things she had to explain to her parents.

The evening after their arrival, the house was quiet, for Grainne had gone to see her youngest son, whose birthday it was, and Hen and Becca had accompanied her. Anne had taken Isabella up to bed, and Hugh and Susannah were dining with Henry Jermyn, so they would not be disturbed. There was mulled wine against the cold, and the shutters and curtains were drawn tight, shutting out the snowy dark outside, and Alathea sat on one side of the fire of the big parlour in which, so terribly, Kit had died, and her father and mother sat at the other. Sandro and Lovell and the new puppy, who had been christened Leone by his two-year-old master, 'because he looks like a lion,' were dozing in an undisciplined heap in front of the flames, warm and scruffy and relaxed.

Thomazine looked at her first grandson and smiled. The boy was a little like his father, but his sunshiny nature and mischievous grin were all his own – very different from the moody, devious Herons, and showing none of the erratic brilliance of both his parents. She was more concerned for Isabella, who had hardly spoken to her, who shied away from men, and whose face was so terribly scarred.

It reminded her of what she must ask. They had been talking of mundane matters, old family jokes, news of Mun, Lucy's attempts to join those that would not be joined, namely, Sophie and Oliver. Thomazine, whose tact had never been her strongest suit, said into a temporary silence, 'Tell us – tell us what really happened to Kit!'

Involuntarily, Alathea glanced down at her sleeping son, so misleadingly angelic with his head on Lovell's shaggy black side and his arms around Leone's plump, feathery middle. This was the moment she had dreaded, the moment when she would have to re-live those appalling events, and see again the terrible figure of her brother, her darker self, her *bête noire*, her *deus ex machina*, wielding his sword to slay both herself and Sandro.

There was Anne to consider, too. Alathea had tried to talk to her about it, and had completely failed to penetrate the awesome power of her cousin's reserve. Anne had turned her head away, when she had asked her gently if she wanted to discuss the matter. The suggestion that it might help to talk with a sympathetic listener had fallen on unresponsive ears, and Hugh's comment, that Anne had appeared halfway to insanity herself, seemed to be coming true. It was as if she had managed to erase the murder of her husband utterly from her mind. Once, chillingly, she had spoken of him as if he were still alive, and in Yorkshire, as if he were still capable of inflicting harm on his wife and child. Alathea could not ask her permission to reveal the truth of the matter to

Thomazine and Francis: she knew too well the blank, bewildered look she would receive in reply. Anne's world had dwindled, obsessively, to Isabella, and she did not know how to bring her out of her withdrawal from reality.

Alathea looked up at her parents' faces. So different they were, her father's long and fair-skinned under his outdoor tan, his hair liberally silvered now but the eyes, shadow-green and ironic, still the same as they had always been, and her mother, small and aquiline and brown, her eyes very large and bright and her thick, wiry hair peppered with grey. They were past fifty, but their minds remained as keen and tolerant and wide-ranging as ever: yet she did not want to have to utter the terrible truth.

It came at last, as it had to, although not quite in the form she had intended. 'He was killed,' she said, her voice sounding abrupt and unnatural in her own ears. Thomazine's fine eyes widened, but her reply had her usual firm directness. 'Who killed him?'

Alathea took a deep breath, let it go, and committed herself. 'It was Anne.'

In the silence, you could have heard a snowflake fall. She saw her mother's eyes fill suddenly with tears, saw her father's look of concern and his quick grasp of her hand. They had a deep and abiding love beside which her passion for Rochester seemed as the brief spark of flame in dry grass, flaring suddenly, and as quickly fading. She was beginning to see that there were many different kinds of love, and that the fiercest was not necessarily the best.

'Tell us what happened,' said her father's deep, dark voice, bereft of its habitual mockery and irony and laughter; and in words thickened by emotion, she told them, bleakly and without evasion or embellishment. There was another long silence when she had finished. Sandro muttered something in his sleep and turned over, displacing Leone, who uttered a brief yelp of complaint and then settled down again, cuddling up to his infant master as if to another puppy.

'And so life goes on,' said Thomazine quietly, staring at them, her eyes more than usually brilliant. 'Oh, Thea – what can I say? All of this was my fault, originally, for I weighed Kit and your father in the balance, and chose your father, thirty years ago – and Kit has paid the price, ever since.' She added, the tears running down her cheeks, 'I wish I could have loved him.'

'I did,' said her daughter, sadly. 'And I could never tell him –

you know I could not, and why. But in the beginning, when I came back to Ashcott from London, he was my friend, we had such happy times together – I could never erase that from my mind. And he died trying to kill me, and Sandro – and I think that if he had succeeded, he would then have killed himself. Anne – what she did – it was like an execution.' And the memory came back, making her shudder: the impassive, unemotional face of the plain girl in the dark dress, swinging the poker in her hands, dealing death to the man who had made her life such a torment.

'It's possible,' said Francis, his voice thoughtful, 'that what happened was for the best. If Anne had not acted, he might well have killed you – there was no one else who could have helped. Anne alone had the strength and the will to save you – and you should remember that. If Kit was indeed mad, and it seems as though he was, then I think death, however terrible, was kinder. He did not suffer, after all: it was a quick and merciful end.'

'An execution,' said Alathea, and found herself weeping.

It was true, she realised in her distress: she had hated Anne, for killing her brother, however justified that murder had been. She should remind herself of what would almost certainly have happened without Anne's deed: it might well have been herself, and Sandro, as well as Kit in that lonely bare grave at St Martin-in-the-Fields. And for the first time, she thought with sympathy of her cousin's true state of mind, the horror of her loveless, brutal marriage, and attacks on herself and her beloved child, and the terrible revenge she had taken.

'Treat her kindly,' said Thomazine, wiping the tears from her own face. 'She has been in hell, I think – and perhaps she has not yet emerged.'

That talk revived Alathea's grief for her brother, yet it also marked one more step along the road to her acceptance of his death, and the manner of it. It was strange to think, also, that Kit's murder marked the beginning of her changing attitude to Jasper. For how could she refuse to take seriously a man who was quite willing to sacrifice his life for her?

She had never accepted his love, either: she had spurned him, scorned him, ridiculed him. She had ruled her own life, her own feelings, until they had turned traitor on her, first with Rochester, and now, with the man who in two days would become her husband. She knew now that she would love Jasper – a different kind of love, assuredly, from the desperate passion with which she had loved John Wilmot, but love nonetheless, gentle and honest and certainly far more long-lasting. And she would be home, in Suffolk where she had been born and bred, and she could paint as the Dutch painted, recording the rich, varied, complex life around her, in all its ugliness and vitality and beauty, without fear of failure or penury, without dissipating the wonderful power of the magic in her hands, in years of drudgery over unsympathetic faces and the conflicting demands of fashion and truth.

She explained this to Thomazine and Francis, and they seemed to understand. She gave them two miniatures she had done, just before Kit had shattered their brief tranquillity, of Sandro and Isabella. The two children stared out of their painted ovals, one smiling and blond, the other wide-eyed and hesitant, the scar only faintly sketched in: Alathea knew that there were bounds beyond which the truth was not permitted. She also gave them the only miniature of herself. It was unfinished, for Samuel Cooper, the greatest limner in the world for a face, had been more than four years dead.

'And you do not regret leaving London?' her father asked her, looking down at the twin portraits of the children.

Alathea emphatically shook her head. 'No. I can paint anywhere, at any time I so desire: all I need is time, and the money to buy what I require. I don't care if I never paint another portrait for money again – I've had enough of fashion and all the pressures it puts upon me and my painting. But,' she added, remembering with a pang of affection and nostalgia those wild-worded afternoons in the studio at Covent Garden, when she had crossed verbal swords with the Wits, and earned their admiration, companionship and respect, 'there are some other things I think I shall miss.'

They came to her wedding, Buckhurst and Fleetwood Shepherd, fat Harry Savile and John Wilmot, Earl of Rochester, back in favour with the King after the past summer's disgrace. There was Aphra Behn, plump and merry, as successful at her art as Alathea had been in hers, and cheerfully unrepentant about her need to earn her own living, to which any more artistic considerations had early been sacrificed. Mistress Behn wrote popular bawdry, and was not ashamed to admit it, but she was also staunch in defence of her independence, and obviously dubious about Alathea's resignation of hers. 'Still,' she said, clapping the younger woman on the shoulder with a broad, ink-stained hand, 'there's still the chance to change your mind, so long as there's no consummation!'

Alathea found herself, to her intense annoyance, blushing. She grinned awkwardly, and intimated that she was, perhaps, looking forward to it. Aphra laughed, and said she did not blame her: the groom was a pleasant-looking fellow, and obviously loved her. 'But he is not like Strephon, is he?' she added, glancing towards Rochester, who was talking to Harry Savile.

Alathea smiled, thinking of the past for once without sadness or regret. 'No,' she said, 'he is not.'

Oh, she had loved John: she could love him still, and for ever, for she knew his heart and his soul and was not deceived by the face he turned to most of the world. But she knew it could never be again, and she had gladly accepted this very different fate.

So she moved amongst her guests, exchanging greetings, reminiscences, laughter: it was a very good-humoured occasion. And with her went the astonishing thought, always at the forefront of her mind, that she was Alathea Heron no longer, but Alathea Sewell: that in the crowded church of St Martin's, she had vowed to love, honour and obey that tall, red-haired man chatting, improbably, to Buckhurst – or the Earl of Middlesex, as he now was. She had seen the smile in his eyes as she promised obedience, and knew that in this marriage at least, the word would be somewhat out of place.

But the deed was done, her boats burned, and she could not retreat to the past, even if she had wanted to. So, she spoke to Aphra, and to Shepherd and Savile, Henry Jermyn and the Beales, who were somewhat out of place in this gathering. Then a late arrival loomed before her, the tall impressive figure of William Wycherley, the playwright with whom she had never felt at ease, a man who had a savagery of wit to rival Rochester's.

'I have brought you a gift,' he said without preamble, and thrust it into her hands, a small leather-bound book. 'I doubt you've seen the play, it has not been performed these two years or so – but since you are in some sort portrayed in it, I thought you should read it.'

'I am in it?' she said, astonished and somewhat apprehensive:

she had no wish to be pilloried on the public stage, even in her absence.

Wycherley laughed. 'Oh, yes, dear lady, you are in it – for is not the name of the heroine, Alathea? And,' he added, with a grin that made him seem, suddenly, much less intimidating, 'she is without doubt the finest character in the play – not that it says a great deal for her.'

'Then perhaps I do wrong to feel flattered.'

'I doubt it,' said William Wycherley, and bowed, and moved on.

It seemed to pass very quickly, that afternoon of celebration. All too soon the hour was approaching when she must bid her friends farewell, and enter into married life in earnest. She kissed all her old companions, even Henry Jermyn, and last of all, came to John Wilmot, Earl of Rochester, who had met her at the very beginning of her career as an artist, and was here too, at the end. She embraced him with love, and sorrow, and friendship, and the look in his eyes would have made the fiery Mistress Barry leaf-green with jealousy, had she seen it.

'Goodbye, my dearest Thea.'

'We shall surely meet again,' she said, and wondered if they ever would: it would be so different between them, if they did. 'I will look after Alexander for you, and you may come and see him whenever you desire – but if you ever write a lampoon about me, do me the courtesy of not letting me know of it!'

'I can't imagine you immured in the country,' he said.

Alathea shook her head. 'You misunderstand. I can paint there, just as I wish, and I cannot do that here any longer. And besides,' she added shrewdly, 'I do not think you find the country as dull as you pretend – Harry has told me all about Woodstock, and your disgraceful naked frolics.'

'Do you plan to emulate me? If you should ever intend riding through the streets of Saint Edmundsbury attired only in your hair like Lady Godiva,' said Rochester, with a smile that at once made her want to laugh and to cry, 'do let me know – I should love to see it.'

She had said farewell to them all at last, and retired upstairs, to be ceremonially disrobed for the wedding-night. Sophie and Bridget were her bridesmaids, Matthew and Oliver her bridemen. She was made ready for bed by the two girls, Sophie laughing and chattering, Bridget, whom she hardly knew, shyly and diligently performing her tasks. Then Math and Oliver appeared, escorting Jasper in his nightshirt, followed by as many of the guests, distinctly the worse for drink for the most part, as could crowd into the little bedchamber that had been hers ever since their move to Jermyn Street. Healths were drunk, stockings were flung, bawdy suggestions were offered, and Alathea, unable to resist it, gave as good as she got until Hen, brisk and practical, drew the bed-curtains around them with a triumphant clashing of brass, and ushered the riotous revellers downstairs to continue their celebrations, leaving Alathea alone with the man whom, so astonishingly, she had married that day for better for worse, richer and poorer, until death should part them . . .

'Hello,' said Jasper, and his eyes, very bright, scanned her pale, fine-drawn face, the flowing tangled mass of her yellow hair falling across her breasts, her long hands clasped over her knees in a characteristic posture. 'Are you happy?'

'I am,' said Alathea, with perfect truth, and smiled at him. 'Are you?'

'Do you need to ask? You have made me the happiest man alive,' said her husband softly. 'And it only wants one more thing to make the day perfect.'

He took her in his arms then, and kissed her; and Alathea, who despite her apparent witty calm was seething with apprehension and excitement, found that her fears were easily cast aside.

She learned also, that night, that love indeed takes many forms, and that though she had perhaps known more passion, there was made here, between herself and Jasper Sewell, more joy, greater pleasure and, afterwards, a serener, more satisfied contentment. For there was no guilt in this, no separation, no insecurity, no danger: and in such a sheltered garden, her love would grow and flower.

The message came three days later, short and stark, in Malise Graham's hand. It was addressed to his wife Grainne, but the news it imparted was for all the Herons to hear, and obey.

Lord Bradfield's illness had suddenly worsened. He knew now the imminence of his death, and desired reconciliation with his family before the end, and so everyone was summoned to Goldhayes, as quickly as possible. 'For,' the letter finished, 'I do not think that he will last the week out, and for his sake I would greatly desire the presence of all of you at Goldhayes, before it is too late. And Hugh and Susannah are not excluded.'

Hugh, hearing the message, could wish that they were: he was well aware of the embarrassing potential consequences of such a meeting, particularly for Susannah. There was, too, the question of her mother. Meraud had also been ill, so Grainne had said, and Lord and Lady Bradfield had lived in virtual seclusion for some time: but ill or not, Hugh did not in the least relish a reunion with his unlikeable mother-in-law – and neither did Susannah.

But they must go, he knew that, and besides, Alathea, obviously, would like his presence in the party. So the coaches were hired, hasty packing completed, and the entire Heron family, save for a few far-flung members – Mun at sea, Nick Graham visiting cousins in Scotland, Mall at her husband's country seat – embarked in convoy on the long, cold, difficult winter journey to the home of their ancestors.

Alathea, sitting in the jolting, uncomfortable coach, huddled against Jasper for warmth and with Sandro pressed close against her other side, closed her eyes and thought of Goldhayes, that she had not seen for – how many years? Not since Rupert's tragic death . . . She worked it out and realised, with some surprise, that it had been nearly twelve years. A long time, to be away from the place she loved best in all the world, better even than the house in Covent Garden, or the Florentine villa that had held such delightful memories: better than Ashcott, her parents' home. She pictured the glowing, red-brick house, reflected in its wide moat, surrounded by trees and garlanded with flowers, and in her imagination walked up the drive once more, over the brick bridge, and into the front court. She read the Latin verse around the sundial, that claimed not to count the hours unless they were sunny ones, and then passed under the porch, opened the great iron-strapped oaken door, and stepped into the hall. Lovingly, she went on to explore each and every room, remembering the furnishings, the view from the window, the associations it had – this chamber had been hers, that parlour was where Mun had fallen off his chair and cut his head on the court cupboard, Mab had caught a rat in the buttery, and dozens in the stable yard – despatching each with a brisk shake of her head. And in her mind-pictures, it was summer, as it always seemed to be at Goldhayes, with every window flung wide and the heady aroma of flowers and hay, sunshine and beeswax polish and strewn herbs colouring the air. How would it look now?

Her eagerness to be there again quite overrode her apprehension about the purpose of their visit. Like Hugh, she did not relish the thought of another confrontation with Lord Bradfield, whatever his desire for reconciliation. She was also concerned for Anne, who had received the news of her father's desperate illness with her usual lack of emotion, and sat now, opposite Alathea, with Isabella tucked into her cloak, staring out of the window at the bleak, wintry landscape.

They were a long time in reaching Suffolk. The roads were dreadful, covered in snow and half-frozen, treacherous mud, and a journey that lasted two or three days in summer now took a week. But at last, ten days after Alathea's wedding, the three coaches lumbered into Bury St Edmunds just before dinner. The ground was awash with thawing snow. They stopped at the Angel for a meal, and then pressed on through the short January afternoon, until they came to Bradfield Tye, and the Home Farm where Malise Graham, big and clumsy and gentle, came out to greet his wife and children and stepchildren and his cousins, and to accompany them up to Goldhayes to make sure of their welcome.

Alathea had dreamed once, long ago, of coming to her beloved birthplace on just such a bleak, chilly, grey afternoon as this, and as their coach, the first in the convoy, rumbled ponderously up the drive, she opened the window and leaned out, contemptuous of the cold. But the sight that greeted her made her heart quail and her courage melt, for it was as if she were back in that nightmare again. There was grass growing in the drive, once so immaculately raked and tended: a tree had fallen across the door fence, obviously long ago, and nothing had been done: another tree, more recently, had partially blocked their path and the coachman had some trouble in guiding the six horses around it. With a terrible sense of foreboding, Alathea ignored her chill fingers and the cheerful complaints of her husband, and watched intently as they turned the bend in the driveway and came in sight of Goldhayes.

And it was as it had been in her nightmare. The house was deserted: there were no lights to greet them, apparently no smoke from any chimney. The flowerbeds in the court in front of the house were ragged and untidy above the scattering of half-thawed snow, and the moat was choked with weed and soft ice upon which a mournful duck padded, searching vainly for a clear space in which to feed.

She found tears, cold on her face. The coach stopped, and she did not wait for the coachman, but opened the door and jumped out. The other carriages, laden with passengers and baggage, were just visible down the drive, but she ignored them: Goldhayes, glorious even in neglect, filled her heart. The coachman knocked thunderously upon the door, but such was the air of desolation around them, that Alathea did not really think that anyone would emerge to welcome them. The house was empty, deserted, dead, inhabited only by its ghosts.

Then, to her surprise, the door opened, very slowly, and an elderly man appeared, very bent and slow. By now the other coaches had crossed the bridge, and Malise Graham, who had ridden up on the box of the last one, jumped off and hurried over to the old man. Words were exchanged, orders given, and suddenly, as if by a miracle, the house sprang to life: lights appeared, and servants, not very many, hastened out to help with baggage and horses. Malise, his face anxious, ushered everyone inside. The sky was rather threatening, and a few fat wet flakes of snow had already fallen.

It was almost as cold in the hall as it had been outside. No fire burned in the huge hearths, and there was a damp, musty smell in the air. The members of the two families, Heron and Sewell, stood wan with tiredness by the great oak table, now dull with dust, that had always dominated the room, and on all their faces was something of the same shock that Alathea felt herself.

Her father was talking to Malise, who was his oldest friend, as Grainne was to Thomazine, and she heard Malise's answer, the Scots accent especially marked, true sign of his distress. 'He wouldna keep the servants on – most of the house hasna been used for years, save for the West Wing. He wouldna spend the money on their wages, he said, and he's been a recluse in the house for five years and more.'

Susannah's high voice carried all round the dark room, fitfully illuminated by candles and the last of the daylight. 'Please tell me – where is my mother? Why isn't she here to greet us?'

Malise Graham stared at her. Hugh's wife had Meraud's knack of always appearing immaculate whatever the circumstances, and her resemblance to her mother was at this moment particularly striking.

'Your mother? Are ye Meraud's daughter, then?'

'I am,' said Susannah. 'Is she here?'

Malise looked at once confused and apologetic. He glanced at his wife, and Grainne nodded. Plainly there was a great deal happening here that did not at once meet the eye, and Alathea, bewildered and apprehensive, turned to seek Jasper and found him just behind her. His long, warm arms about her were a reminder of love and reality, as Malise spoke.

'I dare say ye'll be wondering, all of ye, what's been happening here – and I canna rightly say, for Lord Bradfield didna let me past the door until he fell mortally sick, ten days ago. We did all our business at the Farm, and he never spoke to any o' the tenants. I tried to persuade him to keep up the house, to see some of ye all – but ye ken the Heron ways, and he was no' to be persuaded. As for Meraud – as far as I ken, she's here, but I havena seen her in months. And to be honest, I preferred it that way.'

He glanced at Susannah under his intimidating brows, and Susannah, who knew that he was not nearly so fearsome as he appeared, smiled briefly. 'I understand, sir. My feelings are the same, as are everyone else's here, I think. But surely she is with her husband, even if she has been ill herself? And how is Lord Bradfield? Does he wish to see us tonight?'

'One question at a time,' said Malise, looking harassed. He pushed his straggling, still reddish hair out of the way, with a broad, freckled hand. 'I dinna ken if she be with him or no' – but, yes, she had been very ill herself, I ken that much, so she may no' be. Lord Bradfield is asleep, they tell me, so there's no point in disturbing him tonight, but perhaps Jasper could take a quick look at him?'

With an apologetic smile, and a kiss for his wife, Jasper was escorted through the maze of rooms that he had once known so well, towards the West Wing. At the end of it, in a high beautiful chamber surrounded on two sides by the moat, and on the third by the front court, lay Simon Heron, Lord Bradfield, a man to whom the fates, and his own nature, had been bitterly unkind. The room was warm, a fire blazed in the grate, and a middle-aged maid whose round face he instantly recognised rose to her feet and bobbed a curtsey.

'Isn't it Hepzibah Greenwood?' he enquired, in a hasty whisper.

'Thass right, sir,' said Heppy, who had been Thomazine's maid and companion, who had shared their Oxford exile and who had been much more a friend than a servant. She had married soon after Thomazine and Francis, and had lived in the village with her farmer husband and increasing brood of round-faced children. He had known her all his life, for a sensible, cheerful, practical soul: at least Lord Bradfield would be well cared for.

'How is His Lordship?' he asked, after greetings had been exchanged.

Heppy glanced towards the half-curtained bed, and her kind face creased with sorrow. 'He's sleeping now, Master Jasper, sleeping peacefully enough, and I've given him some of they drops as you towd Master Malise to get for him – but when he wakes, the pain do gnaw him up suffen cruel. I don't think as how thass a-gooing to be very long,' she added, with a sigh. 'And I woon't want him to live in such pain, that I woon't.'

Jasper walked quietly over to the bed, and parted the curtains. The Lord Bradfield who lay sleeping there, his body wasted away almost to nothing, his hair white and straggling, his face sunken back from the great eagle's beak Heron nose, was a terrible travesty of the man who had once wielded such power, and enjoyed such wealth and prestige. His family had defied him, even his children were estranged from him, his second marriage was the general object of contempt, rejected by his friends and neighbours: and so he had retreated into his own world, and spoken only with Malise. Perhaps he had cared about Goldhayes no longer, knowing that the brother he despised would inherit it, perhaps he had been unable to face the censure of the world and of those he had once regarded with at least familial affection. Whatever the truth of it, he had been brought at last to this: the proud scion of a hundred and fifty years of Suffolk Herons, laid low by the indignity of approaching death.

Jasper's experienced eye could see that it was only a matter of time now. He would probably last the night out, but he gave him at most another twenty-four hours of life. The Herons were an obstinate breed, though, and he knew that Simon Heron would hold on tenaciously to this world for as long as possible.

He withdrew, and turned to face Heppy and Malise. There was one more question he had to ask. 'Lady Bradfield – where is she?'

Malise looked unhappy, an honest man caught up in a subterfuge of which he disapproved, but to which he had been forced to accede, on his employer's order. 'She's kept in the upstairs part o' this wing, now. I spoke truth when I said I havena seen her for months. Heppy and her sisters nurse her in turn. But I don't think yon little lass should see her mother, unless she knows.'

Jasper knew. It was a secret that had been on his conscience too long, and he was at once relieved and appalled at the prospect of bringing it at last into the open. He looked round at Hepzibah.

The Suffolk woman, her face sober, shook her head. 'Thass just as you said, Master Jasper, you said right from the beginning as how there woon't be no change in her – and there in't.'

'I will see her later,' said Jasper. After witnessing the shocking alteration in Lord Bradfield, he did not yet feel ready to minister to his lady. He thanked Heppy for her diligent care, and left the stuffy, sour-smelling room, accompanied by Malise. Both men felt a great sadness, a sense of grief for the once-proud man now humbled by terrible illness, the man who had been, not exactly a friend to either of them, but who had dominated their lives for so long. And both had the grim thought, that his last years need not have been so full of bitterness, if he had only been less high-principled, less inflexible, less overbearing, less proud – less himself.

They discovered the rest of the family uncomfortably ensconced in the Long Gallery, around a new, bright and inadequate fire while the butler, ancient and punctilious, served them with wine and refreshments and promised them a speedy supper. Jasper, who had his suspicions about the state of the kitchen, was not sure about the worth of this promise. He sought Alathea and found her, sitting next to her mother and Hen. She welcomed his return with a smile, and quick press of the hand, but he could sense her distress, and knew its cause. At least, however, the neglect of Goldhayes could be remedied with a little time and money: the ailments afflicting its master and mistress were not so easily put right.

For a normally lively, loquacious family, the Herons were remarkably subdued that night. True, there was a tolerable supper, and ample supplies of rather more tolerable wine from the capacious cellars that had once been the crypt of the priory that had stood on this site until a hundred and forty years previously.

But even Lucy, who could normally be relied upon to gloss over awkward circumstances and lend at least a jolly surface to the gathering, was quiet and sad, thinking, no doubt, of her happy childhood here, so early disrupted by violence, war, separation and bereavement. Her eldest brother was dying, and an era was dying with him, and the meat had lost its savour.

There was no music to grace the Gallery after supper as had been the custom till the King, and Simon Heron, came into their own again: cards were unsuitable, no one had brought sewing, talk died in its infancy. Jasper, with the immediate future looming before him like a threatening black wall, was not surprised, nor sorry, when one by one the various members of the family pleaded tiredness and retreated to their allotted chambers. He longed for the time when he could at last be alone with Alathea, but there was something he must do first.

He said as much to her, as they inspected their bedchamber. It was on the east side of the house, as far away as possible from the horror that awaited him. Their nearest neighbours were her parents, in the big room at the end of the East Wing that hung above the moat. It was too cold to look out of windows: theirs was shuttered and curtained against the dark, and the fire blazed brightly. It had not, however, managed to banish the draughts, nor the smell of damp, mould, and decay.

'Is Lord Bradfield dying?' asked Alathea. Her face, contrasting light and shadow in the radiance of one three-branched candle-stick, looked haunted, desolate. He had no way of knowing about that old nightmare that had, so disturbingly, come true, but he could sense her mood of sadness. He nodded, knowing that the truth was what she wanted.

'Yes – he is very near to it now. I do not think he will die tonight – if I did, I would not have let everyone troop off to bed. But it will be tomorrow, perhaps – and sooner would be kinder.'

'Is he in very much pain?'

'He is sleeping now, so, no – but it will be different when he wakes.'

Alathea shivered, as if a ghost had crossed her grave. 'It frightens me, the thought of watching a man dying – watching him slip from life, and not to be able to do anything about it. Like Nell did. And Mab, my little dog Mab, do you remember her? I sat up all night with her, and watched her life just ebbing away, and the light going from her eyes. I've never forgotten it.'

'But Mab was old, she had had a good life.'

'You can't say that of my uncle,' said Alathea, her eyes dark with emotion. 'He's only – how old? Fifty-six, fifty-seven? That's no great age. And his life hasn't exactly been carefree.'

'And a large part of his misery he has brought upon himself.'

'You sound just like the Widow Gooch,' said Alathea wryly. 'I'm sorry, I'm in a strange mood tonight. To see Goldhayes like this, desolate, neglected, I hate it. I want to sing and dance and cry all at once.' She stared unhappily at her husband, and then smiled, with difficulty. 'But I shouldn't be so unhappy, should I? After all, if Lord Bradfield dies, my father will inherit Goldhayes – and this will be my home again.' She swallowed. 'And that's always at the back of my mind – and it shouldn't be.'

'Why not? It's the truth,' said Jasper gently. 'Thea – my dearest love, you can't set the world to rights in a night, still less the Herons – so why not go to bed? Is Sandro asleep?'

There was a truckle bed in the corner for her son. All that could be seen of him was a heap of flaxen curls, and a small hand amidst the sprawled chestnut-and-white of Leone the spaniel – Lovell had been left behind in London.

Alathea nodded. 'Yes, sound asleep, despite the fact that Leone seems to be taking up most of the bed.' She turned away, smiling, after dropping a kiss on the fair head, and saw Jasper by the door. 'Where are you going?'

'I have to see my patient again,' said Jasper, hating himself for his deception. Then, he met Alathea's eyes, clear and direct and dark, and knew that she, at least, could not be deceived.

For a long moment they looked at each other. At last she said softly, 'No – you're going somewhere else, aren't you?'

'I am,' said Jasper unhappily, and Alathea saw the sick look of dread in his face and came to a curious decision.

'Would you like me to come with you?'

Jasper drew a deep, ragged breath and shook his head. 'No – no – you said once that illness frightens you, and if you come with me now, you will see someone who is – who is more than ill.'

'I think I have guessed who it is,' she said. 'And whatever is wrong with her, that sets that look upon your face, I want to share it with you – however horrific the truth may be, I don't think you ought to shoulder it alone. I think you need me, tonight, so please

– let me come with you?'

Reluctantly, with many misgivings, he acknowledged that she had the strength to face it, and held out his hand.

He had a candle. It was the only illumination in the Long Gallery, for the house had settled down for the night. Behind them, their shadows wavered hugely, dipping and bowing with every draught: before them was a tiny oasis of light, and beyond it the dark. Alathea knew the house as well as her own face, knew where the furniture was, could remember the positions of rugs and chairs and stools, but tonight she might as well have been blind. Fear darkened her eyes and she clung tight to Jasper's hand as he led her unerringly down the length of the great Gallery to the door leading to the West Wing.

A light showed underneath. He knocked briefly, and opened it. The room beyond was a maid's chamber, a little ante-room with a truckle bed, and a woman who was obviously a member of the ubiquitous Greenwood family rose abruptly, a little heap of sewing descending on to the floor. 'Why, sir, you startled me suffen shocking! Is suffen amiss?'

'No, Jemima – and I'm sorry if I surprised you,' said Jasper. He took a deep breath and glanced at Alathea, who was still holding his hand. 'Someone is always here, you see: Lord Bradfield insisted on that. She is never left alone. Do you still want to go in?'

'Cowardice is sometimes one of my virtues – but I will,' said Alathea, wondering if what lay on the other side of the door could possibly be worse than her imaginings. Madness, disfigurement, idiocy, all the alternatives rushed through her mind as Jasper opened the further door and walked inside. But she was not prepared for the reality.

The empty, mouthing, slobbering husk that had once been the beautiful, feared and ruthless Meraud Trevelyan lay in the bed, and made nameless noises. Jemima Greenwood, her face kindly and concerned, tucked in the crumpled bedclothes and replaced a wandering leg. It was white, shrivelled, useless, like a very old woman's. Alathea stood appalled, the stench of sickness and decay clogging her nostrils, her gorge rising. She stared, unable to look away, at the shrunken, twisted face, the slack, dribbling mouth, the aimless, twitching hands and the tangled, straying hair that had once, not so long ago, been as lovely as Susannah's. Then something made her look at the eyes. They were as blue as they had ever been, and within them was a dreadful glimpse of intelligence, a spark of awareness and anguish amid the physical ruin. Alathea could bear no more. With a gasp of horror, her hands across her mouth, she turned and fled from the sickroom that was also a tomb. It was all she could do not to vomit. She pressed her head against the cool panelled wall of the maid's room, and pushed her hands across her mouth. But up rose again that dreadful imbecile's face, with those eyes that knew, that understood . . .

Hands touched her gently, and Jasper's voice said with deep concern, 'Thea, oh Thea – are you all right?'

She swallowed painfully, and got a grip on her emotions. Had she not wished Meraud Trevelyan dead, and hated her more than any other? And was not this living death her just deserts?

But no crime on earth could justify that penalty.

She straightened, and turned to face her husband, unaware of the stark white horror on her face. 'I'm sorry – I couldn't bear it. Oh, Jasper, she knows!'

'You saw that too? It's why I – I can hardly bear to look at her either. I'm truly sorry,' said Jasper. 'I should have warned you.'

'No – it was my choice. But tell me, what – what happened to her?'

'She had an apoplectic fit that should have killed her, and did not. It struck four or five months ago, during a quarrel with Lord Bradfield. He had discovered – how, I don't know – something of her true nature, her past, and taxed her with it. She defended herself, tempers were lost, the argument grew more and more heated and then suddenly, in the midst of railing at him, she was struck down. He thought at first that she was dead: it would have been better if she had been. He felt terrible guilt about it, he sent for me in the middle of the night, begged me to use any means I could to cure her. But I couldn't – no man could. It has left her right side paralysed, she cannot use her right arm, or leg, and her face is twisted, and what part of her is not paralysed, she cannot control. But . . . although she cannot speak or feed herself or direct her movements, her mind is still alert, I think – but there's no way of communicating with her.'

Alathea thought of the hell that Meraud was now enduring, and would continue to endure until death, kindly, took her at last. She said, her voice shaking, 'How long – how long do you think she will be like that?'

'Who knows? Herons are a tough breed,' said Jasper. 'And sometimes, too tough. What she suffered would have killed most ordinary people, but she has refused to give up life. Whenever I see her eyes, I wish she would.'

There was a silence. Alathea touched his hand gently, offering comfort. She said slowly, 'Then – did Lord Bradfield order her condition to be kept a secret?'

'I was told to say that she was ill – but not the nature of her illness. I think he was too ashamed. She had no friends, anyway – or no one that you or I could call a true friend – cronies would be a more apt description. So there were no insistent callers. At first I thought she would die: now I think she could exist for years, until another fit carries her off – as it will, sooner or later.'

'I pray it's sooner,' said Alathea grimly. 'Jasper – I don't think Sue ought to see her. I know she's tougher than she looks, tougher than any of us, perhaps. But I don't think she would like to see her mother reduced to that. She must have some feeling for her, despite the fact that Meraud used her quite cold-bloodedly, as a pawn to further her own ambitions.'

But Susannah, informed by a diffident Jasper of her mother's condition, insisted on a visit to the sickroom the next morning, even before breakfast was ready. She went in the circling shelter of Hugh's arm, and returned visibly shaken, though not more than her husband, who had once prided himself on his inability to be shocked. Nor could either of them eat any food that morning, and Hugh's terse, horrified description was quite enough to discourage anyone else from making the journey to the West Wing.

Instead, they ate and drank in a desultory way in the big, bleak dining-hall, served by Robertson, the elderly butler, and two curious maids. Everywhere was the evidence of neglect, and Susannah, shivering in the cold, looked around at the threadbare hangings and dusty floor and grimy windows, and said into the subdued silence, 'And this is what my mother sold her soul for.'

'You remember, it was very different, not so long ago,' Hugh told her. 'And let's hope that it will be again.'

But only after Simon Heron's death: the thought hung glowering in the air, unspoken. Alathea, wan and heavy-eyed after a disturbed night full of bad dreams, looked around at the despondent company, picking gloomily at the food. The news of the sad condition of Meraud, Lady Bradfield, had only increased the lethargic misery visible in most faces, and the apprehension which everyone must be feeling at the prospect of the day ahead.

Malise Graham, grim and solemn, arrived with his wife and family soon after, and ascertained that Lord Bradfield was awake, and ready to receive them. Barely fortified by their repast, the various branches of the Heron family were led by the deferential butler to the room in which his master lay.

It was also the room in which his father had died, thirty-six years ago. Thomazine, looking round at the high, carved ceiling, the ancient and gruesome hangings on the bed, for an instant was transported back to her childhood, and thought that the wasted, gasping figure between the curtains was old Sir Simon, her harsh but fair-minded guardian.

But it was not, of course. It was Simon, Francis's brother, the young man whose obsessional hatred had driven the two of them asunder, whose inflexible principles had forced him into exile and penury, ruining his wife's health and embittering his elder daughter: the man whose bigoted, rigid mind had led him to quarrel with all his family – brother, sister, wife, children, nephews, nieces, cousins – all his family, save Malise, who was generous and had never, ever taken offence.

Malise stood by the bed, a big, gaunt, bear-like man, loved and trusted friend, and beside him, tall and slender still, was Grainne, her face holding that calm wisdom which would endure into old age, when her great beauty had vanished at last. There was Bridget, shy and sweet and very like her mother, and Robin, a far more dependable, solid character than Nick, the elder, who was in Scotland, and Hen, who took after her long-dead father, Henry Sewell, and did not in the least favour her dark-haired mother. Becca did, though. Thomazine had not seen the resemblance in the child until now, but they were very similar in bearing. Becca would not have her grandmother's beauty, but that quality of serious, graceful calm was apparent already.

Thomazine's eyes went to Jasper, the eldest of Grainne's five surviving children, who had his mother's face and his father's colouring, and still that idealistic, far-away look. She was glad that he had married Alathea, for no one else she knew would have suited her unpredictable daughter better, and besides, it kept it in the family. She did not like the look on Alathea's face: a remembered horror lingered in the long, shadowy eyes, and she recalled that her daughter had also seen what had happened to Meraud. It was a fate, apparently, that transcended all their idle hopes of punishment or revenge.

She glanced at Lucy, and saw her dear friend and cousin's round blue eyes filling with tears. Lucy had been the only weeper at her father's deathbed: now, it seemed, she would shed tears here, for her brother. Of all of them, the years had been kindest to Lucy: only a little silver marred the shining perfection of her black glossy hair, her dress was perfectly chosen and fitted her plump figure to exactness. Dan stood beside her, quite white-haired and rather thin and stooped since his illness: he was well past sixty, and looked it. Ros was her usual neat, pretty self, next to her brother: Oliver, bold dashing Oliver, cut a fine figure, a Heron through and through. *But I will* not *let Lucy marry him off to Sophie*, thought Thomazine firmly, *that's a recipe for disaster if ever I saw one.* Sophie would have to marry someone, she was twenty years old and deliciously pretty, but not Oliver. As well set a match to gunpowder.

Her gaze slid past Math and Sophie, the dear figure of Hugh, and his pale little wife who was, so disconcertingly, the image of Meraud but not like her at all, to Anne. She was the only one in the chamber who did not look either bored or apprehensive: her white hand clutched Isabella's, convulsively, and her dark sombre eyes stared fixedly, with horror and grief and something else, at her father.

'They are all here,' said Malise to Lord Bradfield, and the figure in the bed, propped up on pillows, moved, and raised a hand, and spoke.

Simon Heron had had a deep voice, harsh and powerful: the sound that issued from that shrivelled throat was a most terrible travesty. 'I wished . . . to see you all here . . . before I die,' he said, the breath rasping between his teeth. 'All of you . . . my family . . . together.' There was a painful pause while he gathered voice and strength, and then went on. 'We have had . . . differences . . . disagreements . . . and I wanted – wanted to call you here . . . to forgive you.'

There was silence, broken only by the lively crackle of the fire. Thomazine felt tears prick against her eyelids: her nose began to run. *Oh, Simon, dear, stupid, high-minded Simon – why couldn't you have been more like the rest of us? Less stubborn, more tolerant? What possible good to you is a deathbed reconciliation?*

'Hugh?' said that terribly changed voice. 'Are you there? Where is Hugh?'

His young half-brother stepped forward: tall, fair, cynical, a little too heavy, he stopped at the foot of the bed. 'I am here, my lord.'

'You are my brother . . . you have no need to call me that. And Susannah? Where is she?'

Silently, like a lovely ghost, Susannah Trevelyan came to stand by the side of her husband. 'Here I am, my lord . . . I am sorry.'

The old man who had wanted to marry her shook his head, the straggling hair dragging across the pillow. 'No . . . no need. You love him . . . I could not . . . could not have made you happy. It does not matter now,' said Simon Heron, and the brief agony on his face showed everyone who saw it that it still did matter, a great deal. 'You . . . have my blessing. Have you any children?'

It had been nearly six years since their marriage. 'No,' said Hugh. 'No children, yet.'

'There . . . will be, I am sure . . . there will be,' said his brother painfully, and added something incoherent out of which emerged only the word 'Rupert'. Then he added, more strongly, 'My children . . . Mall . . . Mall, are you there?'

'I am afraid she is not,' said Anne's strained bleak voice. She had been so silent that Thomazine, startled, could not at first identify the speaker. Then Kit's widow moved forward, Isabella clinging to her skirts, to take her place by the side of the bed. For a moment, father and daughter, too much alike for comfort, stared at each other, and then Anne gave a stifled sob, and knelt by the bed, and burst into tears. Lord Bradfield's claw-like hand crept from under the bedclothes, and in a gesture that Thomazine found deeply moving, stroked her hair.

The two stayed there for some time. Anne's sobs at last died away, and she said something to her father, and then turned and gently brought the reluctant Isabella to the bedside. Lord Bradfield's hand went out to touch his only grandchild, and the little girl did not flinch away.

They were all summoned to the bedside after that, to make their farewells. Alathea, as reluctant as Isabella, came to the bed with dragging feet. The man whom she had defied stared up at her, the dark eyes exhausted in the sunken grey face, and said something she had not expected. 'Alathea . . . I insulted you most dreadfully when last we met . . . I beg your forgiveness.'

'You already have it,' she said, and the faint remnant of a smile crossed his face. 'I am . . . glad. And you have married young Jasper . . . that is good . . . do you want . . . the pictures?'

She stared at him, bewildered, and then remembered the three Dutch paintings in his study, that she had seen the day that Rupert died. 'The pictures?'

'Yes . . . they are yours . . . I had my will . . . drawn up last week. I remember your face . . . as you saw them.'

'They are beautiful,' said Alathea, shaken and delighted. 'It is so very kind of you, my lord – thank you – thank you so much.'

'One more thing . . . ' His voice was faltering now as his strength failed, and the intakes of breath grew harsher and more difficult. 'Rupert . . . know you tried . . . your best . . . could not have done any more . . . I thank you, now . . . you deserve it.' He fell back, fighting for air, and Alathea, suddenly overwhelmed by this utterly unexpected kindness, turned into Jasper's comforting arms, her eyes full of tears.

And so it went on: there was a pleasant word, an apology for everyone who had been wronged or insulted. Jasper, who had dreaded this day, was greatly surprised, and thought, with sorrow, that it was a great pity that Lord Bradfield had waited until his last days on earth before offering this reconciliation with his family.

At last he was done. Completely exhausted, he sank back on the pillows, gasping with pain and effort, and Heppy Greenwood wiped the sweat from his face and gave him water. Jasper felt for his pulse, found it faint and labouring, and turned to the Herons around the bed. 'He must rest – I think you should leave, for the moment.'

'No,' Lord Bradfield whispered. 'No – not Anne . . . not Isabella.'

So one by one, they trooped out, silent, sad, grieving, and left Anne Heron alone with her dying father. What was said between them, no one ever discovered, but somehow it must have affected her very deeply, for when she came up to the Long Gallery, perhaps half an hour later, the bleak remoteness had gone from her face, and her eyes looked at reality once more.

And then there was nothing to do, but wait.

Neighbours, friends came that afternoon. Malise had sent word about the countryside, and Goldhayes was suddenly full of Jermyns and Gages and Herveys, all curious to see the state of the house and to cast their eye over the man who would inherit it. And Francis Heron, who had had more reason than anyone else to hate his eldest brother, had gladly accepted their reconciliation and stood beside him to help and support and to welcome those who came to say farewell.

In the manner of such things, Lord Bradfield's deathbed had ceased to be a purely private, family affair, and became the social occasion that such an event always was. There were refreshments for the visitors, and gossip, reminiscences and even, mutedly, laughter filled the Long Gallery, and Thomazine played hostess and thought with sadness of her dying brother-in-law below. But at last the final mourners left, and it was curious how, after that first encounter with the dying man, many of his family returned to the sickroom to talk to him, to watch, or simply to be there at the end.

Simon Heron, first and last Lord Bradfield, died peacefully at nine o'clock that night, and with grief and also with much joy, his last remaining brother Francis came into his inheritance. And Alathea, with a heart full of hope and happiness, knew that at last her beloved house was safe, and would always be her home.

EPILOGUE

Goldhayes

Happy is the country life,
Blest with content, good health and ease:
Free from factious noise and strife,
We only plot ourselves to please:
Peace of mind the day's delight,
And Love our welcome dream at night.
(Anon, contemporary songbook)

A thrush was singing, glorious and proud in the tree by the drive: all the delights of spring poured from his liquid throat and filled the air with music. The sun shone, warm and brilliant on her back, and there was the sweet smell of new grass and slightly damp earth. A few feet away, a couple of sulphur-yellow butterflies danced and swooped above the ground, and Alathea wished that she could capture their movement as well as their colour on her paper.

But Goldhayes was her subject today. She had chosen her vantage-point well, far enough away to view the whole house with ease, yet not so far that detail was lost. She had practised the art of perspective-drawing in Italy, and now she was about to employ it in earnest. Using the new soft plumbago, she sketched in the lines of turrets and buttresses, windows and walls until, working over her original faint outline, she was satisfied. Most artists doing this sort of work in Italy, and in Holland, had used a camera obscura: she preferred to trust her eye and her hand, and the tingling flow in her fingers proved her to be right.

Carefully, she selected a brush from the half-dozen or so she had carried out with her, and set up her limning paints in a row of little shell boxes on a wooden tray beside her. It was curious to think that she had never succeeded in portraying Goldhayes from the life before: curious also to think that the last time she had sat here, doing this, had been the day that Rupert had died.

As if in echo of that terrible day, a child shouted in the distance. She looked round, and saw Sandro and Isabella crossing the front court, hand-in-hand, with the two dogs, Leone and Lovell, bounding ahead of them to the freedom of the park. Lovell was a little old now – he was twelve – and stiff of leg and rather deaf, and

Leone could literally run rings around him, but he still made gallant efforts to keep up. She thought of Kit, who had given Lovell to her in those innocent, golden days when she had thought he only offered friendship: and the old pain flared briefly, and was gone.

She mixed up a pale wash of blue for the May morning sky, and began to apply it, humming. Impossible to feel sad on a day like this: impossible to regret the past when the present was so delightful. She guided the brush gently round the outlines of those ridiculous turrets and fantastic, twisted chimneys, and realised that the children were approaching: indeed, Leone, their harbinger, was already frisking dangerously close to her paint-pots.

'Hello, Mama,' said her son. Sandro was almost three, and grew daily more handsome, more intelligent, more charming. He gave her a grin. 'What're you doing, Mama?'

'Standing on my head in a bucket,' said Alathea, grinning in return.

'No, you're not,' said the literal-minded Isabella, as Sandro erupted into giggles. 'I can *see* that you're not.'

'Well, I'm very busy at the moment,' Alathea told her firmly. 'Are you taking the dogs out for a walk?'

'Yes, and we're going to see Becca,' said Sandro. 'Can we?'

'Yes, so long as she brings you back for dinner. Can you please take Leone away before he puts a foot in one of my paint-pots? Go on, Bella, take him away.'

'Come on, Leo,' said Isabella, and Sandro, laughing, ran off through the grass. The two dogs raced after him, and Isabella trotted in pursuit.

How she has changed, thought Alathea with satisfaction, *hardly a trace now of that terrified little phantom. But the scar will be on her face for life*.

Anne, too, had changed: she smiled now, and laughed sometimes, and the past seemed to have lifted from her. But she never spoke about Kit, either in life or in death, and Alathea, despite their growing friendship, knew that she would never ask. It was enough to know that Anne, evidently, had come to terms with her dreadful deed.

She chose a red ochre, mixed with a little Cologne earth, for the rose-red walls of Goldhayes. There had been men working on the roof only two days ago, replacing tiles and repairing gutters. They were gone now, and the house stood proudly again, warm and light and cared for, polished and lovingly tended by a small army of servants, Greenwoods and others, directed by her mother and by Henrietta, who had joyfully offered assistance. There were flowers in the parlours and the hangings had been mended, dust had been outlawed and, to cap everyone's pleasure, the elderly Heron coach had been despatched to Ashcott with Matthew and the Widow Gooch had been brought to Goldhayes and ceremonially installed in a chamber just off the Long Gallery, from whence she could keep a beady eye on all that went on.

There's nothing left to complete my happiness, thought Alathea, putting in the slanting morning shadows in a darker rust-red. *My parents here, at last, at Goldhayes, where they have always longed to be. Math given Ashcott to look after, to practise running an estate, so that he can marry. Who will Math marry, I wonder? Whoever she is, she'll have to like books!*

And Sophie: Sophie had already set staid Suffolk by the ears, had received four proposals of marriage and rejected them all. *I wouldn't be in the least surprised if she ran off to London after all*, Alathea decided, suppressing a grin: *Sophie is just not made for a quiet, married life. One day we'll find she's gone to stay with Hugh and Susannah in Jermyn Street, and the next we'll know, she'll be the toast of the London stage. Whatever happens to Sophie, it will not be ordinary*

Thinking of Susannah brought Hugh's last letter to mind. She missed Hugh very much, but it was not so far to London: they would meet often. And he was delighted, and so was Susannah, for after six years of barren wedlock, she was at last expecting their first child. *Meraud's grandchild*, thought Alathea, and remembered that other, scarce-conceived grandchild that had died with Nell. But Meraud would never know of it, for, mercifully, a chill on the lungs had carried her away from her hideous existence, two months previously. Jasper had made sure she did not suffer, but had done nothing to save her, and she had died surprisingly quickly and easily.

Jasper. She smiled, thinking of what they had done that morning, making love in the soft feather bed of the house they shared in Bury, in a little lane off Abbeygate Street. She had come to love him very swiftly, to admire his idealism, his dedication, to laugh at his jokes and delight in his company, and Sandro loved him too, and called him Papa. Her smile widened as she considered the contrast between her son's real father and his stepfather. *Whatever Sandro becomes*, she said to herself with feeling, *I pray that he is* happy. But she knew that there was small danger of her sunny, sensitive Alexander becoming another tormented, wild, demon-driven genius such as John Wilmot, Earl of Rochester. She doubted she would ever see him again, and beside the sweet joy of sharing her life and her love with Jasper Sewell, in that idyllic little house, that year's passion seemed pale, remote, part of another life and another Alathea.

With just a wash of green trees and grass to point the contrast with the glowing red of the brick, she was finished. She might go over the outlines later with pen and ink, but for the moment she must let it dry. She put the piece of paper, wet and shining, down on the tray, weighting it carefully with a paint-pot at each corner to stop it blowing away in the breeze. She put the tops on the pots, wiped her brushes with a damp rag, and then turned her considering, critical gaze on the painting. After a long moment, studying the perspective, the colour, the light and shade, she was satisfied: Goldhayes lived again on the paper, and she had lost none of her skill nor her magic.

I made the right choice, she thought, and clasped her hands around her knees with a happy sigh. *I chose the right man, the right place, the right way to paint. I could never have done anything like this in London, I'd still be painting fat courtiers and fatter maids-of-honour for a pittance, and losing custom to Lely and that brilliant new German artist Hugh told me about in his last letter, the one that Jasper says he knew in Leyden, and getting less and less pleasure and satisfaction from my work. I* did *succeed: I* did *make my living as a painter: I proved my point and fulfilled my ambition and I have not let it turn sour on me. Alathea the picture-drawer is gone for good – long live Alathea the artist!*

Someone was calling her. She looked up, and saw that it was her father. She waved back, and picked up the tray of paints and her precious picture. He was standing on the bridge over the moat. She walked across to join him, and they stood together, looking at the fruits of her morning's work.

'One day,' Francis Heron said, with the old sense of wonder within him, that his beloved child should have this wonderful gift, 'one day, people will appreciate work as fine as this, and not care for fashion.'

'But then it will be the fashion,' said Alathea, smiling. 'Do you like it?'

'Like it? It's as beautiful as the real Goldhayes,' said her father, smiling. 'Don't stop painting, will you? Not even if you're surrounded by a dozen brats.'

'I shall come and give them to you and Mother to look after, while I live a life of idleness and paint in Bury,' said Alathea, laughing. 'Which reminds me – I haven't told you yet, have I?'

'Told me what?' Her father's face told her he had guessed, but she shook her head, teasing. 'I can't. I'm not sure if you'll survive the news that you'll be a grandfather for the second time, in December.'

'My grey hairs have multiplied already,' said Francis Heron, and took her shoulders and kissed her, noting the unalloyed happiness shining from her. 'How very glad I am, maw – is Jasper?'

'I told him last night – and do you know what he said?'

'What did he say?'

'He said that he had all manner of theories about safe childbirth, and he looked forward to practising them on a patient who wouldn't dare to complain and couldn't refuse to pay the fee!'

And together, with laughter, Alathea and Francis walked across the front court of Goldhayes, and entered the house where they belonged.

Laura Black

Glendraco £2.50

In flight from her grandparents' Edinburgh home, destiny takes Kirstie Drummond up into the Highlands, where her beauty draws the men as surely as her Drummond features remind the local folk of her ill-starred ancestry. It is there that Kirstie sets out to discover the truth about her father's family . . .

'The real thing in romantic adventure' KIRKUS REVIEWS

Strathgallant £2.50

The indomitable old Lady Strathgallant had decided. Her ward Perdita was to be married and to inherit the Strathgallant estate. Rupert would have been the perfect match, but Rupert had fallen in the damned Indian Mutiny. The four Ramsay boys, the great-nephews Harry, Colin, James and John would be summoned to attend Perdita's eighteenth birthday ball. As each arrived, Perdita fell in love with each in turn. Then came Jules Delibes, connected to the family by a French marriage and keen to be the fifth suitor . . .

Daphne du Maurier
Frenchman's Creek £1.95

While the gentry of Cornwall strive to capture the daring Frenchman who plunders their shores, the beautiful Lady Dona finds excitement, danger and a passion she never knew before as she dares to love a pirate – a devil-may-care adventurer who risks his life for a kiss . . .

'A heroine who is bound to make thousands of friends, in spite of her somewhat questionable behaviour' SUNDAY TIMES

The King's General £1.95

A brilliant re-creation of the love shared by Sir Richard Grenvile – at once the King's General in the West and the most detested officer in his army – and Honor Harris of Lanrest, as brave as she was beautiful, during the years when Cornwall echoed to the brisk tattoo of Royalist drums and the alien challenge of rebel bugles.

Jessica Stirling
The Spoiled Earth £2.95

A powerful and exciting love story set against the loyalties and oppressions, catastrophies and ambitions, of a nineteenth-century Scottish mining community. This haunting saga traces the joys and despairs of Mirrin Stalker, radical firebrand and tantalizing beauty, who is unprepared for the directions which her passions take . . .

'Jessica Stirling has a brilliant future' CATHERINE COOKSON

The Hiring Fair £2.50

This magnificent sequel to *The Spoiled Earth* is set in the Scotland of the bleak 1870s. With he father and two brothers dead in the Blacklaw mine disaster, Mirrin Stalker, the restless firebrand of the Stalker family, takes to the road. Through tinker camp and hiring fair she finally emerges on the stage of the music-hall in its bright-lit heyday.